NEXT OF KIN

Sequel to
Conflict of Interest

By

JAE

ePublisher

book

http://L-Book.com

Next of Kin
Sequel to *Conflict of Interest*
Lesbian Fiction: Romantic Crime

Print ISBN: **978-1-934889-42-8**
eBook ISBN: **978-1-934889-26-8**
Audio ISBN: **978-1-934889-46-6**
Audio available only at http://L-Book.com.

First Edition
Paperback Format
First Print: August 2009
Published: November 2008

Paperback and electronic books are published by
L-Book ePublisher, LLC
La Quinta, Ca. USA
Email: info@ L-Book.com
Web Site: http://L-Book.com

Editors: Judy Underwood

Cover Design by Sheri
graphicartist2020@hotmail.com

Acknowledgments

The biggest thank-you goes to my beta reader Pam. She had the patience to work with me on several versions of *Next of Kin*. Pam, thanks for all the time you invested in this story and its prequel.

Thanks to Chris, who beta read *Next of Kin* when I first wrote it, and to Margot, who makes a great test reader. I also want to thank Sheri for three wonderful covers for my books. A special thank-you goes to RJ Nolan—it's great to have the support of a fellow writer.

Dedication

To my "next of kin," especially to Susanne—a great sister, a great friend, and a great woman.

Next of Kin

CHAPTER 1

"*W*HAT ARE YOU wearing?" a sultry voice purred through the phone.

Aiden closed the file she had been reading and tossed it on top of the others that were scattered all over her desk. She pressed the phone against her ear and whirled the desk chair around, trying to obtain a minimum of privacy in a room full of nosy detectives. She cupped a hand around the receiver and lowered her voice. "What am I wearing?" she repeated with a disbelieving smile.

"Ooooh, Carlisle's got an obscene caller!" Jeff Okada announced.

The detectives crowded around Aiden's desk, and she waved at them to go away.

"Yeah," the female voice at the other end of the line answered. "Or rather... what aren't you wearing?"

Aiden tipped her chair back and laughed, relaxing for the first time all day. "You're sexually harassing a sex crimes detective at her workplace? My, my, you're a daring woman, Doctor Kinsley!"

"Daring? No. Concerned? Yes," Dawn answered, giving up on her attempts to sound seductive. "I've seen neither hide nor hair of you for the last three days, and the mountains of mail in your mailbox tell me that you haven't made it home since Thursday."

She hadn't. Aiden sighed. "I'm sorry—"

"No," Dawn interrupted. "I didn't call to make you feel bad. You're doing your job, and you don't have to apologize for that. I just thought you could probably use a change of clothes by now. Unless, of course, the Portland Police Bureau has a new interrogation technique, and you want to get a confession from the perp just because he can't stand to be in the same room with you any longer."

Aiden laughed for a second, then her face once again took on the grim expression she could see on the faces of her colleagues. "We have to catch him before we can force a confession, by offensive smell or otherwise."

"You will," Dawn said quietly. "It just takes a little time."

Time his next victim doesn't have. Still, Dawn's belief in her felt good.

"So do you want me to drive by the precinct later to bring you a change of clothes?" Dawn asked.

Aiden looked around the busy squad room. It was Saturday evening, but there were still two dozen detectives and police officers working on finding a serial rapist. Aiden's sexual orientation and her relationship with Dawn were not exactly a secret, but it wasn't something she talked about a lot at work either. Most of her colleagues hadn't commented one way or the other, and she was loath to rub it in their faces.

Dawn seemed to notice her hesitation. "I could pick up a change of clothes from your apartment and send them by bike courier if that would be—"

"No!" Aiden said, sounding harsher than she wanted to. Her patience had already been wearing thin after working the case for thirty-six hours straight, and she lost what little patience had remained when she heard Dawn's careful response. "No, I want to see **you**, not some bike messenger."

At her outburst, even the normally oblivious Ronny Pratt looked up from his work. A few other detectives gave her curious stares, probably wondering to whom she was talking.

Aiden wearily rubbed her face, trying to hide her blush from her colleagues.

"Okay," Dawn said after a while. "I'll be over a little later. I'm having dinner with my mom, and I'll stop by on my way home."

Aiden's stomach growled. She couldn't even remember the last time she had eaten anything, much less a home-cooked meal. "Tell Grace I said 'hi.'"

"I will. I love you."

"Uh." Aiden glanced around the squad room. *There goes my tough-cop reputation.* "I..."

Dawn laughed. "You don't have to say it. I know that the boys are probably listening to every word you say."

"Yeah," Aiden grumbled. "They're a nosy bunch."

"I'll let you go now," Dawn said after a moment of silence. "See you later."

"Dawn?"

"Yeah? Don't worry. I won't bring your sexy undies to work. I'll search for a pair of sensible granny panties," Dawn said with a giggle.

Aiden's tense features relaxed into a smile. "I love you," she said into the receiver before she put it down.

Ruben leaned across his desk. "How's the li'l doc?"

Aiden looked up, a sharp retort on her lips, but when she saw nothing but sincerity in her colleague's eyes, she leaned back again and rubbed tired eyes. "She's fine." She picked up the file again.

"Don't you know that by heart now?" Ray asked, looking up from his own file and pointing at hers.

Aiden stared down at the crime scene report until the print became blurry. "There has to be something we're missing." She threw down her file and rubbed the back of her tense neck, then trudged across the squad room to the coffeemaker. By now, only coffee, adrenaline, and stubborn determination were keeping her awake.

"Why don't you lie down in the 'dungeon' for an hour or two?" Ray suggested, referring to the claustrophobically small room next to the locker room. "If there's anything in there you're missing, you won't find it while you're this exhausted."

Aiden put down her cup of coffee. She knew Ray was right. "You'll wake me the moment there's a new lead?"

"You'll be the first to know," Ray promised.

With a tired nod, Aiden headed for the nearest bed.

* * *

Dawn stepped off the elevator, surprised to see the precinct's hallway still busy even on a Saturday night. Carefully balancing her armful of bags and containers, she pushed through the glass doors announcing "Sexual Assault Detail" and entered the squad room.

She had visited the squad room before but under very different circumstances. Just six months ago, she had been one of the victims whose pictures were hanging on the dry erase board. A shiver raced across her skin, almost making her drop her packages. She took a deep breath and stepped farther into the room.

"Can I help you, ma'am?" A young plainclothes detective quickly blocked her way.

Dawn nodded. "I'm searching for Detective Carlisle." She pointed over the young Latino detective's shoulder to where she knew Aiden's desk was.

Aiden was nowhere to be seen, but Ray Bennet stood from his desk and greeted her with a warm smile. "It's all right, Moreno," he said to his younger colleague. "She's welcome here anytime."

Dawn knew the reassurance was meant more for her than for the young detective, and she appreciated it.

"Hey, Dawn!" Ruben shouted from across the room. "After having to stare at my partner's ugly mug all day, you're a sight for sore eyes."

Okada ignored him. "Hello, Doctor." He stepped closer, both hands pressed to his stiff back, and peered into the bags that Dawn carried. "Do you come bearing gifts?"

"Yes. My mother and I combined forces to make sure that Portland's finest wouldn't go hungry tonight." Dawn set down her bags on the closest desk and handed out containers of still steaming food. She just smiled at the promises of eternal salvation from half a dozen hungry cops.

The door to Lieutenant Astrid Swenson's office opened. "What's going on?" She frowned as she glanced at her men who were crowding around Aiden's desk. "Is there a new lead?"

Dawn froze. She knew Aiden's friends and colleagues would welcome her anytime, but she wasn't so sure about the lieutenant. Not only was Dawn an outsider in this group of cops, a civilian who shouldn't even be here, but she also knew Aiden had taken a lot of criticism from her superiors for starting a relationship with a former victim.

"No, just an upstanding citizen bringing us nourishment," Jeff Okada answered, undauntedly digging into his food.

The group of cops around Dawn parted as the lieutenant stepped closer, giving her a direct view at Dawn. The frown on Swenson's face deepened for a second when she recognized her. "Doctor Kinsley, right?"

Dawn swallowed and nodded.

"She's just here to drop off a change of clothes for Aiden," Ray came to her rescue. "Susan already dropped off mine earlier."

Dawn suppressed a smile. She knew Ray was telling his lieutenant that she had to respect the relationship between her and Aiden the same way she respected his marriage to Susan. "Yeah, and having done that, I'll go and leave you to your work now."

"Dr. Kinsley," the lieutenant's voice made her turn back around. "I think she's back there, taking a nap. I'm sure she would kill her partner if he let you leave without seeing her, so why don't you go and wake her up before her dinner gets cold?"

Dawn stared at her.

The lieutenant's blue-gray eyes softened, and she gave Dawn an encouraging nod. "Go on." She pointed to one of the doors down the hall.

"Thank you, Lieutenant." Dawn pressed one of her home-cooked dinners into the surprised woman's hands and hurried down the hall before Swenson could change her mind.

"Wow," Jorge Moreno, on loan from narcotics for the duration of this case, said with admiration, "who was that? She's not on the job, is she?"

Ray settled down at his desk to eat his dinner. "No, she isn't. She's a psychologist."

"Huh." Moreno was quiet for a moment. "Is she married?"

Ray almost choked on his dinner. He set down his fork. "Whatever you're thinking—forget it, rookie."

"Why?" Moreno grinned boyishly and dug into his dinner. "She's gorgeous; she holds down a steady job, and she can cook—she's exactly the kind of woman my mama wants me to bring home."

"Your mama might be all right with you bringing her home, but Carlisle might object," Ray answered, pointing his fork at Moreno.

"Why, she her girlfriend or what?" The young Mexican laughed at his own perceived joke. Slowly, his laughter died down when he looked into the smug faces of his colleagues.

Ray merrily stabbed a piece of chicken with his fork. "Yep."

"Oh." Jorge Moreno sat down heavily and scratched his head. "So asking Carlisle out wouldn't be a good idea either, huh?"

"What is this—my squad room, where serious business is conducted, or a dating service?" Lieutenant Swenson shouted from the door of her office. "Go back to work, people!"

* * *

Dawn quietly opened the door the lieutenant had indicated. The room was dark, and she needed a second to let her eyes adjust to the darkness. She silently paused in the doorway, not sure if there was anyone sleeping on one of the cots. Finally, her eyes got used to the darkness, and she could make out a single form huddled under a blanket.

She couldn't see the face, but she didn't need to. She had slept next to Aiden enough times to recognize her even in the darkness. The way she slept on her back, the door within easy view every time she woke, was typical for her cop girlfriend. Aiden was tossing and turning every few seconds, and one of her hands was clutching the blanket.

Dawn didn't need her PhD in psychology to know that Aiden was stressed. This case, like so many others, was getting to her.

Quietly, taking care not to stumble in the darkness, Dawn inched closer. She sat down on the edge of the cot and peered down at her sleeping lover. The shirt that peeked out from under the blanket was wrinkled, and Aiden's short hair was disheveled. There was a frown on her face, even while she slept.

Dawn couldn't resist. She bent down to kiss the frown off her face. Her lips softly touched the corner of Aiden's mouth.

"What?" Aiden jerked upright. She stared at Dawn, blinked, rubbed her eyes, and then looked at her again. "If this is a dream, please don't wake me."

Dawn ran a hand through Aiden's hair, combing the tousled strands back into some semblance of order. "If this were a dream, I wouldn't bring you fresh underwear. I would **be** in my underwear." When Aiden didn't react to the joke, Dawn wrapped her arms around her in a tight hug.

Aiden's breath washed over Dawn's neck as she exhaled. She could feel Aiden's tense muscles relax against her. "Come on," she said after a few seconds, "your dinner is getting cold."

Aiden moved back a few inches to stare at her. "You brought me dinner, and you left it downstairs with the twenty famished cops in the squad room? Do you honestly think they're above petty theft just because they're supposed to uphold the law?"

"No need for jealousy, Detective. I brought enough for everyone." Dawn softly grasped her hand and pulled her up from the cot, enjoying Aiden's sensual, catlike stretches for a few seconds.

Aiden stopped and looked at her. "Sometimes I think this can't be for real," she murmured.

"The case?"

"You." Aiden lifted her hand and touched Dawn's cheek with a single finger. "Us."

Dawn put her hand over Aiden's and pressed it against her face, solidifying their contact. "It is real."

"Yeah. But you waiting around for me, playing second fiddle to my job, and instead of complaining when I don't call you for three days, you come and bring me food and clothes. It just seems too good to be true," Aiden said, her voice almost a whisper.

"My dad, my brother, and my ex-husband were cops—I knew exactly what I was getting myself into when I made a play for you," Dawn said.

Aiden arched a skeptical eyebrow as Dawn had expected her to. "You made a play for me? Excuse me, Doc, but that's not the way I remember it."

Dawn was glad to feel Aiden's mood shift, and she answered her smile with one of her own. "Oh, you mean that lame attempt to ask me out to dinner?" she teased.

"Lame attempt?" Aiden echoed. "If I remember correctly, you agreed quite willingly."

"Aiden!" Ray burst through the door, nearly running them over in the tiny room. "Deming called. There's DNA evidence on the last victim. We got a name and an address."

Dawn watched Aiden transform from gentle lover to determined cop before her eyes.

Aiden bent down to pick up her badge and service weapon from their place next to the cot, and when she turned back around, the formerly gentle, honey-colored eyes were filled with steely determination. "Let's go."

A quick thank-you and one last glance to Dawn and they were gone.

Dawn listened to their retreating steps with a sigh. "Be safe," she whispered into the darkness of the empty room.

CHAPTER 2

$\mathcal{T}$HE UNDERGROUND garage was almost empty. At this time on a Saturday night, most other attorneys and paralegals had long since gone home. The high heels of Kade Matheson's shoes clacked on the concrete, sounding eerily loud in the silence of the night.

The creepy feeling of being watched accompanied her as she crossed the parking level.

Kade gripped the strap of her briefcase tighter and clenched her fist around her car keys. She strode toward her BMW as fast as her skirt and elegant pumps would allow.

A sound echoed through the garage, and she whirled around.

Nothing. The garage was still empty.

"You're becoming paranoid, Kadence Matheson," she murmured. This wasn't the first time she had felt as if somebody was watching her, but whenever she glanced over her shoulder, no one was there.

Reaching her car, she settled into the driver's seat with a sigh of relief. She stared down at the car keys that were still in her hand and remembered a very similar situation that had happened in the same underground garage.

Five months ago...

The underground garage was almost empty.

After another long day in court and an even longer evening pouring over witness statements, crime scene reports, and evidence lists, Kade left the office long after everyone else.

A sound echoed through the underground garage behind her. Kade turned around, expecting to see one of the DA's interns hurrying after her with just one more document she had to review before tomorrow.

Nobody was there.

Kade shivered and lengthened her stride. Leaving the office on her own, walking to her car alone in the darkness had never been a problem for her. Even after working with the sex crimes unit for two years, she was not one to be particularly afraid of being attacked. She had always felt safe, knowing that her Matheson confidence and the pepper spray in her purse would chase away almost every attacker.

But during the last few weeks, that feeling of safety had somehow vanished. There had been no threats—at least not more than usual—and she couldn't put her finger on it, but when she was alone, leaving the office at night or going for her morning run, she felt as if she was being watched lately.

Maybe it's just the trial. Since the beginning of the trial last week, Kade had put herself under a lot of pressure. It wasn't just her usual determination to win. Aiden seemed to have a somewhat personal connection to one of the victims, Dawn Kinsley, and that put Kade under even more pressure to win the trial.

A steel door banged shut somewhere behind Kade. She fished for her car keys, not only to be able to make a quick escape into her car should it become necessary, but also to have some kind of weapon in her hand. She pressed the small button on her car key.

The flash of the BMW's blinkers revealed a dark figure lurking right next to her car.

Kade froze in fear.

The tall person circled around the back of the car and stepped closer, the face still shrouded in darkness.

There was no time for thinking as Kade's fight-or-flight reflexes took over. Her Matheson genes weren't much for running away, so she thrust her keys into the attacker's side and used the seconds while he was cradling his hurting ribs to duck under his arm and grab the BMW's door handle.

But her attacker was faster. A long-fingered hand prevented her from opening the door on the driver's side. "Is that how you usually say hello, Counselor?"

Kade whirled around to face her attacker. The voice was distorted with pain but definitely female. In the grayish light in the underground garage, she could make out the features of a tall Latina woman. She seemed a little familiar, but Kade was sure they had never been introduced. Still, the woman seemed to know her. "Who are you?" Kade demanded to know, bravely trying to keep her voice from trembling.

The tall woman reached into the pocket of her jacket but stopped when she saw Kade's hand reach into her purse, probably anticipating her to pull out a weapon of some kind. "Don't worry. I'm a cop. I just want to show you my badge."

Kade hesitantly let go of her pepper spray that she'd pulled halfway out of her purse. The rest of her fear and tension vanished as she stared down at the gold shield and ID that identified her "attacker" as Lieutenant Delicia Vasquez Montero. Instead, anger stirred. "The police usually make an appointment through my assistant and visit my office when they want to meet with me. They don't usually ambush me in dark and lonely places," she said curtly.

Lieutenant Vasquez gave her a sheepish grin. "Not the best way to introduce myself," she admitted, "and usually I'm a lot smoother, but there's something I have to discuss with you, and Detective Carlisle told me that I'd probably still find you in your office. I didn't want to miss you in case you'd already left your office and were on the way home, so..."

"So you decided to lurk behind my car," Kade finished her sentence.

"I'm sorry if I scared you," Lieutenant Vasquez said.

Kade put her car keys away. "You didn't scare me," she insisted.

"Of course not," Lieutenant Vasquez readily agreed. "Listen, can we talk?"

Kade still didn't know what to make of this strange meeting. She had no intention of talking to this ambushing lieutenant before she had a chance to regain her composure.

"Of course," she said in a businesslike tone of voice, "if you'd be so kind as to make an appointment with my assistant, we can talk all you want."

Lieutenant Vasquez didn't remove her hand from the door of Kade's car. "There's no time to make an official appointment. You're already in the middle of the trial that I need to talk about."

Kade glanced at her through narrowed eyes. "You're not with the Sexual Assault Detail." It was a statement, not a question. She knew every detective who worked sex crimes in Portland.

"No. I'm with the homicide unit."

"The case I'm trying is not a homicide," Kade said with growing irritation. *But this could very well become one if you continue to waylay me!*

"I know. My connection to the case is not a professional one." Dark eyes looked right into Kade's, sending a silent message of urgency.

Kade tilted her head, a bit irritated that she had to look up at the older woman. "What's that supposed to mean, Lieutenant?"

"It means my connection to the case is a personal one— one I don't want to discuss in the middle of a parking garage. Have you had dinner yet?" Del Vasquez asked.

Dinner? Kade suppressed an unladylike snort. She hadn't even had lunch today. She shook her had. "Not yet, no."

"Then let's go to that little Italian place right around the corner," Del Vasquez said. "We can grab a bite to eat, and I can tell you what was so important that I decided to 'lurk behind your car.'"

That sounded sensible enough, and Kade wanted to know what connection this stranger could possibly have to her case. She hated to be surprised in open court. She locked her car and followed Del Vasquez out of the parking garage.

* * *

Del Vasquez nodded a thank-you at the waiter when he set down a spicy pasta dish in front of her. Kade noticed that Del skeptically eyed the mixed salad with slices of chicken she had ordered. She waited for a comment, but Del said nothing.

"So?" Kade said without even having tasted her food.

"Well, with what I'm about to tell you, I think I should start with a proper introduction," Del said with a friendly smile. "I'm Lieutenant Del Vasquez with the North Precinct." She offered her hand across the table.

Kade gripped the offered hand in a firm handshake and returned Del's gaze with confidence. For a moment, she could see the surprise in Del's dark brown eyes. *What, you thought because I'm picking at a salad while you're devouring a three-thousand-calorie meal, I'd have a limp, timid handshake?* It wasn't the first time someone had made wrong assumptions about her based on her appearance or her family. "So, what is this connection to the case you've been mentioning?" Kade asked. She didn't want to waste any more time exchanging pleasantries.

Del set down her fork with a sigh. "I went to the club with Dawn Kinsley on the night she was raped. I want you to call me to the stand so I can testify that she never spoke to Garret Ballard."

Kade took a moment to unfold her napkin and put it on her lap. *So she's gay,* Kade thought, but then reminded herself, *Not every woman who sets foot into a gay bar is necessarily gay.* She studied the woman across from her. With her sturdy, athletic build, the angular features, and short, casually finger-combed hair Del Vasquez wasn't exactly the picture of the feminine, heterosexual woman. *Don't stereotype,* Kade admonished.

"You can just ask," Del said calmly.

"What?" Kade stared at her.

Del grinned. "You're wondering if I'm a lesbian. If you want to know, you can just ask me instead of wasting time speculating about it."

Kade wasn't used to so much openness. Polite silence and speculations behind other people's back was the normal modus operandi in her circles. She quickly recovered and pierced Del with a direct gaze. "Okay," she said, forcing herself to keep eye contact. "Did you visit the gay bar with Dawn Kinsley because you are gay?"

"I went to the gay bar because I wanted to spend some time with Dawn," Del answered without any hesitation. "But, yes, I am a lesbian."

Kade felt a brief flash of admiration for Del's casual frankness but quickly forced her thoughts back to the case. "My detectives tell me that Dr. Kinsley is currently not in a relationship, so what's your connection to her?"

"Why is that important?" Del asked, obviously much more reluctant to reveal information about Dawn than about herself.

Kade leaned forward. "Let me be frank, Lieutenant. I don't like to be surprised by information that comes up during the examination or cross-examination of a witness. If I call you to the stand, chances are that opposing counsel will dig into Dr. Kinsley's love life—and into your own. Are you prepared for that?"

Del squared her shoulders. "I'll do whatever is necessary to put that bastard behind bars," she answered. "And no, I'm not Dawn's lover if that's what you're asking in your lawyerly politically correct way. I'm an old friend of her family. Her father was my partner on the force before he died."

"So if you're an old friend and want to help put Ballard away, why didn't you offer to testify before?" Kade asked.

"I offered to testify a hundred times before," Del said, running a hand through short, black hair. "Dawn always refused. She didn't want to drag me into this messy trial, and I respected her wishes."

"So why come to me now?" Kade asked.

"Well, with the way the trial is going... No offense, I think you're doing a great job as a prosecutor, but still... Too much rests on Dawn's testimony for my comfort." The dark eyes looked at Kade without hiding anything.

Kade accepted the explanation with a nod. "You visited the club with Dr. Kinsley on a regular basis?" she asked.

Del shook her head. "Neither of us is a regular. Some friends of hers talked her into going that night, and I went with them to make sure they wouldn't abandon Dawn for some hotties with beer."

"And?" Kade leaned forward, fully concentrated on Del and her answer. "Did they?"

"No. I did." Del took a healthy gulp of wine as if she was trying to wash away a bitter taste in her mouth.

Kade could sense that Del had beaten herself up over this for the last month. "What do you mean?" Her voice now had the same tone she used to coax a reluctant witness into talking.

"I left the club before Dawn did because all that smoke and the flashing lights were getting on my nerves." Del emptied her wineglass with jerky movements.

"Even if you had personally seen Dr. Kinsley home, it wouldn't have changed a thing," Kade said, giving in to the sudden urge to comfort Del.

Del stabbed at her pasta. "I know." She sighed. "But at least I could have told the jury that Dawn never talked to Ballard the whole time she was in the club. Now I can't attest to that."

"We can work around that," Kade said. "A witness who can testify that Dr. Kinsley never talked to Ballard when she entered the club is better than nothing. And if you are an old friend of the family, you can also testify to the fact that Dr. Kinsley identifies as a lesbian and would never consider a one-night stand with a man." Kade paused. "If you're willing to testify, knowing that it will probably out you to judge, jury, and all the people in the gallery, that is."

Del nodded without hesitation.

"All right." Kade put away her still untouched plate and laid down a legal pad in its place. "Then let's go over the questions I'll ask you on the stand."

When they left the restaurant an hour later, Del insisted on seeing Kade to her car.

Kade settled into the driver's seat and gave her a nod before reaching out to close the door.

"Oh, Counselor?" Del waited until Kade looked up. "Next time," she said, pointing to Kade's car keys that dangled from the ignition, "aim for the eyes."

*

A light tap on the driver's side window brought Kade back to the present. She jumped, almost hitting her head, and clenched her fingers around the car keys that were still in her hand as she whirled around.

A security guard stood in front of her car. He gestured for her to roll down her window. "Everything okay, ma'am?" He studied her. "I saw you sitting there without moving and—"

"I'm fine," Kade interrupted, a little embarrassed at having been caught daydreaming.

"All right." The security guard took a step back. "I just wanted to make sure."

Kade gave him a friendlier nod. "I appreciate it. Goodnight." She rolled her window back up and shoved the key in the ignition. "There'll be no next time, Del Vasquez," she grumbled and started the car.

CHAPTER 3

*D*AWN OPENED THE door to the office's small kitchen, where she found Janet McNamara, her colleague and friend, digging into a piece of cheesecake with almost orgasmic delight. She entered and rummaged through the cupboard in search of tea. "Tough case?" she asked over her shoulder.

"Aren't they all?" Janet answered around a forkful of cake.

Dawn shrugged and sat down at the table while she waited for the water to boil.

"So, what's got you smiling all morning?" Janet asked when she had eaten every last crumb.

An uninterrupted Sunday in bed with the incredible Aiden Carlisle, Dawn thought with a grin. Aiden and her colleagues still hadn't caught the serial rapist they had wanted to arrest on Saturday. By the time they had arrived at his apartment, he had disappeared, but there was an arrest warrant out on him, and Lieutenant Swenson had sent her detectives home, knowing there was nothing else they could do at the moment. They had spent a lazy Sunday with each other, the first uninterrupted date in weeks. "What, I'm not allowed to smile on a Monday morning? Is that an unwritten rule in this office you failed to tell me about when I agreed to work with you back in December?"

Janet threatened her with her fork. "Don't try that with me."

Dawn schooled her features into the innocent expression she had seen on her niece every time the girl had pulled one of her stunts. "Try what?"

"Answering questions with questions," Janet said. "I don't let my patients get away with these cop-outs, and I certainly won't let you get away with it."

Dawn spooned sugar into her tea. "No professional courtesy, huh?"

"Nope." Janet flashed a grin at her. "So tell me, who's the new guy?"

Dawn froze, the cup of tea halfway to her mouth. "New guy?" she echoed lamely. "What makes you think there's someone new in my life?"

Janet shrugged. "Maybe not necessarily new, but there's someone who puts that smile on your face. And don't think I didn't notice that you answered my question with a question again. So?"

Oh, boy. Dawn had gotten back in touch with her old friend from college only four months ago, and she still hadn't told her that she had discovered her romantic interests lay with women, not with men. The last time the topic of relationships had come up in a conversation with Janet, Dawn had still been married.

"Come on, admit it," Janet said. "It's that hot detective that seems to be in and out of here every other day."

Dawn blinked. Had they been that obvious? She had tried to be discreet when Aiden stopped by at her office. "Yes," she answered simply. Janet didn't seem to be shocked, so there was no reason to deny it.

Janet raised a cautioning eyebrow. "You've seen the ring on his finger, right?"

"What?" Dawn sputtered into her tea.

"Don't tell me you didn't know he's married?"

Slowly, Dawn realized that the "hot detective" Janet was talking about was not Aiden, but her partner, who had accompanied her a few times. She laughed. "Oh, no, Detective Bennet's wife has nothing to fear from me. It's his partner I'm interested in."

"His p—" Janet's eyes widened when she remembered who that was. "You don't mean...? You...?"

"I'm in love with her." She had said those words quite often to Aiden in the past two months, but rarely had she told other people about her feelings for Aiden, and it still made her a little nervous to wait for the reaction. She held her breath until Janet relaxed again.

Janet leaned back in her chair to study her colleague. "So you finally found out why you weren't happy in your marriage, huh?"

"That would be one of the reasons, yes," Dawn agreed. She watched her old friend closely, still unsure about her reaction to this revelation.

"Well, in that case..." Janet stood, shoved her chair back, and knelt down in front of Dawn.

Dawn white-knuckled her cup of tea. "W-what are you doing?"

Janet laughed. "I'm not proposing marriage or anything. Don't worry. I'm merely groveling for a favor."

"You know, people like you are responsible for the rumor that psychologists are a bit wacky themselves," Dawn said, shaking her head. "Get up off the floor, you goof. What favor?" she asked when Janet was back on her feet.

"Well, I've just seen this new patient of mine sitting in the waiting room on my way in."

Dawn stared at her. "You have a patient waiting, and you're sitting here, eating cheesecake and interrogating me about my love life?"

"She's half an hour early," Janet defended herself.

Dawn nodded. They both knew that coming to sessions early, late, or not at all was often nothing more than a patient's attempt to show the therapist who had the control over their therapy sessions. Dawn always tried not to get involved in these power games.

"Mrs. Phillips said her mother dropped her off and that she was probably glad to be rid of her for a while," Janet explained wryly.

Dawn nodded. She knew Mrs. Phillips, their office manager and receptionist, had a keen eye and was good at reading people. "Rebellious teenager, huh?"

"Poster child for rebellion," Janet said. "Leather jacket, tattoo, thumb ring, the works. And I have a feeling she would be more interested in your sweetheart than in Detective Bennet too."

Dawn gave her a smirk. "You're not stereotyping at all, are you?"

"Maybe. But I'd rather err on the side of caution. You know there are studies indicating that therapy is often more effective for a gay patient when the therapist is homosexual too," Janet said.

"You're not just saying that because you want to stay in here and eat cheesecake instead of trying to talk to a troubled teen, are you?" Dawn fixed her with a mock stern gaze.

"One piece of cheesecake is enough for me, thank you very much. Some of us are still searching for Mr. Right." Janet patted her stomach. "But seriously, if you have the time, I have a feeling you'd be better equipped to reach this particular patient."

Dawn glanced at her watch. She had more than enough time for an intake interview with the teenager before her next patient arrived. "All right. If it's okay with the girl, I'll take her off your hands."

"Thanks. Maybe I'll eat that second piece of cheesecake after all," Janet said with a grin.

"So we're okay?" Dawn asked, studying her old friend. "You're okay with—"

"With you being gay?"

Dawn nodded.

"Well, it's a bit of a surprise, but when I think about it... I can see you with a woman, and that female detective is no slouch in the looks department. Next time she comes visiting you at the office, you'll have to introduce us," Janet said.

"Sure." Dawn put her empty cup into the dishwasher and went to get the patient's intake form from Mrs. Phillips.

"Evan Whitfield" was scrawled across the blank space titled "name" on the top of the crumpled piece of paper. The date of birth told her that her new patient was sixteen. The girl had checked only the option "other" in the list of problems that she was having and had filled in "shrinks" on the line where she was supposed to describe that "other problem." The names listed under "previous therapy/counseling" read like the who's who of Portland's psychologists.

"Thanks a lot, Janet," Dawn muttered. She straightened her shoulders and walked over to the waiting room. "Ms. Whitfield?"

The only patient in the waiting room didn't look up. The dark-haired girl's head was bobbing up and down to the loud music that blared out of her earphones.

Dawn walked over and pulled one of the earbuds from the girl's ear.

"Hey!" The girl shot up from the chair that she'd tipped back against the wall. Brown eyes glared down at Dawn from under shaggy black hair that was cut short except for long, rebellious bangs. Evan Whitfield obviously enjoyed the fact that she was already taller than Dawn.

"Hello, Ms. Whitfield," Dawn said calmly and extended a hand. "I'm Doctor Kinsley."

Evan Whitfield ignored the offered hand and folded leather-jacket-clad arms across her chest. "So?"

"Why don't you come with me to my office and take a seat?" Dawn continued without paying the girl's provocation any attention.

"Take a seat? I thought I was supposed to lie down on the couch?" Evan asked sarcastically, but at least she followed Dawn as she led the way to her office.

Dawn shrugged. "Whatever works for you is fine with me, but personally, I like to look people in the eye while I'm talking to them."

The girl didn't answer. She had her back to Dawn, her hands shoved into the pockets of her baggy jeans, silently taking in the office.

Dawn suppressed a smile. *Not what you expected, huh?* Dawn knew that her office didn't have much in common with the neat, clinical offices of some of her colleagues. On her old, marred desk, mountains of paperwork warred for space with toys, chocolates, and photos. Her diplomas hung side by side with children's paintings. "Why don't we sit down?" she suggested again.

Evan Whitfield walked around the yellow beanbags and plopped down in the chair in front of the desk, forcing Dawn to sit in her chair with the desk between them.

So she wants to keep her distance. I guess she doesn't want to get too close to the shrink or anyone else. Dawn took a seat and studied the teenager. She knew most patients expected her to start asking questions right away, and they were eager to fill the awkward silence. She had learned the power of silence a long time ago, so she merely sat and watched Evan Whitfield.

Dawn took in the long legs lazily sprawled in front of Evan, the stubborn jaw, and the confident, cautious gaze of the brown eyes. *My God!* she thought with amazement. *That's exactly how I imagine Aiden must have looked at this age.*

She stared at Evan for a second longer, then called herself to order. *Oh, come on, Kinsley, after six months, you'd think you were over that infatuated stage where everything and everyone reminds you of Aiden. Get your mind on the job!* She gently cleared her throat. "So why don't you tell me a little bit about yourself?"

Evan Whitfield continued to stare out the window as if she hadn't spoken.

This is why she had so many other therapists before. She simply refused to talk to them. "Okay, I received your message loud and clear," Dawn said bluntly. "You don't want to be here."

"Damn right, Doc!" Evan's cool façade was destroyed when she glared at Dawn.

Dawn didn't react to the anger in her voice or the abbreviation of her title that was meant only to provoke her. "Here we are anyway," she continued calmly. "Why not cut this childish crap and talk like adults?"

For a second, Dawn could see surprise and something like reluctant respect glimmer in the brown eyes before the mask of anger was back. "Do they allow you to talk to patients like that?" Evan growled at her.

"They?"

"The guys on the ethics committee," Evan answered, her words a silent threat.

How long has she been handed from therapist to therapist to have learned about the ethics committee at the tender age of sixteen? Dawn wondered. "They want me to use the language my patient does so that he or she will feel more comfortable talking to me about their problems."

"I don't have a problem!" Evan Whitfield exploded. "I'm not crazy! I don't need a shrink!"

"Good thing I'm not a shrink, then," Dawn answered softly. "I'm a psychologist. I work with people who are unhappy with some aspect of their lives."

A heavy boot kicked against her desk. "I'm not unhappy!"

"Then why are you yelling?" Dawn kept her voice low and gentle, emphasizing the contrast between their modes of communication. Actually, Dawn didn't care if Evan was yelling as long as she was talking to her. Patients had whispered their most painful secrets in this office, and they had yelled at her at the top of their lungs. In Evan's case, it meant she had succeeded in piercing the cool, bored façade and reaching the swirling emotions beneath.

"I'm not—" Evan shouted, then stopped and deliberately lowered her voice. "I'm not yellin'. And I don't wanna be here."

Dawn nodded. "I know. But since you're here, let's try to make the best of it, okay?"

Evan rolled her eyes and didn't answer.

"So," Dawn tried again, "whose idea was it to send you here?"

Evan ignored her.

"Your mother's?" Dawn asked.

"She's not my mother!" The long, sprawled-out legs tensed as Evan got ready to jump up.

Bingo. "She's not?" Dawn asked in a neutral tone.

"No!" Evan's hands gripped the armrests, barely keeping herself in the chair.

Dawn knew that she needed to change the subject for a moment to lessen the emotional intensity or risk having her patient run from the room and never return. "Okay, before we start, I think you should know our sessions will be completely confidential. Unless you're planning to hurt yourself or someone else, I won't discuss anything you tell me with your relatives, your teachers, or anyone else," Dawn said.

Evan snorted. "Right. Like I believe that even for a second."

"Any particular reason for your distrust?" Dawn asked.

Evan regarded her coolly. "Maybe I just don't like you."

Dawn didn't believe her. Evan's issues with trust ran much deeper than a simple dislike for her. "Listen, Ms. Whitfield." She stopped herself. Calling Evan by her last name didn't feel right. It was just one more barrier Evan could hide behind, and she wouldn't allow that. "Can I call you Evan?"

Evan flashed her a wolfish smile, and for a second, Dawn was once again reminded of Aiden. "Only if I can call you..." Evan craned her neck to be able to read the name on the diploma hanging on the wall. "...Dawn." She met Dawn's gaze, clearly expecting her to back down.

Dawn hesitated, then made a decision. Evan tended to keep herself apart from the rest of the world, and she needed to employ some unusual methods to establish some kind of connection. "All right. You can." Again, an expression of surprise flashed across Evan Whitfield's face before it was quickly hidden again. "On one condition."

Evan groaned. "I should have known." When Dawn just continued to look at her, she finally relented. "What condition?"

"You use my first name with the same respect that I address you with," Dawn bargained.

Evan stared at her. "You're one weird shrink, Doc."

Doc, Dawn silently repeated. *Not Dawn. She doesn't want to be respectful toward me.* "About the confidentiality I promised you... I mean it. Unless you put yourself or others in acute danger, I won't repeat anything you tell me to another person."

"Yeah, yeah, yeah." Evan leaned back with her trademark bored expression as if she wasn't listening to a word Dawn had said.

"Try me."

Evan looked up. "What?"

"If you don't believe me, try me. Tell me one thing about you. If your... the woman who dropped you off doesn't chew you out about it on the way home, you'll know you can trust me."

Brown eyes narrowed. Dawn was sure she would refuse to answer, but then Evan's lips curled into a grin that reminded her once again of Aiden. "You want to know something about me, huh? How about this: I just finished fucking this girl before I came to your office. That personal enough for you?"

Dawn forced herself not to react. *Congratulations, Janet, your gaydar is working just fine.* "So the woman who is not your mother, she doesn't know about this relationship?" she asked, careful to keep her tone neutral.

"Who said it's a relationship?" Evan Whitfield looked Dawn right in the eye, a challenging gleam in her eyes.

"It isn't?" It was clear to Dawn that Evan wanted to shock her, but she wasn't sure if she had really slept with a girl or was just bragging.

Evan leaned back. Her leather jacket creaked as she crossed her arms behind her head, looking like a satisfied, lazy cat. "Just a bit of fun. I don't do relationships."

"Why not?"

"Why should I buy a cow if all I want is milk?" Evan drawled.

Dawn leaned forward, trying to bridge the distance between them. "Let's try not to hide behind lame statements like that while you're in here, okay?"

Evan scowled and removed her arms from behind her head to cross them in front of her chest again.

"So the woman who dropped you off... if she's not your mother, who is she?" Dawn asked, hoping that Evan would answer that question now that she had started to talk.

Evan made a show of examining her fingernails.

All right. Let's try a little provocation of my own. "She's not that one-night stand you just told me about, is she?"

A strand of black hair fell into Evan's face as her head shot up. "Are you crazy? What would I want with an old, pushy broad like that?"

I'll take that as a no. Dawn just looked at her and waited.

Evan tried to stare her down for a long minute, then relented. "She's foster mother number thirty-seven."

Dawn was sure Evan was exaggerating, but the meaning was clear nonetheless. *She grew up in a number of different foster homes. She has no family and no girlfriend. I bet all that rebellious bravado is just to hide how lonely and rejected she's feeling.* "How long have you lived with her?"

A casual shrug. "A while."

"And what's so horrible about it?" Dawn asked.

Evan looked at her with brooding dark eyes. "I never said it was."

"You called her a 'pushy, old broad' and 'foster mother number thirty-seven' instead of just using her name," Dawn pointed out. "Sounds like she's not your favorite person." *Is there anyone in your life you allow yourself to like?* Dawn wondered. *What made you close yourself off from people?*

"She just gets on my nerves." Evan's fingers impatiently tugged on a tear in her jeans.

"About what?"

"Everything!" Evan snapped.

This is going to be a long fifty minutes, Dawn thought, suppressing a sigh. *You better save some of that cake for me, Janet.* "Can you give me an example?"

Evan threw up her hands. "She's constantly naggin' me about school, the way I dress, and who I hang around."

"Sounds like the same stuff every teenager fights over with her parents," Dawn said. Not liking Evan's leather jacket or her friends couldn't be the reason why her foster mother thought she needed therapy.

"They're not my parents!" Evan snarled.

Dawn studied her, well aware that her next question would most likely not be answered. It needed to be asked anyway. "Can I ask why you don't live with your biological parents?"

"You can ask," Evan said in a condescending manner. "Doesn't mean I have to answer."

"I know this might be a difficult topic for you—"

"You don't know anything!" Evan leaped to her feet so fast her chair tumbled to the floor. "You don't know anything about me!" She prowled around the office like a caged panther.

Dawn stayed where she was. "You're right. That's exactly why I need to ask you these questions. I have to get to know you before I can help you. Now would you please pick up the chair and sit down again?"

Evan stopped in midstride to glare at her.

"Please." Dawn pointed at the chair, her voice soft, but her gaze firm and steady, not giving an inch.

Evan picked up the chair but didn't sit down. She stood behind the chair, her hands clenched around its back. "Why do you think you can help a fucked-up kid like me when all the other shrinks couldn't? You think you're the Mother Teresa of mental health or what?"

Dawn couldn't help smiling. *She's more intelligent than she lets on. I bet she could be a straight-A student, but of course that would ruin her tough-girl image.* "Because I don't think you're fucked-up or a kid. You're an intelligent young woman, and you want me to help you."

Evan snorted. "And you're delusional, Doc. What makes you think I want your help? The way I treated your office furniture?" She barked out a laugh, a sound devoid of humor.

"No. The fact that you stayed here and talked to me for the last thirty minutes when you didn't even want to say so much as 'hello,'" Dawn answered with a smile. She turned the small clock on top of her desk around so Evan could see the time.

Evan stared at the clock. Her eyes held an almost panicked expression when she noticed she had, in fact, been lured into a conversation during the last half hour.

"So now that we've established you're not fucked-up and I'm not the enemy, do you think we can give each other a chance and see if we can work together?" Dawn offered her hand again.

Evan ignored the gesture as she had before, but she settled back down into her chair. "If I stay, it's only because I'm bored. There's nothing on TV, and I ran out of weed yesterday."

Dawn just smiled and made a mental note to ask Evan about her drug habit later. "So tell me a little about foster mom number thirty-seven. Does she have a name?"

CHAPTER 4

"*L*IEUTENANT VASQUEZ?"

Del looked up from the paperwork on her desk and found a stranger lingering in her doorway, apparently not eager to enter her office. "Yes?"

"Officer Cassidy Logan," the woman said. "My sergeant told me to meet you here."

Translation: I wouldn't have come if he hadn't ordered me to, Del read between the lines. She could tell Officer Logan didn't want to be here.

Cassidy Logan stood ramrod straight, the gray uniform hat tucked neatly under her arm, and looked at a point somewhere above Del's shoulder. While Del appreciated a professional attitude, this strict, almost military demeanor was not what she expected from a police officer.

"Take a seat," Del said, pointing at the chair in front of her desk.

Cassidy Logan sat down but kept her stiff posture.

Del was instantly reminded of Kade, and she needed a few moments to figure out why. At first glance, Kade and Cassidy Logan had nothing in common but the color of their hair. While Kade's straight red hair fell just beyond her shoulders, Officer Logan's hair was much shorter, curling just slightly around her ears and neck. Kade was a little taller than Logan, and where Kade's body possessed feminine curves and refined elegance, Logan appeared more sturdy.

Finally, Del realized that it wasn't Cassidy Logan's looks that reminded her of Kade. It was the cool, detached air the officer projected like a shield. She appeared cut off from the emotions Del could sense stirring beneath the surface and from the people around her, focusing only on her job. Del was on a mission to change that with Kade, and she hoped Cassidy Logan had someone who reached beyond the surface in her life too.

Officer Logan cleared her throat. It was obvious that she didn't like Del's close scrutiny. "You wanted to see me?" The "why" was clearly heard, if not said aloud. The question was justified since Officer Logan was with the Mounted Patrol Unit and not part of Del's team of homicide detectives.

"It's about Officer Morland," Del said.

Suddenly, Officer Logan's cool detachment disappeared. She lost her perfect soldier stance as she leaned forward, waiting for more information on the edge of her seat. "Any news on the investigation? Did you find—"

"No," Del interrupted, not wanting to give her false hope. "No, there's nothing new, but we're not giving up."

Logan's shoulders slumped for a moment, then the perfectly straight posture was back. "Why did you want to see me, then?" she asked, her almost brusque tone in contrast with her by-the-book stance.

"Your sergeant thought you might find it helpful to talk to someone who lost her partner too," Del said softly.

Officer Logan jerked, but her expression was unreadable. "No, thank you, Lieutenant," she said stiffly. "I don't need any help."

"I said the same thing when my partner was killed, but we both know it's not true." Del studied her, and when Officer Logan didn't answer, she added, "Did you talk to his wife?"

A tangle of emotions flashed across Cassidy Logan's normally controlled face for a second before she carefully schooled her features into a calm, almost bored expression. "I didn't know that was a departmental requirement."

Del thought of Grace, and her temper flared. "It's simple human decency!" She stopped herself. "Talk to her. It might resolve a few things for both of you."

"Anything else, Lieutenant?" Officer Logan asked, once again staring at a point above Del's shoulder.

Del sighed. They both knew she couldn't order her to seek help. "That will be all." She watched the officer turn and walk away. *I can only hope that she has a Grace in her life too. Someone who grabs her by the ear and forces her to talk and deal with her emotions instead of ignoring them.*

Thinking of Grace reminded her that she still had a call to make, and she reached for the phone. "Hello, Tina. It's Del Vasquez. I need a bunch of flowers again.... No, I'll pick them up.... Yes, but yellow this time." For the last twenty years, she had given Grace a large bouquet of yellow roses for her birthday. "The card... um..." Del thought about it for a moment. "Just write 'Thank you.'"

When Del put down the phone, she turned her desk chair, stared out the window, and remembered the last time she had ordered flowers for another woman.

Five months ago...

"We really have to stop meeting like this." Del stepped away from Kade's car and into the flickering neon lights of the underground garage, armed with her most charming smile and a bouquet of long-stemmed roses.

Kade's steps faltered. She gave Del and the roses a wary look. "Lieutenant." She stopped next to her car and nodded a formal greeting at Del.

Del took another step closer and extended her armful of flowers. "These are for you."

Kade made no move to take the roses. She stared at Del.

What is she so afraid of? Del wondered. Most women she knew loved getting flowers. *She told me before that she doesn't like to be surprised. Does that extend to situations out of the courtroom too? Or is it that she's afraid of what the roses might mean?* "They aren't red," she pointed out.

"What?" Kade frowned.

"The roses—they're not red," Del explained. "You probably can't see it in this poor light, but they're a light pink."

Kade shook her head, dismissing the color of the roses. "Why are you giving me roses, Lieutenant? These are from you, aren't they?"

"Of course. Can you imagine anyone else being foolish enough to lurk behind your car twice in a row?" Del asked with a disarming smile.

"No," Kade answered curtly, "that seems to be your specialty alone. So why the roses?"

"I want to say thank you for winning Dawn's case," Del said, looking directly into Kade's eyes. "Therefore the light pink—it conveys gratitude and admiration."

She tried to hand Kade the flowers again, but Kade still refused to take them. "You already said 'thank you' when you bought me a drink after the trial. Flowers aren't necessary. I get paid to do my job."

Del gave her a patient smile and decided to change tactics. "If you won't accept them as a thank-you for a job well-done, then take them as a sign of my personal admiration." She bowed at the waist, hoping to make Kade smile and finally accept the flowers.

"Lieutenant." Kade still hesitated. "I think we should clear up a few facts." Kade sounded like the confident DDA that Del had seen in the courtroom and ignored the fact that they were discussing her private life.

Del inclined her head, willing to listen. "What facts would that be?"

"Well, I don't want you to misinterpret the situation, so I should probably let you know I'm straight," Kade said.

So she knows I'm offering more than a simple bouquet of flowers, and that's what has her so scared. Kade's profession of heterosexuality didn't surprise her, but neither did it diminish her admiration. Del just grinned, totally unimpressed. "And straight women don't like flowers?"

For a second, Kade stared at her. "Of course they do," she said, speaking very carefully and precisely as if she had to take care not to stammer.

"Good." Del pressed the bouquet of roses into her hands.

"Ow!" Kade glanced down at her hand and then glared at Del. One of the thorns had pierced her thumb, leaving a tiny pinprick of blood on the tip of her finger.

Oh, shit! Del rushed forward, encroaching on Kade's personal space that she had carefully respected before. "Let me see."

Kade hid the injured hand behind her back. Clearly uncomfortable with having Del stand so close, she stepped back. She acted as if she was looking for a tissue in her purse, but Del saw through the pretense and didn't try to come closer again. "Don't worry, Lieutenant. It's not a fatal wound," Kade assured her. "I won't sue you for an assault with a deadly weapon."

Seeking refuge in the familiarity of legal terms, huh? Del ran her fingers through her hair and watched Kade sheepishly. *I'm making a mess of things, and instead of getting closer, I scare her away.* "At our first meeting, I almost scare you to death, and now I attack you with a bunch of flowers—real icebreakers, huh?" Del smiled at Kade.

"Lieutenant." Kade held out a hand to stop the conversation.

"I hope you know I'm not out to hurt you," Del said. She looked directly into the blue eyes, letting Kade know that she was talking about so much more than just her pricked finger.

Kade searched for her car keys in her purse and quickly unlocked her car. "No harm done. Thank you for the flowers," she said.

"So, will you go out to dinner with me sometime?" Del asked before Kade could jump into the car and close the door between them.

Kade set the flowers down on the passenger seat and crossed her arms over her chest. "I'm not sure what you're trying to accomplish here, Lieutenant. I just told you I'm straight."

"You still have to eat," Del said.

"At sporadic intervals, yes," Kade agreed.

Del smiled. She liked Kade's dry sense of humor. "Then why not do it with me—eating dinner, I mean. You don't have to answer right now. I'm a patient woman. Just think about it, okay?"

Kade nodded warily and shut the driver's door.

*

Del turned her desk chair back around and stared at the phone. She would have loved to order another bouquet of flowers for Kade to remind her of her continued interest, but she knew it was not a good idea.

With a sigh, Del grabbed her car keys and went to pick up Grace's flowers.

CHAPTER 5

*T*HE FLASHING LIGHTS of two patrol units lit up the night. Ducking her head against the falling rain, Kade strode toward the house that had turned into a crime scene tonight.

"Good evening, Ms. Matheson." The uniformed officer at the front door handed Kade the entry log and lifted the yellow crime scene tape for her to pass through.

Just two years ago, he would have stopped her and asked for the ID that was now tucked away in her purse. By now, most cops knew her and her tendency to show up at crime scenes. It hadn't always been like this. When she had first started working with the sex crimes unit, she had only ever seen a crime scene when she looked at the photos in the case files.

Visiting crime scenes in person hadn't seemed necessary. It had never been necessary in her former job, prosecuting white-collar crimes. Two years ago, the unlucky detective who had dared to interrupt her beauty sleep with a two a.m. phone call had been subject to one of the rare, but famous Matheson temper tantrums. She had told herself that wading through puddles in the middle of a rainy night wasn't her job. It was what her detectives got paid to do.

Now, after hundreds of difficult and sometimes heartrending cases, it was no longer possible to keep that kind of emotional and physical distance to her work. She no longer saw her detectives as lackeys who did the grunt work for her. It had taken a while, but now Kade saw herself and the detectives as parts of the same team, cogs in the machine of justice.

Visiting crime scenes in the middle of rainy nights wasn't beneath Kadence Matheson any longer. She liked to get involved in the cases she would prosecute as early as possible.

She ducked under the yellow tape and entered the house.

Aiden Carlisle looked up from the dead body sprawled across the dining room floor. "Hey, Kade."

Kade stared down at the bloodstains on the formerly pristine Persian carpet. "So this is why the DA found it necessary to interrupt my beauty sleep." Robert Parker, the man lying dead on his dining room floor, had friends in high places. She looked at the gunshot wound to his head. "Doesn't seem like a sex crime to me, so why did the SAD catch this case?"

"His wife was raped before they shot her." Aiden pointed at the door that probably led to the bedroom. "And there's another body in the backyard. We got some backup from homicide to help us work the case."

Kade nodded. "Then I'll go and rub elbows with their DDA. I bet she got a wake-up call from her boss too." Careful not to destroy any evidence, Kade made her way to the backyard.

There was no sign of Stacy Ford or any other homicide DDA outside. A tall detective and two crime scene techs crouched over the body, trying to preserve evidence before the rain washed it away. After a few minutes, the detective straightened and turned around.

Kade froze as she recognized the tall woman. *Del Vasquez.* She hadn't seen Del since Valentine's Day. Kade closed her eyes as she thought back to that dreadful day.

Two months ago...

Kade was late. Not because she hadn't been able to decide what to wear for her Valentine's Day date that wasn't a date. She had changed into the first ensemble that caught her attention, a simple but elegant blue dress, and hadn't allowed herself to obsess about its appropriateness. Paying too much attention to what she was wearing would mean she was dressing to impress Del, and she wasn't ready to admit that just yet.

Her tardiness was the result of an unfamiliar insecurity. She had hesitated until the very last second to leave her condo, and twice she had almost told the cabbie to turn back around. She still wasn't sure if calling Del to finally agree to have dinner with her had been a good idea. It had been one of the rare spontaneous decisions in her life, and she'd only made it after receiving ninety-seven bouquets of flowers and cards signed with "your secret admirer."

Well, Del told you she was a patient woman, but apparently, she's also a very insistent woman. Del's determination to court her scared her a little, but if she was honest with herself, it also flattered her. She had been brought up to expect constant admiration and worshiping from the men in her life, but she had always found reality to lag far behind expectations. Romance had never warmed her heart. Since her halfhearted attempts to date the son of her father's business partner, she hadn't received flowers, and she had to admit that it was nice to come home after a long day at work to find beautiful flowers and sometimes a card waiting on her doorstep.

At the same time, Kade had watched the friendship between Aiden and Dawn Kinsley slowly blossom into something so much more. Aiden had even spent Christmas with the Kinsleys, and Kade was sure they would do some kind of commitment thing on Valentine's Day—all while Kade would sit at home, alone with her case files and law books.

No, she had decided. *Not this year.* In a rare moment of spontaneity, not allowing herself to think, she had called Del.

Now, as she was being led to the table where Del Vasquez was already seated, her stomach was in knots, and she was glad for her cool Matheson façade that she knew was making her appear calm and collected even if she was anything but.

Del stood as Kade approached. She wasn't wearing a dress, Kade noted, or anything else with a designer label. In simple but neatly pressed black slacks and a russet blouse, she didn't look that much different from the witness Kade had questioned on the stand, the quasi aunt who had wrapped a crying Dawn into her arms after the trial, or the lieutenant she had seen at the precinct once or twice.

That's what I like about her, Kade realized with sudden insight. *She's not playing roles. She's just herself, no matter what.*

Del didn't try to pull out Kade's chair for her, silently accepting the boundaries Kade had erected during their phone conversation—Del wasn't allowed to pick Kade up, open doors and pull out her chair for her, or pay for dinner since Kade wasn't ready to be constantly reminded that she was out on a date with a woman.

Del waited until Kade was seated, then grinned up at her from under dark bangs. "So you didn't turn back around after all."

Kade's fingers flexed around the wine list. She knew she was usually not that easy to read, and it irritated her that Del seemed to know exactly what had made her so late. She looked up sharply, directly into Del's eyes. She had learned a long time ago that attack was often the best form of defense. "What makes you think I wanted to turn back around? As you can see, I'm here."

"Yes, to my surprise, delight, and unspeakable relief—I need someone to explain all these different forks and glasses to me," Del answered with a self-deprecating grin.

Kade stared at her, not sure if she was being made fun of. No one in her circles would have ever admitted to not knowing one of the intricate rules of the higher society. Acting superior and not admitting any weaknesses had made Kade a good prosecutor and her mother the envy of her friends, but Kade knew it was also the reason why she had no close friends.

Kade studied the menu even though she had been here often enough to almost know it by heart. At least it gave her something to do other than staring at the woman across from her.

A few minutes later, the waiter came by to take their order. He asked for their wine selection, looking at Del, probably because she was the older woman at the table.

"Don't look at me," Del told him with a smile. "I appreciate a good glass of wine, but I'm not a connoisseur by any means. Why don't you choose for us, Ms. Matheson?"

Kade quickly made her selection, but her thoughts were on Del. The ease with which Del had deferred to her was unexpected. Kade thought back to her last date. Defense lawyer Neill Sutherland had always insisted on choosing the wine they would have even though Kade was convinced he was barely able to keep white and red wine apart and knew she would have done a much better job.

Del seemed completely at ease with herself and her own shortcomings. She didn't feel the need to prove herself to anyone.

When the waiter had brought over their wine and Kade had nodded her approval, Del raised her glass and softly touched it to Kade's. "Here's to getting to a first-name basis."

Kade's glass hesitated halfway to her mouth. She wasn't sure she wanted to take away the old, comfortable roles just yet.

"I admire Deputy DA Matheson, but I want to have dinner with Kade," Del said softly.

The honesty in her eyes took Kade's breath away. Being here with Del Vasquez was so very different from any date she had ever been on—and not just because Del was the first woman with whom she had ever gone out. She was used to compliments, small talk, and flattery, not to this unveiled openness.

"Or do you prefer Kadence?" Del asked when Kade remained silent.

Kade blinked. Some of the men she had dated had called her "Kade"; some had chosen the more sophisticated sounding "Kadence," but no one had ever asked her what she preferred to be called. "Kade," she answered decisively and finally took a sip of her wine.

Del nodded. "Kade it is." She clinked her glass to Kade's again. "Why do you prefer Kade to Kadence? Is there any particular reason?"

Kade stared into the red depths of her wine, then back up into the attentive dark eyes. "Because it's the name I made for myself, not the name my parents gave me." She had never thought about it before, but she knew it was the truth as soon as she had said it. She had inherited the name "Kadence" as she had inherited her trust fund. But being called "Kade," being accepted into the circle of prosecutors and cops, was something she had earned on her own. "What about you?" she asked. "Do you prefer Del or Delicia?"

Two black eyebrows rose. "How do you know the D-word?"

"D-word?" Kade had to smile at Del's expression.

"My dreaded first name," Del explained.

Kade leaned back and allowed an enigmatic smile to curl her lips. "I'm a DDA. I have my sources." When Del continued to look at her, she finally relented. "You showed me your ID when you ambushed me in the underground garage, remember?"

"Oh. Yeah." Del rubbed her ear.

"So why Del?" Kade asked.

Del extended her arms and nodded down at herself. "Do I look like a Delicia to you?"

For the first time, Kade allowed herself to really look at the other woman. She let her gaze wander over the tall, sturdily built body, the muscular forearms that the rolled-up sleeves revealed, and calm dark brown eyes. Del wore no makeup and with her Latin complexion didn't need it. With her small breasts and narrow hips, Del was not one of the voluptuous Latina women, and her features were a bit too rugged to be considered classically beautiful. "No," Kade admitted, "not really."

Del just grinned, and when the waiter returned, she allowed Kade to order for them both.

"So," Del said when she picked up the fork Kade indicated to eat her entrée, "tell me a little about yourself."

Kade delicately picked at a piece of lamb's lettuce. "What do you want to know?"

"Everything." Del's voice was quiet and sincere.

"Well, I've been with the sex crimes unit for a little over two years and before that—"

"I already know the competent counselor, now I want to get to know the woman," Del gently interrupted.

Kade set her fork down and dabbed at her lips with her napkin. "My job with the DA's office is a very important part of my life." She had expected them to converse about their jobs, something they had in common and could use to build a connection. It threw her completely off stride that Del refused to talk shop.

"One part, yes, but there has to be so much more to you than just your job," Del said. She looked at Kade, clearly waiting for her to start talking about herself.

"I spend fourteen hours a day with lawyers, detectives, and criminals, so what more do you expect there to be?" Kade asked soberly.

Del shrugged. "Well, you could tell me what you do with the other ten hours, what kind of music you like, if you have any siblings, and what you're looking for in a man... or a woman."

"Sleep and go for a run, Jazz, one older brother, and I'm not looking," Kade answered, ticking off the answers on her fingers.

Del stared at her for a moment, then burst into laughter. The people at the other tables started to look at them, but Del didn't pay them any attention. "You're very efficient if not detailed, I'll give you that."

Kade smirked and picked up her fork again.

"You're a runner?" Del asked.

Oh, yeah, running from the things I don't want to face is a specialty of mine, Kade thought wryly. Aloud she said, "Yes. I try to run every morning, no matter what else is going on." She tried to picture Del's long, strong legs that were hidden under the table. "Do you run too?"

"I'm training to run the Portland Police Marathon, but I have a feeling you'd run circles around me, Counselor," Del teased.

Kade smiled. It was nice to have dinner with someone who thought her capable of things other than looking beautiful. "You never know," she answered with a grin.

"Unless of course I accompany you on one of your morning runs and find out." Del's dark eyes observed her closely, waiting for her answer.

"Smooth, Detective, really smooth. Are you trying to get a second date when we haven't even made it halfway through the first one?" Del's insistence was flattering even if it scared her a little.

Del circled the rim of her wineglass with a lazy finger. "You said you aren't looking, but if you met a person who could hold your interest, would you give them a chance?"

Kade sighed. She definitely wasn't used to so much openness. "We could be friends."

"Friends?" Del repeated the word as if she was trying to taste it.

"Yes." She knew it wasn't what Del wanted to hear, but she wasn't ready to jump into a relationship with a woman. "For now."

"All right, let's try to be friends for now," Del agreed. She extended her hand over the table, attracting the gazes of their fellow restaurant guests again.

Kade was very aware of their attention while Del didn't even seem to notice. Hesitantly, she reached across the table and laid her hand into Del's warm, solid grip.

They conversed about a variety of topics during dinner, none of them related to their work. Finally, Kade was ready to ask for the check, but Del shook her head. "What about dessert?"

Kade folded her napkin. "No, thanks, not for me."

"Come on, Kade, you can afford to put a little more meat on these bones. Share a piece of cheesecake with me," Del said.

Another first in the history of Kade's dates: no one had ever encouraged her to eat more. Her male dates always seemed to like the elegant, ladylike way she sampled dinner, and her mother had taught her that a woman should never, ever eat more than the man with whom she was dining. *You're not dining with a man,* she told herself. *And your mother isn't here to criticize you—and even if she were, you eating dessert would be the last thing she would comment on if she saw you on a date with a woman.* "Does that mean you think I'm too thin?" she asked, adopting her most stern badass DDA glare.

"It means I think you're denying yourself the opportunity to enjoy life," Del said, not breaking eye contact for even a second.

Kade was speechless again. No one had ever affected her like this before, and she still wasn't sure if it was a good or a bad thing.

"And just for the record," Del said, this time with a smile, "I think you're beautiful just the way you are."

Kade was a veteran at handling compliments with grace, but now she felt herself blush. "Sharing a piece of cheesecake sounds good," she said.

Just a few minutes later, the waiter set down a piece of cheesecake between them.

"Stop nibbling and dig in, or you'll have to make do with the crumbs," Del warned her as she picked up her fork. "I have five brothers. Ladylike restraint wasn't taught at our dinner table."

Kade smiled but inwardly shook her head. *God, this will never work. We couldn't be more different if we tried. We grew up in completely different worlds.* She took a bite of cheesecake and savored it for a long moment.

"So," Del asked around a forkful of cake, "what finally convinced you to go out to dinner with me?"

Kade picked up her napkin to dab at her lips. "I guess your insistence finally paid off," she answered with a shrug. She didn't want to admit that with all the happy couples around her she had felt lonely, like the last remaining spinster on earth.

Del tilted her head and arched one black eyebrow. "Insistence?"

"You wouldn't call ninety-seven bouquets of flowers insistent?" Kade asked with a smile. Even for Matheson standards, that kind of courtship seemed impressive.

"Ninety-seven bouquets of flowers?" Del repeated.

Kade gave a nod. "I kept count."

Del pushed the plate back and leaned forward to study Kade. "I'm not sure what you're talking about. Someone sent you flowers?"

Kade stared at her. Del had been so open and honest before, why was she denying this now? "Yes, you did."

"Are you talking about the roses?" Del asked.

"The roses, the carnations, the lilies, the gladioli..." Kade stopped herself when she saw Del's blank expression. "You didn't send them?"

Del shook her head. "I wish I had, but no, that must have been another admirer."

"Are you serious?" Kade stared at her in confusion, not sure if Del was telling the truth or denying her role in the flower deliveries for unknown reasons. "I was so sure. The flower deliveries and the cards started the day after you gave me the roses, and I just thought..."

"Kade." Del gently laid her hand over Kade's. "Having flowers delivered and sending unsigned cards is not my style. I'd have personally brought you flowers every day if I had thought it would accomplish anything but chase you away."

Kade still couldn't believe this. "But who else would send me all those flowers?"

Del squeezed her hand. "I'm sure there are a lot of people who would go to great lengths to impress you."

"One bouquet of flowers, sure, but ninety-seven?" Kade shook her head. "That's not something your garden-variety admirer would do. Are you sure you had nothing to do with this?"

"I'm a lieutenant with the Portland Police Bureau. I don't make that kind of money, believe me," Del said with a rueful shake of her head.

Kade pulled her hand out from under Del's and nervously folded them in her lap. "In one of your cards you said you grew them yourself."

"I didn't write that card or any of the other ninety-six," Del insisted. "You really have no idea who else could have sent you the flowers and cards? Kade, if this is not just a harmless admirer or an insistent law firm who's trying to lure you over to the dark side, maybe you should have this investigated. Do you want me to—"

"No," Kade said quickly. She didn't want to involve Del in this whole mess even though the thought that anyone else but Del had sent all the flowers was scaring her. Who else would go to all this trouble to get her attention, but then not even tell her his name? In the last six months, no one had given her more than a second glance. No one but Del.

Then another thought hit her. *She didn't send the flowers, probably hasn't even thought about me since we met last November, and I call her to make a date on Valentine's Day! I knew this was a bad idea.* Kade didn't think she had ever been this embarrassed.

"Hey, listen." Del reached across the table to squeeze Kade's hand, but Kade pulled back before their hands could touch. "I didn't send you the flowers, but that doesn't change anything." She looked at Kade with an open gaze. "I'm still interested in you."

*

"Kade?" a voice interrupted her memories. "Kade? Hello?"

Kade looked up and into the dark eyes she had avoided for the last two months. She had rarely seen Del since Valentine's Day, telling herself it would have never worked out anyway. It was better not to start something when nothing could have come of it.

Now here she was, in the middle of a rainy night, trapped in a tiny backyard with Lieutenant Delicia Vasquez, with no way of escaping this awkward situation. She squared her shoulders and put on the practiced smile with which she usually dazzled jurors. "Hello, Lieutenant."

Del just stood and looked at her. She took a few moments to take in all of Kade. Finally, she smiled. "It's Del, remember?"

"Not when we're at work," Kade said. *And not since you witnessed me making a complete fool of myself.*

Del stepped closer, ignoring the still falling rain and Kade's discomfort. "Listen, I know you were embarrassed by your assumption that I was the one who—"

Kade held up a hand, stopping Del's words. She threw a quick glance at the two crime scene techs. She was sure they were paying close attention to every word Del said. "Lieutenant," she warned in a low voice.

"You broke off contact, and I accepted that," Del continued undaunted. "I'm not a stalker."

Kade couldn't stop herself from flinching. *Stalker.* The word echoed through her mind. Since Del had come into her life, the feeling of being watched, of being followed, had become more and more pronounced. By now she was sure someone was stalking her. She didn't need rumors about her being gay to add to all the complications in her life. "Is he a family member?" she asked, pointing at the dead body in the middle of the backyard. Focusing on work had always been her method of dealing with the complicated things in her life, and now was not the time to change that.

Del stared at her for a few seconds longer, then she abruptly turned and walked over to the dead man. "We'll need forensic confirmation on that, but my guess is he's one of the men who broke into the house tonight and raped Mrs. Parker."

"And then he committed suicide in their backyard?" Kade arched a skeptical eyebrow.

"He doesn't even have a gun. I think his partner in crime shot him," Del answered. "Maybe he didn't want an accomplice, or he didn't want to share the money they found in the house. It's even possible that the rape and murder wasn't part of their plan, and they fought about it."

Kade nodded slowly. That sounded plausible. Del seemed to be really good at her job. "Anything you need me for?"

"No, not yet," Del answered. "Maybe a little later when we identify this guy. If he has a record, we might need you to get a search warrant for the apartments of his usual accomplices."

There was no need for her to hang around the crime scene any longer. She could finally leave this more than awkward situation behind. "All right. If you need anything, let my detectives know, and they'll contact me," she said.

"Or I could save them the work and contact you myself," Del said, her eyes probing into Kade's.

Kade bit her lip. "Or you could do that," she agreed after a moment of silence. She had worked too hard to be accepted in her job not to act like a professional in this situation. After one last nod that included Del and the two crime scene technicians, Kade strode back into the house.

* * *

Del stood in the pouring rain, her gaze fixed on the retreating Deputy DA. She had thought about Kade often in the two months since Kade had broken off all contact with her, but every time they had seen each other, Kade had been all business. Even now, Kade had kept their interaction strictly professional. Del knew she should just cut her losses and find herself another, more receptive object of her attentions. *Yeah, right.* She snorted. *Like walking away from Kade Matheson is such an easy thing to do.*

For Del, it had proved to be nearly impossible. From the very first moment she had seen her in the courtroom, the cool, calm, and collected DDA had fascinated her, and she wanted to discover the person behind that mask of professionalism.

With every meeting since then, her admiration had only grown, and tonight hadn't been an exception. Kade's dedication to her job impressed her. None of the homicide deputy district attorneys had shown up at the crime scene yet, but Kade had waded through the puddles in the backyard at three a.m. *And the way her soaked-through jeans were clinging to her body was as impressive as her professional dedication,* Del admitted to herself.

Tonight she could sense that under the soaked-through, distanced exterior, a lot of confusion, uncertainty, and fear were hiding. The fact that Kade had been mortally embarrassed at their almost date on Valentine's Day was not helping either. Kade Matheson was a proud woman, and she didn't suffer humiliation easily. Kade had apparently convinced herself that her initial interest in Del had been a mistake and pulled back.

The question is, do I just stand by and let her? Del stared at the house where Kade had vanished. "Secure the crime scene. I'll be back in a minute," she told the crime techs and hurried after Kade.

Kade was nowhere to be seen, but Aiden Carlisle, Dawn's sweetheart, was riffling through the victim's briefcase.

Great. Del grimaced. She didn't want Aiden of all people to get mixed up in her business with Kade. Her feelings toward Aiden were still a little mixed. She didn't dislike her, but she wasn't sure if the dedicated cop was the right partner for Dawn. *Come on, give her a chance. It's the grasshopper's choice, not yours.*

Dawn wasn't the only issue that existed between them, though. Del hadn't missed the admiring glances Aiden had directed toward the long Matheson legs during the opening statement of Dawn's trial. Kade had repeatedly told her she was straight, but Del thought that under different circumstances, Kade and Aiden might have ended up together.

"Find any ID on him?" Aiden asked, pointing in the direction of the backyard.

"No. We'll probably know more once we run his fingerprints. Is DDA Matheson in the bedroom?" Del asked, trying not to sound suspicious.

Aiden looked up from the briefcase. The glance she directed at Del was all too knowing for Del's liking. "No, she already left. If you want me to, I could call her for you?" She reached for the cell phone clipped to her belt.

"No, it's all right." Del hesitated for a second, then quickly crossed the room.

* * *

Kade stepped around a puddle and tried to make out her car in the darkness. The police cruisers had blocked the Parkers' driveway, so she had parked farther down the street. With all the police officers at the crime scene, she should feel safe. *Unless of course, the stalker is a police officer.* She didn't want to think that about Del but couldn't help wondering.

A cat yowled in an alley somewhere to her right, and Kade could hear quick steps on the wet pavement behind her. She pulled her damp coat tighter around her and quickened her steps.

The footfalls behind her indicated that whoever followed her was falling into a jog.

Kade whirled around. Relief, anger, and fear warred within her when her stalker stepped close enough to identify in the pouring rain. "Jesus Christ! Would you finally stop doing that!" she hissed at Del.

Del lifted both palms. "Sorry, sorry. I just wanted to walk you to your car."

Kade turned back around, away from Del, and ran a hand through damp strands of hair.

"Hey, is everything all right?" Del stepped closer and gently touched Kade's arm, making her turn and face her.

"I'm fine," Kade said distractedly. With Del so close and the worried gaze resting on her, it was hard to believe Del meant her any harm.

Del studied her. "You sure? You seem a little... disturbed about something. I hope it's not me?"

"No. I told you I'm fine," Kade answered again. What else was there to say? She was hesitant to confide in Del. Not only because she was still embarrassed and didn't want to ask Del, of all people, for help. She also wasn't completely sure if she could trust Del. Del could very well be her stalker. She didn't want to believe that, but she had learned to rely on the objectivity of evidence, and there were just too many things that made Del look a little suspicious. Her habit of hiding in the darkness of the underground garage instead of visiting her office in bright daylight, for example, and then the concurrence of her appearance and that of the stalker in Kade's life.

"You might be a good liar but not good enough to fool an old warhorse like me." Del waited for a reaction, but when Kade just looked at her with an inscrutable expression, she sighed. "What happened to 'let's be friends'?"

Kade looked at Del through the raindrops beading on her glasses like tears. "I don't know."

"I'm still searching for a training buddy to help motivate me for the marathon. Tomorrow, six a.m.," Del said. "Let's meet at the Riverplace Marina."

Riverplace Marina? Kade eyed her through narrowed eyes. *Of all the places to suggest as a meeting place why the Riverplace Marina? Does she know I live right next to it, or is this all just a weird coincidence?* "Why Riverplace Marina?" she asked suspiciously.

"Because it's beautiful there early in the morning. We could jog along the river and up to Waterfront Park," Del suggested.

Kade stared at her for a few seconds longer but couldn't detect any ulterior motives. "What makes you think I'd even be up at six, much less go running with you?" she tried to protest. A part of her longed to go running with Del, and that made the other parts of her even more hesitant.

Del studied her from head to toe. "You're not a late riser."

She wasn't. Kade sighed. "Not tomorrow. Make it the day after. I may not be a late riser, but I still need some sleep, and it's already four a.m."

When Kade drove away, Del still stood in the middle of the street, her short hair sticking to her head in the rain. Kade could feel the gaze of the dark eyes rest on her all the way down the street.

CHAPTER 6

*D*AWN JERKED AWAKE with a gasp.

Her gaze flew left and right, trying to pierce through the darkness. Everything was quiet in the apartment. There were no steps coming down the hallway, no rough hands grabbing her, no cold muzzle of a gun pressing against her temple.

Dawn pressed a hand to her heaving chest and tried to calm the frantic hammering of her heart. *You're safe,* she told herself, over and over again. Her gaze fell on the sleeping woman next to her, and finally the terror retreated. Her heartbeat slowed.

She usually slept better with Aiden by her side, but tonight not even her lover's presence had prevented the old nightmare.

Her nightshirt was saturated with cold sweat and stuck to her clammy skin. Dawn turned back the covers and, careful not to wake Aiden, slipped from the bed. Quietly, she opened a dresser drawer and selected a dry sleep shirt. She padded to the bathroom without turning the lights on and changed. She stood on the cold tiles, staring into the mirror. She knew she wouldn't be able to go back to sleep anytime soon and didn't want to wake Aiden by tossing and turning, so she quietly turned back the security lock, pulled up the window, and slipped outside to sit on the fire escape.

She sat there, watching the lights of the city, listening to the cars driving by on the street below. In moments like this, she wished she had taken up smoking.

She had no idea how much time had passed when she heard the window being opened again. "Hey, what are you doing out here in the middle of the night?" Aiden climbed out and sat next to her on the top step of the fire escape.

Dawn shrugged. "Couldn't sleep."

"It's cold out here." Aiden wrapped an arm around Dawn and pulled her against the warmth of her body. "You all right?" she whispered against Dawn's temple.

Dawn cuddled closer and closed her eyes. Nothing could hurt her now. "I had a nightmare."

"Same one?" Aiden's free arm wrapped around her too, holding her even closer.

Dawn just nodded. There was no need to discuss the details. Aiden had been the one to take her statement after the rape—she knew exactly what happened in Dawn's nightmares. While her nightmares had become less frequent during the last few months, she still had one from time to time.

Both of them had had to admit that their love, as wonderful as it was, was not the cure-all that would magically undo Dawn's rape or any of their other problems.

"You're barefoot," Dawn noticed. She half turned in Aiden's embrace and put her socked feet over Aiden's bare ones. They were now huddled as close together as they could be without sharing the same skin.

Aiden kissed her forehead and gently stroked one of her arms. "Hey, what's this?" She moved back a bit to look down at the resistance her stroking fingers had encountered in the bend of Dawn's arm.

Both of them looked down at the small band-aid.

"I went by the hospital today," Dawn said, her voice almost a whisper.

"What? Why?" Aiden's strong arms clutched at her. "What's wrong? Did you feel sick?"

Dawn stroked the tense back. "No, no, everything's fine. I went to get retested for STDs and HIV. It's standard procedure after... after a rape; you know that."

Aiden was silent for a long time, processing what this meant for Dawn and for their relationship. "So that's where the nightmare came from," she finally said.

"Probably." Dawn shuddered, and it had nothing to do with the cool air. The antiseptic hospital hallways had reminded her of having to go through the rape kit examination just six months ago. It had brought back a lot of unpleasant memories.

Aiden lowered her head and pressed a gentle kiss to the band-aid, then kissed the soft skin all around it. "Why didn't you say something? I would have gone with you."

A part of her would have loved Aiden's company, knowing she always felt safe with her, but she knew this was something she had to do on her own. Aiden was stressed enough at work without her adding to it. "It would have been too difficult for you to get a few hours off for a procedure that was over in under five minutes. You're too busy for that with all your new cases," Dawn said.

Aiden let go of Dawn's forearm with one last kiss. "I'm never too busy for you. What happened to sharing our problems and fears? Isn't that what you're so patiently trying to teach me?" She smiled, but her amber eyes were serious.

"Looks like I taught you a little too well, huh?" Dawn rubbed her nose against the underside of Aiden's chin and deeply breathed in her comforting scent. "I think I just wanted to get this over with as quickly as possible. I didn't want it to interrupt our lives."

Aiden nodded in understanding. "When will you get the results?"

"A few days," Dawn said.

Aiden tightened her embrace for a few seconds. "It'll be fine."

Dawn exhaled. "Yeah."

"Come on, let's go back to bed." Aiden pulled her up and helped her climb back inside. She pulled back the covers and waited until Dawn had settled down before she slipped into bed.

The sheets on Dawn's side of the bed were still a little damp from her sweating through the nightmare, and she squirmed closer to Aiden's side.

Aiden helped her adjust the covers and then carefully wrapped her arms around her. "Is this okay?" she asked, indicating the loose embrace.

Dawn loved her for her constant understanding. Aiden never assumed it was okay to touch her in any way she wanted just because it had been six months since her rape. She understood that it wasn't always possible for Dawn to be physically close after having one of the nightmares. "It's wonderful," she answered, wrapping an arm around Aiden's waist. "You're wonderful."

"Go back to sleep, flatterer," Aiden said with a chuckle.

Dawn smiled and closed her eyes, knowing that Aiden might not always be able to keep her nightmares at bay, but at least she would be there for her if she woke up in fear again.

* * *

"Your three o'clock is here, Doctor Kinsley," Mrs. Phillips, her office manager, announced. "Jamie Dean again."

Dawn furrowed her brow. As far as she knew, she had no patient with that name. "Jamie Dean?" she said into the receiver.

Mrs. Phillips chuckled. "The rebellious teen. Her mother is here too, and she wants to talk to you if you have a minute."

Dawn glanced at her watch. Evan Whitfield and her foster mother were early again. "Tell her to come in, please."

Not a minute later, the door to her office opened, and a small woman in her early forties entered. "Jill LeCroix," she said, offering her hand. "Thank you for taking the time to see me."

Dawn gave her a polite nod and shook her hand. "No problem. Now, what can I do for you?" She knew exactly what Mrs. LeCroix wanted her to do for her. She had this kind of conversation almost every week, and it wasn't getting more pleasant.

"I just wanted to make sure Evan has been talking to you. She wasn't exactly cooperative with the other therapists who tried to work with her," Jill LeCroix said. "She doesn't tell me much, so... you agreed to see her, right?"

Dawn nodded. "I'd like to see her twice a week." That was as much information about Evan's therapy as she wanted to share with her foster mother.

Relief washed over Jill's face before her features settled back into an expression of worry. "And did she—"

"I'm sorry, Mrs. LeCroix, but I can't talk to you about this," Dawn said politely but firmly.

Jill LeCroix blinked in confusion. "But... but you just agreed to help me!"

Dawn stood from her place behind her desk, indicating that this conversation was coming to an end. "I agreed to help Evan," she emphasized. She waited a moment to let the difference sink in. "We can't expect Evan to open up to me if she thinks I'm reporting everything she says back to you. I have to earn her trust, so please don't expect regular progress reports from me."

Mrs. LeCroix stared at her with wide gray eyes. After a few moments, she nodded. "I understand. What you say makes sense. It's just that I'm worried about Evan, you know? She's completely out of control, and I'm at my wit's end with her." She shook her head in exasperation. "She's neglecting school, and she hangs around some pretty tough-looking guys, only coming home to sleep. I think she's doing drugs, and I'm worried that she's having unprotected sex. What if she gets pregnant? She's only sixteen, Doctor Kinsley!"

Dawn worked hard to keep her expression neutral. *That's one thing you don't have to worry about,* she thought, but of course she didn't say it aloud. "I'd tell you if she planned something that put her in immediate danger, but with everything else, you'll just have to trust me—and Evan. Don't make her feel like you're only expecting bad things from her. Do you think you can do that?"

"I'll try." A subdued Mrs. LeCroix left Dawn's office.

Dawn took one last sip of her now cold tea and went to fetch her young patient from the waiting room. As she crossed the reception area, she caught a glimpse of Evan Whitfield talking to someone in the waiting room and stopped for a moment to watch.

A slender blond girl of about Evan's age sat in the chair next to Evan, talking animatedly. Dawn had a feeling she had seen the girl before but wasn't sure where. *She's probably one of Janet's patients, and I saw her in the waiting room before.*

Dawn watched as the blond girl gestured while she talked. Evan just sat and listened with her trademark stoic expression. The girl didn't let that bother her. She touched Evan's arm, obviously asking some question about her tattoo.

Dawn expected Evan to scowl and move away from the uninvited touch, but Evan just looked down at the smaller girl with a confident half smile that once again reminded Dawn of Aiden. *Where's that "touch me and I'll bite off your arm" attitude gone?* She clearly remembered how Evan had refused to even shake her hand. *Guess you just have to be young, blond, and attractive. Wait, I am young, blond, and attractive.* She watched the teenagers with a smile. *Face it, Kinsley, you're getting old.*

She stepped into the waiting room.

The blond girl greeted her with a friendly smile while Evan clearly wasn't very happy to see her.

"Hello, Evan," Dawn said. "I'm sorry to interrupt you and your friend—"

"She's not my friend!" Evan growled, ignoring the girl and her hurt expression. "Just a fellow sufferer whose parents think therapy is fashionable." She stood without giving the blond girl another glance and strode toward Dawn's office. "You coming, Doc?" she said over her shoulder. "You're wasting my time and money. I'm your paying customer after all, and she isn't."

She's embarrassed that I saw her being nice to someone, Dawn realized, *and now she has to reestablish her bad-girl persona. It wouldn't do to have me think she was softhearted, after all.* She gave the blond girl an apologetic smile and followed Evan into her office. Evan had chosen her usual chair, so Dawn moved around her desk and sat down behind it. "Why did you hurt her?" Dawn asked, pointing to the now closed door and the waiting area beyond.

"Did I?" Evan shrugged, pretending not to care at all.

Dawn fixed her with a stern gaze. "Do you know her?"

"Not in the biblical sense," Evan answered, "at least not yet." She flashed a confident grin.

Dawn very nearly rolled her eyes. "Do you know her name?" she asked more precisely.

"Lori or Lauren or something." Evan shrugged. "I usually don't ask girls their names. Too much trouble to keep them all straight. No pun intended, of course." She winked at Dawn.

Dear God! If this is what raising a child that's even a bit like Aiden is like, I should probably reconsider my plans for motherhood, Dawn thought with a mental shake of her head. "Who's wasting time and money now?" she asked, looking Evan right in the eyes. "Why did you hurt her? And try to give an honest answer this time. You don't need to impress me with cool repartees."

Evan looked down, studying the knickknacks on Dawn's desk. "It wasn't that bad," she mumbled. "It was supposed to be funny, and if she had any sense of humor—"

"Do you find it funny when people tell you straight out you're not their friend and imply it's a waste of time to talk to you?" Dawn interrupted another lame excuse.

"Hey, you just implied that about me, Doc," Evan pointed out with a grin.

Dawn didn't acknowledge that with an answer. She just looked at Evan.

"Okay, maybe it wasn't all that funny," Evan conceded.

"Why say it, then?" Dawn dug deeper. "Why did you go out of your way to be rude to her? She seemed nice, and I don't think she did anything to deserve that kind of treatment, did she?" She managed to make it sound like a neutral question, not as if she was telling Evan off.

Evan shrugged, still not looking at Dawn. "People don't always get what they deserve. Who said life was fair, Doc?"

"Your life or life in general?" Dawn asked. They were getting closer to the issue now. Evan hated her life, maybe even hated herself, and she tended to take it out on others.

"Both, I guess," Evan answered with another bored shrug.

Dawn nodded thoughtfully. "So what's so unfair about your life?"

"Oh, is this the part where you want me to spill my guts about my unhappy childhood, Doc?" Evan gave her an arrogant smirk, but one of her knees began to bounce up and down, betraying her nervousness.

"Tell me about it," Dawn encouraged without bothering to correct Evan's choice of words. She knew Evan was trying to get her to start a discussion about her provocations, just so she wouldn't have to talk about herself and her feelings. "What were you like as a child?"

Evan threw her head back in an exaggerated laugh. "Oh, I was a sweet little angel. Why else would no one want to adopt me?"

She blames herself, thinks there's something wrong with her. "How old were you when they put you in the foster system?"

Evan glared at her but answered, "Six."

"And before that? Did you live with your mother?" Dawn asked.

Evan roughly shook her head.

"Why not?" Dawn knew she was prying, but she needed to know more about Evan's family history if she wanted to understand her. "Did she... die?"

"I wish." Evan snorted. "Nope. Last I heard, she was still alive and kickin'."

So she's not dead. She somehow chose to give up her daughter. That's where all this anger and secret self-doubts are coming from. "Why couldn't she keep you, then? Did she think she was too young or too poor to be a good mother?" Dawn asked softly.

"She didn't want to be a mother!" Evan was almost screaming at her.

Dawn didn't believe it was that simple. "But she chose to have you anyway. She gave birth to you."

"That wasn't her idea. She would have killed me without a second thought, but my grandmother talked her out of it." Evan's voice was low and empty now, all her anger gone. For the first time, something like respect, if not affection, flickered across her face.

"So you lived with your mother and grandmother until you were six?" Dawn asked, trying to put the puzzle together.

"You think good old Mom stuck around long enough to meet me, huh?" Now the sarcasm was back full force. "Dream on, Doc; she didn't."

"I'm sorry to hear that," Dawn said sincerely. She knew Evan didn't want to hear it, but she needed to say it anyway. She wanted to show Evan that she was allowed to show feelings other than anger about her mother's abandonment of her.

Evan snatched a stress ball from Dawn's desk. For a moment, she looked as if she wanted to throw it at Dawn. "I don't need your sympathy!"

"I'm not only sorry for you. I'm sorry for your mother too," Dawn explained. It was a calculated answer, and it provoked the explosion she had expected.

"What? Why would you feel sorry for her?" Evan squeezed the stress ball until her knuckles whitened. "She got what she wanted!"

Dawn shifted onto the edge of her chair, leaning closer. "I'm sorry for her because she missed out on a lot of things."

"Like what? Paying for the therapy bills of her messed-up daughter?" Evan snapped. "Visiting me in juvie? Having to reheat dinner because I'm stuck in detention again?"

Dawn waited until Evan had calmed down enough to hear her answer. "The way you just said that, you didn't make it sound like accomplishments. You're not as proud of being a badass as you want everybody to believe."

"Hey, it's what I'm good at," Evan tossed back with a grin that didn't quite reach her usual level of confidence.

"I'm sure there are other things you're good at besides breaking the rules," Dawn said. *I'd bet she's a little like Aiden not only in the looks department. She's probably good at every sport she tries. She's physically fit, intelligent, and charming if she wants to be. Now I only have to get her to see herself in that light.*

Evan smirked and opened her mouth for an answer.

"I don't want the smart-ass version," Dawn interrupted before she could say anything. "I want you to think about it and answer honestly." She had a feeling Evan had been about to give her a list of sexual activities or something like that.

"Well, if you put it like that, I guess I'm not good at anything." Evan leaned back, folding her arms across her chest as she had at the very beginning of their first session.

"Then that's your homework," Dawn decided. "Until your next session on Monday, I want you to find something you're good at. Write about it and describe it to me." She handed Evan a notepad.

Evan negligently threw the notepad down at the floor next to her chair. "I'm good at forgetting to do my homework."

"Something positive," Dawn said, slowly pronouncing every syllable. "I want you to find something positive you're good at. And I mean my definition of positive, not yours." She smiled at Evan but kept her gaze firm.

"All right, I'll try," Evan promised vaguely but didn't pick up the notepad.

"So, let's talk about your grandmother," Dawn said.

Evan slid down in her chair and sprawled her legs out until she was almost lying in her chair. "Nothing to talk about. She's dead."

She died when Evan was six. That's why they put her into foster care, Dawn concluded. Talking to Evan was like pulling teeth, and she had to put the pieces of information together on her own. "Was she a good substitute parent?" she asked Evan.

Evan's leather jacket creaked as she shrugged.

Dawn noticed for the first time that Evan had yet to take off that article of clothing. *Layers of protection.* "Can you give a more detailed answer?"

"I guess," Evan mumbled. "She didn't beat me or anything."

"But that's not enough to make a good parent, is it? Otherwise, you'd be a lot happier to stay with your foster parents," Dawn said gently.

Evan looked up, surprise clearly written all over her face for the second it took her to put on her mask of bored stoicism again.

She didn't expect me to question the LeCroixs' qualities as parents when everyone else thinks she's the only one to blame for things not going well. "Why don't you tell me a little about her," she suggested, leaning back in her chair again.

"About Jill or my grandmother?" Evan asked, still looking a little unsettled.

This time, it was Dawn's turn to shrug. "Whoever you want to start with."

Evan eyed her for a few seconds. "You already had a little chat with Jill, so you probably already know everything of interest about her." There was a silent accusation in her voice.

Shit. I should have addressed that sooner. Dawn stood and circled the desk, perching on the edge of it right next to Evan's chair. "Yes, she was here in my office earlier. I'm sorry I haven't told you."

"You're not even denying it?" Evan asked in disbelief.

"Why should I?" Dawn answered as calmly as possible. "I have nothing to hide from you."

"Whooo-hoooo!" Evan whistled lewdly and wiggled her eyebrows.

Dawn knew that only served to hide how hurt she was. "Evan," she said and waited until the teenager looked up. "I made it very clear to your foster mother that I'm your therapist, not hers. Our sessions are strictly confidential. I don't report to her."

Evan snorted. "She's the one who pays your bills."

"I don't care about the bills. I care about you." Dawn cursed herself as soon as she had said it. "I care about helping you," she quickly amended, not wanting to give Evan room for any misinterpretations.

Evan was silent for a long time. When she looked up, the anger and hurt were gone from her face. "Jill hasn't thumped me over the head with her Bible or thrown me out of the house for sleeping with a girl, so you probably haven't told her yet."

"I didn't," Dawn said, keeping eye contact to show Evan that she wasn't hiding anything. "And I won't."

"We'll see," Evan answered noncommittally.

Dawn just nodded. She knew it would take time to earn Evan's trust. "Is there a reason why you haven't told your foster mother that you like girls? You weren't exactly shy about it with me, so why hide it from her?"

"I'm not hiding it," Evan said. "It just hasn't come up. We don't talk a lot."

Dawn could easily believe that. Evan wasn't willing to talk, and Mrs. LeCroix wasn't willing to listen. She wasn't listening to what Evan's rebellious behavior was saying either. Still, Dawn was convinced there was another reason why Evan hadn't thrown her sexual orientation in Jill's face. "Are you afraid to tell her?"

"Afraid? Ha!" Evan slapped her jean-clad thighs.

Dawn shook her head. "Don't laugh it off so easily. Coming out to people you depend on can be a scary thing because you don't know how they'll react."

"I don't care about her reaction or what she thinks about me," Evan protested. "And I certainly don't depend on her. If she doesn't want to live under the same roof with a queer, I'll just be shuffled off to yet another foster home. Who cares?"

"Do you know why Jill wanted to talk to me?" Dawn asked, seemingly changing the topic.

"She's a nosy bitch; that's why!" Evan grumbled.

Dawn ignored the comment. "She's worried about you." She talked right over Evan's sarcastic snort. "She's afraid you're gonna hurt yourself with drugs or partying... and that you might get pregnant."

Evan didn't seem surprised to hear that. "No chance of that," she said, amusement coloring her voice. "My bedpartners lack the kind of equipment you'd need for that."

"Yes, but Jill doesn't know that." Dawn abstained from telling Evan that even if she couldn't get pregnant, STDs were still a concern. That would be a topic for another session. "You purposely let her believe you're sleeping with the boys you hang around."

"I'm not responsible for the stupid assumptions she makes," Evan said, but the gleam in her brown eyes told Dawn she had enjoyed letting her foster mother believe it.

Dawn threw a quick glance at the small clock on her desk. "Our time's up for today."

"Oh, how time flies when you're having fun," Evan commented, the sarcasm very evident in her voice.

Dawn bit back a witty answer and ignored the comment. "Until our next session on Monday, I want you to think about why you enjoy letting Jill worry about you."

"More homework?" Evan groaned.

"Well," Dawn said with her sweetest smile, "you did say you were bored, didn't you?"

Evan's expression didn't change, but Dawn had studied her facial expressions and body language for two hours now. She had the impression that Evan barely managed to hold back an answering smile. "I have to watch what I say around you in the future, Doc," Evan said after a moment of silence.

"No, you don't," Dawn said very seriously. "That's what therapy is all about. You can say whatever you want as long as you try to be honest with yourself."

Evan stood and strode toward the door without answering.

Dawn didn't even need to look to know that the notepad with her homework instruction was still lying next to her chair. "Aren't you forgetting something?"

"You want me to kiss you good-bye?" Evan flashed a grin over her shoulder.

God, I hope there's a special place in therapists' heaven reserved for me for agreeing to take her on. "No, thanks," she answered without batting an eye. She threw Evan the notepad. "See you Monday."

CHAPTER 7

KADE'S SNEAKERS crunched over the gravel as she paced up and down to keep warm. It was five past six, and the sun was slowly starting to rise over the Riverplace Marina, but Del Vasquez wasn't there to see it.

Kade shot a glance back up into the direction of her condo building. *This was a bad idea,* she told herself. *Remember how your last "date" with her ended? Wasn't once enough? Since when are you a glutton for punishment? Five more minutes and I'll go back home or go running without her.*

She had barely finished the thought when the crunching of gravel made her look up.

Del was charging down the path toward the marina at full speed.

Kade pointedly glanced at her watch.

Del skidded to a halt in front of Kade. "Sorry, I—" She stopped and bent over to catch her breath.

Kade watched, alternating between irritation and amusement. "I thought we'd go running together, and here you are, looking as if you already had your morning run."

"No." Del finally straightened and shoved a strand of black hair off her face. "I came straight from a crime scene. Thank God I had my running clothes in my car."

"You could have called me to cancel—"

"No!" Del said quickly. "No, I'd enjoy a good run after being crouched over evidence all night. I'm fine, really, so let's go."

Kade eyed her skeptically. Del looked exhausted, but Kade couldn't help feeling a little flattered at having Del so determined to spend time with her. "Okay," she said. "Then let's go. I promise to go easy on you."

"Ha!" Del snorted as they began to jog along the river. "With all the adrenaline still running through my system, you better hope that I'll go easy on you."

Kade just smiled and picked up the pace.

They ran side by side for a while, evenly matched.

Kade hadn't had a running partner in a long time. She preferred running alone because it gave her the time to go over her schedule for the day or to practice her opening and closing arguments.

Still, as far as running partners went, Del wasn't so bad. She didn't try to make conversation, and Kade appreciated the companionable silence.

A few bikers and two in-line skaters zipped past, but otherwise the path wasn't too crowded yet. Two uniformed officers patrolled the Esplanade, and Del greeted them with a playful salute.

As they got closer to the Hawthorne Bridge, Kade noticed that Del's playfulness and the smiles she gave Kade whenever they made eye contact were replaced by a more serious expression. "You okay?" she asked. "Need a break?"

"What?" Del's head swiveled around to face her. "Oh, no, I'm fine. It's just..." She gestured to the left. "I just noticed that I haven't been here in a while."

"And why should you?" Kade didn't understand. "I think Aiden mentioned you live in St. Johns, so this is not exactly your neighborhood. You probably have a jogging route there." That's why Kade had been surprised and a little suspicious when Del had suggested the marina as a meeting place.

"That's not what I mean." Del pointed again.

Kade looked and finally understood. To their left, she could see the wall of the Portland Police Memorial. *Her partner, Dawn's father, is one of the names on the wall,* she realized.

"I used to go there with Dawn every week," Del said a little wistfully.

"You don't do it anymore?" Kade asked.

Del looked away from the memorial and gave her a smile. "Every once in a while. I think Dawn goes with Carlisle too. She would have loved for her father to meet Carlisle, and this is the only way to make Dawn feel as if she can somehow connect these two parts of her life."

Great. What do I say now? Kade wasn't used to dealing with other people's emotions so early in the morning. "Want to go now?" She added a teasing smile to break the sudden tension. "You look like you could need a break anyway."

Del thought about it for a moment. "No," she finally said. "I appreciate the offer, but Jimmy, my partner, would be the first to kick my ass if I dragged a beautiful woman over to stare morosely at the memorial instead of just enjoying her company."

She wants to live in the present, huh? Kade could understand that. "Okay. So let's see how much you're going to enjoy my company if I kick your ass in a little race," she suggested.

Del flashed her a grin. "All right. You can try. So, what are the terms of the race, and is there a prize involved for the winner?"

"No prize. The first one at Salmon Street Springs wins. Ready? Go!" Kade shouted and raced ahead of her without waiting for Del's confirmation.

"Hey! Wait up, you little cheater!" Del yelled, but Kade could hear the laughter in her voice.

Kade just grinned and picked up her pace.

* * *

Del slipped into the courtroom just as Judge Ruth Linehan banged her gavel, ending the trial for the day.

The observers stood from their benches in the gallery and filed out of the courtroom. Some of them threw Del annoyed glances as they had to move around her, but she stood her ground and just flipped back her jacket, revealing the gold shield clipped to her belt. She looked right past them, her gaze immediately zeroing in on the red-haired woman behind the prosecution's table.

The DA's office employed a lot of young, attractive DDAs, but even without her turning around, Del knew she had found

Kade Matheson. After trying to keep up with those long Matheson legs for an hour just yesterday morning, she would know them anywhere, even from behind.

She let her gaze wander over the well-formed calves and up the rest of Kadence Matheson, taking in the custom-tailored skirt, the expensive blazer, and the perfectly styled hair. *Hmm, I just love a good-looking woman in a power suit!* Kade embodied elegance, style, and confidence. Del watched the slender hands sort files and legal pads neatly back into a leather briefcase.

What's this? Are you suddenly developing a lawyer fetish? Del asked herself, then shook her head. She knew it wasn't like that. In all her years in law enforcement, no DDA, and certainly no defense lawyer, had ever impressed her like that. She did like Stacy Ford, the homicide DDA, but she had never gone out of her way to catch a glimpse of her in court.

You could have had it so much easier if you had been interested in Ford, Del pointed out to herself. *She's a lesbian even if she doesn't advertise it. But no, you just had to be interested in this straight, blue-blooded prosecutor.*

Kade slung her briefcase over her shoulder and turned around.

By now, Del was the only person left in the gallery, so Kade's gaze met hers immediately. With an inviting smile, Del held open the gate that separated the front of the courtroom from the gallery.

Kade strode up to her on three-inch heels, passing through the gate with a casualness that told Del she was very used to having doors held open for her. "Don't they keep you busy enough at the North Precinct, Lieutenant?" Kade asked by way of greeting. There was no smile and no warmth in her voice. Kade was all business, but Del thought she could detect a welcoming light shining in Kade's eyes.

"Oh, yes, they do. I'm actually here for professional reasons," Del said with a smile. "I'm searching for a DDA."

Kade looked at her with curiosity. "And now that you've found one, what are you intending to do with her?"

Del stared at her. *Is it wishful thinking, or is she flirting with me?* "Hmm, maybe I'm gonna drag her off and make her comply with my every wish?" she said with a playful wink.

Elegant hands tightened around the strap of the briefcase, and the kingfisher blue eyes narrowed dangerously.

"Relax." Del laughed. "There's only one thing I want from you right now."

"And that is?" Kade asked a little warily.

"I need a DDA to get a judge to sign my search warrant," Del said.

Kade still looked skeptical. "I'm not a homicide DDA."

Sad but true. Getting to see her at work is not one of my job benefits. "I know, but I couldn't find Stacy Ford anywhere, and I was in the neighborhood, so I thought I'd say hello and ask for a little interdepartmental help," Del answered as smoothly as possible.

A perfect copper-colored eyebrow arched up. "Mixing business and pleasure, Lieutenant?"

Del just shrugged and smiled. "Multitasking can be a good thing."

"Not in my job," Kade said. "A good prosecutor has to concentrate on the case and on nothing else."

"While she's on the job, yes. But you're not trying a case right now, are you?" Del said, gracing Kade with her most patient smile. She could sense that she had to be gentle but persuasive if she ever wanted to have a more than professional relationship with the workaholic DDA.

"No," Kade answered. "But you are. What is so urgent about this search warrant that you have to hunt down a sex crimes DDA?"

With a self-mocking smile, Del gave up on her attempts to get Kade to talk to her on a more personal basis. Within these sacred halls, Kade Matheson was all business. "We just found our main suspect's fingerprints at the crime scene, and I want my detectives to search his apartment for the murder weapon before he decides to take a vacation abroad," she told Kade.

"You have fingerprint evidence, and yet you're not going for an arrest warrant? What aren't you telling me?" Kade asked.

This is one brilliant lawyer. She's not just a pretty face and a hot body. Not that Del had ever assumed otherwise. *So this is where I have to make a decision—tell her the truth and risk losing my chance at a search warrant, or lie and get one?* Looking into Kade's eyes, the decision was an easy one. "Our suspect claims to have an alibi—he was out on a date with the police commissioner's niece."

"So that's why they sent a lieutenant to obtain a simple search warrant," Kade said without even batting an eye.

That and my eagerness to see you again, Del thought but refrained from saying it. She knew Kade was already aware of her feelings. Anything more would just chase her away. "It's a delicate situation," she answered, using her captain's words.

Kade's gaze was stern, totally unimpressed. "Nobody is above the law, not even the police commissioner's niece. Have your detectives questioned her?"

Del nodded. "We can't prove it, but we think she's covering for him. None of her neighbors saw him entering or leaving her apartment."

"Then let's try and get you that search warrant." Kade strode out into the hallway.

Del hastily caught up with her. "Where are you going? There's a judge with two able hands right next door," she said, pointing to the chambers adjoining the courtroom.

"No." Kade resolutely shook her head. "Asking Judge Linehan for a favor with me in tow is not a bright idea."

Del laughed. "What did you do?"

"Do?" The inscrutable lawyer poker face was firmly in place. "What makes you think I did anything?"

"Because that's the same expression you had yesterday morning when you used that little trick to get a head start in our race," Del said with a smile. She actually hadn't minded coming in second because it had given her the opportunity to watch Kade in her tight running pants.

Kade grinned for a second, then the professional DDA was back as she stopped and knocked on a door, motioning Del to follow her into the room.

Judge Thayer? Del groaned internally when she saw the gray-haired, dignified judge who was sitting behind his desk. Henry Thayer wasn't known for making it easy on detectives coming to beg for a warrant. He had shot Del down in three seconds the last time she had knocked on his door. *We should have taken our chances with Linehan.*

"Your Honor," Kade said, very businesslike. "We need you to sign a search warrant in a homicide case."

Couldn't she have at least tried to soften him up with one of those dazzling Matheson smiles I know she's capable of? Del sighed.

The judge moved his glasses higher up on his nose and studied Kade, then his gaze wandered over to Del. "What's going on here?" he asked without answering their demand for a search warrant.

"What do you mean?" Kade could play innocent with the best of them.

"A decorated Portland Police Bureau lieutenant and a sex crimes DDA come to ask me for a search warrant in a homicide? What's going on?" Judge Thayer asked again, this time with even less patience.

Del took a step forward, but Kade lifted a single finger, silently indicating for Del to let her handle it. Del nodded and remained silent.

"The suspect has an alibi witness covering for him who has friends in high places," Kade told the judge.

"Who?" Henry Thayer demanded to know.

Kade looked him right in the eyes. "The police commissioner's niece."

"And you want me to sign that warrant, knowing full well that I play golf with the commissioner tomorrow morning?" Judge Thayer arched one silver-gray eyebrow.

Shit. Del grimaced. *There goes our search warrant.*

Del expected Kade to dazzle the judge with one of her brilliant legal arguments, but Kade just said a single word, "Yes." She laid the unsigned search warrant down on the judge's desk.

Thayer picked up a pen and signed the document without even looking at it.

"Thank you." Kade picked up the warrant and strode from the room.

Del hastily followed. "What just happened here?" she asked as soon as the door closed behind them.

"You got your search warrant," Kade said with just a hint of smugness, handing Del the document.

"He didn't even ask what evidence we had or warn us to tread carefully with the commissioner's niece!" Del shook her head. "That's not the hard-assed Judge Thayer I know. Last time I was in there, he practically made me crawl over shards of glass before he signed that damn warrant!"

Kade didn't answer. A small smile played around her lips as she continued to walk down the courthouse hallway in her busy-lawyer clip.

"Maybe he's the admirer who sent you all these flowers," Del said. He certainly wouldn't be the first officer of the law to fall prey to Kade Matheson's charms.

Kade stiffened and sent a cool glance back over her shoulder. "He isn't."

They reached the courthouse's exit, and Del jogged a few steps to overtake Kade and open the heavy doors for her. "Why are you so sure?" Del didn't think Kade was one to underestimate her own attractiveness. More often than not, she seemed to be very aware of the effect she had on people.

"He's my uncle," Kade said, never stopping on her way down the courthouse steps.

"What? Judge Thayer is your uncle?" Del wanted to slap herself. Calling her uncle a hard-ass was probably not the way to get into Kade's good graces. "I didn't know that."

Kade reached the end of the stairs but didn't stop to look at Del. "Why would you?" she answered calmly.

Yeah, why would I? Kade certainly isn't forthcoming with personal information about herself or her family, Del thought with a sigh.

"And just to make one thing crystal clear..." Kade stopped in her hurried walk down Fourth Avenue and turned to look at Del. "He didn't sign the search warrant because I'm his niece. He signed it because he knows I would never ask him to if there wasn't a solid evidence base."

Del stared into the flashing blue eyes. *This means a lot to her. She made it this far in her career because she's good at what she does and because she works her ass off, not because her family paved the way.* "I'd never think otherwise," she said honestly.

Kade nodded and then continued her brisk walk down the street.

"Has anyone ever told you that it's not a good idea to train for the marathon in high heels?" Del said when she caught up with her. She had wanted to ask Kade to grab a coffee with her, but it seemed Kade was in a hurry to get back to her office or wherever else she was headed.

Kade turned, a frown on her face, until she realized to what Del was referring. "Sorry. It has become a habit lately."

Del almost missed it. She had paid very close attention to every little detail about Kade, had studied her body language, her facial expressions, and the nuances of her voice ever since she had first met her, and now that intense appraisal paid off. There was a certain note of troubled resignation in Kade's voice that had nothing to do with the pressures of her job. "Lately?" she repeated, her gaze never leaving Kade's face. She took a step closer when Kade didn't answer immediately. "Kade, is everything all right?"

"I'm fine," Kade said and resumed her walk at an only slightly slower pace.

What is she running from? Del studied the elegant line of Kade's back. *Is it me?* "Kade..."

"Listen, I have to get back to the office, and you have a search warrant to execute," Kade said, resolutely pointing at the document in Del's hands.

"Right," Del conceded with a sigh, but then decided not to give up just yet. Kade Matheson was worth a little patience. "If we find the murder weapon, I'll invite you for coffee."

Kade calmly shook her head. "That's not necessary. I was just doing my job."

"Well, strictly speaking, you weren't. You're not a homicide DDA," Del said, allowing a small grin to show as she repeated Kade's earlier words and beat her with her own weapons. "Coffee is the least I can do after insulting your uncle."

Kade turned back around. An impish glint warmed her ice blue eyes. "You didn't. Uncle Henry **is** a hard-ass—and so is every other member of my family."

Del laughed. "Present Matheson included?"

Kade simply raised an eyebrow. "What do you think?"

"I think I like hard-asses and that I'll call you about that coffee date." Del lifted the search warrant. "Thanks again. Take care." She turned and walked away before Kade could again refuse her offer to go out for coffee.

CHAPTER 8

AIDEN THREW HER badge down on the coffee table and kicked off her shoes. She reached into the fridge for a beer and guzzled down half of it in one gulp. She knew she should probably be tired and go straight to bed after the eight-hour interrogation they had just finished, but the adrenaline was still pumping through her veins.

After eight long hours of looking into their suspect's smirking face, they had finally managed to provoke him into a confession. When he realized what he had blurted out in his anger, the perp had jumped across the table at her, and Aiden had taken a certain satisfaction in slamming the cruel rapist of a young mother down on the table and cuffing him.

Aiden prowled through the living room, knowing she was too charged to sleep. Six months ago, she wouldn't have gone straight home after leaving the precinct—or if she had, she certainly wouldn't have been alone. A night like this had often resulted in one-night stands. Sex had always been her way of relieving a little tension and dealing with the emotions her job evoked.

Now that she was in a steady relationship, that form of stress relief was out of the question. It was also too late for a workout with her punching bag or a run through the neighborhood. Aiden resigned herself to a sleepless night in a cold bed. She trudged into the bathroom, pulling off her blouse as she went.

She frowned when she couldn't find the T-shirt in which she usually slept where she had left it in the bathroom this morning. *I'm not that tired, am I? I could have sworn I left it right here.* Finally, she shrugged out of her bra and decided not to bother with a T-shirt. She was alone tonight, so no one would object to her choice—or lack—of sleepwear.

She finished her beer and rounded the couch, finding her way to the dark bedroom by sense of touch and memory alone. She slipped under the covers—and almost jumped out of her skin.

Instead of the cold sheets she had expected, she encountered warm skin. She flicked on the bedside lamp.

Dawn was sleeping peacefully right next to her. The covers had halfway slipped off, revealing Aiden's missing sleep shirt. It loosely covered the gentle curves of her lover.

A tingle shot through her, and the happy grin that formed on her lips felt almost unfamiliar after the grimness of her workday. *What's she doing here? Not that I'm complaining.* Aiden turned off the light and slipped under the covers again, immediately snuggling up to Dawn.

Dawn's warm body felt so good against her own, and there was something incredibly sexy about knowing Dawn was wearing her T-shirt—and probably not much else. Aiden pressed her face against Dawn's soft neck and deeply breathed in her enticing scent.

Dawn began to stir against her, turning in Aiden's embrace.

Heat flooded through Aiden as she felt Dawn's breasts press against her own, and she reflexively pulled Dawn even closer.

"Hmmmhm," Dawn mumbled, snuggling even closer. Her lips sleepily skimmed Aiden's collarbone. "Aid'n?"

"Yeah," Aiden answered. One of her hands slipped under Dawn's sleep shirt to draw circles on the soft, warm skin. "I'm home."

Dawn's eyes blinked open. A sleepy grin formed on her lips when she made out Aiden in the darkness.

"What are you doing here?" Aiden asked, very distracted by the sudden discovery that Dawn wasn't even wearing panties. Her sleepover must have been a last-minute decision. Both of them rarely stayed over at the other's apartment on weeknights.

"'s lonely," Dawn murmured, still not fully awake.

Aiden rolled around, covering the pliant body of her lover with her own. "Let's see if we can't change that," she seductively whispered against Dawn's lips.

Dawn lazily returned Aiden's kiss, and her arms came up to wrap around Aiden, not moving, just holding on.

The casual submissiveness ignited an unexpected spark in Aiden. Suddenly, she wanted nothing more than to conquer Dawn, to awaken her passion, and make her come to life. She trailed challenging nips down the soft skin of Dawn's throat, and when Dawn arched up against her, she lifted one of Dawn's legs and wrapped it around her hip.

Dawn's warm hands clutched at her, firing her body temperature up even more.

One hand pressed against the bed for leverage, Aiden began to move against Dawn while her other hand tugged up her sleep shirt until her mouth could meet Dawn's bare breast.

Dawn groaned. Her fingers slid up Aiden's back and tangled in her short hair.

Aiden nipped at an erect nipple with gentle teeth and moved her hand down between their bodies.

"No!"

The word hit her like a slap in the face. Aiden froze and stared down at Dawn, who was stiffly lying there, her chest heaving and her face flushed.

"I'm sorry, but I can't. Not tonight," Dawn whispered. She was looking at the ceiling, not meeting Aiden's gaze.

Aiden quickly rolled off her partner's warm body and onto the cold sheets. She threw an arm over her eyes and closed them tightly. "You all right?" she asked after a few seconds, trying in vain to make her voice gentle. She could hear desire, guilt, and anger roughen her voice, and she knew Dawn could hear it too.

"Yeah." Dawn exhaled shakily. "It just got a little intense there for a second." She rolled around and leaned over Aiden, looking down at her with gentle green eyes. "Hey, are you okay?" She reached out a hand to stroke a damp strand of hair from Aiden's face.

Aiden quickly rolled out of bed. She couldn't stand Dawn's gentleness right now. She didn't deserve the loving touches.

"Aiden?" Dawn called after her, clearly confused by the abrupt departure. "Where are you going?"

Aiden pressed her lips together. Another thing that was different now: she couldn't just get dressed and slip out of her bedpartner's apartment without comment. "I forgot to take a shower," she said. Suddenly, she felt as if she needed one to wash away the guilt and frustration. Half-drunk with emotions, she stumbled through the dark apartment and into the bathroom.

She stood under the scalding hot water, her hands pressed against the cold tiles, and let the water beat down on her back like a medieval instrument of torture. A mental picture of her passionately pressing a female partner against the wall of the very same shower flashed through her mind, and she hit her fist against the tiles. *Stop it!* she yelled at herself. *You're not an animal, only controlled by its needs! You're not like your father!*

The shower curtain was pulled back.

Aiden looked up, sputtering.

Dawn slipped the sleep shirt over her head, let it drop to the floor, and stepped into the shower without a word.

"Dawn..." Aiden said, moving back half a step.

Dawn moved under the water and into Aiden's arms.

Aiden quickly adjusted the water to a more bearable temperature and tried to move out of Dawn's embrace, but Dawn stubbornly held on and pressed her lips gently to one of the red marks the hot water had left on Aiden's shoulder.

"What are you doing to yourself?" Dawn asked, her voice a worried whisper.

"To myself?" Aiden laughed roughly. "You mean, what am I doing to you?"

Dawn pulled Aiden's head around, forcing her to look into her eyes. "You haven't done anything wrong."

Aiden snorted. Even now, Dawn was trying to defend her. "I practically ambushed you!"

"Mm-hm, in a very nice way," Dawn agreed with a smile.

"Oh, stop it, Dawn!" Aiden shut off the water and stepped out of the shower. "You were clearly not in the mood, and I—"

Dawn followed her, stepping close in the cramped space of the small bathroom. "And you were; there's nothing wrong with that. I enjoyed what you were doing. It's just... everything is just so close to the surface tonight, and I suddenly felt so out of control, and I could smell beer on your breath."

Tonight. The sudden realization hit Aiden with force. "You got your test results back today?" With all that had happened at work, she had almost forgotten about it. A cold sweat broke out on her still wet skin, and she felt as if she couldn't force enough oxygen into her lungs.

Dawn nodded. "Don't worry. Everything's fine. It just brought back a lot of memories. Sitting in the waiting room, that feeling of helplessness..."

You're an asshole, Carlisle! Aiden grabbed a towel and roughly dried herself. *An asshole of gigantic proportions!*

"Stop it!" Dawn took the towel away from her and gently dabbed it over Aiden's skin. "Don't punish yourself for wanting to make love to your girlfriend."

"I didn't want to make love! I wanted to have sex!" Aiden snapped before she could stop herself. She abruptly turned and stormed out of the bathroom, gathering her clothes and slipping into them as she went.

By the time Dawn stumbled out of the bathroom, shrugging into a bathrobe, the door of the apartment fell closed behind Aiden.

* * *

Kade closed the thick law book with a resounding "thud." She threw the pen down on her legal pad and leaned back with a groan, looking down at the work she had managed to complete tonight. *Being stalked has its advantages,* she decided with a self-mocking grin. She had stayed late every day for the last week, feeling safer in her office with the security guard downstairs than at home. By now, she was almost caught up with all the paperwork and trial prep—a miracle that hadn't happened since she had started working with the sex crimes unit.

A quick glance at her watch showed her that it was almost midnight. She looked at the small sofa, contemplating staying and sleeping in the office for another night, but then she dismissed the thought. She was due in Judge Trenton's court first thing tomorrow morning, and she hadn't brought a change of clothes.

She packed her briefcase with a few documents she wanted to review tomorrow morning over coffee and picked up a stack of files. She would drop them off at the precinct on her way home so that the detectives would find them when they came in tomorrow morning.

The security guard hardly looked up when she wished him a good night anymore. He had gotten used to her nightly presence by now.

Kade paused on the front steps for a moment, staring into the darkness. Everything was quiet. *Don't be silly,* she reprimanded herself. *No one but a workaholic DDA would voluntarily hang around here after midnight. Even amorous, flower-sending stalkers keep office hours that are shorter than yours.*

She stepped into the darkness and strode to her car without pausing. A few minutes later, she gathered the files from the passenger seat and stepped out of the car.

Two officers from the night shift, leaning against their patrol cars during a cigarette break, greeted her. Kade gave them a stern nod but didn't stop to chat.

She made her way through the still busy squad room toward the Carlisle/Bennet desks that should have been empty this time of night.

Aiden sat behind her desk, staring off into space. She rubbed her neck with one hand while the other played with a pen. Kade had seen her do this a hundred times before, sometimes during a witness interview, sometimes while she studied a crime scene report, but this time, Kade got the impression Aiden wasn't obsessing about her work.

Kade set down her files on Ray's desk. "Aiden?" she asked quietly.

Aiden didn't react.

"Aiden?" Kade said, this time a little louder.

Aiden jumped and whirled her chair around. "What?" she snapped, clearly irritated. Then her gaze softened when she recognized who was standing in front of her. "Oh, hey, Kade. What are you doing here at..." She glanced at her watch. "...midnight?"

"Same thing you're doing, it would seem." Everyone knew that Aiden's workaholic tendencies were surpassed only by Kade's own.

Aiden barked out a laugh and mumbled something that sounded like, "So you're hiding from your lesbian lover too?"

"What?" Kade asked, pretending not to have heard. The truth was that all her years in the courtroom had sharpened her hearing. Being able to understand all the whispered reprimands of sleazy defense lawyers in front of the bench was all the incentive Kade needed to school her hearing.

"I said I just need to finish up a few things," Aiden said, trying to appear hard at work by reading through a witness statement that had already been highlighted.

Kade knew that was not the reason why Aiden was still at the precinct, and she knew Aiden was aware that she knew. But in the past, both of them had always respected those polite little lies. Both had been careful not to cross the boundaries of professionalism. When they talked, it was work they discussed, not their private lives.

But during the last few months, something had changed. Kade couldn't say what exactly it was. They were still the competent detective and the confident deputy district attorney, and the Sexual Assault Detail still worked the toughest cases in Portland, so she had tried to tell herself that nothing had changed. Still, she could feel that something was different.

It had all started when she had confessed to Aiden that she was going out on a date with Del on Valentine's Day. *Interpersonal relationships are like practicing law: once there's a confession, the game is over. There's no going back,* she thought, then raised a skeptical eyebrow at herself. *Oh yeah? If practicing law and interpersonal relationships are so much alike, how come you're so good at one and so very bad at the other?*

She returned her attention to Aiden and noticed she wasn't pretending to read through the witness statement any longer. Instead, she was staring at one of the pictures on her desk, lost in thought.

At first Kade thought it was the photo of Aiden's mother that she had seen before when she had perched on the edge of Aiden's desk, but when she took a closer look, she saw that a new photograph had been added. Dawn Kinsley was smiling into the camera in a way that left no doubt in Kade's mind that Aiden had been the one taking the picture.

Dawn. She was a part of what had changed between Kade and Aiden. Aiden was in a steady relationship now, and that changed the dynamic between them. Not that either of them had ever seriously considered a relationship between them, at least Kade hadn't. Enjoying Aiden's admiring glances had been as far as she had allowed her thoughts to stray.

Aiden was a colleague, a detective working for her, and that automatically excluded her from ever ending up in the "romantic interest" category. Keeping her work and her private life separate had always been Kade's hard and fast rule.

Despite that personal law, her life and Aiden's were not as separate anymore as they had once been. They had slowly started to become more interwoven. Aiden had even called her "Aunt Kade" when she had thought she would start dating Del. Kade had confessed her interest in Del to Aiden, and that sign of trust had started them down a road of cautious friendship when they hadn't been more than friendly colleagues before.

"Can I ask you something?" Aiden's voice interrupted Kade's thoughts.

Kade nodded.

Aiden looked away from Dawn's picture. Her gaze landed on Kade. "What happened between you and Del?"

Kade quickly dragged Ray's chair around the desk and closer to Aiden's. She didn't want the whole squad room to overhear her answer, short as it was. "Nothing."

"Nothing?" Aiden obviously didn't believe that for a second.

"Nothing happened between us." Kade spelled it out as she would for a jury.

Aiden drummed her pen against the desk. "That much I already knew, or Dawn's friend would have let something slip at the Kinsleys' dinner table."

Kade narrowed her eyes and studied her. Why was it that Aiden always sounded a little brusque when she was talking about Del? "Dawn's friend?" she repeated. "Not 'our' friend? I thought lesbian couples weren't supposed to have separate circles of friends?"

"Are you afraid I'll lose my U-haul discount card? What did you do, research lesbian mating habits?" Aiden asked with the charming little Carlisle grin that almost made you forget the casual snark of her words.

Almost. "I thought you and Lieutenant Vasquez got along great?" Kade put a silent question into her words and ignored Aiden's comment. Her mating habits, lesbian or otherwise, weren't up for discussion while they were sitting in the middle of the squad room.

Aiden shrugged. "We do, I suppose."

"Then why are you insinuating that Lieutenant Vasquez would broadcast it to the whole Kinsley clan if anything had happened between us?" Kade put her well-practiced cross-exam stare to good use. Del was a decent, honorable person, and she wouldn't let Aiden insinuate otherwise. *Wait a minute! You thought she might be stalking you, and now you're defending her honor?*

"I'm not insinuating anything," Aiden interrupted Kade's internal monologue. "I'm just saying that any lesbian would have a hard time not shouting it from the rooftops if she had managed to be 'cross-examined' by a certain DDA."

Kade resolutely shook her head. "There was no cross-examination."

Aiden tilted her head. "Why not? I mean Dawn said she hadn't seen Del so interested in a woman in years, and there seemed to be a certain interest on your part too, so why didn't you let something happen?"

Kade glared at two police officers who wandered past Aiden's desk for the third time, making them suddenly remember that they were urgently expected somewhere else. Anywhere else. *Okay, this is clearly going a little too far for our first friendly talk. Is she really asking me why I didn't jump into bed with Del?* When Aiden continued to just look at her, her gaze open and nonjudgmental, Kade sighed. "I dismissed Lieutenant Vasquez from the witness stand when she broke the golden rule of lawyering," she answered, keeping up the lawyer analogies Aiden had started. That way she could pretend they were just discussing a case, and every eavesdropper would think the same.

"The golden rule of lawyering?" Aiden scratched the back of her neck. "That's not that 'Sometimes long legs are better than long legal arguments' thing, is it?"

Kade had to smile. She had told Aiden that a few months ago. *Figures she would remember it.* "No. The cardinal rule is to never ask a question you don't know the answer to."

Aiden nodded. She knew that principle. It was the reason for endless hours of witness preparation. "So Del asked a question she didn't know the answer to?"

"Worse," Kade said. "We both didn't know the answer."

"So that keeps you on equal footing. What's wrong with that?" Aiden looked at her inquisitively.

Kade sighed. "I thought I knew the answer, but it turned out I had completely misjudged the situation."

"You know," Aiden said, shaking her head, "we have to stop with that 'talking in legalese codes' thing, or I'll get lost in the translation. What situation are we talking about?"

There had been a certain playfulness to their conversation, both of them trying to forget that they were talking about some very complicated and very private things. But now Kade sobered. She didn't feel like wading through the minefield that was her private life tonight. If she told Aiden she had thought Del had sent her ninety-seven bouquets of flowers and then found out she hadn't, Aiden would immediately want to know who **had** sent the flowers—and that was another question to which Kade didn't know the answer.

For a moment, she contemplated telling Aiden everything: the flower deliveries, the cards, and the feeling of being followed. She knew Aiden would be willing to help her. *A little too willing, probably. Before I know it, I'd have a protective detail in front of my apartment and two cops following me around the courthouse.* Kade shook her head. She didn't want a private problem, which wasn't even a problem yet, spread all over Portland in triplicate. She wasn't in any real danger, so it was better not to make it official.

"What's this situation?" Aiden asked again when Kade didn't answer.

"It's..." Kade hesitated and then settled for, "complicated."

Aiden shook her finger at her. "That's a cop-out. I'm dating a psychologist, remember?"

So? Kade saw no reason to bare her soul just because Aiden's girlfriend had a PhD in psychology. "She's not here now," she pointed out.

Now Aiden was the one who suddenly looked sober. "No, she isn't."

They stared at each other, both silently re-erecting the barriers of professionalism.

"So anything interesting in this witness statement?" Kade asked.

"So what's with the files?" Aiden asked at the same time. She laughed. "Let's face it, Counselor, we're both awful at girl talk."

Kade smiled at her. "No objection from the prosecution. If you want to talk about the intricacies of romantic relationships, your psychologist girlfriend might be a better choice in conversation partners."

The smile Aiden gave her in return seemed very forced, but they had just agreed to end their ineffective attempt at sharing a sensitive talk between friends, so Kade couldn't very well ask what was wrong with her tonight. She had a sneaking suspicion that

Aiden had fought with Dawn, and Kade had decided early on to stay completely out of anything to do with their relationship.

Kade might not be good at interpersonal relationships, but that didn't mean that she was completely oblivious when it came to matters of the heart either. She had seen the glances Dawn had sent in her direction when she had talked to Aiden at the precinct's New Year's Eve party.

Dawn was clearly worried about Kade's role in her girlfriend's life, and Kade knew she would only make the situation worse if she got involved in any relationship problems they might have. "If you could read over the files before opening statements in the Walker trial," she said, pointing at the files she had laid down on Ray's desk. "I used sticky notes where I need you to clarify something."

Aiden willingly reached for the first file. "Consider it done."

* * *

"Ray?"

Ray took his gaze off the road for a second to glance at his partner in the passenger seat. He had been waiting for her to start talking all morning, but until now, she had only brooded on her side of the car, staring out the window with sleep-deprived eyes.

"How long have you and Susan been together?" Aiden asked.

Ray clutched the steering wheel in surprise. He hadn't expected that question. *What's going on in that busy head of yours, partner?*

"Almost eighteen years." He glanced at Aiden again, but she was staring straight ahead. "Why the sudden interest?" They had talked about his marriage before, but mostly when there was a problem between Susan and him and Aiden was doing some hand-holding or, more often, hitting him over the head for being an inconsiderate jerk.

"In all those years, have you ever wanted something that Susan... didn't?" Aiden asked. Ray got the impression that she was trying very hard to keep her voice neutral and casual.

He furrowed his brow. "What do you mean? Like wanting pot roast for dinner when she wanted to have a veggie jambalaya? Sure, that happens every single day."

"No, I don't mean your different tastes in food," Aiden said, clearly becoming impatient with his lack of understanding and her own inability to explain. "I mean the big things."

Big things? Ray tried to guess what Aiden would consider a big thing in a relationship. "Like moving in together?" That would certainly be a big thing, considering she hadn't lived with anyone all the years they had been partners.

Aiden sighed. "No, nothing like that. I..." She shook her head. "Just forget I said anything, okay?"

Ray was quiet for a moment, concentrating on his driving. When Aiden turned her head to stare out the window again, he quickly stopped her retreat into herself. "You sure? I'm your partner. You can talk to me about anything. You know that, right?"

Aiden nodded but remained silent.

"Something is clearly bothering you," Ray broke the silence again.

"I'm fine," came the standard Aiden Carlisle response.

Ray knew she was lying. "You spent the night in the 'dungeon' even though I know you went home last night, and you've been grumpier than Okada all morning. Doesn't sound like 'fine' to me."

Aiden gave him a glare, then looked away, showing him that she didn't want to talk about it anymore. "Just attribute it to PMS and move on."

Ray smiled and gave her a rueful shake of his head. "Living with five females has taught me that blaming anything on PMS is the fastest way for a man to get himself killed."

That finally made her smile for a second, but the smile was just as quickly gone from her face. "Dawn and I... we had a fight last night," she admitted. "Or at least we would have if I hadn't walked out on her."

Ah. That's what I thought. "About what did you almost fight?" Ray knew his partner was not normally one to start fights at the drop of a hat, and in his eyes, Dawn had to be the most patient woman in the world, so whatever they had been fighting about had to be big.

"I can't tell you that," Aiden said.

Ray looked at her out of the corner of his eye. For a fleeting second, he almost thought he saw a hint of a blush coloring her cheeks. *Oooh! They're fighting about **that** already? No way in hell am I touching that topic with a ten-foot pole!* He tried valiantly not to picture what it could be that his partner wanted and Dawn didn't. He cleared his throat. "Have you tried to talk to Dawn about it?"

Aiden gave a half nod that could equally mean "yes" or "no." "That didn't go over too well. I ended up storming out of the apartment in the middle of the night."

"Ouch. And you haven't talked to her since?" Ray asked.

Aiden shook her head, staring down at the paper cup of coffee she was cradling in her hands.

"Has she tried to call you?" Whenever he and Susan had a fight, she usually ended up calling him at work, worried that something would happen to him and not wanting the last words she spoke to him be angry accusations.

Aiden fingered the cell phone clipped to her belt. "No."

"No?" Ray raised an eyebrow. "I always thought she would be the one to make the first step and start talking it out."

"She usually is," Aiden said with a sigh.

Ray grinned. His partner, who chronically tried to hide from her feelings and the demons with which she lived all her life, being in a relationship with a psychologist was just one of the ironies of life. "It drives you crazy," he said, a statement, not a question.

"She's so mature and levelheaded and in connection with her own feelings—and with mine. It's infuriating." Aiden and Ray traded grins. Then Aiden's self-mocking grin turned into a more wistful smile. "And I love her for it," she added in a voice so low Ray almost missed it over the honking Portland drivers around him.

Ray glanced into the rearview mirror and pulled over. He shut off the ignition and turned to look at Aiden.

"What are you doing?" Aiden asked in exasperation.

"Me? Nothing. But you're going to call your girlfriend," Ray told her. "And I don't think you want to do it with me listening to every word."

Aiden stared at him. "Has anyone ever told you that you're a meddling son of a bitch?"

Ray grinned, unimpressed. "No, first compliment I've had all day."

Aiden put down her empty paper cup and reached out to open the car door. One foot already outside, she turned back around and gave him a genuine smile. "Thanks, partner."

She nudged the passenger side door shut with her hip.

"You're welcome," Ray said.

He watched her press the number one on the speed dial—a position that he had once held on her cell phone—and prowl up and down in front of the car while she waited for Dawn to pick up. She stopped in midstride and spoke hastily into the receiver.

She listened for a few seconds, then her shoulders slumped. She said another few words and returned the cell phone to its position on her belt. A few deep breaths and she was back in the car.

"She hung up on you?" Ray asked in disbelief.

"What? No, no. Her secretary picked up the phone. Dawn's with a patient right now," Aiden said, sounding equally disappointed and relieved.

Ray studied her. "Did you leave a message?"

"Saying what?" Aiden sounded helpless and irritated.

Ray shrugged. "That you're sorry and that you love her? Always works for me."

"Yeah, but you're not a lesbian," Aiden pointed out.

What has that to do with anything? "No, can't say that's part of my resume. But why would it prevent you from saying—"

"Because I don't think she's out to her new secretary. Outing herself in a professional context could be a very bad thing for a psychologist. Patients could request a referral to another therapist because they're uncomfortable with a lesbian therapist, or some could even try to sue her, claiming she made sexual advances during their one-on-one sessions," Aiden explained.

"So you told the secretary...?" Ray prompted.

"That a police officer would come by later to talk to Doctor Kinsley about her unpaid parking tickets," Aiden answered with a deadpan expression.

Ray laughed. "You didn't?"

"Not really." Aiden grinned. "I said I would call again later, and that it wasn't a job-related call. I don't want to scare Dawn on top of everything else."

Ray nodded and started the car.

* * *

Dawn watched her office door click shut behind her last patient. She leaned back in her chair with a groan and rubbed her eyes. Her last patient of the day had canceled, which meant she was free to go home now.

Home... Her empty apartment didn't hold much appeal. Normally, she would have called Aiden, hearing how her day was going, joking and flirting on the phone until she had all but forgotten the worries and problems she had listened to all day.

Not today. Dawn stared at the phone but didn't reach for it. She had started to dial Aiden's number half a dozen times today, but each time, she had hung up before the first ring. For once, she wasn't sure what to say.

The words Aiden had shouted before she had run out on her still rang in her ears: *I didn't want to make love! I wanted to have sex!* Dawn knew Aiden hadn't just said it to hurt her, but it had hurt nonetheless. It made her feel as if she couldn't give Aiden what she wanted, as if she wasn't what Aiden wanted.

"Doctor Kinsley?" Her office manager's voice from the intercom interrupted Dawn's thoughts. "Your next patient is here."

Dawn frowned. "I thought Mrs. Chancey canceled?"

"She did, but I filled her time slot with a walk-in," Mrs. Phillips informed her. "It's a woman, but... well, you'll see for yourself when you read the intake form."

Dawn suppressed a sigh. *Come on, being professional for another hour won't kill you. Then you can fall apart all you want.* "All right. I'll come and get her from the waiting room." She liked the more personal touch of greeting her patients as soon as they arrived, not having them directed to her office by her secretary.

She stopped by Mrs. Phillips' desk to pick up the intake form and glanced at it on her way to the waiting room. She stopped abruptly when she read the name her patient had scribbled into the top blank.

Xena of Amphipolis? She had to laugh. She was used to patients hesitating to give their real name, but no one had ever given a pseudonym like that. *Well, maybe a patient with a sense of humor like that will cheer me up—provided it was a joke and she doesn't believe she really is Xena. Well, let's see what the Warrior Princess needs my help with. Probably PTSD or aggressive behavior.* She looked down at the intake form again. *Relationship issues, huh? Could have told you that. All that repressed desire for the bard can't be good for the soul.*

She took a moment to compose herself and school her features into a neutral expression, then stepped into the waiting room.

Xena, Warrior Princess, was nowhere to be seen. Instead, a sheepish looking Detective Aiden Carlisle rose from her seat and stood silently, just staring at Dawn.

Dawn still wasn't sure what all of this meant, but at least Aiden was here, had sought her out, and that had to count for something. "You know," she said, looking Aiden up and down, "I always imagined the mighty Warrior Princess to be a little taller."

"Sorry to disappoint." Aiden smiled, but there was a regret in her eyes that had nothing to do with not being taller.

"I'm not disappointed, just surprised to see you," Dawn said. "Let's go to my office."

Aiden followed her through the reception area. Her steps were hesitant, not the usual confident stride Dawn was used to. Aiden ignored the couch and the beanbags, instead choosing to sit in the chair in front of Dawn's desk.

Their seating arrangement was a little too much like her therapy sessions with Evan Whitfield for Dawn's comfort, so she dragged her chair around the desk and sat next to Aiden. She didn't want any additional barriers between them for this conversation.

"I called and booked your next hour to make sure you had time to talk to me," Aiden broke the awkward silence.

"I'm glad you did, even if it makes me feel a little like a high-priced call girl," Dawn tried to joke.

Neither of them laughed.

Dawn winced. *Genius! Considering the way you left off, making a joke about her paying you for sex is not a good conversation starter!*

Both of them sat, awkwardly looking at each other, neither knowing where to start.

Finally, Dawn cleared her throat. "Well, Ms. Amphipolis, what can I do for you?" *Maybe it'll be easier for her... for both of us, if we keep up that little role-play she started for a while.*

Aiden smiled and took a moment to think of an answer. "Well, you see, I travel around with this beautiful and very talented little bard."

So she still thinks I'm beautiful and talented, huh? Dawn suppressed a grin. "I've heard of her. You're lovers, right?"

"Not according to the official scripts, but if you promise not to tell..." Aiden lowered her voice to an almost whisper and looked deeply into Dawn's eyes, "...she's the love of my life."

Dawn swallowed. Aiden had never told her that before, and she hadn't expected to hear it now. "So what's the problem?" she asked after a while.

"Well, you see, last night, after fighting this week's bad guy, I had a severe case of... bloodlust, and when I found Gabrielle in my bedroll, I started to ravish her." Aiden looked down, examining her hands with fake interest.

Dawn almost reached out to touch those hands, but she forced herself to remain where she was. "I take it the bard didn't react too well?"

"No, no, she reacted... her reaction was absolutely appropriate," Aiden quickly defended "Gabrielle." "She... I..."

"Aiden..." Dawn couldn't keep up this Xena/Gabrielle role-play any longer. "Let's go for a walk. If we talk in here, I feel like I'm doing couples therapy with myself as part of the couple. It would be too weird."

Aiden stood so fast that it was clear she was not keen on talking in a psychologist's office either. "Well, at least you could be sure the therapist was on your side," she said with a forced smile.

"There are no sides, Aiden," Dawn objected. "We're having problems, yes, but we're not enemies in a war. I still love you."

Her hand already on the doorknob, Aiden turned around. "I love you too."

And I think that might be part of the problem, Dawn thought but remained silent until they were out of the office. *Casual sex is no longer an option.*

Usually, when they were walking next to each other, they held hands, but now Aiden shoved her hands into the pockets of her long, tan suede jacket. Dawn could see that she was full of nervous energy and had to force herself to adjust her long stride to Dawn's shorter steps.

"Thanks for being the one to take the first step," Dawn said, putting her hands into her own coat pockets.

Aiden nodded. "Why didn't you?" she asked, sounding merely curious, not accusing.

Since the beginning of their relationship, Dawn had always been the one to search Aiden out and force her to talk when things got difficult, so Aiden's question was justified.

"The other times, it was about you, about your issues. This time, I felt like it was about me. Like I was the one at fault," Dawn admitted. At times, she was still angry and frustrated with herself and her body's inability to distinguish between the cruel groping of her rapist and Aiden's passionate but still loving touches. Being left behind just when she needed Aiden most had added feelings of hurt to her already turbulent emotions, but she didn't want to start out their conversation by pointing it out. Aiden was already feeling guilty enough.

"You're not to blame for any part of this whole fucked-up situation!" Aiden protested, almost wildly.

Oh, yes, of course! The blame is all yours, as always. Oh, no, I won't let you do this again! "If I had made mad, passionate love to you last night, there wouldn't be a problem, right?" She stared at Aiden until the older woman looked away. "So maybe 'blame' is not the right word, but I'm part of this whole fucked-up situation as much as you are."

"I shouldn't have done that to you," Aiden grumbled, kicking out at a can somebody had thrown on the sidewalk. "I should have just stayed away."

Dawn caught up with her in two quick steps and grabbed her by the shoulder, roughly dragging her around to face her. "I'm the one who crawled into your bed. Stop blaming yourself!"

"If neither of us is to blame, why did... last night happen, huh?" Aiden hurled at her. Her amber eyes glowed with anger that was mainly directed at herself.

Dawn sighed. She knew that as a cop, Aiden often tended to see situations as black/white, good/bad things. In her world, you were either guilty or innocent, with very few options in between. "Last night, our needs simply clashed. I needed you to hold me after that whole test results thing, and you needed me to get rid of all the tension and emotions of your job. It was just bad timing, that's all."

"Bad timing?" Aiden repeated, clearly not believing the answer could be so simple.

Dawn nodded calmly. "We love and respect each other, but we're still two very different people with very different needs and very different ways of dealing with our emotions. I usually want to talk things out while you tend to work out your feelings in a more physical way." Aiden had used the bloodlust analogy as a joke, but now that Dawn thought about it, there was a kernel of truth in it.

She thought back to the many times she had found Aiden punching a heavy bag within an inch of its life after a particularly rough case, and she had long since suspected that Aiden had used sex as another way to exorcise her demons before they had started a relationship.

Aiden couldn't argue with that. "Yeah, but sex is no longer an appropriate way to let off some steam, now that I'm in a relationship," she said, very strict with herself. "That has to change."

"And maybe it will, but not in such a short time." Finding alternative ways to deal with her emotions would take some time and a lot of patience from both of them.

Aiden raised both eyebrows and stared at her. "I hope you're not insulting me and yourself by suggesting we start having an open relationship?"

"No!" Dawn was almost shouting. Then she calmed herself. Aiden didn't seem to have any desire to see other people either. "Just for the record, I'm a firm believer in monogamy."

Aiden nodded. "So am I."

"Isn't it ironic?" Dawn said, smiling wistfully. "You're finally in a committed relationship, and you're having less sex than before."

"Well, according to Ray, that's normal," Aiden said with a shrug.

Dawn shook her head. "Not for a relationship with Aiden Carlisle. I have a feeling you're a very passionate and sexual person."

Aiden stared at the tip of her sensible cop shoes. "I guess," she mumbled.

"That's not a crime, you know." Dawn gently touched her arm, getting Aiden to look up from the ground. "Don't beat yourself up for desiring me. I'm flattered, really. Waiting for you in your bed like a half-naked surprise present, I should have expected you wanting to make love."

"I didn't want to make love. I wanted to have sex," Aiden repeated her words from last night, now a lot gentler, like a confession, not an accusation.

Dawn slowly shook her head. "I don't think that's true. There are many different ways to make love, Aiden," she said, finally entwining her fingers with Aiden's. "Making love, having sex—that's just terminology. As long as it's done with love, it's the same thing."

Aiden still looked a little doubtful.

"Just because you'll sometimes get a little more... energetic doesn't mean you don't love me anymore, does it?" Dawn asked.

"Of course not!" Aiden confirmed without hesitation.

"We only started sleeping together a few weeks ago, so it might take us a while to feel entirely comfortable with each other. That's only normal, especially after I was raped." Dawn forced herself to say the words, to get it all out in the open. "So just because it's mostly been very tender between us so far doesn't mean that it'll always be that way. Sometimes one or both of us will feel like bed-breaking, hot, sweaty sex. Sometimes our sexual clocks will tick synchronously, and sometimes they won't."

"What does that mean for our relationship?" Aiden asked, relaxing a bit. The guilty look on her face finally faded. "I mean, our sexual needs will probably clash again at some point in the future."

Dawn nodded. She was sure there would always be days when Aiden would be on an adrenaline high or unable to get rid of the stress and emotions of the workday in any other way. "You could ask me for what you need," she gently suggested.

"No." There was a finality in Aiden's voice. "I won't do that. I don't want you to sleep with me because you feel obligated."

Dawn shook her head in frustration. Discussing emotional issues with Aiden was more draining than every single fight with both of her exes put together—but also more rewarding, she reminded herself. "It's not about obligations. It's about finding a compromise."

"Compromise?" Aiden repeated skeptically. "Dawn, sweetie, maybe you didn't notice, but sex is kind of an 'all or nothing' thing. Either you have sex, or you don't. Not much room for compromise."

Dawn had to laugh at the expression on Aiden's face. "Oh, I noticed, sweetheart, believe me, I noticed," she said with a grin. "But we could compromise on the way we have sex. For instance, I don't mind giving you a little... relief whenever you need it even if there are times when I don't want to be touched."

Aiden helplessly shook her head. "You don't understand. An orgasm isn't really what I'm after in those situations. At least not always. I want to make my bedpartner wild with wanting me. I want to get her off. Getting touched in return is just icing on the cake."

"You, dear Xena," Dawn gently touched the tip of Aiden's nose, glad and impressed that Aiden felt comfortable enough to disclose her desires, "want to be the conqueror sometimes."

Aiden had to laugh at that effective and humorous summary. "Yeah. Without all the gory and violent parts. I'm not into that," she said vigorously.

"I know." From the very beginning, Dawn had felt safe with Aiden. She knew that Aiden would never hurt her physically. "I know you're not that kind of person, so please stop feeling guilty about last night."

"I can't," Aiden murmured, shuffling her feet against the asphalt. "I feel bad to have hurt you."

Dawn looked into Aiden's troubled eyes. Now was the time to be honest and add her own feelings to the discussion instead of just helping Aiden deal with hers. "I won't deny that you hurt me," she said, quickly touching Aiden's cheek and directing her gaze back to hers when she wanted to look away. "But not the way you probably think."

Aiden swallowed. "How?" she rasped.

"What hurt the most was not the passion you put into your lovemaking. It overwhelmed me for a moment, but that's all." Dawn pulled Aiden to a stop next to her, making sure that she heard every word. She wasn't sure she would be able to say it twice because it hurt as much to say it as it probably did to hear it. "What hurt much more than that was the way you walked out on me just when I needed you to stay, to talk, to give me a little comfort."

Aiden blanched. She suddenly looked nauseated. "I didn't mean to hurt you. I was just... I was too angry to stay."

"So what could have happened if you stayed anyway, angry as you were? We would have fought and yelled at each other and maybe cried and said a few hurtful things—so what? I would have preferred a fight to being left behind to restlessly roam around your apartment all night." Dawn sniffled a little and riffled through her coat pockets in search of a tissue.

Aiden wordlessly handed her one. Her hand was trembling. "I'm sorry," she whispered. "I let my feelings of guilt, anger, and frustration get in the way. I couldn't deal with them, so I just ran away."

"That's the point I'm trying to make," Dawn said, quickly drying her tears. "The problem isn't only our different attitudes toward sex. We also have very different reactions to stress and emotional issues. Most often, I won't feel better about things until I've talked about it with someone else. I don't want to be left alone to lick my emotional wounds. You, on the other hand, ignore your emotions and run away until there's too much bottled up inside of you and you have to find physical relief in some way."

"You're right," Aiden said slowly, almost sadly. "We couldn't be more different if we tried."

Dawn forced a smile. "That's not a bad thing. Differences make life so much more interesting. But if we want our relationship to last, we have to find some compromises."

Aiden was silent for so long that Dawn started to worry, afraid Aiden was shutting her out again. But then Aiden looked up. "It hurts to think of another fight, but I know there'll be others, so maybe we could try this: If I feel like running away from an intense situation, I'll go and get us some coffee. That'll give me half an hour to feel a little more in control of my emotions, and then I'll come back with a caramel cappuccino for you, and we'll stay up for as long as it takes to talk things out." She looked down expectantly, waiting for Dawn's reaction.

"Better make it decaf," Dawn said with a smile.

Aiden looked puzzled for a moment, then she laughed. "You mean you'll have to drink a lot of coffee in the years to come, huh? You're probably right."

"Only at the beginning. You'll get better at staying and talking, and I'll get better at letting you go without flipping out." Dawn reached out and tenderly combed a strand of short hair back behind Aiden's ear. "I'm proud of you."

"Proud!"

"You were the one who sought me out to talk, and you were the one to find a compromise for any future heated discussions we might have," Dawn said. "Talking about emotional issues might not come easy for you, but you can do it if you try."

Aiden shrugged her agreement. "I never had a good enough reason to try. The other women and men I've been with didn't grab me by the ear and tell me off if I acted like an insensitive jerk."

"I won't grab you by the ear either. I'm not in this relationship to act like a parent, to criticize and change you, but I won't let you trample all over my feelings either," Dawn said, very seriously. The last year of her marriage had been an emotional hell, and she had sworn right then and there that she would never allow it to happen again.

"I'll try to be more sensitive to your feelings," Aiden promised. "Had I stopped to think about what kind of day you probably had, I wouldn't have tried to ravish you as soon as I walked in the door."

Dawn entwined her fingers with Aiden's again. "On most days, I wouldn't have a problem with being ravished. Just give me a heads-up next time you set out to conquer Greece, all right?" Dawn said with a wink.

"More communication, hmm?" Aiden drew Dawn's hand up and kissed her palm.

Dawn hummed a confirmation. "Tell me what you want instead of just... doing it. I know it takes the spontaneity out of it, but I think I'll need it for a while. Give me a little time to fully wake up before the ravishing starts. And skip the beer."

Aiden nodded earnestly. "I can do that."

"Voila, another compromise." They grinned at each other. Both knew there would probably be times when it wouldn't be enough, but it was a good start, and they both were willing to work on it.

They turned around and strolled back in the direction of Dawn's office. "So now that you've cured the Warrior Princess, are there more patients back at the office, waiting for you to work a miracle?" Aiden asked with a smile.

"No, the miracle-working bard is free to go home now," Dawn answered. She held her breath, hoping Aiden wouldn't try to back away from her after the emotional intensity of their discussion.

"Well, in that case... Would you mind if I stayed over at your apartment tonight?" Aiden bounced on the balls of her feet like a teenager with too much nervous energy. "I'd love to just hold you. So, would you like some company?" She directed a hopeful puppy-dog look down at Dawn.

"No. I mean, yes, yes, I'd love to have you over," Dawn corrected quickly, "but I have self-defense class tonight, remember?"

"Oh. Right. No problem. Guess we'll see each other on the weekend anyway." As always, Aiden was quick to hide her hurt feelings.

"I won't be home 'til ten, but that doesn't mean you can't come over. You have a key," Dawn reminded. "Or I could come over to your apartment after class." After last night, Dawn thought it might be important for both of them to go back to Aiden's apartment instead of staying over at Dawn's and avoiding the memories of last night.

Aiden looked down at their hands, stroking Dawn's fingers with her thumb. "You really don't mind? If you need some space... I don't want to be clingy."

Dawn laughed. "You don't have a clingy bone in your body, Aiden Carlisle. I'll come over as soon as I've mastered that 360-

degree spin kick, okay?" she asked, using an old inside joke from a time when they had still only been a victim and a detective to each other.

"All right. I'll get rid of the beer and the Warrior Princess attitude before you arrive," Aiden promised, giving her hand a squeeze.

"Avoiding beer would be a good idea, but I like an adventurous woman every once in a while." Dawn winked at her. "Maybe this time, I could wake you up by ravishing you, hmm?"

Aiden leaned down to kiss her, not caring who might see them. "Mm-hm, I'd like that."

"Great." Dawn lightly patted her partner's irresistible butt. "Now, Xena, where did you park Argo, your trusted horse?"

CHAPTER 9

THE PHONE RANG for the third time in less than half an hour.

Kade opened tired eyes with a groan. She struggled to throw off the damp covers and sat up. She held her hand over the receiver, waiting for her head to stop spinning and debating with herself whether to pick up.

The last two calls had been hang-ups—and they weren't the first. The calls had started a few days ago. As soon as she got home from the office, her phone would ring. When she picked up, her mystery caller would say nothing. No threats, no profanities, just soft breathing until Kade slammed the receiver down.

The mysterious flower deliveries and the feeling of being watched had been on her mind a lot lately, but she hadn't been too worried. Kade didn't intimidate easily. Pissing off people who had a lot of criminal energy was what she did for a living after all. In her two years with the sex crimes unit, she had received enough hate mail, death threats, and detailed descriptions of sick fantasies to wallpaper her entire two-bedroom apartment. She didn't pay them any more attention than the seventeen letters of admiration or the two marriage proposals she had received via mail.

But now she was sick, helplessly chained to her bed, and she felt as if the situation was escalating out of control. She was not just being paranoid. She had an unlisted phone number, but her stalker was resourceful enough to get it anyway.

Kade tentatively lifted the receiver to her ear. "Hello?"

Nothing. Silence. Then breathing.

Kade quickly ended the call and dialed *69, only to be told that the caller had withheld his number and couldn't be reached in this manner.

The phone started ringing again.

Kade's pounding head threatened to explode. Only the thought that it could be her office, trying to get some last-minute advice on the case she'd had to hand over, made her pick up again. "Hello?"

"Hey, Counselor, it's Del Vasquez. I'm calling to invite you out for that long-overdue coffee I still owe you," Del's cheerful voice announced.

Kade turned away for a second to blow her nose. "Oh, hi. So you found the murder weapon in the suspect's apartment?" she asked, ignoring the coffee invitation for now.

"Yes. And we got a confession. Case closed, no work for the DDA," Del reported, the smile evident in her voice. "Hey, you sound a little... are you sick? Your office said I could reach you at home."

"Just a little cold. I'll be back behind the prosecution table come Monday," Kade answered, willing it to be so. She had no time—and no patience—to lie in bed and be sick.

"Do you have enough to drink? To eat? Medicine? Someone to take care of you?" Del asked in a rapid staccato that made Kade's head hurt even more.

"Yes," Kade said, answering at least one of Del's questions honestly. She wasn't one for being coddled.

Del was silent for a second, then she drawled, "Why do I get the feeling there's only a cup of lukewarm tea and a bunch of tissues on your bedside table?"

Kade turned her pounding head to look at her bedside table. *Because there is?* Del was so good at reading her that it made her a little uncomfortable. *Is it a cop thing, or is she just able to read me like this? Or maybe she's my stalker, and that's why she knows every little thing that's going on in my apartment.* Most times, Kade didn't believe that, but maybe it was better to err on the side of caution than to be overly trusting.

"Listen," Del said when Kade remained silent. "I'm coming over with a giant bowl of chicken soup."

"No! There's no need to—" The beeping of the phone interrupted her. Del had hung up. "Great!" Kade sank back against the pillows. *When did I lose control over my life?*

* * *

"Gracie?" Del trapped the cordless phone between her chin and her shoulder and rummaged through her cupboard for a pot. "Do you have a minute for your best friend?"

Grace laughed. "When you start a conversation with a reminder of your 'best friend' status, you usually end up confessing something that will take more than a minute."

"Not this time," Del said. "I just need you to tell me how to make that delicious chicken soup of yours."

For a few seconds, there was only silence. "You want to cook something? You?"

Del straightened to her full height. "I can, you know? I just usually don't have to with all the talented Kinsley women around. So, what do I need for the soup? I already have the pot, now what do I put in it?"

"You don't even like chicken broth," Grace said. "What's going on, Del?"

Del sighed. *She knows me too well.* "Kade is sick," she said as if that would explain everything. She was reluctant to tell Grace too much, too soon, not knowing how her old friend would react. Grace had been the only woman in her life for so long, and even if they had never been romantically involved, it was a big change for both of them.

"Kade? Who's Kade?" Grace was clearly confused.

Kade was not exactly a rare name, but in Del's mind, there was only one Kade, so she hadn't bothered to clarify. "Kade Matheson. She was the deputy district attorney in Dawn's case, remember?"

"This isn't a free-food program for the DA's office, is it? So why are you trying to make chicken soup for DDA Matheson?" Grace asked.

Del hesitated only a second. She owed her old friend the truth. "I'm kind of courting her, and now she's sick, and I don't think she has anyone to take care of her."

"You're courting her?" Grace's surprise was very obvious. "Is she even... you know?"

Del shrugged, almost dropping the phone in the process. "Don't know. Don't care. A woman like Kade is worth finding out, though."

Grace gave her a noncommittal "Hmm."

"Grace?" Del asked when the silence between them grew. "Are you still there?"

"Yes, of course," was all Grace answered.

"Sorry to spring this on you out of the blue." For the last few years, Del hadn't shown more than a fleeting interest in a woman, and the sudden revelation had clearly caught her friend unawares. "I should have come over and told you in person. Although there's not much to tell so far." She sighed.

Grace chuckled. "The DDA giving you a hard time?"

"Very hard, yes," Del said with a relieved smile. Grace seemed ready to accept this new development in her life. "Maybe I could bring her over to dinner one night, and you could sing my praises and make her agree to date me."

"Let's start with trying to impress her with the chicken soup, huh?" Grace said.

"Okay." Del knew that Grace probably needed a little more time before she was ready to accept Kade at her dinner table and into her life. She picked up a pen. "So tell me what I need for this magical chicken soup."

* * *

"Del Vasquez. I'm here to see Kade Matheson," Del announced to the rare Portland doorwoman in the foyer of Kade's condo building.

The tall, stony-faced doorwoman shook her head. "Ms. Matheson is not receiving visitors tonight."

"It's important," Del urged. *Come on, sister, how about a little compassion for a fellow dyke?* She was pretty sure that the muscular woman was gay.

"I'm sorry, but Ms. Matheson said she doesn't want to see anyone tonight," the doorwoman insisted. It was obvious that she took her job very seriously and would not allow Del to slip through to the elevators of the condo tower.

Del reached into her jacket and flashed her badge. "Urgent police business!" She stared the doorwoman down, pretending the pot of chicken soup she had tucked under one arm was a secret police weapon and nothing unusual for a cop on duty at all.

After a few more seconds, the doorwoman stepped aside, and Del rushed to the elevator before she could change her mind. Minutes later, she knocked on the door of Kade's condo.

It took a long time, but finally she heard Kade's slightly hoarse voice through the still closed door. "Who is it?"

"It's me, Del Vasquez. I have your chicken soup." Del stepped closer, waiting to be let in, but Kade didn't open the door.

"I'm fine," Kade said. "It's very kind of you to come over, but I don't need chicken soup or any other help."

I should have known she would do that. Kade Matheson is clearly used to taking care of herself. She doesn't want me to see her so vulnerable, Del concluded. "Come on, just let me in for a second. I only want to say hello."

"You could have done that over the phone," Kade pointed out.

Even sick, her logic is as impeccable as ever. "Okay, if you don't want to let me in, I'll just sit here on your doorstep and wait for your neighbors to come home. Maybe they'll be interested in a little soup. That is, if they don't run away screaming and calling for the police when they see me lurking in the stairwell."

"That's blackmail!" Kade protested.

"You can indict me as soon as you're back at your office, but for now, please let me in." After a moment, the door opened an inch, and Del quickly pushed it open and stepped into the apartment.

Kade had already disappeared down the hall, so Del closed the door behind her and took her time looking around. The elegant condo near the Riverplace Marina fit Kade perfectly. Del carefully walked across the shining hardwood floor and past the gas fireplace in the living room. The apartment was tastefully furnished, with a few paintings and sculptures that Del knew Dawn would have appreciated more than she did. When she reached one of the floor-to-ceiling windows, Del took a moment to enjoy the view of the Willamette River and the snow-white yachts in the marina before she crossed the hall and knocked on the door of the room where Kade had vanished. "Kade?"

"Just leave the soup in the kitchen," Kade said instead of the expected "come in." The exasperation was clear in her voice. "First door to the left."

Del wasn't here to see the kitchen. She wanted to see Kade and make sure she was okay. She set the pot down on the kitchen's granite counter, then knocked on Kade's bedroom door again. "Kade? Can I come in for a second?"

"I'm in my bathrobe," Kade protested.

"I've seen women in bathrobes before," Del said with a smile.

Kade didn't give an inch. "Not this woman."

Del leaned against the closed door. "Kade... Do you really think I came all the way from St. Johns to take advantage of your weakened state and ogle you in your bathrobe? Is that what you think of me?" She knew she was putting Kade on the spot. If Kade answered with a yes, she would leave the soup, wish her a speedy recovery, and leave. She was crazy about Kade and willing to be patient with her, but she wasn't a masochist.

Finally, she heard Kade's frustrated sigh through the door. "Just for a second," Kade demanded.

Del slowly opened the door.

Kade was sitting up in her queen-sized bed, her knees pulled up and her arms slung around them. Instead of the impeccably dressed, not-a-hair-out-of-place counselor, Del found a bathrobe-clad, slightly disheveled Kade Matheson with a reddish nose and glassy eyes.

"Hi," Del said, almost whispering. "How are you?"

"I'm—" Kade sneezed. "— fine."

Del nodded. "Clearly. You're the picture of health," she agreed dryly. "Have you seen a doctor?"

"I don't need a doctor!" Kade's argument lost a good deal of her usual conviction because of her stuffed-up-sounding nose. "It's a simple cold. It takes a week with a doctor's help and seven days without. You know how it is."

Del looked at the reddish hue of the normally fair skin. "You look like you're running a fever." She resisted the urge to touch Kade's forehead to judge her temperature. Kade looked as if she would rip off her arm if she invaded her privacy any more than she already had.

"I just need a good night's sleep; that's all," Kade said before she noisily blew her nose.

Del smiled to herself. *Maybe this fascination with the perfect Kadence Matheson will lessen a bit now that you've seen she's a mere mortal.* "Do you want me to bring you a bowl of soup? It's probably still warm enough to eat."

"I'm not hungry," Kade said, and then, when she noticed how harsh she had sounded, she added more gently, "but thanks."

Before Del could think of an answer, the phone began to ring.

Kade jumped. Her gaze flew to the phone, wildly staring at it as if she could make it stop ringing just by the power of her will.

"Aren't you going to pick it up?" Del asked, not bothering to hide her amusement or her confusion. She had never seen Kade act so out of sorts.

"I'm out sick. That means I don't have to answer my phone." Kade was suddenly playing the pouting patient.

Del furrowed her brow. *The hardworking, diligent DDA refuses to pick up her phone? What's going on here?* She directed a questioning gaze at Kade. "Didn't you just tell me it was just a simple cold?" She suspected that normally, not even pneumonia could keep Kade from working. There was something else going on with Kade, not just her cold.

Kade abruptly looked away and snatched up the receiver. "Yes?" she barked into the phone, making herself cough. "Oh! Mother!"

Oops! Del hadn't imagined the first time she had any kind of contact with Kade's mother, indirect as it might be, would be while she was standing in the bedroom of an only half-dressed Kade.

Kade seemed as surprised as Del was. Del noticed that she sat up straighter.

Del pointed at the door, mouthing "Should I go?"

As adamantly as she had tried to get Del to leave earlier, Kade shook her head now. "No, no. Stay." She listened for a few seconds. "No. No, it's not a him. No. No man. Just a... friend. Yes, a female friend." Kade looked up. The gaze of her blue eyes met Del's.

Friend... Del smiled. *Well, that's a step in the right direction.*

"Yes, Mother," Kade continued to talk into the phone. She pressed her hand against the receiver when another coughing spell shook her slender body. "No, just a cold. Yes, Mother, I will call her to congratulate her on getting married." Finally, after a few more assurances to her mother, Kade put the phone down. She exhaled sharply and sank back into her pillows.

Her mother wants to know in detail if there's a man in her apartment, but she doesn't even ask her if she's all right when even a deaf man could hear she's coughing up a lung? Del silently shook her head. "You okay?"

"Yeah. That was just my mother. She takes it upon herself to call me whenever one of my high school friends gets married," Kade said with a wry face.

"Just a friendly reminder that you're still not married, huh?" Del smiled at her.

Kade returned the smile. "Sounds like you know my mother."

"No, but I've dated a few women who had mothers like yours," Del answered. *Not as rich or as influential, of course.*

"I take it your mother isn't like that?" Kade quickly directed the attention away from her family. She took a sip from her cup, then shuddered. The tea had long since gone cold.

Oh, yes, she is. Del's mother had always wanted a Latino husband, a splendid wedding, and a gaggle of kids for her daughter. That dream would never come true, though. "I haven't talked to my parents for a long time—or rather they haven't talked to me," Del said.

Kade looked at her for a little longer. Del could practically feel that there were a lot of questions lingering on the tip of her tongue, but Kade held them back—quite a feat for a woman who asked questions for a living. *She doesn't want me to think she's interested in my private life because then she would have to reciprocate and answer my questions.*

When Kade looked away from her, Del let her gaze wander and noticed she had been right about the items on the bedside table. "I'll heat up a little soup for you," she announced, not reacting to Kade's protests. She slipped out of the bedroom and into the kitchen, where she had left the pot of chicken soup and the bag she had brought with her.

Fifteen minutes later, she returned to the bedroom, quietly opening the door in case Kade was asleep.

Kade wasn't. She was still sitting up, heavily leaning back against the headrest, the covers tightly wrapped around herself. Her eyelids were drooping, but she stubbornly refused to close them while Del was still in her apartment.

Del slowly walked over to the bed and carefully set the tray she had found in the kitchen down on Kade's lap.

"What's all this?" Kade croaked, trying to shove the tray away. "Did you rob a drug store?"

Del held on to the tray, keeping it in place until Kade noticed that she was no match for her strength in her weakened state and gave up her attempts to refuse Del's offerings. Del rearranged the steaming bowl of chicken soup, the cup of herbal tea, the toast, and the bottle of cough syrup on the tray. "Here. Eat. It'll make you feel better." She handed Kade a spoon.

Kade leaned forward, skeptically trying to sniff the soup through her stuffed-up nose.

Del used the opportunity to plump up the pillow against which Kade had rested.

"Stop fussing over me!" Kade ordered as sharply as her hoarse voice allowed.

Del stopped and straightened, looking down at Kade. "What are you so afraid of, Kade?" She studied the pale features. Even with blotchy cheeks and a running nose, Kade was still beautiful. "Are you afraid you'll owe me?"

Kade didn't answer the question. Instead, she had one of her own, "Why are you doing this?"

Del smiled. She had expected that question. "Are you searching for a motive to fit your neat little theory, Counselor? This is not a case, and I'm not a suspect. I don't have any ulterior motives. I'm a very up-front person. All I want is to help you feel better and maybe get to know you better in the process. That's all."

"I don't understand you," Kade said, her voice not only rough from the cold but also from frustration.

Kade Matheson not understanding something! I bet that doesn't happen very often. "Then ask me. I'm always willing to explain," Del said.

"I told you I'm straight and not interested in dating you, but you continue to... woo me. What do you expect to gain by it?" Kade asked, clearly puzzled.

"You're not all that uninterested," Del objected with a smile.

Kade raised two perfectly arched eyebrows and stared at her. "You're assuming that based on what evidence?"

"If you really didn't want me here, I'd still be sitting outside on the stairs with my soup," Del said, and when Kade opened her mouth to object, she added, "You went out to dinner with me, on Valentine's Day I might add, and you didn't send back the flowers and cards you thought were from me."

"All circumstantial," Kade said, still hiding behind the familiar legal terms.

Del smiled. For a moment, she allowed herself to imagine Kade whispering sweet, legalese nothings into her ear after a passionate night of lovemaking. "I don't want to convince a judge or a jury," she answered. "I only want to convince you."

"And if you fail to convince me?" Kade asked, still searching for Del's motives.

Del shrugged. She knew that was a distinct possibility. Kade Matheson was just too stubborn for her own good. "Then I hope to at least gain a friend. And judging from the fact that you're suffering alone in your apartment, you could use a friend too."

The ringing of the phone startled both of them.

A pale Kade laid down her spoon and turned to reach for the phone.

Del was faster. "I'll get it. Eat your soup before it gets cold." She reached over Kade with one of her long arms and snatched up the receiver. "Hello," she said, praying it wasn't Kade's mother calling again.

No one answered.

"Hello?" Del repeated, a little louder this time.

Again, there was only silence.

"Asshole," Del muttered and replaced the receiver. She turned back around to face Kade. "How's the soup?"

Kade wasn't eating the soup. In fact, she wasn't doing anything but staring at the phone. Except for the reddened tip of her nose and the feverish blotches on her cheeks, her face was even paler than before. There was an expression on her face that Del had never seen on the confident DDA before, so it took her a moment to realize what it was: fear.

"Kade?" Del worriedly tried to get Kade's attention.

When Kade looked up, the fear was gone from her face, the arrogant-lawyer mask firmly in place. "Yes?"

Del took the tray and lifted it from Kade's lap, setting it down on the floor.

"The soup will get cold," Kade protested.

"I'll reheat it later," Del promised even though she knew that it wasn't the thought of the soup getting cold that was bothering Kade. "After you've told me what's going on with you."

Kade tilted her head, rendering a nearly perfect performance of clueless innocence. "Going on?"

"Something is bothering you. Don't tell me it's nothing," Del said before Kade could open her mouth, "or that you have no idea what I'm even talking about. I know something has got you tied up in knots, and it's not just this annoying cold."

Kade hesitated.

"Whatever it is, you can trust me. Please." Del reached out a hand but stopped just short of touching Kade's hand. A woman who didn't want anyone to cook her chicken soup when she was sick probably wasn't too fond of hand-holding during emotional confessions either. Del also didn't want to add to Kade's emotional burden by reminding her of her romantic intentions. *Be a friend first and a love interest later.* She sat down on the edge of the bed but kept a healthy distance. "Tell me."

* * *

Kade stared at her visitor. *How did I get myself into this situation?* So far, she had avoided telling anyone about feeling she was being followed. She knew she could trust Aiden and her colleagues, but telling the detectives with whom she worked would mean an official investigation sooner or later. Kade didn't want that. She didn't want anyone to think she was using professional connections and her position in the DA's office to get special treatment. She had always kept her professional and her private life strictly separate—and it had been easy, mainly because there hadn't been much of a private life. Nevertheless, she didn't want anyone snooping around her private life, as little of it as there might be.

Now someone had noticed without her saying anything, and Kade had a decision to make. Should she confide in Del or send her away once and for all? Her instincts told her she could trust Del. *She's a decorated lieutenant and Dawn Kinsley's most trusted friend. She has been nothing but direct and honest from the moment you met her,* Kade reminded herself. *You were the one constantly hiding your thoughts and feelings and acting defensive.*

"Tell me," Del said again.

Kade took a deep breath. "Do you remember how I thought you sent me a daily bouquet of flowers?"

"Of course I remember. Those mysterious flower deliveries were what made you run away from me," Del answered, once again very direct and honest.

One of many, many reasons, Kade silently agreed but ignored the other reasons for the time being. *Opening one can of worms at a time is enough.* "Around the same time the flower deliveries started, I began to feel like someone was watching me, following me around. Maybe my job has made me a little paranoid, but..."

"I don't think it can be explained away that easily," Del said. There wasn't even a second of hesitation in believing Kade. A deep worry line formed between dark eyebrows. "You've also been getting hang-up calls."

It was a statement, not a question, but Kade answered anyway. "Yes. They only started last week. He doesn't say anything, but I can hear him breathe."

"Do you have missed phone calls or voicemail messages when you come home at night?" Del asked, her cop training taking over.

Kade shook her head. "He only calls when I'm at home." That was what was so scary about it. It meant the stalker was observing her closely and knew exactly where she was and what she was doing any minute of the day. Kade suppressed a shiver and pulled the covers tighter around herself.

Del inhaled sharply. Her dark eyes looked at Kade with an expression of hurt and accusation. "Why didn't you tell anyone?"

"A prosecutor can't afford to be intimidated that easily," Kade said as reasonably as possible. "I can't request a protective detail every time a suspect looks at me the wrong way."

"That's not the same, and you know it." Del looked her right in the eyes, not willing to accept the reassuring lies Kade had told herself. "This is personal. You could be in real danger."

Kade hadn't wanted to believe it, but she knew Del was right. She nevertheless felt the need to object, "There's no evidence. You know stalking is nearly impossible to prove."

"How much evidence do you need before you're willing to get help? Did you want to wait until he attacked you before you'd have told anyone? Why didn't you tell me?" A hint of anger crept into Del's normally calm voice.

Wait a minute! We don't know each other all that well. I don't owe you anything. Kade opened her mouth to tell Del exactly that, but Del was faster.

"All right," she said with a deep breath, quickly reining in her anger. "I can understand that I wasn't your first choice to talk to, but why didn't you at least tell Carlisle?"

"I have a feeling she already has enough to deal with at the moment without me adding to it," Kade answered. She knew Aiden would instantly start watching her apartment at night if she told her. Aiden had gone weeks without seeing her own apartment in similar situations before, but back then, she hadn't been in a relationship. Kade didn't want to add another problem to a relationship that already seemed to be going through a few difficulties.

Del frowned. "What exactly does she have to deal with at the moment?" she asked suspiciously. "This doesn't have anything to do with her relationship with Dawn, does it?"

Kade knew the expression on Del's face all too well. Aiden wore the same overprotective expression every time she insisted on walking Kade to her car after a late-night search warrant execution or a visit to the detectives' favorite bar. *If I tell her Aiden slept at the station one night this week, she's gonna hunt her down as soon as she leaves here.* "They're drowning in unsolved cases," Kade said. She didn't have to lie even though her workload was not the main reason Kade didn't want to add to Aiden's burden. Kade knew that Dawn felt at times threatened by Aiden's former infatuation with her, so she didn't want to give Dawn the impression that Aiden would drop everything and come running the moment Kade asked for a favor.

"The Sexual Assault Detail is always drowning in unsolved cases," Del said.

Kade grimaced inwardly. She had forgotten that Del wasn't just an admirer; she was also an experienced cop and knew the detectives weren't any busier than usual.

"All right," Del said when Kade remained silent. "If you don't want your own detectives to handle this, let me see what I can—"

"No!" Kade reached out and stopped Del's hand as it reached for her cell phone. She touched Del's warm fingers and quickly retreated. "If at all possible, I want to avoid an official investigation. I don't want a report on the details of my private life."

Del looked at her for a long time. "Okay. We'll keep it under wraps for as long as possible. But if I get the feeling things are escalating, I'll have no choice but to make this official. I'd rather you lose your privacy than your life."

Lose my life... Kade swallowed against her sore throat. "Do you really think my life is in danger?"

"Not while I am around," Del promised, her eyes glowing with steely determination.

Kade shook her head but stopped when the move made her temples pound. "Stay out of this."

"You tell me your life might be threatened and expect me to stand back and do nothing?" Del shook her head. "That's not gonna happen."

"It's not your duty to protect me. You're not Kevin Costner, and I'm not Whitney Houston," Kade reminded her. *This is not going to end with you getting shot—or me in your bed!*

Del managed a half smile. "That's where you're wrong."

"I'm not," Kade said. "You look nothing like Costner, and I can't sing to save my life." She winced when her attempt at lightening the mood reminded her once again that her life might be threatened.

"You're not wrong about that, but it is my duty to protect you," Del said, briefly flipping open her badge to indicate her duty to serve and protect.

"You just agreed to keep this unofficial for now, so you can't refer to your professional duties when it comes to this," Kade said logically.

Del shrugged. "Okay. I wanted to spare you the embarrassment, but if you insist... My determination to keep you safe has nothing to do with my job. I'd want to stand guard in front of your apartment at night even if I were a kindergarten teacher."

The intensity of her gaze made Kade's already overheated cheeks flush even more.

"Do you still have the cards that came with the flower deliveries?" Del asked after a few seconds.

"Just a few," Kade said. "I threw away the later ones." She cringed when she realized she had practically admitted to having kept the cards she had thought were from Del.

Del just smiled but mercifully didn't comment. "I'll take them with me for fingerprinting. Who knows, the guy might have missed a few CSI episodes and left behind a nice fingerprint to identify him."

Kade nodded but knew it probably wouldn't be that easy. "What else can we do?"

"You may want to review a few files once you're back at the office," Del said. "Look for anything unusual from the time shortly before the flower deliveries and the cards started."

Kade laughed bitterly. If she went through every unusual case they'd had in the last few months, her stalker would have died of old age by the time she had gone through every one of them.

"We could put a tap on your home and office phone, but I don't think the calls last long enough to trace them," Del said as honest and open as she had always been. She never tried to sugarcoat anything.

Kade held back a sigh. *In other words, there's nothing we can do.* She wanted to close her eyes, feeling very tired and frustrated.

"I'd like to arrange some surveillance. Just for your apartment at night," Del continued. She directed a careful gaze at Kade, clearly knowing there would be some protest.

Kade shook her head. "How would you justify that to your superiors without making it an official case?"

"I don't need to justify it—not when I'm the only cop doing the surveillance." Del held Kade's gaze steadily.

Kade didn't feel ready to make Del a daily part of her life in any way. She firmly shook her head, then grimaced and pressed a hand against her throbbing forehead. "I can't allow you to do that. You work during the day, so you need to sleep at night, not hang around in front of my apartment."

"Allow me?" Del was not happy with that choice of words. "Kade, I respect your opinion and your wishes, but this isn't something you can allow or forbid."

"Yes, I can! This is my life we're talking about, so I make the decisions!" Kade could feel her temperature rise even more as anger bubbled up inside of her. She always hated the feeling when someone else was trying to run her life.

Del took three deep breaths. "All right. It's your decision. Please, just don't make it for the wrong reasons. If you refuse to let me protect you just because you're afraid to let me be part of your life..." Del stopped and shook her head. "I didn't offer to help in order to impress you or to guilt-trip you into going out with me. I just want to know you're safe."

Kade bit her lip. *It's hard to say no to Miss Altruistic. She's very convincing. She should have been a lawyer.* "You don't have to do this," she tried one more time. "My building even has a doorman, so I'm not completely unprotected."

"I got by her without a problem even though you told her you didn't want to see anyone," Del said calmly.

"One night," Kade conceded. She raised her finger, pointing it at Del to make her rules very clear. "You watch my apartment for one night, and if everything stays quiet, we'll just assume the stalker is not nocturnal, and you'll go home."

Del hesitated, but then seemed to sense that this was as far as Kade was willing to go for now. She finally nodded. "Defense lawyers must hate to sit down at a table for a plea bargain with you," she said, a grudgingly admiring smile on her lips. She rose from the bed. "I'll go and bribe someone from fingerprints to take a look at the cards, and you should finally eat some soup. Want me to heat it up again?"

"No." Kade held on to the bowl when Del tried to pick it up. She didn't want Del having to play nursemaid. "It's fine. It's still warm enough."

"Okay," Del said. "I'll bring you more when I come over to watch the apartment tonight."

The bedroom door clicked shut behind Del before Kade could answer. With a sigh, Kade got up and went to lock the front door. When she returned to the bedroom, she picked up the bowl of chicken soup and lifted it into her lap. She tried the first spoonful and grimaced. Del had clearly used a little too much salt. *I hope she's a better protector than a cook*, she thought as she set the bowl on her bedside table and closed her eyes.

CHAPTER 10

*A*IDEN NODDED WITH satisfaction. Dawn's sardine can was still in its parking space. *Let's see if she's up for going to a club and letting off a little steam on the dance floor.* Ten long hours at work lay behind her, but Aiden was still too keyed up to go home right away. She swung open the door to the joint practice and stepped inside.

Dawn's office manager was still there, leafing through the appointment book, but the waiting room was empty. Mrs. Phillips looked up when Aiden stopped in front of her desk. "Oh, hello. Are you back to make another appointment? I'm afraid the doctor is on her way out and can't see you tonight. But I could pencil you in on—"

"What?" Aiden stared at her, but then she remembered: she had booked one of Dawn's hours yesterday, so of course her secretary would assume she was one of Dawn's patients. "Oh, no, no, that's all right. I don't want another appointment with 'the doctor.' Could you just tell her that Aiden is here?"

"Oh!" Mrs. Phillips shut the appointment book. "You're Aiden? Nice to meet you. Dr. Kinsley told us so much about you."

Aiden blinked. "She did?" She had assumed that Dawn hadn't told her new colleagues and the new office manager about their relationship. Aiden wasn't exactly in the closet at her workplace, but she wasn't advertising her sexual orientation either. She never talked about Dawn or their relationship with anyone but Ray. There were still too many cops who would react with scorn and derision or maybe even outright hostility to a lesbian in their ranks. Obviously, psychologists were a lot more open-minded—or Dawn just didn't care.

"Oh, yes, of course!" Mrs. Phillips' head bobbed up and down. "She seems quite proud to be friends with a female detective."

So Dawn hadn't told her colleagues how close their "friendship" really was. Aiden nodded at the office manager. "You said she was on her way out?"

"She wanted to leave half an hour ago, but I think she fell asleep on her own couch." Mrs. Phillips leaned over her desk to whisper conspiratorially, "She seemed a bit upset after her last session."

Upset? Aiden frowned. *I hope they didn't have her counsel a rape victim again!* "Can I...?" She pointed at the door to Dawn's office.

"Yes, of course. Now that you're here, I'll leave for the day. I waited because I didn't want her to have to walk out alone after... well, you know what happened to her." Mrs. Phillips looked at her with sad eyes.

Another surprise. Dawn had obviously told her colleagues about her rape. It continued to amaze Aiden how open Dawn was about it. She knew it wasn't easy for her, but Dawn forced herself to talk about it and set an example for other victims, encouraging them to speak up about what had happened to them. "That's very kind of you. I appreciate it." Aiden gave Mrs. Phillips a sincere nod. It felt good to know the people around Dawn cared about her and looked after her when Aiden couldn't be there to do it.

She left the reception area behind and quietly slipped into Dawn's office. The room was almost dark, just one single standard lamp throwing its light onto the unmoving form on the couch.

Dawn was stretched out on the small couch, her blouse wrinkled and her hair falling in disarray around her face. Her shoes were next to the couch, leaving her feet bare, and her skirt had slipped halfway up her thighs.

Aiden quietly sat down on one of the beanbags and watched Dawn sleep.

Suddenly, a jerk went through Dawn's slender body. Her eyes snapped open as if she had somehow sensed the intruder in the quiet room.

"Hey, sweetheart, it's me, Aiden," Aiden announced herself immediately, not wanting Dawn to be afraid for even a single second.

Dawn sat up and sleepily rubbed her eyes.

Aiden smiled as she watched her. *God, she's adorable.* She wanted to cross the room and kiss her awake, but she was determined never to ambush Dawn again while she wasn't fully awake.

"You don't have to add your name," Dawn said when she was awake enough for decent conversation. "Currently, there's only one woman—except for my mother—who would call me 'sweetheart.'"

"Currently?" Aiden lifted a teasing eyebrow as she sat down on the couch next to Dawn.

Without hesitation, Dawn leaned against her shoulder and buried her face against Aiden's neck.

Aiden closed her eyes for a moment, enjoying the sleepy warmth and innocent trust that Dawn radiated. What she and Dawn shared was so different from the things she experienced at work, and she didn't know how she had ever lived without it. "Hey, sweetie." She wrapped both arms around Dawn. "Everything all right?"

She felt Dawn nod against her.

"Really? Mrs. Phillips said there was a session that seemed to upset you." Aiden looked down at the woman in her arms. She wasn't used to Dawn being reluctant to talk about what troubled her. "I know you have to keep confidentiality and can't talk about details, but can you tell me why that patient's case is hitting you so hard?"

"It's not a patient," Dawn said. She sat up but took care to stay within Aiden's embrace.

Aiden frowned. "No? But Mrs. Phillips said..."

"It was a co-vision session," Dawn explained. "That's like supervision, only with a colleague instead of someone with more experience. We normally meet twice a month to talk about tough cases or issues from our private lives that influence our work."

Aiden instantly wondered about what "issues" Dawn might talk during these sessions, but then shoved the thought aside. "What was so troubling about today's session?" she asked, rubbing Dawn's back.

"This colleague, she's a friend of mine," Dawn said. "We've known each other since college, but she went into police psychology."

"Uh, a department shrink!"

The playful expression of horror on Aiden's face made Dawn laugh, and Aiden answered the smile with one of her own.

"Don't act as if I just told you she was a professional torturer!" Dawn pinched her playfully, but then the serious expression returned to her face. "My friend is having a difficult time coming to terms with the fact that she's falling in love again."

"What's so troubling about falling in love?" Aiden asked. "I, for my part, enjoy being in love very much."

Dawn pressed her lips to Aiden's for a second. "She lost her husband, a cop, just a year ago."

"Oh. And now she's probably feeling guilty about falling in love with another man, huh?" Aiden had seen it with the wives of colleagues who had died in the line of duty before. "I can imagine it's very hard for her, but if something happened to me, I wouldn't want you to stay alone for the rest of your life."

She felt Dawn clutch at her shoulders, pulling her even closer as if to make sure no one would take Aiden from her. "Would you want me to spend it with Ray?" she asked after a while.

"Uh... Ray? Why Ray? Is there something going on between you and my partner that I should know about?" Aiden asked with a mock stern gaze.

"No." Dawn slapped her on the shoulder. "But that friend of mine... she thinks she's falling in love with her late husband's partner on the force."

"Oh." Aiden tried to imagine what that must feel like for both of them.

"His female partner," Dawn added.

Aiden exhaled sharply. "Wow. What's that saying? If you think shrinks don't have problems, you're crazy." She whistled and shook her head. "I can easily see why that would give your colleague some sleepless nights, but why is it upsetting you so much?"

Dawn ran a hand through her tangled hair. "My friend is dealing with a lot of different issues at once—falling in love with a woman after a lifetime of nothing but heterosexual relationships, feeling guilty for loving anyone but her dead husband, and she's also very afraid to open herself up to loving a cop again. I'm over the first one, luckily didn't have to deal with the second one, but the third issue is something that hits a little too close to home," she quietly admitted.

A sudden feeling of guilt knotted Aiden's stomach. She didn't know what to say, realizing there wasn't anything she could say to allay Dawn's fears.

"I lost my father and my brother to their jobs; I had to visit my ex-husband in the hospital twice during our marriage, and I don't even want to think about how I felt when Del told me you had been shot. I know how very real the dangers of being on the job are," Dawn said, her voice barely above a whisper. "I thought about it a lot during the last few months, and I don't think it's a coincidence that I picked an art gallery owner for my second relationship. The worst that ever happened to Maggie at work was having paint spilled all over her designer clothes."

Aiden nodded thoughtfully. She had only met Dawn's ex-girlfriend once, but she had noticed right away that she and Maggie couldn't be more different and still belong to the same species. Maggie was sophisticated and elegant. She had never come in contact with the horrors and the violence that were a part of Aiden's life.

Until now, she hadn't given a lot of thought to what might have attracted Dawn to the gallery owner. Maggie Forsyth was breathtakingly gorgeous after all, so she hadn't searched for other explanations. *Part of the attraction was Maggie not being a cop,* Aiden suddenly understood. *Dawn needed to have someone in her life who couldn't be taken from her in the blink of an eye.* Aiden cleared her throat. "I know my job scares you, and I'm sorry you have to go through all the worrying again. But... that's what I do. It's who I am. I can't just turn in my badge because—"

"And I don't want you to," Dawn said quickly. "But I think it's time for us to deal with some hard realities."

Hard realities? Aiden didn't like the sound of that. They had dealt with a lot during the last few weeks, and she was ready to just have some fun and enjoy the good times for a while. *Apparently not tonight.* "What do you mean?" she asked reluctantly.

"You could be hurt in the line of duty again," Dawn said, staring down at the gun Aiden still wore on her hip. "Or worse. We haven't prepared for that possibility in any way."

"Prepare?" Aiden repeated, not quite sure how she could prepare herself for being shot other than making sure to wear her bullet-resistant vest.

Dawn nodded, finally looking up from the badge and the gun on Aiden's belt. "We can't get married, and the law doesn't protect our relationship. We have to do it. Otherwise, if anything happened to you, I'd be treated like a complete stranger with no right to visit you or make any decisions for you."

Aiden had never thought about things like that. Up until a few months ago, she'd never had a reason to. There had never been a woman she wanted to have any long-term rights in her life. Now she had Dawn.

"There's a lot to think about," Dawn continued. "Right now, it's just the two of us, but what if we decide we want to have a child... or even more than one?"

Aiden could only sit and stare at her. Her head was spinning. *I came here to ask her out to a nightclub, and she's talking about having children. We're clearly not on the same page tonight.* "I'll ask around," she promised vaguely. "Maybe Kade knows a lawyer who specializes in gay rights."

Dawn nodded, stood, and smiled down at Aiden. She seemed to sense that Aiden wasn't up for tackling all these difficult issues tonight. "So, what brings you to my humble workplace tonight? Not a relapse into your Xena persona again?"

"No. Tonight, I'm searching for a Cinderella who will go out and dance with me 'til the midnight hour," Aiden said with a grin. "Or do you still have some peas and lentils to sort out?" She nodded at the files on Dawn's desk.

"The peas and lentils could wait, but I don't think I'm up for going to a club tonight. Frankly, I'm exhausted and just want to curl up on my couch for a while," Dawn said, guiltily looking up at Aiden from under honey-colored lashes. "But if you're willing to take a rain check, I'd be willing to make room on the couch for you."

Aiden nodded slowly. Curling up on the couch with Dawn was a nice thought even if it wasn't what she wanted tonight.

Dawn tilted her head and looked up into Aiden's eyes, studying her intently. "If you really want to go, I'll come with you," she offered.

Now Aiden was the one to stare into Dawn's eyes. With a frown she realized they had never been to a club together. Dawn hadn't gone out to a club or a gay bar since she had been raped, and she was clearly not up to making that difficult step after her hard day at work. "You know what? Curling up on the couch with you sounds like a perfect evening." *I'll just go on an extra long run tomorrow morning. That should take care of any excess energy,* Aiden decided.

* * *

Dawn woke with a frown. The space next to her in the bed was cold and empty. "Aiden?" she called and sat up, rubbing her eyes.

Aiden stepped out of the bathroom, already dressed in her running clothes. "Hey, good morning." She bent down and gently kissed Dawn.

Closing her eyes, Dawn wrapped her arms around the strong neck and tried to drag Aiden back into the bed. She had missed cuddling with Aiden in the mornings during their busy week.

"Ah, ah!" Aiden gently resisted. "Come on, lazybones, get out of bed and come running with me!"

Dawn nestled herself deeper into the warmth of the covers. Today was her day off, and she didn't want to start it by running around the park like some lunatic. She didn't want to start her day at all. Not before ten o'clock. "Running? Me?" She shook her head.

"I'm not a runner. If you want somebody to accompany you on your morning runs, you should get a dog or find yourself another girlfriend."

Black hair fell onto Aiden's forehead as she shook her head. "Considering the hours I work, getting a dog wouldn't be fair to the poor animal, and I'm quite satisfied with the girlfriend I have, thank you very much—except for her lack of willingness to go on a run with me," Aiden said with a challenging grin.

"Hey, maybe you could convince Del to be your running partner!" Dawn sat up with a bright grin. She had tried for months to come up with something that would make her partner and her oldest friend spend some time together but hadn't been very successful at it.

Aiden didn't seem very taken with the idea. "I don't know."

"I know she's always searching for someone who can keep up with her. Unless you think she's out of your league. Del is training for the marathon. That might be a little too much for you." Dawn innocently looked up at Aiden. She knew how competitive Aiden could be, especially when it came to Del.

Aiden folded her arms over her chest. "Give her a call. She's probably not even up yet."

Dawn grinned and reached for her phone. She dialed Del's home number, but only the answering machine picked up, so she tried Del's cell phone. It rang a few times, and Dawn was about to give up when it was finally answered.

"Yeah?" Del's voice was rough as if she had just woken up.

Dawn raised her eyebrows. *She's not at home, and she's just waking up?* For as long as she had known Del, she had never stayed at anyone's apartment until the next morning. "Del? Did I wake you? Where are you?"

"Grasshopper?" Del cleared her throat. "Is that you?"

Dawn smiled at the old childhood nickname. "Yes. Sorry to wake you."

"You didn't."

"Liar," Dawn said with a smile.

Del chuckled. "It's a good thing you woke me up anyway. I think I was about to be arrested for loitering with intent. There's a uni coming my way who looks like he didn't have his morning coffee yet."

"What? Where are you?" Dawn asked again.

"Enjoying a quiet morning in South Waterfront," Del answered, then Dawn heard her exchange a few words with the uniformed cop she had mentioned.

South Waterfront? As far as Dawn knew, Del had no friends in that neighborhood, and it wasn't exactly close to her apartment in St. Johns. She pressed the receiver against her blanket-covered shoulder for a moment and looked at Aiden. "Where does Kade live?" she asked with sudden inspiration.

"South Waterfront. She has this posh apartment overlooking the marina," Aiden answered, looking up from the task of tying her running shoes. "Why?"

Dawn didn't answer. She was too shocked to find her hunch confirmed. Del had spent the night at Kade Matheson's apartment. *Wow!* "Del?" she said into the receiver. "Do you want to go for a run?"

"With you?" Del laughed, not even trying to hide her disbelief.

"Thanks," Dawn grumbled. "No, with Aiden."

"Ah." Del was silent for a few seconds. "I thought I'd give it a rest for today and maybe start up again tomorrow."

Dawn drummed her index finger against the receiver. Del didn't seem any more eager than Aiden to spend time together. "Del, I know Aiden is a few years younger than you, but that's no reason why you shouldn't run with her. I could ask her to pace herself if you want." She barely held back a grin, knowing Del would hear it in her voice.

"Tell your sweetheart to have a hearty breakfast. She's gonna need it," Del growled. She gave Dawn the time and place where she would meet Aiden and hung up.

When Dawn replaced the receiver and looked up, Aiden stood there watching her with her hands on her hips. "You have that woman wrapped around your cute little finger," Aiden said, shaking her head.

"Both of you," Dawn corrected with a charming grin. She knew she was shamelessly manipulating Del and Aiden, but they were both too stubborn to spend any time together and get to know each other otherwise. "Aiden, listen. I know I shouldn't be doing this. I shouldn't get involved, but it would mean a lot to me if Del and you got along."

"We do," Aiden said.

Dawn sighed. Yes, there seemed to be a certain understanding between them—mainly the understanding that each of them would stay out of the other's way. "You're polite strangers with only me and your jobs in common. I want you to be friends. Do you think you could try? For me?"

"For you, I'll even let her win," Aiden promised as she straightened and bounced up and down on the balls of her feet a few times.

"Win?" Dawn echoed. "It's not a competition. You're just gonna keep each other company on your morning run." She was beginning to think she had made a grave mistake.

* * *

Aiden glanced to her right where Del Vasquez was jogging up the slope next to her. Del wasn't even breathing hard, and her strides were even. Aiden noticed with satisfaction that her own legs still felt strong and her breathing was rhythmic.

They silently ran next to each other for another mile. Their pace wasn't too fast, still neither of them had said a word since the "let's go" when they had met. They were running together, yes, but that wasn't exactly what Dawn had in mind. *Come on, you know Dawn is going to ask what you talked about. Just "hi" and "bye" won't cut it.*

"How far do you go on your morning runs? Five miles?" she asked.

Del turned her head in Aiden's direction. "Fifteen on most mornings. More than that on the weekends."

Hmm. I should add a few miles to my training regimen. Aiden was silent for another few steps, waiting for Del to keep up her part of the conversation.

Del didn't.

Okay. One more try at friendly conversation, then I've fulfilled my duties to Dawn. "Do you have a regular training partner?" Aiden asked.

"No. Mostly, I run alone." Just when Aiden thought Del would leave it at that short answer, Del said, "I went on a run with your DDA last week, though."

Aiden's legs slowed without her conscious decision, and she quickly lengthened her stride to catch up with Del again. "You went on a run with Kade?" she repeated, just to make sure she hadn't misunderstood. *I thought Kade had given Del her marching orders?*

Del confirmed with a nod. A slight smile softened the serious expression.

"I hope you took pity on her," Aiden said. Kade was in great shape, but Aiden couldn't see her keeping up with the intense Del Vasquez.

"You've clearly never been on a run with her," Del said with an only slightly out of breath laugh. "She was the one who took pity on me."

Aiden worked hard to keep the frown off her face. Del's answer was surprising on so many levels. Not only had Kade proven to be faster and to have more endurance than Del, but the competitive lieutenant had taken it so well. Del looked as if she had taken it for granted that Kade could beat her. *Seems she has a very different image of Kade than the rest of us. I wonder how much time they spent together for her to see the more hidden side of our DDA.* "So is she going to be your regular running partner?" she asked in an attempt to find out more about how far the relationship had progressed.

"I doubt it. Kade prefers to run alone," Del answered. Her voice was carefully neutral, not betraying what she thought about that.

"She told you that?" Aiden asked. *Ouch, Kade, that was a blatant rebuff.*

Del turned off to the left and shook her head. "She didn't need to. I could sense it. Other prosecutors practice their opening and closing statements by reading them out loud in their office or trying them on their assistants. Kade goes over them during her morning runs. With every step she takes, she leaves more and more of Kade behind and becomes DDA Matheson."

Aiden almost stumbled over a root as she stared at Del. *I've worked with Kade every day for the last two years, but I never knew that about her. How come Del knows all the little details?* An unexpected wave of something that felt close to jealousy overcame her, followed immediately by anger at herself. *What are you doing? Stop it right now! There was never anything between you and Kade—and even if there were, you have Dawn now.*

She looked at Del, who was a step ahead of her by now. Quickly, she picked up her pace until they were running side by side again. The rhythmic breathing helped her to calm down and focus on her emotions. A few more even strides and she realized she wasn't jealous of Del because she might be embarking on a romantic relationship with Kade. She was jealous because Del had been privy to the more private, vulnerable side of Kade while she had mostly encountered the cool, calm, and collected DDA Matheson.

"You okay?" Del asked.

"Of course," Aiden said immediately. She didn't want Del to think she was tired already just because she had been distracted by her thoughts. "Pick up the pace?" She flashed Del a challenging grin.

"You bet! Just because your DDA ran me ragged doesn't mean I'd let a lowly detective beat me!" Del called as she lengthened her stride and raced ahead of Aiden.

With a curse, Aiden picked up her pace.

CHAPTER 11

AIDEN WATCHED Swenson's office door close behind the lieutenant. "Shit." *There go my plans for the evening.*

"What?" Ray asked, looking up from the files on his desk with a grin. "You don't look forward to spending eight hours in a small car with a defective heater, not allowed to drink coffee because it might make you have to pee?" He grinned when she glared at him. "Well, it's not exactly how I pictured my ideal Friday evening either. You had plans with your favorite shrink?"

Aiden nodded morosely. "We have invitations for an art exhibition."

Ray whistled. "Art exhibition? My, my, you're moving up in the world!"

Aiden held back a sigh. Art exhibitions were not usually how she spent her time, but Dawn had asked, so she had said yes. Now Dawn would think she was using work to back out of an event she hadn't wanted to go to in the first place. She waited until Ray was on the phone with Susan, then quickly dialed Dawn's office number. "Hi, Mrs. Phillips," she greeted Dawn's office manager. "It's Aiden Carlisle. Is the doc with a patient right now?"

The office manager still thought they were nothing more than friends, but by now she knew exactly to which doctor Aiden was referring. "No, she's between patients. You have six minutes. I'll put you through."

"Hi, sweetie," Dawn said brightly. It seemed as if her day was going better than Aiden's.

"Hey." Aiden took a breath. There was no way to make this sound better than it was, so she decided to come right out and say it. "Dawn, about tonight. I won't be able to make it. We have to help out narcotics with surveillance. I'll probably be gone all night."

There was a moment of silence. "Oh. All right. Call me when you get home, okay?"

Aiden knew Dawn well enough by now to hear the slight disappointment and the worry in her voice. "It could be in the middle of the night," she warned her. "I don't want to wake you."

"Call," Dawn insisted, putting a lot of intensity behind the one word.

"Okay," Aiden finally relented.

Dawn cleared her throat. "Will you be able to catch an hour or two in that room you call the 'dungeon' before you head out?"

Aiden stared down at the files on her desk. "Probably," she said even though it was doubtful. She didn't want Dawn to worry. "Listen, I'm sorry I can't go with you to the art exhibition."

"That's one of the perils of your job; we both know that," Dawn answered, doing a good job at hiding her disappointment.

Aiden bit her lip. She had wanted Dawn to have a nice evening out, but now she would sit at home alone, worrying. Aiden brightened when she saw Kade entering the squad room. Kade's family was a well-known supporter of the arts, so it stood to reason that Kade would be interested in going to an art exhibition. "What if I could offer a replacement?" she asked, grinning at her own brilliant idea.

"No one can replace you," Dawn said.

Aiden could practically see the impish, affectionate grin on Dawn's lips. She smiled. "Well, all right, she won't be able to replace me, but at least she could accompany you to the art exhibition. She probably knows a lot more about art than I do anyway."

"Who?" Dawn asked.

Aiden looked across the room to where Kade stood talking to Okada, the strap of her briefcase slung over her shoulder, indicating that she was probably ready to go home for the day. "Kade."

"Kade? Kade Matheson? You want me to go to an art exhibition with Kade Matheson?" Dawn asked, her voice ending in a disbelieving squeak. "Does she even know you're offering her company?"

"She's standing right here," Aiden said, answering the question without lying but also without telling the whole truth.

But Dawn knew her too well. "You haven't even asked her."

"But I will. And I bet she'll want to go," Aiden said.

"She's probably too busy," Dawn said.

Aiden shrugged. "I'll just ask her. You'd go with her, right?"

Dawn hesitated. "I don't know."

Aiden frowned. Dawn was not a shy person. She loved people, and people loved her. But when it came to Kade, Dawn sometimes seemed oddly self-conscious. "You tricked me into going for a run with your friend Del, now it's your turn to spend a little time with one of my friends." She stopped and listened to the echo of her words. *Friends...* Yes, she admitted, Kade was becoming a friend even though they hardly ever socialized or talked about anything but work.

There was a knock on Dawn's office door. "I have to go." Another second of hesitation. "Have Kade give me a call if she wants to go to the exhibition."

"Great." Aiden grinned.

"Be careful, please. I love you," Dawn said as she always did when it was time for Aiden to return to her job.

Aiden smiled. She knew how important that little ritual was for Dawn, and she was beginning to like it too. "I will," she answered. Out of the corner of her eye, she saw Kade stopping next to her desk. "And..." She gave herself a mental kick. "...I love you too."

She replaced the receiver and looked up at Kade, who was gazing down at her with an unreadable expression. *Now I only have to convince Kade.* "On your way out?" she asked, pointing to the briefcase resting over Kade's slender shoulder.

Kade nodded. "If you don't have anything else that needs my attention."

"Nah. We're going out for a fun night with the guys from narcotics later," Aiden said, making a face. "Should be a quiet night for you."

Kade gave her a businesslike nod.

Aiden couldn't tell if she was looking forward to her night off or not. It was hard to read Kade sometimes. *Del probably could.* The thought flashed through her mind, annoying her. "Do you have plans?"

Kade eyed her with something that looked like surprise. The detectives normally didn't ask about her private life. "Not really," she answered vaguely.

"Are you interested in art?" Aiden asked before her courage could fail her. It felt strangely like trying to ask Kade out.

"Art?" Kade repeated slowly.

"Yes, you know, paintings, sculptures... that kind of thing," Aiden said with an awkward grin.

Kade grazed her with a small, superior smile. "Thank you, Detective, I'm aware of the definition of art, but why are you asking?"

Aiden picked a pen off her desk and played with it. "Well, I'm stuck at this surveillance tonight, so Dawn has no one to accompany her to the art exhibition she wanted to go to. I thought you might be interested."

Kade shifted her briefcase to her other shoulder, a simple tactic intended to buy her a little more time to mull over the question. "You want me to go to an art exhibition with your..." Kade looked around the busy squad room. "...with Dawn Kinsley?"

Aiden found herself getting a little defensive. "She's not a persona non grata in this squad room, you know? Her case is long since closed. There's no reason why you shouldn't be allowed to socialize with her—unless you don't like her, of course." She studied Kade, waiting for her response.

"I don't know her well enough to form an opinion one way or the other," Kade answered.

That carefully neutral answer gave Aiden the opening she needed. "Then why not go with her to the exhibition and get to know her a bit better?" she suggested gently. She knew Kade would not react well to too much pressure.

Kade smoothed nonexistent wrinkles out of her skirt. "If she doesn't mind being left behind in a hurry, in case you call me away for a search warrant or any other legal assistance."

"Don't worry; Dawn is used to that. She's an old hand at being left behind in a hurry," Aiden said. They had been interrupted on romantic evenings out more times than she could count.

Kade hesitated for another second, then she straightened her shoulders. "It's been a while since I've been to an art exhibition, so why not?"

"Great." Aiden quickly scribbled Dawn's cell phone number on a piece of paper and shoved it at Kade before she could change her mind. She took her jacket from the back of her chair and shrugged into it as she stood. "Have fun."

"You're setting Kade up on a date with your girlfriend?" Ray chuckled as they walked to their car.

Aiden rolled her eyes. "Get your mind out of the gutter, Ray. They're going to look at a few oil paintings while they sip champagne and nibble on cheese and crackers; that's all."

"And talk about you," Ray said with a wide grin.

Aiden stopped with her hand on the door of their unmarked car and turned to face her partner. "What?"

Ray laughed. "Don't look so surprised. What else do they have to talk about? Dawn is a psychologist from a middle-class family, and Kade is a blue-blooded lawyer. They only have one thing in common—you." He laughed again and clapped her on the shoulder. "I guess that's one conversation where you'd like to be a fly on the wall."

Aiden grimaced. It was a conversation she not only didn't want to overhear—she wanted to stop it before it went too far. She had thought this evening would be about Kade and Dawn getting to know each other better. What she hadn't counted on was that they would bond over exchanging information about her. She didn't want Kade to tell Dawn about the dangerous situations she had gotten into while on the job, and she didn't want Kade to find out about the softer, more private side of Aiden Carlisle. But she had given Kade Dawn's number, and it was out of her hands. "Give me the keys," she ordered. "I'll drive." That was one thing over which she still had control.

* * *

Dawn shuffled her feet and breathed into her hands. It was a rather cool night for the end of April, but the gesture was more one of nervousness than because she was cold. *Come on!* she gave herself a pep talk. *Kade hasn't even arrived yet. Why are you so intimidated by her? She's only human, with as many flaws and insecurities as the rest of us.* She knew part of her nervousness when it came to Kade Matheson was because she had been just a helpless victim and Kade had been the competent prosecutor when they had met.

That's no reason to be nervous, she told herself. *Aiden has seen you on the worst day of your life, but that didn't make you uncomfortable around her, did it?* It was different with Kade somehow. Maybe because she had been able to sense Aiden's compassion and admiration from the start, whereas it was much harder to discern what Kade was feeling and thinking.

"Dr. Kinsley?"

Dawn turned around—and found herself staring at Kade Matheson. She wasn't the only one. In her tight, elegant, pine green dress that formed a striking contrast to her hair, Kade attracted the attention of every man and almost every woman who was heading into the gallery. She was moving toward Dawn with a graceful confidence that told Dawn she was used to the admiring glances.

Dawn sighed. That was another difference between her and Kade. Dawn had been a shy, slightly overweight teenager and had only lost the last of her puppy fat during the last five or six years.

Next to the classically beautiful Kade Matheson, she still felt like the ugly duckling. *Oh, come on! Aiden is getting over her infatuation, and you have to get over it too.* Belatedly, she reached out her hand to greet Kade. "Hi. It's Dawn, not Dr. Kinsley. I'm glad you could make it."

Kade took her hand in a gentle yet firm grip. "Kade," she said with a smile. "Thank you for the invitation. Shall we?" She nodded at the gallery's entrance.

They stepped inside and wandered from painting to painting for a while, commenting on style and colors. Both of them conversed easily with the other guests and a few of the artists. Kade was clearly very much at home at an event like this.

"Dawn!" An elegant hand slipped down Dawn's arm and came to rest on her elbow in a familiar gesture.

Dawn turned away from the painting at which she had been looking. "Hi, Maggie," she said with a smile. She had expected to meet her ex-girlfriend at the exhibition—it was her gallery, after all, and if she wasn't mistaken, a few of the works across the room were hers too.

"Good to see you haven't abandoned the arts just because you left me," Maggie said with a wink.

Great. Now Kade knows she's my ex before we've even said more than a few polite words to each other. Her failed relationship with Maggie wasn't the first thing she had wanted Kade to learn about her.

"And you also haven't given up on women," Maggie added. Her startling blue eyes threw admiring glances at Kade. "What happened to that cop, though?"

Dawn sighed. As elegant and cultured as Maggie was, she would never be a diplomat. She took being an artistic free spirit much too far sometimes. "Aiden has to work tonight. This is Kade, a... friend," she said after a few seconds of hesitation. She wanted to make it clear that she was still in a relationship with Aiden even though Maggie was obviously convinced that it hadn't lasted and Kade Matheson was a much better match than a cop for her. Dawn looked at Kade, wanting to see her reaction to being called a friend by a woman who had been a former witness.

Kade didn't even blink. She just looked at Maggie with a pleasant smile as if she had accompanied Dawn to a hundred art exhibitions before.

Maggie looked from Dawn to Kade. Her smile brightened when she realized Kade wasn't Dawn's new girlfriend. She reached for Kade's hand, but instead of shaking it, she lifted it to her mouth for a hinted-at kiss. "Enchanté."

Kade looked startled only for a split second, then she accepted the compliment with the same grace that she would a man's attention.

"Maggie," Dawn drawled warningly.

"What?" Maggie flashed her a charming, innocent smile.

Dawn sternly shook her head. The time when she couldn't resist Maggie's charms was long over. "We're here to admire the art—not the artist."

"Can't you do both?" Maggie quipped, her gaze never leaving Kade.

Another artist who sidled over for a few questions captured Maggie's attention.

Dawn quickly used the opportunity to direct Kade away from her.

"So," Kade said while she picked up a glass of champagne from a tray, "that was Maggie Forsyth, right?"

Dawn wasn't surprised that Kade had made the connection. Kade knew a lot of people, who knew a lot of people. "That was Maggie Forsyth," she confirmed and chose a glass of sparkling cider from the tray, "and yes, she's my ex, in case you're still wondering what that charming little greeting was all about."

Kade just nodded, but that relative lack of reaction made Dawn even more nervous and made her prattle on, "I know, I know, she's a British version of Bette Porter... with a toned down alpha-female attitude, of course."

That finally got her a bit of a reaction. Kade lowered her champagne glass and raised both eyebrows instead. "Bette Porter?" she asked. "You're not referring to Councilman Porter's wife, are you?" Kade clearly wasn't used to not knowing the important people.

Dawn almost choked on her sparkling cider when she burst into laughter. She finally felt herself relax around Kade. "No, no.

Bette Porter isn't someone you would know. She's just a fictional character from a TV show." *Just because Kade spent the night with Del doesn't mean she's an educated member of our team now,* Dawn reminded herself. *They didn't spend the night preparing for a lesbian pop culture exam, after all.*

Kade gave her a nod. "I didn't think Councilman Porter's wife would be that smooth in trying to pick up other women," she commented dryly.

Dawn laughed again. *Who would have known... Kade Matheson has a great sense of humor, and she's much more comfortable around lesbians than I thought.* "Oh, yes, I bet Maggie can be so much smoother than Mrs. Porter."

"How did you meet her?" Kade asked between elegant sips from her glass of champagne. "At an art exhibition?"

Dawn nodded and thought back to that day with a smile. "It was almost five years ago. I stood looking at a painting, and this beautiful woman stepped up behind me and asked my opinion. I told her I didn't like it. It wasn't until later that I found out she was the artist who had created that painting."

Kade laughed, and Dawn realized she had never heard her laugh out loud before. The sound of Kade's laughter also made Maggie look up from her own conversation and smile at Kade.

"I'm afraid you picked up a new not-so-secret admirer," Dawn said and watched with astonishment how the smile vanished from Kade's face. "Are you uncomfortable with it? Do you want me to tell Maggie to back off?"

"No, I can handle it," Kade said confidently. "If it gets to be too much, I'll just tell her I have a boyfriend."

Dawn studied her. She still found it hard to read Kade. She didn't appear uncomfortable being admired by a lesbian, but she had cringed when Dawn had told her she had a new admirer in Maggie. "Do you?" she asked, deciding it was time to take the more direct route.

"Have a boyfriend?" Kade was unperturbed by the question. It probably was something she had to answer quite often, and her answer was a practiced one. "Well, according to the courthouse rumor mill, I'm having a torrid affair with Judge Yates, but at the end of the day, I have neither the time nor the energy for it."

So she's basically telling me her job leaves her no time for a private life. Doesn't tell me much about her interests. "I know the feeling. Aiden wanted to take me out to a nightclub last week, but I was just too exhausted," Dawn said.

Kade nodded her understanding but didn't pick up that topic of conversation.

Dawn had thought that they would talk about Aiden for most of the night because it was the one thing they had in common, but so far, Kade had successfully avoided that topic. *Is she uncomfortable thinking about her detective being in a relationship with me?* She was sure it wasn't because Kade was uncomfortable talking about lesbian relationships. She had asked her about Maggie without hesitation. "Aiden seems to have so much more energy than I do sometimes," Dawn continued, carefully watching Kade's reactions. "I've been trying to get her to go on a run with Del, but I'm not so sure that was a good idea."

"Why?" Kade asked immediately, obviously much more willing to talk about that subject. "Del is a well-trained runner, and from what I've seen of Aiden when she chases down a perp, they should be evenly matched."

Ah. Dawn started to understand. Kade would discuss Aiden, and she would discuss Dawn's past relationships, but she had obviously decided to stay out of her present relationship. Dawn's respect for Kade grew. "They are, and that's the problem. They're both so competitive, not willing to give an inch. Aiden came home from that run totally drenched and exhausted, and I bet Del didn't look any better."

"Del is not particularly competitive," Kade said. "She didn't even bat an eye when I beat her in our little race."

Dawn hid her surprise at the revelation that Kade and Del had been running together. *Obviously, they spent more time together than I was aware of.* Dawn realized somewhat guiltily that she had been so busy with her own problems lately that she hadn't kept up with what was going on in Del's life. She promised herself to change that. "She's not competitive with me either," she answered and then added with a laugh, "Not that she would need to be. I'm not a runner, and I couldn't keep up with her or Aiden. I think Del is only competitive with some people. Aiden definitely brings the competitive streak out in her. My dad did sometimes too."

"They were partners on the force, right?" For the first time all night, Kade appeared really interested, not just like someone who was merely engaging in polite small talk.

Dawn thought of her earliest memories of her father and Del playing basketball in the backyard. She smiled wistfully. "They were more than that. They were almost like siblings even though Dad was ten years older than Del. Del spent more time with my dad than his own family. In some ways, losing him was harder on her than it was on us."

"Why?"

Dawn noticed that Kade asked short questions intended to keep her talking. She smiled. Obviously, their jobs had some things in common. "My dad was killed in a traffic stop. Del was right next to him, but neither of them saw it coming in time to prevent it. Del felt guilty for a long, long time. She didn't know how to face us, so she started to avoid us until Mom yelled at her that losing one member of the family was enough."

Kade nodded thoughtfully. It was obvious she had never thought the strong, reliable Del could have once been so vulnerable.

"What about your family? Are you close?" Dawn asked. She was willing to open up and try to build a friendship with Kade but only if Kade was prepared to do the same.

Kade set down her not yet empty glass on the nearest tray. Her steel blue gaze met Dawn's, and they just looked at each other for an endless second. This time, Dawn refused to be intimidated by the cool confidence Kade projected, and for a moment, she could glimpse the woman behind the DDA. "My father died a few years ago, and my mother lives in Ashland, near the Californian border. We don't see each other a lot," Kade answered, her voice calm, giving away none of her feelings.

"Your father... was he a lawyer too?" Dawn asked.

Just a quick clenching of her hands showed Kade's surprise. "How did you guess?" She forced a practiced half smile. "You're not using your psychic abilities, are you, Doctor?"

Dawn returned the smile, but only for a moment. It seemed cops weren't the only ones who used humor to hide their true feelings. "I'm a psychologist, not a psychic, and I think this would be the right time to give you the little speech I give all possible friends. So, just for the record, I'm not here to counsel or treat you. If I talk to you about emotional issues and if I give you advice regarding your private life, I do it as Dawn, not as Dr. Kinsley. This is friendship, not psychotherapy."

"Is it?" Kade asked slowly.

"Friendship?" Dawn waited for Kade's nod of confirmation. "As far as I'm concerned, it could be. You're one of very few friends Aiden has and the woman my best friend is dating, so I'd like to get to know you better."

Instead of opening up now, Kade suddenly appeared even more guarded. Dawn could almost hear the steel doors slam shut. "What makes you think I'm dating Del Vasquez?" Kade asked. "Is that what she told you?"

"Del didn't tell me anything about you," Dawn said with a shake of her head. "She's one of those honorable gals who doesn't kiss and tell."

But instead of soothing Kade's ruffled feathers, it seemed to infuriate her even further. "We didn't kiss, so there is nothing to tell!" She managed to hiss and still keep her voice low enough not to carry beyond the two of them. Kade looked left and right, clearly uncomfortable with discussing her private life in public.

Dawn made a quick decision. "You know what? I think I've had enough art for one evening. How about we head back to my place for a cup of coffee or something more substantial to eat?"

For a moment, she thought Kade would reject the offer, but then one corner of Kade's mouth curled into a smile. "Is that a proposition, Dr. Kinsley?"

Dawn blinked and barked out a surprised laugh. Kade's sense of humor and her witty repartee always came a bit unexpected. "Is that a yes, DDA Matheson?" she asked in the same tone of voice Kade had used.

Kade hesitated, then nodded. "All right. One cup of coffee and I'll be on my way."

* * *

"Make yourself at home while I make some coffee," Dawn called, already heading for what Kade assumed was the kitchen.

Kade wandered through the living room, taking in the shelves full of books, photos, stuffed animals, shells, and other small trinkets. The coffee table looked as if it were covered with smallpox scars, and the colors of the easy chair were a little faded. The couch was clearly the only new piece of furniture in the apartment.

Her parents wouldn't have been impressed with this modest little apartment and its motley collection of furniture, but Kade realized that she liked it. It had a cozy, lived-in feeling that her interior decorator had never achieved even with all the designer furniture.

She stopped in front of the bookcase to look at Dawn's photos. The biggest picture showed Dawn with a baby on her hip while Aiden embraced both of them from behind. A little girl was grinning into the camera in front of them. Kade had seen Aiden with kids before, but they had always been traumatized victims or scared witnesses. This was something else. The children in the picture looked happy—and so did Aiden.

A hissing sound made Kade look away from the picture and down into eyes that were as blue as her own. A chocolate- and cream-colored cat stared up at Kade, her long hair standing on end.

Kade respected cats, but she didn't have much experience, so she preferred to simply stare back until Dawn returned to the living room.

"Oh, I see you've already met the mistress of the house," Dawn said when she set a tray down on the coffee table.

Kade and the cat still eyed each other. Kade hadn't known Dawn had a cat. *Or do they own it together? Aren't cats supposed to be the golden retrievers of lesbian couples?* "I never saw Aiden as someone who would share her life with a cat," she said. Actually, she had never imagined Aiden sharing her life with anyone.

"Oh, she wasn't too cat-crazy at the beginning, but Kia quickly convinced her otherwise," Dawn said with a grin.

Kade looked at the cat. It flicked its tail once and then strode from the room, happily ignoring Kade. *I fail to see how an animal with this kind of attitude can win anyone over.*

"She's not always this reserved and arrogant. Once you get to know her a bit better, she's a real sweetheart," Dawn said, once again guessing Kade's thoughts.

Is she still talking about the cat, or is this how she really sees me? Kade wondered.

"I'm going to change into something more comfortable," Dawn said. "Do you want a change of clothes too?"

Kade quickly shook her head. She didn't intend to make herself that much at home. "No, I'm fine. Go ahead."

"Your dress is beautiful," Dawn said, giving the dress in question one last admiring glance, "but it has been designed for standing around at dinner parties, not for curling up on a couch. You can't have a decent conversation in a dress like that."

Generations of Matheson women had taught Kade otherwise. Her mother had never owned a pair of jeans or, God forbid, sweatpants. Custom-tailored slacks and a silk blouse were as casual as she got.

"Come on; I'll get you a pair of sweatpants," Dawn offered.

Dawn was as persistent as her adopted aunt, but Kade knew she could easily match her stubbornness. "We're not exactly the same size," she said, pointedly looking down at the smaller woman. Dawn was four or five inches shorter than she was but more rounded in other places. "I doubt anything you have would fit me anyway."

"Oh, no problem," Dawn said, already on her way to the bedroom. "I'll give you one of Aiden's sweat suits. I think you're roughly the same size."

Kade grimaced. Wearing Aiden's clothes was the last thing she wanted. Somehow, it appeared much too intimate. However, not wanting to explain the reasons for her refusal to Dawn, she remained silent.

A few minutes later, Dawn reappeared in a baggy pair of sweatpants that had once been black but now appeared more gray. The sleeves of her sweatshirt were pushed up, and she was barefoot. "I left a change of clothes in the bathroom for you," she said.

Kade rose with a sigh.

The bathroom was as small and cozy as the rest of the apartment. Kade noticed there were two toothbrushes resting in the glass next to the mirror. She slipped out of her dress and into the sweatshirt Dawn had provided. The sweatpants were a little baggy but fit well enough if she pulled the strings tight.

When she stepped out of the bathroom, Dawn handed her a cup of coffee and a plate of what Kade guessed to be homemade cookies. *How domestic,* Kade thought. *It must be nice for Aiden to come home to this. Having a wife has its advantages.* She grinned at her own thought as she sipped her coffee. She was glad Aiden had found that safe haven. Over the rim of the mug, she studied Dawn.

Dawn was sitting cross-legged on the couch, both hands curled around her cup of tea. From time to time, she wriggled her bare toes. She appeared so free, so comfortable in her own skin that Kade found it hard to believe she had been raped just six months ago. She seemed so much more content with herself and her life than Kade had ever been. Kade had always wanted to have more, to achieve something higher, to be better than she was now.

Dawn didn't live with that kind of pressure. She was content with what she had and who she was.

"Do you want anything to eat?" Dawn asked. "Other than the cookies, I mean."

Kade shook her head. "No, thank you." She had nibbled on some canapés at the exhibition, and that would tide her over.

"Are you sure? We could make lasagna or something," Dawn said.

Kade stared at her. *Is she really suggesting that we go into the kitchen and prepare a meal together?* Any of her friends, if you could call them that, would have suggested they go out to dinner or order in, but no one had ever wanted to cook with her. "You don't want me anywhere near your kitchen, believe me," she said with a laugh.

"You can't be worse than Del or Aiden," Dawn answered with confidence.

Kade smiled to herself. *Oh, yes, Del's soup was motivation enough to get better quickly before she came back with another pot of the salty broth.* She didn't mention Del's culinary adventures, though. "I wouldn't be so sure. My mother thinks hiring a good cook and reading a menu is all a woman has to know about cooking."

"And my mother wouldn't have let me move out of her home before I could cook every single dish in Granny's old cookbook," Dawn countered. She stood and grabbed Kade's hand, pulling her up from the couch. "Come on. It'll be fun."

The unexpected touch startled Kade, and she allowed herself to be dragged into the small kitchen. "Maybe I should just watch," she said as Dawn pulled out the ingredients for lasagna.

"Oh, come on, Kade!" Dawn set down an ovenproof dish with more emphasis than needed. "You're not a watcher. You're a doer."

Kade couldn't deny that. Standing at the sidelines had never been her thing. "All right. Anything I can do without spoiling the dish?"

"You're not gonna spoil it. I don't expect the perfect masterpiece of haute cuisine. It just has to be edible." Dawn handed her a grater. "Here, you can grate the cheese. But watch your fingers. I don't want to get sued by some overzealous lawyer."

She's teasing me, Kade realized. *She's trying to become my friend.* It was an unfamiliar experience. Not that making friends was a new thing. Kade had a wide circle of acquaintances. There were always people who tried to get on a friendlier basis with her, but most of them had ulterior motives. Some were aiming to help her spend her trust fund; some wanted to make a profit from her family's influence, and some just wanted to have a beautiful woman on their arm or in their bed.

Dawn clearly wasn't one of those people. She made a good living with her practice, but from the look of her apartment, money or power had no real importance to her. And she already had a beautiful woman in her bed. She was trying to befriend Kade just for the sake of friendship.

Kade picked up the piece of cheese and began to grate it. "How come you never tried to teach Del how to cook?" she asked after a while. If she was stuck here for the evening, she might as well use the time to learn more about Del from the woman who knew her best. Gathering information before planning your tactics was the lawyerly thing to do after all.

"Who says I didn't try?" Dawn shot back, looking up from the ground meat she was browning.

"Del's sad attempts at chicken soup," Kade answered before she could censor herself. She realized too late that she had let down her guard.

Dawn turned, spatula in hand, and studied her until the sizzling from the pan made her turn back around. "Del has always respected me just the way I am, so I try to do the same with her. If she doesn't like to cook, I won't force her to," she said over her shoulder, mercifully not commenting on what Kade had let slip.

"How come you're forcing me, then?" Kade demanded to know.

"Because you have to try it first before you know if you like to cook or not," Dawn answered.

Valid point, Kade had to admit and started to grate the cheese again.

"Can I ask you something?" Dawn asked while she cut up a tomato with rapid moves.

Kade stiffened. *Great. Here it comes.*

"Don't worry," Dawn said, lightly touching her arm in the close quarters of the small kitchen. "I won't ask you what's going on between you and Del. I'm curious and a little worried about my best friend, yes, but I respect your privacy. I won't bring up that topic unless you want me to."

Kade grabbed a new piece of cheese. She felt relieved but also a little guilty. Dawn was willingly opening up to her while she was holding back and not telling her anything about herself. As a lawyer, Kade understood the principle of quid pro quo only too well. "In that case, ask away," she said with false cheerfulness.

"Why was there never anything between you and Aiden?" Dawn asked quietly and then added, "Assuming there wasn't."

The sharp edges of the cheese grater scratched over Kade's fingers when she used a little too much force. "Ouch." She quickly pulled back her hand and stared down at the drop of blood running down her index finger.

Dawn grabbed her wrist and pulled her over to the sink.

No one had encroached on Kade's personal space with Dawn's casualness in quite some time. "It's just a small scratch," Kade protested but held still while Dawn placed a band-aid on her finger.

"I'm sorry," Dawn said, her greenish eyes expressing honest regret. "That was a bad time to ask that kind of question."

There is no good time for a question like that. "I told you I wasn't good at cooking," Kade said, pretending the startling question had nothing to do with her little accident.

Dawn turned back to her sauce.

Something told Kade she wouldn't try to ask that question again. *Now I feel obliged to bring it up. Is that a trick they teach psychologists in college?* She sighed. "Just for the record, there was never anything between Aiden and me, and there never will be."

Dawn pulled the pan from the stove and turned back around. She nodded, and Kade could see that she believed her. "Why not?" Dawn asked. Curiosity and just a hint of insecurity shimmered in the depths of the gray-green eyes.

"What happened to 'I respect your privacy'?" Kade asked in an attempt to avoid an answer. The question about her and Aiden wasn't any easier to answer than the question about her and Del.

Dawn bit her lip. "I know this is a very private question too, and I'm aware that you're a very private woman, but I feel like this... thing between you and Aiden will forever stand between us," she pointed from Kade to herself, "and between me and Aiden if we don't address it and clear it up once and for all." Dawn looked up at Kade, ignoring her half-prepared lasagna. "Since I've met Aiden, I've always felt like..." She stopped and searched for words.

Kade waited, worried and curious about where this was going.

"Have you ever watched Star Trek?" Dawn asked, out of the blue.

"What?" That was the last thing she had expected Dawn to say. "What does a sci-fi show have to do with all this?"

Dawn smiled sheepishly. "Well, there were a few episodes about alternative realities. At some points in your life, you make a decision, and that decision changes the course of your life. A different decision would lead to a different life."

"Okay, I'm following you so far," Kade said, trying hard to be patient, "but I still don't see what it has to do with Aiden and you and... me."

"In an alternative reality, Aiden could have very well ended up with you instead of with me," Dawn said very honestly.

Kade shrugged. "In alternative realities, she could have ended up with hundreds of other people." She wasn't sure how much Aiden had told Dawn about her past relationships, so she avoided pointing out details.

"I know Aiden slept with a lot of people before we met, but somehow, for some reason, the only relationship in her life that feels a little threatening at times is her relationship with you," Dawn admitted.

God! Kade mentally groaned. *Why did I agree to come back to her apartment?* "Dawn," she began, looking her right in the eyes, trying to be as convincing as possible to clear this up once and for all, "I told you there was never anything between us. There's nothing to feel threatened about. Aiden loves you."

A wistful smile flitted over Dawn's face. "I know. I don't doubt her feelings or her loyalty. That's not what this is about. I know she loves me, but on bad days, I'm still not sure that I'm the ideal mate for her. Under different circumstances, I could see her with you, you know? You'd have been a good match. You could give her everything I can't."

Kade's first reaction was to deny it or laugh it off, but she knew Dawn was too stubborn, too persistent to let her off the hook that easily. She leaned against the counter and allowed herself to think about it for the first time. Could she imagine herself being with Aiden in an "alternative reality"? There were still a lot of unresolved issues about her sexual orientation and the possible consequences for her career. When she shoved those thoughts aside for a minute, though, she could see herself having a romantic dinner with Aiden. She could even see herself being kissed goodnight. She purposely skipped over the sex part and concentrated on the long-term picture. *What would happen in that alternative reality? A house, a dog, 2.5 kids? Is that what Aiden wants?* Kade wasn't sure, but she knew her own long-term goals didn't involve a white picket fence. *If that is what Aiden dreams of, we'd have a problem. And if it wasn't... we'd still have a problem.* "It wouldn't have worked," Kade concluded. "Even ignoring the fact that I've never been with a woman and didn't plan on ever being with one, I don't think Aiden would have been as happy with me as she is with you. We're both too focused on our jobs to have a healthy relationship together."

"I have a job too," Dawn said, her expression very serious, "and it's important to me too."

"It's one of the things that's important to you," Kade said. "But your life doesn't revolve around your job."

Dawn nodded. "Yeah, but priorities can change."

"Not mine," Kade said with determination. "Aiden deserves better than to play second fiddle to a job that's not exactly nine to five."

Dawn still didn't look convinced.

Kade had admired and almost envied her because she appeared to be so comfortable in her own skin, but she was beginning to see that Dawn had her own insecurities. It was time to be completely honest with Dawn and open up a little. "The first time Aiden told me about her... connection to you, I was livid." She held up her hands when she saw the questions in Dawn's eyes, stopping her from asking them. "My reaction had nothing to do with being jealous or homophobic. You were a victim and our key witness, and Aiden was the detective working the case. I've never known her to risk a case because of personal feelings before, and I was worried about the case and about Aiden's career."

"I would never—" Dawn started to protest, but Kade stopped her again.

"I'm no longer worried that your relationship will hurt Aiden or her career," Kade said. "I've heard a few derogatory or suggestive remarks around the squad room, but overall, your relationship has been nothing but good for Aiden. She's so much happier and more balanced than before."

"She needed someone in her life," Dawn murmured with a gentle, loving expression that made it obvious she was thinking about Aiden, imagining her face right now.

Kade slowly shook her head. *Come on, you've convinced entire juries, so convincing one woman shouldn't be a problem.* "She needed **you** in her life," she corrected, meaning it. "I don't pretend to know you well, but even I can see that you're a nurturer—and that's what Aiden needs. She needs someone who shows her love without holding anything back and who helps her to open up and love without reservation. I know I could never be that woman." There was only a tiny hint of regret in Kade's voice. She had long since dealt with the fact that she was not one to experience that kind of love.

"Without holding anything back," Dawn whispered, almost to herself. She dabbed at her eyes with the sleeve of her sweatshirt, then roughly shook her head. "That's exactly it. I can't love her without holding anything back. I'm just not... after the rape..."

Kade wrapped her hands around the edge of the counter, imagining it was the rail of the jury box. At this moment, she would have chosen Judge Linehan's court over Dawn Kinsley's kitchen. She didn't want to talk about the couple's sex life. She didn't even want to think about it.

"I'm sorry," Dawn said, quickly composing herself. "I embarrassed you."

Kade stood looking at her. She realized that this was one of the decision points that would lead to the alternative realities Dawn had described. She could just nod and change the subject. It would spare both of them a lot of awkwardness, but they would never be more than casual acquaintances. Or she could bite the bullet and try to make a new friend feel better about her own perceived shortcomings. She took a deep breath.

"Listen, Dawn, I can easily imagine that things are not always easy for you... or for Aiden." In her two years with the sex crimes unit, she had seen the devastating effects rape could have on the victims and their loved ones. "But you love each other, and that's so much more important than everything else. What good would it do her to be with a woman who could give her nights of incredible sex but not her whole heart?"

Dawn exhaled and gave Kade a tremulous smile. "I know it's silly."

"It's not," Kade interrupted. "You're wondering if you can give Aiden everything she needs or if she wouldn't be happier with another woman. Just the fact that you're worrying about it should be answer enough."

Dawn gave her a questioning look, full of hope and fear.

"You're thinking about what Aiden wants and needs first and foremost. Not that I have any firsthand experience with it, but I would think that's a sign of true love," Kade said with a small smile.

Dawn didn't answer. She just looked at Kade, and slowly her expression changed. She took a step forward, stopping directly in front of Kade. "I still think you could give her everything—great sex, true love, the whole package. Despite what everyone thinks of you, you can be a very lovable and warmhearted woman."

Warmhearted? Lovable? Kade quirked a skeptical brow. She had heard a lot of adjectives describing her, some of them quite colorful, but lovable and warmhearted had never been among them.

"Yes," Dawn confirmed with a smile, "you delivered proof just now. You didn't want to talk, or even think, about the possibility of a relationship between you and Aiden, but you did it anyway because you knew I'd forever worry about it otherwise. Thank you."

Kade tilted her head in silent acknowledgment, glad that the topic was finally closed. "Glad to know my lawyerly skills of argumentation worked. You are the best thing that could have happened to Aiden." For once, there was no need to pretend she believed in her argument—she really did.

Dawn shook her head. "Sorry to attack your lawyerly ego, but your argument didn't convince me," she said with an impish little smile. "Not totally, at least. I still think you'd have been a great partner for Aiden, but I've decided that for once, I'd like to be just a little selfish, so I'm glad Aiden ended up with me and not with you."

Kade didn't know what to say to that, so she just gave a nod. She admired Dawn's openness and her honesty. She had willingly revealed her emotional insecurities, something Kade had avoided all her life.

"Come on, Chief Cheese Grater!" Dawn bumped Kade's shoulder with her own. "This lasagna isn't gonna make itself."

* * *

"What a waste of time," Aiden murmured as she entered Dawn's apartment. She quietly laid down her badge and gun on top of the dresser in the hallway, careful not to wake Dawn should she already be asleep.

After her surveillance duty had ended early, she had decided to come over and see if Dawn was still up instead of possibly waking her with a call. She knew Dawn would be glad if she could see for herself that she was okay, but Aiden had selfish reasons for coming over too. She had missed Dawn, and she couldn't imagine a better end to her frustrating day than to go to sleep wrapped around Dawn's familiar warmth.

Kia, Dawn's Balinese, intercepted her in the hallway and herded her to the kitchen with demanding "Mrrrows." Aiden filled her bowl with cat food and gave the cat's neck a few gentle scratches. When she straightened, her gaze fell onto the microwavable container on the counter. She lifted the lid and inhaled deeply. *Mmm, Dawn made lasagna.*

It was Aiden's favorite dish, and she knew Dawn had prepared the contents of the container for her. She picked up a fork, ready to dig in, but then shook her head. *Kisses now, food later,* she decided with a grin.

She kicked off her shoes and padded through the hallway. Soft voices came from the living room, and Aiden grinned affectionately. *Dawn probably fell asleep in front of the TV again.* She opened the door and froze in the doorway.

Dawn wasn't asleep—and she wasn't alone. Right there, on the couch next to Dawn, sat what looked like Kade Matheson. She had one leg curled under her and was holding a half-empty wineglass in one hand. There was an empty plate on the coffee table in front of her. Kade looked more relaxed than Aiden had ever seen her.

Aiden's eyes widened. *Are those my sweatpants she's wearing? And my shirt?*

"Hey, Aiden." Dawn had looked up and noticed the silent woman leaning in the doorway. "I thought you'd be out on surveillance all night?"

Aiden nodded. "That's what I thought too, but an hour ago our guy drove to the airport for an unexpected trip to Vegas. Now some poor guys from the LVPD have to take over, and we got to go home," she explained, staying exactly where she was. Normally, she would have crossed the room by now to kiss Dawn hello, but with Kade in the room, she wasn't sure about the public display of affection. She didn't know what to make of the whole situation in the living room. Sure, she had known Dawn and Kade would go to the exhibition together, but this looked a great deal cozier than she had expected.

Dawn stood and rounded the coffee table. "Hi," she said when she had reached Aiden. She lifted up on her tiptoes and brushed her lips against Aiden's.

Aiden's brows shot up. Not only was Dawn kissing her while Kade was watching, but she could also taste the red wine on Dawn's lips. She could count the occasions on which Dawn had taken even a single sip of champagne on two fingers. Dawn had never been a big drinker, and since her rape, she had avoided alcohol altogether. Not tonight, it seemed.

What have these two been up to? Aiden wondered.

"Are you hungry?" Dawn asked as she sat back down. "There's food for you in the kitchen. Kade and I made lasagna."

"You made lasagna?" Aiden looked from Dawn to Kade. Dawn was the best cook she knew. Kade's talents lay in the courtroom, though, not in the kitchen.

Kade set down her wineglass. "Dawn made lasagna. I just grated the cheese."

Aiden shook her head. DDA Kadence Matheson performing the mundane task of grating cheese... She still couldn't see it.

"It's late. I should go," Kade said. She stood and walked toward Aiden.

It took a few seconds for Aiden to realize she was blocking the way to the bathroom, where Kade had probably left whatever she had worn to the art exhibition. She quickly stepped out of the way.

Kade closed the bathroom door behind her.

Dawn wandered over and wrapped both arms around Aiden's waist, taking advantage of the fact that they were alone for the moment. "Hey, you okay?"

Aiden rested her hands on the familiar curves of Dawn's hips. "Yeah, I'm fine, just a little surprised." She nodded in the direction of the closed bathroom door.

"I hope it's okay that I brought her here?" Dawn asked cautiously.

"Of course it is. This is your apartment, Dawn," Aiden said. "You can invite whoever you want."

Dawn pressed her cheek against Aiden's shoulder. "Not if you're uncomfortable with it. I want my apartment to be Aiden-friendly," she mumbled against Aiden's skin.

Aiden chuckled and rested her chin on Dawn's strawberry blond hair. "You've been watching that TV show with the girlie bloodsucker killer again," she accused, poking Dawn with one gentle finger. "The APA really shouldn't allow its psychologists to watch so much TV."

Dawn just giggled.

The bathroom door opened, and Aiden reluctantly removed her arms from around Dawn and stepped back.

Kade emerged from the bathroom in a dress that almost made Aiden drop the clothes Kade handed her.

This time, Dawn poked her in the ribs. "Thanks for accompanying me to the exhibition," she said to Kade.

"Thanks for the cooking lesson," Kade answered with a smile.

Aiden stood watching. She had a feeling that there was a lot that the two younger women weren't saying as they smiled at each other. "I'll drive you home," she offered in Kade's direction.

"No," Kade said immediately. "You just finished your shift plus overtime. I'll take a cab."

"It's no trouble, really," Aiden tried again. She didn't want to leave Dawn so soon, but she also didn't want Kade walking around on her own at night. "I'm on my way home too, and it's practically on my way, so..."

It wasn't, and they both knew it.

"You didn't come over after a fifteen-hour shift to drive me home," Kade said. She looked at Aiden, then pointedly at Dawn.

Aiden sighed. It was hard to win an argument against someone who argued for a living. "All right. I'll see you tomorrow."

* * *

No! Aiden opened her eyes with an annoyed groan when the cell phone on the bedside table next to her began to ring. *It can't be more than half an hour since I went to sleep.*

Next to her, Dawn stirred as Aiden sat up. "M'ne?" she mumbled sleepily.

Aiden smiled despite her frustration at being pulled from sorely needed sleep. Dawn's lack of coordination when first awakened was adorable. Years of being woken at odd hours had taught Aiden to clear her sleepy mind within two rings of the phone, but Dawn didn't have the same training. "No, it's mine. Go back to sleep." She smoothed back a strand of blond hair from Dawn's forehead while her other hand reached for her cell phone. "Carlisle," she said.

"Aiden, it's me." It was Ray's voice.

"Hold on a second." Aiden rolled out of bed, not wanting to wake Dawn, and padded through the dark bedroom. Her still sleep-fogged mind tried to remember if Ray had been on call tonight. "All right, talk. What is it?" she said when she had closed the bedroom door behind her.

She could hear Ray take a deep breath and instinctively braced herself for what might be coming.

"There's been a rape," Ray said.

Being called in at night because a rape had been committed was nothing new, but the hint of tremor in Ray's voice was. A cold numbness spread through her body. "Who?" she asked, already dreading the answer.

"The victim's name," Ray said, stopping to clear his throat, "is Matheson."

Kade. Aiden's hand with the cell phone fell limply to her side. *No. That's not possible. She was just here, not even an hour ago. She was fine. Not Kade. God, I should have insisted on driving her home!* She sank against the nearest wall. Finally, she lifted the cell phone to her ear again. "What happened, Ray?" she asked and realized that her voice was now trembling too.

"They didn't tell me much. An old buddy from Central Precinct called me. One of his friends was the first officer on scene," Ray said.

Only secondhand information. We have to get there. "I'll meet you at Kade's." Aiden hurried back into the bedroom to pick up her clothes.

"No. They gave me another address," Ray said.

Another address? I thought Kade was heading home. Where did she go at this hour? Aiden wondered.

"Stay where you are. I'll come and get you," Ray said. "I'm already halfway there."

Aiden struggled to pull up her jeans one-handedly. "I'm not at home."

"I know. I tried calling you at home. I'll pick you up at Dawn's in ten minutes." Ray ended the call, neither of them in the mood for further conversation.

Dawn flicked on the light and sat up groggily. "Do you have to leave?"

"Yes." Aiden shoved her gun into its holster. She was trying to stay in cop mode and pretend this was just another call out.

"Aiden?" Dawn crawled across the bed and reached out a hand to touch her.

Aiden jerked away. She stopped in her frantic dressing and looked down at Dawn for a moment. "Kade has been... attacked," she said, the whisper still much too loud in the silence of the bedroom.

"What? What happened?" Dawn was fully awake now. She scrambled off the bed.

"I don't know. Ray's picking me up." Aiden slipped the nearest sweatshirt over her head and then bit her lip when she realized it was the shirt Kade had worn just a few hours ago.

"I'll come with you," Dawn announced. She began to search for her own clothes.

Aiden stopped her with a single touch. "No. This is police business."

"But—"

"No," Aiden said with finality. She didn't want Dawn anywhere near whatever had happened. She wanted her safe in her apartment. "I'll call you as soon as I know anything, okay?"

"O-okay." Dawn stood and watched her snap the handcuff case to her belt. She silently followed Aiden through the hallway and handed her the badge she had left on the dresser next to the door. "Be careful."

Aiden touched her hand before it could retreat, wanting to take one last reminder of what was good in her life with her to the ugliness of the crime scene that awaited her. "I will."

CHAPTER 12

*T*HE SHRILL RINGING of her phone woke Del. She flopped onto her back and, for a moment, debated whether to pick up the phone or throw it against the wall. She hadn't had a good night's sleep in over ten days. Either work or her private Kade Matheson surveillance project had kept her busy at night.

She had spent more time in front of Kade's apartment than in her own bed lately. After seeing nothing out of the ordinary for a few days in a row, she had decided to take a break before Kade could become suspicious and notice that she hadn't stopped watching her apartment after the one night on which they had agreed.

The phone rang again.

Del flicked on the light and glanced at the phone's display. She recognized the number immediately. *Dawn!* She snatched up the receiver. "Dawn?" she said, a little panicked. She hadn't received a phone call from Dawn in the middle of the night in a long time. *Since she met Carlisle,* she realized. "Are you okay?"

"What? Yeah, yeah, I'm fine," Dawn said, sounding everything but. "I'm sorry to call you so late, but..."

"It's fine," Del said. "You know you can call me any time, grasshopper. Tell me what's going on."

The clanking of a pot could be heard over the phone. Dawn was either making tea or cooking. Either meant she was upset and trying to calm herself. "Aiden just got a call from her partner," Dawn said.

"She'll be fine." Del had said a similar thing to Dawn or Grace so often it had almost become a reflex by now. She knew that losing Carlisle to her job was the biggest fear Dawn had to live with. "You know these late-night call outs to crime scenes are part of her normal job routine. Nothing to worry about. The crime scenes are always well secured by the time the detectives arrive and—"

"I'm not worried about Aiden," Dawn interrupted. "I mean... of course I am, but that's not why I'm calling you. There's been an attack. I know you've both been trying to keep it quiet for now, and I tried to respect that, but now it means no one knows and no one's gonna call you."

What on God's green earth is she talking about? Del's confusion grew with every word. For a woman who made her living with words, Dawn wasn't making much sense. "Dawn, Dawn, calm down and start at the beginning, please. I don't understand what you're talking about."

Dawn's shuddering breath echoed through the phone. "I know you didn't want anyone to know about the relationship yet, so you're probably not one of the people she gave to notify in case of emergency."

All Del had understood so far was that someone had been attacked and she hadn't been notified, which made sense because the only two people to whom she was close enough to be listed as a contact in case of emergencies were Dawn and her mother. *And unfortunately, I'm still not in a relationship.*

"I'd come over and keep you company while you wait for news on Kade," Dawn was talking so fast her voice almost cracked, "but Aiden said she would call as soon as she knew anything and—"

"What?" *News on Kade? She's talking about Kade?* For some reason, Dawn seemed to think that she and Kade were in a relationship they had kept secret. Del's mind worked overtime to catch up with Dawn's words—and then she realized what they meant. "Kade has been attacked?"

"Yes, that's what I've been telling you the whole time," Dawn said.

Icy fear paralyzed Del for a second. "Is she all right?" she asked the only question that was important to her right now.

"I don't know, Del," Dawn said, her voice tender and compassionate like a caress. "I hope so."

"I have to go. Call me on my cell phone if you hear anything from Carlisle." Del hopped out of bed and dressed with trembling fingers. Thirty minutes and three frantic phone calls later, she stopped her car with wailing sirens in the driveway of a house whose address had been provided by one of her friends on the job.

She was still cursing herself while she kicked the driver's side door shut and stormed up to the house. "Stupid, stupid, stupid!"

The uniformed officer who stood guard at the edge of the property wasn't one of her own people, but he recognized her and knew better than to try stopping her when she was this angry.

Her anger wasn't directed at the uni, but at herself. *God, I shouldn't have agreed to keep this under wraps! I should have made it official, tried to get her a protective detail!* But she hadn't, and now something had happened to Kade.

Del wasn't even sure what, and the not knowing was driving her crazy.

At the front door, she almost collided with another person who had hurriedly gotten out of a car. "Get out of my way!" Del ordered without slowing down or even trying to look at whom she was ordering around. At the moment, she didn't even care if it was the police commissioner.

"Let me through!" the other person demanded.

Del threw an angry glare at her. She finally realized it was Aiden Carlisle who had tried to beat her into the house. Detective Bennet followed behind Carlisle but wisely stayed out of the way of the two women, silently hovering behind his partner.

For a second, Del and Carlisle stood face-to-face, both half in and half out of the door, knowing only one of them could pass through at a time. Neither of them wanted to step back and grant the other the right to be the first at Kade's side.

Del didn't want to waste another second. "Move, Detective!" she yelled, emphasizing Carlisle's rank. When it came to Kade, she was not above pulling rank.

Bennet tugged on his partner's leather jacket, pulling her back so that Del could enter the house in front of her.

"What do we have?" Del asked the young uniformed cop in the hall, trying to at least sound businesslike.

The young officer straightened and looked as if he might salute. "We caught the rapist," he announced, his chest swollen with pride.

Rapist! Del almost shouted it. *Kade has been raped? No, not her. Not her too.* She shook her head, again and again, until she almost felt dizzy.

Carlisle silently stepped next to her, her face very pale. Del could see that she was thinking the same thing. Another woman she cared about had been raped.

"Where's Kade... DDA Matheson?" Del demanded to know. The rapist's whereabouts didn't interest her at the moment. She would deal with that bastard later. For now, only Kade mattered.

The officer pointed to one of the doors. "She—"

Del didn't have the patience to listen to his explanation. She practically pushed him out of the way in her haste to reach Kade. At the last possible moment, she hesitated with her hand on the doorknob, almost afraid of what she would find behind the door. She could feel Bennet's and Carlisle's presence behind her. Straightening her shoulders, she opened the door.

The distressed sobbing of a woman could be heard, almost drowned out by an angry male voice.

Del stormed into the room.

Kade was nowhere to be seen. A crying woman sat on the couch, and a red-faced man was pacing across the large living room.

Are they Kade's friends or family members? Has Kade been visiting them? Del wondered but didn't stop to make polite conversation. "Where is she?" she asked and flashed her badge to force an answer.

"She locked herself in the bedroom. She..." The rest of the woman's words were unintelligible due to her renewed sobbing.

Del quickly crossed the room and listened to the sounds that were coming from behind the only other door in the room. She wasn't sure, but she thought she could hear muffled sobbing and quiet, soothing murmurs. *Good. At least they got somebody in there with her.* "Kade?" she called softly. "It's me, Del. I know you probably don't want to talk right now." *Especially not to me,* she added with a new wave of guilt. *God, I really fucked up! I shouldn't have let her out of my sight for even a moment after she told me about her stalker. I should have pushed her to make it official.*

The door opened, and a pale Kade peeked out.

"Oh, Kade," Del whispered, not knowing what to say to her. She resisted the urge to take Kade into her arms. Kade wouldn't have wanted that under normal circumstances, and she sure as hell didn't want it now. "What happened?" she asked.

"That's what I'm trying to find out. She refuses to tell me, and her parents didn't have any luck either." Kade ruffled her red hair in frustration.

Del stared at her. "Huh? Whose parents?"

"They didn't tell you? I thought that's why you're all here?" Kade looked from Del to Carlisle and Bennet. "My niece has been raped."

"Your niece?" Del was still staring. "You're not...? You weren't...? You're fine?"

"Of course I'm fine," Kade said impatiently. "Well, as fine as one can be in the middle of all this confusion. Uff!" She stopped talking when Del's unexpected hug squeezed the air from her lungs for a moment.

Del quickly caught herself and let go of Kade. "Sorry. It's just... I thought... They told us you had been raped."

Kade snorted haughtily. "I would have strangled that little pup with the straps of my briefcase."

Del couldn't look away from Kade. She drank in her face, making sure she was all right. Finally, she forced herself back into cop mode. "Maybe one of us should try to talk to your niece?" she suggested. "It's possible she'd be more comfortable talking to someone who's not so emotionally involved."

Kade shrugged. "At this point, I'm ready to give anything a try. She did nothing but sob, and I couldn't understand a single word she said since my brother called me."

"Ray and I are gonna take care of the perp," Carlisle announced grimly, her hand clenched around her belt next to where her gun rested.

Del gave her a nod. She wanted a face-to-face with the rapist too, but it had to wait.

"I want this by the book!" Kade called after the two retreating detectives. "Do everything you legally can to get a confession, but no thumbscrews just because the victim is my niece!"

When they were alone, Del turned to Kade, studying the pale, patrician features. "Are you okay? When Dawn called me, I thought the stalker—"

"This has nothing to do with that," Kade quickly hushed her. "This is about my niece and nothing else."

Del nodded, reluctantly accepting that Kade didn't want to talk about the stalking situation or about how worried Del had been for her. "Shouldn't you remove yourself from the case? The defense could claim a conflict of interest if this goes to trial."

"We don't even know if this is a case yet. For now, I'm just a worried family member," Kade said with determination.

Del had to smile. *A family member with a horde of cops doing her every bidding.* "All right. Then let's talk to your niece."

Kade nodded with grim determination and reopened the door to the girl's bedroom.

Del entered behind Kade. She made sure to stay right next to the door so the girl wouldn't feel threatened by her presence.

"Laurie," Kade said, her voice softer than Del had ever heard it. The tenderness in her voice had a powerful effect on Del, and she hoped it would work on Laurie too. Kade carefully sat down on the edge of the bed.

The bundled-up form under the blankets moved, and a blond head peeked out. Red-rimmed blue eyes looked from Kade to Del. Laurie was sobbing uncontrollably, not even able to utter a single word of explanation.

Del blinked, startled for a moment. Except for the different hair color, Laurie Matheson was the spitting image of her aunt. She looked like a younger, more vulnerable version of Kade. "Hey," Del said softly. "I'm Lieutenant Vasquez."

The blond head retreated back under her blanket.

"Her name is Del," Kade said. "She's a friend. Can you tell her what happened?"

"I c-can't," Laurie sobbed. "I don't want to talk about it. Send them all away, please, Aunt Kade."

Del met Kade's gaze. It was clear Laurie was too scared to talk to the police.

Kade nodded at the door and mouthed, "Let me try again."

With a sigh, Del retreated from the room.

* * *

Aiden walked up to the young uni. "Where's the perp?" she asked without preamble. She was impatient to get to the bottom of this case. Even though it had turned out that Kade's niece, not Kade, was the victim, this case still hit a little too close to home for her liking.

"Outside, in one of the squad cars," the uni answered eagerly.

"Has he been mirandized?" Aiden asked. Kade wanted this done by the book, making it impossible for her niece's rapist to walk on a technicality.

The uni nodded. "She," he corrected.

"What?" Aiden stared at him. "You mean the perp is a woman?" Aiden wasn't ignorant. She knew better than anyone else that rape was more about exerting power and control than about sexuality. She knew women could be rapists too, but experience had taught her that in ninety-nine percent of the cases, the perp was male.

When the officer nodded, she pushed past him and strode to the squad car parked in the driveway.

A lanky young woman, barely more than a teenager, lounged in the backseat, her arms crossed over her chest, her head defiantly thrown back against the headrest. The look of boredom on her face made Aiden's blood boil.

Aiden jerked the car door open, making the young woman almost fall at her feet because she had casually leaned against the door. She scowled up at Aiden, her dark eyes flashing. "Hey! Watch out, you...!"

"Yes?" Aiden drawled. She hoped the young perp would take her up on it and add insulting a police officer to the list of her charges.

"Ha! You think I'm stupid, huh?" The young woman leaned back again and proceeded to ignore Aiden.

"Did you hear that, Ray?" Aiden asked, glancing back over her shoulder. "Did she just call me stupid?"

Ray stepped closer to stare down at the woman in the backseat. "Nope. She called herself stupid—and she must be because raping the niece of a Multnomah County deputy district attorney is not a clever thing to do."

Only Aiden could see that the smug grin on his face was fake. She knew he was thinking about Kade's niece. She was close in age to his own daughters, and he was probably thinking it could have very well been one of them.

"I didn't rape her, goddamnit!" their perp raged. "I don't need to rape anybody, man! I have enough willing girls throwing themselves at me."

"Yeah, right!" Aiden snorted and shut the door in her face. She wanted the young woman to repeat her bragging and her lies in the more official surroundings of an interview room at the precinct. *By the book,* she reminded herself, trying to calm her still seething anger.

She pounded on the roof of the car. "Get this piece of work to the precinct!" she shouted at the uni in the driver's seat.

* * *

Ray leaned back against the wall of the interrogation room, watching the stare down taking place in front of him.

Their perp sat behind the small table in the middle of the room, her long legs lazily sprawled out in front of her. She coolly returned Aiden's gaze.

Finally, Aiden threw the wallet with the ID they had taken from Evan Whitfield, their suspect, down at the table. "You don't look like you're nineteen."

Evan Whitfield just shrugged and grinned. "Good genes, I guess. When I'm your age, I'll be thankful to look a few years younger."

For a moment, Ray thought Aiden would jump across the table and strangle the young woman, but she only leaned forward and pinned Evan with a challenging stare. "Why did you sleep with a fifteen-year-old, then?"

"Who says I did?" Evan shot back.

Their suspect was a cocky braggart, but she wasn't stupid. Either she wasn't admitting to anything out of principle, or she knew they could charge her with statutory rape if she admitted to sleeping with a fifteen-year-old.

"Let me tell you what happened," Aiden said, her voice sharp, yet calm. "You conned your way into the bedroom of a young, naïve girl under the pretense of friendship, and when she didn't give you what you wanted, you raped her."

Evan Whitfield stared at her for a moment. This time, she didn't yell or declare her innocence with threats and curses. She just looked at Aiden with a smirk. "Is that a fantasy of yours, Detective?"

Ray quickly moved away from the wall and laid a restraining hand on his partner's shoulder. He knew Evan's remark had hit a nerve, and he didn't want Aiden to do something stupid. "Come on. Let's get a pop while Miss Whitfield thinks of something more original to say." He pulled Aiden up and away from the table.

Aiden jerked out of his grip and stormed out of the room.

Ray followed at a more sedate pace. He found her pounding and kicking at the vending machine in the hallway. "Hey, hey, take it easy! Okada is not gonna be happy if you destroy his steady supply of candy." He reached inside, jerked a few times, and pulled out Aiden's pop. "Here."

"Thanks," Aiden grumbled, looking as if she wanted to have something much stronger than a soft drink.

"Don't let her get to you, Aiden," Ray said. He wasn't sure why this suspect was affecting Aiden so much. Usually, she was a lot more restrained than that. He had seen perps hit her or spit at her without Aiden going off the deep end. Granted, Aiden didn't have the experience with annoying teenagers that he did, so maybe that was part of the reason.

Aiden gulped down her pop. "I have to call Dawn, tell her Kade is okay." She turned away from him and walked a few steps down the hall.

Ray waited, watching her as she paced the hallway with the cell phone pressed to her ear. He couldn't hear what she said, nor did he know what Dawn answered, but after a few minutes, Aiden stopped her agitated pacing and leaned against one of the vending machines, nodding a few times as she listened to what Dawn had to say. Her expression was calmer now, and Ray saw a gentle smile on her face. *Oh, yeah. Dawn is really good for her.*

He turned away, not wanting to interrupt the private conversation, and used the opportunity to call Kade and get an update on the situation at the Matheson residence.

* * *

"Dawn?" Aiden pressed the cell phone to her ear, pacing the hallway with her back to Ray for a little privacy. "It's Aiden."

"Aiden! How's Kade?"

Aiden could hear Dawn's voice trembling. The situation probably reminded her too much of her rape just six months ago. She took a deep breath, forcing her own churning emotions back. "Kade is fine," she said quickly. "She's not the victim. It's her niece."

Dawn paused for a moment. "The one we met when she was out shopping with Kade?" she asked. "The cute, kind of shy little thing who has a crush on you?"

"What?" Shocked, Aiden stopped her pacing. "Yeah, we met when she was Christmas shopping with Kade, but she doesn't have a crush on me." She shook her head. Sometimes Dawn had an overactive imagination.

"How is she?" Dawn asked. "God, to go through this at fifteen..."

Aiden bit her lip. "I don't know. I haven't seen her yet. We're giving her a little time while we're trying to get a confession from the perp." She sighed.

"Are you okay?" Dawn asked, her voice soothing. "You sound a little... agitated."

Aiden sighed and leaned her back against one of the vending machines. "Our perp drives me crazy."

Dawn didn't ask any questions. She never had. She knew Aiden couldn't discuss open cases. "You'll get him," she said, and Aiden could hear the unshakable belief and trust in Dawn's voice. "But it might take a little time. Just take it step by step. I know it's hard when someone you know is the victim."

Aiden swallowed. "Yeah."

"If it gets to be too much, please hand over the case to someone who isn't as emotionally involved," Dawn said softly.

Aiden knew she wouldn't do that, but it was good to hear someone worrying about her emotional well-being nonetheless. She'd never had that in her life before. "I'll talk to you soon."

"Take care. I love you."

A small smile flitted over Aiden's face. "I will. Ditto," she answered, knowing Ray was right behind her and probably listening to every word she said. When she ended the call and returned to Ray's side, he was just putting away his own cell phone.

"You okay?" he asked.

"Yeah. Sorry about that." Aiden gestured back to the interrogation room. Normally, she was the one who kept her cool while Ray sometimes had a difficult time controlling his anger when he was with a perp who had hurt a child or teenager. This time, it was the other way around. "It's just... something about her just rubs me the wrong way. A young girl's innocence was destroyed tonight, and that bragging smart-ass is acting like that's something to be proud of!"

Ray nodded and gently patted her shoulder. "Come on, let's swab and fingerprint her. Trying to get a confession can wait until we have something on her."

"Was that Kade?" Aiden asked, pointing to his cell phone.

"Yeah. She's at her brother's, but her niece is still too distraught to talk. We'll wait until tomorrow," Ray said. "By then, we should have some DNA evidence from the crime lab. They're processing the sheets from Laurel Matheson's bed. Kade did have something else for us, though. It looks like Evan Whitfield's got a juvenile record."

Aiden shook her head in frustration. "Juvenile records are sealed. You know that."

"Yeah, but Kade called in some favors. She won't be able to use it in court, but we might find something interesting nonetheless. She's faxing the records over right now." Ray stepped over to the fax machine, waiting impatiently until it spat out the documents they were waiting for.

Aiden was faster. She snatched up the sheet of paper and studied it. "Bingo!"

Ray tried to read over her shoulder.

"She did time in juvie," Aiden read out loud, almost triumphantly. "Shoplifting, auto theft, drug possession, that kind of thing. No history of violent crimes, though."

Ray stared at the piece of paper. "Shit. Look at the date of birth."

Aiden did. "That means she's sixteen. Her ID is fake. Which means we won't get her for statutory rape. We have to prove the sex was nonconsensual, or she walks," she said grimly.

CHAPTER 13

DAWN CLOSED THE last of her patient files. Normally, she tried to take Saturdays off, but she knew Aiden wouldn't leave the station until she got a confession from Laurie Matheson's rapist, so she might as well get some work done too.

She stretched and wandered out into the reception area to get a cup of tea.

Mrs. Phillips was on the phone but motioned for Dawn to wait in front of her desk. She said her good-byes and ended the call. "That was Mrs. LeCroix," she told Dawn. "She called to cancel Evan Whitfield's session on Monday. Evan won't be able to keep her appointment."

Dawn frowned. *I thought we'd made some progress. What's going on now?* "Did she give a reason?"

"Yes." Mrs. Phillips nodded dramatically. "She got arrested by the police."

Shit! Dawn knew Evan was still hanging around the wrong crowd, but she had begun to see some positive changes in Evan and had hoped she wouldn't do anything to sabotage her own future. "Did Mrs. LeCroix tell you what happened?"

"No. But she was crying, so it can't be good." Mrs. Phillips stared up at Dawn from her place behind the reception desk, obviously waiting for Dawn to work a miracle.

Dawn chewed on her lower lip, then made a decision. She reached across the desk and picked up the phone.

Instead of Jill LeCroix, it was her husband who answered the phone.

Dawn quickly adjusted and told him her name. "I don't know what exactly happened, Mr. LeCroix, but if I can help in any way..."

"It's too late for that," Mr. LeCroix said. His voice was frosty.

God, what did she do? I hope she didn't kill somebody. Dawn hadn't thought Evan capable of committing a violent crime, but obviously they weren't just dealing with a minor offense like shoplifting. "Why? What happened?"

"That good for nothing..." Mr. LeCroix roared, then stopped himself. "She raped a girl! So tell me, Doctor, how can you help with that?"

For long seconds, Dawn couldn't answer. She held the phone in a limp grip, staring at the wall, her thoughts racing. *Oh, God! Evan Whitfield is not a rapist... is she?* Suddenly, she wasn't so sure anymore. *Did I misjudge her so badly? Did I just not want to see it because she reminded me of Aiden?*

"...excuse me now," Mr. LeCroix's voice interrupted her tumbling thoughts. "We have to head down to the station."

"Wait!" Dawn said quickly. "Can I come and talk to Evan?" She needed to find out if she really had misjudged Evan so badly.

"Do whatever you want." Mr. LeCroix sighed in resignation. "That girl has me at a point where I just don't care anymore."

* * *

A dozen different emotions churned through Dawn as she entered the squad room. She was still shocked and in a state of disbelief, hardly able to believe that Evan Whitfield could have raped anybody. *What if she really did it?* Dawn had never wanted to face another rapist, and she wasn't sure she could maintain her objectivity. Her professional and her private life were colliding in more ways than one. There was a good chance this was one of Aiden's cases, but there was no time to talk to her, to give her fair warning.

A uniformed officer opened the door of the interrogation room for them.

Dawn stepped into the room behind Evan's foster parents.

Evan was sitting behind a small table, her pose as rebellious and confrontational as ever. She didn't even look up as they entered.

Dawn looked at Evan's foster parents. Jill was crying, and her husband's jaw was clenched. Both of them looked almost physically unable to utter a single word. Dawn stepped forward. "You know, you take avoiding our sessions a little too far."

Evan's head snapped up. Surprise and something like hope flickered in her eyes when she recognized Dawn, but then the cool, bored expression was back. "Hey, Doc. What's a girl like you doin' in a place like this?" She indicated the sterile interrogation room.

"I should ask you that question," Dawn answered as calmly as possible. "What happened, Evan?" She didn't ask the question the police and her foster parents had probably already asked Evan: what did you do? She knew Evan needed someone to believe in her, to give her the benefit of the doubt, and she was determined to be that person even if she secretly harbored her own doubts.

The door opened again before Evan could answer.

CHAPTER 14

"*A*ND?" AIDEN ASKED urgently as Ray put the phone down.

"DNA results aren't back yet, but Deming promised to have something for us within the next hour," Ray reported. He stood and picked his jacket up from the back of his chair. "Come on. Let's see if our suspect is a little more cooperative today."

A uni waved at them as they headed toward the interview room. "We put your suspect in the bigger interview room," he told them. "She's got company."

Aiden nodded. It wasn't unexpected. "She lawyered up?"

"No. Her parents are with her," the uni said.

Aiden gave another nod. Now that they knew Evan Whitfield was a minor, they were no longer allowed to question her without her parents present.

"And her shrink," the officer added.

"Her shrink?" Aiden echoed. "Don't tell me she's going for an insanity defense?" *Kade won't like that.*

The uni shrugged and opened the door to the interrogation room for them.

Aiden immediately zeroed in on Evan Whitfield as she entered the room. The teenager still looked as cocky as ever, even after spending the night in custody. Aiden's gaze wandered over the angry looking bearded man and the crying woman who were probably Whitfield's parents and then landed on... "Dawn? What are you doing here?" She gaped at her lover.

"You know her?" Evan's mother blurted out, clearly surprised that Dawn would "fraternize with the enemy."

Evan Whitfield howled with laughter.

Aiden shot her a murderous glare, but Evan didn't stop.

"Stop it, Evan," Dawn ordered with an authority Aiden had seldom heard from her gentle partner.

Evan Whitfield stopped laughing but continued to smirk at Aiden.

"Can I talk to you for a minute?" Aiden wanted to know what was going on as fast as possible. "Outside." She pointed at the door.

Dawn followed her out of the room without protest.

Aiden stopped and turned to Dawn as soon as the door had closed behind them. "What the hell are you doing here? Why are you connected in any way to a person," she spat out the word, "like Evan Whitfield?"

"She's my client," Dawn answered quietly.

"What?" Aiden pressed both hands against her temples. She didn't even want to imagine Dawn alone in a room with a rapist. Evan Whitfield might be just a teenager, but she was already taller and heavier than Dawn and could probably overpower her easily. "I don't want you to counsel her any longer!"

Dawn shook her head. "That's not your decision to make."

"She's dangerous, Dawn!" It was getting difficult to keep her voice down in the desperate attempt to make Dawn understand the situation.

"She needs help," Dawn said, "and I'm the one who can give it."

Aiden roughly massaged the back of her neck. "You can't—"

"Aiden?" Another voice interrupted them.

Annoyed with the interruption, Aiden whirled around. "What?"

Irene Deming, their medical examiner, froze in midmotion. She clutched a thin folder and studied Aiden with a disapproving glance.

"Sorry," Aiden mumbled. "You have the results?"

The medical examiner nodded. "Do you have a minute?"

Aiden glanced at Dawn, then back at Irene Deming before she nodded.

"Is there somewhere we can talk without being interrupted?" Deming asked.

Aiden frowned. She didn't plan on having a long conversation with the ME. "You could just give me the results," she suggested. After all the years with the Sexual Assault Detail, she had learned to make sense of DNA results.

"No, I can't." Deming's dark eyes met Aiden's. There was something in her gaze that made Aiden's stomach churn.

"All right," Aiden relented. She looked at Dawn. "I'll be back in a minute. Wait here, please?" She managed to make it a request, not an order. When Dawn nodded, she turned and led Deming to the smaller interview room.

Deming moved to one of the chairs and gestured for Aiden to take the other.

Aiden didn't move. She didn't want to sit down. She was impatient to get back to Evan Whitfield and, most of all, to Dawn, in order to clear up this weird situation. "Just tell me the results. I have a suspect waiting in the interview room."

"What I have to tell you has to do with that suspect, but it's going to take more than twenty seconds. Aiden, would you please sit down for a moment?" Deming pleaded.

Aiden sat. "So?" She gestured impatiently to the file with the DNA results.

"The swab from Evan Whitfield was a match to the fluids we found on Laurel Matheson's sheets," Deming said, laying a sheet of paper on the table in front of Aiden.

Aiden picked up the results and stood. "Thanks." It didn't necessarily prove rape, but at least it proved that there had been a sexual contact.

"That's not all," Deming's voice stopped her before she could reach the door. "Please sit back down."

Aiden returned to the table but didn't sit. "What's going on, Irene? Why are you so secretive all of a sudden?" Normally, their ME wasn't one to beat around the bush.

"We also ran her DNA through the system to see if she's connected to any other crime," Deming said.

"And?" Aiden squinted at the medical examiner.

Deming leafed through the file for another sheet of paper. "There was a match."

Aiden nodded with grim satisfaction. "So she's committed other crimes?"

"No. It was not a hit in CODIS. It was a partial match to a sample in the state system. You know that all law enforcement personnel are put in the database for elimination purposes, right?"

Aiden nodded. Of course she knew. She had often cursed what Okada called "Murphy's Law of Police Work": the least competent person on the force was always the first to arrive at the crime scene—which meant they often had to eliminate the fingerprints, shoe prints, and DNA evidence their own officers had left behind at the crime scene. "So?" She waited impatiently to see where Deming was going with this.

"The sample from Evan Whitfield and the DNA in our database have five alleles in common," Deming said seriously.

"So you're telling me she's related to a cop?" Aiden grimaced. *Figures. Her father is a cop, and my girlfriend is her shrink. How much more complicated can this case get?*

Irene Deming nodded, her lips a tight line. She slowly slid the second sheet of paper across the table. "Aiden, she's your sister."

Aiden stared at her, then at the piece of paper. The graphics and numbers on the page didn't make any sense at the moment. Nothing made sense anymore.

"I personally ran her DNA through a kinship analysis," Deming said, breaking the deafening silence. "I did it twice, just to make sure. She's your half sister."

Aiden slowly pushed the chair back under the small table and turned to the door.

"Aiden..."

"Not now." Aiden couldn't deal with this revelation and its implications right now. She opened the door and mechanically walked out into the hallway.

Dawn's soft grip around her wrist pulled her out of her daze. "Hey! What happened?" Dawn stared up at her in alarm.

Aiden didn't want to talk. She didn't want to say out loud that she might be directly related to not one, but two rapists. She didn't want Dawn to know. "Not now," she repeated, not knowing what else to say.

But Dawn didn't loosen her grip and continued to look at her with a very concerned gaze.

Dawn's behavior in the middle of a busy hallway began to draw attention. Okada walked over and looked from Dawn to Aiden. "Everything all right here?"

"Okada, go and help Ray in the interview room, please." Aiden knew she couldn't face the young woman who was her half sister. She didn't want to be in the same room or even the same building. Somehow she was convinced her colleagues would know as soon as they saw them together. She gently freed herself from Dawn's grip and strode down the hallway, trying to leave everything behind.

* * *

Aiden didn't bother to turn on the light. She passed the mirror in the hallway without checking out her reflection. Never even taking off her jacket, she slowly walked through the dark apartment and flopped down on the couch.

"Hi."

The unexpected voice from the bedroom made Aiden shoot up from the couch. "Dawn! God! You scared me half to death!"

Dawn leaned in the doorway, studying her. "Well, you gave me a key, so I thought that meant it's okay for me to be here even if you aren't."

"It is," Aiden confirmed gruffly. *Just not now,* she wanted to say but didn't.

Dawn slowly came closer, her movements almost cautious.

Is she afraid of me? The depressing thought shot through Aiden's mind. *Is she afraid that I'm like Evan... like our father? Like father, like daughter, right?* But then she shook her head. Dawn didn't know about her being related to Evan Whitfield, and Aiden didn't know how to tell her—or if she should tell her at all.

"What's going on with you?" Dawn asked, gently helping Aiden out of her leather jacket.

Aiden pressed her lips together. She could barely stand the gentle touches.

"Everyone at the precinct was worried about you," Dawn continued when Aiden didn't answer her question. She touched Aiden's hair, which was still a little damp. "Where have you been? It's not raining, is it?"

Aiden shrugged. "I don't know." She probably wouldn't have noticed even if tennisball-sized hailstones had fallen from the sky.

"Where did you go after you left the squad room?" Dawn asked again. She leaned in to sniff Aiden's skin and her clothes. "You went to a bar?"

Aiden nodded slowly. She had downed a whiskey in one big gulp and had raised her hand to order a second shot, but then she had changed her mind. She didn't want to fall into her mother's old habit. It was bad enough that her father's inheritance had reared its ugly head. She didn't need to inherit her mother's alcohol problem too. "I'm not drunk," she said, knowing Dawn wouldn't have liked that.

"I know." Dawn's fingers slid through the damp hair at Aiden's neck. "It feels more like you bathed in that stuff. Where were you?"

It was the third time Dawn had asked her that question, and Aiden knew she couldn't withhold an answer any longer. Dawn had patiently tried to teach her to talk about her feelings and problems, and Aiden knew that stubborn silence would destroy all the work each of them had invested into their relationship. "The Portland Police Bureau has an indoor swimming pool," she said, knowing that was no real explanation.

"You left work to go swimming?" Dawn was clearly confused.

Aiden hadn't planned to end up in a swimming pool. Her mind was too busy with nagging thoughts and self-doubts to have any room left for making plans. After leaving the bar, she had driven around aimlessly, and when she ended up in front of the PPB training center, she decided to go in. "I was on the swim team in college," she offered another useless explanation. Swimming endless laps had helped her deal with a lot of things in her life back then. The water drowned out the rest of the world until Aiden could think clearly again.

This time, it hadn't been enough, though.

"Talk to me," Dawn begged. "Tell me what happened. Why did you leave so abruptly? Was it because of me? I know I should have tried to let you know I was involved in your case before you walked into the interview room, but everything happened so fast and there was just no time to—"

"No," Aiden stopped her. "This has nothing to do with you. I wasn't overjoyed to find you in that interview room, but I'm not angry with you."

Dawn bit her lip and let tense shoulders drop. "What is it, then? It has to do with Evan Whitfield, right? I know you're worried about me and don't want me to work with someone who could be dangerous, but I can't believe Evan would hurt me. She's a very troubled teenager with a lot of issues and bottled-up anger, yes, but I don't think she raped that girl. I think she's innocent, Aiden."

"She is? I mean... did she say anything that makes you believe she is?" Aiden asked, hanging on Dawn's every word.

"You know I couldn't tell you even if Evan had told me about it. I'm her therapist, so everything she tells me is confidential." Dawn regretfully shook her head.

More than frustrated with that answer, Aiden ran her hand through her damp hair. How could she tell Dawn that it wasn't the ambitious cop who was asking for that information? How could she tell her it was just a desperate woman, grasping for any information that might indicate that her sister was a decent human being, despite all indications to the contrary?

With a sigh, she gave up all attempts to get her tumbled thoughts back into order. "Can we talk about this later? I'm exhausted and just want to go to bed." It wasn't a complete lie. She was exhausted, but she knew she wouldn't sleep.

She lay awake long into the night, gently holding on to Dawn.

* * *

Someone was touching her. A hand was gripping her shoulder. Dawn jerked awake.

"Dawn?" Aiden's familiar voice whispered.

Dawn took a few deep breaths to calm her racing heart. She sat up and flicked on the lamp on her side of the bed.

Aiden was sitting up too. She looked as if she hadn't slept a single minute. "Sorry," she murmured. "I didn't want to startle you."

"What's wrong?" Dawn reached across the remaining space between them and gently touched one bare arm.

Aiden blew out a breath. "I need to talk," she said.

A wave of worry, mixed with relief, hit Dawn. She knew something had troubled Aiden all day, and she was glad Aiden was finally ready to talk about it. She had started to worry that Aiden was pulling away from her until she couldn't reach her any longer. She trailed her hand down Aiden's arm and gave her hand an encouraging squeeze. "Tell me."

"I don't know how," Aiden said, not meeting Dawn's gaze but entwining her fingers with Dawn's. "Talking to you about this... it's hard."

Dawn frowned. "Because I'm Evan Whitfield's therapist? This is about the case, right?"

"Yes. No. I mean... it has to do with Evan Whitfield, but it's not about you being her therapist although it doesn't make it any easier." Aiden sighed.

"Would it be easier for you to talk about this with someone else?" Dawn wanted Aiden to trust her with whatever troubled her, but what she wanted even more was for Aiden to feel better. If that meant Aiden confiding in someone else, she would accept it.

Aiden leaned her head back against the backrest. "I could tell Ray, but I don't want to go into details about how this affects our relationship with him."

"What about Kade?" Dawn asked. A few weeks earlier, she would have avoided anything that might push Aiden in Kade's direction, but now she was starting to get over seeing Kade as competition for Aiden's love.

"Kade?" Aiden ruefully shook her head. "No, with her niece being the alleged victim, she's too emotionally involved in this. And Kade is even worse at talking about emotional issues than I am."

Dawn smiled a little. "Yeah, I noticed that. So that leaves only me, huh?"

"Don't make it sound like you're the best of bad choices. It's not only that I need to talk. I need to tell **you**. You've got a right to know with whom you're sharing your life and your bed," Aiden said. The old expression of self-recrimination was on her face.

Dawn crawled closer and possessively hooked her leg over one of Aiden's. "I already know that, and I like that person. In fact, I love her, and nothing you tell me will change that. It won't change the way I see you."

Aiden idly trailed her fingertips over Dawn's leg. "But it changes the way I see myself," she said.

"Tell me what it is. What hit you so hard?" Dawn pulled Aiden's hand in her lap and gave it another squeeze. "Tell me. Please."

Aiden gently disentangled her fingers from Dawn's and rolled out of bed.

Dawn could only stare at her back as she moved away from her. A lump of emotions formed in her throat, and she had to blink back tears of frustration, hurt, and loss.

Within a minute, Aiden was back. "Hey, hey." Her steps quickened as she hurried around the bed and knelt in front of Dawn. "What's wrong? Are you crying?"

"No. I..." Dawn swallowed with difficulty.

"You thought I was running away again," Aiden said with a sigh. "Not that I blame you for assuming that. I did it before, and I'm sure I'll do it again, but I promise no matter how far I run, I'll always turn back around eventually. That's our deal, right?"

Dawn quickly wiped her eyes and forced a smile. "I believe our deal also included a caramel cappuccino."

"Do you want one? I could...?" Aiden pointed at the door.

"No." Dawn quickly stopped her. Aiden was here and apparently still willing to talk, and she'd never risk that by sending her away. "I'm sorry. I should have had more trust in you, but when you just got up and walked away without another word..."

Aiden sat down on Dawn's side of the bed. "I was searching for this." She handed Dawn a creased piece of paper. The usually steady hand Dawn loved so much was trembling.

Dawn took the sheet of paper and carefully unfolded it. She stared down at the numbers and graphs on the page. "It's the results of a DNA test, right?" Why was Aiden showing her this? "Is it Evan's?"

Aiden nodded. Her jaw clenched and unclenched. "This one is her DNA profile." She pointed at the upper half of the page. "And this one," she indicated the results at the bottom, "is mine."

"Yours?" Dawn blinked in confusion. Why would the crime lab analyze Aiden's DNA? She stared at Aiden. The tousled black hair, the toned body, her defensive stance. "Oh my God," she whispered with sudden insight. "She's your sister!"

The amber eyes widened. "How...?" Her voice failed her.

Jesus, it's true! Dawn shook her head to clear it. "How did I guess?" she helped Aiden finish her sentence.

Aiden nodded numbly.

"From the moment Evan Whitfield stepped into my office, I couldn't stop thinking she reminded me of a younger Aiden Carlisle," Dawn said with a shaky smile.

"We're not that alike," Aiden protested.

Dawn sobered. *So that's what's troubling her so much. She doesn't want to be anything like Evan, whom she suspects of raping someone. She's afraid Evan could have inherited her father's violent tendencies, because that might mean she has inherited them too,* she realized. "I thought I was just imagining similarities and seeing you in everyone I met because I was head over heels in love with you," she admitted with a touch of embarrassment.

"Was?" Aiden repeated.

"I still am," Dawn reassured her. "I told you: nothing you tell me will change the fact that I love you."

Aiden leaned closer until they were sitting shoulder to shoulder. She was silent for a while. "Did Evan tell you anything about her parents... her father?" she asked.

Dawn bit her lip. "You're putting me in an ethical dilemma. I'm not allowed to talk about Evan with you."

"Great!" Aiden jumped out of bed and began to pace. "I'm not allowed to talk about the most shocking, troubling thing that happened to me in years with the person I love and trust most! I know your job has its rules, just like mine, but where does that leave me?"

Dawn stood and stopped Aiden's pacing by wrapping her arms around her. "You're allowed to talk to me about anything you want. You're not a psychologist, so there's no confidentiality clause for you. I can listen; I can hold your hand, and I can even give you advice about coming to terms with this shocking revelation. But what I can't do is tell you what Evan might or might not have told me in one of our sessions."

"This is so awkward," Aiden mumbled, her body tense in Dawn's arms. "My girlfriend is counseling my half sister."

"Not anymore," Dawn promised.

Aiden lifted her face from where it had been buried in Dawn's hair. "I thought you were so determined to be the one to help her?"

"That was before you told me she's your sister. Now that I know, I can't continue as her therapist. Multiple relationships with a client are a big no-no in my job," Dawn said.

"Multiple relationships?" Aiden asked, finally having calmed down a little.

Dawn nodded. "That means you can only ever be a therapist to your client. You're not his or her friend, love interest, or relative. Now that I'm practically her sister-in-law, I can't be her therapist any longer."

Aiden blinked, startled, and then rubbed her temples.

Shit. I guess calling her my sister-in-law was a bit too much to take in. Going from being an only child to having a sixteen-year-

old sister in just one day is hard enough, but she also has to deal with that whole "violence gene" thing. Dawn soothingly stroked Aiden's back. "How do you feel now?" she asked quietly.

"At a loss," Aiden said. She stood passively in Dawn's embrace, without even lifting her arms to hug back. "I don't know what to do or say or even think."

"You don't have to figure it all out tonight." She rubbed Aiden's back, trying to warm up the cool skin. "Let's get back under the covers and maybe try to sleep a little. We'll try to get to the bottom of this tomorrow."

Aiden made no move to get into the bed. "Do you think he raped her mother too?" she asked instead.

"I don't know," Dawn answered simply. *But given what Evan told me about her mother and her plans to abort Evan, I think it's a distinct possibility.* It wasn't something she was allowed to tell Aiden, and even if she were, this was something Aiden and her half sister had to discuss between them.

Finally, Aiden moved back to her side of the bed and lay down, every one of her movements as if in slow motion. She crawled under the covers and pulled them up to her chin.

Dawn slid down and got settled next to Aiden, close enough to see her face and feel the heat of her body but not to touch her. She knew Aiden might prefer some physical distance right now. She waited a few seconds, but when Aiden didn't say anything, she turned off the light. She tried to get comfortable enough to sleep but couldn't. Dawn was a cuddler by nature, and though they mostly stayed over only on weekends, she had gotten used to Aiden's close proximity while she fell asleep.

She sighed with relief when Aiden moved closer and gently pulled her into her arms.

"How many more are out there?" Aiden whispered against Dawn's skin.

Oh, sweetie, don't torture yourself with thoughts like that. "I don't know," she answered, pulling Aiden even closer. "Chances are, you and Evan are the only ones. But even if there are more half siblings out there, I bet they're all decent human beings."

"You don't know that," Aiden objected, a resigned bitterness making her voice rough.

"I know you," Dawn emphasized. "You're a decent person, a wonderful partner, and a good cop. The circumstances of your conception can't change that."

"He's my father," Aiden said, very matter-of-fact. "You can't escape genetics. Whether I want it or not, I have inherited a few things from him—and so has Evan. If we resemble each other at all, it's because we have the same father. We resemble him."

Dawn reached behind herself and flicked the light back on. She knew Aiden was right. She had seen pictures of her mother, and Aiden didn't look like her at all. "I think about it sometimes too," she admitted.

She felt Aiden stiffen against her. "And? What do you think exactly?" she asked with bated breath.

"After I was raped, I saw Garett Ballard everywhere. Not him as a person, but little parts of him—a voice that sounded like his or a man with his build or his hair color. But then, after a few months, I realized that a voice or a hair color doesn't make someone a violent person. I see your hair," Dawn gently combed her fingers through a few black strands, "or your hands," she kissed Aiden's palm, "or your eyes, and I know there's a good chance you inherited them from the man who raped your mother. But in the end, it doesn't matter. They're your eyes, your hands, and your hair—and I love them. I love you, exactly the way you are."

Aiden tightened her embrace. "Thank you," she whispered.

"No thanks necessary, just promise me you won't beat yourself up over things that are out of your control," Dawn said seriously. "No matter what Evan Whitfield or your father did or didn't do, it has no bearing on you... on the kind of person you are. Okay?"

"I'll try." Aiden laughed shakily. "Old habits die hard, you know?"

Dawn rested her head on Aiden's shoulder in her favorite sleeping position. "That's why you have me. I'll remind you a few times along the way. You won't have to go through this alone."

Aiden reached over Dawn and turned off the light again. "That's the only good thing about this whole mess."

CHAPTER 15

"SHE'S STILL TOO distraught to talk about it," Eleanor Matheson said, dabbing at her eyes.

Kade shook her head at her sister-in-law. "We can't wait any longer. I already gave her over twenty-four hours." She was neither able nor willing to give Laurie more time just because she was a member of the Matheson family. "Laurie has to give a statement now." She indicated a clearly uncomfortable Del, who had insisted on accompanying her today. Kade had a sneaking suspicion that Del had spent the night in front of her house and hadn't let her out of sight since Friday night.

Her brother rose from his place on the couch. "What if we don't want to press charges?"

Kade stared at him. "What?" Victims and family members not wanting to testify out of fear or embarrassment was what she had to deal with every day in her job. She hadn't expected to encounter it within her own family too. "Ignoring it won't make it go away. I won't make it go away." She fixed her sharpest prosecutor gaze on her brother, making it very clear that the influence of their family would not help him in this situation. "If Laurie was raped, I want to—"

"Rehash the gory little details in open court, for all our friends, neighbors, and my patients to hear," Doug interrupted. "Think about the consequences."

"So you decided to let your daughter's rapist walk because it might be detrimental to your practice to make it common knowledge what happened to Laurie?" Kade couldn't believe it. "Could you be any more selfish?"

Doug stopped his pacing and placed himself directly in front of her. He had their father's athletic build even though he had never done manual labor for even a single day in his life, and he used his height and weight advantage to try and intimidate her.

Kade smiled coolly. *Scarier men than you have tried and failed, big brother!*

"Selfish?" Doug repeated, managing to keep his voice calm and cultured but to still sound angry. "I'm not doing this for myself. I'm doing it for Laurel. I have a family to think of—not that you would know anything about that!"

It was a low blow, but Kade schooled her features and didn't even blink. "Laurie is part of my family too."

"Coming over with a trunk full of gifts on birthdays and on Christmas is not what I'm talking about," Doug lashed out at her again.

Kade folded her arms and stared at him. "I thought this was about helping Laurie through this situation. Why are you making this about you and me?" She didn't want to have this discussion in front of Del. When her brother didn't answer, she drove the urgency of the situation home again. "I have to talk to her. She has to tell us what happened. We don't even know how Evan Whitfield got into the house."

"I don't know what she was thinking!" Doug paced through his living room again. "To take a strange girl up to her room without us knowing about it! Where does she even know her from? That girl sure as hell doesn't move in the same circles Laurel does!"

"Doug." Kade lifted her hand to stop her brother's tirade, but he didn't listen. "Douglas!" she interrupted him with more force. "Calm down and stop shouting, or I'll have Lieutenant Vasquez escort you from the room!"

Del dutifully took a step toward him even though Kade knew her well enough by now to see that she was hesitant to get involved into a family argument.

"You wouldn't!" Doug sputtered indignantly, but Kade didn't let him continue.

"I would," she told him calmly. "We're here to help Laurie, and your anger isn't helping at all. You're scaring her." Kade had a feeling that was one of the reasons why her niece still refused to talk.

Doug folded his arms across his chest. "What do you suggest we do?" he asked, a hint of defiance in his voice.

"I'll try to talk to her again, but this time, you're going to take a walk while I do it," Kade demanded, jerking her thumb in the direction of the front door. "I don't want her to feel pressured because she knows you're lurking right behind her door."

Doug opened his mouth, no doubt to object. He had inherited the traditional Matheson stubbornness. His wife, Eleanor, quickly laid a hand on his arm. "It can't hurt for her to try, Douglas. Please." She softly stroked his forearm until Doug relented.

"You don't resemble him at all," Del said when they had left the room. "Well, apart from your pigheadedness, of course," she added with a small grin.

Kade shot her a quick glance, but there was no real heat behind her glare. She knew Del was right and appreciated her honesty. "Doug is the spitting image of our father while I look more like my mother's side of the family." She moved to the door Laurie was still hiding behind. She listened to the sounds behind the door for a moment, then turned back to Del. "This could take a while. It's okay for you to go. This is not an official police interview."

Del made herself comfortable in one of the easy chairs. "I'll stay."

Kade nodded. She didn't want to admit it, but just knowing Del would be in the next room made her feel calmer. She knocked on the door and entered slowly. "Laurie?"

Her niece sat at her desk, her back to Kade. She didn't turn around when she heard Kade enter.

I wish Aiden was here to do this. She's so much better with victims than I am. But this was **her** niece, and Kade had never been one to shirk her responsibilities. "Hey." She carefully perched on the edge of Laurie's desk, wanting to be able to see her face while she talked to her. "How are you?"

"I'm fine," Laurie murmured without looking up.

Oh, yes, of course. The standard Matheson answer, taught at a very young age. Kade sighed. "I sent your parents away," she said.

That finally made Laurie look up. She stared at Kade with wide eyes, clearly not used to someone ordering her father around.

"I thought a little fresh air would maybe cool your father's temper," Kade said with a smile.

Laurie giggled, then quickly pressed her hand over her mouth and stared down at her desk again.

What's going on here? Kade wondered. She knew there were many different ways people reacted to a trauma like rape, but somehow, Laurie didn't seem like a distraught rape victim. Still, she couldn't be sure. While she had known her niece her entire life, she had to admit that she didn't really **know** her.

Laurie was too shy and Kade too busy with her work to get to know each other.

"Laurie, do you know Evan Whitfield?" Kade gently asked her first question.

The girl's head jerked around. "You know her name?"

"I'm a prosecutor, Laurie," Kade reminded. "My detectives told me." She waited, but when Laurie said nothing, she urged, "Tell me what happened, please."

Laurie pressed her lips together and shook her head.

"Laurie, this is important. If she forced you in any way, if she pressured you to do anything you didn't want to..." She took a deep breath, trying to control her anger at the thought of her niece being raped.

"Nothing happened," Laurie finally whispered.

"That's not true, and you know it. Your mother found you half-naked, with Evan Whitfield on top of you." Kade forced herself to be frank for a moment. She knew she couldn't spare the girl's feelings even if she was her niece.

Laurie began to sob again. She covered her face with both hands, but big teardrops continued to leak from under her fingers.

Kade sighed. She had never been good at giving comfort. Apparently, neither were Laurie's parents, and the girl needed someone to be there for her. Giving herself a mental kick, Kade moved forward and wrapped gentle arms around her niece.

The sobbing became even louder as Laurie burrowed her face against Kade and wept.

"Hey, hey, it's okay. You're safe." Kade smoothed her fingers over Laurie's hair. "She can't hurt you anymore."

"She didn't," Laurie said, her voice muffled against the fabric of Kade's blouse.

Kade gently moved her niece back a bit so she could look into her eyes. "Tell me what happened," she said again. When Laurie didn't answer, she decided to back up a bit and start with a question that wasn't as threatening. "You know her, right?"

Laurie gave a reluctant nod.

"Where did you first meet her?" Kade immediately asked the next question, not wanting to give Laurie an opportunity to retreat into her silence again.

"When I went to see Dr. McNamara." Laurie's voice was barely audible because of her sniffling.

Kade dried the girl's tears with her own handkerchief. "Dr. McNamara? Is he your family doctor?"

"No. She's my therapist," Laurie answered, dabbing at her eyes with the sleeves of her shirt.

Kade raised her brows. She'd had no idea her niece was seeing a psychologist. *God, have I been so out of touch with my own family?* "Why are you seeing a therapist?"

Laurie shrugged.

It was her parents' idea, Kade realized. "And you met Evan Whitfield at the psychologist's office?"

"Yeah. She was nice. She showed me her tattoos," Laurie said, still sniffling.

Kade held back a frown. *Nice indeed.* "Has she been to your house before?" she asked.

Laurie wildly shook her head. "I didn't think Mom and Dad would approve of her."

She's right, of course. Evan Whitfield isn't the kind of girl who is fit company for a Matheson heir, Kade thought sarcastically. Her parents had carefully picked her own friends until the day she had moved out. "But you did spend time together before?" Kade asked, trying to get closer and closer to the truth of what had happened.

"She bought me ice cream last week." Laurie looked at Kade as if she expected her aunt to show her disapproval.

Kade kept her expression carefully neutral. "And Friday night?" she asked gently.

"Evan climbed in through the window," Laurie said, her voice barely above a whisper.

That still didn't tell Kade what had happened. Rapists came in through windows, but so did amorous teenagers. "Did you open the window for her?" she asked, watching her niece closely.

Laurie didn't look at her. "I'm not allowed to have guests up here without Mom and Dad knowing," she answered evasively.

"That doesn't answer my question, does it?" Kade asked softly. She didn't want to treat Laurie like a hostile witness and bully her into a confession. When Laurie didn't answer, she gently stroked her shoulder. "Laurie, I'm your aunt. I know we're not as close as we could be, and I'm sorry for that. But I hope you know you can trust me. I won't judge you, no matter what happened."

Laurie's gaze flitted up to meet Kade's. She searched her face, clearly hesitant to believe her.

"Laurie, if Evan hurt you, I want her to pay for it. But if she didn't, you have to tell me or Evan could go to prison for something she didn't do."

"Prison?" Laurie's blue eyes grew almost comically wide.

Kade nodded gravely, a little surprised by her niece's naivety. "If she touched you without your consent, it's a very serious crime."

Laurie whispered something. It sounded like "She didn't," but Kade wasn't sure.

"What?" she asked, but Laurie didn't repeat it. "Laurie, it's okay if you've... been with her because you wanted to. It's okay to like her... to like girls, you know?" She had never thought it possible that her niece might be gay, but if she was, Kade wanted to be as supportive as she could.

Laurie snorted. "Yeah, right! That's so not okay in this family! A Matheson has to be perfect. Like you."

Kade couldn't breathe for a moment. *Is that how she sees me? Perfect Aunt Kade?* She took a deep breath. It was time to be supportive Aunt Kade. "It's okay to be a lesbian or bisexual or even not to be sure yet if you like girls or boys," she insisted once again. "Even for a Matheson."

"Being gay is a deadly sin in Grandmother Sophie's book," Laurie objected bitterly. "Oh, yeah, it might be okay for her interior decorator to be gay but not for her only granddaughter!"

Kade sighed. "Your grandmother is a little old-fashioned in that regard. She was born in another time. I'm not sure how she'll react, but you should know that there are a few members of this family who will love you and support you no matter what."

"You?" Laurie asked with a hint of skepticism.

Kade nodded seriously. "Yes. I'll support you whether you're straight, gay, or bisexual. It doesn't matter," she promised.

Laurie didn't answer, but it was easy to see what she was thinking, even for Kade. Her words were just empty promises from the "perfect Aunt Kade" for Laurie.

Sighing, Kade pinched the bridge of her nose. Telling Laurie she was supporting gay rights and that she had a few gay friends wouldn't mean anything to Laurie. Other lesbians didn't have to deal with the Matheson family and their high-flown expectations. Kade knew she had to make a decision right now: keep up her image of perfection or help her niece. How hard it was for her to make this decision was a good indication for how hard this whole situation had to be for Laurie. "I know I haven't been a big part of your life until now, but that could change if we both want it," Kade said. "We might discover that we have a lot of things in common."

Laurie looked even more skeptical now. "You're confident, beautiful, and successful, and I'm just a shy, awkward kid. What could we possibly have in common, huh?"

Kade hesitated. Her thoughts raced as she desperately searched for some last-minute inspiration. In court, a sudden, brilliant idea had often saved her neck, but this time, there was no artful trick to pull off the impossible. There was only one way to support Laurie in this situation. *It's now or never.* Kade lifted her head and looked Laurie right in the eyes. "Well, for one thing, it's possible we might have a similar taste in romantic interests."

Laurie blinked, then stared at her. "What do you mean?" she asked suspiciously.

Kade realized she had to be frank even if saying it out loud went against every instinct she had. *I'm not ready for this, but here we go.* "You are not the only Matheson woman who might be interested in women."

"No way! You mean... you? You are... a lesbian?" Laurie laughed giddily, overjoyed with that revelation.

Kade hesitated, but then nodded. She knew that pointing out she was technically still straight or bisexual at best would not help her niece. There was no doing this halfway.

A still laughing Laurie almost bowled her over with an exuberant hug. "Do you have a girlfriend? It's not..." Laurie lowered her voice. "...Detective Carlisle, is it?"

"What? No, no, she's not my girlfriend." Kade threw her hands up in exasperation. *Why does everybody always think that there's something between Aiden and me?*

"Oh." Laurie looked half-relieved, half-disappointed to hear that. Her cheeks were flushed.

Oh my God! Kade didn't know whether to laugh or to cry. *I think my niece has a crush on Aiden!* She rubbed the bridge of her nose. *God, this is getting complicated!*

"Then it's the tall Latina outside?" Grinning, Laurie pointed to the door leading to the living room, where Del was still waiting.

So she did pay attention to what is going on in the rest of the house. "No. I don't have a girlfriend," Kade quickly ended the discussion. "Laurie, we can talk about me later. For now, please tell me what happened with Evan Whitfield."

Laurie blushed and ducked her head. "We made love," she said with a dreamy smile. "At least we would have, but Mom interrupted."

Made love? Kade had seen the tough-looking Evan Whitfield being led away by two police officers. She doubted Evan was one for love or steady relationships. "Are you sure she didn't take advantage of you in any way?"

"She would never do that," Laurie said fervently. "But of course Mom had to assume the worst as soon as she saw us. She would rather believe that Evan raped me than that I was gay and in love." She began to cry again. "What do I do now? I can't tell them!"

Kade reached out and stroked Laurie's blond head. "You have to, Laurie. This whole misunderstanding has gone on for too long. You have to clear it up. Evan has been dragged out of here in handcuffs; she spent the night in jail, and she's probably in a lot of trouble with her foster parents."

Laurie stared at her in shock. "I didn't want that," she said meekly.

"I know you didn't," Kade said. "But every minute you wait and don't tell your parents what happened only makes things worse for Evan. I know it's not easy to face your parents, but I promise to come with you and support you." *Let's hope she won't parade "perfect Aunt Kade" around as a prime example of the successful lesbian in front of the whole family.* At the thought, her stomach did a nervous flip she hadn't experienced in years. For a few seconds, Kade thought about asking Laurie not to mention what she had just told her. If Laurie mentioned Kade's sexual orientation to anyone else in the family, things could get complicated, and she wasn't sure she was ready to deal with it. Still, Kade knew making the request would only send the message that homosexuality was something you had to hide. She decided against asking Laurie to keep it to herself even though she knew the consequences it might have for herself. *God, I'm really in for it now.*

Laurie sniffled. "Can I come live with you if they throw me out?" she asked in all seriousness.

Only years of practice in keeping a neutral expression kept Kade from staring at her in shocked horror. She was determined to play a more active role in her niece's life in the future, but she wasn't ready to raise her. "They won't throw you out," she said, hoping she was right.

* * *

"You didn't have to drive me home," Kade said for the third time. "It's just a few blocks to my apartment."

A few blocks too many for Del's liking. After the scare on Friday night, she didn't want to tempt fate a second time. She stopped her car in front of Kade's building. "I told you it's not a problem."

"Oh yeah, I'm sure witnessing the Mathcson family drama was exactly how you wanted to spend your Sunday," Kade replied sarcastically.

To tell the truth, Del could have done without all the yelling and crying, but the way Kade had stood up for her niece had been pretty impressive. If nothing else, it had proven that Kade, though from a very traditional family, was a fierce and well-informed defender of gay rights and in no way narrow-minded. "Well, for a second I thought I might have to restrain your brother, but all in all, they took it well. Compared to my parents' reaction when I came out to them, they were downright giddy about Laurie's confession."

"If you think that was giddy..." Kade shook her head. "What did your parents do? Tar and feather you?"

"My mother cried and prayed for a cure, and my father tried to 'beat it out of me.' Neither had a lot of success," Del said with a chuckle.

Kade didn't laugh. "That's awful! Was there no one to stand up for you?"

"Nope. There was no brave Aunt Kade in my family," Del said, smiling. She didn't want to scare Kade with her coming out story, knowing that Kade was having enough trouble coming to terms with the possibility of being attracted to a woman as it was. She didn't need to be reminded of the consequences. "It's okay, Kade. I have a new family now even though we're not related by blood."

Kade just nodded, deeply in thought.

"You really made a difference for your niece today," Del said, trying to cheer up Kade, who had been strangely silent, worrying about something, since they left the house. "It took a lot of courage for her to face her parents and tell them she's gay. After she didn't give us a single sentence of explanation since Friday night, I didn't think she ever would. How did you get her to admit the truth?"

Kade turned her head, her blue-eyed gaze meeting Del's. "I told her she's not the only Matheson woman who is interested in women."

Del was glad that she had already stopped the car. Kade's statement was a surprise, as was the calm she projected. Del was convinced it was just an act. She couldn't believe Kade would be so cavalier about coming out to a member of her conservative family. "You're not talking about some distant cousin or something, are you? You really came out as bisexual to your niece?" Del asked, just to make sure.

"It was the only way to get her to tell the truth and to make her feel better about being a Matheson and gay," Kade said.

Del knew she was right, but still, she hadn't thought Kade would admit to even the remote possibility of finding another woman attractive. Maybe to herself or to Del, but not in front of her family. Hearing that Kade had taken that step was a pleasant surprise, but at the same time, it made her worry about Kade. "Are you ready to deal with the consequences?" she asked softly.

"No, I'm not," Kade admitted, her jaw a hard line as she gritted her teeth. "But it doesn't matter. Helping Laurie is all that mattered. I'm old enough to deal with whatever happens next, but she isn't. Not on her own." She reached out to open the passenger side door. "Thanks for driving me."

"Kade! Wait a minute, will you? There's something I want you to have." She had to laugh at Kade's almost scared expression.

"Don't worry. It's not jewelry or another romantic gesture." Del leaned toward Kade and opened the glove compartment. "Here."

Kade stared down at the gun Del laid into her hands. "A gun?"

"It's the smallest and lightest nine millimeter ever made," Del explained. "It only weighs twenty-one ounces and has a ten-round magazine."

"Nice," Kade said and moved to hand it back.

Del refused to take it. "This is not an attempt to charm you with my weapons collection. I want you to keep it."

Kade studied it with a frown. "I'm a lawyer, Del, not a cop."

"A lawyer who is being stalked. If things escalate, I want you to have the means to defend yourself." After Friday night, Del was determined to do everything necessary to keep Kade safe.

Kade politely but energetically shook her head. "I appreciate your concern, but—"

I don't want your appreciation or your politeness. I want you to take the goddamn gun! "Kade, forget your pride for a moment," Del demanded. "Your pride won't protect you if push comes to shove. This gun will."

"I don't even have a permit to carry a concealed weapon," Kade said, still not picking up the gun that rested on her palm.

"I'll take care of that for you," Del promised.

"That's exactly what I don't want!" Kade exploded. "That's why I didn't want the police to know about this secret-admirer situation. I don't want anyone to think that I'm taking advantage of my position in the DA's office. I'm not above bending the rules to win a case, but I'm not willing to do it for private reasons."

Del felt anger bubble up in her too. Usually, she found Kade's stubbornness adorable, but right now, it was threatening her life. "You want this strictly by the book?" she asked, her voice barely controlled.

"Yes!" Kade's voice was sharp and definite, like a judge's gavel coming down for the final ruling.

"You want to take a firearms safety and training course, fill out a long and complicated form, submit it to the Sheriff's Office along with all the other paperwork they require, then you'll have your fingerprints and photo taken, and after that you'll wait for up to forty-five days for them to make a decision?" Del's fist hit the steering wheel in frustration. "It takes time to do this by the book—time you might not have!"

Kade tilted her head and looked down at the weapon in her hand. "You could get in trouble over this," she said quietly.

Del didn't hesitate. "That's why I only want you to use it if you have no other choice. If it can save your life, I'll gladly get in trouble for it."

They stared at each other for a few seconds, then Kade reluctantly curled her slender fingers around the gun's grip. "I've never fired a gun," she admitted.

Del breathed a sigh of relief, glad that Kade seemed to be giving in. "That's not a problem. I'll show you," she promised.

"When?" Kade asked.

"Right now?" Del was in no hurry to leave Kade. Not only did she enjoy spending time with Kade, but she also knew she'd only end up sitting in her car, watching the apartment, if they said good-bye now.

Kade raised an eyebrow at her. "Now?"

Del shrugged. "No time like the present, right?"

Finally, Kade nodded. "All right. I'll just have to make a quick call to Aiden."

She calls Carlisle on a Sunday? Del couldn't help it. Even knowing Aiden was in a committed relationship and Kade was nowhere near ready to act on her attraction to women, she felt a little jealous.

Kade flipped open her cell phone. "Aiden? Sorry to call you at home, but I have important news. I just talked to my niece." Kade listened for a few seconds, then frowned. "Call Ray? Why can't I tell you?" Again she listened, and her frown deepened. "What? That's just what I wanted to tell you. No, listen for a second, there **is** no case. It turns out all it was is two teenagers getting caught making out. Laurie was just too scared to tell her parents."

Kade explained a few details, then closed her cell phone. "That was weird," she murmured, more to herself than to Del.

"What?" Del asked as she started the car.

"Aiden didn't want to talk about the case. She told me to call Ray instead of her."

Del shrugged. "Maybe she just wants to spend a quiet, work-free Sunday with Dawn." *Good for her. She better treat Dawn right and not neglect her.* She had promised herself to keep an eye on Carlisle and make sure she made Dawn happy.

Kade shook her head, still frowning. "No, that's not it. She said she had taken herself off the case. I've never known her to do something like that, and God knows we've had our fair share of tough cases."

That's odd, Del silently agreed. If Carlisle was anything like Del, she would never willingly hand over one of her cases—and definitely not this case. "She didn't tell you why?"

"No, but she seemed very relieved to hear that the case is closed and all charges dismissed," Kade said, deep in thought.

"Well, with her caseload, one less case is a good thing, right? Especially since it means your niece isn't the victim of a horrible crime. Of course Carlisle would be glad about that. That woman cares about you, Kade." *Sometimes maybe a bit too much for my liking.*

That comment clearly made Kade uncomfortable, and she quickly changed the topic. "So where are you taking me?"

"Our first stop is the shooting range," Del said even as she stopped the car in front of the building.

Kade didn't get out of the car. "First stop?" she repeated.

"Well, after your first shooting lesson, I'm gonna take you out to lunch." Del had been with Kade all day and knew she hadn't eaten a single bite. She didn't like what she had seen of Kade's eating habits so far. Kade never took the time to eat. Del would bet her paycheck on the fact that Kade's breakfasts consisted of a hastily gulped-down coffee while she went over her notes for the day's trial. Midday recesses were used for preparing witnesses for their testimony, and her working lunches with other lawyers were ninety-nine percent work and only one percent lunch.

Kade indignantly stared at her over the rim of her glasses. "You're gonna take me out to lunch? Excuse me, but don't I get a say in the matter?"

Don't give her the feeling of being driven into a corner, idiot! "Of course you do. You get to choose where we go. That's only fair since you're going to pick up the check as a thank-you for your shooting lesson," Del said with a charming grin. There was no way Kade could refuse now without appearing impolite and ungrateful. And if Del had learned one thing about the Matheson family today, it was that they taught their children to uphold appearances.

Kade pointed an accusing finger at her. "Don't think I didn't notice your clever manipulation. You're a sneaky woman, Lieutenant."

"Yep." Del grinned. *All is fair in love and war.*

* * *

Kade followed Del into the building, taking in the unfamiliar surroundings. She had never been at a shooting range before.

In contrast, Del felt very much at home. She greeted people left and right as they walked down a hallway, and more than a few knew her by name.

"Do you come here often?" Kade asked after it had happened a few times.

A mischievous smile spread over Del's face. "Is that a pick-up line?"

Kade couldn't hide her blush. She searched for an answer.

"Hey, relax." Del chuckled and quickly reached out to squeeze her forearm. "I'm only teasing."

Kade shot her a gaze. She wasn't angry with Del, though. She was annoyed with herself. *What is it about Del Vasquez that makes you, the eloquent DDA, speechless on a regular basis?*

"You know, apart from your job, there is only one thing in your life right now that you should take deadly seriously—the man who's stalking you. Everything else is not a life-or-death matter, so don't take me—or yourself for that matter—so seriously all the time." Del smiled at her. "You have to learn how to let go a little."

Kade stopped her fast clip down the hallway. She knew Del was right, but still, it irritated her that Del was always trying to get behind the walls she had erected. Everyone else usually knew enough to back off when she aimed a cool glance at them, but Del only answered with one of her unwavering smiles. "Who says I have to? No one's forcing you to stay if you don't like the company of my somber self."

Del stopped next to her. "I do like your company, and that cool, calm, and collected lawyer façade is sexy as hell, but frankly, it has to get rather exhausting after a while—for you, not for me," she said with that brutal honesty Kade liked and hated with equal parts. Then Del added almost wistfully, "I'd like to see you smile or hear you laugh every once in a while."

"Not much to smile or laugh about at the moment," Kade grumbled.

Del took her hand and squeezed gently, then quickly let go before Kade could pull away. "I know. Okay, then let's at least try to make you feel a little safer."

Kade followed her to one of the shooting booths.

"Put these on," Del ordered, handing her a pair of earmuffs and Plexiglas safety glasses.

Kade felt a little silly but did as Del told her. She slid the earmuffs down to rest around her neck so she could still hear Del's explanation.

Del held up the small gun she had given Kade in the car. "It's a semiautomatic," she explained. "You slap the magazine into place and chamber the first round. Never point the gun at yourself or anyone else while you load it." She demonstrated, her movements slow enough for Kade to follow them and then handed over the gun for Kade to try.

Del watched and nodded. She let Kade repeat the loading and unloading process a few times before she took over the gun again. She pressed a button, moving the black silhouette-shaped target forward to the fifteen-yard line. "Now comes the fun part. You spread your feet for balance and hold the gun like this."

Kade let her gaze wander down Del's long legs, then up to the steady hands that held the gun in the two-handed grip she had often seen with her detectives. She took the gun when Del handed it to her and tried to imitate Del's stance. "Like this?" She looked over her shoulder at Del.

"Lift your arms a little higher and straighten your firing arm." Del stepped closer until Kade could feel her body heat directly against her back. She felt Del's gentle fingers on her hands as they corrected her grip. "Don't forget to breathe, Kade," Del said directly into Kade's ear before she pulled the earmuffs up to cover Kade's ears.

Kade took a deep breath and told herself her nervousness was only due to handling a weapon for the first time in her life, not because of Del's closeness.

"Your left hand supports the other like this." Del almost had to shout for Kade to hear her with the ear protection on and above the noise from the other shooting booths. She gently moved Kade's left hand a little farther down. "Your index finger stays outside the trigger guard until it's time to shoot. Never touch the trigger before you've sighted your target, and never aim the gun without being fully prepared to fire it."

Kade quickly rested her index finger along the side of the weapon.

Del turned Kade's whole body a bit to the right. "Now you line up the sights. Focus on the front sight of the gun. When you're ready, squeeze the trigger gently and gradually."

Del's arms disappeared from around her, making Kade lose sight of her target for a moment. She quickly called herself to order and refocused her attention on the black silhouette in front of her. She fired once and stopped to critically inspect the target, noticing that the bullet had only grazed the lower left part of the target. "What am I doing wrong?" she asked and turned to look at Del.

"You're pulling the trigger, not squeezing it gently, and you flinch in anticipation of the recoil." Del stepped a little closer again, her voice gentle, not reprimanding. "Don't jerk the trigger, or it'll throw your aim off. Apply a steady pressure, and let the gun surprise you when it goes off."

She wants me to give up control even in this matter, huh? Kade turned back to the target and lifted the gun again. This time, she concentrated only on the sight and moved her finger back with a more constant pressure. She fired once, then corrected her aim a little before she emptied the rest of the magazine. When it was empty, she turned to look at Del.

"Not bad for your first time," Del said.

"Not bad?" Kade repeated incredulously. She pushed the button to bring the target to them. As far as she could see, she had hit the black paper with every single shot.

Del grinned. "Even you can't be perfect at everything, Counselor." She laughed at Kade's expression. "Relax, I'm just teasing. You're a natural. If we train regularly, you'll soon be able to outshoot your detectives."

If we train regularly? We? Kade arched her eyebrows. "Is this some clever ploy to get me to spend more time with you?" she asked skeptically.

"No ploy," Del promised, her expression now completely serious. "We're here to make sure you can defend yourself should the need arise. But if that should cause us to spend more time together, it would be a pleasant side effect, don't you think?" she said with a twinkle in her eyes.

Kade laid the gun down and looked at her. Yes, she silently admitted, Del was a good person to spend some time with. She was intelligent and had a great sense of humor. She kept Kade on her toes, but at the same time, she felt as if she could trust and relax around Del. Instead of answering, she extended her hand, palm up. "New magazine, please."

Del laughed. "I thought you'd see it my way."

* * *

Kade looked up as Del stopped the car. She knew they were somewhere in St. Johns, but she had never been in this part of the city. "This is not a restaurant," she said, lifting an aching hand to point at the row of nearly identical looking apartment buildings in front of them. Every muscle in her arms, shoulders, and her back was starting to hurt after two hours at the shooting range.

"No, it's my apartment. I thought after the day you had, it would be nicer if we ordered in and didn't have to venture out into public again," Del said, resting her hands on the steering wheel and calmly waiting for Kade's reaction.

Kade bit her lip and looked from the three-story apartment building to Del and back.

"Come on." Del laughed. "I'm not dragging you back to my cave to have my way with you!"

Her frankness shocked Kade for a moment, but she quickly regained her composure. "All right. But I'm still paying for dinner."

They entered the building, with Del politely holding the door for Kade.

A small, silver-haired woman was trying to wrestle her mail from a dented mailbox without much success.

"Hi, Mrs. Rios," Del said with a smile. "Can I help you with that?" She took over the small key and finally handed the mail to the elderly woman.

"Oh, thank you, Clarice!" The elderly woman beamed up at Del and patted her hand.

"Clarice?" Kade asked as they stepped into the elevator.

Del chuckled. "She thinks I'm with the FBI."

Kade still didn't understand. "What does that have to do with—"

"Mrs. Rios is a big Jodie Foster fan," Del said with an affectionate smile. "One day, after I finished helping her with a few things around the apartment, she sat me down and made me watch The Silence of the Lambs with her. She has been calling me 'Clarice' ever since."

She's helping her elderly neighbor? God, this woman is too good to be true! The women Kade usually socialized with donated to charities, went to fund-raisers, and might even be seen helping out in a soup kitchen once a year, but they always made sure to get publicity for all their good deeds. Del just helped out, without being asked and without expecting more than a thank-you.

Del opened the door to her apartment. "Come in and make yourself comfortable."

Comfortable was the last thing Kade was feeling when she stepped into Del's living room. She was curious to see how Del lived, but at the same time, it seemed strangely intimate to be here, and it made Kade uncomfortable.

"Coffee?" Del called from the kitchen. "Do you like Chinese?"

"Yes to both." At least the coffee would give her something to do with her hands until their food arrived.

"I always take egg rolls and chicken and cashew nuts with fried rice. Want to take a look at the menu to see what you'd like?" Del called.

Kade hesitated only for a moment. It was time to show a little trust in Del even if it was just ordering dinner. "No," she answered. "Egg rolls and fried rice sounds great. Go ahead and order two of everything."

She turned back around and studied Del's living room. There was a comfortable looking leather couch against one wall, but Kade was not ready to sit down without an explicit invitation. She wandered through the living room, glancing at a few photos on top of the bookshelves.

One of them showed a smiling, younger Del leaning against a squad car next to a slightly older man, both of them in uniform. Kade had never seen Del in uniform before, so she took a moment to admire the way Del looked in the Portland Police blues before she forced those thoughts from her mind.

She grinned at a picture of a pigtailed, chubby-cheeked Dawn, showing off her braces as she smiled at the camera. *Del saw her grow up,* she realized again. *That's why she's so protective of her. Aiden, my friend, you better take care never to hurt Dawn, or you're gonna have one very pissed-off adopted aunt on your hands.*

Kade put down the photo and looked at Del's vast collection of books. She turned her head sideways to read the titles on the spines but didn't recognize any of them. Curious, she pulled a random book from the shelf to look at it.

On the top half of the cover, a few glass chess pieces were depicted.

Just as Kade turned the book around to read the description on the back, Del cleared her throat behind her.

Kade hastily put the book back and took the mug Del handed her. "I didn't know you were a chess player," she said, embarrassed to have been caught snooping through Del's books.

Del smiled at her over the rim of her coffee mug. "I am, but this one," she pointed to the book that Kade had looked at, "is actually not a book about chess. It's one of my favorite lesbian romance novels."

"Oh."

"Don't look at me like that!" Del almost spilled her coffee, she was laughing so hard. "I said it's a romance, not the lesbian <u>Kama Sutra</u>."

Kade didn't answer. She just sent her a reprimanding glare.

"You can borrow it if you like," Del continued her teasing.

Kade already had a flippant "No, thank you" on her lips, but then she met Del's challenging gaze. If Kade had one weakness, it was her inability to back down from a dare. "I'd love to, thanks," she purred and plucked the book from the shelf.

For the first time, Del was the speechless one, and Kade enjoyed it immensely. After a few moments, Del laughed at herself. "So, wanna play with me?" She nodded down at the book in Kade's hands.

Now Kade didn't know what to say to that blatant offer. *Is that how it's going to be? Us taking turns rendering each other speechless?*

"Chess, Kade. I'm talking about chess." Del laughed. "I told you to relax around me. If anything should ever happen between us, it'll be because you make the first move. As long as you don't give me a clear signal, I'll be a perfect gentlewoman. I'm not into chasing straight women."

Could have fooled me, Kade thought but admitted to herself that Del's gentle insistence was flattering. "Okay, let's see if you'll put your money where your mouth is."

Del sputtered, almost choking on her coffee. "Excuse me?"

"Chess, Del. I'm talking about chess." Kade smirked at her. Turning the tables at Del was fun. "Let's play." She nodded at the chessboard she had spotted on the coffee table.

"You want to play for money? That hardly seems fair—you're stinking rich, and I'm just a lowly lieutenant," Del complained, a playful twinkle in her eyes.

Money had been an issue in a lot of Kade's relationships, but if Del's relaxed joke was any indication, it would never be an issue between them. "So what do you suggest? We just play for the honor?"

"Where would be the challenge in that? No, let's play strip chess," Del said.

"Strip chess?" Kade shook her head at her, hiding her amusement. "There's no such thing as strip chess, Delicia Vasquez!"

Del shuddered dramatically at the use of her full name. "Of course there is," she said with a grin. "Regular rules, with one addition: for every piece you lose, you lose an article of clothing. The first one who is checkmated or completely naked loses."

Kade didn't hesitate for more than a second. She sat down in front of the white pieces. "Okay."

"Okay?" Del stared at her. She clearly hadn't expected Kade to take her up on her offer.

"Yeah," Kade drawled. "Let's play."

"We could wait," Del said. "The food will be here in about thirty minutes."

Kade shook her head. "No. This won't take long."

"Uh-oh! Someone is very confident about her skills on the chessboard." Del sat down across from her.

Kade shook her head. "I haven't played in years." Not since her father had died. She moved one of her pawns to e4. "Earlier, at the shooting range, you were very good at that." Kade had emptied a few more clips, and after each one, they had stopped and gone over Kade's mistakes. Del never ran out of patience, no matter how often she had to correct Kade's stance or answer her questions. Kade doubted she would have had Del's patience.

Del laughed easily and moved her pawn to face Kade's. "Well, I'd hope so. Even lieutenants have to submit to the annual firearms requalification, so getting out of practice is a bad idea."

"No, I don't mean shooting although you're certainly good at that too. I mean you're a good teacher. You should consider a change in careers." It was not a serious suggestion, of course. Even if she tried, she couldn't picture Del as anything but a cop.

Del nodded thoughtfully. "I almost did once."

Oh. Kade looked up from the chessboard. That was a surprise. Del seemed to put her heart and soul into being a cop. "You thought about quitting the force?" *Probably after her partner's death,* Kade speculated. She knew that asking too many questions about Del's life was probably not a good idea because it might encourage Del's interest in her, but she couldn't help herself.

"No. I thought about applying for a job teaching at the Portland Police Academy," Del said. "I was in a long-term relationship back then, and we started to talk about having a baby. I didn't want my family to go through what Jim's family had, so I thought about applying for a position that would take me off the streets."

Kade moved one of her knights. She found herself more surprised with every word. She knew a woman of Del's age had probably been in a few long-term relationships, but she had never thought Del would be the type to seriously think about having a baby. Maybe she was judging Del by her own standards, but she had always thought Del was putting her career over thoughts of love and family. *Well, apparently she did—she's a lieutenant, but she has neither a baby nor a long-term partner, so calm down.*

Del captured one of Kade's pawns with one of her own and looked up at her with an expectant grin. "Strip!" she ordered.

Kade had to laugh, finally relaxing a bit. "You wanted to say that for a while, didn't you?" she teased.

"Yes, so get on with it, woman!" Del leaned back with a satisfied grin and watched her.

"No, sorry, but I won't even take an earring off for that." Kade gestured at her captured pawn. "Strictly speaking, a pawn is not a piece. You should have clarified." She sent Del a triumphant smirk.

Del groaned. "Playing chess with a lawyer was a bad idea."

Kade grinned and moved her other knight to cover the gap her captured pawn had left in her pawn structure. "What happened?" she asked at last. "I mean... why didn't you go through with your plans of motherhood and changing your job?"

"We split up, and after that, I concentrated on my job and on Grace and her daughter," Del answered. She moved her bishop, threatening one of Kade's knights.

Concentrating on her job... Now Kade found herself back on familiar, safe ground again. Instead of moving her knight back and losing momentum, she captured Del's bishop with her queen. "So you gave up your plans of having a baby?"

Del smiled and shrugged, taking off one of her shoes without comment. She didn't appear uncomfortable talking about her private life with Kade at all. "It was not a conscious decision, but in the last few years I wasn't in a situation to think about it seriously, and now... Well, I'm a little too old for having a baby."

"There are a lot of forty-year-old women having babies nowadays," Kade objected, not sure why she was doing it. Maybe she just didn't want Del, who was so encouraging to her, to give up her dreams. "And besides, I thought that was one of the advantages of being a lesbian. Your partner could be the one to have the baby."

"Provided that I prefer younger women," Del said with a smile while she started attacking Kade's pawns on one of the wings, at the same time making room for her rook to move forward.

Kade felt a blush creeping up her cheeks, and she pressed her lips together in annoyance. "Yes, provided that." She decided against capturing Del's pawn, because that would have made her end up with a double pawn, and moved her queen instead. "Check."

"And that my hypothetical partner would want to have kids," Del said, the smile still present on her lips as she moved her queen between Kade's and her king.

Kade nodded again but didn't say anything. Maybe it was better if she kept her mouth shut. She thought for a moment and then captured Del's queen with her own.

Del kicked off her other shoe and took Kade's queen with her king.

Kade slipped out of her left sneaker. "So not wanting to have kids would not be a deal breaker for a hypothetical mate?" she asked, studying the board before she made her next move.

"No." Del took one of Kade's pawns with her knight. "I like kids, but I found out that I'm not one of those women who need children to be happy in life. I think what I found so appealing about having a child was that it meant having a family, someone to belong to. If my hypothetical partner wanted to have kids, I wouldn't say no, but if not, that's not a big deal. We could take turns acting childishly." She winked at Kade.

Kade laughed and captured Del's knight.

Twenty minutes later, Kade took Del's last rook and leaned back with a satisfied grin. "Checkmate," she announced.

Del stared down at the board. "Damn, you're good," she said, not even a hint of annoyance in her voice, only open admiration. "Who taught you to play like that?"

"Why?" Kade smirked. "You want to take lessons?"

"Yeah, might be a good idea," Del said ruefully. "If someone had taught me how to play like that, I wouldn't be sitting here in my underwear while you're merely barefoot."

Kade looked at Del, taking in the ripped wifebeater that showed off sleekly muscled shoulders, before she quickly looked away again. "Well, you're a few years too late."

"Your father taught you," Del said, a statement, not a question.

Kade nodded, not surprised that Del had guessed. Del always seemed to have good instincts when it came to her. "Other fathers taught their kids how to play Parcheesi. My father taught me chess."

"I'm surprised you beat me so easily," Del said.

It hadn't been that easy. Del's game was solid. "Well, then it seems you underestimated me."

"No, it's not that. I assumed you'd be good. I just thought... I didn't expect you to play that aggressively," Del said. "I assumed you'd employ a more defensive strategy."

Kade shook her head. She had learned the hard way that a defensive player hardly ever won a game against someone who could play well. "Playing it safe is not always a good tactic. You can't win if you're always reacting instead of acting, always one step behind."

"Seems like a good life philosophy," Del said.

"I'm talking about chess, not life," Kade objected.

Del simply smiled. "How about a rematch?"

"Not so fast! You haven't taken something off for losing your rook yet." Kade pointed at the captured piece.

"You really want to see me naked, don't you?"

This was a nonthreatening opportunity to literally see more of Del, but Kade didn't want to admit to that. "It wasn't my idea. You made the rules, now you have to follow them."

"Okay. What do you want me to take off? The undershirt..." Del teasingly lifted it up, revealing her navel. "Or the pants?" She reached for her zipper and waited for Kade's decision.

"You know what? Let's have that rematch now," Kade quickly decided. "There might be a few minutes left before our food arrives."

Del laughed. "Chicken." She made clucking noises.

"I'll make you take them off in the next game," Kade promised.

Del started placing the pieces back on the board. "No. This time, you'll be the one who ends up in her underwear."

CHAPTER 16

AIDEN'S STEPS slowed as she neared the door to the interview room. She glanced back at Dawn, glad she had given in and let Dawn come with her.

Dawn stepped next to her and gently touched the small of her back. "Ready?"

"Not really, no." Aiden took a deep breath. She had faced Evan Whitfield and had stared her down before without a problem, but she hadn't known she was her sister then. Now that Evan was no longer a suspect, she didn't know what to say to her.

"I'll be right beside you," Dawn promised, rubbing her back. "You don't even have to tell her right now if you're not comfortable with it. Let her get to know you a little better first and find out what she knows about her father."

With this new perspective, it was a little easier to open the door.

Evan Whitfield looked up as they entered. Anger sparked in her eyes. "Why did you drag me in here again? It's been almost forty-eight hours. You have to let me go!"

"We are," Aiden answered quietly. "Laurel Matheson told us what happened between you two. You're free to go."

"That's what I told you from the start, but you stupid cops wouldn't believe me!" Evan shot up from her chair and strode over to the door. It was clear she didn't want anything to do with Aiden.

Dawn quietly stepped next to her and touched the arm that was reaching for the door handle.

Oh, oh! Dawn! Aiden quickly strode over to them. She wasn't sure if touching the angry teenager right now was a good idea. Evan looked ready to rip Dawn's arm off. Sister or not, Aiden wouldn't tolerate her lifting a single finger against Dawn.

To her surprise, Dawn's touch seemed to have the same calming effect on her sister that it had on her. Evan whirled around, but when she realized it was Dawn, her angry gaze softened. "What?" she asked gruffly.

"We'll drive you home," Dawn said.

"We?" Evan repeated. "Why we? Didn't you hear? I'm innocent. My business with the cops is finished."

Aiden waited, letting Dawn decide what she would tell Evan. Dawn seemed to have a much better rapport with Evan. Despite the shared genes, she still found Evan irritating. She sometimes stretched Aiden's patience to the limit.

"Aiden is my partner," Dawn said.

Evan frowned at her. "Partner? You're not a cop. You're a shrink, Doc."

Dawn smiled patiently. "There's more than one kind of partner. Aiden is my life partner."

Evan looked from Dawn to Aiden and back. An almost lewd smirk appeared on her lips. "So you're family, huh?"

Family! If you only knew! Aiden forced herself not to react to Evan's suggestive tone of voice. For now, she would let Dawn handle Evan.

Dawn nodded calmly. "Now you know why your attempts to shock me with your tales about your imaginary lesbian love affairs were futile," she said with an impish smile.

"Imaginary?" Evan bristled. "I'd say me being here would prove that they're not—"

"Calm down," Dawn interrupted. "You've got nothing to prove. Let's get you out of here."

They made the trip to Evan's home without much talking. Aiden didn't know what to say to the stranger who was her sister, so she kept silent and concentrated on her driving. She felt Dawn's gaze on her, and Dawn laid her hand on Aiden's thigh once, giving it an encouraging squeeze. Aiden quickly looked into the rearview mirror, a little embarrassed with the display of affection in front of Evan.

Dawn smiled and withdrew her hand.

"Will I see you tomorrow for another one of our torture sessions?" Evan finally broke the silence, talking only to Dawn as she had from the moment they had entered the interview room.

Dawn uncomfortably cleared her throat. "I wanted to talk to you about that. Evan, I can't be your therapist any longer. I think it would be best if I refer you to one of my colleagues."

"Great!" Evan didn't attempt to hide her bitter sarcasm. "So you're givin' up on me too? I thought you were different, Doc, but I guess you're just another hypocrite." She fell silent and stared out of the window.

Dawn turned in the passenger seat and helplessly looked at Evan. "I'm not giving up on you. That's not the reason I can't work with you any longer. It's not anything you've done."

"Yeah, right." Evan snorted.

"Evan..."

"Shut up and save it for someone who is interested in what you have to say. I don't care. I didn't want to go to stupid therapy in the first place!" Evan snarled at her.

Aiden threw a warning glance back over her shoulder. "How about a little more respect, please!" No one was insulting Dawn in her presence.

"How about you shut up too?" Evan shot back. "This is between me and the doc. It has nothing to do with you."

"It has everything to do with me! I am the reason she can't be your therapist anymore." Aiden had said it before she could stop herself. It seemed she and her sister were very good at pushing each other's buttons and provoking each other. *Shit.*

Evan looked at Dawn contemptuously. "You let her tell you what to do? She forbid you from seeing me again because she thinks I'm scum!"

"I make my own choices," Dawn told her much more calmly than Aiden could have. "I don't need Aiden to tell me what's right or wrong."

"Yeah, but why is continuing as my therapist wrong, huh? Not that I'm crazy about having to talk to a shrink, but compared to the others you were tolerable. And cute," Evan said with a small smile.

"I won't see another shrink. If even you think I'm hopeless, why bother at all?"

Dawn shook her head in desperation. "You're not hopeless. I told you my decision has nothing to do with you."

"Yeah, right." Evan rolled her eyes.

Aiden couldn't stand it any longer. She knew nothing Dawn said would convince Evan. "Actually, her decision has to do with you. With me and you," she said and clutched the steering wheel with clammy hands. Dawn's concerned glance told her this might not be the best of times, but she knew there was no ideal moment to tell Evan. She had to do it now before she chickened out.

"You and me? There is no you and me. Apart from you arresting me because that red-haired bitch—"

"Shut up and listen!" Aiden's patience was wearing thin. "We ran a sample of your DNA."

Evan shrugged. "So what? I'm not denying I slept with Laurie."

Aiden stopped the car in front of the LeCroix residence.

Dawn's calming hand returned to Aiden's thigh. Aiden took a deep breath. "The DNA analysis showed that you and I... we're sisters. Half sisters."

Evan Whitfield laughed hysterically. "You're crazy. I don't have any sisters." She turned to Dawn. "Doc, I think your girlfriend needs therapy more than I do. She's one can short of a six-pack. I think she watched one too many soap operas, and now she thinks I'm her long-lost sister!"

"No, Evan. I know it sounds crazy, but it's true," Dawn said.

"You're lying!" Evan jumped out of the car and slammed the door.

Aiden cursed. "That went well."

Dawn rubbed Aiden's leg. "She's angry and confused. Give her some time to calm down, and then try again. Come on, let's go and tell them we brought their foster daughter back."

There was no sign of Evan as they walked up the driveway and rang the bell.

Evan's foster father opened the door.

"We're bringing Evan home," Aiden said, vaguely pointing in the direction of the garage, where she assumed Evan was hiding. She had to concentrate to keep herself from fidgeting. Her mother had been her only living relative, so dealing with her half sister's foster parents made her more than a little nervous. "The girl she was accused of raping finally gave a statement, and she confirmed that Evan didn't hurt her in any way. It was all a misunderstanding."

"You're bringing her back?" Mr. LeCroix asked without opening the door farther to let them in. "Detective, I'm not sure that my home is the right place for Evan to stay anymore."

Aiden looked from him to his wife, who was weakly leaning against the wall of the hallway, looking close to tears. "You don't understand, Mr. LeCroix. She's innocent." It had been such a relief to find out that her half sister was not guilty of rape, not only because she was glad for Kade's niece, but also because it made her hope that they hadn't inherited their father's violent tendencies.

"You're the one who doesn't understand. This whole drama has just been the latest in a long row of incidents. Wild parties, drugs, shoplifting, hanging around with criminal thugs, coming home drunk or stoned at all hours of the night." Mr. LeCroix ticked it off on his fingers. "And now we find out she's been having sex with girls!"

For a moment, Aiden lowered her head under Mr. LeCroix's burning gaze, feeling somewhat guilty for the sins of her sister as she had always felt guilty for the sins of her father.

It was Dawn who courageously stepped forward, preventing Mr. LeCroix from closing the door in their face. "Being gay is not a crime, Mr. LeCroix, and neither is acting on it. I'm a lesbian, and I know how hard it is to be true to yourself and come out at her age. If anything, you should be proud of Evan's courage and support her in any way you can."

"But she didn't come out," Mr. LeCroix said. "She never told us she was gay!"

Dawn stood her ground. "Why should she? Why should she trust you with that very personal information when you don't even show a little trust in her? You chose to believe the accusations against Evan as soon as you heard them—without even asking Evan for her side of the story first!"

Aiden stared at her usually gentle, soft-spoken partner. She couldn't help admiring Dawn's fire, her passionate defense of Evan, and her courageous honesty. *God, I love this woman!*

"She never gave us any reason to trust her," Mr. LeCroix said after a few moments of shocked silence. "From the very first day she—"

"Evan grew up in foster care," Dawn interrupted, her voice like cutting steel. "Do you know what that means?"

"Of course," Mr. LeCroix immediately defended himself. "I—"

Dawn didn't let him finish. "It means she never had anyone who loved her unconditionally. It means she never had anyone who believed in her. No one to understand her, to comfort her, to help her with her problems — and there were bound to be problems when you consider her family background." Dawn pushed the door open a little more and now stood directly in front of Evan's foster parents. "Evan never learned to ask for help, so she had to make sure to get a little attention in other ways."

"By starting down the road to becoming a career criminal?" Mr. LeCroix asked incredulously.

"She's not a criminal, Mr. LeCroix. Evan acts tough and uncaring, but that's only to hide her true feelings. She has to protect herself against the constant rejections of people like you," Dawn told him bluntly.

Mr. LeCroix stood stock-still, caught between feeling angry and ashamed.

"Don't you understand that this is a vicious circle?" Dawn continued hotly. "You expect her to fuck up, so she does. You agreed to take on the role of her parents, so it's on you to break that vicious circle. Start showing a little trust in her."

"She's right, Roger," Jill LeCroix finally whispered. "We can't just throw her back into the system just because things are not as easy as we imagined them to be. If we try harder and Doctor Kinsley continues to work with Evan, it will eventually get better."

Aiden and Dawn exchanged a long glance. *Shit. We were almost there, but we can't keep this from them.* "Dawn... Doctor Kinsley can't continue as Evan's therapist, Mrs. LeCroix," Aiden said. She didn't want Dawn to have to stand on the front line alone. She wasn't ready to think, let alone talk about it, but if she wanted the LeCroix family to be a part of Evan's life, they had a right to know.

Roger LeCroix stubbornly raised his chin. "Since when are the police allowed to make treatment decisions?"

Aiden worked hard not to adopt a similarly defiant stance. "I'm not saying it as a police officer, Mr. LeCroix. I'm saying it because Dawn is my partner... my girlfriend."

"I assume she has been your girlfriend before last week. It didn't stop her from being Evan's therapist then," Jill protested while her husband stared at them.

"Last week." Aiden cleared her throat. Last week, everything had been different. "In the course of our investigation, our medical examiner found out that Evan is my half sister."

Jill and Roger LeCroix stared at her. "But... how is that possible?" Jill asked, her face a mask of shock.

"We're not sure yet, but we probably have the same father." That was as much as Aiden was willing to tell them. The details were only for her and Evan to discuss.

Mr. LeCroix folded his arms across his chest. "If you are her sister, why don't **you** take her in?"

Aiden felt herself go pale. *Me?* She swallowed. *Oh, no, that's not a good idea. We would kill each other within a week.* But of course she couldn't tell them that.

"Evan needs stability in her life, not to be handed over to yet another person," Dawn came to her aid. "I think it would mean more to Evan if she lived with someone because they want her to and choose to have her be a part of their family instead of someone who has no other choice because they're related."

Wow. That sure sounds better than "I'm too scared to take her in," Aiden thought with relief.

"We'll let her stay for the moment," Jill LeCroix said before her husband could decide otherwise. "Where is she, by the way?"

Aiden sighed. "She took off when I told her we're sisters. I'm not sure she believed me." If Irene Deming hadn't shown her the DNA results, she wouldn't have believed it either.

Dawn's arm wrapped around her waist. "A part of her knows it's true. That's why she took off. She can't handle it right now. We have to give her time."

The four of them awkwardly said good-bye. Aiden and Dawn walked back to their car, still not seeing a sign of Evan.

"Damn," Dawn muttered as she sank into the passenger seat. "I blew it!"

"What?" Aiden turned and stared at her. "You didn't blow it. You were wonderful. If I'd been here on my own, Evan would be on her way to the next foster family by now."

Dawn insistently shook her head. "I was unprofessional. My role is—or was—to counsel Evan, not to tell her foster parents off!"

"Hell, they needed it!" Aiden saw no reason for the guilty expression on Dawn's face. "The way you defended Evan... it gave me a lot to think about. Her irritating, smart-assed attitude was grating on my nerves, and I admit that even after I found out she's my sister, I had no patience with her. What you said made me think about what it was like for her, growing up in the foster system. That could have easily been me." If her mother had decided not to keep her but to give her up for adoption, she could have ended up in a similar situation. *Despite the way I was conceived, I was lucky,* Aiden realized. *No matter how many times I got into trouble at school, my mother never judged me. She never openly compared me to my father or threatened to give me into foster care.*

"Yes," Dawn quietly confirmed. "You're very much alike in some ways. She's like a younger, more aggressive version of you."

"I wouldn't go that far," Aiden said. She wasn't ready to admit they had much more in common than the man who had fathered them.

"Don't worry. You're still my number one." Grinning, Dawn leaned over and kissed her.

Aiden deepened the kiss for a few moments, inspired by the passionate fire Dawn had shown when she had confronted Evan's foster parents. After a while, she moved back and grumbled playfully, "I better be!"

* * *

"This is nice," Dawn murmured. She wrapped the blanket around the two of them and cuddled even closer.

"Yeah, it is," Aiden agreed and found to her surprise that she really meant it. In past relationships, she had never been one for cuddling—except maybe as part of foreplay or right after sex. Now she was completely content to just lie here and hold Dawn close. *I wonder if that's a good or a bad sign.*

Dawn began to trace the silver necklace Aiden wore. Her finger slid gently down Aiden's neck and over her chest until it came to rest on the oval pendant.

Aiden craned her neck and looked down at herself. She swallowed a lump of emotion when she saw Dawn stroke the good luck charm with the same reverence with which she had caressed Aiden's skin. "Why did your father give it to you?" she suddenly found herself asking.

"Hmm?" Dawn looked up at her.

"I mean... your brother was a cop too, and Saint Michael is the patron saint of police officers, so why didn't your father give the good luck charm to Brian?" She smiled down at Dawn. "I bet you were his favorite, huh?"

Dawn shook her head. "No, I wasn't."

Aiden tickled her gently. "Oh, come on! I've seen pictures. You were lethally cute. There's no way you weren't his favorite."

Dawn chuckled. "Well, maybe I was," she conceded. "But that's not why he gave me the good luck charm instead of giving it to Brian."

"So what was the reason?"

"A few months before my father died, I was in a serious car accident," Dawn said.

Aiden felt all her muscles tighten. She stared down at Dawn. She knew there were no big scars hiding under Dawn's sleep shirt. "Were you hurt?"

Dawn bit her lip and nodded. "I was in the passenger seat of a friend's car when another driver ran a red light and hit our car from the side. My head hit the passenger side window pretty hard. I don't remember any of it, but I was in a coma for three days, and the doctors said it was touch and go."

"W-what?" Aiden's arms clutched at Dawn, pulling her closer. "You never told me about any of this! What happened?"

"I only know what my parents told me about it. Mom says it's the only time she had ever seen my dad cry. When I woke up after three days, the first thing I saw was Dad's good luck charm. He had placed it in my hand," Dawn said and gently touched the silver pendant again. "When I got home from the hospital a few weeks later, I wanted to give it back to Dad or give it to Brian, but they both refused. They said the good luck charm clearly worked for me, so I should keep it."

Aiden didn't know what to say. It was hard to think that Dawn could have died. She pressed her hand against the one resting on the good luck charm. "But now you gave it away. Your father and your brother clearly wanted you to have it." She suddenly felt guilty for accepting the good luck charm.

"They wanted it to protect me from being hurt—and if it helps to keep you safe, it's doing exactly that. Nothing in the world could hurt me more than losing you," Dawn whispered.

Aiden lifted Dawn's hand to her lips and kissed it, silently accepting that Dawn wanted her to have the good luck charm even though it was a family heirloom. "That accident..." She swallowed as a picture of a younger Dawn smashing against the car's window flashed before her eyes. "There were no lasting effects? You're fine, right?"

"I'm fine," Dawn confirmed with an encouraging smile. "I have a little scar, but other than that—"

"Where?" Very gently, Aiden's fingers slid into the strawberry blond hair and felt along Dawn's scalp.

Dawn reached up and directed Aiden's hand with her own. "A little more to the right... there."

"Jesus!" Aiden carefully stroked the scar that was hidden under Dawn's hair. "That's not a 'little' scar!" She shook her head in disbelief. *Why did I never notice it before?*

"It's not so bad," Dawn assured her. "It can be a little sensitive every once in a while, but normally it doesn't hurt at all."

Aiden looked into the gray-green eyes. *God, she's been through so much in her life... and still here she is, trying to make me feel better. In a way, she's so much stronger than I am.* "You're amazing," she said.

Dawn grinned. "So you like women with scars?"

"I like one woman with one scar, so don't get any ideas about acquiring more scars," Aiden told her firmly.

"It's not on my to-do list," Dawn said.

"Good." Without disentangling herself from Dawn, she finally closed her eyes to get some sleep, hoping she wouldn't have nightmares about Dawn and the car accident.

CHAPTER 17

𝒟EL SET A PAPER cup down in front of the doorwoman. *I've seen so much of her lately, maybe I should start dating **her**.* Del chuckled to herself.

"What's this?" The tall woman looked up with a frown.

"Coffee," Del said with a smile. "It's for you." She was not above simple bribery when it came to Kade. Getting into the good graces of the woman who guarded Kade's front door seemed like a good idea. "Don't bother calling up. I'm going to surprise her," she called as she strode past the front desk with the other two coffee cups she was carrying.

A woman with a baby-stroller, chatting with an older woman who was loaded down with shopping bags, blocked the way to the elevator, and Del spontaneously decided to take the stairs. At least that would give her some time to think about how to explain her sudden visit to Kade. She couldn't very well tell her "I was getting bored down there in the car, watching your apartment" when Kade didn't even know she was there. *Kade would probably accuse me of treating her like a child that needed babysitting and shoot me with my own gun.*

She still hadn't found a convincing argument for her presence in Kade's apartment building when she reached Kade's floor. She energetically rounded the corner. A bit of coffee spilled over, burning her hand. Del cursed and fumbled to get a better grip on the paper cups.

Without warning, pain exploded in the back of her head. The last things she saw were the falling paper cups before she crashed on top of them.

* * *

Kade threw her pen down on the legal pad when she heard the piercing scream. Her neighbor's shrill voice had interrupted her work often enough in the past to identify her easily. *Don't tell me her Chihuahua escaped again.*

She stood and stretched before she slowly made her way to the door. She opened the door and peeked out carefully. Under no circumstances did she want the Chihuahua trying to find sanctuary in her apartment.

Her elderly neighbor stood in front of her apartment door, wildly waving her hands about. "She's dead! Oh my God, she's dead!"

"Your dog?" Kade asked, trying to show a little compassion even though she had never been a big fan of the little rat whose yapping regularly interfered with her work.

"No!" The older woman pointed a trembling finger. "That woman!"

Kade turned her head in the direction indicated.

A motionless figure lay in a puddle of what looked like coffee.

"Call 911," Kade ordered calmly. She took her keys from the side table right next to the door and stepped out into the hallway. Her calm disappeared when she recognized the unconscious woman. "Del!" She rushed toward her and fell to her knees next to Del. "Del?"

There was no sign of life from Del. She was very pale. Blood mixed with the coffee on the floor.

"Oh, God! No, no, no! Del, come on! Come on, you have to be okay! Del?" Kade tried to feel a pulse, but she was trembling so much and her heart beat so loudly, she wasn't sure if it was Del's pulse or her own hammering heartbeat.

Del groaned.

"Del!" Kade leaned closer, not caring if she got blood and coffee all over her clothes. "Del, can you hear me?"

Del rolled onto her back before Kade could stop her. Her eyelids fluttered open. "K-Kade?"

Kade reached out a trembling hand and combed back a strand of hair that had fallen onto Del's forehead. "Yeah, it's me."

"Uh." Del moaned as she tried to sit up.

"No, don't try to get up just yet." Kade gently pressed her back down. "Help is on the way. You'll be fine." She willed herself to believe it.

Del sank back, her head now cushioned against Kade's lap. "What happened?" she asked, looking up at Kade with wide, confused eyes.

A new wave of fear shot through Kade. *She can't remember?* "I'm not sure," she said. "You shouldn't even be here."

"Wanted to bring you coffee," Del murmured.

Kade looked down at the puddle she was sitting in. "Did you fall? Did you feel dizzy?"

Del frowned, still looking confused. "I don't know. I don't think so."

"It's all right." Kade smoothed her hand over Del's brow. "You don't have to figure it all out right this minute. Are you in pain?"

"No, feels great," Del said, looking up at her with a lopsided grin.

It took Kade a few seconds to realize Del was talking about the small caresses she was bestowing on Del's face. "You are impossible," she said without any real annoyance.

The doors of the elevator pinged open, and two paramedics rushed out, a stretcher in tow. "We've got it now. Move away from the patient and give us some room, please," one of them told Kade.

Kade reluctantly relinquished her place next to Del to the paramedics. She watched anxiously as they told Del to move her hands and feet and shone a light into her eyes.

Del protested as they fitted a brace around her neck and lifted her onto the stretcher. "I can walk."

"No, you can't!" Kade answered. She quickly grabbed her purse from her apartment and followed the paramedics and the still struggling Del to the elevator. "Now stop struggling before I club you again!"

The paramedics stared at her. "You did...?"

"What?" Kade realized how that must have sounded. "No! No, of course not!" She wearily rubbed her face but stopped when she realized her fingers were covered in Del's blood. Her stomach nearly revolted.

"Ma'am?" One of the paramedics gripped her elbow. "Are you all right?"

Kade shook his hand off. "I'm fine."

The elevator came to a stop.

They wheeled the stretcher past the staring doorwoman and outside to the ambulance.

"I'll ride with her," Kade decided.

The paramedic closest to her shook his head. "That's not allowed. I'll tell you which hospital we're taking her to, and you can—"

"I'm a deputy district attorney, and she's with the Police Bureau. I'm riding with her," Kade said with her most determined voice. She flashed her ID at him and pulled back Del's jacket to reveal the badge clipped to her belt.

They lifted Del into the back of the ambulance, and Kade climbed in before they could protest again.

One of the paramedics started the ambulance. Kade was glad that they didn't turn on the sirens. She hoped it meant that Del was not that badly hurt and would soon be fine. She looked at Del, who was lying strapped in on the stretcher, nearly immobilized. There were no windows, so all Del could see were the roof of the ambulance and the medical equipment surrounding her.

"Kade?" Del raised her voice over the sounds of traffic.

"Yes? I'm here," Kade said quickly.

Del cleared her throat. "I'd like to hold your hand, but... well... I'm a little tied up at the moment."

The paramedic looked from Del to Kade, then smiled and moved out of the way.

A little embarrassed, Kade moved closer and laid her hand on top of Del's. Cold fingers squeezed her own, and she gently rubbed them, trying to get some warmth back into them. "How are you doing?" Kade asked softly.

"Fine," Del answered, and Kade was relieved to hear that her voice sounded a lot stronger than it had when she had been lying in front of her apartment. "This wasn't necessary."

"It's their job to decide that, not yours." Kade pointed to the paramedic, who smiled and nodded. What she didn't tell Del was how scared she had been and that she would be able to relax only when she heard from a doctor that Del was fine.

"Which hospital are you taking me to?" Del asked.

The paramedic looked up from examining Del's head wound. "The Garfield Memorial Hospital."

"Wonderful," Del groaned.

Before Kade could ask for clarification, the ambulance stopped. Within seconds, they were wheeling Del through the doors of a hospital. Del disappeared behind a curtained-off area, and Kade was asked to stay back and wait.

She wearily settled down on an uncomfortable plastic chair and stared down at her blood- and coffee-soaked sweatpants. No one had ever seen Kadence Matheson in public in such a state of disarray, but right now, Kade didn't care. She couldn't have cared less about what she looked like. What she cared about was that Del's blood on her clothes meant Del was injured and in pain—and there was nothing Kade could do about it.

It seemed like hours, but her accurate sense of time told Kade it was just a few minutes before a doctor stepped out from behind the curtain. He looked barely old enough to be a doctor, and Kade frowned. She wanted only the best care for Del.

"Ms. Vasquez tells me you found her?" the young doctor asked without much preamble.

"Yes." Kade shot up from her seat, eager for news. "How is she?"

The doctor tilted his head. "She has a concussion, but so far, I think she'll be fine."

So far? I think? That wasn't good enough for Kade. Not where Del was concerned. *Maybe I should call Doug and have one of his doctor friends check Del out.* "You think?" she repeated, not even trying to hide her skepticism.

"I'd like to do a CT, just to make sure there's no bleeding under the skull," the young doctor said, looking too tired to care about what Kade thought about his competence. "And I need you to answer a few questions."

Kade nodded briskly. "Ask away."

"Did she lose consciousness after her fall?" The doctor looked down at his clipboard.

"Yes." Kade was sure she would never forget those heart-stopping moments after finding the motionless Del.

"For how long?" the doctor asked.

How long? Kade knew it had probably felt longer than it had actually been. "Not long. Couldn't have been more than a minute after I heard my neighbor scream for help, but I can't be sure how long Del had already lain there until my neighbor found her."

The doctor scribbled more notes on his clipboard. "Did she seem confused when she regained consciousness?"

"A little. She couldn't remember what happened, but she recognized me immediately." *That's good, right?*

The doctor thanked her, and Kade settled back onto her uncomfortable seat for more waiting. Kade hated waiting.

A woman in a nurse's uniform hurried down the hallway and skidded to a halt in front of Kade. "DDA Matheson?" she asked, looking confused and upset.

Kade looked up into her face. She frowned at the stranger until she remembered where she had seen her before. The woman was Dawn's mother. "Mrs. Kinsley..." She didn't know what to say to Del's best friend.

"One of the ER nurses told me they brought Del in. Is she all right? What happened?" Grace Kinsley was not even pausing for breath between her questions. She stared at the blood on Kade's clothes. "Oh my God! Is she...?"

Kade quickly stood and pressed Grace onto the chair she had vacated. "The doctor said she should be fine. They're just doing a few more tests."

Grace slumped back against the wall. "What happened?" she asked, a little calmer now.

"Del doesn't remember, but it seems she wanted to bring me coffee and fell right in front of my apartment door." Kade felt guilty for that although she hadn't even known about Del's intentions to visit her. "Maybe she tripped with the coffee in her hands, or maybe she got dizzy because she hadn't eaten." The paramedic had given her Del's jacket to hold on to, and she had found two squished muffins in the pockets.

"Tory," Grace called out to another nurse walking down the hallway. "Can you find out what's going on with Del Vasquez? She's a friend of mine."

Grace and Kade waited in tense silence until the nurse returned with information on Del. "They're just getting her settled into her room," she reported. "It's room 1019."

Kade silently followed Grace through the maze of hospital corridors to room 1019. Kade, unsure how to act, lagged behind as Grace strode directly toward Del's bed.

"Del." With just that single word, Grace bent down and took her friend in a full body hug, kissing her cheek with a tenderness that made Kade stop right next to the door. The hot wave of jealousy surprised her. It was a completely unfamiliar feeling to Kade. She had never been jealous about anything or anyone before. In most things in her life, she had always been the uncontested number one, and when one of her lovers had shown an interest in someone else, it was mostly her pride that had been hurt. Kade had simply moved on without a lot of heartache.

"They told me they'd rushed you into the ER, bleeding," Grace said, her voice shaking. "Suddenly, it was Jimmy all over again."

Del's hands made soothing circles on Grace's back. "It was nothing like that. I wasn't even on duty. Clumsy old me just fell; that's all."

"You're not clumsy," Grace said, finally moving out of Del's arms to look at her. "Tell me what really happened."

"I don't remember how it happened, but I probably just slipped and fell," Del said.

Grace studied her. "What are you hiding?"

Hiding? Kade stared at the pale woman in the hospital bed. She hadn't noticed Del hiding anything, except in how much pain she was. *But I guess Grace knows her a lot longer and better than I do. They have so much shared history. How could I ever compete with that?* For the first time in her life, Kade was coming in second.

"Nothing," Del said, winking at them. "You can't exactly hide a lot in these flimsy hospital gowns."

Del's nod directed Kade's attention downward. For the first time she realized that Del was indeed only wearing one of the unattractive hospital gowns. It made the usually strong Del look strangely vulnerable.

Kade listened to Grace and Del's conversation while the three of them waited for the results of the CAT scan. It took longer than Kade had expected, and she began to get nervous and impatient.

Finally, the young doctor from before stepped into the room with a patient file in his hands. "The CT is clear," he told them.

"See?" Del gave all of them an exasperated glare. "I told you I was fine."

"Yes, but I'd like to keep you overnight for observation anyway, just to make sure that no unforeseeable problems develop. I'll send in a nurse with your pain medication." The doctor turned to leave.

"I'm fine," Del repeated with more determination. "I want you to release me."

The young doctor turned back to her with a frown. "Do you live with someone who can keep a close eye on you for the next twenty-four hours?" he asked.

"I'm sure I can find someone," Del said even though she lived alone.

The doctor looked at Kade. He probably thought Grace was one of the ER nurses. "Make sure she gets a lot of bed rest and enough fluids. I'll prescribe a mild pain reliever for her. You have to wake her every hour tonight. If you have trouble waking her up, or if she's not able to give a coherent response to questions or her headache or nausea keep getting worse, immediately take her to the nearest emergency room."

Grace nodded while Kade just stood there passively for a change. The complications that the doctor had described sounded serious, and she didn't want to take on that kind of responsibility for Del's well-being.

When the doctor finally left, Grace softly touched Del's hand. "You'll have to wait here a little longer while I try to find someone to take my shift. If I can't, I'll call Dawn and ask her if—"

"No," Del said. "Let Dawn enjoy her weekend. Kade is going to stay with me."

Years of experience in the courtroom and at the Matheson dinner table had taught Kade how to keep a poker face, but this time, her impressive self-control failed. She stared at Del in disbelief, not sure if Del was joking or not. "I am?"

"Yeah, sure, it's the perfect solution," Del said casually.

"I think your head injury is more serious than we thought! How is this a perfect solution?" Kade energetically shook her head. "It's crazy, Del! Grace is a nurse. She's trained to watch over injured people. I'm a lawyer. The only thing I know about concussions is that they can be the result of assault and battery!"

"You don't have to do much," Del quickly soothed. "Just wake me every hour and chat a little. Everything will be fine. I've had concussions before, so I have more than enough experience for the both of us."

Kade stared at her in confusion. Why was Del insisting on her playing nurse when she had a real, qualified nurse as a best friend?

Grace leaned across the bed and looked at Del from a distance of mere inches. "Are you sure that's how you want to do this?"

"Very sure." Del smiled at her old friend. "Go back to your work, nurse. I'm in the best of hands."

Grace still looked a little doubtful, and Kade couldn't blame her.

"Look," Del said, giving Grace's hand a reassuring squeeze, "Kade can work from my apartment, but your work is here. Kade staying with me is the most logical choice. You don't mind, do you, Kade?"

Mind? Kade minded a lot, but of course, after all Del had done for her, she couldn't tell her that. Del had been injured while bringing her coffee, so how could she turn her back on Del now? Kade silently cursed a long row of Matheson nannies, who had drilled the importance of politeness into her. "I don't mind," she said through gritted teeth. She would bring up the subject again when they were alone.

Grace glanced at her watch. "Okay, if you're sure, I should get back to pediatrics. I'll call you later to make sure you're okay." She kissed Del again and left.

Kade took her place in front of the bed and stared down at Del. "Why are you doing this?"

"I thought you didn't mind?" Del smiled calmly.

"I don't. But it's still not a good idea. Grace would have been better suited for this job. If any complications develop, I can't help you." Kade felt herself get more and more agitated with every word. In her mind, she replayed the endless minutes of sitting helplessly next to Del without being able to help her in any way. She wasn't used to feeling so uncertain and helpless.

"Hey." Del sat up with a groan and reached for Kade's hand. Kade didn't move away. "No one expects you to pull a Dr. Weaver and miraculously save my life. You just have to keep an eye on me and call 911 if you think I'm in trouble. You can do that, right?"

Kade nodded reluctantly. Still, she didn't like this. "I'll let it go this time, but don't you ever put me on the spot like this again," she warned. "You should have asked me in private before you announced to Grace that I would stay with you."

"I know it wasn't fair, but I had my reasons. I'll explain later," Del promised. "Let's get out of here first. Would you hand me my clothes?"

Kade turned around and spotted Del's clothes on a small table next to the wall. She picked them up and carried them to the bed. When she looked up, Del was just slipping out of the hospital gown. With a small sound of surprise, Kade quickly turned back around.

"What?" Del laughed. "You've already seen me half-naked twice, so why the sudden shyness?"

Kade slowly, deliberately turned back around. No one had ever called her shy, and she wouldn't stand for it from Del. "Maybe I just like looking at you better when you aren't bruised and battered?" she shot back with a lingering, challenging smile.

Del gaped at her. She hadn't expected that comeback. "Do you?" she asked, her smile now gone.

"Of course. Cuts and bruises are not a particularly attractive sight." She got enough of that at work, and she didn't like seeing Del injured.

"No, I mean... do you like looking at me when I'm not bruised and battered?" Del asked. The teasing smile that Kade had expected to accompany that question was missing. Del's dark eyes looked at her with a serious expression.

Kade shifted the bundle of clothes in her arms and nervously licked her lips. "Yeah, well, the dancing mice boxer shorts were cute," she tried to avoid the answer with a joke.

Del simply continued to look at her.

Kade finally nodded. Looking at Del's half-naked body across the chessboard had been worth all the long hours studying the game in her childhood. "You're an attractive woman," she said.

"Do **you** find me attractive?" Del dug deeper.

"Yes." She had no problem admitting that much. She might have been straight all her life, but that didn't mean she had been blind. Besides, Matheson women were supposed to look at other women, if only to judge the competition. Granted, in Sophie Matheson's eyes Del probably wasn't much competition for a Matheson woman, but Kade ignored that for the moment.

Del looked as if she wanted to ask another question, but then just nodded and took the clothes from Kade's hands.

* * *

Dawn jumped out of her car and almost forgot to lock it in her haste to reach Del's apartment building. She hurried across the street and pressed the buzzer.

"Yes?" an unfamiliar voice answered after long seconds of silence.

Dawn frowned. Only then did she remember that Kade had offered to stay with Del. "Hello, Kade. It's Dawn Kinsley," she said quickly.

Kade buzzed her in, and Dawn took the stairs, not wanting to wait for the tiny, slow-moving elevator.

When she reached the third floor, Kade was waiting at the open door. Kade greeted her without a word and let her into the apartment. She followed Dawn back into the living room but didn't make herself comfortable or offer Dawn a seat. It was clear that Kade felt out of place and not comfortable yet in Del's apartment.

Or maybe it's me, Dawn thought. *Maybe she's uncomfortable with me seeing her here.* "How's Del?" she asked.

The door to Del's bedroom opened, and Del appeared in the doorway. "I'm fine. Would everyone please stop acting as if I'm at death's door?"

Dawn rushed over to her for a careful hug. "You're really okay?" she asked when she finally stepped back. She looked at Kade for confirmation.

"She's playing the hero," Kade said curtly. "She checked herself out of the hospital against the doctor's advice."

Since she had grown up around cops, Dawn wasn't surprised. She rolled her eyes at Del. "At least sit down and rest," she ordered.

Del trudged over to the couch and sank onto the worn, comfortable leather.

"I'll leave you two to talk," Kade said and disappeared into the kitchen, closing the door behind her.

Kade in the kitchen. Dawn remembered the cheese-grating incident and hoped Kade wasn't trying to cook anything for Del. "Offering to take care of you was really nice of her," she said. She knew taking care of other people didn't come naturally to Kade.

"Well..." Del grinned and turned her head a little so that the small dressing on the back of her head wasn't pressing against the couch. "She didn't exactly offer. I told your mother that Kade would look after me, and Kade graciously agreed."

"Graciously?" Dawn could imagine how Kade reacted to other people making decisions without asking her first. **Graciously** wasn't the first word that came to mind for describing that reaction. "Del, really, why didn't you call me? You know I would have come right away. Send the poor woman home and let me stay with you."

Del shook her head, then grimaced and stopped. "No. I know you would be there for me, and I appreciate it, but... no. Kade is staying."

"Delicia Vasquez!" Dawn eyed her old friend. "You're not using your injury to force Kade to spend time with you, are you?"

Del looked at her with a serious expression. "My intentions are honorable."

Dawn smiled and softly touched Del's arm. She had never doubted that. Del was nothing if not honorable. "I know that."

"But I admit I'm killing two birds with one stone," Del added with a grin. Then her expression became more serious. "There are other reasons why I want Kade to stay, but I can't go into them right now. And I think it will be good if Kade feels she can be there for me too. She's very independent, so she'll never accept a one-sided relationship."

That seemed like a sound strategy for building a relationship with Kade. It had been more than a decade since Dawn had last seen Del so serious about anyone. "What is it about Kade Matheson that has you so interested?" she asked.

Del gave her a knowing smile. "Don't you mean really what is it about Kade that had me and Carlisle so interested?"

"No. I know exactly why Aiden was interested in her," Dawn said. "And please stop calling her Carlisle. She has a first name, you know?"

Del shrugged and grinned.

Dawn knew she didn't plan on stopping to call her "Carlisle" anytime soon.

"So, what is it that had your girlfriend so interested in Kade?" Del asked.

"I think it was the image Kade projects. The confident, aristocratic, and a little unapproachable DDA. Aiden knew she could never have her, and that was what made her so interesting. She could safely admire her from afar, without taking the risk of emotional involvement," Dawn explained. "And, of course, it also doesn't hurt that she's really beautiful." She glanced at the kitchen door to make sure it was still closed.

"No." Del smiled softly. "It sure doesn't."

Dawn tilted her head. "But I take it you're not attracted to Kade for the same reasons why Aiden found her so interesting?"

"My reasons are just the opposite," Del said.

"The opposite?"

"Not that I don't admire Kade's confidence or her aristocratic bearing, but mainly I like what I see when I look a little deeper. And I don't just want to admire her from afar," Del said with confidence.

Dawn had only caught a few glimpses of what lay beneath Kade's cool exterior, and it was obvious that Del was determined to get behind Kade's defenses and see more in Kade than the rest of the world did. A sudden thought struck her. "Do you want me to invite her to your birthday party?"

Del blinked innocently. "What birthday party?"

"Oh, don't try that puppy-dog look with me." Dawn laughed. "The surprise party we had for you every year for the last twenty years, of course."

Del chuckled. "Does that mean I can stop acting so surprised every year?"

"No. It's your duty as the birthday girl to act surprised," Dawn told her. "So? Do you want me to invite Kade or not?"

"Well, I wouldn't mind having her jump out of a cake." Del winked at her. She leaned over and kissed Dawn's cheek. "That's very thoughtful of you. Thank you."

The kitchen door opened. Kade stepped out with a tray. "I made coffee," she said. With a nod in Dawn's direction, she added, "And tea."

She's been paying attention, Dawn noticed, once more impressed by Kade. "Thank you, but I have to go. When my mother called, I left my office in disarray." She softly touched Del's shoulder and stood.

Kade politely escorted her to the door.

Dawn turned back around to face Kade. "Take good care of her."

A faint glimmer of nervousness flashed across Kade's face, then the confident expression was back. "I will."

* * *

Del jerked awake when someone touched her shoulder. After years of being single, she wasn't used to having company in her apartment. In the light of the lamp on her bedside table, she could make out Kade's face.

How does she do it? It's after midnight, and she has been running around in circles all day, yet she still looks perfect. Not a hair out of place. Even that old shirt of mine that shrunk in the dryer looks classy on her. "Hey," she said, her voice rough from sleep and emotion. "Time for my first wake-up call?" She patted the bed next to her.

Kade sat down on the edge of the bed and peered down at her. "Yes, time to test your verbal and motor responses. So, tell me your name. The full name."

"Torturing an already injured woman, DDA Matheson? How cruel of you." Del leaned her head back against the pillow. She still had a bit of a headache, but she didn't want to worry Kade by admitting it. "Okay. My full name is Delicia Vasquez Montero. At least I don't have a middle name, thank God!"

Kade smiled. "Now squeeze my hand."

Oh, finally an excuse to touch her. Del didn't hesitate. She gently wrapped her fingers around Kade's, feeling the softness of her hand and the calluses on her middle finger, where her pen usually rested when she wrote.

"I said squeeze, not caress," Kade scolded but didn't move her hand away.

Oops. Del gently squeezed Kade's fingers, then released them. "So, how do I rate, Doctor Matheson?"

"You don't get the top score because I had to repeat the verbal command, but it's good enough not to drag you back to the ER," Kade said and stood up. "Go back to sleep."

Before Del could say anything, Kade had disappeared back into the living room. Del closed her eyes with a smile.

The next time Kade woke her, she didn't jerk. Her head was pounding, and she wasn't exactly overjoyed at having her sleep interrupted again, but Kade was the one person in the world at whom she didn't want to snap. "Hey," she said, patting the empty space next to her again. She eyed Kade's sweatpants, the rumpled T-shirt, and the red hair that fell loosely to her shoulders. It seemed Kade had finally made use of the sofa bed.

"Do you want more ice for your head?" Kade asked as she sat down.

Kade's hip pressed against Del's side, and she breathed in Kade's scent. *Hmm, if you keep that up, I might need the ice to cool down other body parts!* She shook her head, then quickly stopped when it made her dizzy. "So, what's the question of the hour?"

"Why did you want me to stay with you tonight instead of Grace?" Kade asked.

Del groaned. "Aren't you supposed to ask me who the president of the United States is or something like that?"

"You promised you would explain later," Kade said. "Now is later."

Del sat up gingerly. "Okay, let's talk about it." She eyed Kade. "Do you want to get a blanket?" She had noticed that it was always warmer in Kade's apartment than in her own. Kade got cold easily.

"No, I'm fine." Kade couldn't be distracted from their discussion.

Del settled a part of her covers over Kade's lap, ignoring the protests. "I insisted on you staying with me because I didn't want you to stay in your apartment alone." She quickly held up her hand when she saw Kade getting ready to interrupt. "I still can't remember what happened this morning. The last thing I remember is entering your apartment building with the coffee."

"The doctor said loss of short-term memory is not unusual with a concussion," Kade said, her voice soothing like honey.

"I know. That's not what I'm worried about. But Grace was right—I'm not the clumsy type. The last time I fell was when I got a little drunk on Dawn's bachelorette night. Even then, I was able to break my fall." Del shook her head. "And now, in full possession of my faculties, I slip on even ground and land directly on my head? Something doesn't add up."

Kade stared at her. "You mean...?"

"I'm not sure, but I think someone hit me over the head. The position of this charming little laceration on the back of my head is more consistent with a blow than a fall." Del reached around Kade and took her hand. "I think your stalker is coming after me now."

Kade's fingers jerked in Del's loose grip. "What? But why would he... why would he want to hurt you? It's me he's after!" Kade sounded shocked and angry.

"We know he's watching your apartment. Apparently, he thinks I'm spending a little too much time with you, and he doesn't like it," Del answered calmly. She knew it would upset Kade, but it needed to be said.

"You haven't spent that much time in my apartment," Kade said.

Del idly rubbed the tender skin of her stomach, where the hot coffee had burned her. "Maybe not in, but in front of your apartment," she admitted, ducking her head a little.

"What?" Kade's blue eyes drilled into her like lasers. "Don't tell me you spent your free time watching my apartment! We had an agreement, Del! One night, not one month!"

Del sighed. "I know."

"No 'I'm sorry'?" Kade pressed.

Del began to feel like a hostile witness being cross-examined on the stand. "I'm sorry for not telling you. But I'm not sorry for trying to protect you."

"What about protecting yourself? I don't want you to get hurt because of me. This is my decision, Del. Mine!" Kade withdrew her hand from Del's and gestured energetically, stabbing her finger at her own chest.

"You can't prevent people from caring about you, Kade," Del said, struggling to stay calm. This discussion was adding to the headache she already had. "Don't be so afraid to accept a little help from your friends." She took a deep breath. "I think we should start an official investigation."

"I told you I don't—"

"Keeping it quiet is no longer an option, Kade," Del interrupted. "It was okay as long as he was only sending you flowers, but I'm afraid I made a mess of things. Instead of protecting you, I only made it worse. The stalker thinks I'm competition, and he'll take more active steps to claim you as his."

Kade stood abruptly and strode to the window, staring out into the darkness as if she could detect the stalker and strike him dead with just once lethal glare. "What if you're wrong? What if it was just a fall, without anyone attacking you?" she asked without turning around to face Del.

Del threw the covers off and, after finding her balance, stepped up behind Kade, very close but not touching. "What do your instincts tell you?"

Kade turned around. They looked into each other's eyes from a distance of mere inches. Both of them stood without moving. "He's escalating," Kade said in a rough whisper.

Del slowly crossed the remaining space between them and wrapped her arms around Kade, pulling her against her body.

She felt Kade stiffen in surprise, then Kade's slender arms came up and wrapped around Del.

Del ignored the pain caused by Kade's body pressing against the tender skin on her stomach and the bruise on her hip. She turned her head and pressed a kiss to Kade's forehead. With their bodies so close, Kade's heat and her intoxicating perfume surrounding Del, the urge to kiss Kade was almost irresistible, but Del held herself back. She knew this was not the time. "We'll get through this together, okay? Aiden and Ray will help. There won't be strangers invading your privacy if we can help it."

Kade nodded. With one last squeeze, she let go and stepped back. "Your motor responses are satisfactory," she told Del.

It took a moment for Del to calm her rebellious body enough to understand to what Kade was referring. "Good to know," she said with a grin. She felt a little woozy but wasn't sure if Kade's closeness was to blame or if it was just an effect of her concussion. She settled back down under the covers with a sigh of relief. "You know, now I'm almost afraid to go back to sleep. I'm already scared of what you might ask me the next time you wake me up."

Kade leaned in the doorway and grinned down at her. "You'll just have to wait and see."

CHAPTER 18

OKAY, IF SHE isn't here, I'm giving up. Dawn had already searched for Evan at three different skate parks all over the city. Her growling stomach had made her want to give up half an hour ago, but the thought of how alone Evan must feel kept her going. They hadn't heard from Evan since they had told her she was Aiden's sister more than a week ago.

Dawn still wasn't sure if being here, searching Evan out, was the right thing to do. Establishing a relationship with a former patient, even a strictly platonic one, was not exactly a stellar example of ethical behavior for a therapist. Dawn knew that some of her colleagues would frown upon it, not to mention the APA's ethics committee. Dawn had thought about it long and hard and had finally decided that there was no way of escaping some kind of relationship with Evan. She was Aiden's half sister, so she would be part of Dawn's life, no matter what. Holding on to the rules of her job couldn't change that, and she was convinced that staying away would do Evan more harm than good.

Dawn got out of her car and started across the parking lot toward the half-pipe. No one seemed to be using it at the moment, but a few kids were racing around on in-line skates or trying out tricks with their skateboards. A group of teenagers lay around under a tree, smoking something Dawn didn't want to examine closely. She started toward them when she caught sight of a lone figure sitting on top of the half-pipe, dangling her skate-clad feet from the edge of the platform at one end.

Without even seeing her face, Dawn knew she had found Evan. She slowly made her way over to her. "Hello, Evan."

Evan turned around. She didn't remove the cigarette that lazily dangled from the corner of her mouth when she saw Dawn. "Doing house calls now?" she asked with heavy sarcasm. "I thought you didn't want to be my therapist any longer?"

Dawn had expected that kind of hostility. Evan felt rejected by her, by her foster parents, and by the whole world, and now she was acting out again. "Can I sit down?" she asked, pointing at the concrete next to Evan. She was on Evan's turf now, so this conversation would take place by Evan's rules.

She took Evan's lazy shrug as an invitation. She climbed up onto the platform and sat down, taking care not to encroach on Evan's space. "I **can't** be your therapist any longer. There's a difference," she said gently. "And it doesn't mean that I never want to see you again. We can see each other—just not as therapist and patient."

"Why else would we want to see each other? And don't even try to give me that bullshit about us being sisters-in-law." Evan flicked her cigarette stub onto the half-pipe and immediately lit the next cigarette.

"Aiden is your half sister, but let's forget that for the moment, all right? I'm not here because of Aiden. I'm here because of you." Dawn met Evan's skeptical gaze without blinking. She wanted Evan to get to know Aiden and form some kind of bond with her, but for now, she knew Evan needed her more than she needed Aiden. Aiden was basically a stranger, but she had been Evan's therapist and her only ally. If Evan felt she had abandoned her, she would cut herself off from the rest of the world too.

"Well, I'm here because I want to hang out with my friends," Evan said, pretending not to care about Dawn's presence at all.

Dawn looked down at the kids with the skateboards and at the pot-smoking teens under the tree. A few glanced in the direction of the half-pipe, but all of them kept their distance from the brooding Evan. "They're down there, and you're up here. Not much hanging out going on."

"Even better. Then I have the half-pipe all to myself." Evan flashed her a wolfish grin that couldn't quite hide the hint of loneliness in her eyes.

"Not much skating going on either," Dawn said, indicating their seated position.

Evan stubbed out her cigarette and stood. "You just caught me at a cigarette break. Now it's back to the skating business, so unless you want to join me, you better go."

"I don't even have skates," Dawn said but didn't get up to leave.

"You can have mine," Evan offered.

Dawn looked down at Evan's feet. They were already at least two sizes bigger than her own. "They wouldn't fit me."

"Hey, Joe! Give me your skates," Evan called down to one of the boys.

Dawn watched with interest as the boy complied. *They respect her. She acts tough, and they give her what she wants. Easy to see why she would rather hang around these bad boys than stay at home with her foster parents.*

"So what's it gonna be, Doc? Skating or going?" Evan pointed in the direction of Dawn's car. The expression on her face said all too clearly that she expected Dawn to back down and retreat.

Dawn took the skates from her. "I guess it's skating."

Evan folded her arms and watched as Dawn put on the skates. "Once from one end of the half-pipe to the other," she demanded.

Dawn closed the last buckle and straightened. She reached for Evan's shoulder to hold on to as she tried to find her balance. She looked down the half-pipe, then at the thin fabric of the elegant slacks she had worn to work today. *This could really hurt.* She was nervous, but she knew she had to do this to earn Evan's respect again. She took a deep breath and let go of Evan's shoulder.

"Do me a favor and try not to break your neck, Doc," Evan said, trying to sound gruff.

"Thanks for the concern," Dawn mumbled while she stared down the half-pipe.

Evan snorted. "I'm not concerned about you. I'm concerned about me. Your cop girlfriend will wring my neck if you come home with a few broken bones."

"I don't intend to break anything, and I don't intend to tell Aiden about this," Dawn answered and stepped off the platform. She tore down the steep wall of the half-pipe, barely holding back a scream as she nearly lost her balance. Then she reached the flat part of the pipe and tried to build up enough momentum to reach the platform on the other side of the half-pipe.

She made it halfway up the other side, but then noticed she wouldn't make it. Gravity made her begin to roll back down even though she was still facing the other direction. She tried to turn around, but she had too much speed.

She landed hard on the concrete and slid down the rest of the way on her backside.

Evan was by her side before she stopped moving. "You okay, Doc?"

Dawn looked up at her. *That elegant landing probably didn't impress her much.* "Never been better, thanks," she answered in a breathless voice.

The cell phone in Dawn's pocket began to ring. For a second, Dawn thought about ignoring it, but she knew it could be a patient, so she quickly reached for it. "Kinsley."

"Hey, Dawn. It's me." The warm tones needed no further identification. It was Aiden. "Where are you?"

"Oh, just sitting around." Dawn grinned up at Evan, who was trying to look as if she wasn't tempted to grin back.

"Where?" Aiden asked. "I could come and sit with you, keep you company."

Dawn kept grinning at Evan. "I already have company, thanks, darling."

"Anyone I should be worried about?" Aiden asked, obviously teasing.

Dawn playfully eyed Evan. "Well, she's attractive, but a bit young for me." She chuckled when she saw Evan's eyes widen before she quickly feigned disinterest in Dawn's conversation.

"Jamie?" Aiden guessed with a laugh.

"Not that young."

Now Aiden stopped laughing. "You're not with Evan, are you?"

Dawn frowned. Aiden didn't sound very enthusiastic about it. "Yes, I am."

"Without even telling me first?" Aiden sounded annoyed.

"Listen, let's talk about this later," Dawn tried to end the discussion before Evan could realize that they were arguing about her.

Aiden sighed. "You should have told me. She's my sister. I should be the one to talk to her. She's my responsibility now."

"This has nothing to do with you," Dawn said. She hated fighting with Aiden, but she was fully prepared to stand up to her if Aiden thought she could dictate Dawn's relationship with Evan.

"How can you say that? You're my lover, and she's my sister! This has everything to do with me!" She could hear Aiden start to pace around.

Wonderful. I guess I should have told her beforehand. "Are you at home?" she asked instead of continuing their discussion.

"Yeah."

"Then I'll come over later. We'll talk about it then," Dawn said.

"Fine. See you later." Aiden ended the call.

Dawn put the cell phone away. When she looked up, she saw Evan reaching out a hand to help her up. "Thanks." She tried not to smile as Evan demonstrated her strength by practically lifting her to her feet.

"I didn't think you'd actually do it," Evan said when they took off their skates and climbed back up onto the platform.

"Well, I'm reasonably good at ice-skating, and I figured it couldn't be that different. Guess I was wrong." Dawn chuckled and patted her backside.

Evan lit another cigarette and leaned back.

Dawn wrinkled her nose as the smoke drifted in her direction, but she didn't comment. *You're not her therapist. You're not her mother, and you're not her sister. You're trying to be her friend, and that means accepting her decisions even if you think they're bad decisions.*

"That was your cop girlfriend," Evan said, pointing at the cell phone in Dawn's pocket.

Dawn tilted her head. "Her name is Aiden Carlisle, and yes, that was her."

Evan flicked the ash off the tip of her cigarette. "She's the jealous type, keeps you on a short leash, huh?"

"No," Dawn said as calmly as possible. "There's no reason for jealousy. She knows that I would never cheat on her." *And certainly not with her teenaged half sister!*

"But she doesn't like you talking to me." Evan was not stupid. She had understood the gist of their phone conversation.

Dawn thought about her answer for long moments. She decided to tell Evan the truth and treat her like an adult. Only then could she expect Evan to do the same. "No, she doesn't," she admitted, "but it's not for the reasons you think."

"Yeah, right." Evan snorted. "A blind man could see that she wants to keep her precious girlfriend away from trash like me."

Dawn energetically shook her head. "That's not it at all. She doesn't think you are trash and neither do I." *And you shouldn't think it, either.* "Aiden just thinks that she, as your sister, should be the one to talk to you."

Evan spread her arms, indicating the skate park around them. "Then why isn't she here, huh?" she asked, an aggressive edge in her voice and stance.

"Because she's afraid," Dawn said quietly.

Evan laughed. "Good one, Doc."

"I'm serious. Just because she acts confident and tough doesn't mean she's not afraid sometimes." Dawn watched as Evan quickly looked away, studying the tip of her cigarette with exaggerated interest. *Message received.* "Aiden never had a sister. She doesn't know how to handle this situation or what to say to you. I can imagine that you might feel the same."

"How can I even be sure she really is my sister?" Evan said instead of talking about her feelings. "How do I know she's not just fucking with my head?"

Dawn shrugged. "You could have Aiden show you the scientific proof," she said. "Or you could just look me in the eyes and trust me when I tell you there's no doubt in my mind. You are half sisters."

Evan slowly turned her head and stared directly into Dawn's eyes. She quickly broke eye contact and threw her only half-smoked cigarette onto the half-pipe. "Whatever. Even if it's true, I don't care. I never had a sister, and I sure as hell don't need one now." She stood and climbed down from the platform.

"Don't," Dawn said. "Don't throw this away without thinking about it."

Evan didn't even turn back around.

Dawn quickly caught up with her. "Do you know who taught me how to ice-skate?"

Evan rolled her eyes. "Oh, let me guess: your beloved cop."

"No." Dawn had to laugh as a mental image of Aiden on the ice-skating rink flashed through her mind. "Aiden is really bad at ice-skating."

Evan grinned, visibly pleased with that answer.

Dawn held back a grin. *She's denying any interest in Aiden or that she even is her sister, but she's already experiencing sibling rivalry.* "It was Brian, my brother. He was five years older than I."

"Was? So he's dead now?" Evan asked, acting as if she didn't care at all.

Dawn bit her lip. "Yes. He was shot ten years ago. I still miss him."

"What has that sob story got to do with me?" Evan impatiently demanded to know.

She's trying to hurt me because she's hurting, Dawn realized. "You've got an older sibling now too. I know it's not the same for you—"

"Damn right it isn't—and that's the last thing I want to say on the subject. Don't you have an impatient girlfriend to go home to?" Evan took the skates from Dawn.

"She can wait," Dawn decided. "I earned the right to hang out with you when I risked my neck on the half-pipe, and I intend to make the most of it. Want to go and get some ice cream?" She knew it was better to drop the subject of Aiden for now.

Evan looked at her down her nose. "Ice cream is for kids."

That tough-gal image is very important to you, isn't it? "Then I guess I'm a kid because I love it. Will you at least keep me company while I indulge in that childish treat?"

"I can do that," Evan said without showing any enthusiasm. "At least Jill and Roger won't get on my ass for being late if I tell them I hung out with you."

They got in the car, and Dawn drove them to the nearest ice-cream shop. "Are you sure you don't want anything?" Dawn asked when they sat down. "It's my treat."

"I don't need charity. I have my own money," Evan answered gruffly.

"I know. I just thought it would be fair for me to pay because I suggested it. You're welcome to pay next time." Dawn held her breath, waiting for Evan's answer.

Evan's long fingers played with the ice-cream menu. "Well, I guess I deserve a little something for showing you how to skate, huh?"

Dawn's first instinct was to agree, but then she stopped herself. Evan wanted to be treated like an adult, not like a kid she was humoring. "Showing?" she repeated incredulously. "You didn't show me anything, Evan. You just shoved the skates at me and told me not to break my neck. If you want to earn anything for teaching me how to skate, you have to try a little harder than that."

A hint of a smile played around Evan's lips, but she quickly forced it down. "You don't want me to teach you how to skate. Not really."

"What? Are you a mind reader now? If I say I'm interested, then I am interested. I'm a decent ice-skater, so I guess with the right teacher, I could be proficient at skating in no time. Unless, of course, you're not up to the job." She looked at Evan with a challenging twinkle in her eyes.

"Depends on what's in it for me," Evan said frankly.

"You mean money?" Dawn shook her head. "I don't pay my friends for doing me a favor. But how about this: you help me pick out a pair of skates and all the other equipment and teach me how to skate, and I'll pay for a new pair of skates for you."

"Any pair I want?" Evan asked with a furtive grin.

Dawn laughed. "Oooh, let me guess—you've got expensive tastes, huh?"

Evan gave her a lopsided grin.

"Any pair you want," Dawn confirmed. "So, do we have a deal?" She offered her hand across the table.

Evan looked at the hand, then at Dawn's face. "I am the teacher? I get to call the shots?"

Oh, you're enjoying this role reversal, aren't you? Dawn was willing to give up the dominant position in their relationship. It might even help them form a relationship that had nothing to do with their former roles of therapist and patient. "You are the teacher," she agreed. "You call the shots."

Evan firmly gripped her hand. "Then we've got a deal."

* * *

A key jangled in the lock.

Aiden hastily put down the book she had held in her hands without reading for the last half hour. "Dawn?" she called, then mentally slapped herself. *Who else would it be?* Dawn was the only person who had a key to her apartment, and she was well aware of that, but she was too impatient at the moment to wait for Dawn to search her out and start a conversation in her own time.

Dawn entered the living room and went directly to the couch, where Aiden sat. "Hey, Aiden." She leaned down to kiss her hello.

Aiden wasn't in an affectionate mood, but she forced herself to return the gentle kiss. She didn't want to make Dawn feel as if she wasn't loved, just because she was angry with Dawn, with herself, and with the whole complicated situation. Withholding her love was what her mother had done when she was on one of her drinking binges, and Aiden didn't want to repeat the sins of either of her parents. "How is Evan?" she asked when Dawn sat down next to her.

"A little better, I think." Dawn shifted on the couch. "Next time, I want to start convincing her to accept a referral to another therapist."

Aiden was glad Evan seemed to have calmed down since running away from them last week. She had been worried, wondering where Evan had gone and with whom she was, but she had no idea what to do. She had the feeling that no matter what she did it would only end up driving Evan further away instead of helping her. "Next time?" she repeated with a frown. "Sounds like you have regular meetings planned even though you're no longer her therapist." She couldn't quite keep the reproachful tone from her voice.

"I thought about it all day. Normally, I would never try to get involved in the life of a former patient in any way, but with Evan... I think it would do her more harm than good if I stayed away." Dawn shifted again and softly touched Aiden's knee. "I know you think I'm trying to take your place in Evan's life and—"

"No." Aiden quickly covered Dawn's hand with her own. "What I said on the phone was stupid. I didn't mean it. Not like that. It makes me proud that you're reaching out to her like that."

Dawn looked at her. "But?" she prompted.

Aiden sighed, then grinned self-mockingly. *Who would have ever thought that one day a psychologist would get to know me so very well?* "But," she said, rubbing Dawn's hand to take the sting out of her words, "at the same time, it makes me feel guilty, inadequate, and angry because I know I can't do it. I can't reach her like you can."

"You shouldn't expect yourself to," Dawn said. "Shared genes aside, you're strangers and know absolutely nothing about each other. You can't go from being the enemy who wanted to put her behind bars to beloved sister in one big leap."

"I know." Aiden let her head fall back against the back of the couch. "I know I can't get there in one big leap, but I feel like I don't even know the first tiny step."

"Try being her friend first," Dawn suggested.

Aiden inhaled and exhaled deeply. "Easier said than done. I don't know how to befriend a rebellious teenager, and she doesn't make it easy on me."

"Why should she? Evan never had it easy, so she doesn't make things easy for anyone else either. You have to remember that you're only dealing with finding out you have a sister, but she has to deal with so much more at the moment—there's Laurie Matheson and almost getting charged with rape, the constant arguing with her foster parents, and even the fact that I told her I won't continue as her therapist." Dawn ticked it off on her fingers. "Try to put yourself in her shoes."

That's what's making this so hard. "I've done nothing but put myself in her shoes since I found out she's my half sister." Aiden stared at the wall as the familiar "what ifs" started in her mind. "What if my mother had decided she couldn't stand to keep me around? What if she had given me up for adoption? What if I had grown up in a dozen foster homes? What if I had never known my father was a rapist?"

"That's the point: you didn't grow up like that. Evan did." The greenish-gray eyes looked at Aiden very seriously. "I know the revelation that you have a sister raises a lot of questions about yourself and your father, but for now, try not to make this about you. Make it about Evan."

Aiden groaned and rubbed her face. "I know you're right, but it still doesn't help me to face Evan. I don't know how you do it. You're so frustratingly good with people." She gently poked Dawn to show her she was only teasing. The admiration and the envy she felt were real, though.

"You're good with people too." Dawn reached out and trailed two of her fingers down Aiden's jaw.

A tingle ran down Aiden's body, almost making her forget the conversation for a moment. She cleared her throat and corrected, "I'm good with victims."

"Yes, you are." Dawn gazed deeply into Aiden's eyes, and in her gaze, Aiden could read the gratefulness of a woman who had once been a rape victim in one of her cases.

"Yeah, but that approach won't work with Evan," Aiden said. That was the only thing she was sure of.

Dawn smiled. "Evan wouldn't like being treated like a victim, that's for sure. You have to find another way to relate to her."

"For example?" Aiden wasn't above accepting advice from her psychologist girlfriend.

"Find some common ground, something you have in common," Dawn said without even having to think about it.

One thing came to mind immediately. "Having a violent father?" Aiden asked sarcastically. She didn't even know if Evan had been told about the way she had been conceived. *Hell, I'm not even sure if she **was** conceived by rape. Maybe that old bastard settled down and started a family!*

"Something positive," Dawn rebuked her gently.

"Being in love with you?" Aiden suggested with a grin, already anticipating Dawn's reaction.

Dawn pinched her thigh, making Aiden jump and rub the affected body part. "Evan is not in love with me!"

"Okay, it's not love, but she has a teenage crush on you." Aiden was finally relaxed enough to laugh about something that had to do with her half sister.

Dawn stubbornly shook her head. "It's not a crush. If anything, it's what my psychoanalytical colleagues call transference. She still sees me as her therapist, not as the person behind that job. It's easy for a patient to fall for his or her therapist—or to think they are. You know what Evan's childhood and home life were like. Now imagine suddenly having someone focus entirely on you and show you concern."

"I know what you mean. So that common ground is out too, huh?" Aiden sighed. "What else do we have in common? I'm a cop, and she's on the fast track to becoming a criminal."

"Get that out of your head right now! If you think about her like that, you'll never have a relationship with your sister!" Dawn's voice was surprisingly hard and angry.

Aiden knew Dawn was right. If she continued to think about Evan as a misguided hoodlum, she would probably treat her accordingly. She couldn't blame Evan if she wanted nothing to do with a person who treated her like that, sister or not. "I know you're right, but it's hard to see anything we might have in common." She rubbed her neck in resignation.

"That's because you're more than twice her age and at a very different point in life," Dawn said, now calm again.

Now that helps to make me feel better. Aiden made a face.

Dawn laughed. "I didn't say you were Methuselah. Imagine yourself at Evan's age for a second. What were you interested in at sixteen? What did you want more than anything else?"

Aiden leaned forward and stared at the coffee table without seeing it. *Sixteen.* She remembered trying to spend as little time as possible at home when her mother barricaded herself into her studio to paint. She remembered her mother's drinking, the shouting, and the good times when her mother had stayed sober and hadn't been so busy with her art. *What did I want more than anything else?* "To get away from it all," she said out loud.

"And how did you do that when you were sixteen?" Dawn asked.

"I accepted a marriage proposal," Aiden said and laughed at the expression on Dawn's face.

Dawn stared at her long enough to make sure Aiden wasn't joking. "Wow. We want to find things you have in common with Evan, and instead we discover that **we** have more in common than we thought. What happened?"

"I broke it off when I realized marrying a man I didn't love wouldn't give me the independence I wanted," Aiden said. *Thank God!*

Dawn sighed. "Then you were more mature than I was."

"Hey, don't beat yourself up." Aiden stroked Dawn's cheek with the back of her hand. "After your father and your brother died, you needed the security and the feeling of belonging somewhere."

"Yeah, and I searched for it in all the wrong places." Dawn sighed again, then smiled and wrapped her arms around Aiden, cuddling against her side. "But it doesn't matter anymore. I finally got it right. Tell me, how else did you try to achieve your independence when you were sixteen?"

Aiden groaned when the memory resurfaced. "I stole my mother's car and drove around for hours. So Evan and I both were little thieves. I thought we're searching for a positive thing we have in common?"

"That's not what I mean. Evan takes her skates everywhere, and I suspect she hitchhikes. I don't think she has her driver's permit yet." Dawn looked at her expectantly.

"Oh, no! You don't mean...? You want me to let her drive my car?" Aiden didn't like the idea.

Dawn nodded with amusement. "Help her get her driver's permit, and then supervise her driving. I don't think that's an offer any sixteen-year-old would turn down even if it comes from someone she's not all that fond of yet."

"Hmm." Aiden rubbed the back of her neck.

Dawn nudged her with an elbow. "Come on! What do you have to lose?"

"My car?" Aiden didn't like the thought of giving her car into the hands of an impulsive teenager.

"What's more important—your sister or the car?"

Dawn's frank words made Aiden wince. "You're right. The car is just a replaceable thing. So what if it gets a few scratches, right?"

Dawn chuckled and curled her legs under her, then quickly stretched them out again. "Who are you trying to convince—me or yourself?"

"Myself," Aiden said with an embarrassed grin. She knew she sounded as if she cared more about her car than about her sister, but she couldn't help herself. She had seen Evan on her worst behavior, and now it was hard for her to trust her with her car and with her life. Still she was determined to try.

Aiden frowned as she watched Dawn continue to wriggle and shift her position, as she had done since she'd sat down on the couch. "I thought I made it clear it wasn't really you I was angry at? Do I make you nervous for some reason?"

"I'm not nervous," Dawn said.

"You're wriggling around like a fish on a hook," Aiden said, pointing at Dawn as she did just that.

Dawn made a face. "Nice comparison. It's just... I just can't seem to get comfortable on this couch."

Something was off here. Dawn had always felt quite at home on Aiden's couch, and as far as Aiden could tell, it hadn't developed any sudden lumps. "Want to sit on my lap?" She winked and patted her thighs in invitation.

Dawn smiled. "Normally, I'd love to, but..." She sighed. "Well, I fell, and I think I have a few scratches and bruises on my ass."

"You fell?" Aiden looked at her in sudden concern. *Why is everyone suddenly so accident-prone? Didn't Kade say Del took a fall too?*

"Nothing too bad. It could have been worse, considering I had never done something like that before." Dawn stared off into space, shaking her head at herself.

Aiden wasn't sure what she was talking about. "Hadn't done what before? Falling on your ass?"

"Maneuvering up and down a half-pipe on in-line skates," Dawn said, ruefully rubbing her backside.

"And here I thought my job was dangerous. What kind of therapy is that?" Aiden shook her head in disbelief.

Dawn laughed. "It's not a therapy... although it works quite well for downsizing a therapist's inflated ego. It's what I was doing with Evan when you called. You missed my graceful landing by mere seconds."

Aiden let her gaze wander over Dawn's body, checking for further injuries. Anyone who had ever spent any time with Dawn knew she was not into sports. She looked fit and healthy, but she was not an athletic woman. Aiden couldn't see her racing down a half-pipe on skates. "You've never skated before, have you? You took a risk on that half-pipe!" She still couldn't believe it. She had done a few stupid things in her life because she refused to back down from a challenge, but Dawn was usually not like that.

"Price of admission," Dawn said with a shrug. "When I was Evan's therapist, I made the rules. Now it's her turn."

"Yeah, but you have a Hippocratic oath or something like that, and she doesn't. Evan risked you getting hurt. I don't like that at all." Anger stirred again.

Dawn raised herself up on her knees and then climbed onto Aiden's lap, straddling her. She looked her right in the eyes. "It's not for you to approve or to disapprove. I'm an adult, and it was my risk to take. I appreciate that you care about my well-being, but it was my decision, not yours and not Evan's. Are we clear on that?"

Dawn's index finger pressed into Aiden's chest in a playful manner, but the expression in the gray-green eyes was very serious. What Dawn demanded of her went against every instinct Aiden had. She was a protector at heart, and she had been more protective of Dawn than of anyone with whom she had ever been involved. She still wasn't entirely sure if that was because she loved Dawn more than anyone before or because she had met Dawn at a time when she was very vulnerable and needed the protection.

Dawn's insistence that she let her make her own decisions and be her own protector made her feel frustrated, worried, and proud at the same time. Despite her gentle nature, Dawn was not a woman who would let Aiden dominate her—and she secretly liked that.

"We're clear on that," she answered very seriously too. "It won't stop me from worrying, but I know it's your risk and your decision."

Dawn nodded with grim satisfaction. "Good. Now that we cleared that up..." She started to get off of Aiden's lap.

"Hey, not so fast." Aiden gently held her back by resting her hands on Dawn's hips, her grip not strong enough for her to force Dawn to stay, but firm enough to encourage her. "Don't you want me to kiss it and make it better?" She gently ran one of her hands over Dawn's hip and down her ass.

"You'd have to be a contortionist to be able to kiss my booboo from your position," Dawn answered with a teasing grin. She leaned forward until Aiden could feel her body heat. Aiden's own body temperature shot up when Dawn's breasts pressed against hers. "But it's already beginning to feel better." Dawn moaned.

"We could change positions," Aiden suggested, preparing to roll out from under Dawn and cover Dawn's body with her own, but Dawn threw her weight forward.

Her body weight pressed Aiden against the back of the couch. "What if I like this position?" Dawn's voice was playful, but there was something else in her eyes.

"R—" Aiden had to clear her throat as she looked into Dawn's now smoky-gray eyes. She hadn't expected to encounter the sudden passion. "Really?"

"Yeah." Dawn leaned forward, pressing even more of her body against Aiden's.

Aiden shuddered as gentle teeth nipped her earlobe. She slid her hands around the small of Dawn's back and pulled her in closer.

Dawn fell against Aiden for a second, but then quickly braced herself with both hands on top of Aiden's shoulders. "Lean forward," she commanded.

Aiden's brows rose in surprise. She wasn't used to Dawn giving orders and taking the initiative in their lovemaking, but she wasn't about to argue. She quickly leaned forward, away from the back of the couch.

She felt the tips of Dawn's fingers trail down her back until they slipped under her sweatshirt and traced circles over bare skin. Aiden held her breath as Dawn quickly unhooked her bra. As Dawn's hands circled around to the front of her body, she could no longer stay still. She surged forward and captured Dawn's lips in a passionate kiss.

Dawn's mouth melted against her own, soft and pliant, but after a few seconds, Dawn broke away with a gasp and took charge again.

Dawn's insistence on challenging her for the lead in their lovemaking fueled Aiden's passion. She kissed Dawn again, only wrenching her mouth away when Dawn ripped the sweatshirt over

Aiden's head and separated their lips for a second. Aiden slipped out of her bra and dropped it, not caring where it landed.

Dawn started to rock her hips. Aiden could feel Dawn's warmth against her abdomen. She tensed her muscles and pulled Dawn closer, not directing her movements, but encouraging them.

Dawn's hips picked up a faster rhythm.

Aiden squirmed under her. She wanted to feel more of Dawn's skin against her own. She began to undo the buttons of Dawn's blouse, but her fingers were trembling with excitement and not fast enough for her liking. With other partners, she would have just ripped the buttons off, but with Dawn, she forced herself to take the few extra seconds. Finally, she opened the last button and slipped the blouse from Dawn's shoulders, careful not to trap Dawn's arms in the material. Sharing this experience with Dawn was wonderful, and she didn't want it to end in a flashback and a panic attack.

She leaned forward and kissed a rounded shoulder, tracing the freckles with her tongue.

Dawn's fingers slipped into her hair and pulled Aiden even closer.

Aiden leaned back a bit, making room between their bodies for her to reach down, unbuckle Dawn's belt, and pull down the zipper. Dawn mumbled her protest when Aiden's mouth left her skin, but Aiden quickly soothed her by kissing her again. She smoothed her hand down the soft curves of Dawn's belly. When she reached the edge of Dawn's panties, she stopped and looked up, searching for Dawn's hazy gray eyes. "Yes?" she asked.

"Yes," Dawn answered without hesitation.

Aiden kissed Dawn, swallowing her moan, as she slipped into her.

They rested against each other for a few moments, panting. Then Dawn shifted and moaned. Passion exploded.

Dawn buried her face against Aiden's shoulder as she rocked against her.

Dawn's teeth raked over her skin. Aiden surged forward, driving deeper into Dawn without thought.

"Aiden!" Dawn gasped.

Aiden would have pulled back in panic, but Dawn's enthusiastic movements made it clear that it had been a moan of passion, not of pain. She let Dawn set the pace, intoxicated and enchanted by the way Dawn took her pleasure from her. Dawn's frantic rocking against her continued to press the seam of her jeans against Aiden's clit, but she held back and forced herself to concentrate on Dawn.

She created a path of openmouthed kisses down Dawn's chest and stopped to taste the salty skin between her breasts.

Dawn threw her head back with a moan, pressing her breasts against Aiden's face.

Aiden turned her head and captured a nipple between her lips through the satiny material of Dawn's bra.

"Oh! God, Aiden!" Dawn's rhythm faltered for a moment, then became even faster as Aiden sucked on her nipple. Dawn thrust her hips against Aiden's fingers, once, twice, before she cried out and collapsed against Aiden.

A hot wave shot through Aiden. Blood rushed through her ears, almost blocking out Dawn's moans. Her whole body was pounding, so it took her a few moments to realize that some of it was pain, not just pleasure. Dawn had bitten her on the shoulder, and her hand was starting to cramp in its awkward position.

She gently withdrew and eased both of them down to lie on the couch, their bodies still plastered together.

Dawn's hand started to slip down her body, but Aiden quickly caught it and held it against her belly. "Give me a moment, please," she said breathlessly.

Dawn raised herself up on her elbow and gazed down at Aiden. Her face was still flushed, and her red lips begged Aiden to kiss them again. "You mean you...?"

"I'm not sure, but I think your little love bite drove me over the edge." Aiden laughed shakily.

Dawn lay back down, snuggling against Aiden. "Love bite?" she asked drowsily.

"Yeah." Aiden tugged her T-Shirt aside and craned her neck to look at the teeth marks on her shoulder.

Dawn's gaze followed hers. Her eyes widened, and her fingers flew up to gently touch Aiden's shoulder. "God! I didn't even notice I had hurt you! I'm so sorry!" Her fingers stroked the red marks on Aiden's shoulder as if she could heal them by touch alone.

Aiden laughed. "It didn't hurt at that moment, believe me. Quite the opposite."

Dawn traced the mark with trembling fingers.

"Hey, it's no big deal." Aiden directed Dawn's gaze to meet hers. "In fact, I think I like it. It's a sign of your love and your desire for me, so that's a good thing, right?" She tenderly stroked Dawn's face.

"Right," Dawn said, but she still didn't look fully convinced.

"You didn't even leave your little stamp of possession in plain sight for Ray and the guys to tease me about it for days," Aiden continued, trying to make Dawn feel better about the bite marks.

"I totally lost control," Dawn said, still looking amazed. Then she smiled hesitantly. "I think that's a good sign, don't you?"

Aiden kissed Dawn's throat, where her pulse was still pounding. "A very good sign," she hummed against the damp skin.

CHAPTER 19

"**Y**OU KNOW THIS is blackmail, right?" Kade glared at Del. Her well-practiced glare usually worked on even the most hardened criminals, but Del met her gaze without flinching.

"No, this is me caring about your well-being," Del answered calmly, gesturing for Kade to take a seat on the couch next to her. "At this point, we have to assume that the stalker found a way to get into your apartment building, so until you tell a few of your detectives and we start an investigation, it's not a good idea for you to stay in your apartment alone."

Kade stopped her pacing and finally sat down at the other end of the couch. She knew Del was right. She knew this had already gone on for too long. She had to do something now, or she would risk getting hurt. *Or someone else being hurt because of me.* She still felt guilty every time she glanced at the now healing laceration on the back of Del's head. Still she was hesitant to approach the detective she trusted most. "I can't bother Aiden with this right now. She has enough on her plate as it is."

"Why? What happened?" Del frowned, and Kade could see that she was already beginning to speculate about the possible problems Aiden could have with Dawn.

"Before I got Laurie to tell me the truth about what happened, our ME ran Evan Whitfield's DNA," Kade said.

Del shrugged. "Yeah, that's standard procedure."

"But the results were not." Kade hesitated. Should she tell Del? She knew it wasn't her place to tell her, but at the same time, Del deserved to be trusted. She had been involved in the investigation beyond the call of duty, and she wasn't just a colleague to Aiden. She was practically her aunt-in-law. "The DNA analysis confirmed that Evan Whitfield is Aiden's half sister."

Del leaned forward and stared at her. "What? How is that possible?"

"It's not my place to tell you that. Needless to say, it threw Aiden for a loop. I don't want to bother her with my problems on top of everything else she has to deal with." Compared to what Aiden had to deal with, Kade's own family issues seemed minor.

"All right. I'll accept that for the moment—under the condition that you stay with me until you get a more official investigation started." Del's dark eyes pierced into hers, waiting for her decision.

Kade folded her arms across her chest. "What if I say no?" She knew Del was right, and she would probably end up taking her advice, but the way Del had formulated her condition was igniting the famous Matheson stubbornness.

"Then I'll start watching your apartment from my car again," Del answered calmly. "Of course, it would be ill-advised with me not having fully recovered from my concussion, but I'll do it if I have to." She put on a pathetically brave expression.

Despite her annoyance, Kade had to bite back a laugh. "This is blackmail!" she said again.

"No, this is you caring about my well-being." Del grinned. "So, will you stay?"

"I'll think about it. How's your head?" They had just returned from a checkup at the hospital when Del had decided that Kade shouldn't stay at her apartment alone.

"Well, that depends on whether you find people with bald patches attractive." Del winked and turned her head, showing off the spot on the back of her head where the doctor had shaved off a bit of her hair.

Kade didn't care about the attractiveness of bald spots. She had been too worried about Del to think about anything else. She didn't say that to Del, though. "Sorry, that has never been one of my fetishes."

"No? Haven't you heard that bald men are supposed to be more potent in bed? I'm sure the same is true for women with bald spots," Del said with a smug grin.

Kade tilted her head to shoot Del a cool glance over the rim of her glasses. Del was clearly challenging her, and Kade wasn't about to back down. "And how, pray tell, would I benefit from that theory?"

Del stared at her in surprise, but before she could answer, the doorbell rang. "Shit." Del stood and pointed a finger at Kade. "Hold that thought. I want a chance to answer that question in detail."

As Del walked away to answer the door, Kade rubbed her face and cursed herself. *Uh-oh, you're in for it now, but no, you just couldn't let it go.*

"Kade," Del called from the door. "I think it's for you."

Kade frowned. No one knew she was here. Her friendship with Del was not common knowledge. She stood and walked to the door, craning her neck to see around Del.

Hesitating in the doorway was Laurie, tears in her eyes and both of her hands clutching the straps of her backpack.

"Laurie!" Kade strode up to her and pulled her into the apartment. "What are you doing here? How did you even find me here?"

Laurie shuffled her feet. She bit her lip in an attempt not to cry. "I went to your apartment, but the doorwoman said you had just left in a cab. Luckily, she remembered the address you gave the cabbie. One of her neighbors," she pointed at Del, "let me into the building, and when I described you, she said you were Clarice's friend and told me which apartment Clarice lives in."

"Her name is Del, not Clarice," Kade murmured, still shocked to find herself face-to-face with her niece.

"Impressive detective work," Del said, giving Laurie an encouraging smile. "You'll make one hell of a detective one day."

"Or a first-class prosecutor," Kade said absentmindedly. It took her a second to realize she was putting Laurie under the same kind of pressure her parents did. There were more professions than just being a lawyer, even for a Matheson. "She'll be first-class in whatever she chooses to do," she added.

Laurie turned her head to throw a cautious look at Del, then whispered to Kade, "Can I talk to you?"

"I'll leave you two alone," Del said.

"It's your apartment," Kade protested. It seemed hardly polite to have Del stay out of her own living room, especially since she was still supposed to take it easy and do nothing but relax. On top of that, Kade wasn't looking forward to having a conversation about whatever had happened to Laurie. *I could use a little help from someone who knows more about what Laurie is going through than I do.*

Del was already on her way to the kitchen. "I don't mind," she said over her shoulder. "I'll make us something to eat."

Kade shook her head in amusement. *Every time I see her, she's trying to feed me.* Then she sobered and turned back to Laurie. "Come on. Let's go to the living room." She directed Laurie to the couch and took a seat next to her. "Now tell me what happened."

"It's horrible! They're ruining my life! I won't go back! Ever!" Laurie sobbed.

Kade hadn't felt so helpless since she had found the unconscious Del in front of her apartment. *That was only two days ago,* she reminded herself. Lately, her life seemed to spin out of control. "What happened?"

Laurie looked up, her tears now replaced by anger. "They forbid me from ever seeing Evan again. And when I called Evan to tell her about it, she said it's probably for the best! She said it's getting too complicated, and it's just not worth it." She began to cry again.

Oh, God! Why do I have to be the one to deal with her first broken heart? "Laurie, calm down!" She rubbed Laurie's back when she started to hyperventilate. "You're making yourself sick. Do you want a glass of water?"

When Laurie nodded, Kade hurried into the kitchen, glad to escape from the living room and the tense situation for a moment. "Can I have a glass of water for Laurie?" she asked.

"Sure." Del handed her two glasses. "Everything all right out there?" she asked.

"No! Nothing is all right!" Kade slumped against the counter. "She has homophobic parents and a girlfriend who I think just broke up with her—and she comes to me for advice. Suddenly, I've become the spokesperson for all lesbians! The gay Dr. Ruth! I can't do this, Del."

Del turned away from the stove and wrapped an arm around Kade's shoulder, pulling her against her comforting warmth for a second. "You can."

"But she thinks I'm an experienced lesbian—and I'm not!" Kade filled a glass with water and then drank it herself before she filled the second glass for Laurie.

"You don't have to be. Just be yourself. Don't try to be someone else." Del gave her an encouraging nod. "And if she has specific questions you can't answer, you can always defer to the more senior lesbian." She winked at Kade.

Kade took a calming breath and returned to the living room. She pressed the glass of water into Laurie's trembling hands and thought about what to say. Her first instinct was to tell Laurie that everything would be okay, that it was not as bad as it seemed, but then she remembered Del's words. *Just be yourself. Don't try to be someone else.* Dawn and Aiden were good at giving emotional comfort, but it was not Kade's forte. Kade was good at taking action, so she did. "Is there anything I can do to help?"

"Can I stay with you?" Laurie begged, clutching Kade's sleeve.

Kade had to fight down rising panic. Raising a teenager was not on her top ten list of things to do in the near future. She also didn't want Laurie to stay with her while a possibly dangerous stalker was watching her apartment. "Laurie, it's not that I wouldn't love to have you over a little more often, but I can't just let you stay without your parents' consent. I know it probably doesn't seem like it right now, but they're your parents and they care about you."

Laurie snorted. "Oh, yeah! They care about me so much that they threatened to send me off to a boarding school if they catch me seeing Evan one more time!"

God, this is a mess. I'm not equipped to deal with this. How can I sit here and tell her that her parents will learn to accept her when I avoided exploring a possible attraction to women because I knew it was not acceptable for a Matheson? Kade desperately searched for something to say.

"Need more time to talk, or are you ready for some pancakes?" Del asked, sticking her head around the doorjamb.

Laurie looked up with red-rimmed eyes. "Pancakes are breakfast food," she said, sniffling.

"They're also one of three things I can actually cook." Del came in and set a tray with pancakes and maple syrup down on the coffee table.

"I'm not hungry," Laurie said, hunching down and crossing her arms over her stomach.

Kade had also lost her appetite, but she was glad to have Del's company anyway.

Del began to set the table. "I can understand that. I didn't feel like eating after my parents threw me out either."

Laurie's head shot up, and she stared at Del. "Your parents threw you out? Because you...?"

"Because they caught me with another girl, yes," Del answered with casualness that Kade could only admire.

She was glad that Del had come in and was now taking over this difficult conversation. Del had more experience from which Laurie could gain.

"Did it ever get better?" Laurie asked with hope in her eyes.

"My parents are not like yours, Laurie," Del said quietly. "They grew up in Puerto Rico and were raised to believe that homosexuality is a mortal sin. They didn't just sit me down and yell at me after they found out I was gay. My father beat me black and blue while my mother said one Hail Mary after the other. I haven't seen them since."

Kade forgot Laurie for a moment and just looked at Del in shock.

"Wow, that's awful! I'm sorry that happened to you," Laurie said. "At least I don't have to worry about that. My parents are too genteel to ever lay a hand on me. They deal with their problems by sweeping it all under the rug." She turned curious blue eyes on Kade. "It's a wonder they didn't tell me I couldn't see you again, too. How did they take you being gay? How come no one ever told me? I haven't heard even one peep about you being gay from anybody!"

There it is. Kade had known the question would come sometime, but it didn't make it easier to answer now. How could she tell Laurie the truth without making it feel like a betrayal? "That's really... complicated, Laurie."

Laurie looked at her with a bitter expression on her young face. "Why is everything I want to talk about 'too complicated' in this family?"

Kade sighed. Laurie was right. She had heard the "that's complicated" excuse much too often growing up too. She looked at Del, who gave her a nod and mouthed, "Tell her."

"Your parents don't know that I... that I'm interested in women." Every single word was hard to say. "In fact... no one in the family knows."

Laurie leaped to her feet, almost toppling over the coffee table. "You forced me to tell my parents while you stayed safely in the closet?"

Kade lifted her hands in an appeasing gesture. "It's not like that, Laurie." *Isn't it?* she asked herself. *Is that not exactly what you've been doing?* She stared helplessly at Laurie, not knowing what she could say.

"I thought I could trust you!" Laurie grabbed her backpack and ran to the door.

"No." Del quickly blocked the way to the door. "You're not leaving like that. Not before you hear what your aunt has to say." She gently but firmly dragged Laurie back to the couch.

That's the problem—I don't have anything to say. Nothing that could reestablish her trust in me. She looked from Laurie to Del, silently asking for a little help.

"Coming out to someone you know will probably react badly is not an easy thing to do," Del said. She was looking directly at

Laurie, but Kade could feel that her words were directed at her too. "It should be an individual choice whenever possible. With you, it just wasn't possible. If you had kept quiet about what happened between you and Evan, she would have gone to prison. I know you wouldn't want that."

"Of course I didn't!" Laurie forgot her shyness when she snapped at Del.

Del only nodded calmly. "Do you think it would have helped the situation if Kade had told your parents that she's not straight either?" Laurie immediately opened her mouth, but Del cut her off. "Take a moment to think about it. How would your parents have reacted?"

"They would have kicked her out of the house for being a bad influence on me," Laurie said, the sarcasm in her voice barely hiding the bitter sadness.

Kade stared at Del. *She makes it sound like it was the rational thing to do. But was it really? Wasn't it just cowardice?*

"Okay, so maybe Sunday was not the right moment," Laurie finally conceded, "but why didn't you tell them before? You didn't just start being a lesbian on Sunday!"

Kade barely resisted the urge to get up and pace around the room. "You're right. My sexual orientation didn't change overnight. I've noticed women all my life. I also noticed men," she added slowly, watching Laurie for her reaction.

Laurie just looked at her, waiting to see where she was going with that explanation.

"For a lot of years, I didn't act on either attraction. Relationships seemed like too much of a distraction. My job... my career has always been the most important thing in my life. I never met a woman who seemed worth the risk." Kade fell silent, listening to the echoes of her own words. She could feel Del's gaze on her but avoided turning around to face her. She didn't want to tell Del she could be the woman who was worth the risk even though she admitted to herself that she was beginning to think more and more in that direction.

Laurie frowned. "What are you saying?"

Kade sighed. She knew Laurie would take it as a rejection of her own sexual orientation, as a betrayal by her one ally, but she had to say it anyway. "My interest in women never played an active part in my life, so I never thought it necessary to come out."

"You're not a lesbian?" Laurie jumped up again. She stared down at Kade, trembling with anger, confusion, and feelings of betrayal. "B-but you said —!"

Del gently cleared her throat. She stepped between the two Matheson women. "Laurie, contrary to what some people think, sleeping with another woman is not what makes you a lesbian. Your feelings are. Some people seem to know they're only attracted to people of the same sex from a very early age, and they come out to everyone and their dog before they're even through high school. Others take a little longer, and some may never explore these feelings at all. Sexuality is a very complicated thing." She gave Laurie a smile. "And I'm not just saying that because I don't want to talk about it. I promise you can always talk to me, whenever you want, about whatever you want."

Kade exhaled. The tension in the room seemed to dissipate slowly. She knew Del had basically offered to be Laurie's lesbian mentor, and Laurie seemed to accept. She could just leave it at that, but she knew it would be the easy way out. "Just because I chose a different path from yours doesn't mean I'm not willing to support you in any way I can. Do you want me to talk to your parents?"

Laurie shrugged. Now that her anger was gone, tears reappeared in her eyes. "Could you talk to Evan? Convince her to see me again?" she begged.

God. Kade rubbed her eyes. *Just when I thought this situation couldn't get more complicated.* "I'm not sure if that's a good idea, Laurie. I was involved in getting her arrested and almost charging her with rape. I might not be the best person to talk to her. For now, let me concentrate on your parents, okay?"

* * *

Kade had almost forgotten how uncomfortable she could feel in a Matheson home. *Is this how Laurie feels in her own home?*

She sat on the edge of her chair, playing with her teacup while she waited for her brother to come home.

Her sister-in-law kept her company, but they didn't have much in common, and Kade wasn't in the mood for small talk. As a result, they sat in silence.

When Doug finally arrived, he politely kissed Kade's cheek before he sat down for a cup of tea. "Where's Laurel?" he asked his wife.

"That's what I came to talk about. She came to my apartment an hour ago," Kade said. There was no sense explaining why Laurie hadn't found her there and where she was now.

"She's not in her room?" Doug's teacup rattled as he swiftly set it down. "She went out even though I grounded her for the week?"

Kade stared at him. She felt her cheeks grow hot as anger bubbled up. "You grounded her?" She couldn't believe it. "Punishing her is not going to change the fact that she's gay, Douglas. It won't just go away. That's something you have to deal with."

"She's not gay!" Doug boomed. "She's just confused right now."

How can he just dismiss his daughter's feelings like that? "Confused?" she repeated. "Like you were confused at seventeen when you fell in love with each other?" She looked from Doug to Eleanor. At least her sister-in-law had the decency to lower her gaze. "Laurie might be confused about your reactions, but she's old enough to know her own feelings."

"She is confused," Doug insisted. "She's so confused that she sees homosexual people everywhere. She even thinks you are gay!" He laughed and lifted his teacup to his lips.

Kade froze. *She told them. Of course she did. I expected she would at some point.* She shook her head at the irony. She'd had sleepless nights about her family's reaction, and now that they knew, they didn't believe it. "Laurie is not confused," she told him once more, very quietly, trying to keep control of her voice and her emotions. "I told her I'm a lesbian." She actually hadn't said those words to Laurie, but the distinction was too subtle for her brother to understand. Kade took a deep breath. She had said it, and now she was waiting for the inevitable explosion.

But it never happened. Doug just stared at her with a disapproving frown. "Why would you tell her that?" he asked, clearly confused.

He still doesn't understand. He doesn't want to understand. "Because it's the truth," Kade answered quietly.

"What the...?" Doug's chair scraped over the parquet as he jumped up. "What kind of stupid game is this? You are not gay! You dated my best friend in high school and—"

"Technically, I'm bisexual," Kade said before Doug could list all her former boyfriends, but then stopped herself. *Wait a minute, why am I defending myself? I'm acting as if I'm a suspect, as if I've done something wrong.* She squared her shoulders and raised her head to stare them right in the eyes. *You're a prosecutor, so prosecute! Take the offensive!* "I'm not here to talk about me. I'm not even here to talk about Laurie. I'm here to talk about you!" She stabbed her finger at both of them. "There's nothing wrong with me or Laurie. You are the ones with the problem!"

Doug bristled. "I don't have a problem! I'm just trying to do what's best for my daughter, and I don't need my single, childless, younger sister to help me with that!"

Kade ignored the dig and took a step closer, getting into her brother's face. "You think you're acting like a good father?"

"Of course, I—"

"You're treating Laurie like our father treated you!" Kade noticed that Doug went pale, but she didn't stop. "You were a good kid with fantastic grades, a bright future, and a lovely girlfriend, but it wasn't enough in the eyes of our father. Your plans and dreams meant nothing to him because he wanted you to become a lawyer and marry the daughter of one of the partners in his firm. He never acknowledged any of your achievements over the years. He barely even commented when you opened your own clinic—and I know you suffered all these years."

"Oh, like you even noticed!" Doug shouted back. "You were too busy being paraded around as Daddy's little darling, the bright star of Harvard Law!"

Kade bit back an angry retort. Her own life hadn't been as easy as Doug made it sound, but she wasn't here to discuss that. "I noticed," she said. "I just never did anything about it. Don't make the same mistake with Laurie."

"It's not the same," Doug protested, a little calmer now.

"You have a healthy, beautiful, intelligent daughter. She has good manners, a kind personality, and good grades, but still you're not happy with her because you don't agree with her life choices. Because she's not like you or how you want her to be." Kade stopped to let her words sink in. "Now tell me that doesn't sound exactly like what our father did to you!"

Doug's chest was heaving. His jaw clenched, and for a moment, he looked as if he wanted to hit Kade, but then he whirled around and stormed from the room.

Kade stood staring after him.

"That was harsh," Eleanor whispered.

Kade slowly turned toward her. She had almost forgotten that her sister-in-law was even in the room. "It was the truth—and he needed to hear it." *And so did you.*

"Is Laurel okay?" Eleanor asked after a moment.

Two decades of living under her father's roof almost made Kade answer with a polite, socially accepted, "She's fine." She stopped herself from the automatic Matheson response, though. It had been an evening of hard truths for all of them, so she wouldn't start lying now. "She's pretty upset," she said. "Imagine how you would feel if the person you think is the love of your life breaks your heart and your parents abandon you."

Eleanor pressed a hand to her mouth to hold back her sobs. "Where is she? At your apartment?"

"No. Del took her out for ice cream." She hadn't wanted to leave Laurie alone right now, and Del had volunteered to keep her company until Kade returned.

"Del?" Eleanor blinked in confusion.

Kade only noticed how casually that name had dropped from her lips when she saw Eleanor's confused expression. Del had slowly become an important part of her life, so gradually she hadn't even noticed. "She's the lieutenant who came with me when I talked to Laurie yesterday."

"Oh." Eleanor nodded and seemed to accept that explanation without question. Then suddenly, her eyes widened. "Oh! Is she your...?"

"My friend?" Kade knew it wasn't exactly the word Eleanor had been looking for, but she could play innocent with the best of them. If Eleanor wanted to know something, she would make her ask. She had no intention of giving away information on her private life or making it easy for her brother and his wife.

Eleanor traced the pattern on her teacup with her finger. "Yes... no. I mean... is she your... lover? Is that the right word to use?"

At least she's admitting her ignorance. "Maybe you should ask your daughter what expression she'd like you to use when you refer to Evan Whitfield. I suspect it's not any of the swear words Doug shouted across the house yesterday."

Eleanor sniffled. "This isn't easy for us."

"No one expects you to jump for joy because you found out your daughter is gay. Just don't make Laurie feel like she's doing something wrong, or she'll only hide it from you," Kade warned her, hoping she was reaching at least her sister-in-law if not her stubborn brother.

"Like you hid it from all of us?" Eleanor asked quietly.

That question from her quiet sister-in-law completely blindsided Kade. She hadn't expected it, and she wasn't ready to answer it. "I wasn't exactly hiding," she said slowly, trying not to squirm under Eleanor's interested gaze. "There never **was** anything to hide."

"I don't understand. You're not a lesbian or a... bisexual? But you said...?"

"I know what I said," Kade interrupted her nervous stammering. "Those labels have nothing to do with the reality of how I lived my life. I could love a woman, yes, but I never allowed myself to." She realized that she had hid from herself. She had shut herself off from a lot of options because she had only considered men proper dating material.

Eleanor bit her lip but didn't discuss the subject further. Not that Kade wanted her to. "Do you think Laurel could stay with you until tomorrow?" Eleanor asked, directing a pleading gaze at Kade. "I think her father needs a little time to calm down after what you said to him."

After hearing it phrased like that, Kade knew she couldn't say no. She had been the one to upset Doug, and now she would have to be the one to keep his daughter away from him until he had calmed down. Normally, that wouldn't have been much of a problem, but with the stalker probably still lurking around her apartment, she didn't want Laurie to stay there. "I'm not sure," she started.

"Please." Eleanor softly squeezed Kade's forearm.

Kade sighed. She would have to find a way. "All right. She can stay with me tonight."

* * *

Del met Kade at the door.

Kade's patrician features were even paler than normal, but the ice blue eyes were flashing with determination. Kade had been through a lot the last couple of days, and Del's admiration for her grew in leaps and bounds.

"How did it go?" Del asked as she let Kade into the apartment and took a pink backpack from her that probably held a few of Laurie's things.

Kade licked her lips and looked around. She seemed nervous for some reason. "Where's Laurie?"

Del grinned. "Don't worry, she'll probably be busy for the next few hours. She found my collection of lesbian fiction."

"Lesbian fiction?" Kade arched an eyebrow. "You're not letting her—"

"Oh, don't worry. I only gave her access to the G-rated stuff." Del winked at her.

Kade looked too tired to even grin.

Del reached out and gently squeezed her shoulder. "How did it go?" she asked again.

"I got into a shouting match with my brother. I'm not sure if it did any good, but it at least gave him something to think about." Kade walked down the hallway and peeked in on Laurie without announcing her presence. "Her mother wants her to stay with me until tomorrow. I couldn't tell her no, so now I have a problem."

"You could stay here," Del suggested without hesitation. She had wanted Kade to stay anyway, and she found Laurie to be good company. She reminded Del of a younger, shyer version of Kade.

"You have a one-bedroom apartment," Kade reminded in her logical DDA voice.

Del shrugged. "It's only for one night. You and Laurie could share the bed, and I could sleep out here on the couch." She wanted there to be no misunderstandings. She wasn't doing it to cleverly arrange a situation in which they had to share a bed. This was about protecting Kade first and foremost.

A thin line was forming on Kade's normally smooth brow. "I can't ask that of you."

It was always a struggle to get Kade to accept help, and this time was no exception. "You're not asking. I'm offering. Come on. Say yes. I'd like the company."

"I'll have to ask Laurie," Kade hedged. "I'm not sure she'd be comfortable staying here."

Laurie had been a little shy and hesitant to talk to Del at the beginning, but that hadn't lasted long, so Del was confident in Laurie's reaction.

"Hey, Laurie," Kade said quietly as she entered the living room.

Laurie immediately laid her book down and looked up with wide, cautious eyes. "How did it go? What did they say?"

"They didn't say much, but I hope I got them to listen. They need a little time to digest what I told them. You'll stay with me tonight... if that's okay with you?" Something in Kade's voice and the way she interacted with Laurie made Del think she hadn't been close to her niece before.

"Great!" Laurie was visibly relieved. "I'd rather stay at your apartment than go home; that's for sure."

Kade bit her lip. "We're not staying in my apartment. We're staying here because..." She searched for something to say without revealing that she might be in danger.

"Because I just had a concussion, and your aunt generously offered to stay and watch over me," Del quickly came to her aid. It wasn't the truth, but it was not a complete lie either.

"Concussion?" Laurie repeated. "You're hurt?"

The concern in her voice warmed Del's heart. *This is what Kade must have been like before her family taught her to hide her feelings behind a mask of stiff politeness.* "It's not too bad," she answered. "The doctors already cleared me. Kade is just staying to make sure I'm really okay."

"Staying here is even better," Laurie said with a shy grin. She glanced at her aunt. "Have you seen all the books she has?"

Del had to smile at the overwhelmed expression that appeared on Kade's face for a second before the mask of confidence was back. "Yeah, I've seen them. She even lent me one of them, but I haven't found the time to read it."

Del grinned to herself. *So you didn't even peek at the love scenes, huh?*

"It's getting late," Kade said, "and you have school tomorrow. You should probably go to bed now." Kade was clearly uncomfortable with her new role as a substitute mother, but Del thought she handled it well.

When Laurie reappeared from the bathroom, Kade and Del were making up the couch for Del to sleep on. "You know," Laurie said, looking at the ground with red-tinged cheeks, "you don't have to do this because of me." She gestured at Del and the couch. "I'm not a kid. I have eyes."

Kade turned toward her with a frown, clearly not understanding to what Laurie was referring.

Del laughed. "Did you hear that, sweetie?" She stepped next to Kade and teasingly patted her butt. "We don't have to hide our love from your niece. The clever girl found us out."

Kade slowly turned around. She narrowed her eyes at Del. "Stop touching my ass, or I'll have yours for sexual harassment!" she threatened, seemingly dead serious, but as she turned back to Laurie, she casually pinched Del's butt. "Laurie, I told you she's not my lover, and I meant it. She's not just sleeping on the couch because of you."

"Oh." Laurie lowered her head. "I thought... I'm sorry."

"You don't have to be sorry. You Matheson women are a beautiful bunch, so being mistaken for your aunt's lover is not exactly an insult." Del chuckled as she watched Laurie blush at the compliment. Kade stayed seemingly cool, but Del had learned to see behind the controlled façade.

Kade wrapped her arm around Laurie's slender shoulder. They looked good together, more like sisters than aunt and niece. "Come on, Laurie. Let's go to bed before this one tries her lame compliments on us again." With a playful toss of her head, Kade majestically strode from the room.

CHAPTER 20

THE FAMILIAR clacking of Kade's high heels stopped in front of her desk. Aiden could still identify the sound, but it didn't have the same effect on her blood pressure that it had a year before. "Hey, Kade," she said before she had even looked up.

"Aiden." Kade planted her briefcase on Aiden's desk and sat down in one of the chairs.

Aiden felt her eyebrows rise. *She's sitting in a chair? Is there suddenly something wrong with the edge of my desk?* She studied Kade's serious expression. "Everything all right? I haven't seen you all week."

"I was swamped with arraignments, and Tenley's lawyer kept me busy with all the paper he wasted on last-minute motions." Kade made a dismissive gesture, letting Aiden know that most, if not all, of the motions had been dismissed by the judge. "Do you have a minute?"

Aiden leaned back in her chair, stretching and rubbing the back of her neck. "Sure." She always had a minute for Kade.

Ray looked up from the file he was reading but continued to work when he noticed Kade's question was only directed at Aiden, not at him.

"Is one of the interview rooms free?" Kade asked.

Aiden hid her surprise. She would soon learn why Kade was so secretive. She rose and led Kade over to the smallest interview room. When she passed Okada's desk, Okada waggled his eyebrows at her, gesturing at Kade behind her back. Aiden threw her pen at him.

Kade firmly closed the door behind them. "I know this is unusual, and you're probably wondering what's going on, but this is not about our jobs, and I didn't want to discuss it in front of the crowd."

"Okay," Aiden said slowly, trying to catch up with what Kade had said and what it implied. If it wasn't about their jobs, what else was there to talk about? A sudden thought occurred to her. *Del? Does she want to talk about Del?* She hoped Del hadn't done anything to upset Kade—not only for Del's and Kade's sake but also for her own. She knew from Dawn that something was developing between Kade and Del, but she wasn't prepared to give relationship advice to Kade Matheson. "So what is it you want to talk about?"

"I want you to talk to your sister for me," Kade said straight out.

That was the last thing Aiden had expected. "Talk to my sister?" she repeated. What interest could Kade have in that?

"Not just talk. I want you to talk to her about what she's doing to my niece," Kade said.

Oh, God. This is the "Make your sister stay away from my niece" talk! Aiden couldn't believe that Evan hadn't been staying away from Laurel Matheson. *She doesn't know with whom she's dealing. Messing with a Matheson is not a good idea.* Laurie Matheson was way out of Evan's league as Kade had always been out of her league. It had made Aiden stay away from Kade, and she had hoped that Evan was smart enough to stay away from Laurie too. Aiden was convinced that, in the long run, a relationship between them would never work out, and trying would only cause more problems for Evan. "Well, I can try, but to tell you the truth, Evan is not exactly eager to listen to her big sister. We haven't spoken more than a few words with each other since Deming told me I have a sister."

Kade leaned against the edge of the small table in the interview room and studied Aiden. "It must be difficult for you."

"I always wished for a sister growing up, but now that I have one, I don't know what to do with her," Aiden said. She had stalled, putting off calling or visiting Evan for the last few days, simply because she didn't feel ready. "Having to tell her to stay the hell away from your niece is not going to make it easier," she said with a sigh.

Kade looked up sharply. "I don't want her to stay away."

"What? But I thought..." *Now I'm confused.* She would have bet her entire paycheck that the influential Matheson family would find ways to keep Evan away from their daughter.

"My brother and his wife would probably like that, but it's not what my niece wants. Laurie is bawling her eyes out because Evan refuses to see her again." A gentle sarcasm resonated in Kade's voice, but Aiden could see that she truly cared for her niece. "I would appreciate it if you could do something about that."

"My half sister and your niece." Aiden shook her head to clear it.

Kade shot her an understanding glance. "I know. Scary thought, huh?"

Aiden nodded. *Oh, yeah.* "So you want me to tell Evan...?" she prompted, wanting to be very clear on the subject.

"Just make sure that she didn't break up with Laurie because my overprotective brother scared her away," Kade said. "Let her know that not all Mathesons are arrogant, controlling, pigheaded snobs."

"They're not?" Aiden asked with her most innocent expression.

Kade smirked. "Laurie isn't."

"Oh, right. We're talking about Laurie." Aiden grinned, then sobered. "I'll talk to her, but no promises. The way things are going between us, she'll probably do the exact opposite of what I tell her to do."

"It's worth a try. If she wants nothing to do with Laurie, at least I'll know it was her decision and not my brother who destroyed Laurie's first relationship."

Aiden sighed and leaned back against the wall of the interview room. *Now I really have to talk to Evan. No more putting it off. Shit.* She gave Kade a nod and turned to leave the interview room.

"Aiden?" Kade called.

She turned back around. "Yeah?"

Kade hesitated.

With a frown, Aiden returned to her side. "Anything else you wanted to talk about?" Whatever it was, judging from Kade's expression, it wasn't something pleasant. Aiden couldn't think of any subject that would be even more awkward than talking about the relationship between her sister and Kade's niece.

"Actually, yes. There is this... situation I could use your help with." Kade's words were slow and hesitant.

Aiden knew what it had to mean for the proud woman to ask for help. "Anytime, you know that, Kade," she said. "Tell me about this situation."

"Well, it seems I have a secret admirer," Kade said. "Six months ago, someone started sending me flowers and sappy cards."

Aiden frowned. *Why is she telling me this? The Kade I know wouldn't come running because of a bunch of flowers. Surely she doesn't think they're from me?* "And the problem with that is...?"

"It's not just the flowers and cards. I often feel like someone is watching me, and I get a lot of hang-up calls even though I have an unlisted phone number." Kade's calm mask slipped for a single second, showing Aiden the fear in her eyes.

"Kade! That's not just a secret admirer. You have a stalker!" Aiden couldn't believe it. How could Kade, a DDA prosecuting sex crimes, not take this kind of situation seriously?

Kade bit her lip. "I know. And I think he's escalating."

"What? What happened?"

"I can't prove it, but it's possible that Del's fall wasn't an accident," Kade said quietly, no longer holding Aiden's gaze. She looked down with a guilty expression.

Aiden gripped the back of a chair. She wanted to throw it across the room but held herself in check. "People are getting attacked right in front of your apartment, and you kept it to yourself all this time? You could have been killed, and you didn't think it necessary to ask for help? To tell anyone?" She knew shouting at their DDA was not appropriate, but she didn't care.

"I didn't keep it to myself," Kade said defiantly. Then her voice lowered as she realized what she had just admitted. "I told Del."

The words she had wanted to shout died in Aiden's throat. *Del. She told Del. Not me.*

"It's not that I trust her more than I trust you," Kade said, guessing Aiden's thoughts. "When I had that cold, she answered my phone and realized it was not a normal hang-up call. I had to tell her."

"When you had the cold... that was two weeks ago! She knew for two weeks, and she did nothing?" Aiden resolved then and there to have a heart to heart with Del Vasquez. *If she wants to take over the role of Kade's protector, fine. But she better do her job!*

Kade took a quick step closer, encroaching on Aiden's space. "Del did exactly what I wanted her to do. The last thing I want is an official report on my private life."

And certainly not now that she's finally starting to have something like a private life, Aiden finished what Kade hadn't said. From the day Kade had joined the sex crimes unit, she had made it clear her ambitions didn't end with being a DDA. Kade was aiming high, and being outed in an official police report would not help with that.

Aiden took a deep breath. She forced herself to change from worried friend to professional cop modus. "Do you still have the cards the stalker sent?"

"Some of them. Del already had a friend from the lab check for fingerprints. Nothing. Local flower shops were a dead end too." Kade blew out a frustrated breath.

Well, at least Del didn't sit idly and wait for the stalker to attack Kade, Aiden conceded. "I'll call Del and have her bring me up to speed. We'll investigate this semiofficially for now. No reports until it becomes necessary to take more official steps," she promised.

Kade touched her forearm for a fleeting moment. "Thank you."

Aiden shifted her weight from one foot to the other while she waited for the door to open. She had felt more comfortable at the front door of serial killers she was about to arrest. At the moment, she would have preferred the serial killer to having to face her half sister. She quickly put on a smile as Jill LeCroix opened the door. "Hi," she said, "is Evan home?" She half hoped, half feared that Evan wasn't.

"Yes. She's in the garage. Come on in. I'll tell her you're here." Evan's foster mother enthusiastically waved her into the house. "It's so great that you're here to see her. I think she could use a big sister."

Mrs. LeCroix continued to talk, but Aiden didn't listen. She was already overwhelmed with the expectations Jill LeCroix was putting on her. The silent implication of Mrs. LeCroix's words was that she would continue to spend time with Evan, would make enough of a difference in her life to stop all of Evan's problems, and would make life better for her and her foster parents. *I can barely keep control of my own life and wrestle my own demons, how can I take on Evan's too?*

Suddenly, she felt under too much pressure, as if she would suffocate in the house. She wondered if Evan sometimes felt the same. "If it's all right, I'd rather go and join Evan in the garage," she said quickly.

"Sure." Jill LeCroix smiled and pointed her in the right direction.

Aiden walked around the house and to the garage in the back. The door to the garage was open. Loud music blared out of a CD player, interrupted only by a rhythmical thumping.

Aiden stepped closer and looked inside.

Evan was hammering away at a heavy bag that hung in the back of the garage. It was the first time Aiden had seen her out of her ever-present leather jacket. Without it, Evan looked lanky and more vulnerable, like the teenager she was. Aiden watched for a while, mentally correcting Evan's stance or applauding a clever feint and quick footwork.

Something must have alerted Evan to her presence. She abandoned the bag and whirled around.

"Hi," Aiden said, feeling very awkward.

"Hi," Evan mumbled. She held on to the punching bag with both gloved hands, stopping its movements, but she didn't step closer to greet Aiden or invite her in. She clearly didn't share her foster mother's enthusiasm about seeing Aiden.

Aiden nodded at the punching bag, the first topic of conversation that came to mind. "You box?"

"Nah, just playin' around." Evan shrugged casually.

Oh, yeah, right. Don't show any interest in anything, Aiden thought sarcastically. *It would make it too easy for me to find a common ground, and of course we can't have that.* "So this is not what you had planned for the afternoon?" Aiden decided to beat her with her own weapons.

Evan shrugged again. "No, not really."

"Then maybe you'd like to come downtown to the DMV office with me?" Aiden suggested. "I thought we could take care of the paperwork today and see what else you need to do to get your driver's permit." She dangled the word in front of Evan like a carrot in front of a mule.

Evan's cool, uninterested expression didn't change. "I already have my driver's permit."

Shit. Now my one good idea is gone. Aiden felt like an actor without a script. She had no idea what to say. "Oh. I assumed you hadn't gotten it yet because Dawn said..." She stopped and rubbed her neck. "So I guess your parents are already teaching you how to drive?"

"They're not my parents!" Evan gave the punching bag another forceful hit, making the chains rattle. "You of all people should know that!"

Aiden wasn't sure if she should be embarrassed or angry. She settled for diplomatic. "I'm sorry. Of course I know. I just didn't know what to call them."

"Try their names. Novel idea, huh?" Evan mocked.

Aiden took a deep breath and pictured Dawn's gentle green eyes. *Don't react. Don't let her provoke you. She just wants to keep you at arm's length.* "So Jill and Roger are taking you out to practice your driving?" she repeated her earlier question.

"Yeah, they took me out every once in a while," Evan answered.

"Took?" Evan's use of the past tense hadn't gone unnoticed. Something had happened to stop the driving lessons. Aiden's mind immediately started providing a dozen scenarios about what Evan could have done, but she stopped herself. Dawn was right—she needed to stop assuming that everything that went wrong was Evan's fault.

Evan casually hooked her arm around the punching bag. "They overreacted to me borrowing the car one night."

Borrowing the car? Aiden had to bite back a laugh. She didn't want Evan to think she was making fun of her or agreeing with her behavior. *Ooops. It seems Dawn was right. We do have some things in common.* "You could practice with my car," she said, acting as if it was no big deal.

"Your car?" Evan repeated suspiciously.

"With me in it, of course," Aiden hastened to say. She didn't want Evan to "borrow" her car for a solo spin.

Evan still didn't jump up and down at that offer. She eyed Aiden with distrust. "Why are you doing this? Don't think you owe me anything just because your father couldn't keep it in his pants with my mother."

Aiden worked hard not to react to those provocative words. "I owe it to myself," she said. "I did wrong by assuming you hurt Laurie Matheson, and I want a chance to make it right. What do you say?" She withdrew her car keys from her pocket and held them out to Evan.

"That's not the key to the doc's miniature version of a car, is it?" Evan asked.

Aiden laughed. "No, don't worry. I have my own car, and it's adult-sized."

Evan looked back and forth between Aiden's face and the car key. Finally her interest in driving won out. "Okay, why not?" She started to remove her gloves with the help of her teeth.

"Here, let me help," Aiden said.

Evan pulled away. "I managed on my own before I met you." They both knew she meant so much more than just opening her gloves. Without another word, she took the car key from Aiden.

Aiden quickly hurried after her. She felt more and more uncomfortable as she settled in the unfamiliar position in the passenger seat. She watched as Evan eagerly turned the key in the ignition. "Seatbelt," she reminded, barely holding herself back from listing a dozen other rules Evan had to follow while she drove the car. For now, she would trust Evan to know and follow the important rules and only intervene when she had to, even though it was driving her crazy.

Evan pulled out of the driveway much faster than Aiden was comfortable with, but she bit her lip and said nothing. She could sense that this was a mutual test—she was testing Evan's driving skills, but more importantly, Evan was testing Aiden's patience and her willingness to start a relationship on more equal footing.

On their way through the city, she repeatedly grabbed onto the door handle and stole glances at the speedometer. Each time she found Evan was not going as fast as she had suspected. It only seemed that way to her, now that she was in the helpless position in the passenger seat.

"Want to practice parking?" she finally asked after an hour of constant tension and silent driving. She pointed at a parking lot ahead of them.

Evan gave a short nod. Aiden noticed that she changed her pronouncedly casual grip on the steering wheel and took a firmer hold. She silently picked a parking space and began to maneuver the car backward.

Aiden tensed. Evan had turned the wheel the other way too late, and Aiden could already sense that Evan would end up much too close to the car to her right. Aiden pressed her foot against the imaginary brake. "Um... you're getting a little close to that car."

"I'm not blind. I noticed," Evan snapped. She put the car into forward again, pulled out of the parking space, and quickly corrected the position of the wheels before she navigated backward again. This time, the car ended up in the parking space with enough distance to the cars on the left and right.

Aiden finally relaxed a little. "That's good," she praised her. "Let's shut off the engine for a minute and take a break." She wasn't so sure that driving lessons had been a good idea. Not only would her tense muscles hurt tomorrow, but the driving took Evan's complete concentration, making it impossible to have any conversation. "So... how's it going?"

"The driving? Great of course! You couldn't tell?" Evan was beginning to look irritated.

"No, not the driving. The rest of your life," Aiden clarified. "How's that going?"

Evan coolly crossed her wrists over the steering wheel. "Didn't commit any crimes this week if that's what you're asking."

Aiden sighed. *We can't even make small talk. A simple "How are you" could quickly become an ugly argument.* "It's not what I'm asking. Let's stop always assuming the worst about each other, okay?"

Evan didn't react to that peace offering. "So what are you asking?"

Aiden had promised Kade to talk to Evan about Laurie, and this might be the only opportunity to do it. "Are you still seeing Laurie Matheson?"

"No. You can tell her parents they don't need to worry. I broke up with her." Evan fiddled with the radio, feigning total indifference toward Laurie and what had happened between them.

"I don't report back to her parents." Aiden knew she had to make that very clear if she wanted Evan to trust her.

"You report back to her aunt," Evan shot back.

She's not stupid. "I'm Kade's friend, yes, but I'm not her spy," Aiden said. "I just don't want you to break up with Laurie for the wrong reasons. If you don't want to see Laurie again, that's fine, but don't do it because her parents scared you away."

Evan sat up straighter. "I'm not scared!"

"Then why end it so suddenly?" Aiden asked.

Evan shrugged, playing it cool. "Maybe I just got bored with her."

Aiden barely held her temper in check. She didn't like anyone talking like that about Kade's niece. "From what her mother says, you didn't look bored with her that Friday night two weeks ago." It was out of her mouth before she could hold it back. *Shit. I wish I had Dawn's patience and her ability to just talk to Evan, without the undercurrent of tension and mutual accusations that seems to linger between us.*

"It was a one-time thing, okay? I don't do relationships." Evan glared at her until Aiden nodded her understanding.

She doesn't want to get close because getting close means getting hurt. We do have more in common than I realized, Aiden admitted to herself. "Does Laurie know that?" she asked as gently as she could. Evan was her sister, and Aiden knew that should automatically make her take Evan's side, but she couldn't help worrying about Laurie, who looked so much like a younger, more vulnerable version of Kade.

Evan shrugged again.

"If you're not ready for a steady relationship, that's fine." God knew she hadn't been ready for a long-term relationship at sixteen. She laughed at herself. *You weren't even ready at thirty.* "If you want to break up with Laurie, that's fine too. But please be nice about it. Don't break her heart; that's all I ask."

Evan didn't answer. She stared through the windshield, still acting as if she didn't care and wasn't even listening.

Aiden turned in her seat to be able to see Evan's face. "Before I met Dawn, I was a lot like you." She heard Evan's snort but ignored it. She hadn't wanted to believe how alike they really were either. "I slept with people and then told them it meant nothing the next day. I was an inconsiderate asshole, and I'm just glad I got my head out of my ass in time not to do it to Dawn."

That finally got a reaction. Evan scowled at her.

Hmm, look at that. Seems like she doesn't like the thought of anyone hurting Dawn either. Dawn, avoiding intimacy, and borrowing cars—that's three things we have in common. Despite all her toughness and bravado, she has a soft spot for Dawn. Aiden had to suppress a smile.

"Can we drive back now?" Evan asked, clearly fed up with talking.

"Sure. You're the one in the driver's seat." Aiden was uncomfortably aware that she was handing over the control over more than just the car to Evan, but she did it nonetheless. "Just start the car and pick the route."

Evan turned the key in the ignition without comment.

* * *

Aiden closed the last file and threw it into the out box on her desk. "You got plans for tonight?" she asked, looking across their joined desks at her partner.

"No. Want to grab a beer?" Ray obviously took it as an invitation or a request for his company.

Aiden shook her head. "That's not why I'm asking. If you don't have anything planned, I could use your help." She had waited all day for an opportunity to talk to Ray, and now that most of the other detectives had already left for the day, it was finally time.

Ray furrowed his brow. They both knew she didn't ask for help very often. "What is it?" he asked with an openness that said he was willing to help no matter what.

"Actually, it's not me you'd be helping. It's Kade." Aiden looked around the nearly empty squad room and took a deep breath. Her fingers wrapped tightly around the pen in her hand. "She's being stalked. Flowers, letters, feeling watched, hang-up calls, the works. And she thinks he's escalating. It's possible that he attacked Del Vasquez when she visited Kade's apartment." She got out the information in a rush, not wanting to linger on the words or think about what they could mean for Kade.

Ray's eyes grew wider and wider with every word. He stared at her in disbelief. "Why is she only coming to us with this now? It sounds like it has gone on for weeks or even months. Kade of all people should know better than to think it would just go away!"

Aiden nodded grimly. She forced down growing annoyance, knowing Kade had only taken the risk to protect her privacy, not because she didn't trust them. "That's what I told her too. She says she didn't want an official report on the details of her private life."

Ray barked out a laugh. "Not much to write about. Kade doesn't have much of a private life."

"I think she's starting to have one—and she's afraid it could hurt her political ambitions. That's why she told only Del Vasquez about the stalker."

"What could be so destructive about our resident ice queen's private life?" Ray asked, using the good-natured nickname Kade had earned within the Portland Police Bureau. "She doesn't eat the politically correct brand of cereals or what?"

Aiden didn't laugh. "Think about it. What rumors could make it hard for Kade to go after the DA's seat?"

"Apart from the political nuances I won't even pretend to understand... that she's bribable, incompetent, or gay." Ray ticked it off on his fingers.

"Exactly. Everybody knows that Kade doesn't need more money than she already has, and her closure rate is above reproach, so that leaves...?" She looked at her partner expectantly, knowing he would connect the dots.

"Oh, come on, Aiden!" Ray flicked a crumbled-up piece of paper at her. "You don't expect me to believe... Kade?"

Aiden nodded slowly.

"Kade Matheson is a lesbian?" Ray still couldn't believe it.

Aiden quickly held up a hand. "I didn't say that. I just think that she's beginning to explore other possibilities, and she doesn't want to read about it in a police report or in the newspaper."

"Wow." Ray rubbed the back of his neck. "Stacy Ford, you, now Kade... are there any straight women in this place?"

Aiden chuckled. She knew Ray was surprised but not upset. "Well, if it makes you feel any better, I never got any vibes from Judge Linehan."

"Oh, now that's a real consolation!" Ray grumbled good-naturedly while he stood and slipped into his jacket. "So what do you have planned for tonight? Staking out Kade's apartment?"

"Finding out how he got into her apartment building. I called Vasquez. She's meeting us at Kade's." Aiden grabbed her keys and took the gun from its place in the bottom drawer.

Ray held the door open for her. "So Lieutenant Vasquez and Kade...?"

"Oh, no, I'm not answering that question." Not when she wasn't sure what was going on between Kade and Del. She wasn't even sure Kade knew. "If you want to know, you have to go directly to the source—ask Kade."

Ray held up both hands, palms forward. "Thanks a lot! I want to live long enough to see my kids graduating from college." He grinned deviously. "I'll just let the rumor slip when I'm having lunch with Okada. You know he can't help investigating when he smells a mystery. Let him ask our DDA."

Aiden smiled inwardly at his reasoning but didn't return his grin. "No. No spreading rumors about this, Ray," she warned him. "No rumors, no reports, no squad room jokes. Nothing. Can you do that?"

"I've been doing it for you, haven't I?" Ray answered seriously. "I never joked about you and Dawn, not even when you came in with hickeys the size of Madagascar."

Aiden's hand crept up to her shoulder, but she quickly stopped the movement before Ray could suspect she had told them a lie about wearing a scratchy shirt when she had repeatedly fingered the bite marks on her shoulder. "I know, Ray, and I'm very thankful for your support." She realized that she had never told him this. "I didn't want to imply that you'd—"

"I know. Come on. Let's get going." Ray ushered her out of the door.

* * *

Del Vasquez was already waiting when they pulled up in front of Kade's building. She was leaning against her car and lifted a hand in greeting but didn't smile when she saw them.

"So Lieutenant Vasquez, you, and me—we're the new Lesbian Case Squad, huh?" Ray joked as they got out of the car. "Don't I get a special badge or diploma for that?"

Lesbian Case Squad? Aiden didn't want to encourage her partner's antics, but she had to laugh at that. "Why don't you ask the lieutenant?" she suggested, knowing Ray wouldn't repeat his question in front of the stern Del Vasquez.

Del took a step toward them, greeting them with a nod. "Thanks for coming."

She's thanking us? Like she's Kade's oldest friend and confidant, and we're the new acquaintances helping her out! Her old resentment toward Del crept up again. She was still not completely over Kade telling Del about the stalker weeks before she had mentioned even a word to Aiden.

"So where do we start?" Ray asked, deferring to Del more easily than Aiden would have.

"There's still a minute right before the attack missing in my memory, but I remember seeing a few people in the foyer of Kade's building before I went up. We should talk to them and find out if they saw anything of interest," Del said. She unconsciously rubbed the back of her head, where a small bald spot showed a healing gash.

As they entered the marbled foyer of Kade's building, a tall woman stepped out of the doorman's office. "Let me do the talking," Ray said with a grin. "I'm a pro at handling doormen."

Aiden and Del tolerantly stayed back.

"Hi. I'm Detective Bennet, and these are my colleagues, Lieutenant Vasquez and Detective Carlisle." Ray flashed his badge and a charming grin.

Aiden held back a smile. *Oh, Ray, my friend, if my gaydar is in working order, your charms are wasted on this one.*

"We're investigating an incident that happened...?" Ray threw a questioning gaze at Del, who smoothly supplied the correct date. "...last Saturday morning," Ray repeated. "We were wondering if you would do us the professional courtesy of answering a few questions?"

Professional courtesy? Ah, he's trying the "We're practically colleagues" approach! Really clever. A lot of the security personnel and doormen they encountered had at one time in their lives dreamed of becoming a police officer, and many of them liked to pretend that their jobs had a lot in common.

The doorwoman didn't give Ray the flattered smile most of her colleagues would have. Instead, she directed a level gaze at him. "I'm not a cop, so professional courtesy doesn't apply."

Aiden held back a grin at the expression on her partner's face. *You might be a pro at handling doormen, but you're not doing so well with doorwomen.* "Then how about helping out a fellow female working in a traditionally male job?" she suggested. She knew they couldn't afford to alienate the doorwoman. She and whatever colleagues she might have spent the most time around Kade's condo building and might have seen something.

"I can do that." The doorwoman nodded.

"So what did you see last Saturday morning?" Aiden asked.

The doorwoman pointed at Del. "She went up with two cups of coffee, but she had done it before, so I didn't think much of it."

Just how often does she visit Kade? Aiden wondered. "Was anyone else around at that time?" she asked.

"Mrs. Meyers and Ms. Giavelli were standing in the foyer, chatting away for hours, like they always do," the doorwoman reported.

"You didn't see anyone else that morning?" Aiden asked. "Anyone who doesn't live in the building?"

The doorwoman thought for a moment. "There was a young man, smoking one cigarette after another on the sidewalk. He was there for at least half an hour, but when I went outside a little later to let the EMTs in, he was gone."

A young man lurking around Kade's apartment building... *Could this be the stalker?* "What did he look like?" she asked.

"Late twenties, brown hair, tall—about my height. He was wearing a baseball cap and didn't look up, so I can't describe his face," the doorwoman answered.

That's more than most witnesses can give us, but it still fits half of Portland! Aiden would ask Kade later if that description fit any of her more recent cases, but she didn't hold out much hope.

Del turned around and walked out of the building.

"Hey!" Aiden quickly thanked the doorwoman and followed Del. "Where are you going?"

Del crouched down right next to the building. "I'm collecting evidence. She said he was smoking, so maybe he left his cigarette stubs behind."

She's very good at her job, Aiden had to admit. She silently bent down too and started to search for cigarette stubs.

Ray joined them, mumbling, "You know, I thought working on this new squad would be more fun."

CHAPTER 21

*T*HE SHRILL RINGING of her phone made Kade flinch. She threw down her pen and cursed. Since Del had put a tap on her phone, the hang-up calls had stopped. It should have calmed her, but it did exactly the opposite because it meant the stalker was aware of their half-official investigation. He was still watching her apartment.

The phone rang again, and she reached for it. "Matheson."

"Hi, Kade. It's Dawn Kinsley."

Kade had expected it to be Laurie or one of her detectives. Dawn calling her was a surprise, and she didn't know what to make of it. "Hello, Dawn," she said, hiding her surprise. "What can I do for you?"

"You probably know that Del's birthday is coming up."

Actually, I didn't know that. "No, Del hasn't mentioned it," Kade answered with a frown.

Dawn chuckled. "She's trying to ignore it because it makes her feel old. Anyway, it's next Thursday, and we're having a big surprise party for Del. I'm hoping you could come?"

A birthday party. The thought was a little overwhelming. She did want to spend the day with Del and celebrate with her, but she wasn't sure if she was ready to meet the family and friends, all of them at the same time. "Who will be there?" she asked instead of a direct answer.

"Well, you know Aiden, of course, and I think you met my mother. The rest of the family is coming too," Dawn answered lightly.

"Family?" Kade repeated. She knew Del hadn't been in contact with her own family for more than two decades. "Yours or hers?"

"It's the same thing, Kade," Dawn said. "And she wants you to be a part of that group too. So will you come?"

Kade hesitated for a few more seconds, then mentally slapped herself. *Del has done so much for you. She gave you shooting lessons; she let you and Laurie sleep over at her apartment; she even got hurt playing bodyguard. So what if coming to this party might be a little uncomfortable for you! It's the least you can do.* "I'll be there," she promised.

"Great!" Kade could hear the bright smile in Dawn's voice.

"Can I bring anything?" Kade asked. Being a polite guest had been part of the Matheson upbringing.

Dawn laughed. "I'd say a salad, but we didn't cover that in our cooking lesson, so I'll let you off the hook. You don't have to bring food, but you could bring your niece."

"Laurie?" Del and Laurie got along very well, but Kade wasn't sure why Dawn wanted to invite Laurie to Del's birthday party. She wasn't even sure she wanted to bring her—Laurie was already convinced that Kade was in a relationship with Del. Bringing her to Del's party would only encourage that assumption. "Why do you want me to bring Laurie?"

"I thought it would be a great opportunity to introduce Evan to the rest of the family, and if Laurie is there, Evan wouldn't be the only teenager and would have someone to talk to," Dawn reasoned.

"You're not playing matchmaker, are you, Dr. Kinsley?" Kade asked with mock suspicion. She had learned a few things about Dawn in the last few months, and she knew Dawn had a talent for connecting people.

Dawn chuckled. "Me?"

"Playing innocent is not going to work with me," Kade told her sternly. "I'm a DDA. I know the difference between being and acting innocent."

"Okay, okay. I think Evan would like to see Laurie again, but she's too proud and too stubborn to take the first step," Dawn said.

Sounds like she has a lot in common with her big sister. Who knows what would have happened if Aiden had taken the first step and had been as insistent as Del is with me? Kade quickly shoved the thought back. "All right. I'll ask Laurie if she wants to come."

* * *

Aiden stuck her head out of her closet. "Is it okay for me to wear pants to Del's party?" she called out to Dawn, who was getting ready in the bathroom.

"Why shouldn't it be?" Dawn called back. "You know that Del is not too fond of skirts and dresses either."

Yeah, Aiden thought, *at least not when* ***she*** *has to wear them. On Kade it would probably be another matter.* "I'm not asking because of Del. I want to make a good impression on your family," she admitted, albeit a little embarrassed.

"Oh, come on! You know my mother is not big on formality," Dawn said.

Aiden smiled at the memory. "Yeah, I remember. You're not the 'napkin at the dinner table' kind."

"Exactly. So there's no need to impress my mother by wearing an elegant gown," Dawn said, still from her place in front of the mirror in the bathroom.

"Your mother is not the Kinsley woman I'm trying to impress." A few months earlier, that would have been the case, but by now she had shared enough relaxed dinners with Grace to know she only needed to treat Dawn well to earn Grace's support.

Dawn came out of the bathroom in the light green dress that always seemed to turn her eyes the color of emeralds. Before Aiden could take the time to admire her, she stepped closer and wrapped her arms around Aiden. "The other Kinsley woman is already impressed by you." She kissed Aiden, her lips just skimming over Aiden's. "Very..." she kissed Aiden again, "...very," another kiss, "very impressed."

Aiden pulled her closer and captured her lips in a longer kiss. "I'm talking about your grandmother," she said when she finally came up for air.

Dawn laughed. "My grandmother is not big on formality either. You could wear an elegant gown, ripped jeans, or a

Hawaiian grass skirt, and Grandma wouldn't care one way or another."

For some reason, Aiden hadn't heard a lot about Dawn's grandmother in the last six months, and now she felt ill prepared to meet her for the first time. She had never met her own grandparents or spent much time around old people. "So she's a liberal old lady?"

"She's not old-fashioned at all, but don't let her catch you calling her old." Dawn pointed a warning finger at her.

Aiden grinned and made a mental note to avoid all comments about anyone's age tonight. At least her not being old-fashioned sounded encouraging. "So she was cool about you being gay?" Her mother's parents had died before Aiden was born, so she didn't have any experience with grandparents and how they might react to their grandchild's coming out.

"Well..." Dawn handed Aiden her earrings, silently asking for help with putting them on. "To tell you the truth... she doesn't know yet."

Aiden dropped one of the earrings. "What? How is that possible? I thought everyone in your family knew." She bent down and picked up the earring, holding it numbly in her hand.

"Everyone but Grandma," Dawn said with an embarrassed little grin.

"How come?" Dawn had never been hesitant to tell people she was a lesbian. Even her ten-year-old niece was well aware of it.

Dawn took the earring from Aiden and put it in her own ear. She took Aiden's now free hand and slowly traced circles into her palm while she thought about it. "My mother and Del didn't seem to be too fond of Maggie, and even with Del's help, it took my mother a while to feel comfortable with my sexual orientation, so I thought I'd wait a bit before I told my grandmother."

"But you never did?"

Dawn shook her head. "Before I could summon up the courage, Maggie and I broke up, and I concentrated on my work. I never had another girlfriend until I met you, so it never became necessary to tell her."

"And after you met me?" Aiden asked. It had been almost eight months since they had met, after all.

"Grandma was in and out of the hospital for most of last year. I also didn't want to tell her on the phone. I know it sounds like lame excuses, but..." Dawn sighed. "I want her to like you. I wanted to wait for the right moment."

Aiden entwined her fingers with Dawn's. "Are you worried about her reaction?"

Dawn shrugged. "We never talked about it, but I don't think she's homophobic or anything. After my marriage, though, I think she would be a little skeptical no matter who I brought home."

"She didn't like Cal?" Aiden could understand that. He seemed like an okay guy, but she wasn't overly fond of him either.

"She liked him well enough at the beginning. He's a cop, like her husband, my grandfather," Dawn said.

Aiden brightened. "I'm a cop too! Is that an extra point for me?"

Dawn laughed and teasingly tugged at Aiden's ear. "Why do you think you need the extra points so desperately? It certainly didn't help Cal."

"What happened?" Aiden asked. For some reason, they hadn't talked much about Dawn's marriage and her ex-husband. Dawn had told her why she had married Cal, but not much about their marriage itself and why it had ended.

Dawn pulled her over to the couch as if she expected the conversation to last a while. "The first year of our marriage was fine," she began.

"Fine?" Aiden repeated. She hoped Dawn used other words to describe their relationship. "That doesn't sound like marital bliss."

"It wasn't," Dawn confirmed. "We would have been better off as friends, but I didn't realize that back then. I knew there was something missing, but I didn't have enough experience with men or relationships to know what."

It always humbled Aiden when she remembered that Dawn had only been with two people before her.

"The second year was an emotional hell," Dawn continued, her voice rough and her gaze far away.

Aiden felt herself stiffen. "Why? What happened?" The thought of what Cal might have done to make Dawn's life a living hell made Aiden furious.

"He never laid a hand on me," Dawn said, knowing Aiden well enough to almost read her thoughts. "He just humiliated me and trampled all over my feelings."

"Yet you stayed for another year?" That was a surprise. Dawn had always come across as a person who stood up for herself and never allowed Aiden or anyone else to walk all over her.

Dawn nodded, worrying her lip.

"Why?" Aiden simply asked.

Dawn looked down at their joined hands. "Cal was trying so hard to hold on to what he thought we had, but I had already begun to realize I had feelings for women. I felt so bad for him, so guilty."

Aiden lifted Dawn's hand and kissed the palm, looking at Dawn with compassionate eyes.

Dawn smiled and gently touched Aiden's cheek. "Don't worry. I got over it."

"But your grandmother never learned the reason for your divorce?" Aiden asked.

"She just saw that I wasn't happy with Cal," Dawn said quietly. "That was enough for her. She never asked any questions."

Having a grandmother like that sounded nice, but Aiden still felt unsure about meeting the oldest Kinsley woman. She was a little afraid of being thought of as the "woman who turned my granddaughter gay."

"Ready to go?" Dawn asked.

Aiden wasn't, but she nodded anyway.

* * *

Grace led them into the living room, where a lot of strangers already sat, laughing and talking. Kade didn't know anyone in the room. Del wasn't here yet and neither were Dawn or Aiden. They had been sent to pick up Del for her surprise party.

Kade had never felt uncomfortable at parties. She had learned to make small talk and mingle at her parents' big receptions when she was a child, but this was something else. These people weren't just smiling politely while they nibbled on hors d'oeuvres. They were laughing and hugging and seemed genuinely happy to see one another again.

Kade looked over her shoulder at Laurie, who seemed even more uncomfortable than she was. The girl's blue-eyed gaze was flitting from guest to guest, and her shoulders slouched when she didn't find Evan.

Before Kade could think of something encouraging to say, a girl who looked remarkably like a ten-year-old version of Dawn ran up to Laurie and lured her away with the promise of hot chocolate and ice cream.

Kade watched them go with an amused smile.

"Hello."

Kade turned around at the voice greeting her. A small, gray-haired woman stood in front of her. Her face was weathered and full of wrinkles, and the hand that offered Kade a glass of champagne was mottled, but the old woman's eyes twinkled with life.

"You were looking a little lost, and I thought I'd come over and introduce myself," the old woman explained with a kind smile. "I'm Margot Kinsley."

The gray-haired woman looked nothing like Dawn, but her kindness did remind Kade of Aiden's girlfriend. "You're Dawn's grandmother?"

Margot Kinsley smiled. "Yes. And proud of it. Are you one of Dawn's friends?"

Am I? Kade wondered. "I'd like to think so," she answered and then noticed that she hadn't even introduced herself. A social faux pas like that wouldn't have been tolerated in her parents' home. Margot Kinsley just smiled. "I'm Kade Matheson." She carefully shook the older woman's thin hand.

"Do you work with Dawn?" Margot Kinsley asked.

Kade almost choked on a sip of champagne. "Oh, no. I'm not a psychologist. I work with Aiden. I'm a deputy district attorney."

"Aiden?" The elderly woman cocked her head as if she had never heard that name before.

Is she having problems with her memory? Kade wondered. Then another thought occurred to her, and her eyes widened. *Maybe she doesn't know about Aiden! God knows I wouldn't be eager to introduce my girlfriend, should I ever have one, to my family.* "Um... she's... another friend," she hastily said.

"Oh." Margot Kinsley looked around but only saw familiar faces. "You'll have to introduce her when she arrives."

Kade avoided an answer by taking another sip of champagne. *Oh, no, Dawn can do that on her own. I'm not getting involved in this. I have enough on my plate with my own coming out.*

Del's arrival spared Kade from having to answer.

Two dozen guests rushed forward to congratulate and greet a surprised looking Del. Kade stayed back and watched. She had to laugh when Dawn's grandmother hugged Del. With their height difference, Del had to bend far down to be able to hear what Margot Kinsley wanted to whisper in her ear.

When Dawn's grandmother let go of Del, the next guest, a tall, attractive brunette, stepped forward. She enthusiastically threw her arms around Del and wrapped her in a full-body hug.

Kade didn't laugh as she watched this particular hug. The tender kiss Del placed on the younger woman's cheek evoked feelings in Kade she didn't want to examine too closely.

Then Dawn's niece and a blond toddler almost toppled Del over with an exuberant group hug, and Kade lost sight of her in the mass of guests.

"Hey, Kade." Aiden quietly sidled up to her.

"Hi, Aiden." She and Aiden hadn't spent a lot of time together off the clock, but she was glad to see Aiden nonetheless. At least it was one familiar face in the room, and she would also offer a welcome distraction to the sight of the brunette in Del's arms.

"Do you want me to introduce you around?" Aiden asked.

As trained in the art of small talk as she was, Kade didn't feel up for it right now. "No, thanks. I assume Del will want to do that later. Do you know everyone here?" It was hard to believe that the reclusive Aiden Carlisle, who had never had many friends outside of the job and no family, suddenly had a large extended family.

Aiden looked around. "Most of them, yes."

"So who's that?" Kade asked, pointing in the direction of the brunette next to Del as casually as possible.

Aiden turned to look. A knowing grin appeared on her lips. "She's beautiful, isn't she?"

Kade narrowed her eyes at Aiden. *Is she trying to annoy me, or does she want to find out my taste in women?* She had to admit that, yes, the brunette was beautiful, but Kade wasn't interested in her. She arched an eyebrow, silently repeating her question.

"That's Eliza," Aiden said, "Dawn's sister-in-law."

"Her sister-in-law?" Kade had always assumed Dawn was an only child. "Dawn has a brother?"

Aiden pressed her lips together. "Had. He died ten years ago."

"Oh." Kade was sad to hear that but glad to realize the brunette was probably just another family member to Del. "So the blond girl who kidnapped Laurie from my side, she really is Dawn's niece?" She now remembered having seen the girl in a photo in Dawn's apartment.

Aiden nodded absently while she looked around the room again.

"What or who are you looking for?" Kade asked. "Dawn?"

"No," Aiden answered, still craning her neck. "Dawn is in the kitchen, helping her mother. I'm looking for Evan."

"You actually convinced her to come?" Kade hadn't thought Aiden would succeed.

Aiden shook her head. "It was Dawn who convinced her. Dawn has a way of talking to her that I still have to master." She sighed. "Did you bring Laurie?"

"Convincing her was actually very easy. I was prepared to dazzle her with a well-thought-out argument about why she should come, but I only had to mention Evan would be here to convince her." Kade smiled wryly.

Aiden smirked. "Well, that's the charm of the Carlisle/Whitfield sisters. Women just can't seem to resist us."

Kade slowly raised both eyebrows, looking at Aiden over the rim of her glasses with a gaze that was more than skeptical. "Oh, I think I managed to resist you just fine, Aiden Carlisle."

* * *

"Auntie Aiden! Auntie Aiden!" Dawn's niece practically ran Kade over in her haste to get to Aiden.

"See?" Aiden smirked at Kade as she caught Jamie before she could fall. "What did I tell you about our effect on women?" She leaned down to Jamie. "What's wrong, sweetie?"

"I was playing outside, but my Frisbee got caught in a tree, and I can't get it down!" Jamie gestured wildly. "Can you come and get it down for me, Auntie Aiden?"

Aiden always enjoyed the casualness with which Jamie came to her for help. She loved the honorary aunt title Jamie had bestowed on her—that is until she caught sight of a small, silver-haired woman, who could only be Dawn's grandmother, staring at her.

Oh, shit! Dawn had wanted to tell her grandmother about her sexual orientation and new relationship in a quiet minute, after she had introduced her to Aiden. Now Jamie had inadvertently spilled the beans or at least made it necessary for Aiden to do some quick damage control.

Without looking away from Margot Kinsley, Aiden bent down and told Jamie, "Go ahead. I'll be there in a minute." When Jamie ran off, Aiden straightened and turned to face Dawn's grandmother.

"Hello," Margot Kinsley said with a curious smile. "My great-granddaughter called you 'auntie,' but I'm pretty sure I don't know you. Please tell me I'm not getting so senile that I forgot I have another granddaughter?"

The old woman was clearly kidding. Aiden saw Kade hide a smile behind her hand, but she was too tense to find it funny. She nervously fumbled with the good luck charm she wore on a chain around her neck.

Margot Kinsley's gray eyes widened. She took a step toward Aiden and reached out a trembling hand, almost touching the silver pendant. "Where did you get that?" she asked, her voice a little shrill.

Aiden automatically looked down and stared at Saint Michael, the patron saint of law enforcement. She remembered what Dawn had told her about the good luck charm. It was one of a kind. Dawn's grandmother had it made for her husband, who had been a cop too. Of course Margot Kinsley would recognize the pendant. *Oh, shit. How do I explain this?*

"I gave it to her for Christmas," Dawn's voice suddenly came from behind Aiden.

Aiden turned, very relieved to see her girlfriend.

Dawn was staring at her grandmother, the plates of food in her hands forgotten. "Aiden is with the Portland Police Bureau too," she said as if that would explain everything.

Her grandmother was still shaking her head in disbelief. "You gave away your grandfather's good luck charm? You know your father wanted to keep it in the family; that's why he gave it to you even though you're not a police officer."

Dawn set down the plates of food on the table before she could drop them. She stepped next to Aiden and laid her palm over the pendant in a gesture so tender and intimate that it made Aiden's cheeks flush. "That's why I gave it to Aiden, Grandma," Dawn said, her voice shaking with tension. "I want her to belong to the family."

Margot Kinsley sighed, then her lips formed an affectionate smile. "You're a good girl, Dawn, and you have your father's big heart. If it's important to you, then I'll consider your friend a part of the family, just as I do Del." She gave Aiden a friendly nod.

Is it really that easy? Aiden looked at Dawn. For a moment, she almost hoped Dawn would leave it at that. Dawn's grandmother would go back to her home in Spokane tomorrow, and Aiden didn't want to cause any trouble between them in the little time Dawn had with her grandmother.

"No. I mean yes, I want you to consider Aiden a part of the family, but not for the reason you think," Dawn said as Aiden had known she would. In matters of the heart, Dawn was so much more courageous than she was. "Aiden is not just any friend to me. She's my girlfriend."

Margot looked from Dawn to Aiden. "Of course she is," she said, clearly not understanding what Dawn was talking about.

"Not a friend who's a girl, Grandma," Dawn explained patiently. Aiden could see the nervousness in Dawn's expression, though. "My girlfriend. The woman I love."

Margot stared at Dawn's hand that still rested over the pendant on Aiden's upper chest. "Oh."

Aiden looked away and rubbed the back of her neck. She could feel the other guests beginning to look over at them. This scene was exactly what she had wanted to avoid.

"You mean... you're... like Del?" Margot asked still wide-eyed.

Like Del? Aiden hadn't expected her to put it that way. Then she remembered the warmth with which Margot had embraced Del, and hope began to burgeon. Margot Kinsley obviously knew about Del's sexual orientation but accepted her as a member of the family anyway.

Del wandered over. She casually wrapped one arm around Margot and the other around Dawn. "No, Mama Kinsley, she's not like me. She's much prettier, wouldn't you say? It runs in the family."

Aiden relaxed a little when Margot smiled and slapped Del's arm. "Flatterer. You know exactly what I mean. Is she...?"

Del said nothing. She knew it was Dawn's answer to give.

Dawn's fingers closed around the pendant as if for good luck. "Yes, Grandma. I'm gay."

"And you are...?" A gnarled finger pointed between Aiden and Dawn.

"We're a couple," Dawn confirmed, waiting nervously for her grandmother's reaction.

"Oh," Margot said again. She took a firmer hold on Del's arm. "I think I need to sit down."

Kade quickly dragged a chair over, and Del and Dawn helped the elderly woman into it.

Aiden watched helplessly. Her stomach felt queasy. She wasn't used to all this family drama.

Dawn crouched down next to the chair and gently reached for her grandmother's hand. "I didn't want to upset you, Grandma, but I also don't want to lie and hide who I am. I love Aiden, and I want to share my life with her."

Wow. Aiden had known that was what Dawn wanted, of course, but she had never heard her put it into one simple, yet overwhelming sentence.

Margot looked down at her granddaughter's slender hand she held in her lap. "I'm not upset. I just need a little time to... I need a little fresh air." She looked up, right into Aiden's startled eyes. "Would you be a dear and accompany me on a little walk around the neighborhood?"

Me? Aiden's mouth was too dry to answer.

"Grandma," Dawn protested.

"Oh, don't worry, child. I'm not gonna take her out behind the house and shoot her," Margot said resolutely. She stood and directed a questioning gaze at Aiden.

Someone, probably Kade, softly nudged her, and Aiden finally stepped forward. "Um... yes, of course." She offered the older woman her arm to hold on to and slowed her steps as they walked across the room. Her heart beat faster with every step as Aiden anticipated what Margot would say to her once they were alone. She hoped for her own sake—and for Dawn's—she would be able to make a good impression.

Jamie ran toward them as they left the house. Aiden suddenly remembered that the girl was waiting for her to fetch her Frisbee down from the tree. Maybe it was a way to avoid the awkward conversation with Margot for a while. *I'd rather climb a giant redwood than walk around the neighborhood with Dawn's grandmother.*

But Margot Kinsley had other plans for her. "I'm sorry, Jamie, but your old great-grandmother needs Aiden's help more than you do. Why don't you wait for us to come back or get one of the other young folk to help you?"

Jamie pouted but ran off, leaving Aiden alone with the Kinsley matriarch.

Aiden swallowed nervously.

Margot waited until they reached the sidewalk before she asked the first question. "When did you first meet Dawn?"

"Last September," Aiden answered. It had only been eight months, but Aiden couldn't even imagine going back to the life she had once led.

Margot had counted in her head too. "You were the detective working Dawn's case."

It was a statement, not a question, so Aiden had no choice but to nod. "One of them, yes." She could only hope that Margot wouldn't think her unprofessional.

But Margot's next question went in a completely different direction. "Do you think...?" She bit her lip and interrupted herself. "You're a lovely woman, and I don't want to insult you, but... do you think Dawn would have been attracted to you if she hadn't been raped?"

Oh, God! She told herself that Margot Kinsley's generation just hadn't heard a lot about homosexuality when she was growing up. *But why do I have to be the one to educate Dawn's grandmother about lesbianism?* "It doesn't work that way, Mrs. Kinsley," she said as patiently as possible. "You don't just become gay because you had a bad experience with a person of the opposite sex."

Margot seemed to think about it for a few seconds. "Are you saying you aren't the first woman my granddaughter has... been with?" Disbelief colored her words.

"I think that's something you should discuss with Dawn." Aiden didn't want Margot to think she was refusing to talk to her or had anything to hide, but she also didn't feel comfortable making Dawn's decisions for her. She knew Dawn wouldn't have liked it.

"So that's a yes," Margot Kinsley concluded. She patted Aiden's arm when she started to protest. "You don't have to answer that. I'll talk about it with Dawn later. I'm just a little surprised. I never thought Dawn could be..." She shook her head. "I could understand it with Del. Don't get me wrong, she's a sweetheart, and all these years after Jimmy's death, she's been like a daughter to me. But she's not very..."

Aiden cocked her head and watched Margot search for the right word.

"She's a little..."

"Butch?" Aiden suggested.

Margot nodded hesitantly. "I think that's what you young folks call it."

"Being gay is not about how you look. Some of us look like Del, some look like me, and others look like..." Aiden hesitated. She wanted to add Kade's name to the list but knew it was not her place to do it.

"Like Dawn," Margot surprisingly finished her sentence.

Aiden looked up and met Margot's gaze. What she saw in the gray eyes looked already close to acceptance. "Yes," she said quietly. She looked at Margot with amazement.

"I won't insult Dawn's intelligence, or my own, by asking if she's sure about this. She obviously is, or she wouldn't have given you this." Margot slowly lifted her hand and touched the pendant around Aiden's neck with one gnarled finger.

Aiden could see a lot of sad and happy memories flash across Margot's face, and she immediately felt guilty. She lifted her hands to the clasp, starting to open the necklace. "I'm sorry Dawn gave it away without asking your opinion first, and I can give it back if you want."

"No." Margot placed her hand over Aiden's. "Stop. Dawn wanted you to have it, so it's yours."

Grace came out of the house and joined them. "Is everything okay?" she asked, worriedly looking from her mother-in-law to Aiden.

"You could have told me a little sooner," Margot immediately accused her.

"I needed time to come to terms with it myself," Grace defended herself.

Margot intently stared at her. "And?" she asked. "Did you?"

Aiden wished herself far, far away, but at the same time, she wanted to hear Grace's answer. Grace hadn't been a big fan of her relationship with Dawn at the beginning, and Aiden wasn't sure how she felt about it now. Grace had acted supportive but never voiced an opinion about Aiden or her relationship with Dawn.

"If I'd had to pick a spouse for Dawn, it would have been one of her male colleagues," Grace spoke to her mother-in-law but looked at Aiden. "I didn't like Dawn being in a relationship with a cop or with a woman."

Aiden swallowed. She had sensed that, but now Grace had said it out loud for the first time.

"Both for the same reason," Grace continued pensively. "I want Dawn safe and happy. I knew sharing her life with a person who's a woman and works in a high-risk job could end up hurting Dawn."

"Yes, it could," Margot agreed. The worried frown added a few wrinkles to her face.

It already has, Aiden thought. Dawn had been raped just because of her sexual orientation. Thinking about it still made her stomach roil.

"But then I watched them together, and for the first time in years, Dawn seems happy," Grace continued. "In the last ten years, I can count the number of times when I've seen Dawn really happy, not just content, on one hand. First Jimmy died just a few months after Dawn's car accident, then Brian. She lived through an unhappy marriage and an ugly divorce. She struggled with coming to turns with her sexual orientation, and her first relationship with a woman was a disappointment to her, so she stayed alone and concentrated on her work. Then, just when she seemed to have found her stride, she was raped."

"I... I didn't know she was unhappy." Margot looked horrified and close to tears.

Aiden stood silently staring at Grace, not able to utter a single word. She had known about all the bad, sad, and disappointing things that had happened to Dawn in the last decade, but she had never thought of Dawn as an unhappy woman. Even right after the rape, Dawn's inner strength had always seemed unbroken.

Grace shook her head. "You know Dawn. She was pure sunshine from the day she was born. It's not that she was unhappy with her life. She just wasn't happy."

"But she's happy now?" Margot asked, hope in her voice and in her gray eyes.

Grace looked directly at Aiden, capturing her gaze while she answered. "She's happy, healthy, and in love. What more could a mother want for her child?"

To be a happy, healthy, straight woman in love with a man? Aiden's skeptical inner voice answered.

"Nothing," Margot answered. "It's exactly what I want for Dawn. But still, it's hard to wrap my mind around... this." She looked at Aiden almost apologetically.

"I know. For now, you don't have to understand it; you just have to accept it. Give yourself time," Grace told her mother-in-law what Del had told her a few years ago. "A year from now, you'll be at a point where you can't imagine Dawn with anyone else but Aiden."

Aiden was startled to feel Grace's arm slip around her, wrapping her in a supportive half embrace.

Margot sighed. "I promise to try."

That promise was enough for Aiden because she had expected a much worse reaction. She just hoped it would be enough for Dawn too.

Margot began to walk again. "Once more around the block?" she asked.

Uh. Aiden looked longingly back to the house. Not only did she want to escape this awkward situation, she also didn't want Dawn to worry if they didn't return to the house immediately. "Dawn—"

"Can have you back after we talk a little," Margot interrupted resolutely.

Grace laughed at the expression on Aiden's face. "Don't worry. She put me through the same interrogation when Jimmy brought me home to meet her for the first time."

It made Aiden feel better, if only a little.

"So tell me about your family," Margot began with what she probably thought was a harmless conversation starter. She couldn't know it was anything but harmless for Aiden.

Aiden opened her mouth for the "I don't have a family" answer she had gotten used to after her mother's death but stopped herself just in time. That answer didn't feel right anymore. Dawn was her family now. *And there's Evan,* she reminded herself. "My mother died almost two years ago, but I have a half sister." She said it out loud for the first time, and suddenly, it was almost overwhelming. There was someone who shared her blood and probably also shared the circumstances of her conception.

"What about your father?" Margot asked curiously. "He's not around?"

Aiden looked at Grace, but nothing in her face revealed if Dawn had told her about Aiden's father. Knowing Dawn, she probably hadn't. "I never knew him," she answered truthfully. She didn't want to lie, but she also didn't want to reveal the whole truth. Dawn's grandmother had enough to deal with for now.

"Grandma? Aiden?" Dawn's voice came from around the corner.

Aiden longed to turn around and run toward her, but she held herself back.

Margot studied her for a few seconds, then smiled. "Go before she thinks I hit you over the head with my cane and gagged you with my support stockings."

Aiden walked away with a smile.

CHAPTER 22

*D*EL LEANED BACK in her chair. After Margot had cornered Carlisle, her guests had finally diverted their attention away from Del. They were staring out of the window or talking to each other, speculating about what Margot might be saying to Carlisle. It gave Del the opportunity to focus on her favorite guest.

Kade had been standing next to Dawn, directing a few calming words toward her. Now that Dawn had gone to make sure her grandmother didn't torture Carlisle, Kade looked a little forlorn. Before Del could move in her direction, Kade started for the door to follow Dawn.

"Oh, no!" Del quickly blocked her way. "Not you too. I invited you to keep me company and celebrate my birthday with me, not to run around outside."

"It's a surprise party. You didn't invite me at all," Kade pointed out.

Del grinned. She loved Kade's annoyingly analytical mind. "All right. But I still want you to keep me company. If Carlisle needs more backup, she'll call for help." She pointed at the gift-wrapped, rectangular present that Kade had laid on the table when she arrived. "Is that for me?"

"Yes," Kade answered. Her raised eyebrows added a silent, "Stupid question."

"Will you give it to me?" Del asked with a smile.

Kade looked around the room. Most of the other guests were staring out of the windows, trying to find out what was going on with Carlisle and Dawn's grandmother. "I want to take the opportunity to thank you for everything you've done for me in the last few weeks," Kade said with an atypical emotional openness.

Del gently squeezed her hand. "Anytime." She looked deeply into Kade's eyes, trying to make her see how sincere that promise was. "Whatever you need."

Clearly uncomfortable, Kade broke their eye contact when she handed Del her gift.

Del carefully shook it and tested its weight in her hands. "A book?" she guessed.

Kade didn't confirm or deny it. "Open it and find out."

Del removed the wrapping paper. It was indeed a book. She turned it around to find out the title and author, half expecting a crime novel.

At first glance, it seemed to be. A yellow crime scene tape stretched across the bottom of the cover. But one glance at the name of the author told Del she was holding a lesbian romance novel in her hands. She looked at Kade in surprise.

"I hope you don't already have it. I didn't see it in your collection when Laurie and I stayed over at your apartment," Kade said, almost babbling in her nervousness.

Del smiled. *A nervous Kade Matheson... isn't that adorable?* "No, I don't have it, and I haven't read it. I always wanted to but never got around to it." Kade giving her that book meant a lot to her. Only two weeks before, Kade had known nothing about lesbian fiction. She had even mistaken one of Del's favorite romances for a book about chess. It was obvious that she had done some serious research in the field of lesbian fiction.

"I'm glad you like it," Kade said. She looked down at Del's hands holding the book.

"What's not to like? It's a story about a sexy butch cop seducing her hot, formerly straight colleague." Del flashed her a challenging grin, waiting to see if Kade would take the bait or ignore the remark.

Kade looked up. Her arctic blue gaze met Del. "It's fiction," she said sternly.

Del laughed and gave up. "Thanks for the book, Kade."

They were distracted when Carlisle, Dawn, and the two older Kinsley women came back inside. Dawn had her arm around Carlisle, stubbornly demonstrating her love and support.

"Everything okay?" Del asked when Dawn reached them.

"Yes, I think everything's fine. Sorry for making your birthday party a Kinsley family drama," Dawn said.

Del gently chucked her under the chin. "My birthdays would be boring without it. Do you remember when you fell into my cake face first when you were ten?" Sometimes it was still hard to believe that Dawn was a grown woman now and didn't need her protection anymore.

"How did you manage to do that?" Carlisle asked.

Dawn flushed and rubbed the eyebrow she had singed back then. "I think I fell over my own feet. Speaking of cake..." She pointed in the direction of the kitchen.

When Del turned, she saw Grace carrying a big birthday cake with a sea of burning candles over to her.

"Oh my!" Kade laughed. "Tell me, Del, how many candles are on this cake?"

Del chuckled ruefully. "A lot more than on yours, I'm afraid." She didn't need to count to know that Kade would only have two thirds of the candles on her birthday.

"You're not feeling insecure, are you?" Kade teased.

"Nope." Del watched Grace place the cake on the table in front of her. "Not insecure. Just old." She looked at Grace. "Did you have to put all the candles on the cake? A few symbolic ones would have been enough."

Grace gently pinched her. "Don't complain. I'm older than you. Now shut up and blow out the candles before they burn the house down!"

"Yes, ma'am!" Del bent down and took a deep breath. She felt a gentle hand in her hair, keeping it from getting too close to the burning candles. To her surprise, she realized that the hand belonged not to Grace or Dawn, but to Kade. She quickly blew out the candles before Kade could notice what she had done without thinking.

Her guests clapped and hollered.

"Del!" Grace shouted over the chaos. She reached over the table and handed Del the cordless phone. "Your brother is on the phone for you."

Del shook her head. Her brothers hadn't called her for over twenty-five years. *Must be one of the clowns from the station.* She took the phone and walked away from her noisy guests.

* * *

Evan leaned against the tree in the Kinsleys' yard, hiding in its shadows. This way she could watch without being watched. Totally bored with the party inside, she had come out here to have a smoke. *I shouldn't have let that damn shrink talk me into coming to this lame-ass party.*

She regretted it now. Being at the party made her feel like growing up in the foster system had always made her feel. She was on the outside looking in, not really part of the group.

Not that I'd want to be, she quickly told herself. *It has been hard enough to avoid Laurie all evening.*

She watched as the front door opened. The doc's grandmother stepped out, her steps resolute despite her cane. A more hesitant Aiden Carlisle followed. Evan couldn't hear their conversation, but Aiden looked clearly uncomfortable. *The old lady is interrogating her!* Evan realized. *And the cop doesn't like a taste of her own medicine.*

As she watched Aiden uncomfortably follow the old woman down the street, Evan thought back to what Dr. Kinsley had told her. It seemed the doc had been right about her girlfriend. *So the big, bad cop can really be afraid, huh?* She took another drag on her cigarette.

"Hey." The sudden voice right next to her almost made Evan drop the cigarette.

Laurie Matheson had walked up to her, her blue eyes and the pale skin almost glowing in the near darkness beneath the tree. "What are you doing out here?" Laurie asked.

Hiding. Dying of boredom. "Smoking," Evan answered. She casually flicked the ash off the tip of her cigarette. She didn't say anything else, not knowing what to say to Laurie. The last time they had seen each other had ended in a disaster, and the last time they talked to each other on the phone, Laurie had ended up in tears.

"Oh." Laurie stepped closer and leaned next to her against the tree. "Can I have one?"

Miss Goody Two-shoes wants to smoke with me? That was a surprise. Evan wasn't sure if it was a pleasant surprise. For some reason, she didn't like the thought of Laurie smoking.

"This is a cigarette, isn't it?" Laurie asked when Evan didn't answer or offer her a cigarette from her pack. "It's not a joint, right?"

Nope. Those are in my other pocket. Evan had thought about it, but with the house full of cops, she didn't want to risk it. One of them was sure to notice something, and then all hell would break loose. "It's a regular cigarette, but I don't think your aunt would like it if I gave you one anyway," she finally answered.

"Just like your sister wouldn't like it if she saw you smoking," Laurie answered with an uncharacteristic boldness.

"I don't care what my sister likes or doesn't like." Evan growled at her. She didn't care if Aiden caught her smoking. If Aiden got angry and lost her temper with her, it would only prove she wasn't the perfect sister she pretended to be. "How do you even know she's my sister?"

Laurie shrugged. She looked at Evan from under blond lashes. "I eavesdropped on my aunt," she admitted, flushing a bright pink.

Laurie stepped even closer, making Evan decidedly uncomfortable. She had nothing against being physically close to a pretty girl, but it had to be her choice, not the girl's attempt to have an intimate conversation. "So Detective Carlisle really is your sister?" Laurie asked.

Evan shrugged. "I suppose."

"Wow! That's so cool!" Laurie enthused.

"No, it's not!" It wasn't cool at all. Maybe if it had been the cute little doc, but Aiden Carlisle was just a pain in the ass.

"Hello?" a small voice called. "Is someone out there?"

Evan rolled her eyes as she realized the doc's niece had followed Laurie. *Speaking of pain in the ass.* She quickly put out her cigarette and threw it away.

"Hey, Jamie. We're under the tree." Laurie stepped out from their hiding place and waved the girl over.

Great. There goes my peace and quiet. Evan watched in resignation as the ten-year-old sidled up to them. "Why don't you go back inside?" she asked, and when she realized it sounded a little harsh, she added more friendly, "I hear there's cake."

"But it's so boring inside with all the adults," the girl complained.

Yeah, welcome to the club. Evan smirked.

"You can keep us company," Laurie offered.

Evan groaned. *How did I end up babysitting with Miss Goody Two-shoes? Next time, I'll go for a bad girl.*

"Can you help me get my Frisbee down from the tree?" Jamie asked, pointing up into the tangle of branches and twigs.

Evan had no intention of getting her leather jacket all scratched up. She looked down, about to tell the girl no.

"Auntie Aiden said she would help me, but now she's walking with my great-grandmother and said I have to wait," Jamie reported with a sad pout.

"We don't need the great Auntie Aiden to get the Frisbee down from this stupid tree," Evan impulsively decided.

Jamie looked up at her in awe. "Are you going to get it down for me?"

Evan straightened. "Of course. No problem."

"Oh, thank you!" Jamie hugged her around the waist.

Evan felt her cheeks burn, and she stepped back with a growl. "Don't get overexcited, kid. It's not down yet." Still, the fact that the kid never doubted even for a second that she could get the Frisbee down felt strangely good.

Now I only have to get the damn thing down. Evan looked up into the tree. A small, pink piece of something peeked out from between two branches higher up in the tree. Getting to that point looked impossible, though, because the branches only began higher up. The tree trunk down here was smooth, without branches or other handholds.

"I could help you," Laurie said.

Evan wanted to decline. She wanted to do this on her own, and she didn't want Laurie to get hurt, but she realized it would be impossible to get the Frisbee down on her own.

"Do you think you could lift me up?" Laurie asked.

In comparison to her, Laurie was small and slender. "Sure," Evan said with more confidence than she felt. "If you're not afraid of heights."

"Oh, no, don't worry," Laurie said quickly. "I'm a cheerleader. I've climbed on people before."

Evan grinned and wiggled her eyebrows, enjoying Laurie's blush. When Laurie had recovered, Evan shrugged out of her leather jacket and handed it to Laurie. "Here. Put it on," she said with a sigh. The tree's twigs and foliage were very dense, and she didn't want Laurie to get all scratched up. She grimaced when she thought about the damage the twigs might do to her jacket. *Better the jacket than Laurie's skin. At least the jacket doesn't have an aunt who could sue me for bodily harm.*

She held back a grin as she saw the smaller girl in her heavy leather jacket.

"You're letting me wear your jacket—does that mean we're going steady?" Laurie asked with a grin that reminded Evan of Laurie's more confident, but equally sexy aunt.

"It means I don't want to get in trouble again because you got hurt," Evan grumbled. She leaned against the back of the tree and folded her hands, forming a makeshift step for Laurie. She heaved Laurie up and suppressed a groan as her muscles protested. She grimaced when Laurie climbed onto her shoulders, leaving earthy footprints behind on her shirt. Laurie's weight was heavier than expected, and just when she thought she couldn't hold on any longer, the Frisbee dropped down into the grass next to her.

Laurie slid down Evan's body, landing in the circle of her arms.

Evan had promised herself she would stay away from Laurie Matheson and her family. She had told herself Laurie wasn't worth getting into trouble again. But now the cute blonde was looking up at her from mere inches away. Evan suddenly leaned forward and captured Laurie's lips with her own.

Only Jamie's happy dance around the recovered Frisbee made her remember they were not alone. *Shit! The kid! She's going to freak out and run inside to tell her parents.* She gently disentangled herself from a breathless Laurie and stared down at Jamie.

The ten-year-old didn't appear freaked out at all. She was grinning and triumphantly waving the Frisbee. "Thank you!" she said again, hugging both Laurie and Evan.

That's right. She's the doc's niece. She must be used to seeing her and Aiden kiss. Evan shook herself at the thought of watching her half sister and her former therapist kiss.

"Jamie?" A tall brunette stepped outside the house.

"Mama, look! Evan and Laurie got my Frisbee down from the tree!" Jamie held out the Frisbee for her mother to see.

The brunette stepped under the tree. If she smelled the smoke on Evan's clothes, she didn't comment. "That was nice of you. Thank you."

Evan didn't want to like the doc's and Aiden's family, but she had to admit that all of them had treated her with respect, not as if she was only Aiden's dumb kid sister. "It's okay," she answered gruffly.

"Jamie, you have to come inside and say good-bye now. We have to go," the brunette told her daughter.

"But I want to wait until Auntie Aiden comes back!" Jamie whined.

She's totally crazy about Aiden. And so is Laurie. What's so special about her? Evan wondered. All she had seen was a strict cop and a woman who tried to assuage her guilty conscience by acting like a caring sister.

"She's already back inside," Jamie's mom said. "Now come and say good-bye."

Evan watched them go. She didn't want to turn and look at Laurie.

"I'm sorry," Laurie said suddenly. Evan could hear her sniffle. "I'm so sorry about getting you in trouble. I should have told you sooner, and I came out here to tell you—"

Evan finally turned around. "Stop crying," she ordered. Tears didn't change what had happened.

"I was so stupid," Laurie said, still crying. "I really thought my parents would just calm down and tell the police it was all a misunderstanding. I thought it would all just go away."

Evan just looked at her, stunned by that naivety. Laurie's naïve optimism had been one of the first things she had noticed about her—and for some reason, it had been one of the things she liked about her. Maybe because it meant Laurie never assumed bad things about anyone, not even Evan.

"I didn't know you had to spend the night in jail or that the arrest would appear on your record, even after they finally believed you were innocent." Laurie wiped red-rimmed eyes. "I could talk to my aunt. Maybe she can get your arrest record expunged."

"Don't bother," Evan told her, trying not to feel sorry for the sniffling girl. "It's not the only arrest on my record, so what's one more?"

Laurie finally stopped crying and stared at her. "B-but... don't you care that your employers will be able to find out you were suspected of... rape when you try to get a job? My aunt says that this is what could happen."

"Of course I care!" Evan suddenly found herself yelling. "Do you think I want people to think I'm a rapist?"

Startled, Laurie began to cry again. "I didn't want that to happen."

Evan sighed. "Would you just stop crying? It's done, and tears won't change it."

"But maybe I can help to make it right. I could talk to your foster parents and tell them what really happened and that you're not to blame for anything," Laurie offered.

That was a courageous offer from the girl who had been so afraid to tell her own parents. "You don't have to do that," Evan told her. "The doc and Aiden already talked to them. They're not too pleased about me being a lesbian on top of everything else, but at least they didn't kick me out."

Laurie's hand shyly slipped into her own. "I'm sorry," she said again.

Evan sighed but didn't ward off the contact. She didn't like girls that were the clinging sort and thought one night was a promise of forever, but she also didn't want to see Laurie cry again. For now, she would tolerate Laurie's displays of affection.

They were both silent for a while.

"Will you come inside with me?" Laurie asked, her voice almost a whisper. "Del said there'd be dancing later."

Del, huh? Seems like Laurie is already a part of the family. "I don't dance. At least not to what they call music." She didn't know how to dance, but Laurie didn't need to know that. Evan didn't want to appear stupid in front of Laurie.

"Then come inside with me anyway. The food is good," Laurie tried again.

Evan sighed. She knew she couldn't hide out here all night. At some point, the doc would come looking for her—or worse, she would send Aiden. "All right. But only for the free food."

* * *

Kade leaned back and took a sip of wine. She had nursed the same glass for the last hour. She often felt a little out of control around Del, and she didn't want to add to that feeling by drinking too much.

She watched Aiden and Dawn slowly move across the improvised dance floor, their arms around each other and their bodies softly touching all along their lengths.

Dawn was not a good dancer. Her slightly awkward movements wouldn't have held up to the polished Matheson standards, and Kade had seen Aiden dance much more spectacularly with other dance partners at the annual police ball. Despite that, Aiden and Dawn looked perfect together.

Even Dawn's elderly grandmother, who had been shocked to see her granddaughter in the arms of a woman at first, had commented on how good they looked together. Kade could only wish her own family were so open-minded.

The thought made her gaze wander over to Del, who was twirling Grace around on the dance floor. Grace wasn't a better dancer than her daughter, but together they made as nice a couple as Dawn and Aiden did.

Finally, a breathless Grace escaped back to the table, and Del wandered over to Kade. She bowed with a grin and held out her hand. "May I have this dance, please?"

Kade hesitated. She had danced with women before, but they had been her cousins or female friends when there weren't any male dance partners around, nothing that could compare to this situation.

"Come on." Del nudged her. "I'll even let you lead."

Now that's a helpful comment. Instead of encouraging Kade, it only reminded her that she would be dancing with a woman. *With Del.*

"As my guest, it's your solemn duty to fulfill my birthday wish," Del told her. "And this," she pointed at Kade, then at the dance floor, "is what I wished for when I blew out the candles."

"You're not supposed to say your wish out loud, or it won't come true," Kade objected.

Del just smiled. "If I didn't say it out loud, how would you know what to do to make my wish come true?"

Kade had to admit it was a sound argument. Reluctantly, she laid her hand in Del's and let herself be led to the dance floor. They struggled for a few awkward moments about who would lead, but then Del relinquished control and followed Kade's steps across the dance floor.

Kade was glad her mother had insisted on drilling dance steps into her until she could do it in her sleep. She was too preoccupied with wondering how they appeared to the onlookers to think about what her feet were doing. Del's arms around her, her body so close Kade could feel the heat, and Del's unmistakable and slightly musky scent were distracting to say the least.

"Relax," Del said. "This is supposed to be fun."

Fun. Oh, yeah. Kade bit her lip. "Sorry."

"No need to apologize. You're a great dancer."

Kade was used to smooth compliments like this, but she could see Del meant it. "Still you seemed to have more fun with Grace." Kade couldn't help noticing.

Del studied her. "You're not jealous, are you?" One corner of her mouth curled into a delighted smile.

"Of course not!" Admitting feelings of jealousy would mean admitting she had romantic feelings toward Del, and Kade wasn't ready to face that. But she also couldn't completely forget about it. "It's just... Well, you looked very... comfortable together."

Del nodded. "Of course we're comfortable with each other. Grace is my best friend, Kade. You're comfortable with your best friend too, aren't you?"

Kade thought about it for a moment. She had never danced or joked around with anybody like that. "I don't think I have a best friend." She had never thought her life lacking because of it, but now she did.

"What about Carlisle?" Del asked.

"Why do you always have to call her 'Carlisle'?" Kade asked in exasperation. Aiden wasn't really her best friend, but of all her acquaintances and colleagues, she came closest. Kade wouldn't tolerate Del's strange attitude toward Aiden any longer.

Del shrugged. "It's what we cops do."

It was more than that. "You don't call me Matheson," Kade said.

"It's not the same thing," Del protested.

Kade twirled her around. "Does Aiden call you 'Vasquez'?"

Del thought about it. "Mostly she avoids addressing me directly, so she doesn't call me anything."

"Aiden is Dawn's life partner and a part of your self-proclaimed family, and yet the two of you seem to avoid each other. Why is that?" Kade asked.

"It's not that I don't like her," Del said reluctantly. "I like her better than I ever liked Dawn's ex-girlfriend or her ex-husband. Maybe that's part of the problem." Del looked as if she had just realized it for the first time. "Cal and Maggie never were worthy partners for Dawn. They never took over my role in Dawn's life."

Kade nodded. "But Aiden does."

"It's like a strange role reversal. She's Dawn's protector and confidant now, and I'm the one who's interested in you," Del answered in her usual open, direct way that always left Kade speechless.

"It must be a little awkward for you," Kade agreed after a few moments of breathless silence.

Del gently tightened her hold on Kade's shoulder. "Sometimes I think we're a little too much alike—and I hope you're not just interested in me because I remind you of her."

Kade stopped dancing. She stood staring at Del in the middle of the dance floor. She decided to ignore Del's matter-of-fact assumption that she was interested in her and concentrated on the other aspect of her comment. "You don't remind me of Aiden," she said resolutely.

"Oh, come on, Kade! Two take-charge, tall lesbian cops with dark hair and dark eyes, both more than a little smitten with you—don't tell me you can't see the similarities!" Del's expression held equal parts amusement and exasperation.

"Yes, you and Aiden have some things in common, and I started to trust you because of that," Kade said. "But the better I got to know you, the more I realized how many differences there are, and now I respect you for your own sake."

Del tilted her head and grinned down at her. "So tell me: what are the differences you like about me?"

"You're more... solid," Kade said for lack of a better word.

"Solid?" Del seemed to taste the word in her mouth. "Now that sounds sexy!"

Kade shrugged. "You don't have Aiden's troubled edge. You're more relaxed and self-assured. You always seem to be so at peace, so content with yourself and your life."

"I am content with my life," Del agreed, but then corrected, "Well, I could use someone to share it with. I'm working on that." She smiled at Kade.

Kade quickly began to dance again, interrupting their eye contact. She knew Del would take it as a sign to back off for the moment.

"So, now that we discussed me and Aiden," Del said, emphasizing her use of Aiden's first name, "let's talk about you and Grace."

"There's no problem between me and Grace. I like her," Kade said, and she was telling the truth. It was impossible not to like Dawn's friendly mother. She was warm, genuine, and kind—the exact opposite of Kade's own mother.

Del grinned. "So you're not jealous?"

"No!"

"Good, because you have no reason to be," Del said calmly.

Kade still wasn't fully convinced of that. Del had practically taken over the role of Grace's husband for the last ten years. Grace and Del had shared everything but their beds and their bodies. "Because she's straight?" she asked skeptically. "That's what I told you about me, and it hasn't exactly diminished your interest."

Del chuckled. "Right, it hasn't," she admitted freely. "But only because I'm convinced you're not as straight as you made yourself believe all those years. You know, there are not only perfect zeros and perfect sixes on the Kinsey scale. I'm pretty much a six, and I'd say Grace is a one. You, on the other hand, would fall more toward the middle of the scale if we leave out social and professional implications."

"The middle?" Kade repeated with raised eyebrows. "I'm a Matheson. I'm not allowed to be average in anything. We don't do middle ground." During the last few weeks, she had come to realize that Del was probably right about her, but for now, it was easier to joke about it.

"Oh, so your family would rather have you be a perfect six?" Del asked with a smile.

No, that's one perfect attribute they'd never want me to have. "Anything other than a zero is not acceptable for a Matheson," she answered.

"Even if it means ignoring a part of yourself?" Del asked, keeping her voice carefully neutral. Kade recognized it as her "I'm helping you figure it out" tone.

"Ignoring a part of ourselves is a Matheson legacy," Kade said dryly. "My mother ignored my father's affairs, my father ignored his own son, and my brother ignores his daughter's sexual orientation."

Del looked her right in the eyes, the intense gaze almost like a physical touch. "And what are you ignoring, Kade?"

That a potentially dangerous man is stalking me. That it's just a matter of time until my mother hears about what is going on in my life. That I like dancing with you way too much. "That you tried to take over leading for the third time right now," Kade said with a smile that was only a little forced. She knew Del would accept the answer even though she knew there was more to it. It was one of the things she liked about Del. Del was one of very few people in her life who didn't pressure her to do what they wanted her to do.

"Well, maybe I don't like where you're leading us," Del answered playfully.

Despite the teasing words, Kade could sense a silent question lingering between them. *Where are we going with this?* "You don't?" she asked, reminding herself to breathe while she waited for the answer.

"Actually... I do." Del grinned down at her from the two-inch height advantage she had despite Kade's high heels. "It's a slow waltz, but I can live with that."

"Well, you'll have to because I'm not ready to foxtrot," Kade said seriously.

Del didn't stop smiling. "Waltzing is fine with me."

* * *

"Oh, no, Delicia Vasquez!" Grace took a pile of dirty dishes from Del's hands. "It's your birthday, and you're not helping in the kitchen today."

"I always help with the dishes," Del said. "I don't mind."

Grace shook her head. "Nope. You sit here and keep us company. Kade is gonna help me, right, Kade?"

Kade set down the tray of empty glasses. "Right." *At least Del is not leaving me alone to be interrogated by Grace Kinsley.*

Grace picked up one of the dishtowels and leaned against the counter while she waited for Kade to wash the first dishes. "You're a little quiet," she said to Del. "Everything all right?"

"Well, I'm another year older now, as a friend of mine so helpfully pointed out with her horde of candles. Guess I get tired more easily," Del answered with a smile.

Kade turned away from the sink to glance at Del. Now that Grace had pointed it out, she realized Del had indeed been unusually quiet for the last few hours.

"You're forty-three, Del, not ninety-three," Grace answered while she took the first washed glass from Kade's hands.

Forty-three, huh? Kade smiled to herself. Del's secret was finally out. *Maybe the age difference should upset me, but somehow, it's the least of my concerns.*

"Thank you so much for pointing it out to Kade," Del grumbled.

Grace didn't answer with the expected joke. "That call you got... that wasn't really your brother, was it?"

Kade stopped all movement when Del didn't answer immediately. "Yes," Del said after a few tense moments, "it was."

Kade turned around. "I thought you said you hadn't talked to any member of your family for the last twenty-five years? And now your brother calls out of the blue to congratulate you on your birthday?" It didn't make sense to Kade's logical mind. There had been twenty-five birthdays without any calls, so why call now?

- 337 -

"He didn't call because of my birthday," Del said. Her words were slow and her body stiff. "He called to tell me our father is dying."

The dishcloth sank to the bottom of the sink as Kade's nerveless hands let go of it. "Del." She wanted to rush to Del, to touch her in a reassuring way, but she was elbow-deep in soapy water and Grace was watching them. "I'm so sorry."

"He wants to see me before he dies, but I'm not sure I want to see him." Del's face was a stony mask.

Kade remembered clearly what Del had told her about her parents. Del's father had beaten her and thrown her out of his house when he realized his daughter was gay. He had never contacted her again. He had acted as if she was dead to him, and now that he was dying, Kade could understand why Del wasn't rushing to his sickbed.

Kade wasn't sure what to say. She didn't know how to make this easier for Del. She looked at Grace, Del's oldest friend, hoping she would know what to do and what to say.

But Grace just handed her the dishtowel and remained silent.

She's letting me handle this, Kade realized. *She's handing over the responsibility for Del's emotional well-being.* She quickly dried her hands and sat down next to Del while Grace took the place on Del's other side in silent support. "Will you go see him?" Kade asked quietly.

Del looked down at the table. "I'm not sure. Would you?"

Would I? It was a question Kade had asked herself for years. "My father never asked for me."

Del's gaze flew up, meeting Kade's with sudden realization. "Your father and you... you were estranged when he died?"

Kade had never liked talking about family issues with non-family members. Actually, she had never liked talking about it with anyone. Now she was determined to do it anyway if it could help Del make a decision in this situation. "My father was a proud and stubborn man," she began.

"Like father like daughter, huh?" Del said it without accusation or judgment.

Kade smiled ruefully. "It's a family trait," she said. "He was a politician and a senior partner in an influential law firm."

"Matheson, Sutherland, & Bryce, right?" Del had already connected the dots.

"It's just Sutherland & Bryce now," Kade said without regret.

Del studied her. "Your father wanted you to join his firm." It wasn't hard to guess.

"He had ambitious plans for his only daughter. Joining the firm, marrying the son of one of his partners, and following him into politics one day." Somehow it all seemed so far away as if she were talking about somebody else's life. Still, the pain belonged to her.

"You're an ambitious woman too. I take it you didn't share the same ambitions?" Del asked.

That was putting it mildly. "Some of our dreams weren't all that different. I can see myself going into politics or taking over the DA's seat one day too."

"There are easier and faster ways to achieve that than being an underpaid, underappreciated Deputy DA," Del said, again without judgment. Kade understood she was just playing devil's advocate.

"That's what my father said too. We never saw eye to eye on the path to that goal. I didn't want to tread the beaten tracks," Kade admitted for the first time. "I wanted to go my own way. I was passionate about the law, not about the paycheck or defending clients who might or might not be innocent. My father didn't care about my reasons." After Doug had chosen to go into medicine instead of law, their father had put all his hopes in Kade. He wanted her to follow in his footsteps and fulfill his every expectation. "When I took a job with the DA's office, we had a huge fight. A year went by without us talking, but before we could reconcile, my father died of a heart attack."

"You think I should go and see my father before it's too late," Del assumed.

Kade shook her head. "That's not what I'm saying. I just don't want you to have the same regrets I do."

Del sighed. "I'll think about it."

Kade hesitantly reached out and, very aware of Grace's gaze resting on her, quickly laid a hand on Del's shoulder. "Let me know if I can help in any way, okay?" It felt good to extend the same offer of support Del had always given her.

Del laid her hand on top of Kade's. "Thanks. I will," she said without hesitation.

CHAPTER 23

AIDEN LOOKED UP when Ray set a paper cup of aromatic coffee down on her desk. After drinking squad room sludge all day, this was a real treat. "Thanks, Ray." She reached for the coffee with her left hand while she continued to thumb through a file.

"Did I miss a memo?" Ray asked, pointing at the mountains of files on her desk. "Is there a new case I'm not aware of?"

"It's Kade's case," Aiden said in a low voice. It was late, and most of their colleagues had already left for the day, but she still wanted to be careful.

Ray sat down across from her. "So what's this?" he asked, gesturing with his paper cup in the direction of the files.

"I went through the cases that Kade was working on or had just signed off on when the flower deliveries began." She nodded down at the stacks of files on her desk. "Chances are that whoever is stalking her has a connection to one of Kade's cases from that time." At least they were hoping for a connection because if he was just a crazy stalker who had randomly picked Kade for his next victim, they would never find him.

"And?" Ray leaned forward in anticipation. "Did you find anything?"

Aiden swallowed a mouthful of still too hot coffee. "Three of them roughly match the description of the man the doorwoman saw lurking outside Kade's apartment building." She took a smaller stack of files and handed them to Ray.

"Three?" Ray fanned out the files. "There are four files in this pile." He flipped open the file on top and began to read. "Gary Ballard?"

Aiden knew she didn't need to remind him Ballard was the man who had raped Dawn. "Yeah."

"You think he has something to do with Kade being stalked?" Ray didn't bother to hide his skepticism.

"I know it looks like I'm overreacting because of Dawn, but it's a possibility we should check out. Ballard's case ended right before the stalking began," Aiden said. She had hesitated to add Ballard to the list of suspects because she knew it made her look unprofessional and too emotionally involved. In the end, she had decided to risk that rather than risk overlooking the possibility and endangering Kade.

"Yeah, but the case ended with a conviction—which means Ballard is in prison now," Ray said.

"That doesn't mean anything. He could have hired someone. Men like him always have enough friends, paid lackeys, or sick admirers to do the dirty work for them. Remember how Kade provoked him during the trial?" Kade had tried to provoke him by questioning his masculinity because they knew he would lose control if they hit him in his weak spot. More than once, it had looked as if he wanted to attack Kade right there in the courtroom, but he had kept himself in check until the very end when they had dragged him from the room and he had shouted threats and obscenities. "Maybe he wants revenge. And if he found out Kade is not as straight as we all thought..."

Their gazes met in alarm.

"If Ballard is behind all this, it would explain why he had Lieutenant Vasquez attacked. He has a history of feeling threatened by lesbians," Ray said. "Now that the attack failed, Kade might be in real danger."

And not only Kade, Aiden realized. *What if he wants revenge not only against the prosecutor but also against the women who testified against him? Dawn's testimony was what put him behind bars.* The sudden urge to call Dawn, to race home and make sure she was all right almost overwhelmed Aiden. A lot of thoughts shot through her head. *What if the trashing of Dawn's car back in January was not a coincidence? What if Ballard was behind that too?*

"Hey, you all right?" Ray frowned. "You look a little pale all of a sudden."

"I just realized that Dawn might be in danger too." Aiden's voice was a whisper as if saying it aloud would make it true.

"And you," Ray added seriously.

She almost wished Ballard or his lackey would go for her. "I'm not worried about me. I'm a big girl with a big gun." She grinned at Ray.

"So is Lieutenant Vasquez," he warned. "It didn't do her any good when she was surprised from behind."

Aiden pointed her pen at him. "Yeah, but she didn't have you to watch her back. Are you up for paying Ballard a little visit tomorrow?"

"Uh... um, yes, of course. Meet you at the precinct?" Ray asked casually, but Aiden had noticed his hesitation.

"You have plans," she said, making it a statement, not a question.

Ray looked almost embarrassed. "It's just that I promised Susan an uninterrupted weekend just for the two of us. No kids, no work. She thinks we need it."

"Hey, you don't need to apologize for having a private life." Now that she had Dawn, she could understand the need for time off better than she ever had.

"I'm not apologizing. I just don't want you to go alone. I'll come with you." Ray's decision sounded final.

Aiden rubbed the back of her neck. "You know what? I'll ask the third member of our lesbian case squad. I'm sure Del would love to go visit that bastard with me."

Ray frowned. "Is that a good idea?"

"Both of us have worked cases without male supervision before, Ray," she said, even knowing it was not what Ray meant.

"You're both close to one of Ballard's victims." There was a warning tone in Ray's voice.

Aiden raised an eyebrow at him. "Are you afraid we'll run amok and kill him in his cell without you there to hold us back?"

"Are you sure how you'll react when you're alone with the man who raped the woman you love?"

Ray's quiet question robbed Aiden of breath. She hadn't allowed herself to think about it that way. "No," she answered. "I don't know how I'll react. But I'm not gonna do something stupid."

Ray looked at her, his eyes probing into hers. After a few seconds, he nodded. "Will you tell Dawn that you're going to visit Ballard?"

Aiden groaned. She hadn't thought about that. "I don't know." On one hand, she didn't want to bring back painful memories now that Dawn had finally found some peace, but on the other hand, she didn't want to hide the truth from Dawn. If there was even the remote possibility that Dawn might be in danger, she had to warn her. Aiden knew she had a lot to think about on her drive home.

* * *

"Who would have thought," Dawn said, leaning back in her chair, "Del Vasquez lying on a shrink's couch—of her own free will."

Del stretched out on the couch in Dawn's office, reminding Dawn of a lithe panther. "I hope you're not expecting me to pay you for your advice."

"No. I'm talking to you as a friend." Dawn didn't answer with a joke. Making this distinction clear was always a very serious thing for her.

"So what is your friendly advice?" Del asked. "Should I go and see my father or abandon him like he abandoned me?"

Dawn sighed. "I'm afraid I can't give you objective advice about this. I know that I'd give anything to be able to talk to my father again just one more time."

"It's not the same thing. Your dad was wonderful; mine was an asshole," Del summarized it in ever-efficient cop style. Then her gaze softened, and she asked, "If you could, what would you like to tell your dad?"

Dawn looked at the photo of her father that hung on the wall opposite her desk. "I'd love to introduce him to Aiden, and I'd..." She breathed deeply. "Sometimes, I wonder what he'd say to some aspects of my life."

"What aspects?"

"Well, the gay aspects, mainly," Dawn said. She had only discovered that part of herself after her father had died, and she had often wondered if he would have accepted her. She knew her dad had grown up with a very strict father, and in many regards, he had been a typical cop. She wasn't sure about his attitude toward homosexuality. "How did he react when you told him you're gay?" she asked Del. She realized that they had never talked about it before.

Del put her arms behind her head and stared at the ceiling with a feint grin on her lips. "Well... I didn't exactly tell him."

"You were in the closet? You?" Dawn asked in surprise. She couldn't imagine the out and proud Del being anything but up-front about her sexual orientation.

"It was another time," Del said. "Twenty years ago, the force was still the good old boys club. As a female rookie, it was hard enough to get any respect without outing myself."

Dawn could understand that. Being a newbie and being a woman had been enough of an obstacle, so Del had preferred not to be out at the job. "So how did Dad learn about it if you didn't tell him?" she asked, suddenly curious.

"My first week in training with your dad, we had to interview a witness—who turned out to be a woman I'd had a short fling with." Del grimaced as she remembered. "When she saw me in my uniform, she told anyone within hearing distance in graphic detail what she'd like me to do to her with my handcuffs and my nightstick."

Dawn couldn't help it. She had to laugh.

"I hope you don't do that when your paying patients tell you about the dramatic moments of their lives," Del complained, pretending to pout.

"Sorry," Dawn said, finally calming down. "I take it Dad heard what she had to say?"

Del nodded grimly. "He and half the department."

"How did he react?" Dawn didn't laugh now. Del's answer was too important for that.

Del sat up to look at the photo of her mentor and friend. "He turned around and with the most deadpan expression said: 'If only all our witnesses were that eager to help out Portland's finest.'"

Dawn's eyes widened. She hadn't expected her father to react so casually to the sudden revelation about his partner's sex life. "He really said that?"

"Yep. Not everyone else reacted with such nonchalance, though. I later found out that your dad had some run-ins with a few jerks who had something against 'dykes in uniform.' He always had my back, and finding out I'm gay didn't change that." She smiled at Dawn. "Jim would have been fine with you being gay. I wish my father could be more like him." Del sighed, and the cloud of depression settled back over her.

"Maybe he changed," Dawn said softly. "Maybe he wants to apologize, and that's why he wants to see you."

"Maybe," Del said. She didn't sound as if she believed it. She stood and reached for her jacket. "Come on. I kept you long enough. Let's get out of here."

Janet and Mrs. Phillips were already gone, so they were the last ones to leave the office and walk across the dark parking lot. Dawn jerked in fearful surprise when she saw a shadowy figure leaning against her car. Only Del's presence kept her calm.

Del's cop instincts took over. She shoved Dawn behind her own body. "Hey!" she shouted to the stranger lurking in the parking lot.

The person quickly stepped into the light of the only street lamp.

"Aiden!" Anger, relief, and delight at seeing her lover warred within Dawn. When the emotional chaos within her quieted, she stepped next to Aiden and kissed her hello. "What are you doing here? I thought we said we'd meet at my place?" Not that she was complaining. She enjoyed every extra minute with Aiden.

Aiden shrugged. "I was in the neighborhood and saw your car still in the parking lot."

Dawn narrowed her eyes. It had taken her a while, but by now she could read between the lines and fluently translate what Aiden didn't say. "Being in the neighborhood" usually meant Aiden had been her usual overprotective self and had worried about her being alone at the office late at night. Dawn found it sweet and annoying all at the same time.

"See you later." Now that her other protector had arrived, Del started to walk away.

"Lieutenant... Del!" Aiden's shout quickly stopped her. "Do you have plans for tomorrow?"

Dawn couldn't believe it. Aiden wanted to do something with Del on her day off. Dawn wanted to hug and kiss Aiden, but she knew it would only make Aiden self-conscious about her offer to spend time with Del, so she acted nonchalantly and waited for Del's answer.

"No, not yet," Del answered slowly, almost carefully. "You have something in mind?"

Aiden's gaze flitted toward Dawn. She hesitated.

Del's stance shifted. "Why don't I meet you at Dawn's? Nine o'clock?"

Aiden nodded. A silent understanding seemed to pass between them.

Dawn narrowed her eyes and looked from one woman to the other. For the first time, she noticed that neither of them was relaxed. These weren't two friends making casual plans for the weekend. These were two cops planning a joint operation. "What's going on here?" she demanded to know.

Del looked at Aiden, leaving the decision on what to answer to her.

"Kade is being stalked, and we're investigating a few leads," Aiden said matter-of-factly.

Dawn couldn't believe what she was hearing. "Kade is being stalked? I just spent the whole evening with her at Del's party. Why didn't she say anything?" If she were in Kade's shoes, she knew she would be scared out of her mind, but Kade had acted completely normal as if everything was all right.

"She doesn't want the spotlight an official investigation would put on her private life." It was Del who answered this time, not Aiden.

Dawn could understand that. Kade was a very private person, and now that she was slowly growing closer to Del, she didn't want the whole city to know about it. "Not wanting an official investigation and not telling her friends are completely different things," she said, a little disappointed that Kade still didn't seem to trust her as a friend.

Del reached out and squeezed Dawn's arm. "It's nothing personal. It's just how Kade is. She deals with personal issues by ignoring them for as long as she can. She didn't even tell Carlisle... Aiden."

"Yeah," Aiden grumbled.

Dawn could tell she was clearly irritated about it. *Seems like Kade told Del before she told Aiden.* She almost had to smile. *It's time to accept that you're not Kade's number one cop anymore, darling.* "Is there anything I can do to help?"

Aiden and Del exchanged another quick glance.

Okay, I wanted them to bond, but not over hiding something from me. "What are you not telling me?" she demanded to know.

Aiden rubbed the back of her neck, always a clear sign she was stressed, feeling helpless, or nervous about something. "One of the leads we're investigating... we think the stalker might be someone involved in one of Kade's cases. Maybe a suspect she put behind bars at the time the stalking started or a family member of a suspect."

That made sense. Kade made a lot of enemies as a prosecutor. Chances were the stalking was connected to her job. She nodded her understanding. "I'm following so far, but what does that have to do with me? It has to do with me, doesn't it?"

Aiden uncomfortably cleared her throat. "It's just one of many possibilities. It's probably a dead end anyway, but I don't want to take the risk."

Instead of answering Dawn's question, that answer confused her even more. "What are you talking about?" she asked, starting to feel exasperated.

"One of the cases that ended around the time the stalking started was Gary Ballard's." Aiden bit her lip as she looked at Dawn.

Dawn sucked in a breath. She had hoped to never hear that name again in her life. "You think he might be behind Kade being stalked?" She held her breath, hoping for a reassuring answer.

"It's just one of many possibilities," Aiden repeated as if she had told herself the same time and again. "We want to rule it out, just to be sure. And until we do, it would be better for you not to stay late and leave the office on your own."

Hot anger replaced the cold numbness Dawn had felt since Aiden had uttered Ballard's name. "Is that why you came to my office tonight?" She directed an annoyed gaze at Del. "So you could act as my police detail?"

Del quickly held up her hands. "No. I told you the truth. I wanted to talk to you. I didn't even know about Ballard until Carlisle... Aiden mentioned it right now." She threw an accusing gaze of her own at Aiden.

Dawn consciously relaxed her tense muscles. She knew Del wouldn't lie to her. "If I'm in any danger, I want to know about it," she said, trying hard to keep her voice steady. She looked from Aiden to Del until both of them reluctantly nodded. "And I want to make the decisions about what to do about it. If I think I need a bodyguard, I'll tell you. No self-appointed superheroes risking their lives for me, all right?"

Both cops sighed but nodded.

"So what is this secret operation you had planned for tomorrow?" Dawn asked. After her rape, she had promised herself that she would never again allow someone else to control her life and make her decisions for her, not even out of love and good intentions.

"We want to pay Ballard a visit in prison, see if he has anything to do with the flower deliveries or the attack on Del," Aiden answered.

Dawn looked up sharply. "Attack on Del? I thought you fell! What else are you hiding from me?" She angrily looked at the two women, but neither would meet her gaze. Dawn sighed. "Do we have to go over the same old thing again and again and again?"

"It wasn't our decision to make," Del defended the both of them. "Kade is the one being stalked, so she should—"

"Bullshit!" Dawn interrupted. "You were the one attacked, so it was your decision to tell me that or lie to me."

"I'm sorry, but... What good would it have done to tell you?" Del said. "You couldn't have done anything about it, and you only would have worried."

Dawn sighed. That was how Del, Aiden, and most other cops thought, and she would never change it. Their protective instincts were too strong. *Accept it; hope they'll tell you next time, and move on.*

Aiden shifted uncomfortably when Dawn didn't say anything for a minute. "Do you want us to stay away from Ballard?" she asked, showing Dawn she would let her make the decision.

Dawn didn't want Aiden anywhere near the man who had raped her. She knew it would only upset Aiden. "If it's what you have to do to protect Kade, then do it. Just don't hide it from me."

The two cops exchanged another glance, then both of them nodded. "We won't," Aiden promised.

* * *

Aiden felt every muscle in her body vibrate with tension as they stopped in front of the visitor room and waited for the prison officer to open the door.

"Do you want to question him, or do you want me to take over?" Del asked, turning toward Aiden.

Officially, Del had the senior rank, so the decision should have been hers. Aiden appreciated Del leaving the decision to her. "I'll do it. Just hold me back if it looks like I'm gonna jump across the table," she said, only half joking.

"If you do the same for me," Del said.

They looked at each other, and for the first time, there was a complete understanding between them. Aiden suddenly felt that Del could become a friend—if she wasn't already. They grinned at each other but quickly sobered when the prison officer opened the door and stepped back.

Aiden took a deep breath and entered the room with resolute strides. She didn't want to give Gary Ballard any indication that this meeting was making her nervous.

The man in orange looked up as they entered. "Well, well, well! If it isn't the dyke detective with the glass jaw."

It was an allusion to him hitting her when she had arrested him back in October. Aiden didn't react to the provocation. She sat down across the table from Ballard even though a part of her hated sitting down with Dawn's rapist.

"I see you brought company," Ballard said when Del sat down next to Aiden. "She your girlfriend?" He didn't seem to remember Del from the trial.

Either Ballard had good gaydar, or he thought every short-haired female cop was a lesbian. *Or he's the one who is responsible for stalking Kade, so he knows exactly who and what Del is,* Aiden thought. "I'm not here to talk about me or my colleague. Let's talk about you. What have you been up to for the first of fifteen very long years, huh?" She knew Ballard wasn't stupid. He wouldn't tell them anything as long as he was in control of his emotions. She had to try to provoke him without making it too obvious.

The handcuffs around Ballard's wrists rattled as he leaned back. "Not a lot to do around here, Officer," he answered almost cheerfully.

Aiden ignored his use of the wrong title. "Yeah, I can imagine that. But I bet you're making plenty of new friends. Most of the inmates probably think your ass looks pretty sweet in prison orange." She gave him a suggestive wink, leaving no doubt about the meaning of her comment.

Ballard jumped up from behind the table. "What are you implying, you stupid bitch?"

"Sit down, or this visit is over!" the prison officer shouted from his place against the wall.

Ballard hesitated, and Aiden began to fear she had gone too far and he would end their conversation. Then Ballard glared at her one last time and sat back down. His red face slowly took on a more normal color.

Okay, calm down, Aiden ordered herself. *Control yourself. It might feel good to drive him up the wall, but you're not here to avenge Dawn. You're here to do your job.* "Hey, don't take it personally," she said casually. "I just thought with no contact to the outside world..."

"They could lock me up for the rest of my life. I'd still never allow a guy to touch me," Ballard spat out with contempt.

Hmm. That wasn't the defiant admission that he still has some contact to the outside world that I expected. Either he's more clever than I gave him credit for, or he didn't send the stalker. Aiden studied the man across from her but didn't find the answers she was looking for in his face.

"Why are you here? You don't just want to brag in front of your lover, do you?" Ballard jerked his head in Del's direction.

He's not having Dawn watched, that much is clear, Aiden thought with satisfaction, *or he'd know that Dawn is my lover, not Del.* When she had last seen Ballard, Dawn hadn't been more than a victim and a woman whose strength she admired. "I'm here to find out if you felt the sudden need to send some flowers," she said and looked into Ballard's glacier blue eyes to watch his reaction.

"Me? Sending flowers?" Ballard roared with laughter. "That's for girls and sissies! Even in this shithole, I need my money for more important things."

Meaning drugs, huh? Aiden resolved to suggest a surprise drug test and tossing Ballard's cell to the prison officer before they left. If she could do anything to make sure Ballard got no time off for good behavior, she would.

"So, who got the unwanted flowers?" Ballard asked.

Aiden hesitated. She didn't want to drag Kade into this conversation, but on the other hand, if Ballard was responsible for the stalking, he already knew much more than just Kade's name. "The DDA who was responsible for getting you convicted," she finally answered.

Ballard grinned without even a hint of sympathy. "Someone is going after her, huh?"

Del shifted in her chair, her muscles tensing, but to Aiden's relief, she kept her emotions in check and remained quiet.

"Maybe someone you know?" Aiden asked, looking him right in the eyes.

Ballard laughed. "You're accusing me? Believe me, if I went after someone, it would be the blond bitch whose whoring dyke ways put me behind bars."

You goddamned son of a bitch! You're blaming Dawn for what you did to her? The chair under Aiden creaked as her weight shifted forward. She felt Del's fingers clamp around her thigh, keeping her in her seat.

"And believe me, I wouldn't send her flowers!" Ballard continued without even noticing Aiden's reaction.

Aiden had enough. She couldn't face the man who had raped Dawn any longer. She gestured to the prison officer and quickly walked from the room without looking back.

Outside, Aiden and Del leaned against the wall, shoulder to shoulder, both of them quiet for long moments.

"I don't think he's responsible for stalking Kade," Del finally said. "Either he's a stellar actor, or he doesn't know anything about Dawn's or Kade's private lives. Flowers and love letters are not his style or the style of his cronies. He would send someone to kill Kade, not to court her."

Aiden would have liked nothing better than to add to Ballard's years in prison by charging him with another crime, but she had to admit Del was probably right. Kade would not be Ballard's choice of victim, and sending flowers was not his style. She would check out his visitor logs, but she had a feeling Gary Ballard was just another dead end. They were quickly running out of leads.

* * *

"Do you have time to grab a drink?"

At the unexpected question, Aiden turned and stared at Del. Del had never before suggested spending time together, so she wasn't sure what to make of this. "Uh... I rarely drink these days," she answered carefully.

"Then let's go for coffee or something else. It's not like I want to ply you with alcohol to learn your intentions toward Dawn anyway," Del pointed out.

"It's not? I mean... you don't?"

Del sighed. "I know I'm a little overprotective when it comes to Dawn. You'll understand if you ever have kids."

Having kids... Let's stay away from that topic. Aiden had no desire to discuss it with Del of all people. "Do you really think of Dawn as a daughter?" she asked instead.

Del leaned against the car, which was parked in front of the prison. She thought about it for a while. "No, not really. From the very start, Jimmy—Dawn's dad—treated me like his younger sister. That role stuck, so I guess I'm something of an aunt for Dawn. But I didn't want to talk about Dawn."

Aiden could see only one other thing they had in common. "You want to talk about Kade."

Del smiled. "I admit that she's my favorite topic these days," she said with an openness Aiden could only admire. "But no, I don't want to talk about Kade either. I suggested drinks because I have a feeling there's a lot going on in your life right now—and I'm offering an ear if you want to talk about it."

Aiden could only stare at her. This was the last thing she had expected from Del.

"So? How about that drink?" Del asked again. "There's a small bar and grill right around the corner."

There was no way to politely decline, so Aiden nodded.

Neither of them made conversation as they got into the car and drove to the restaurant.

Del pointed to a small corner table. "Let's sit there."

They reached the table at the same time and almost collided with each other as both of them tried to take the seat that would allow them to sit with the back against the wall.

They looked up, both of them tense for a moment.

Then Del smiled. "That's why I never date other cops. Too much fighting at the dinner table."

Aiden echoed the smile and finally stepped back, allowing Del to slip into the coveted seat.

The server came over and looked at them expectantly. "What can I get you?"

After coming face-to-face with Dawn's rapist, Aiden didn't have much of an appetite. "Nothing to eat for me, but... can I get a Club House sandwich and a Deli sandwich to go, please?"

The waiter raised an eyebrow but nodded. "Sure. What kind of bread do you want?"

"White bread for the Deli and rye for the Club House, please," Aiden ordered. She knew Dawn would sit at home and wait for her, too tense to eat while she knew Aiden was with Ballard.

Del shook her head as the waiter looked at her. "What can I get you to drink? We have a dozen different beers on tap." He pointed proudly at the large bar.

Aiden and Del exchanged a quick glance. "Just coffee," Del decided, and Aiden gave a nod.

"I assume the Deli is for Dawn?" Del asked as soon as the waiter had walked away.

Aiden nodded.

"Good." Del gave her a look of appreciation.

Aiden understood that she had the Aunt Del seal of approval for thinking of Dawn and knowing exactly what she would order.

The waiter set down their coffee in front of them and disappeared again.

Del leaned back and studied her. "So Evan Whitfield is your half sister, huh?"

The unexpected statement almost made Aiden spill her coffee. She quickly set down her cup, blinked, and tried to act unaffected. "You don't beat around the bush, do you?"

Del shrugged. "Why waste your time or mine?"

"Who told you?" Aiden asked. "Kade?"

"Yes. But please don't be angry with her for—"

Aiden held up a hand. "I'm not angry. It's just..." It was a little disconcerting to have Del know about her private issues. *What else has Kade told her?* she wondered. Knowing Kade suddenly had someone in her life whom she trusted enough to tell her these things was equally disconcerting.

"Have I ever told you that I have five brothers?" Del asked, surprising Aiden again. "No, of course I haven't. We never talked much with each other, huh?"

She has five brothers... so what? Aiden neglected to see what it had to do with her own situation.

"I haven't seen any of them for over twenty years. They're practically strangers to me, so I imagine if I met one of them now, I wouldn't know how to act around him either," Del said.

Aiden looked at her through narrowed eyes. "Who says I don't know how to act around Evan? Did Kade—"

"No. Kade said nothing, just that you found out Evan Whitfield is your half sister. So you want to tell me that, after growing up as an only child, you know exactly how to treat the sister you never even knew existed?" Del smiled in a way that said she didn't believe it for a second.

Aiden sighed and finally gave up her attempts of trying to appear strong and confident in front of Del. "I don't have a clue how to act around her," she admitted. "Whatever I do or say seems to be the wrong thing. I just can't seem to win her trust."

"Don't I know that feeling," Del said with a self-mocking laugh.

"You? You have experience with teenagers?" Aiden found that hard to believe.

Del nodded. "When I first met the Kinsley family, I was just a young rookie fresh from the academy. Dawn was eight and she loved me from the start, but her brother Brian... he was almost fourteen... and, boy, did he give me a hard time!" She rolled her eyes as she remembered.

Aiden leaned forward, suddenly interested in what Del had to say. "What did you do?"

Del shrugged. "I waited him out. Just let him know that I was his father's partner and the new adopted aunt, so I wasn't going anywhere. It took a while, but he finally seemed to understand that I was not a threat to him in any way."

Aiden sighed. "So there's no miracle cure? No little trick that can make it happen overnight?"

"Afraid not." Del gave her a sympathetic smile.

The waiter delivered the ordered sandwiches to the table.

Del pulled out her wallet. "Come on," she said to Aiden. "Let's drink up and bring Dawn her sandwich."

Minutes later, they were on their way to the car. "See? Talking to me didn't hurt after all," Del pointed out with a smirk.

"Not much," Aiden admitted, grinning. "But next time, I get the corner seat."

CHAPTER 24

"*I* APPRECIATE you helping me with this on your day off," Dawn said to her mother as the two of them clicked the last food container shut.

Grace waved her hand. "I did it for your dad, for Brian, for Cal, and for Del often enough, so why not do it for Aiden and her colleagues?" she said casually. "If she has to work Sundays, the least we supportive citizens can do is make sure Portland's finest don't starve to death."

Dawn smiled happily. Her mom had really come around during the last six months. In the beginning, she had been very skeptical about her relationship with Aiden, but now she went out of her way to make sure she treated Aiden with the same respect she had given Dawn's husband.

"Besides, it gives me an opportunity to spend some time with you," Grace said. "I don't get to see a lot of you lately."

She said it without any accusation, but Dawn felt a little guilty anyway. Her mother was right. During the last few months, they hadn't spent as much time with each other as usual. "I'm sorry," she said immediately. "I didn't realize... with my new job and Aiden and Evan..."

"You don't have to apologize," Grace interrupted, giving her hand a quick squeeze. "You have your own life, and that's how it should be."

Still... Dawn realized that a lot was changing for her mother. Not only was her only child busy with a new job and a new relationship instead of spending every weekend at Grace's, but at the same time her best friend was slowly pulling away too. Del had always given Grace a lot of attention and support, but now she was starting to spend more time with Kade and less time with Grace. Dawn wondered if her mother might feel lonely.

"Did you ever consider starting to date again?" Dawn asked, surprising both of them.

Grace gestured for her to leave the dirty pots and sit down at the table with her. "No, not really. Where did that question come from?" she asked with a shake of her head.

"Now that I have Aiden and even Del might start to date, I don't want you to be alone." Dawn was almost embarrassed to realize she had never thought about whether her mother might feel lonely.

Grace reached across the table and laid her hand on top of Dawn's. "I still miss your father, but I'm not alone. I already experienced the love of my life, so I'm not searching anymore. Maybe that'll change one day, but for now, I'm content with being happy for you and Del."

They had never talked about the growing relationship between Del and Kade. Dawn realized she didn't know how her mother felt about it. "Do you like Kade? I noticed the three of you spent some time in the kitchen after Del's party. Do you think they would make a good couple?"

"Of course I like Kade," her mother answered. "She's smart and cultivated, and if you manage to look behind the distanced façade she puts up, she's a kind woman and a good friend."

Dawn waited, but her mother didn't add anything. She seemed to consider the subject closed, but Dawn didn't. "What do you think about her relationship with Del?" she persistently dug deeper.

Grace shrugged. "I'm not sure. Del isn't exactly forthcoming with information about this."

"Did you expect her to be?" Dawn asked gently, not surprised to hear the concern in her mother's voice.

"No. I know Del had a few lovers over the years, but she hardly talked about them and never introduced them," Grace said. She was only telling Dawn what she had already known.

"But it's not the same with Kade, is it?" Dawn asked, watching her mother closely.

Grace put her hands on her hips. "Are you trying to shrink your mother, young lady?" she asked in her best scolding mother voice.

Dawn had to laugh. Her mother hadn't used that voice on her for years. "Not really," she lamely defended herself.

"You are!" Grace playfully dug her index finger into Dawn's arm.

"I just want to know how you're dealing with Del's possible new relationship, and you're not making it easy on me." Her mother was withholding her emotions, and Dawn had used the tools of her trade by pure instinct.

Grace looked at her with a very serious expression. "If Kade can make Del happy, I'm fine with it."

Dawn could practically feel the "but" in the sentence. "But?" she prompted.

Grace bit her lip and hesitated.

"You doubt that she can make Del happy?" It wasn't easy for Dawn to voice that doubt, but if she was honest with herself, she had sometimes shared it.

"I don't want to appear petty or jealous." Grace hesitated for a few more seconds, then looked directly at Dawn. "I'm afraid Del is going to end up hurt. She and Kade are not on the same page at all regarding their relationship."

Dawn couldn't refute that.

"Kade is your age, and Del is a dozen years older." Grace worriedly shook her head.

"Age differences never stopped true love," Dawn said, wanting it to be true. She, of course, knew that it was only part of the truth. Age differences didn't make a successful relationship impossible, but they also didn't make it easier.

"It's not just the number of candles on their birthday cakes. Their age difference means that they are at different points in their lives. Del is ready to settle down, and Kade... not that she said anything about it to me, but I got the feeling she's just starting to explore her sexuality." Grace directed a sorrowful gaze at Dawn. "I've been told that a newly out woman will never stay with the first woman she has been with. The first is just a portal for new experiences."

Dawn arched her eyebrows. Her mother had been supportive after her coming out and about her relationship with Aiden, but they had never discussed the particulars of her sexual orientation. *Where is that little gem of information coming from?* she wondered. "Who told you that?"

"Del," Grace said, looking down. "You had just brought home Maggie for the first time, and I couldn't see you spending the rest of your life with her. That's when Del told me you probably wouldn't. And she was right."

Dawn felt her cheeks grow hot. "Not because Maggie was my first girlfriend!" she protested sharply. "Maggie is great, but she's just not the right person for me. I'd like to think I'd have stayed with Aiden had I met her first."

"And are you sure Kade will do the same? Are you even sure she won't pull back and decide she's not gay after all?" Grace looked at her daughter with equal parts hope and doubt.

"No. I can't be sure about it. It's a very real possibility." Dawn had to be honest with herself and her mother. "But don't you think Del is aware of that? She was the one who pointed out to you that most women never stay with their first girlfriend after all. So if she's willing to try with Kade anyway, she must think Kade is worth the risk."

Grace nodded. "You're not just so eager to see Del fixed up with Kade because Aiden had a crush on Kade, are you?"

Dawn sank against the back of her chair. She stared at her mother in surprise.

"Just because I don't comment on the particulars of lesbian relationships doesn't mean I'm blind to them," Grace said with a laugh, much too amused for Dawn's comfort.

"How...?" Dawn asked, then stopped to clear her throat.

"I saw her watch Kade in court back when..." Now Grace was the one who didn't finish her sentence.

"When Aiden was still single, and I was nothing more to her than a victim in one of her cases," Dawn supplied. She had known from the beginning how important it was to call things by their name and talk openly about her rape. It hurt, but she knew if she tried to avoid it, she would be running forever.

Grace nodded without looking her in the eyes. "Yes."

"Not that I'm above petty jealousy or insecurities, but no, that's not why I'm hoping Kade will end up with Del," Dawn answered her mother's original question. "If I wanted to make sure nothing could ever happen between Kade and Aiden, I would encourage Kade to keep fishing on the heterosexual side of the big dating pool, don't you think? I would try to set her up with Del's brother, not Del."

Grace grimaced. "Now that would be a good fit," she said sarcastically. "Del's brother was as cold and businesslike on the phone as Kade sometimes pretends to be."

"How did he know to call your house anyway?" Dawn asked. She had wanted to ask before but had forgotten all about it because of all the agitation over Ballard and Kade's stalker.

"He had no phone number for Del and wasn't sure where she lives, but he remembered our name from reading Jim's obituary notice. He probably thinks I'm Del's life partner." Grace chuckled. It wasn't the first time people had made that assumption, and it had stopped bothering her long ago. "He just looked me up in the phone book."

Dawn hadn't thought it was that easy. "I thought he'd maybe hired a private investigator to find his sister."

"No." Grace shook her head. "I don't think he would have gone to that trouble. He only called because his mother asked him to."

He hasn't seen his sister for twenty-five years. Given that Del is the oldest, he probably doesn't even remember her all that clearly. How can he give up on his sister just like that? Dawn wondered. She sighed, knowing she was influenced by losing her own brother and by what Aiden was going through in her attempts to get closer to Evan.

"Did Del talk to you about her father?" Grace asked, clearly worried about her best friend.

"A little." Dawn knew that there were a lot of things Del hadn't said. Del was a typical cop in that regard: always willing to lend a helping hand or a strong shoulder but very reluctant to talk about her own emotions, fears, and weaknesses. "I hope she's talking to Kade about it."

Grace looked more than skeptical. "Kade is the woman she wants to impress. She won't want to risk driving her away by revealing her ugly family history."

"Kade doesn't scare easily. She's at least as stubborn as Del. She's going to dig until Del tells her what's going on with her," Dawn predicted, hoping she was right about Kade.

Grace stood without further comment. "Come on. Let's drive over to the precinct before the food gets completely cold."

* * *

Kade shut her cell phone with a sigh and massaged her temples for a second. "My mother," she said to Del, who was patiently waiting next to her, a pizza box in her hands. "She wants me to come home for her big dinner party."

"And you don't want to go?" Del asked. She balanced the pizza box against her chest and used one hand to unlock the door to her apartment building.

"Not particularly, no. I already know that I'll spend the evening making small talk with half a dozen eligible bachelors my mother will invite." She flashed Del a self-mocking smile. "My mother thinks I need a little assistance in catching a husband at the spinsterly age of twenty-nine."

Del was quiet while they stepped into the elevator. For a moment, Kade thought Del would suggest she tell her mother she was not interested in finding a husband, but Del said no such thing. "I'm sorry she's putting so much pressure on you to be and to behave in a certain way," Del told her instead. "I know how hard that can be."

Kade suddenly felt contrite. Her own tense, distant relationship with her mother was nothing compared to the problems Del had with her own family. "Have you thought about what you're going to do about your father?" she asked gently.

"I don't think me going to see him will accomplish anything. It's better if I stay away." Del's statement sounded as if it was the last thing she wanted to say on the subject.

Kade knew from personal experience that ignoring an issue wouldn't make it go away. It would only fester beneath the surface. "Better for whom?" she asked softly. "For your father, for your mother and your siblings, or for you?"

Del didn't look at Kade, but in the mirrored walls of the elevator, Kade could see her dark and turbulent eyes. "It's the best for all of us."

The elevator doors pinged open. Del resolutely stepped forward, wanting to escape the confines of the elevator and the discussion, but Kade quickly blocked her way. They stood very close, almost touching in the close quarters of the elevator. Kade's skin started to tingle, but she ignored it. "Talk to me, please." She reached out and gently touched one of Del's hands that were clenched around the pizza box. "You've been there for me, and now it's my turn to be there for you. Isn't that how a relationship, romantic or otherwise, should work?" *If you want us to be friends, or maybe, one day, something more, you sometimes have to let me be the strong one too, Del Vasquez.*

The elevator doors closed again, with them still inside.

"I feel like a bottle of champagne someone shook a little too hard," Del whispered into the confines of the elevator. "All the bottled up feelings inside of me... if I go see my father, I'm afraid they'll explode out of me, and I don't want to yell at a dying man. Or maybe the exact opposite will happen. Maybe I won't be able to utter a single word because I don't know what to say to him."

Kade smoothed her thumb over the back of Del's hand. Del's hand was cold, despite the warmth of the pizza box. "I don't think it's important what you say or if you say anything at all."

"Then what is important?" Del asked, not moving away from Kade's touch.

"To face your past and your father and to say good-bye to both. You have to let go of your old feelings to make room for new ones." Kade wished someone had told her that before her own father had died.

"I already have let go of my past," Del said.

Kade shook her head. "No, you haven't. If you had, this wouldn't hurt you so much. I don't have the best relationship with my own family. I'm not close to anyone, and maybe I'm not the best person to ask for advice about this, but one thing is becoming clearer and clearer to me: you can never escape blood ties. Your father will always be your father, no matter how much he or you dislike it."

"So you're saying I should go and forgive him because he's the man who fathered me?" Del didn't sound convinced.

"No. This isn't about forgiveness," Kade said, still holding on to Del's hand. "Well, maybe it is, but not for your father's sake. You'll have to live with your feelings long after your father is gone. If there's a chance you could bury the anger, the hate, and the resentment, maybe you should do it. For your own sake."

Del squeezed her hand, then pulled away to press the button that opened the elevator doors. "You're probably right, but... I just need a little more time." She stepped out of the elevator and looked back at Kade.

Kade smiled and walked toward her. "That's all r—" She stopped abruptly and stared at the door to Del's apartment. "Jesus! What happened here?"

Del whirled around.

Someone had sprayed "She's mine!" and "Leave her alone!" in bold, blood red letters on Del's door. The wall next to it was now decorated with a skull and crossbones and other symbols of death.

"Shit. Stay back!" Del threw down the pizza box and pulled the gun that she always seemed to carry these days. She reached out to Kade with the other hand, forcing her back while she protected her from whoever might lurk in the corridor with her own body.

Kade leaned against the wall. Her fingers wrapped around the small gun in her purse. Her eyes never left Del, feeling at least marginally safe as long as Del was in her line of sight.

Del checked the stairwell and the corridor before she returned to her apartment door. She carefully touched the paint and looked at her fingers. The paint was dry. The stalker was long since gone. Del exhaled sharply, her whole body tense. Slowly, she put away her gun. "Your stalker is getting creative."

"Creative? He's threatening you!" Kade shuddered as she stared at the death's head. "Hitting you over the head when you visited my apartment was a warning. Next time, he won't let you live. I should go." She turned back around toward the elevator.

Del hurried after her. "You're not going anywhere!" she shouted.

Kade turned slowly and fixed Del with her coldest stare. "What did you just say?" she asked with lethal gentleness. She knew the tense situation had both of them on edge, but she didn't appreciate being yelled at and ordered around like a naughty child.

Del took a deep breath. "Kade..." She ran her hand through her hair in frustration. "I'm not ordering you around, but I don't think you should go anywhere, at least not alone."

"If you don't stay away from me, you're a target!" A picture of Del lying unconscious and covered in blood in front of her apartment flashed through Kade's mind. She never wanted to experience something like that again.

"And if I stay away, **you** are a target!" Del shot back. "Don't you see that this is what he wants? I bet he knew you'd come here with me tonight. He knew you'd see his little message to me. He wants you to order me to stay away so he can get to you."

Kade forced herself to calm down and think about it. What Del said made sense. "He's not your average run-of-the-mill stalker," she finally said with dread.

"No. This is one clever son of a bitch." Del stared at her apartment door with narrowed eyes.

Kade bit her lip. "What are we going to do?" She had no intention of just waiting to see what the stalker would do next. Not when it put Del at risk.

Del bent to pick up the pizza box. "We're going to enjoy our dinner, and then I'll call one of my friends from CSU over to dust for prints and take some photos. Not that I expect to find anything, but it's worth a try. My apartment building doesn't have any cameras and no doorman, so prints are all we can hope for."

"And after that?" Kade asked. She didn't like having no plan at all. As a prosecutor, she never stepped into a courtroom—or any other situation—without a precise plan of action.

Del unlocked her apartment. She waved at Kade to stay back until she had made sure nothing had been disturbed inside, then she firmly closed and locked the door behind them. "I think it would be best if you left the city for a few days."

"Leave the city?" Kade resolutely shook her head. "No. I won't run away from this sick bastard! And I can't just up and leave anyway. I have three arraignments first thing tomorrow morning; the Wright trial starts later this week, and if I don't turn in my motions in the Finlay case by Wednesday, Linehan will—"

"Kade," Del interrupted. "Is your pride or your job worth getting killed over?" Her dark eyes seemed to burn with intensity.

Is it worth getting Del killed? The thought shot through Kade's mind, and there was just one answer for it. *No.*

"This can't go on like before, Kade," Del continued. She still looked at Kade imploringly as if she could convince her just by the power of her concerned gaze. "We're no closer to catching this guy than we were when you told me about him. He holds all the cards. He knows where I live and where you live. He could hurt either or both of us in the blink of an eye."

Kade sighed. She hated to back down, but she knew Del was right.

"It's only for a few days until Aiden and Ray can find out more about the stalker's identity. I know they're investigating some leads right now. Maybe one of them will turn something up," Del said, unaware that Kade had already made her decision.

"Okay," Kade said.

Del turned in the middle of her living room to look at her. "Okay?" She raised her eyebrows in surprise.

"We Matheson women can be reasonable if we want to," Kade said with a half smile. "Maybe I could take a little road trip and visit my mother." If she was honest with herself, she knew a visit was long overdue. *Or do you really want to wait until your mother confronts you with what she heard from Laurie about your newly discovered sexual orientation?* She thought about what she had told Del about playing chess: you can't win if you're always reacting instead of acting, always one step behind. *Maybe it's a good life philosophy after all.* She sighed. "I'll handle the arraignments tomorrow and then try to hand over the rest of my cases before I hit the road."

"Before we hit the road," Del corrected.

"We?" At no point had there been a mention of Del coming with her.

Del grinned at her. "I'm inviting myself along," she said.

Kade gave her a skeptical look. "Just like that? Can you even take the week off on such short notice?" It wasn't that she didn't want Del's company, but it was hard to believe that Del could— and would—drop everything else just to drive all the way across the state with her. In her own life, very few things had priority over her job, and to see Del so willing to put everything else aside for her was a little scary.

"I haven't taken off more than two days in a row for the last two years. The captain has been on my case about taking some time off anyway." Del shrugged casually. "So if you don't mind, I'll tag along when you visit your mother."

"Isn't it a little early in our relationship to meet the parents?" Kade asked, playfully arching her eyebrows at Del.

Del coughed, surprised by the bold answer. "I'm not coming along to meet your mother. I'm accompanying you for safety reasons. But if you want to introduce me as your live-in lesbian lover, that's fine with me."

Now that would go over well with my mother. Kade tried not to picture that scene. "For now, I'll just introduce you as my friend if that's all right."

"Very all right." Del smiled warmly. "At least then I can eat my dinner without being afraid it's poisoned."

Poison? No, much too obvious. My mother could find a hundred much more creative ways to destroy you or chase you out of my life. Kade sighed. At least Del would be safe from the stalker in Ashland.

"So we're starting on Tuesday?" Del asked.

Kade just nodded.

Del grinned. "A road trip with Kade Matheson. Yay!"

CHAPTER 25

"So..." DETECTIVE Jorge Moreno shifted in the driver's seat of the unmarked car they were sitting in. He fingered the plastic top of his coffee cup. "Do you still have that hot partner?"

Aiden widened her eyes in mock surprise. "Why, Moreno, I didn't know you're batting for the other team, but Ray will be flattered you think he's hot," she said tongue in cheek.

"What? Oh, no, no, no!" Moreno quickly lifted his hands. "I meant your life partner... your girlfriend, not your work partner. I just saw her dropping off food for you and the rest of the squad earlier, and I thought..."

"That she's hot," Aiden finished the sentence for him. *Not that I don't agree.* But she enjoyed the young cop's discomfort too much to let him off the hook.

"No. Yeah. I mean—"

Aiden sharply nudged him with an elbow. "Hey! Our target is getting some action." She pointed at the man standing in front of a coffee shop. He was part of the drug dealer ring they were after. Aiden looked across the street at the other inconspicuously parked car, where Ray and a narcotics detective waited.

They watched as the drug dealer casually took a bundle of money from a young man and handed him a small bag in exchange.

Aiden reached out to open the door.

"Wait!" Moreno's voice stopped her. "He's just a small fish. We're waiting until he meets with his supplier, who's a little higher up in the food chain. An informant tipped us off."

"All right." Moreno was young and a little overeager, but he was good at his job. He was the narcotics expert, so Aiden was willing to trust his word.

They continued to watch the coffee shop. Aiden knew it could take hours. It was beginning to look as if she wouldn't see Dawn today. She suppressed a sigh. At least it gave her some time to think about the progress they had made on Kade's stalker. *Or rather, the lack of progress.* They had checked out two of the three suspects from last October's cases who fit the doorwoman's description. The first one had died in a prison fight last month. The second had been in and out of courtrooms so often that it was hard to see why he would stalk Kade but none of the other prosecutors.

Aiden almost hit her head on the side of the car when her cell phone began to ring. *Shit.* She had forgotten to turn it off before beginning the surveillance. With a sheepish grimace, she flipped the phone open. "Carlisle."

"Aiden? Hi, it's Kade."

"Hey, Kade. Do you need something?" Probably the arrest report that was still lying unfinished on her desk. "The lieutenant didn't tell you we're helping out narcotics again?"

"No. I'll call you later," Kade said quickly.

A little too quickly, Aiden thought. *This must be important. Kade doesn't just call me because she's getting bored on a Sunday evening.* "No, I have a moment," she said with a quick glance at Moreno, who nodded tolerantly.

"I just thought I should tell you that I'm going out of town for a few days. Ford will take over the Wright case for me, but don't worry, I'll bring her up to speed before I leave," Kade said as if she did things like this on a daily basis.

Aiden shook her head in bewilderment. The Kade Matheson she knew wasn't spontaneously going on vacation in the middle of a trial. "What's going on, Kade?" she asked suspiciously. "Is everything all right?"

Kade was silent for a few seconds. "The stalker... he left a nice little message on Del's apartment door. Del thinks it's best if I leave the city for a few days until things calm down a little. It'll give you some time to find out more about the stalker," Kade said, sounding much calmer than she probably felt.

Aiden sucked in a breath. The stalker was escalating, so that meant they had to pick up the pace of their investigation. Instead, she was sitting here, caught up in a drug surveillance. She stared out the window in frustration. "I'll talk to the lieutenant. Maybe I can get a few days off on short notice and come with you. I don't feel comfortable letting you leave the city on your own." She knew Kade would probably protest and resolutely refuse to be babysat, but she was equally determined to get her some police protection.

"That's not necessary," Kade said as she had expected her to.

"Oh, yes, it is!" Aiden said forcefully. "We know he's watching you seemingly twenty-four/seven, so it's possible he'll be aware of you leaving the city. Going alone, without any protection, could be exactly what he wants you to do."

To Aiden's surprise, Kade didn't object. "I know. I won't go alone."

Oh. Aiden finally understood. *Del is going with her. Kade is allowing Del to go with her.* Aiden stared out the window, trying to think of something to say. "Oh. That's... good." *It is good,* she told herself. *Del will keep her safe while Ray and I are going to speed up the investigation.* Still, it was hard to get used to not being the one Kade came to for protection anymore. "Be careful," she said to Kade. "And tell Del to be careful too. She's a target now too."

"We'll be careful and take every precaution to make sure he doesn't follow us when we leave the city," Kade promised.

Outside, on the street, another man was strolling toward their target.

"That's the supplier," Moreno said into his walkie-talkie. "Get ready."

"Kade, I have to go." Aiden hastily ended the call. Then she saw another person walking toward the drug dealer and frowned. Something about the tall, lanky figure with the confident stride was oddly familiar. The person looked around to see if anybody was watching before handing money to the dealer, and Aiden caught a glimpse under the hood of the sweatshirt. *Evan! Shit!*

Aiden let go of the cell phone and jumped out of the car just as the command to move came from the walkie-talkie. Chaos broke out. Half a dozen detectives from narcotics and SAD and a DEA agent rushed toward the drug dealer, his supplier, and Evan.

One of Moreno's colleagues pushed Evan against a wall and pulled his handcuffs from his belt.

"Stop!" Aiden ordered. She grabbed his arm and pulled him away from Evan.

The narcotics detective pulled away from Aiden's grip. "What are you doing, Carlisle?" he asked, very irritated that a sex crimes detective had stopped him from doing his job.

Evan struggled against the detective's grip but said nothing.

Aiden had to think fast. "She's my..." Aiden stopped. Confessing that Evan was her sister wouldn't stop him from booking Evan. "She's my informant," she told him as firmly as possible.

"Your informant?" the narcotics detective repeated very skeptically.

Jorge Moreno came over to them. "Problems?" He looked from Aiden to his colleague who still had the struggling Evan in his grip.

"She," the narcotics detective angrily pointed a finger at Aiden, "says that she," he now jabbed his finger at Evan, "is her informant."

"Jorge..." Aiden knew she couldn't beg Moreno to help her. Not in front of the other narcotics detective. *Come on, Jorge!* she mentally beseeched. *I let you call my girlfriend "hot." Now you have to do something for me.*

Moreno looked at her for a few moments, then he shrugged. "If Carlisle says she's her informant, we better let her go." He gestured to his colleague, silently ordering him to remove his grip from around Evan's arm and to put his handcuffs away.

Ray came over to them. "Hey, what's going on?" He stared under Evan's hood. "Isn't that...?"

"Yes. That's our informant," Aiden said hastily, giving Ray a long glance. "We better take her with us for a briefing." *And better make it quick before someone gets her ID and runs her through the system.*

"All right," Ray quickly agreed. "Let's go. We'll fax over our report later."

Aiden herded Evan to Ray's car and pulled open the door with more force than strictly necessary. "Get in!"

Evan set her jaw and met her eyes with a defiant gaze, but with one final look at the narcotics detectives, she slipped into the backseat of the car.

* * *

"Hey." Del watched Kade with a frown, taking in the slender fingers that were gripping the cell phone. "You all right? Aiden didn't give you a hard time, did she?"

Kade jumped when Del gently touched one of the tense shoulders. "What? No. No, she didn't."

"What is it, then?" By now, Del knew Kade well enough to know she was upset about something even though the courtroom poker face was firmly in place.

"Well, it seems narcotics needed some help from my detectives again. They're on surveillance, and Aiden had to end the call rather abruptly," Kade explained.

Del watched her pace the length of the room. "You're concerned about her," she voiced the emotions she could sense behind Kade's matter-of-fact explanation.

Kade stopped her pacing for a moment to stare at Del. "I just don't like it when I'm left out of the loop about what's going on."

"Do you want me to call a few of my friends from narcotics?" Del offered. "If they got involved in a shooting or something like that, one of them will know."

"No, that's not necessary." Kade quickly shook her head. "I don't want my detectives to think I don't trust them to do a good job."

"You don't want them to think you care," Del corrected. "You don't want me to think you care about Aiden. Kade." Del stepped closer, directly into Kade's path of pacing. She forced down a wave of jealousy. "It's okay to care. You're allowed to have feelings, just like everyone else." She looked deeply into the stormy blue eyes.

For a few seconds, Kade just stared at her, then the tension in her slender frame finally lessened, and she sat down on the couch.

Del sat down next to her, silently waiting for Kade's decision.

"Make the call," Kade finally said.

Del gave Kade's hand a quick squeeze, then reached for her cell phone.

* * *

"Stop the car, Ray!" Aiden ordered when they were safely around the next corner.

Now what? Evan couldn't see Aiden's face, but her voice sounded sharp and angry. *If she wants to give me a good beating where none of her colleagues can watch, she's in for a surprise.* Evan had been in a lot of fights, and she was determined to hold her own.

Aiden got out as soon as the car stopped. She jerked open Evan's door. "Get out!"

The athletic cop loomed over Evan. Anger smoldered in her amber eyes. A spark of fear began to grow in Evan. *It's not fear,* she told herself. *I'm just cautious. I know her cop partner will cover for her if push comes to shove.* "No, thanks," she told Aiden as calmly as possible. "I like it in here just fine. Very comfy." She patted the backseat.

Pressing her lips together, Aiden grabbed Evan's arm and dragged her from the car.

"Ouch! Hey, that's police brutality!" Evan protested sharply. Aiden's grip didn't hurt, but she still didn't like being manhandled.

"Shut up. If I were acting as a police officer, you'd be in a holding cell by now." Aiden stared at her with a burning gaze. "What the hell were you thinking? Buying drugs!"

Evan just shrugged. "I don't have to explain myself to you. You're not my mother," she answered coolly.

"I'm your sister!"

"So?" The louder Aiden got, the calmer and more indifferent Evan acted. She had learned that it would drive Aiden up a wall and make her lose her self-control. If she weren't in trouble, it would have been a lot of fun to watch.

Aiden stared at her through narrowed eyes. She looked as if she wanted to hit something. "I care about... what happens you!"

Oh, yeah. You care about your stupid supercop reputation! Can't have a cop's sister busted buying drugs, right? Evan didn't acknowledge Aiden's statement with an answer.

"Don't you know what would have happened if I hadn't been there to stop them from arresting you?" Aiden asked, shaking her head.

"I'd have gotten away. I'm faster than you cops," Evan said, knowing fully well it was a lie. The cops had surprised her, and if Aiden had come just a second later, they would have cuffed her. Evan forced back feelings of gratefulness. *She did it for herself and for her stupid rules.*

"And then? Even if you had gotten away, which I doubt, you'd have taken the drugs and later bought new ones, and so on. It's a vicious circle, and before you know it, you're in too deep to just stop even if you want." Aiden hit the roof of the car with her fist, making her partner in the car jump. "I lost my mother to alcohol. I don't want to lose you to another goddamn addiction! I can't just stand by and watch you self-destruct too!"

Evan wanted to yell back and tell her that a little recreational pot wasn't making her an addict. Her gaze fell on Aiden, and she stopped and just looked at her for a moment.

The anger was gone from Aiden's features. Now she just looked helpless and embarrassed. She was trembling with frustration. She obviously hadn't planned on saying that. It had slipped out in anger, and now Aiden looked as if she would love to take it back. She hadn't wanted to tell Evan about her mother. *So her perfect life isn't so perfect after all, huh?* Evan tried to hold on to her sarcasm but found it harder now that she had glimpsed Aiden's vulnerability. Dr. Kinsley had hinted at it, and after seeing Aiden with Dr. Kinsley's grandmother, Evan finally started to believe it.

She's putting me on the same level with her mother, naming us in the same breath. It made Evan angry to be compared to a drunk, but maybe Aiden hadn't meant it like that. *She wouldn't look embarrassed over calling me an addict, would she? I'm sure she's secretly called me much worse. She looks embarrassed because she admitted... she cares for me like she cares for a family member!*

For long moments, they just stood and stared at each other, both of them at a loss for what to say.

"What happens now?" Evan asked when she couldn't stand the silence any longer.

Aiden shrugged, looking as uncomfortable as Evan felt. "We wait and hope that the guys from narcotics don't question my story about you being my informant."

"What if they do?" Evan asked. The cop who had wanted to cuff her didn't look very convinced about the informant story.

"Then I'll deal with the consequences," Aiden said quietly.

She's putting her job on the line for me, Evan realized. *Shit. Now I owe her.* She had liked it better when she could yell at Aiden instead of talking to her. She sighed. "You're not going to tell my... Jill and Roger, are you?"

"No."

Good. Evan nodded in satisfaction. *This was all the family sensitive chat I can take for one day.*

"You will tell them," Aiden said.

Like hell I will! I'm not that stupid. Evan didn't answer, but Aiden could obviously read it in her expression.

"I'll deal with the consequences of my actions, and you have to deal with the consequences of yours," Aiden said, looking her right in the eyes. "That's what being an adult is all about."

Shit. Evan knew she couldn't back out when Aiden said it like that. "What if they throw me out?" It wasn't that she loved her foster parents or anything, but she had grown used to them, and compared to others they were tolerable. "Would you take me in?"

For a second, the look of panic that Evan had expected flashed across Aiden's face, but then she straightened her shoulders. "I would if it's the best option for you. But for now, I think your foster parents would be willing to forget about it if you admit to your mistakes and try not to repeat them. Provided you're willing and able to give up taking drugs?" Aiden fixed her with an intense stare.

"I'm not a junkie!" Evan bristled. Of course she was able to give up drugs. "I only smoke a little pot when..."

"When?" Aiden prompted when Evan trailed off.

Evan shrugged. "Every now and then." *When I'm pissed off, frustrated, or bored.* It had happened a lot more often lately, she noticed. Maybe giving the pot a break for a while wouldn't be such a bad idea after all. "But I can stop anytime."

"Then promise me you will." Aiden held out her hand but didn't look down. She gazed steadily into Evan's eyes.

Evan hesitated. She didn't want to limit her own options by accepting Aiden's rules. At the same time, she couldn't ignore Aiden's outstretched hand because it meant that Aiden was willing to accept her handshake and her word at face value and trust her to keep her promise. No one but Dr. Kinsley had ever done that before. She took Aiden's hand, gripping it firmly because she didn't want Aiden to think she was weak in any way. "I'll stop smoking pot for now," she promised.

Aiden gazed at her. For a moment, Evan thought she would start to argue about the "for now," but she nodded and shook Evan's hand one last time before letting go. "Great. Then let's go. You have foster parents to talk to, and I have a report to write."

CHAPTER 26

"...*A*ND THEN HE asked the medical examiner how many autopsies she had performed on dead people—as if there was any other kind of autopsy," Kade finished her tale as she smoothly changed lanes.

Del leaned back in the comfortable passenger seat of the BMW and chuckled. "Ouch."

Kade smirked. "That's what the judge said."

Smiling contentedly, Del continued to watch Kade. She liked the way Kade's slender hands looked handling the wheel. She had enjoyed their trip so far. With each mile, the distance between them and the stalker was growing, and Kade was beginning to relax as they left the threat of the stalker and the stress of her job behind. For the last hour, she had regaled Del with hilarious little anecdotes from the courtroom.

"How about another coffee break?" Kade asked as a sign came up on the side of the road.

Del nodded. They'd had lunch in a little roadside restaurant a few hours ago, but coffee sounded good. She stepped out of the car as soon as Kade had found a parking spot, glad to stretch her long legs after hours in the car. "Join me in the ladies' room?" She nodded in the direction of the restrooms.

Kade looked at her with a glint in her eyes that made Del's heart jump. "Is that an immoral offer, Delicia Vasquez?"

"Only if you want it to be, Kadence Matheson," Del said, thoroughly enjoying Kade's playful mood. She didn't want to tell her that she was still reluctant to leave her out of her sight, even for a moment, afraid that the stalker had followed them. *Better safe than sorry.* They had gone to a lot of trouble to make the stalker, should he be watching, believe that Kade had only been driving to work this morning and was still there. Del had even insisted on them driving in the opposite direction for a while before turning back around when she was certain no one was following them.

Kade seemed to sense even what Del didn't say. "It's fine, Del. I feel safe here. I'm sure he didn't follow us. Ashland is not that interesting."

Give her a little space. Don't scare her with your overprotectiveness. "Okay. Then you get the coffee while I go to the restroom."

Fifteen minutes later, they were on their way back to the car. "I can take over the driving for a while," Del offered.

Kade didn't hesitate to entrust her car to Del. She handed over the car keys without further comment.

Del hadn't thought it would be that easy. Usually, Kade was hesitant to let others take the wheel—literally and figuratively. Del grinned, taking it as a sign of Kade's growing trust in her. She adjusted the seat for her longer legs and started the car. "Hmm, nice," she hummed as it smoothly accelerated.

"That's what all the men I date say," Kade commented without thought.

Del looked away from the road for a moment to throw a quick glance at Kade's face. "About the car?" she asked with a smirk.

Kade punched her in the thigh. "They usually use more exciting adjectives to describe me," she threw back.

Del smiled. She loved Kade's confidence. Others might mistake it for arrogance, but for Del, it was just a woman who knew her worth. "So you comparing me to 'all the men' you dated, does that mean you consider us being... being more than friends?" she took the opportunity to ask.

"Not you too," Kade moaned. "I'm going to get enough matchmaking from my mother this week."

"Yeah, but I doubt she'll try to set you up with me, will she?" Del gave her voice a teasing tone, masking the fact that she had been quite serious about her first question.

Kade laughed, but sarcasm vibrated in the sound. "No. She has a very specific picture of the person she wants me to marry. Being male is one of the prerequisites."

"Is she really that meddling?" Del had left home before she had reached the age at which she would search for a life partner, and she knew Grace had never actively influenced her daughter's choice in partners, so matchmaking mothers were completely unfamiliar to her.

"She wasn't at the beginning. There were unvoiced expectations about what kind of boy I could bring home, but she didn't try to set me up with someone specific," Kade said. She closed her eyes as she leaned her head against the headrest. "But since my father died, the unmarried state of her daughter has turned into Sophie Thayer Matheson's personal crusade."

Del glanced back and forth between the traffic and Kade's face. "With all her efforts, there was never someone who met her expectations... or yours?" she asked carefully, hoping to learn more about Kade's past relationships and why they hadn't worked out. Kade was usually so tight-lipped about her private life that she didn't want to miss out on this opportunity.

Kade opened one eye, lazily blinking into the afternoon sun. "There aren't many men who want to be in a long-term relationship with someone who works twelve hours just to come home and continue working. No one is very understanding when I get called away from a romantic date or have to leave in the middle of the night because my detectives need a search warrant or want me to take a look at a crime scene," she answered matter-of-factly.

"Maybe you just haven't looked in the right places?" Del suggested.

Kade tilted her head. "Maybe. But it's not just the job. It's me." She opened both of her eyes now to watch for Del's reaction. When Del nodded her encouragement, she continued, "I never searched for happiness in my personal relationships. I always searched for fulfillment in my job. I had a handful of relationships I was mostly content with, and the sex was okay, but I was never head over heels in love." Kade shrugged. "I guess I'm just not a mad, passionate love kind of person."

"Who told you that?" Del asked. She didn't want to believe that Kade was unable to feel true love and be passionate about someone or something other than the law.

"Experience," Kade answered simply.

Del studied her. She could see it was something Kade had accepted as an unchangeable fact long ago. "Just because it has been your experience before doesn't mean it has to stay that way," she said.

"You mean I just haven't met the right person yet?" Kade asked with the teasing little smile that Del always found devastatingly cute.

"Oh, maybe you have already met her," she teased back.

Kade casually reached out and pinched her thigh.

"Hey! Keep your hands to yourself, woman! I'm driving here!" Despite her protests, Del was happy to see that Kade felt relaxed and comfortable enough around her to touch her in playful, little ways. She smiled at Kade for a few more seconds, then looked back to the thankfully empty road in front of her. "It could be a matter of meeting the right person, but I think it's more about allowing yourself to love with your whole heart and soul, without holding anything back."

Kade searched for something in the glove compartment. She finally found her sunglasses and put them on, hiding her blue eyes from Del. "Have you ever loved like that?" she asked from behind the safe barrier of her sunglasses.

"Once or twice," Del answered, allowing Kade to direct the attention away from herself.

"But it never worked out?" It was more Kade pointing it out than a real question.

Ever the relationship pessimist. Del chuckled to herself. "Not yet." She reached over and pulled Kade's sunglasses down just enough to be able to look into her eyes. "But I'm hopeful for the future."

"Ouch!" She jumped when Kade pinched her again. "By the time we reach Ashland, I'll be black and blue. Your mother will think you're beating me up."

"My mother won't get to see you in your underwear, so she won't know it, even if you are black and blue," Kade said and pulled the sunglasses back up on her nose.

Del laughed. Kade's logic was as impeccable as ever. "And? Will you?"

"Beat you black and blue?" Kade asked seriously. Del was sure her eyes were twinkling with mischief behind the sunglasses. "Only if you deserve it."

"See me in my underwear," Del emphasized.

Kade folded her arms behind her head in a gesture of total casualness. "Old hat," she said, pretending to be bored with the prospect of seeing Del half-naked again. "I've already seen you in your underwear three different times."

"I haven't been on top of my game those times," Del protested. "The first two times, you had just thoroughly trashed my ego by defeating me at chess, and the third time, I had a concussion."

"Details, details." Kade gestured at a road sign. "Take the next exit."

Del maneuvered the car into the next lane. "We're already there?" she asked in surprise. The time she spent with Kade always seemed to go by much too quickly. Two hundred eighty miles didn't seem like a large distance when traveling with Kade.

"Starting to panic?" Kade teased.

"Do I have a reason to?" Del asked.

Kade lost her teasing grin. "Not really. My mother is the perfect hostess, and I'm sure she'll treat you with nothing but politeness."

Del could sense there was something Kade wasn't saying. "And you?" she asked. "Is there a reason why you are so nervous?"

"When I'm visiting my mother, I usually know exactly what to expect and why I'm there. I fulfill my obligation to take part in family functions, and after that, I leave and return to my own life." Kade took off her sunglasses and slowly, methodically folded them. "This time, I don't know what will happen. Maybe nothing. Maybe the big family blowout I've been trying to avoid since my father died."

Del knew the situation had to be especially hard on Kade. Kade hated having no control over a situation. "I can't tell you what will happen. I can tell you one thing for sure, though. No matter what, I'll be there for you. You have backup, okay?"

Kade gave a small grin at hearing the cop jargon. "Okay."

* * *

Del waited next to Kade for the front door to open. *Front door? More like a portal.* Del looked back over the perfect lawn, surrounded by majestic elms. Meeting the parents of a girlfriend— or a prospective girlfriend—had never been a relaxed affair, but Del couldn't remember when she had last been so nervous. The intimidating Matheson estate with the mansion, the rose garden, and its own tennis court wasn't exactly making her feel more at ease. *At least they have tight security,* she thought with a glance at the high fence around the property, the security cameras, and the password-protected gate.

Finally, the front door opened. A gray-haired woman stood in front of them. She smiled when she saw Kade.

Is that her mother? Del wondered.

"Hello, Bernice," Kade said, answering Del's silent question. "Good to see you again. Is my mother home?"

"Yes, Ms. Matheson, she is," the woman answered. She looked at Del. "Can I help you with the bags?"

She's the maid, Del realized, feeling as if she had stepped into a strange world. *They probably have a cook and a butler too.* She quickly shook her head. "No, thanks. I have it." Del followed the two of them into a marbled entrance hall. She gripped her bag tighter and held up one of Kade's suit bags at shoulder height, careful not to knock over one of the antiques that decorated the marbled hall. She knew she could never afford one of the pieces, even after more than twenty years on the force.

A slender woman came down the stairs that led to the second floor. "Kadence," she said, looking down at them. "I didn't expect you so early. I just came in from the tennis court, and I'm not dressed for guests."

Guests? Del wondered if Kade constituted a "guest" to her mother. She looked at the elegant woman. Sophie Thayer

- 384 -

Matheson was wearing an expensive blouse and tan slacks that were clearly tailored for her delicate frame. A cashmere sweater was arranged over her narrow shoulders, and whatever she had done on the tennis court hadn't gotten her sweaty or out of breath.

"We made better time on the interstate than we expected," Kade answered in the same overly polite tone her mother had used.

Sophie Thayer Matheson reached the entrance hall and kissed her daughter's cheek. Her embrace entailed hardly any body contact. "Hello, Kadence."

"Hello, Mother," Kade answered formally.

God, what is this? An audience with the queen or a mother welcoming her daughter home? Del wondered but said nothing.

"I see you brought a guest," Kade's mother said, finally noticing Del. "Hello. I'm Sophie Thayer Matheson. You are welcome in my home."

For a moment, Del almost thought Mrs. Matheson expected her to curtsey, but then she offered Del a delicate hand.

Del put down her bag and gently wrapped her fingers around Sophie's. "Delicia Vasquez Montero. I didn't know Kade has a sister," she said with her most charming smile. She didn't even have to exaggerate much. With her smooth porcelain skin and her slender frame, Sophie Matheson looked barely old enough to have a daughter of Kade's age.

Sophie looked confused at being complimented like that by a woman. After a second, a flattered smile flitted across her face. "I see good manners are still being taught, even in Portland," she said. She was facing Del, but her words were clearly directed at Kade.

She doesn't like Kade living in Portland. She wants to have her home, Del understood. "Thank you for having me," Del said. She noticed that the Mathesons' formality was contagious.

"You're welcome," Sophie Matheson answered.

Despite that graceful answer, it was very clear to Del that Kade hadn't told her mother she was bringing someone with her. It was equally clear that, even if Kade had told her, Sophie wouldn't have expected someone like Del. Sophie Matheson was hiding it well, but Del sensed she was being scrutinized from head to toe. Del knew she was very different from other friends Kade might have brought home before. *I'm not a twenty-something, rich, white lawyer, but a forty-three-year-old, middle-class Puerto Rican cop. Not exactly the kind of guest Sophie Thayer Matheson is used to.*

"Bernice," Sophie Matheson addressed the maid, "please see our guests to their rooms and help them get settled while I change."

Del tried to imagine a young Kade living in this mansion of a house while they were making their way up the stairs to the second floor. She got a peek at an extensive library, but there was nothing in the house to keep a child entertained, and Del couldn't see Sophie Thayer Matheson getting down on the floor to play with her daughter. *I bet Kade was expected to act like a little adult from a very early age.*

Meeting her mother and seeing the house in which Kade had grown up gave Del a whole new understanding of Kade as a person. *No wonder she's always so controlled. Showing emotions just isn't done in this house.*

Suddenly sad for the child Kade had once been and the woman she was now, Del wanted to say something to her but didn't know what. The presence of the maid added to the awkwardness of the situation.

The maid opened the door to the guestroom for Del, and Del noticed with satisfaction that Kade had the room right next to hers. This way, she could keep an eye on Kade should the stalker have found out where she was despite their best efforts.

She entered the large guestroom and looked around while she set down her travel bag and laid down Kade's suit bag on the bed. The furniture was tasteful and expensive, but it looked more like a museum than a comfortable home. Del sighed. Maybe coming here hadn't been such a good idea after all.

A knock on the door that connected her room to Kade's made her look up. Kade's copper-haired head appeared in the doorway. "Is the room okay?" Kade asked.

"Yes, of course." Del would have slept in a broom closet if necessary to keep Kade safe.

Kade walked farther into the room. She left her bag and her laptop bag in her room. "It was my nanny's room when I was growing up," she said as she looked around.

"You had a nanny?" It was a strange concept for Del. There had been a lot of children in her family. Not one of them had ever had a nanny. Older siblings, aunts, or friends had babysat, but no child had been raised by a stranger.

"I had half a dozen of them over the years," Kade answered matter-of-factly. It was probably the most normal thing in the world for her.

Half a dozen? That means she probably didn't have the chance to get close to one of them. Del shook her head. *Seems like a very lonely way to grow up.* She couldn't look back at her childhood and her family without bitterness, but at least she had never been lonely growing up. Until the day she had been thrown out of the house, someone had always been there for her.

"What was that downstairs?" Kade asked. "You didn't try to flirt with my mother, did you?"

I'd rather flirt with her daughter. "No, I didn't. I just paid her a compliment—and I didn't even have to lie about it. Jesus! I'm closer to your mother's age than yours," Del said with a shake of her head. *You're a woman; you're not a blue-blooded socialite, and you're almost her mother's age—three strikes, you're out.*

"She looks younger than she is," Kade answered. "Good genes, I hope, and a good beautician."

Kade was probably right. Sophie Matheson never had to juggle a stressful job and raising half a dozen kids on very little money. She didn't have the work-worn look or the worry lines of Del's mother. Still, one thing was very clear to Del. "There's no way she could have a son of your brother's age," Del said. Douglas Matheson junior was at least ten years older than Kade.

"That's one of the Matheson family secrets everyone knows but nobody talks about," Kade said. "Doug is my father's son from his first marriage."

Once again, Del was reminded how private Kade usually was. She was sure that none of her colleagues and friends knew Doug was only her half brother—if they knew about his existence at all.

Del was glad to see how freely Kade answered her questions. "Your father got a divorce?"

"No. Mathesons don't get divorced. They have unhappy marriages, but no divorces. Make each other miserable, but never leave—that's the unwritten rule," Kade said with a touch of bitterness. "Doug's mother died shortly after his birth. My father remarried two years later."

"So you did grow up together. Is Doug close to your mother?" Del asked. She could see how being half siblings and the weight of their father's expectations had caused a lifelong rivalry between Kade and her brother. Maybe Kade's mother had added to that.

Kade picked up her suit bag that Del had laid on the bed. "Not particularly," she said, no emotions coloring her words. It was just a fact of life for her.

Neither are you, Del thought. Kade and her mother had been polite and friendly toward each other, but there had been no real warmth in their interaction.

Another knock came, this time on the door that led to the hallway.

Kade quickly took her suit bag, gave Del a small, conspiratorial smile, and disappeared through the connecting door back into her own room.

"Yes?" Del called.

The maid opened the door. "Mrs. Matheson had a light supper prepared. If you want to join her in the dining room..."

"I'd love to," Del said with more enthusiasm than she felt. She had a feeling dinner with Sophie Thayer Matheson could be a stiff and boring affair. At least she would have Kade's company, and that made it worth it.

Del followed the maid down to the dining room. Kade was nowhere to be seen, so Del took her time, not wanting to be alone with Mrs. Matheson for too long. Her gaze wandered over the oak panels on the walls and the chandelier above the table that was much too big for just three people. There was a lot of space between the three place settings, and Del couldn't help thinking it was a symbol for the emotional distance between the people in this family.

Sophie Matheson was already seated at the head of the table, now wearing even more elegant clothes.

Del hesitated in the doorway. She wasn't sure where to sit or what to say to Mrs. Matheson. A light touch to the small of her back made her turn around.

Kade had finally arrived downstairs. She had changed out of her comfortable traveling clothes and into a pair of well-tailored pants and a light blue silk blouse that flattered her slender build and brought out the blue of her eyes.

I should have changed before sitting down to have dinner with them, Del realized. Between the very refined Sophie Thayer Matheson and her equally elegant daughter, Del felt like a mongrel among pedigreed poodles. *Come on. Where's your confidence? If Kade doesn't mind your wearing blue jeans to dinner, why would you try to impress her mother? I think it's an impossible feat anyway. Kade is as close to perfect as one can get, but her mother still doesn't seem entirely satisfied with her.*

Del waited until Kade had chosen a seat, barely holding herself back from pulling the chair out for Kade, before she sat down. She noticed the large portrait on the wall in front of her. An imposing man with sand-colored hair and ice blue eyes was sternly looking down at her. *Kade's father.*

"Tell me, Ms. Vasquez, how do you know my daughter?" Sophie Matheson asked while the maid brought in the soup.

No one called Del "Ms. Vasquez." *I'm a cop, not a schoolteacher, for heaven's sake!* She was used to being called Del, Lieutenant, or just Vasquez. "Please, call me Del," she said.

"Del?" Sophie Matheson's eyebrow lifted in exactly the same way Kade's did when she heard something she didn't approve of.

Looks like the proper Mrs. Matheson doesn't like to shorten names. She calls Kade "Kadence" too. "Or Delicia," she reluctantly amended.

Kade gave her a surprised look, and Del shrugged in answer. *The sacrifices I make for you.*

Now Sophie Matheson nodded but didn't return the offer to call her by her first name. "Then tell me, Delicia, how do you know my daughter?"

Del internally winced at being called "Delicia."

Kade didn't look up from her soup, but Del could see her fingers tightening around her spoon at her mother's question.

Don't worry, Kade. I won't tell her anything that might get you in trouble. Del gave Kade a reassuring smile before she turned to Mrs. Matheson. "I'm a lieutenant with the Portland Police Bureau's homicide division, so we occasionally meet through our work. Kade also prosecuted the rapist of a very good friend of mine last year," Del continued. She decided not to use the longer version of Kade's first name. Sophie Matheson might have preferred it, but Del knew Kade didn't. "She won the case, and for that I'll be forever grateful to her."

Kade looked up. Her gaze met Del's, and her features relaxed into a smile.

Mrs. Matheson wistfully gazed at the portrait of her late husband. "Kadence is an excellent lawyer," she said as if Kade weren't sitting right next to her. "Her father always said that. He was convinced that her talent is wasted in the DA's office." The look on her face said she thought the same thing.

Del laid down her spoon. "I can assure you that it isn't. Her conviction rate is way above the national average for a prosecutor. Kade is bringing justice to a lot of women and children who would otherwise see their tormentor go free," she said with passion.

Both Matheson women looked at her with various degrees of astonishment. Under the table, a foot touched Del's in a silent gesture of gratefulness.

"Good to see that at least your talents are appreciated by the people you work with," Sophie Matheson finally said, now directly addressing Kade for the first time.

Oh, I appreciate a lot more about Kade than just her lawyering talents, Del thought, suppressing a smile.

"Tell me a little about yourself." Mrs. Matheson turned to Del again. "Are you married?"

Del nearly choked on her soup. *That won't happen unless a few laws change.* "No, I'm not," she answered as neutrally as possible.

"But you do have a boyfriend, don't you?" Mrs. Matheson inquired. Most people would have suspected Del was gay by now, but Kade's mother was still blissfully unaware.

"I'm single," Del answered. She wouldn't lie if Mrs. Matheson asked her directly, but for now, she saw no reason to come out to Kade's mother. If Mrs. Matheson knew Del was a lesbian, she would probably start to question Kade about their friendship, and Del didn't want that. She wanted Kade to be able to relax for a while.

"If you—" Mrs. Matheson began her next question.

"Mother," Kade interrupted sharply. "I don't think our guest likes being interrogated about her private life." Her facial expression was the same Del had often seen in court when Kade passionately objected to something the defense attorney had said.

Del looked at her appreciatively. She had a feeling it wasn't very often that Kade openly put her mother in her place.

"I was just trying to get to know your friend better," Mrs. Matheson answered indignantly. "It's not very often that you bring someone home."

Yeah, and I now know the reason for it. Del gently cleared her throat. "It's all right, Kade. I don't mind the questions. My life is an open book—but I'm afraid it's not very interesting," she told Mrs. Matheson with a friendly smile. "I spend most of my time at work."

Mrs. Matheson sighed. She looked from Del to Kade. "I always tell Kadence she's working too much. I appreciate her ambition, but it leaves her no time to go out and meet someone. Building a relationship takes time, but how can you do that if you're always working?" Her gaze ranged over her husband's portrait, and for a moment, Del could see sadness and regret in her eyes—the first true emotions she had seen on Kade's mother since they arrived.

"If I met the right person, I'd make time for a relationship," Del said, trying very hard not to look at Kade while she said it.

"But until that happens, putting my energy into a job I love and can make a difference with is not a bad alternative, is it?"

Sophie Matheson looked startled to be put on the spot like this. They both knew Del wasn't only talking about herself. She was talking about Kade too. "Well, no, I suppose it's not a bad alternative," Mrs. Matheson finally had to admit. She picked up her spoon again, effectively ending the conversation.

Kade still wasn't eating, though. She looked from Del to her mother with an expression of amazement on her normally controlled face. She probably didn't have a lot of success trying to get her mother to concede to the exact same thing she had said right now.

Del gave her a smile before she quickly bent her head to eat her soup.

CHAPTER 27

*A*IDEN BOUNCED ON the balls of her feet. She could hear footsteps in the house, but it took forever until the door was opened, making Aiden even more nervous than she already was. She had hoped it would be Evan who opened the door, but now she came face-to-face with Roger LeCroix.

He didn't smile when he saw her.

Aiden grimaced internally. *Shit. It just had to be the stricter parent opening the door.* "Hi," she said, trying to figure out if Evan's foster father was looking so surly because Evan had told them about her near brush with the law or if something else had annoyed him. In case Evan hadn't said anything, she didn't want to get her in trouble by saying the wrong thing now. "Is... is Evan home?"

"Yes," he answered shortly.

This is usually easier if I have my badge and can force them to be a little more forthcoming with information, Aiden thought grimly. "Is it okay if I take her out for another driving lesson?" she asked. The two other times she had picked Evan up for driving lessons, Jill LeCroix had been the one to open the door, and she had always greeted Aiden with enthusiasm.

"No," Roger LeCroix growled. "Evan is grounded for the rest of the month. No driving lessons for her." He started to close the door.

"Wait!" Aiden quickly put her foot in the door, preventing it from closing. "She told you?" To be honest, despite her promise, Aiden hadn't been sure if Evan would tell her foster parents.

LeCroix nodded grimly. "She did."

"And?" Aiden asked carefully.

Evan's foster father snorted. "What do you think? Drugs are not tolerated in this house! Neither are drug addicts."

Oh, oh. This didn't sound encouraging. "You're not going to make her leave and put her back into the system just because of this, are you?" Aiden had to know.

"We haven't made a final decision yet, but..." Roger LeCroix shook his head. "I have to admit that our patience was already stretched to the max before this happened. And now she comes and tells us over dinner that she was almost arrested buying drugs."

"But at least she did tell you. That took a lot of courage," Aiden said. She was finally beginning to see Evan in a more positive light, and she wished Evan's foster parents would do it too. "She's taking responsibility for her behavior, and she promised me she's giving up drugs. What more can we expect of her right now?"

Roger LeCroix had no answer for that.

"Can I come in and see her for a minute?" Aiden asked when he kept silent.

He hesitated, still blocking the door, but after a few seconds, he stepped back and grudgingly allowed Aiden to enter. "She's upstairs. Her room is the first one on the right," he said.

Aiden slowly took one step after another, trying to think about what she would say when she reached the top of the stairs. A part of her felt guilty to have forced Evan into this tense situation with her foster parents even though she knew she couldn't just let Evan off the hook. Evan had to learn that actions had consequences before it was too late. Dawn had wholeheartedly agreed and told Aiden she had done the right thing. Still, it was hard to face Evan for the first time since her near arrest.

Taking a deep breath, she knocked on the door to Evan's room. She listened but heard only loud music coming from the other side of the door. She knocked again, just in case Evan hadn't heard her, and then slowly opened the door. "Evan?"

"What?" was the gruff response.

Aiden opened the door wider and entered the room. "Hey, it's me," she said unnecessarily.

Evan was lounging on her bed, doing nothing but staring at the wall. "Come to visit me in my cell?" she asked sarcastically.

"Cell?" Evan's room wasn't exactly luxurious, but it wasn't Spartan either. "This room is too messy to be a cell," Aiden said with a grin. A creased T-shirt was lying on the floor next to the bed; a stack of folded clothes balanced precariously on the desk, and a few CD casings next to it left no room to do any schoolwork.

"They're holding me prisoner here," Evan complained. "No phone, no TV, no access to the computer or the Internet for two weeks, thanks to you!"

Oh, no, I won't let you blame this on me! Aiden stepped closer to Evan, looking down at her through narrowed eyes. "Thanks to me? Correct me if I'm wrong, but I think you were the one who was trying to buy drugs. If you got into trouble, it's because of that, not because of me."

"Yeah, yeah, yeah," Evan said, but she lowered her gaze and guiltily looked down. "So, did you get into trouble over busting me out, or did they believe your story about me being an informant?" she asked after a while.

Aiden suppressed a smile. *What do you know... she does care about me.* "A few of my colleagues suspect there's more to the story than I told them, but they trust me enough not to ask about it." Aiden hoped Evan would learn to open up to friendship and trust like that someday. "Can I sit down for a moment?"

"Sure." Evan gestured to her desk chair. A stack of magazines and books was piled on it.

Instead of removing the items from the chair, Aiden sat down on the bed next to Evan. *No more keeping each other at a distance.*

Evan looked at her in surprise. She clearly wasn't used to people who didn't keep a physical distance to her. She didn't protest, though, so Aiden stayed where she was.

"How did your foster parents react when you told them what happened?" Aiden finally asked.

"Hello? I'm here in my room, with no TV, no phone, and no computer—that should tell you they weren't exactly pleased about it," Evan answered sarcastically. "I think they're down there, having a family powwow to discuss my future. I wouldn't be surprised if they sent me away."

Aiden resolutely shook her head. "I won't let that happen. You stood up for your mistakes, and now you're trying to do better. That should be enough to make them give you another chance."

Evan eyed her suspiciously. She seemed to mistrust Aiden's support and the positive words about her, but when Aiden just looked at her with a serious expression, she shrugged. "Yeah. Tell it to them."

"I already did," Aiden answered. She could only hope Roger LeCroix had listened to her.

"You did?" Mistrust, surprise, and hope warred in Evan's voice.

Aiden nodded. "I encouraged you to tell them, and I appreciate that you kept your word and did it. That takes a lot of guts." She gave Evan a nod of admiration.

"I knew you'd tell them if I didn't, so it's not like I had a choice," Evan grumbled, immediately shrugging off Aiden's praise, but not before Aiden had seen the blush on her cheeks.

"But you were the one who told them—and in the end, I'm sure it will make all the difference," Aiden said, willing it to be so. She would do everything she could to make sure Evan wasn't punished for taking responsibility for her mistakes. Being grounded for trying to buy drugs was fine with her, but getting Evan thrown out of her foster family was not her goal.

Evan didn't answer, so Aiden chose to change the subject.

"Now that you're under house arrest and are not allowed to use the phone, is there anyone you want me to call for you?" Aiden asked, trying to make it a little easier for Evan.

Evan shrugged. Aiden had noticed before that she always acted as if there were no one in the world she cared about even a little. "You can tell the doc I need to give her a rain check for our skating lesson," Evan finally answered.

She cares about Dawn, Aiden realized and tried not to smile. *Like sister, like sister.* Aiden nodded. "I'll tell her that. She's sending her best wishes, by the way."

"Oh, yeah. I bet that's what she said when you told her about that drug bust, huh?" Evan snorted. "You did tell her, right?"

"Yes, I did. I try not to have any secrets from Dawn," Aiden said.

Evan pressed her lips together. It was clear to Aiden that Dawn's opinion was important to her. "So what did the doc say about my little adventure?" she asked, acting casually.

Dawn hadn't been surprised, but Aiden didn't want to tell Evan that. She didn't want Evan to believe that Dawn had lost faith in her. Dawn hadn't. She was just realistic and knew that Evan's problems wouldn't stop all of a sudden just because she now had a big sister who cared about her. "She was worried about you," Aiden answered truthfully.

Evan hung her head for a moment. When she became aware of Aiden watching her, she quickly looked up again and jutted her chin forward. "Nothing to worry about," she grumbled. "I'm not an addict or anything!"

"Dawn knows that, but it doesn't mean you don't have a problem. She... we worry about you," Aiden emphasized.

Evan didn't answer. Her long fingers plucked at a hole in the knee of her faded jeans.

"So," Aiden cleared her throat, "is there anyone else I should call for you?"

"Like who?" Evan raised a lazy brow.

Aiden hesitated for a second, but when Evan just looked at her, she answered, "Like Laurie Matheson, for example. Won't she get worried and wonder what's going on if you don't visit or call her?"

Evan just shrugged.

"What does that mean? You haven't seen her since Del's birthday party?" After Dawn's niece Jamie had come running into the house, telling everyone that Evan and Laurie had been kissing under the tree in the Kinsleys' front yard, Aiden had assumed Evan was now dating Kade's niece.

"Oh, yes, I did," Evan purred with a provocative stance. "I even had the ovaries to visit her at her house." She relaxed her tightly folded arms when Aiden just chuckled instead of rebuking her for seeing Laurie or for her choice of words.

Aiden gave her a smile of encouragement. "How did her parents take that?" she asked.

Evan rolled her eyes. "Her father wasn't there, but her mother acted like some chaperone from the Middle Ages who had to protect a fair maiden's virtue. She even told Laurie to leave the door open when we went to her room!"

"At least she's letting you see Laurie. That's progress, right?" Aiden tried to cheer her up.

"I guess," Evan reluctantly agreed. Suddenly, she chuckled. "Laurie's aunt set them straight—no pun intended. Having an aunt who's a lesbian too really made things easier for Laurie."

Aiden grabbed a handful of bedclothes as she stared at Evan in surprise. "What makes you think Laurie's aunt is a lesbian?" She knew Kade was finally beginning to admit an attraction to women in general and Del in particular, but, as much as Del probably wished for it, they were not a couple yet, and Kade was bisexual at best. Kade's behavior and her facial expressions were too controlled for Evan to be able to just pick up on Kade's interest in women.

"Laurie told me," Evan answered. She didn't seem to have any doubts about it.

Aiden couldn't believe Kade would be so casual about it and come out so easily to her family after years of letting everyone think she was completely straight. "And how would Laurie know?" she wondered.

"Her aunt encouraged Laurie to come out to her parents and tell them I didn't force her to sleep with me. When Laurie chickened out, her aunt told her she's a lesbian too." A superior smirk appeared on Evan's face as she studied Aiden. "You didn't know? Never tried your luck with her?" She flashed Aiden a wolfish grin.

A harsh answer lingered on the tip of Aiden's tongue. She wanted to tell Evan to mind her own business. *No. Don't shut her out just because her questions make you uncomfortable. If you do, she'll never trust you.* "We're friends," she said neutrally.

"Because you're involved with the doc?" Evan asked. In contrast to her usual pretense of disinterest, her eyes were now bright with curiosity.

It would be so easy to just say yes and leave it at that. Still, Aiden didn't want to burden the fragile relationship with her half sister with a lie. "No. I was working with Kade long before I ever met Dawn."

"But you never...?" Evan made a few lewd gestures.

Again, Aiden had to hold back sharp words of reprimand. She knew Evan was only trying to provoke her, but this time, she was determined to have an adult conversation with her. "No, never. I always believed Kade to be straight."

"She's good at playing the part," Evan agreed.

Aiden looked at her in surprise. She hadn't thought Evan would be a good judge of character. Evan always seemed to concentrate on herself too much to have any insight into other people. *She knows a lot about playing roles and wearing masks to protect herself,* Aiden realized.

"Evan!" Roger LeCroix's voice drifted up the stairs. "Come downstairs. We want to talk to you."

Evan stood with a sigh. "The jury's in," she said, grimacing.

And she's expecting to be found guilty and be given the maximum sentence, Aiden realized. "Do you want me to stay?" she asked.

"No. If they throw me out, I'll just turn up on your doorstep," Evan threatened with a brave grin.

"Evan!" Roger LeCroix shouted again.

Aiden stood quickly, not wanting to annoy Evan's foster parents any further, and walked down the stairs while Evan lagged behind a few steps.

Roger LeCroix leaned in the doorway of the living room. He looked at her with an impenetrable gaze.

"She deserves another chance," Aiden said in a low voice when she walked past him.

Evan's foster father didn't answer.

Aiden reached the front door and turned back around. She made eye contact with Evan, who was trying to hide her nervousness. Her tense shoulders and the hands that were clenched into fists in the pockets of her baggy jeans betrayed her. "I'll come back to visit you tomorrow," Aiden promised, sending a silent message to Jill and Roger LeCroix. *Evan better still be here!*

One last glance, then the door closed behind Aiden.

CHAPTER 28

"**N**ICE PARTY," a male voice said from behind her.

Kade turned her head, looking away from Del, who was on the other side of the room, talking to someone. She saw Mathew Haygood sidle up to her and nodded noncommittally, accepting the glass of champagne he held out for her.

A few years ago, she would have agreed with more enthusiasm. It was a nice party. Her mother had invited all of her old friends from high school who still lived in the area, along with every eligible bachelor in her circle of acquaintances. Sophie had spared neither effort nor expense to make this the most talked-about dinner party of the month.

There was good music, expensive food, and decent conversation. The lawyer jokes Mathew had told her all evening were even halfway amusing. A few years ago, she would have enjoyed the evening, but now it seemed like a waste of time to her.

I think Del is partly to blame for that, she thought, again glancing at her friend at the other side of the room. Lately, she had spent the majority of her free time in Del's company. She had grown used to Del's honesty, to her sincere interest in her. With Del, there was no polite small talk and no pressure to act in a certain way. Del challenged her, and she made her laugh. She could relax and be herself, not the carefully cultivated public image of Kadence Matheson.

"Who's that?" Mathew asked, having followed Kade's gaze.

It wasn't difficult to guess that Del was not an offspring of one of the wealthy families with whom the Mathesons usually socialized. Del stuck out of the crowd of guests like a sore thumb. She was probably the only woman in the room who didn't wear a dress.

It had earned her a few questioning gazes from Sophie, but Kade secretly admired Del for not bending to her mother's unspoken wishes or other people's expectations. She liked that Del was still herself and not willing to act as if she were one of the Mathesons' very sophisticated, very feminine, very well-dressed friends.

She doesn't need to. She's wonderful in her own way—and she looks fantastic! Kade had secretly admired the way the neatly pressed, but still comfortable black slacks fit Del's long legs and athletic frame. The white dress shirt she wore with it contrasted nicely to her coffee-colored skin and jet-black hair.

Mathew lightly touched Kade's bare arm when she failed to answer. "Who's that?" he asked again.

Kade half turned under the pretense of turning back to look at him, making his hand slip from her arm. He had touched her with fake casualness all evening, and it was beginning to irritate Kade. "That's Del Vasquez," she answered. "A very good friend of mine."

"Hmm." Mathew didn't seem to know what to make of that statement—or of Del. "So... you didn't bring a man home with you," he said with a hopeful grin.

Kade had been out on a few dates with Mathew her senior year of high school, and he still seemed to think she would someday come home and marry him. "I brought Del," Kade answered, secretly amusing herself because she knew Mathew would never grasp the true meaning of these words.

Mathew dismissed it with a grin. "But you don't have a boyfriend?"

"No, there's no man in my life," she told him, smiling to herself.

* * *

Del stood with her wineglass in hand, half listening to an amusing anecdote one of Sophie Matheson's guests was telling. Mainly, she was watching Kade from across the room.

Kade was surrounded by half a dozen men, who complimented her, kissed her hand, and offered to fetch her drinks.

It looked like a scene from an old fairy tale. *The admiring underlings are waiting upon the heir to the Matheson throne,* Del thought with amusement.

Del hadn't exchanged more than a few words with Kade since the dinner party started. Every time one or both of them finished a conversation, another guest wandered up to them and occupied them for another few minutes, keeping them apart.

It seems Mrs. Matheson's matchmaking attempts don't stop at her daughter. One or two of the male guests had tried to charm her, something that hadn't happened to Del in a long time. She had taken it in stride. After a few minutes of talking to them as an equal, not a flattered female, they had stopped acting like admirers and were now talking to her like old pals.

When she saw the latest man at Kade's side wander away, Del quickly excused herself and made her way over to Kade. "Having fun?" she asked with a smile.

Kade moved her head in a half circle that could equally mean yes or no. "I've had better evenings," she admitted after making sure no one was within hearing distance.

"For example?" Del asked, immediately interested in what Kade would consider a pleasant evening.

"Your birthday party was a lot nicer than this matchmaking festival," Kade answered, "and I had a lot of fun playing chess with you."

So she likes spending time with me more than she likes going to the classy events she was raised to participate in, huh? A wave of proud giddiness swept over Del at the realization. "So you liked getting naked with me, hmm?" she teased.

Kade gave her a stern look, but a hint of blush on her fair skin gave her away. "I didn't get naked," Kade reminded her. "You were the one who lost all her clothes."

"You were barefoot," Del said.

"So?" Kade was unimpressed. "If you think there's no difference between taking off my socks and taking off the rest of my clothes, then you have clearly never seen me naked." She threw back her head with a confident smirk.

Del's mouth went dry. She blindly reached for a glass of champagne that a nearby waiter offered on a tray. Lately, Kade had begun to flirt with her, and Del loved the sexual confidence she displayed. "Oh, I'm sure there's a big difference." Del laughed and teasingly stared at Kade's chest.

Kade looked at something directly behind Del. "Hello, Mother."

Del felt the color drain from her face, then suddenly rush back as she blushed in mortification. Very slowly, she turned around to face Kade's mother—only to realize that Mrs. Matheson was nowhere to be seen.

"Got you!" Kade smirked.

Del whirled back around. "You! You...!" She pointed her index finger at Kade, at a loss for words at the moment. "That was..."

"Mean?" Kade helpfully supplied. "Well, commenting on the size of my... differences wasn't exactly ladylike either."

Del tried to act hurt but quickly gave up. She liked Kade's rarely shown playfulness and the fact that Kade didn't let her get away with anything. An involuntary smile curled her lips. "Touché. If I promise to abstain from such comments in the future, you have to promise not to scare me like that again."

"It's a deal." Kade nodded gravely as if she had just negotiated a plea bargain.

"I can still compliment you on your looks, can't I? Because you look very beautiful tonight," Del said with honest admiration. Her gaze wandered over the tight black dress Kade wore. It left Kade's arms and shoulders bare, revealed just a hint of cleavage, and dipped teasingly low in the back.

"Thank you." Kade accepted the compliment with the grace of someone who had been told the very same thing a thousand times before.

Del held her gaze. "I really mean it," she said seriously. She wanted Kade to know that she was not just one of her many smooth-talking admirers. She truly appreciated everything about Kade—her beauty, her intelligence, and her personality.

"Thanks," Kade said, giving a nod of understanding. "You look wonderful tonight too."

Del looked down at herself, then back at Kade. "I know I can't keep up with the rest of your guests." She pointed at the other people in the room. Each and every one of them wore clothes that were worth more than Del's old, battered car.

"You don't need to," Kade said. "It's the fact that you're not like one of them that I like about you."

Del stared at her. *Is it just wishful thinking, or did Kade really open up to me over the past few weeks? She's not holding back her emotions so much anymore.*

A little uncomfortable, Kade broke their eye contact by glancing at the buffet. "I think I need a few of these roasted shrimp before they're all gone. Do you want any?"

Smiling, Del shook her head. She allowed Kade to retreat without comment, knowing Kade needed a moment alone to compose herself. In the meantime, she consoled herself with watching Kade's graceful form stride toward the buffet in the backless dress.

* * *

Kade heaped more shrimp than she really wanted to eat on her plate. She could feel Del's gaze resting on her back, heating up her bare skin. She knew most of the other people in the room were stealing glances at her too, but Del's dark eyes were the only ones that didn't leave her unimpressed.

A little uncomfortable with her growing awareness of Del, she was almost glad when her mother walked up to her.

"Are you enjoying your party?" her mother asked.

My party? Kade repeated silently, holding back a grimace. She knew this party served Sophie's needs first and foremost. The party wasn't about Kade's enjoyment, but about Sophie parading around her successful daughter and trying to find an acceptable son-in-law. "Yes, of course I am," she answered politely.

"Have you talked to Thomas yet?" Sophie discreetly nodded toward a man in his early forties who was an investment banker and talked about nothing else every time Kade saw him.

So far, I've managed to avoid it, Kade thought. "Not yet."

Sophie turned fully toward her, fixing her with a strict gaze. "I saw you talking to Delicia."

Kade set down her plate as a mixture of anger and nervousness made her fingers tremble. *Does she suspect anything?* "What's wrong with that?" she asked defensively.

"Nothing. I'm sure your friend is very nice."

Matheson language for "too common and not worthy of your attention," Kade bitterly translated.

"...but wouldn't you rather mingle with your other guests?" Sophie managed to make her question an order.

"Male guests," Kade said what her mother really meant. Usually, she faced her mother's attempts at matchmaking with her courtroom poker face, but tonight she had no patience for it. "Mother, please, stop trying to set me up," she demanded with barely restrained annoyance.

Her mother gave her the indignant look she had perfected over the years. "I wouldn't need to set you up if you—"

"What a wonderful party, Mrs. Matheson," Del interrupted, smoothly stepping between the two Matheson women. "Thank you for inviting me."

She didn't exactly invite you, Kade thought, still annoyed with her mother and this impossible situation. Del's presence calmed her, though. She could practically feel her blood pressure return to normal.

Sophie looked at Del in surprise. They all knew she hadn't invited Del, but Del continued to dazzle her with a bright smile, so Sophie had no choice but to react with the formal politeness that had been drilled into her. "You're welcome," she said stiffly. "I hope you're enjoying yourself."

"How could I not since I'm in the company of our charming hostess." Del smiled so warmly and honestly that Sophie blinked.

Her cool formality slowly melted away and was replaced with a hesitant smile. Sophie gave Del a nod, pointedly looked at Kade, and then walked away.

"Phew," Del groaned even though she was still grinning. "Thought you could use someone to bail you out."

Normally, Kade would have been annoyed at anyone playing the knight in shining armor, charging in to rescue her, but this time, she was glad for Del's intervention. She'd had enough of her mother's meddling, and she knew her mother wouldn't stop just because she told her so.

Del was probably the only person in the room who could get Sophie to back off. Sophie wasn't used to the warmth and sincerity Del projected in her smile. She didn't know what to make of Del, so she had retreated rather than face someone who was so different from all her acquaintances.

"How did you do that?" Kade grumbled. "Call my mother a charming hostess with such sincerity? She hasn't given you the time of day all night, and she told me in no uncertain terms that I should stop wasting my time with you and talk to all the eligible bachelors instead."

"I was looking so sincere because I meant it," Del said with a grin. "You invited me to come home with you, so **you** are the hostess to me."

Del winked at her, and Kade finally felt herself relax.

Del casually stole a shrimp from Kade's plate. "Come on. Let's go make your mother happy and mingle with the crowd."

CHAPTER 29

*J*AMIE SCRAMBLED up from her place on the couch next to Dawn when a key jingled in the front door. "That's Auntie Aiden!"

"Give her a minute, Jamie," Dawn said. She knew Aiden always needed a few minutes after coming home to turn off her cop mode. She had her little rituals, putting away her gun and her badge, that helped her with it, and Dawn had learned not to disturb her.

Jamie didn't listen, too eager to be the first one to greet Aiden. She raced across the living room.

"Must be the Aiden virus," Eliza said with a smile as she watched her daughter disappear around the corner. "I hear it's contagious."

Aiden strolled into the living room, her hand firmly clasped by both of Jamie's. "Hey," she said, clearly surprised to find the visitors in Dawn's living room.

Tim, Dawn's fifteen-month-old nephew, looked up from his building blocks. When he saw Aiden, he immediately reached for her and loudly demanded, "Up!"

Aiden looked a little overwhelmed, but she gamely bent down and picked him up.

"Oh, yeah." Eliza smirked. "Highly contagious."

Dawn stood too and leaned over Jamie to kiss Aiden hello. "How did it go?" she asked. "Find anything?" She knew Aiden and Ray had checked out another suspect who matched the description of Kade's stalker.

Aiden shook her head. Weary frustration showed in every one of her movements, and Dawn regretted inviting her mother, Eliza, and the kids over for dinner. It looked as if Aiden needed a quiet evening and a little pampering from Dawn.

"Is that a real gun?" Jamie asked, curiously touching the holster on Aiden's hip.

Aiden quickly put her free hand on the gun, preventing Jamie from getting her hands on it. "Yes, it is. It can be dangerous, so I want you to always remember that it's not a toy, okay?"

When Jamie nodded seriously, Aiden let go of the gun and gently ruffled Jamie's hair.

Dawn and Eliza exchanged a glance and a smile. *She's so good with Jamie,* Dawn thought with pride.

With Tim perched on her hip, Aiden walked out of the room to put away her gun and then toward the kitchen to greet Grace, who was preparing their dinner.

Jamie ran to catch up with her. From their places on the couch, Dawn and Eliza heard her ask, "Did you ever shoot anyone?"

Eliza groaned. "I'm sorry. I'm sure she gets that inquisitiveness from your part of the family."

Dawn didn't bother to dispute it. "Don't worry. Aiden can handle it."

"She's great with the kids," Eliza agreed. She put her chin on her hands and studied Dawn. "Have you ever talked about having kids?"

Every time Dawn saw Aiden with children, she had to think about what a great mother Aiden would be, but she knew Aiden had some issues with that subject, so she hadn't brought it up. "Well, we had the general 'What do you think about having kids' talk when we were still just friends, but we never seriously talked about having kids together," Dawn answered, her voice almost a whisper. She didn't want Aiden or Grace to overhear.

Eliza nudged her, looking down at her with an affectionate grin. "But you'd like to raise children with her, right?"

It was hard to keep a dreamy smile from her lips and answer matter-of-factly, "Eventually, yes."

Eliza slung one arm around her in an exuberant hug. "I'm so happy for you. I know this is what you wanted for yourself even back when you were still married."

Dawn nodded. She had thought about having a baby when she had been married to Cal but had eventually decided against it. Not only had she barely been twenty back then, but she had also known something was missing in their relationship, and she hadn't wanted to bring a child into that situation.

Jamie came skipping back into the living room. She was chatting incessantly with Aiden, who still carried a shrieking and laughing toddler. The sound level in the room suddenly went up a few decibels.

Eliza good-naturedly rolled her eyes. "You want kids?" She threw a mock self-pitying glance at Dawn and Aiden. "Take mine."

Aiden's eyebrows crept up, but she didn't ask why Eliza thought they wanted children.

Just then, Dawn's mother called for Dawn to set the table, and Dawn forgot what they had been talking about.

* * *

Dawn closed the door behind their visitors.

Aiden stacked the last of the dirty dishes in the sink and plopped heavily onto the couch, stretching her legs out with a groan. She leaned her head back and closed her eyes. It had been a long and frustrating day, and she wanted nothing more than to just go to sleep and forget all about it.

Dawn sat down next to her and gently rubbed her thigh. "You're beat, huh? I'm sorry I didn't ask you if it was okay to have them over for dinner."

Aiden shook her head. She kept her eyes closed, enjoying Dawn's soothing touch. "You don't have to ask me. It's not like you need my permission to have your family over."

"I want to ask you," Dawn emphasized. "You're the most important person in my life, so you should have a say in my decisions."

"Yeah, but having the family over for dinner is not a major decision," Aiden said. She never asked Dawn if it was okay to go out for a beer with Ray after work. She usually just called to say it would be a little later or she wouldn't come by tonight at all. *Does Dawn want me to ask?* she wondered.

"No, it's not," Dawn agreed. "But you had a hard day at work and with the kids clinging to you like limpets, you couldn't relax."

Aiden didn't deny that it had been a little overwhelming. It made her feel off balance to suddenly be around the two kids when she hadn't had any time to transform from the frustrated detective to the relaxed playmate. "If it had gotten to be too much, I could have gone home," she said, not wanting Dawn to feel guilty. She let her hand drift down onto Dawn's leg, stroking it softly.

Dawn leaned her cheek against Aiden's shoulder. "But I don't want you to have to go home," she protested softly. "When we decide to move in together at some point, you won't have that option either."

Moving in together? Aiden abruptly stopped the soft touches she had bestowed upon Dawn's leg and opened her eyes. *First she tells her sister-in-law she wants to have kids, and now she's talking about moving in together?*

Dawn's cheek moved away from Aiden's shoulder as Dawn leaned back to look at her. "Did I say something wrong?" she asked timidly.

"Wrong?" Aiden shook her head. "No." She had known from the beginning that Dawn wanted the whole white-picket-fence scenario. Dawn had always been the commitment type. Aiden had never been like that. No matter with whom she had been over the last dozen years, she had always insisted on keeping her own place. She liked their relationship just the way it was now and wasn't prepared for any changes.

"What is it, then?" Dawn asked and tentatively stroked Aiden's leg again.

Aiden wasn't up for this discussion. Not now. "I'm just tired," she said with a sigh.

But Dawn knew her too well to believe it. "It's because I mentioned wanting to have kids to Eliza, isn't it?"

Aiden rubbed her neck, kneading the tense muscles. "I'm just not ready for that," she admitted.

"Neither am I," Dawn said to Aiden's surprise.

"But you said—"

"That I'd love to have a baby with you, yes," Dawn confirmed.

The certainty in her voice made Aiden's stomach churn. Aiden wasn't certain about it at all, and knowing that they were on different pages and that it could cause serious problems in their relationship was putting even more strain on her already overtaxed nerves.

"But not right here and now," Dawn continued, her voice soothing as if she could sense the subject had Aiden on edge.

Aiden forced a smile. "Well, right here and now would have been a little hard to handle anyway," she said, gesturing down her body, "because you and I both lack the necessary equipment."

Dawn tenderly ran her fingers through the hair on Aiden's neck. "You're being a true cop—making jokes when a subject hits a little too close to home and you don't know what to say." There was no sharp reprimand in her voice, just affectionate resignation. "I meant what I said. Our relationship is not yet at a point where we'd make serious plans to have a baby."

Not yet, Aiden silently repeated. "But it's what you'd like to happen in... in a few years?" she asked even though she already knew the answer.

"Yes," Dawn confirmed. She squeezed Aiden's thigh in encouragement. "But there are a lot of steps in our relationship before that happens."

"Steps?" Aiden didn't like the sound of that. There was no doubt in her mind that she wanted a relationship with Dawn. She was happy with the way things were going, and she didn't want to endanger that by changing anything.

A smile played around Dawn's lips. "You could move in with me," she suggested. "I'd love to come home to you every night."

Dawn had made that suggestion before, but back then, the offer had included a "someday." Aiden had been fine with the thought of moving in together when it had been just one day in the far future, nothing that turned her life upside down in the present.

Aiden tried to imagine what it would be like to live with Dawn. Coming home after an eight-hour interrogation, with clothes stained with the blood of a victim she had been unable to protect. She couldn't imagine being around anyone when she was in a mood like that. "I know keeping two separate apartments in a city like Portland is highly impractical, not to mention expensive," she said hesitantly. "Sharing an apartment would—"

"No." Dawn vigorously shook her head. "I don't want you as a roommate. I want a life partner. I don't want you to move in for practical or financial reasons. I want to share my life and my home with you."

There was so much passion and emotion in Dawn's voice that Aiden didn't know how to answer. She stared helplessly at Dawn.

"You really are beat," Dawn realized. She tenderly stroked a few strands back from Aiden's face. "We should go to bed. We can talk about this later."

Aiden felt the sudden urge to tell her she would sleep at her own place tonight, but she knew she couldn't give a reason that wouldn't hurt Dawn, so she just nodded tiredly.

"Come on." Dawn took her hand and tugged her up from the couch.

Feeling a little numb, Aiden followed her to the bedroom.

CHAPTER 30

"So THAT'S HOW the upper crust lives, huh?" Del lazily dangled her feet in the pool and turned her head to look at Kade, who sat in the shadow of the patio and was tapping away at her laptop.

Kade stopped for a moment, her slender fingers lingering over the keyboard. She lifted a single eyebrow at Del. "I don't know what you're talking about," she stated with playful indignation. "You're the one who's lazing around while I'm working my ass off."

Del laughed. "Okay, you got me there."

The patio doors opened, and Sophie Matheson stepped outside. "Ah, here you are hiding. I'm about to get ready for a round of tennis. Would one of you girls want to play?"

Girls? Del turned her face away to hide her grin. It had been a lot of years since anyone had called her a girl.

"No, thank you," Kade said with the polite but distanced tone she always took with her mother. "I'm working."

Sophie turned questioning eyes on Del, who suddenly froze. "Uh..."

"I'm going to get changed," Sophie said. "Just come over to the tennis court if you want to play. If not, I'm sure Margery," she pointed to the villa next door, "would be happy to join me." She closed the patio doors behind her.

Kade closed her laptop and turned to Del with an amused grin. "So, are you going to play with her?"

"What makes you think I even know how to play?" Del asked. "Just because I'm a lesbian doesn't mean I'm good at tennis. There's no such thing as a Martina gene, you know?"

"Afraid to lose?" Kade teased.

Del folded her arms over her chest. "Why don't you play with her? She's **your** mother after all."

"Oh, I played with her a thousand times already," Kade said with a superior toss of her head. "There's just no challenge anymore."

Del thought about it. She knew it would be impolite to refuse Mrs. Matheson's offer, and it was not as if she had anything else to do. *How hard can it be to hit a couple of balls back and forth over the net with a fragile high society woman like Sophie Thayer Matheson? Come on, be a good guest and go make nice with Mom.*

She stood and walked across the patio. Stopping in front of Kade's chaise lounge, she bent down and offered her cheek to Kade. "Kiss for good luck?" she asked with her most charming smile.

Kade quickly looked at the patio doors, making sure no one was watching them. She grabbed Del's shirt and decisively directed her closer.

Del followed willingly. Warm lips caressed her cheek, skimming over the corner of her mouth before moving away. Tingling electricity hummed through Del, and she leaned back against the armrest of the chaise lounge.

"There," Kade said, visibly fighting down a blush. "Now go and play."

Playing tennis was the last thing on Del's mind, but when Kade hid behind the screen of her laptop again, she straightened and walked to the patio doors. "Do I get another kiss if I win?" she asked when she reached them and stopped to look back.

Kade looked at her over the rim of her glasses. "Sure," she nodded easily, "if my mother is willing to kiss you for beating her."

"Shouldn't the winner get to choose her prize?" Del asked.

Suddenly, Kade visibly shut down. The smile disappeared, and she looked at Del with a deadly serious expression. "I'm not a prize, Del. At least not when it comes to relationships. I'm stubborn, independent, and impossible to live with."

Del didn't bat an eye. "Who needs easy when they can have Kade Matheson?" She gave her voice a teasing lilt, knowing the jury was still out on whether she could have Kade.

When she saw Kade maintaining her serious expression, she sobered. "Kade, I had relationships with women who were very easy to get along with. They were accommodating, friendly, and eager to please. As you can see, it didn't work out anyway." Del walked back to where Kade sat. "I can be pretty stubborn, independent, and impossible to live with too, and the older I get, the more set I become in my ways. I need a partner, not a servant. I need a woman who has a strong sense of herself and doesn't just go along with what I want."

"You're not stubborn," Kade said, for the moment ignoring that Del had just told her she would be a perfect match.

"Oh, I'm not?" Del chuckled. "You told me not once, but twice that you're straight and not interested in a relationship with me—yet here I am, about to impress my future mother-in-law."

Kade's eyes widened, but then she smiled too. "Try calling her that to her face, and you'll see how impressed she is."

Del strode to the patio doors. "I think for now I'll just dazzle her with my tennis game." She closed the doors behind her and looked back through the glass, making eye contact with Kade. They smiled at each other, and Del felt a ball of warm happiness spread inside her.

Finally, Kade turned back around, and Del went inside. She met Sophie on her way upstairs to change and told her she would play with her. Ten minutes later, she hesitantly stepped onto the tennis court.

Sophie Matheson was sitting on a bench, wearing a pleated tennis skirt and an elegant polo shirt that looked as if it had been tailor-made for her. She stood and smiled politely even though Del was sure she had secretly hoped Kade would be the one to come outside and play with her.

Sometimes it seemed to her as if Sophie wanted to make a connection with her daughter but didn't know how. Kade wasn't making it easy on her, for she had written off that relationship a long time ago.

Del felt Sophie's critical gaze wander down her body, from her sleeveless T-shirt to the simple shorts she was wearing, but Sophie didn't say anything. She just handed Del a racquet and told her to stretch. Del studied Sophie while she did her own stretches. She looked at Sophie's delicate frame and remembered that Sophie hadn't even been out of breath when she greeted them after coming from the tennis court.

Clearly, tennis wasn't a strenuous affair when you played with Sophie Matheson. *Strolling around the court, chatting a little, hitting a few balls... I can do that. Maybe I should even let her win. If she's as competitive as her daughter, beating her wouldn't be good for staying in her good graces.*

Finally, Sophie straightened, and they both took their positions on opposite sides of the tennis court. Sophie hit the first ball over the net. It came at Del in a slow pace, and she had no trouble hitting it back with a forehand. Del had played tennis before even though she was not an experienced player. She was in good shape and had no trouble keeping up with Sophie's leisurely game. *This isn't so bad,* she thought.

"All right," Sophie called after a few minutes. "If you are warmed up enough, let's begin."

Begin? Del thought. *I thought that's what we were doing?*

Then she didn't have time to think anymore because Sophie tossed up the ball and sent it spinning toward Del with a power she hadn't used before.

Del hastily ran back to reach the ball and lobbed it back over the net with little finesse.

Sophie reached the ball with a sudden burst of speed. Instead of hitting it back with great force, she softly tapped the ball so that it fell down just on the other side of the net.

Del had no chance of reaching it in time. She stopped running and stared at Sophie, who calmly took up her place behind the baseline again.

After an hour of trying to run down Sophie's cleverly placed backhands and unexpectedly powerful forehands, Del had lost the game in straight sets. Gasping for breath, she walked toward the net and shook Sophie's hand. "You Matheson women are really,

really bad for my ego!" she wheezed. "First Kade beats me in chess, and now you make me look silly on the tennis court."

"Kadence still plays chess?" Sophie asked, not even out of breath.

Del nodded. She wiped away the sweat on her forehead with a corner of her shirt. "She's brilliant," Del said, not bothering to hide her admiration.

Sophie smiled wistfully. "Her father taught her how to play."

"I know."

Sophie turned to look at her. For a second, surprise was written all over her face.

Is she surprised that Kade talks about her father at all—or that she talked about him with me? Del wondered.

Sophie put her racquet away and gestured for Del to sit down next to her on the bench. "Kadence and her father... they were very much alike."

Del still couldn't read Sophie's expression. The older Matheson woman had a tight grip on her emotions, so she couldn't figure out if it was pride, grief, or regret that made her voice falter for a moment. It seemed to Del that Kade had been a daddy's girl all her life, and now that her father was dead, her mother didn't know how to relate to her. "Well, Kade has a lot in common with you too," she carefully pointed out. "Kade is a brilliant strategist in the courtroom, and you're a brilliant strategist on the tennis court. Jesus, you gave me a workout like I haven't had in quite a while! You could do this for a living."

"I considered it when I was much younger," Sophie said. She lifted a hand to smooth back a strand of hair from her face. Only now did Del notice the wiry strength in the slender arm.

"What happened?" Del asked, very interested in hearing more about Sophie and what had made her the woman she was today.

Sophie waved dismissively. "Oh, my parents didn't think it was a suitable profession for a young woman of my standing."

Del sighed. *So history repeats itself. Doesn't she realize that she's doing to Kade and her brother what her parents were doing to her? She's trapping them with her expectations. Why is it so hard to just accept the choices your children make?*

"What is it?" Sophie asked at the sigh.

"Uh..." Del hesitated only for a second. Maybe it was time someone talked to Sophie about this. "I was just thinking about parents and the unrealistic expectations they have of their children."

Sophie shook her head. "Actually, I now believe my parents were right. Back then, I was just too young to see it. Always practicing, playing, or traveling—that's no life."

Oh, yeah. But sitting at home, waiting for your husband to come home from the office or one of his mistresses, living up to the expectations of high society, and becoming so closed off from your own emotions that you can't even relate to your own child, that's a life? Del shook her head. She didn't think it wise to discuss this any further because it would inevitably lead to a discussion of her own parents and their expectations, which would lead to her coming out to Sophie. Kade's mother would start questioning her relationship with Kade, and Del didn't want that. More importantly, she knew Kade didn't want that.

Del stood with a groan. "I think I'll head back inside. You still look fresh as a daisy, but I need a shower," she said, bowing playfully to her victorious opponent.

Sophie gave her a smile that held a little more warmth than before. "Well, we Mathesons are not allowed to have perspiratory glands," she said with a straight face.

Del stopped and stared down at her, totally baffled by the unexpected comment. *Who knew... Sophie Matheson actually has a sense of humor!*

* * *

Kade impatiently drummed her fingers on the side of her laptop. She was nearly caught up with all the work she had brought with her. Her mother and Del still hadn't returned. *What is taking them so long? Mother should have thoroughly beaten her by now.* She closed her laptop with a snap and stood.

Just then, the patio doors slid open, and Del stepped outside. Her hair was damp and disheveled, and her sweat-soaked T-shirt clung to her torso, making Kade take a second look.

"Hey." Kade cleared her throat and forced herself to look away from Del's athletic body. "How was the tennis match?"

Del folded strong arms over her chest. "Humiliating," she answered dryly. "Your mother is one hell of a tennis player. I thought you said playing with her wasn't a challenge anymore?"

"I said there's no challenge anymore," Kade corrected with a sly grin. "There isn't—for my mother. So you lost, huh?"

Del nodded. "Like you knew I would."

"No kiss for you, then," Kade said with mock regret.

Del sauntered up to her.

She was so close now that Kade could feel the warmth of her overheated body and smell the musky odor of sweat. To her surprise, Kade found that it wasn't an unpleasant experience at all. It was different from the way men smelled, and Kade had never consciously realized that before.

"Not even a consolation peck?" Del pretended to pout.

"I don't do consolation pecks," Kade said. "When I kiss someone, I mean it."

Del stared at her, and Kade couldn't look away from the intense dark eyes. They seemed to draw her in.

"Nice match," Sophie said behind them. Neither Kade nor Del had heard the patio doors slide open.

Kade quickly moved away from Del, suddenly very conscious of their closeness.

"Thank you," Del said lamely in answer to Sophie's compliment. "I'll go and have that shower now." She strode away, and Kade self-consciously kept her gaze off the long, muscular legs.

"Your friend..." Sophie began. "How long have you known each other?"

Kade looked at her in alarm. *Why is she asking about Del? Did she see? Does she suspect anything?*

But her mother didn't seem upset, just deeply in thought.

"A few months. Why are you asking?" Kade regarded her suspiciously.

"Oh, I thought it would be longer than that. She just... she seems to know you so well," Sophie said, looking at the point where Del had disappeared around the corner.

Compared to you, even the janitors in my office building know me well. Still, her mother was right. In just a few months, Del had gotten to know her well. "She does. Del made every effort to understand and accept me." Only lately had she begun to realize how important that was to her—how important Del was becoming.

"It's a good thing to have in your life," Sophie said, much to Kade's surprise. "I need a shower too." With that, she quickly walked away, leaving a baffled Kade behind.

CHAPTER 31

*A*IDEN TOOK A sidelong glance at Dawn as they slowly walked toward the house. They had never visited Evan together before. Dawn had spent at least one afternoon each week with Evan, and Aiden had gotten better at visiting her too, but until now, they had never gone to visit her as a couple.

It shouldn't have been a big deal, but Aiden felt strangely self-conscious about it. She was unsure how to act toward Dawn in front of Evan. She didn't want to give Evan any room for wisecracks about their relationship by indulging in PDAs, but she hadn't said anything to Dawn, afraid of hurting her. Also, visiting a family member together and accepting Evan into the family seemed to be one of the "steps" toward a long-term commitment about which Dawn had talked.

"Stop worrying," Dawn said, picking up on Aiden's mood. "Evan will still be here. Her foster parents decided to give Evan another chance, and I doubt they are going to change their minds, especially after you called them to talk about it again."

That wasn't what Aiden had worried about. She had finally convinced Jill and Roger that punishing Evan any further or throwing her out would only encourage her to hide things better and make sure not to get caught in the future. They had agreed to give Evan another chance and start again with a clean slate.

Dawn reached for Aiden's hand and squeezed it encouragingly as they stopped at the front door.

Stop being so goddamn self-conscious! Aiden scolded herself and gently squeezed back.

Jill let them in.

Aiden barely resisted asking her how Evan had been and if she had caused any more trouble since they had last seen each other. *Trust her not to fuck up again,* she repeated to herself what Dawn had told her a dozen times.

"Evan is upstairs in her room," Jill told them. She wasn't as enthusiastic to see them as she had been at the very beginning, but she was also not as resigned and skeptical as she had been just a few days ago.

Aiden felt Jill and Roger were finally beginning to develop a more realistic outlook on Evan and on the big sister of whom they had expected so much. At the beginning, they had been overjoyed to find out Evan had a sister because they had thought it would instantly change things for the better. They had expected Aiden to work a miracle, and when it didn't happen, they were disappointed—in Evan, in Aiden, and in themselves. Only now were they beginning to realize Evan needed time and trust from them too, not just from Aiden.

"I know she's still grounded, but it's such a nice day outside. We wondered if you would make an exception just for this afternoon and let her go out for a few hours under our supervision?" Dawn asked with the soft smile Aiden could never refuse.

Jill thought about it for a moment. "I suppose she deserves a little reward. She voluntarily gave up the last of her marijuana yesterday. We didn't even know she had another bag hidden somewhere. Yes, taking her out for a few hours would be okay," she decided with a smile.

Aiden and Dawn exchanged a grin, glad to hear Evan was doing the right thing even without any outside pressure. They made their way upstairs and knocked on Evan's door.

Evan was lounging on her bed again, lazily flipping through a book without reading much of it. She grinned when she saw Dawn and gave a more reserved nod to Aiden.

"Hey, you," Dawn said. She stopped and directed an expectant glance at Aiden, letting her do the talking.

"We thought you might like to go for a walk or do something else with us," Aiden said. She still felt a little awkward and insecure interacting with Evan. She was good with kids, but talking to teenagers didn't come naturally to her. "Jill already okayed it."

Evan didn't look as happy as Aiden had expected. "Go for a walk?" she repeated, looking as though they had suggested a walk over glowing embers.

"Or do something else," Aiden said again. Apart from the driving lessons, she didn't know what to do with Evan.

"We could go skating," Dawn said. "I have my skates and the rest of the equipment outside in the car."

Evan still didn't seem overly enthusiastic, and Aiden was almost glad about it. She wasn't exactly eager to go roller-skating either.

"I bet she doesn't even have skates," Evan said, pointing at Aiden.

"No, 'she' doesn't," Aiden confirmed with a sarcastic undertone, letting Evan know she didn't appreciate being talked about in the third person.

Dawn was unimpressed by their objections. Her enthusiasm was unbroken. "I thought she could borrow your old ones," she said to Evan.

"Old ones?" Evan's brow furrowed. "I only have one pair."

A mischievous smile deepened the dimples on Dawn's cheeks. "Not anymore. I drove by that little shop yesterday and got you the skates you said you wanted when we were there to pick out mine. I hope that's okay?"

Evan blinked. "Yeah, it's... it's great, of course, but I didn't fulfill my part of the deal yet, and I don't want charity," she said gruffly.

Deal? Aiden wondered. *She's acting like they're businesswomen, not friends.*

"Oh, you mean I haven't learned how to skate yet?" Dawn gave her a challenging grin. "You'll just have to wait and see. I'll skate circles around you today."

"Ha!" Evan snorted but didn't say anything else.

Dawn moved closer and sat down next to her on the bed. "I thought you'd be happy to get out of here for a while," she said quietly, almost sounding a little disappointed.

It tugged at Aiden's heartstrings, and she suspected it didn't leave Evan cold either. Maybe Evan didn't want to go skating with her. Maybe she wanted it to be something she only shared with Dawn. "You two could go skating without me," she suggested. "I've never been skating before and would only slow you down."

"You've been ice-skating," Dawn said.

"Oh, yeah—exactly twice in my life. Remember our first date? It's a wonder you wanted anything to do with me after the way I humiliated myself on the ice that day." Aiden exaggeratedly shook her head.

Dawn grinned. "You were cute."

Evan abruptly stood. "Do you want to reminisce about the happy days of your courtship, or do you want to go skating?" she asked with a gruffness she often displayed when feeling a little uncomfortable.

Aiden could understand that. She didn't want to hear the intimate details about her sister's possible relationship with Kade's niece either. That thought made her think of something. "We can even drive by Laurie's and see if she wants to come with us, then you don't have to be alone with us old grannies," she offered.

"Hey, speak for yourself, sweetheart," Dawn protested. "I'm still young and spry."

Half an hour later, they put on their skates at the edge of the almost empty skate park. While Aiden was still trying to figure out the buckles and get used to the stiff plastic that didn't allow her to bend her feet, Evan and Dawn were already racing around in wide circles. *Jesus Christ! Is that what they have been doing all month?* It seemed a little dangerous and made her worry about Dawn, but she could hear Dawn's laughter as she raced along side by side with Evan, her blond hair trailing in the wind behind her. *My God, she's so beautiful, so full of life and joie de vivre,* the sudden thought shot through her mind. *I hope I never do anything to make her lose that.*

"They're really good at this," a timid voice said next to her, interrupting Aiden's brooding.

Aiden turned to look at Laurie Matheson. It was strange to see the familiar Matheson features with such a timid expression. She

- 425 -

had never seen these self-doubts on Kade's face. *Because she never lets you see them, not because she doesn't have them.*

"If we try hard enough, I bet we could be just as good in a few weeks," Aiden tried to encourage her. She offered Laurie her hands, and they struggled to their feet, awkwardly balancing each other.

Dawn expertly came to a stop next to them. "Need a little help?" She pointed over her shoulder. "Evan is an excellent teacher. She'll have you skating in no time."

A slight blush crawled up Evan's face. She was visibly pleased about Dawn's compliment, but at the same time, she looked a little uncomfortable at being handed the job of teaching a whole class of skating novices. "First, I need you to let go of each other. You can't skate if you cling to each other like scared rabbits."

Aiden looked at Laurie with a shrug and slowly let go of her.

"Now lean forward a little. Not too much, just bend at the waist." Evan corrected Laurie's position with a hand on her back but didn't touch Aiden. "Bend your arms too. You use them to build up momentum. Now step off with one foot and just skate in a slow rhythm." She demonstrated it.

Laurie was the first one to try it. It went well enough until she wanted to stop and didn't know how. She flailed her arms, overbalanced, and fell. "Ouch," she mumbled as she rubbed her backside.

Evan helped her up. "Now you," she ordered, nodding at Aiden.

"Did I mention that I don't like skating?" Aiden grumbled. "Ice-skating was bad enough, but at least falling on the ice was not so bad. If I fall now..." She stared at the rough, hard concrete. "This could really, really hurt."

"Falling might hurt, but it doesn't mean you should let that keep you from trying," Dawn said calmly.

Aiden stared at her. *Is she talking about skating or about commitment?* she wondered.

"Come on, fearless Warrior Princess, try it!" Dawn prodded.

Aiden sighed and carefully pushed off with one foot. Quickly, she put it back on the ground and skated along with both feet firmly on the ground for about a yard.

"Push off again!" Evan called. "Alternate your feet."

Evan looked entirely too amused for Aiden's liking. *Calm down,* she told herself. *Don't get angry at her just because she enjoys being better than you at something.* Dawn had told her it was good for Evan to realize others weren't infallible either and could still be loved.

Aiden pushed off again and began to skate. *Left, right, left, right. Hey, this isn't so bad after all!*

"Don't look at your feet!" Evan ordered.

Aiden looked up. The movement shifted her balance, and she fell backward.

Strong hands grabbed her flailing arm and kept Aiden upright.

When she had found her balance again, Aiden looked up and into Evan's brown eyes. "Phew! Thank you."

Evan quickly let go of her and gave a short nod.

They skated for a while, and after landing on her ass or her kneepads a few times, Aiden's fear of falling finally lessened.

"Are you two okay alone for a few minutes? The doc wants to try the half-pipe again," Evan finally announced.

Aiden's eyes widened, and she stared at Dawn in disbelief.

Dawn gave her a brave grin. "Relax. I did it before."

"You fell when you did it before," Aiden said with concern.

"She'll be fine," Evan said, softly touching Dawn's arm. "I wouldn't let her try it if I thought she couldn't do it."

Aiden was touched and also a little amused by the tender care Evan bestowed on Dawn. "All right. We'll watch from over here. Be careful, please," she said to Dawn.

Dawn nodded, her face already a mask of concentration. She followed Evan over to the half-pipe and climbed onto the platform.

Aiden felt all her muscles tense as she watched Dawn inch toward the edge and look down at the steep ramp. Evan took up position right next to her. She spoke to Dawn and pointed at the half-pipe, obviously explaining something. Finally, Evan gave one last nod and moved back a little.

Visibly nervous, but equally determined, Dawn rolled closer to the edge.

Aiden's fingernails drilled into her palm. She only dully noticed it, her whole concentration on Dawn.

Dawn gave a little hop and raced down the ramp.

A crashing sound and a pained cry pierced the silence.

Aiden froze. After a second, her training kicked in, and she forced herself to look away from Dawn—who had safely reached the flat part of the half-pipe—and searched for the source of the cry.

Laurie, who had circled around the half-pipe to get a better view when Aiden had last seen her, was lying on the ground now, whimpering in pain.

Evan raced down the half-pipe, almost falling herself in her haste to get to Laurie. "Hey, you okay?" She very gently helped her sit up.

Only seconds after Evan, Dawn knelt down next to Laurie and examined her with fingers that were a little shaky.

Aiden, who had to circle around the half-pipe, was the last one to reach them, just as Laurie sat up. She saw the blood that dripped from an abrasion on Laurie's forearm, right between where the wrist guard and the elbow pad protected her arm. Sucking in a breath, Aiden moved toward Laurie.

Quickly, Dawn stood and blocked her way. "No." She put a hand on Aiden's shoulder. "I don't think she's badly injured. Let Evan handle it."

Aiden looked at her through narrowed eyes. "Does she even know what to do?" Staying back, doing nothing was not Aiden's forte. She was used to taking charge in situations like this.

"We're at the skate park—that means Evan is in charge, not you. If she wants or needs your help, she'll tell you," Dawn said firmly.

Sighing, Aiden watched Evan gently strip the protective gear off Laurie's hands, knees, and elbows. She pressed a tissue Dawn handed her to the bleeding scrape on Laurie's forearm and brushed tiny pieces of gravel and dirt off Laurie's jeans, softly talking to her the whole time.

Dawn is right. She's handling this well, Aiden realized with a little bit of pride. There was nothing she could have done to help Laurie that Evan wasn't already doing.

Finally, Evan looked up, her lips a thin line. "I think her wrist is broken," she said, sounding upset.

Oh, shit! Aiden looked down at Laurie, who by now was crying tears of pain and fear. *And I'm the one who gets to tell her parents—and Kade. Great!* "We better take her to a hospital to check it out. Can you walk?" she asked the distraught girl.

Dawn nudged her. "She hurt her wrist, not her legs, sweetie."

Evan took off Laurie's skates and looked up at the two adults. "Can one of you get her shoes from the car?"

Once again impressed by her younger sister and how she handled the situation, Aiden nodded, but then glanced down at her own feet.

"I'll go," Dawn offered and skated over to the car to get their shoes.

When Dawn returned, Aiden and Evan took off their skates and put their shoes back on, then helped Laurie with hers. While Aiden helped Laurie with the right shoe, Evan slipped Laurie's left foot into the other. Their gazes met over Laurie's outstretched legs, and Aiden gave her a nod of appreciation.

Evan gently helped Laurie up. With Evan on one side of Laurie and Aiden on the other, they slowly made their way to the car. Dawn trailed behind them, carrying the skating equipment.

Taking the fastest route to the nearest hospital, Aiden glanced in the rearview mirror a few times. Laurie was pale but had stopped crying. Next to her, Evan looked at least as grim. Her face was a stony façade of guilt and anger at herself that Aiden knew only too well.

The only person in the car who at least looked calm was Dawn. *I didn't realize she was that good in a crisis.* Aiden took a second sidelong glance at Dawn and slowly realized Dawn wasn't as calm and unworried as she appeared to be. Her face was relaxed, but as a psychologist, she was good at hiding her own emotions and keeping a neutral expression. It was the tension in her hands, holding on to the side of the passenger seat much tighter than necessary, that gave her away. *She acts like there's nothing to worry about, because she knows Laurie will pick up on what she's projecting and will calm down. And Evan is already feeling guilty enough without her secret hero acting like she did some irreversible damage to Laurie.*

Aiden reached out for Dawn's hand and gave it an appreciative squeeze. When they got out of the car and walked into the ER, she took hold of Dawn's hand again, knowing Dawn was always a little uncomfortable in hospitals.

"We need your parents' consent and some proof of insurance. Do you want me to call your parents?" Dawn asked Laurie as they all settled down on the uncomfortable chairs in the waiting area.

Evan got to her feet. "I'll do it," she bravely offered.

God, we clearly underestimated her—all of us, except for Dawn, Aiden admitted to herself. *She's taking responsibility for Laurie and for the accident even though she knows the Mathesons won't be too pleased with her. How great is that?*

"No!" Laurie's usually soft voice suddenly sounded firm and determined. "No, you won't. My parents have barely begun to get over thinking you're someone who's bad for me. I don't want to destroy that progress by having you call them to tell them I'm hurt. I'll call them myself."

Look at that! She sounds like Kade. Aiden realized she had underestimated both teenagers.

Laurie wandered over to the nearby pay phones.

Dawn changed seats to sit next to Evan in the waiting area. She squeezed her shoulder in an encouraging gesture. "You handled the situation really well," she complimented Evan.

"Really well?" Evan snarled. "I let her out of my sight even though I knew she hadn't learned braking yet. I handled it really badly!"

This could be me, Aiden realized with sudden clarity. *This is how I react to situations like this.* She began to understand what Dawn had always told her about them being very much alike. She leaned forward, putting her elbows on her knees, and looked directly into Evan's sullen brown eyes. "Accidents happen, Evan," she said beseechingly. "You couldn't have prevented it even if you had been standing right next to Laurie when she fell. You're not to blame for any of it, and you handled everything just the right way after she fell."

"Yeah, I'm sure her parents are gonna give me a medal!" Evan grumbled. "Or Jill and Roger..." She groaned as she thought about her foster parents' reactions to this latest incident.

Evan had acted as if she didn't care at all whether the LeCroixs threw her out and back into the foster system. She had pretended not to want to be a part of that family or any family at all.

It's just an act. She does care, Aiden realized. "I'll come with you when you tell your foster parents. It's my responsibility as much as it's yours."

"Hey, lighten up, you two!" Dawn clapped both of them on the shoulder. "She broke her wrist, not her neck. I broke my arm twice when I tried to keep up with my older brother and his friends, so I know it can happen in a blink of an eye. Let's all just take a step back and treat it like the accident it was. No one is responsible, and no one is to blame." She looked from Aiden to Evan until both of them nodded. "Next time, we'll just start with the braking lesson."

"Next time? You think Laurie wants to go skating with me ever again?" Evan shook her head doubtfully.

"I bet she does," Dawn replied with confidence. "You took very good care of Laurie. The first time I broke my wrist, my brother yelled at me the whole way home, but you didn't freak out. You kept her calm. I'm sure Laurie appreciates that. You should be proud of yourself. I know I am."

Aiden cleared her throat. "Yeah, me too."

Evan looked at them, not able to hide her astonishment. "You're freaking me out," she finally mumbled. She was used to scolding and accusations, not to people telling her they were proud of her.

Dawn laughed. "Get used to it."

CHAPTER 32

KADE FURROWED her brow and listened. There it was again: a low moan from behind the door that connected her room to Del's. She stepped closer to the door, still listening intently.

Another moan came.

A shiver raced through Kade. *She's not doing in there what I think she's doing, is she?* She shook her head. *And if she is, what are you doing standing here, listening?* Still, she didn't move away from the door.

A new sound from behind the door answered Kade's questions. This time, it was more of a pained groan, definitely not a sound of pleasure.

Kade gently knocked on the door. "Del? You okay?" she called through the still closed door.

"I'm fine," Del called back. "Just a little..."

Kade knocked again and opened the door an inch. "Can I come in?"

"Sure. Come on in," Del said without hesitation.

When Kade entered, she saw Del sitting on the edge of the bed, one of her hands pressed to her back in a supporting position. "What's wrong?" she asked worriedly. "I heard you... um... moan."

"I'm just a little sore from being chased around the tennis court all afternoon." Del said with a dismissive shrug. As soon as she had moved her shoulders, she grimaced.

"A little?" Kade raised an eyebrow at her.

"Yeah. I'm just not used to swinging a racquet; that's all." Del tried to downplay it.

Kade knew exactly how irritating sore muscles could be. "Now you know how I felt after going to the shooting range with you, firing a semiautomatic for the first time. The next day, I could hardly hold a pen, my fingers, wrists, and shoulders hurt so much," she remembered.

Del frowned. "Why didn't you say anything? I hope you know you never have to pretend with me."

Kade knew that. Since she had met Del, she had learned to take off the masks, roles, and protective walls that had become second nature to her. With Del, she felt comfortable enough to be herself. "I hope you know the same is true for you?" She studied Del intently. "If you're sad or in a bad mood or in pain, you can come to me too."

"Well, actually..." Del looked her in the eyes and gave her a lopsided smile. "I'm in a little bit of pain right now. I think I strained a muscle in my back or something." She looked at Kade with trusting eyes.

Okay... Now it's up to me to help her. Where's my brother, the doctor, when I need him? She wasn't sure if applying heat or cold was the way to treat a strained muscle, but maybe a massage would help loosen Del's muscles. "If you want, I could massage it for you," she offered.

"Hmm, I never said no to that kind of offer." Del immediately moved toward the bed, getting ready to lie down.

"Stop," Kade said quickly.

Del froze. "I hope you know this is not some kind of trick to lure you into bed," she said, only half joking.

Kade rolled her eyes. "You would still be in the underground parking garage, waiting for a chance to talk to me, if I thought you were trying to trick me into anything, Del Vasquez! I just wanted to suggest we go into my room since I have the bigger bed. And take off your shirt before you lie down."

"You do want to see me naked," Del began the old, playful argument again.

Actually, I wouldn't mind, Kade thought and grinned to herself. "If you prefer, I'll let you leave your shirt on and proceed to rub your skin raw. Your choice," she said with an indifferent shrug, playing it cool.

Del grinned and tugged the shirt over her head with one hand. Without any haste, she walked through the connecting doors, moved to the bed, and turned back the covers, giving Kade ample time to study the athletic body in the black sports bra.

This time, Kade didn't avert her eyes. She took in the defined muscles of Del's shoulders and stomach and the softness of her breasts. It was a contrast she found very enticing. She frowned when she saw the thin scar that ran along one of Del's ribs. "What happened here?"

Del looked down at herself. "This?" She touched the scar. "Oh, just a nervous Deputy DA who attacked me with her car keys in a parking garage," she said, smiling merrily.

"What?" Kade stared at her. She dully remembered jamming the keys into Del's ribs. Suddenly, she felt nauseated. "You mean I... I did this?"

Del took Kade's hand and pressed it against her warm side for a second. "No. Calm down. I was just kidding. It's an old scar from a knife wound."

Kade pinched Del's side and withdrew her hand. "That was really—"

"Mean?" Del just grinned. "Well, I still had to get revenge for you making me think your mother was standing behind me while I made comments about your breasts."

Kade had to smile. It was more a sense of relief than finding Del's joke funny. The thought of Del being injured was unpleasant enough, but thinking she was the one who had caused that pain... Kade hadn't liked that at all. *Not that I like knowing she has been attacked with a knife any better.* She shuddered at the thought that Del could be hurt doing her job every day. "Lie down," she ordered.

Del flopped onto her belly and groaned when the movement jarred her strained muscle. She turned her head and expectantly looked at Kade.

Kade looked back down at her. *Now how am I going to do this?*

"The most comfortable way for you to reach the muscle is probably by straddling me," Del said, easily guessing Kade's thoughts.

Kade eyed the smooth skin of Del's lower back and the muscled buttocks under the snug-fitting jeans. *I wouldn't exactly call it "comfortable," but all right. Here we go.* She swung her left leg over Del and slowly lowered herself. It seemed as if she could feel Del's heat through each and every one of her pores. Very gently, she put her hands on Del's back and applied pressure to different muscle groups. "Which one is the troublemaker?"

She felt Del chuckle under her, then wince as she hit the right spot. "Yeah. There it is." Del groaned.

Kade slowly stroked and kneaded the area around the strained muscle, making smaller and smaller circles with her thumbs. It wasn't the first time Kade had given a massage. Former boyfriends and law review partners had been athletes and had sometimes asked her for a massage. Kade seldom offered it on her own. It just hadn't occurred to her. She was not a very touch-positive person, so giving massages had always been a rather clinical process for her.

Not this time. This time, it wasn't just tendons and muscles under her hands that needed medical attention. She was very aware to whom those muscles and tendons belonged. Kade had trouble keeping her touch strictly clinical. She admired the curve of Del's shoulder blades, the smoothness of the coffee-colored skin, and the play of the lithe muscles beneath that skin whenever Del shifted a little. *Oh, come on. You're not a hormonal teenager!* she chided herself.

She kneaded the affected muscles with a little more strength and bit her lip when Del began to moan and groan. "Have I thanked you for coming to Ashland with me?" she asked, trying to keep her thoughts on a more rational plane.

"No thanks necessary," Del replied sincerely. "I doubt the stalker knows where you are, but I just don't want to take that chance."

Kade shook her head even though Del couldn't see it. "I don't just mean protecting me from the stalker. I'm talking about staying in the same house with my mother for a few days. At least you could shoot the stalker."

Del's laugh rumbled through Kade. "Your mother is not that bad."

"Liar," Kade gently accused.

"No, really," Del insisted.

Kade experimentally scraped her nails lightly along Del's spine. She smiled when she felt Del shiver under her and went back to rubbing her shoulders. "Well, if she was constantly trying to set you up with some bachelor, you would sing a different tune," she predicted.

"Your mother just can't understand why you're still single. She thinks her daughter is a great catch—and so do I, by the way." Kade could hear the smile and the sincerity in Del's voice.

Kade sighed. "Why can't she just let me live my life?"

"I think she's lonely," Del said, craning her neck to look up at Kade.

Kade stopped her massage for a moment. "Lonely? The woman is on every neighborhood committee; she organizes more dinner parties and charity functions than the First Lady, and no one in the family would dare to even sneeze without her permission. How can she be lonely?"

"She gave up her hopes and dreams and built her whole life around the expectations others—her parents and her husband—had for her. Now that they're dead and she's the matriarch, she doesn't know what to do with her life anymore. She forgot how to relate to people without the roles and masks." Del turned over under Kade, forcing her to lift up a bit until she practically sat in Del's lap. Del looked up at her with her deep brown eyes. "She probably wouldn't admit it and maybe she doesn't even realize it, but she's lonely—and she doesn't want you to end up lonely too."

Kade had never thought about why her mother acted the way she did. It was the way her mother had always acted, and she had just accepted it as an unchangeable fact of life. What Del said made sense, though. Her mother was as much a product of her circumstances and her upbringing as she was. Kade stared down at

Del, taking in the open features with wonder. "How on earth did you figure her out so quickly? My mother had a dozen therapists over the years, but to my knowledge, no one has ever understood her issues after knowing her for just a few days."

"I may have only known her since Tuesday, but I've known you for over six months," Del said calmly.

"Is that your way of telling me I'm a younger version of my mother and will end up exactly like her?" It wasn't a pleasant thought.

Del gave a half nod. "You do have some things in common, but don't worry; you won't end up like her."

"What makes you so sure about that?" Not one of Kade's relationships had been a success. On bad days, she could easily imagine ending up as the lonely spinster aunt. The thought had only recently begun to bother her.

Del looked up at her, her smile as soft as the skin of her shoulders on which Kade was balancing her hands. "Well, your mother didn't have someone like me in her life."

And I do. Kade heard the unspoken message. *If I want to.*

"If you stick with me, there's no need to wear a mask and hide behind walls. You don't need to follow anyone's expectations but your own. You won't lose yourself, and you won't have a relationship that consists only of polite small talk at the dinner table," Del promised passionately.

Kade swallowed. She had never allowed herself to want what Del offered. The price had always been too high. "Del," she began, not knowing what to say, but knowing she had to respond in some way. Del had taken huge risks and had put her emotions and intentions out there for Kade to see. Kade appreciated it even if she couldn't yet respond in kind.

Del softly touched her index finger to Kade's lips. "I just wanted to lay my cards on the table. It doesn't mean you have to do the same or that you have to up the ante. As long as you don't fold your cards, it's all right with me."

When Kade nodded, Del took the finger away from her lips. Kade was grateful that Del wasn't forcing the issue. Del was one of very few people in her life who never put any pressure on her to act a certain way. She shook off her thoughts and allowed herself to think about her mother's relationship instead of her own. "I can't believe my mother discussed her marriage with you."

"She didn't have to. I saw the way she looked at your father's portrait in the living room." Del shook her head. "That wasn't a grieving widow looking at a picture of her late husband. It was a woman looking back at the regrets and missed opportunities of her life. She's not just lonely because your father died. I think she was lonely in her marriage too."

Kade knew she was right. *The question is: do I want that for myself? Do I want a safe, nonthreatening marriage with a socially acceptable man—or do I risk everything I ever believed in, my career, my political future, the shaky relationship with my family, my emotional control... just to be with Del?*

When Kade didn't say or do anything for a long while, Del cocked an eyebrow at her. "Getting comfortable?" she asked, nodding down at herself with a smile.

Kade was too aware of Del's close proximity to feel comfortable and relaxed. She could feel the warmth of Del's belly under her thighs and the strength of her shoulders under her hands.

Del didn't try to move closer or touch her in any way. Her hands and arms were resting on the bed. She didn't even lift her head. She just looked at Kade with her warm brown eyes.

For once, Kade decided to voice the thoughts running through her mind. "Comfortable isn't the first adjective that comes to mind right now."

"No? What is a more fitting adjective?" Del's voice and smile combined humor and tenderness in a mix that was typical for her.

Contemplating the right word, Kade trailed a finger down Del's arm until she stroked the soft skin at the bend of her elbow. Goose bumps erupted all along Del's arm. Kade could feel the tingling sensation too. "I feel like... a live wire," she finally confessed.

"That's not an adjective," Del playfully objected.

"Shut up," Kade ordered and leaned forward, her hands still pinning Del's shoulders to the bed.

Del's lips parted—maybe about to answer, maybe in expectation of what Kade might be doing.

Kade didn't wait to find out. She firmly pressed her lips to Del's, cutting off whatever she had been about to do or say. It wasn't a gentle kiss. Now that Kade had finally plucked up the courage to kiss Del, she wanted to taste her, to experience her all at once. For once, she didn't want to be the overly controlled Kadence Matheson.

Del's mouth opened under hers, and Kade deepened the kiss. She moaned when Del's tongue painted hot patterns over hers.

Del slid long fingers into Kade's hair while her other hand sensually stroked Kade's neck. She pulled Kade close until their bodies were touching all along their lengths.

God. Kade's eyes fluttered shut.

"Kade..." Del groaned against Kade's lips, after moving away half an inch.

"If you—" Kade had to take a few deep breaths until she was finally able to continue. "If you ask me whether I'm sure, I'm going to slap you!"

Del looked startled for a moment, then she laughed. "That's not what I wanted to say. You told me you only kiss someone if you mean it, remember?" She grinned in elation at what this meant for her. "I just wanted to express my appreciation for your kissing technique." She lightly traced Kade's kiss-swollen lips with her fingertips.

This time, it was Del who leaned up and captured Kade's lips with hers. The kiss was less forceful, but the passion behind it was the same.

Kade stopped thinking about the significance of the kiss and started to just enjoy it.

"Kadence, your brother—" Sophie stopped abruptly, the handle of the door she had flung open without knocking still in her hand.

Oh, shit! For a few seconds, panic shot through Kade. She tore her lips away from Del's. Hastily, she scrambled off Del and off the bed. "Mother!" She stopped, not knowing what to say. She felt like a diver who had come up to the surface too fast and was now feeling disoriented.

"What... what's going on here?" a very pale Sophie stammered uncharacteristically. "What is... this?" She jabbed her finger in Del's direction, then slowly pointed at Kade too. She was clearly unwilling to believe that Kade had been an eager participant in the kiss.

Family expectations and the standards of her childhood weighed heavily on Kade. The most important thing had always been to make the right appearance, to have the right friends, and to date the right men. Kade had always lived by the unspoken rules of her family. Only once had she rebelled against her parents' expectations—when she had decided on the DA's office instead of the cushy job in her father's law firm. With that, her quantum of rebellion had been used up once and for all. Straying from the Matheson path again hadn't seemed worth it—until now.

"Mrs. Matheson..." Del tried to find a way to calm Sophie down. She hastily put her shirt back on.

"I'm not talking to you," Sophie snapped at her, forgetting her good manners for a moment. "I'm talking to my daughter!"

Slowly, Kade straightened her shoulders. She was not going to let Del take her mother's wrath. "I kissed her," she said in a low voice.

Her mother looked at her in utter disbelief. "Nonsense!"

Kade felt her temper rise. *Of course she would think Del practically attacked me, but I won't let her live with that convenient delusion.* She looked her mother right in the eyes. "I kissed her," she repeated, "because I wanted to."

Sophie stubbornly shook her head. "That doesn't make any sense, Kadence. You are not... homosexual!"

"And how exactly would you know that?" Kade took the offensive. "You don't know who I am and what I want. You never did."

Instead of recoiling and acting hurt, her mother acted as if Kade hadn't even spoken. "Is this some kind of joke? First Douglas calls to tell me Laurel broke her arm when she was skating with her... girlfriend, and now you..."

Oh, God. Kade wasn't sure if she should laugh or groan. *Poor mother. She's getting it with both barrels. What a bright day for the Matheson dynasty!* "Is Laurie okay?" she asked.

"Yes, just a hairline fracture," Sophie said tersely. It was clear that she didn't want to discuss Laurie's injuries. There were other things on her mind.

"I'm sorry you had to find out like this, but it's not a joke," Kade answered. "I ignored it for a lot of years, just like you're ignoring it now, but I'm finally at a point in my life where I can admit I'm bisexual."

"Bisexual?" Sophie pressed her fingertips to her temples. She looked as if she was about to faint. "But that means... you... you still like men?" Hope glittered in her eyes, and Kade could practically feel her determination to steer her daughter back in the right direction.

"At the moment, I 'like' Del," Kade answered simply.

Sophie turned accusing eyes at Del, who was standing next to Kade, close enough to be supportive, but far away enough not to scandalize Sophie even more.

"Stop it, Mother!" Kade ordered. "I'm warning you. Don't start plotting a scheme to get Del out of my life." She knew her mother's way of dealing with things. "It wouldn't change anything. Del is not the reason why I'm bisexual. The only thing she did is to encourage me to be myself."

Del's cell phone began to ring in the adjoining room.

Del didn't move away from Kade's side.

After a few seconds of tense silence, the ringing started again.

"Answer it," Kade said, giving Del a gentle nudge.

Del hesitated.

"Go on. I'll be fine," Kade said. For the first time in her life, she felt motivated and strong enough to stand up to her mother.

With one last glance back, Del strode from the room.

* * *

Kade wasn't eavesdropping, but in the oppressive silence between her mother and her, it was impossible not to hear Del's increasingly upset tone of voice from the room next door. Then there was silence, indicating the call had been finished. Del still didn't return.

Is it the stalker? Did they find him? Has he hurt somebody? "Excuse me for a minute." Kade quickly strode past her baffled mother and entered Del's room.

Del was sitting on the bed, staring at the wall. Her fingers were clamped around the cell phone.

"Del?" Kade sat down next to her and gently took the cell phone away from her. "Hey, what happened?"

Del looked up. The fire was gone from the dark eyes. Now they looked numb. Del shook her head as if to clear it. "My father... they say if I don't visit him now, I'll never see him again," she said roughly.

"I'm so sorry." Kade took Del's right hand in both of hers. "Are you... are you going to visit him?"

Del stonily shook her head. "I can't leave you here on your own."

"Don't worry; I can handle my mother. It's not as bad as I imagined," Kade said. In a way, it was true. She'd never had a close relationship with her mother, and she had realized there was nothing her mother could take from her. She didn't need her money, and she felt as if she'd never had her love anyway.

Del was still shaking her head. "Not only because of your mother. There's still the stalker to worry about. Ray and Aiden haven't had any luck in their investigation. I won't leave you without any protection until we catch that bastard."

"Okay—then I'll come with you," Kade decided. She took in Del's surprised expression. "If you want me to?"

"Yes," Del simply said.

Kade lifted Del's stiff hand to her lips and kissed it. It surprised her just how easy that little loving gesture of encouragement came to her. "All right. Sit tight. I'll go and pack my stuff."

Her mother was still there when Kade marched back into her room. "We're leaving," Kade told her. She threw her suitcase on her bed and began to pack.

"What? No! I won't let you leave like this! Not before we've talked this out!" Sophie protested.

You mean not before you've talked me out of being bisexual, huh? Kade's mind sarcastically supplied. "We don't have time to talk now. Del's father is dying, and she has to leave now if she wants to see him one last time," she told her in no uncertain terms.

Sophie stood stock-still. Memories darted across her face like shadows. Kade knew she was thinking about Douglas Senior's death and Kade never having a chance to say good-bye. "You are going with her?" Sophie finally asked.

"Del has been there for me and helped me through a lot of difficult situations. Now it's my turn to be supportive of her," Kade firmly defended her decision.

Sophie didn't answer. She watched as Kade picked up her suitcase and grabbed her keys. "I'll get the car and then come back for the other things," Kade said on her way out of the room.

* * *

Del folded the last pair of jeans and put it into her duffle bag. She closed the zipper and looked around the room. Despite the tense atmosphere in the house, she was a little sad she had to go. It had been a safe hiding place for her and Kade, away from their jobs, the stalker, and all the responsibilities they had in Portland. Kade had opened up to her, had even initiated a kiss. *God, and what a kiss!* Del closed her eyes as she remembered the kiss.

Now reality was intruding. She had to go and face her past. She opened her eyes, shouldered her bag, and walked out of the room.

The door to Kade's room opened. Sophie stepped out. "I'm sorry to hear about your father," she said very formally.

"You don't have to be sorry. We're not close. I haven't talked to him for more than twenty years," Del said, trying to be as matter-of-fact about it as Sophie.

"Oh." Sophie clearly hadn't known that. "May I ask why?"

Is she trying to find out my weaknesses so she can get me out of Kade's life? Del wondered. She decided to answer anyway. Maybe it would help Sophie come to terms with her daughter's sexual orientation if she told her about the consequences of her own coming out. "My parents couldn't accept me for who and what I am. When my father found out I'm a lesbian, he beat me and threw me out of the house." Del looked directly into Sophie's eyes as she told her story.

"Good God!" Sophie was visibly scandalized at the uncivilized action of Del's father. Beating someone up was not how the Mathesons dealt with things.

"The bloody lip and the bruises healed within a few weeks. The words and insults he hurled at me hurt far more than his fists ever could," Del said frankly.

Sophie looked at her in dismay. She had understood the message in Del's words. "This is not the same situation," she said. "This is a lot more... complex and complicated."

"Is it? I think it's actually very simple: either you love your daughter unconditionally, like a parent should, or you don't." Del knew it wasn't her place to say anything, but she just couldn't take it anymore. Seeing the distance between Kade and her mother had hurt all week even though Kade had acted as if she didn't care.

"Of course I love my daughter," Sophie bristled, "but—"

"No!" Del interrupted sharply. "Unconditional love doesn't have any 'buts.' Your love is conditional—you only love her if she's the perfect Kadence Matheson, with a perfect job, a perfect husband, a perfect life. You won't tolerate any departures from what you consider right for her."

The usually very controlled Sophie Matheson was flushing crimson with anger. "You have no right—"

"I know I don't." Del looked intently into the outraged blue eyes. "I just don't want you and Kade to end up where I am with my parents. Please don't do that to Kade—or to yourself. Take a big step back, and think about what is important in life—is it Kade marrying the man you want her to or is it Kade's happiness?" She didn't wait for an answer. She lifted her bag up onto her shoulder again and walked away, leaving Sophie to think about it.

When she reached the end of the hallway, she saw Kade standing frozen at the bottom of the stairs. Kade was gripping the banister, and one foot was already on the first step, but she made no move to climb the stairs.

Del's steps faltered for a moment. *She heard what I said to her mother,* she realized. Slowly, she made her way down the steps and set her bag down next to Kade. "I'm sorry. I shouldn't ha—"

Kade's fingers on her lips stopped her. "Don't apologize for standing up for me."

"I know you don't want or need me fighting your battles," Del said cautiously. She had known from the very beginning that Kade was an independent and self-reliant woman.

Kade nodded her head in silent agreement. "Still, for once it's nice not to fight the battles alone. Not being a part of the family, you see things more clearly. I never could have said to her what you did—even though it's exactly the right thing to say," Kade openly admitted. She reached around Del and picked up her bag. "Come on. Let's go."

"Don't you have to say good-bye to your mother?" Del asked, pointing back over her shoulder. She didn't want to be the cause of any further estrangement between Kade and her mother.

"No. I like your parting words better. I'll give her some time and call her later." Kade directed them out of the house without looking back.

CHAPTER 33

*T*HIS IS A NIGHTMARE, Aiden thought as soon as she walked through the door and onto the crime scene. *Or déjà vu— very bad déjà vu.*

Through the half-open bedroom door, she could see a crumpled sheet and a chaos of items scattered all over the floor. A small lamp had been knocked over during a struggle. It was almost a copy of what Dawn's apartment had looked like the night of her rape—with one very important difference.

Alannah Hendley was not sitting in the living room, holding on to the blanket around her shoulders with trembling hands. She was lying on the bed in a pool of blood.

"Didn't have a chance. Multiple stab wounds to the chest and abdomen. She bled out in a matter of minutes," Irene Deming told them. She got up from her crouched position, finally allowing Ray and Aiden a glance at the victim.

Sightless green eyes, almost hidden by tangled blond hair, stared up at Aiden.

Bile rose in her throat. Aiden pressed a hand to her mouth. She quickly shouldered past Ray, making it outside just in time before she lost her lunch.

When she straightened, Ray silently handed her a paper towel and a bottle of water. "Hey, you all right?" He studied her with a concerned gaze.

Yeah, sure, I throw up at crime scenes every day, no big deal. Aiden held back the sarcastic remark. Ray was just worried about her. He didn't deserve to be the target of her bad mood. "Yeah. I'm fine." She took a cautious sip of water.

"Are you sure?" Ray looked more than doubtful.

They both knew they had seen worse crime scenes without even blinking. It was part of their job. Normally, Aiden was completely professional, but the parallels between this case and Dawn's had pierced the protective walls that separated the tough cop from the woman.

"You're not pregnant, are you?" he joked, trying to ease the tension.

Aiden didn't find it funny. "Yeah, you found me out," she replied with heavy sarcasm. "My lesbian lover got me pregnant. How did you find out?"

Ray folded his arms over his chest and regarded her steadily. "Maybe it's the fact that you've been grouchy as hell all morning?"

Aiden sighed. "Sorry. It's just... you... what you said and... all of this," she gestured back at the apartment, "it hit a sore spot."

"I can imagine that." Ray nodded seriously. "The crime scene and Alannah Hendley, they look a lot like—"

"Yeah," Aiden said, quickly interrupting him. She didn't want him to say Dawn's name, probably because it would make it more real and force her to realize once again how close she had come to losing Dawn before they even got a chance to get to know each other.

Ray studied her. "But it's not just that, is it?" he asked after a few seconds of silent appraisal.

He knows me too well. Aiden sighed again. "Did you ever feel like it would have been better for your relationship in the long run if you and Susan hadn't gotten married so soon?" she asked, more comfortable with directing the attention away from her private life while still not really changing the subject.

"I don't regret marrying Susan, and I don't regret that we had Rebecca, but yeah, the timing could have been better," Ray readily admitted. "I mean, Susan was barely seventeen, and she had never even kissed another guy before me. We hadn't been together all that long, and suddenly we weren't just a couple—we were parents!"

"Yet you never hesitated to move in together, to get married, and start a family?" Aiden asked.

Ray laughed. "Never hesitated? I was in a constant state of panic for the first year of our marriage. Being responsible for a wife and a kid wasn't exactly what I dreamed about when I was twenty." He looked at Aiden. "This isn't really about me and Susan, is it? What's going on with you, Aiden?"

Aiden took a deep breath. "Dawn asked me to move in with her."

"That's great!" Ray beamed at her. When he saw her expression and her tense stance, his smile weakened. "Isn't it? I mean... Dawn is wonderful. You've known her for nine months; you get along great with her family, and I know you love her. So what's the problem? You're a lesbian, remember? You're supposed to move in together after the second date, so you're way overdue."

"I'm... I'm just not ready, Ray." Aiden leaned her shoulders and the back of her head against the wall and rested her gaze on Ray, waiting for his reaction.

Ray shrugged. "Then tell her," he said. "She's a very understanding woman. I'm sure she'll give you all the time you need. She'll wait for you."

Aiden didn't want Dawn to have to wait. She wanted her to be happy and have what she wanted **now**, and she was angry with herself for not being able to give her that. Her anger only made matters worse, and she tried to shake it off and think clearly. "I'm not sure time is the issue here," she finally admitted.

"Now I'm confused," Ray mumbled. "Then what is the issue? She loves you. You love her. In the last few months, you've been happier than I've ever seen you."

"That's just it—why change things if they're perfect just the way they are?" Aiden looked at him for an answer even though she knew it was not a reasonable question.

"Aiden," he said in the tone of voice she had heard him use with his kids. "You don't mean that. You're just afraid of moving forward and getting hurt."

That was only one of the things Aiden was afraid of, but she nodded and pushed off from the wall. "Come on, let's get back. We have a case to solve."

* * *

Del looked at the sliding doors of the hospital. With the dangers of her job and with her best friend being a nurse, she had been in hospitals a lot, but never had they seemed as intimidating as this one was now.

"Do you want me to wait in the car?" Kade asked beside her.

Del turned to look at her. "No." She honestly couldn't imagine a situation where she wouldn't want Kade's company. Even after driving the three hundred miles to Sacramento without stopping, pale from lack of sleep, and with creased clothes, Kade was a sight to behold. She was not too proud to accept the support if Kade was willing to give it. "As long as you're comfortable being seen walking in there with me, I'd love the company."

Del knew her family had hammered it into Kade how important appearances and what people thought were. It wasn't an easy thing to overcome after all these years. It seemed as if Kade had finally come to terms with being attracted to women, at least when it was just between them. Making a public announcement, even when it was just walking into a hospital where nobody knew them, wouldn't be as easy for her.

"I'll stay as long as you want me to," Kade promised.

They entered the hospital side by side, finally being directed to the right room. Walking down the sterile corridor, Del could see her mother and two men who had to be her oldest brothers standing in front of one of the doors. They were talking to a doctor.

God, she has gotten old! Startled, she realized how long it had been since she had last seen her mother. *The last time I saw her, she was praying to God to forgive me my sins and make me "normal" again.*

Her mother looked as if she was praying now too, looking up at the physician with a desperate expression.

The doctor walked away just before Del reached the group. Kade stayed back a little as Del stopped right in front of her mother. Del didn't say anything. She gave a nod to her mother and a sidelong glance to the two brothers she hardly knew. They had been little boys when she had last seen them. She didn't know how to greet them after twenty-six years.

"Delicia!" Her mother clutched her hands to her chest when she recognized her only daughter. "You came! Your father will be so happy."

Oh, yeah, right. He'll be overjoyed to see his daughter and find out she's still a lesbian. Instead of saying it, Del turned to Kade. "Kade, this is my mother, Rosita Montero Benítez, and my brothers, Ismael and Ricardo. This is Kade Matheson. She came with me from Oregon."

Rosita stared at Kade. "Are you...?" She turned to Del, her cheeks flushed with embarrassment. "Is she... your...?" She gestured helplessly in Kade's direction but didn't finish the sentence.

"My girlfriend?" Del glanced at Kade, who was now blushing a little too. "No, she's not." *Not that I don't want her to be.* But officially, they were still nothing more than friends, and Del didn't want to assume too much just because of one kiss. She would be proud to call Kade her girlfriend one day, but not without Kade's explicit consent. For now, she wasn't sure if Kade was ready to make a public announcement, so she would follow Kade's lead.

"Oh." Her mother visibly relaxed. "So you're not...?" This time, she gestured in Del's direction.

Del knew exactly what she was hoping for. "Sorry to disappoint you, but I'm still gay. That's not something that changes just because you want it to," she said frankly, not willing to hide who she was just to make her parents feel better. She pointed at the door. "Is he in there?"

Rosita nodded and pressed a handkerchief to her face. "The doctors say he probably doesn't have long," she whispered.

Del's brothers bowed their heads in silent grief, but all Del could feel was numbness and dull disbelief. It was hard to believe that the strong, dominating man she had known could ever die. "Are you sure he wants to see me?" she asked, feeling like the scared sixteen-year-old again. She wasn't sure how she would react to seeing her father—or if she wanted to see him at all.

"Oh, yes, of course!" Her mother urged her toward the door. "Go on in."

Del hesitated.

"Do you want me to go in first and talk to him?" Rosita asked.

Del was impressed almost against her will—it was the first time in forty-three years that her mother had stepped protectively between Del and her father. When he had beaten her all those years ago, she had done nothing. *Maybe a few things have changed,* Del conceded. For now, though, she would remain skeptical. "No, it's all right. I'm going in to talk to him. I don't have anything to fear. There's nothing he can take from me anymore," Del said. She inhaled deeply, mentally preparing for the task ahead.

Kade moved a step closer and squeezed her hand for just a moment before letting go again. "I'll be right here, waiting outside, if you need me," she whispered.

Nodding, Del took another deep breath and knocked on the door before she entered.

"I already told the damn nurse I don't want any more painkillers!" the man in the bed ranted before the door was even halfway open.

Del wasn't sure what she had expected, but the patient in the hospital bed was a shock. Her father had gotten old, and he looked as if he had lost forty pounds even though he had never been overweight. His cheeks were hollow and unshaven and his skin thin and mottled.

An oxygen tube, an intravenous line, and various wires connected him to the beeping machines and blinking monitors all around the bed.

Del felt an overwhelming wave of emotions crash down on her—regret, hurt, anger, compassion. It almost choked her and condemned her to speechlessness.

Héctor Vasquez Calderon returned her stare, and Del realized that he didn't recognize her. This realization hit her like a blow in the solar plexus even though it probably shouldn't have surprised her. She wasn't a scared sixteen-year-old anymore, but a mature, confident woman.

Without saying a word, she stepped closer to the hospital bed.

His former strength gone, Héctor sat up in the bed with difficulty. He narrowed his eyes. "Do we know each other?"

Del bit her lip. A lump of emotions burned in her throat and left a bitter taste in her mouth. Her father not knowing her, his own daughter, was almost worse than an angry rejection. "It's me," she said and almost hated herself for the tremor in her voice. She had promised herself years ago to never again show any weakness in front of her father. "Del."

The terminally ill man who was her father gasped. "D-Delicia?" His gaze fluttered over her face in disbelief. "Yes, it's you. You look a lot like me—at least how I looked before this damn cancer made me a drooling, old geezer!"

Del said nothing. She had always preferred to believe that she resembled her kind grandfather, not her despotic father.

"So your mother found you," Héctor murmured. "I knew she would search for you as soon as she had the house to herself. After you left, our marriage slowly broke apart too. Somehow, throwing you out... it always stood between us even though we never talked about it."

Only when she had to gasp for air did Del realize that she had held her breath. "That almost sounds like an apology... as if you regret how you treated me." Torn between hope and mistrust, she looked down at her father.

Héctor rubbed his stubble with one of his thin hands. "Regret?" he said slowly. "Do I regret that I'm lying here, about to make a not very glorious exit as a lonely and practically divorced man? Yes, of course." He coughed but struggled to continue. "Do I regret that your mother and I, after forty-five years of marriage, have only our sons and a daughter I banned from our lives in common? Yes, I think so."

Del stared at him. "You admit how you treated me was wrong?"

"It wasn't the right way, but..." Héctor lifted a hand, and for a moment, Del could see the tyrant from her past. "...it was only for your own good. I thought if I forced you to face reality and showed you how wrong such... perversions are, you would come to your senses sooner or later."

"Perversions," Del repeated quietly and bitterly. No, her father hadn't changed his attitude toward people who didn't share his way of life. "I'm sorry to inform you that I haven't come to my senses," she told him stiffly. "What now?" What did he expect of her?

"Your mother would like to see you again. Maybe she can somehow overlook your... lifestyle, but I... I just can't accept it—and I don't have the time to maybe come to terms with it someday. Sorry." His narrow shoulders moved up and down under the hospital gown like the wings of an exhausted bird.

For the first time, Del didn't only hear hateful reproach for his "perverse daughter" in his voice but also an admission of his own inability to accept her as she was. It wasn't much. Still, it was more than she had expected from him. She cleared her throat. "What am I doing here? Why did you want to see me? Just to tell me that?"

"Maybe because I didn't want my last memory of you to be that of a crying teenager with a black eye and a bloody lip," he said quietly.

Del shrugged with false casualness. "That healed long ago."

"Really?"

Del knew he hasn't only talking about a few bruises. "No," she said honestly. "Wounds like that leave scars. You almost did the worst thing someone can do to their child—you almost made me hate myself. That's not something you forget."

Her father was silent for a long time. Maybe he sensed that nothing he could say would undo what he had done to Del. Maybe he didn't want to undo anything, because he still believed he was right. Finally, he lifted his tired gaze up to look into Del's eyes. "Will you give me your hand before you leave?" he asked quietly.

Del looked down at her own long, strong fingers—the competent hands of a cop—and then at her father's skinny hands that had lost their former, sometimes brutal strength.

It wasn't only the heart monitor and the bed rail that stood between them. A deep rift separated father and daughter—Héctor couldn't accept his daughter's sexual orientation, and Del couldn't accept her father's homophobia.

Del stared down at him. Finally, she took a hesitant step and slowly reached out her hand. She gently closed her fingers around the punctured back of his hand. She could feel the rapid thumping in the veins that carried shared blood.

His bony chest heaved, but his face was almost expressionless. "Thank you," he said quietly.

"You're welcome." Del gave his fingers a soft squeeze before she slowly let go and turned to walk out of the room and out of his life.

* * *

Dawn was sitting on the front steps of Aiden's apartment building, waiting for her, when Aiden got out of her car.

"Hey," Aiden said in surprise. "What are you doing here?" Not that it wasn't nice to see Dawn. After looking into the lifeless eyes of a woman who could have been Dawn, it soothed her to see the familiar green-gray eyes alive with emotion—even if that emotion was worry.

"Two of my patients canceled, so I called your cell to see if you wanted to join me for an early dinner. When you didn't answer, I called the precinct. They told me you had gone home." Dawn stood from her place on the steps and came closer to study Aiden's face. "You rarely do that in the middle of the day. Is everything all right?"

Aiden sighed. The last thing she wanted was to explain to Dawn why Ray had been so insistent on sending her home for the remainder of the day. That was why she had turned off her cell phone. "We have a new case, and the lab results are not in until tomorrow. Ray thought it would be a good opportunity for me to relax for a few hours." It was the truth, but not the whole truth.

"Can I come in?" Dawn asked cautiously when Aiden searched in her pocket for her keys.

"Of course you can," Aiden said. "You could have gone on in without me, you know? You have a key." *God, did my refusal to move in with her make her so unsure about herself... about us? Or is she just trying to be considerate?*

"I know, but I was worried about you, and I wanted to see you the moment you approached the apartment building," Dawn confessed. "I know there's more to why you went home early than just waiting for the lab results." She quickly held up her hands. "It's okay if you don't want to talk about it, but please, don't lie to me."

Sighing, Aiden rubbed her neck. "It's just... It's a tough case for me. Ray thought I could use a few hours to get my emotional equilibrium back. I'd love to have dinner with you, but I want to take Evan out for another driving lesson first."

"I don't mind waiting a bit. I brought a novel," Dawn said as they entered Aiden's apartment. "You won't even know I'm here."

Aiden stopped in the doorway, very close to Dawn in the cramped space. "I'll always know when you're here—and I'm glad about it." Finally, she allowed herself to do what she had wanted to do since she had seen Dawn sitting on her doorstep. She stepped closer and pulled Dawn into a tight embrace, closing her eyes and breathing in Dawn's scent.

Dawn melted into the embrace. "You okay?" she whispered into Aiden's ear.

Aiden let go and slowly stepped back. "Yeah. I'm fine now."

Clearly, Dawn didn't believe her, but she said nothing. She sat down on the couch and, as promised, began to read her novel. After a moment, she kicked off her shoes and curled her legs under her.

Aiden sighed. She knew she couldn't relax now. She was too keyed up from what she had seen at the crime scene and too worried about visiting Evan. She went to the bathroom, checked her messages, and then went to the refrigerator to get them something to drink. Restlessly, she prowled her small apartment. Aiden felt Dawn's gaze following her around the room. It made her feel even more like a caged tiger in a zoo.

"Hey, what's the matter?" Dawn asked as Aiden passed her for the third time. "I thought you took the afternoon off to relax, but now you're pacing."

"I took the afternoon off to spend it with Evan," Aiden corrected.

Dawn raised her brows. "And that's not relaxing?"

Aiden shrugged. Lately, she had begun to relax around Evan. "Not today."

"Why? You're not still nervous about handing over your car to Evan, are you?" Dawn asked with a tiny bit of amusement. With the exception of her sardine can, which had been a present from her father, cars were just cars to Dawn—things that were a necessary evil, but not something you cherished.

"No, it's not the car." Aiden had quickly gotten over that. "Evan is not a bad driver."

Dawn nodded with a satisfied grin. She was visibly proud of her protégé. "What is it, then?"

"I've been debating with myself."

"About?" Dawn prodded.

Aiden took a deep breath and prepared to say it out loud for the first time. "About whether or not I should talk to her about... our father."

Dawn put down the book she had still held in her hands and immediately gave Aiden her full attention. "Why today?" she asked.

"You think I shouldn't talk to her about this?" Aiden asked.

"That's not what I said. I'm just wondering about your timing." Dawn looked up at her with a worried frown. "With work and everything you already have a lot on your plate at the moment."

She's right. There's a lot to deal with in my life, so why am I taking this on now too? Am I using Evan as an excuse not to have to deal with my other problems? Aiden thought about it and shook her head at herself. She knew that wasn't it. *I know I can't deal with everything else that's going on in my life and move forward with Dawn until I somehow deal with my past... and Evan and our father are a big part of it.*

Dawn was still waiting for her answer.

Aiden cleared her throat. She didn't want to reveal all of her reasons for wanting to talk to Evan. It would only make Dawn start to hope for something Aiden wasn't sure she could achieve. "It feels like the right moment," she hedged. "I feel like Evan and I... we finally established some trust between us." Seeing Evan take care of Laurie yesterday made Aiden realize again what a good, caring person Evan could be when she lowered her protective walls. She wanted Evan to see herself that way too.

"Okay." Dawn nodded slowly. If she suspected that there was more to it, she didn't say it. "Have you made a decision about whether to tell Evan about your father?" she asked, her voice carefully neutral.

"Don't use your shrink voice with me, please," Aiden gently admonished, tapping her lightly on the nose.

"Shrink voice? I have a shrink voice?" Dawn cocked her head in interest.

Aiden nodded. She knew Dawn was mostly unaware of using it in her private life, and there were times when she even appreciated it, but this time, she wanted an honest opinion and maybe even someone to make the decision for her. "Yeah. It's friendly and shows sufficient interest, but it's carefully clear of any judgment or emotion."

Dawn thought about it and then nodded to herself. "You're right. I do that, huh? I put off my emotions to give you room for yours. I just don't want to influence a decision that is so unique and personal that only you can make it," she explained.

Sighing, Aiden sank onto the couch next to Dawn. "I wish someone would tell me what the right thing to do is in this tricky situation. If she doesn't know about her... our father, telling her might throw her back into crisis. But if she knows about him and I don't tell her, she'll feel isolated, like an aberration that should never have existed."

Dawn took her hand and entangled their fingers. "Do you think she knows?"

"I have no idea. I can't very well ask her if she knows her father is a serial rapist, can I? That would defeat the purpose." Aiden let her head fall back against the couch in frustration.

"You could ask her what she knows about her father," Dawn said.

Aiden looked at her doubtfully. "And you think she'll tell me if she's aware he's a rapist?"

"What would you tell her if she asks you about your father?" Dawn asked. "And for the record, I'm not using my shrink voice. I'm honestly interested in and nonjudgmental of your answer," she added with a smile.

Aiden grinned and allowed herself to relax a little before she thought about the answer. "I'm not sure," she finally said. "That's exactly what I'm struggling with. Should I tell her, or would it be better to forget about it?"

"Can you forget about it?" Dawn sounded doubtful and not therapeutically neutral at all. "I don't think a day goes by that you don't think about it."

"I work with the Sexual Assault Detail. Of course I think about it. I'm confronted with rape every day," Aiden said matter-of-factly.

"You chose that job," Dawn reminded. She held up her hand when Aiden started to answer. "I'm not criticizing your choice of profession. I'm proud of it and of you."

Aiden relaxed her tense shoulders. She could remember a few dozen similar conversations with her mother, but Robyn Carlisle had never supported her choice of jobs. She knew her mother only meant well, but it had always felt like a criticism of her, not just her job. It felt good to know Dawn was one hundred percent behind her.

"You chose that job," Dawn repeated softly. "It was your choice to be confronted with rape every day."

My choice. Aiden had never thought about it like that. It was true, of course, at least to a certain extent. She could have become a teacher, an artist, like her mother, a scientist, or a mechanic. Or she could have at least picked another specialty within the Portland Police. She'd had offers from vice and from homicide, but she had always said no. *Maybe it is about choice. Maybe I had to take control where my mother had none.*

"Then again, maybe it's not a choice at all," Dawn continued, tilting her head, deeply in thought. "Even without the job, I'm sure you'd think about rape every day of your life anyway—because you can't help thinking it created you and made you what you are."

"I wouldn't even exist without it," Aiden threw in. Thinking about the dilemma of her existence made her head throb.

"Maybe it's the same for Evan," Dawn speculated. "Maybe she thinks being conceived of rape is what decided her fate and determined her personality. That would explain a lot about her, wouldn't it?"

Aiden shook her head. "The 'violence gene' theory is not an excuse for bad behavior."

Dawn squeezed her hand. "I didn't say it was. It's not about genes or heredity. It's about making assumptions about yourself." She looked deeply into Aiden's eyes, her green irises glowing with intensity. "If Evan thinks she's bad and unworthy of trust, respect, and love, she'll act accordingly, and it'll cause people to treat her with distrust, frustration, and loathing. It's a self-fulfilling prophecy."

Could this be the cause of all of Evan's problems? Aiden wondered. She knew better than to ask Dawn if Evan had talked about it in therapy. She knew how hard it could be to feel conflicted about yourself and your sheer existence. It had caused a lot of problems in her life, and only since Dawn was a part of it had she begun to feel more balanced and content with herself. "So you think I should talk to her about... our father?"

"Don't make a decision yet," Dawn advised.

Not a problem. Putting off decisions... that has become a specialty of mine lately, Aiden thought grimly.

"Feel her out first," Dawn continued. "If she doesn't trust you enough yet to talk to you about what she knows about her father, maybe it's not the right time to tell her—if you want to tell her at all."

Aiden nodded and closed her eyes, slightly leaning her shoulder against Dawn's.

"Speaking of right times..." Dawn said quietly. "There's something I wanted to tell you, but with Laurie's accident, it was a little hectic yesterday. Do you have the time—and the nerve—

now? If you'd rather not think about anything else, now that you're worrying about Evan, we could do this later."

There it was: the offer to gracefully back out of the conversation Aiden had been dreading since Saturday. *It would be so easy, but it wouldn't be fair to Dawn. I'll only hurt her if I reject her when she wants to talk.* She sighed inwardly. That was one of her dilemmas. No matter what she did, it could lead to hurting Dawn and maybe even losing her. If she dragged her feet and refused to make all the steps of commitment Dawn wanted her to make, Dawn would begin to think that she didn't love her or at least that her love was not enough. If she made all the steps, moved in with Dawn, and shared her whole life with her, she could just as easily hurt her or scare her away with her little bad habits, major bad moods, and the demons of her past and her job.

"Now is fine," she finally said. "Evan won't be home from school for an hour anyway."

"It's nothing bad," Dawn said, picking up on Aiden's hesitation. "It's not a big discussion. We don't need to actually talk about it. I just wanted to apologize for cornering you on Saturday about moving in together and having kids."

Aiden could only sit and stare at her. The last thing she had expected from Dawn was an apology. Dawn had always clearly communicated her needs and had stood up for what she wanted, without trampling another person's rights or feelings to get it. It was one of the things Aiden admired so much about her. "You don't need to apologize," she assured Dawn. "You were honest about what you want, and I appreciate that." *Unlike me,* she added silently. She hadn't given Dawn much explanation about her reluctance to move in together.

"I'm not apologizing for wanting to build a life with you or for being honest about it," Dawn clarified. "I apologize for my timing and for not taking into consideration what you want. I sprang my plans of commitment on you without warning, after a very busy day. I shouldn't have done that, and I'm sorry."

Instead of making Aiden feel better, the sincere apology made her feel even guiltier. "It's all right," she said quickly.

"Really?" Dawn looked a little doubtful.

"Yeah. I just... it threw me for a loop. I think things are going great between us, so I guess it never occurred to me to change anything." Aiden gave a helpless shrug.

Dawn looked down and stroked Aiden's fingers. "I don't want to pressure you into anything you don't want," she said.

"I want it. I want you. It's just..." Aiden rubbed her face in frustration. How could she explain her complex feelings and unreasonable fears to Dawn?

"Hey, I told you we don't have to talk about it now. I just wanted to apologize for my very bad timing, okay?" Dawn ducked her head to look into Aiden's face.

Aiden nodded. "Okay." For now, it was better to let it rest. Her brain already felt like ground meat from the emotional grinder it had been through today. "I think I should go now. Driving to Evan's during rush hour might take me a while, and if I don't do it now, I'll chicken out."

Dawn leaned over and slid her arms around Aiden.

Aiden closed her eyes and enjoyed the warmth and the feeling of Dawn's breasts pressing against her. She wrapped her arms around Dawn and inhaled deeply.

After a few seconds, Dawn moved back a little and kissed her. "Is it okay if I stay here until you get back, or do you think you'll want to be alone after talking to Evan?" Dawn asked cautiously after their lips separated.

"No, please stay. It gives me something to look forward to." She playfully leered at Dawn, earning her a laugh and another kiss.

* * *

Aiden could hear the animated young voice from the living room as Roger led her into the house. It didn't sound like Evan's bored drawl.

"...and then she gently wiped away the blood and dirt from my arm and practically lifted me off the ground," Laurie continued her tale as Aiden and Roger entered the living room.

Look at that! Aiden thought, taking in the scene in front of her. Laurie was sitting at the place of honor, the head of the table, the glowing white plaster held like a prize in front of her. Jill LeCroix sat next to her, visibly impressed by the vivid picture the girl painted with her words. *So there is a little bit of Kade in Laurie after all. That's exactly how most jurors look at Kade during closing arguments.*

Only one person in the room didn't seem overly impressed. Evan sat at the other end of the table, rolling her eyes. For the first time, she showed real enthusiasm when she saw Aiden. "Great, you're here already! We better go. I want to drive while it's still light outside." She grabbed her jacket from the back of her chair, kissed the blushing Laurie, and sauntered from the room, practically dragging Aiden with her.

"Hey, maybe I wanted to say hello to Laurie and your foster parents," Aiden protested.

Evan didn't react. She kept walking until they had reached Aiden's car. "Keys," she ordered and then added more softly, "Please."

Aiden tossed them over to her. "So you introduced Laurie to your foster parents, huh?" *Not as afraid of taking the steps of commitment as your big sister, are you?*

With more force than strictly necessary, Evan fastened her seat belt. "That wasn't my grand idea. Laurie just came over, and the rest was inevitable. Did you hear what she told them about what happened Sunday? She told her parents the same fairy tale."

"Fairy tale?" Aiden repeated.

"Yeah. With me in the role of Prince Charming, rescuing the fair maiden," Evan said with a grimace. "I'm not a goddamn hero."

Aiden had to think of the journalist who had picked her as the subject of his article a few months earlier. She hadn't been pleased either when she had seen the sensational headline depicting her as a hero. She had given the same reason for being grumpy about the article all day: I'm no hero. Dawn, of course, had protested, calling Aiden her personal hero. "Looks like you're a hero to Laurie," she said, using the same words Dawn had used with her.

Evan grimaced again and started the car.

Aiden didn't try to make much conversation during their drive through the city. Evan needed to concentrate, and she needed time to think of an inconspicuous way to ask about Evan's father.

When Evan finally stopped the car at their usual spot, Aiden didn't suggest they practice parking as usual. Instead, she asked, "You want to walk over there and get a coffee?" She nodded at a little coffee shop at the corner. She didn't want to be confined to the cramped space inside the car for this conversation.

Evan gave the half nod, half shrug that was so typical for her, and they slowly walked toward the coffee shop.

Aiden was still searching for the best way to broach the subject when Evan broke the silence, "How's the doc?"

Aiden looked at her in surprise. Evan wasn't normally one to ask questions like this. It wasn't that she didn't care. She just didn't want to let people know she cared. "She's fine," Aiden answered. "Probably curled up on the couch with her nose in a book." She grinned indulgently.

"Did she... say anything about skating practice?" Evan asked cautiously.

Why is she tiptoeing around this? Having a rapist for a father is the problematic subject here, but skating? Why is she afraid to broach that subject? Aiden tried to remember what Dawn had said about skating. "I think she mentioned something about 'kicking your sorry little ass' the next time you run a race," she reported.

Evan grinned widely. Aiden had never seen anyone appear so happy about the prospect of getting her ass kicked. "Oh, she said that, did she?" Evan laughed.

"It's an exact quote," Aiden confirmed. She studied Evan, curious to find out what made her so happy about it. "Did you think she wouldn't want to skate with you anymore after Laurie's accident?"

"Well, she gave me the new pair of skates we had agreed on as payment, and she made it down the half-pipe like a pro, so that means the skating lessons are over." Evan was trying hard to sound indifferent about it, but Aiden saw through the act quite easily. In her opinion, no one who knew Dawn was indifferent about spending time with her.

"Evan, I'm sure Dawn enjoys skating, as hard to understand as that is for me." Aiden gave an exaggerated shudder. "But what she really likes about these afternoons is spending them with you. She could be the world's best skater, with nothing left to learn anymore, and she'd still want to spend time with you."

Evan didn't look entirely convinced. "Did she say that?"

"She doesn't have to. It's the same for me. I'm not here because I enjoy being stuck in a car. I'm here to spend time with you," Aiden said.

Evan snorted, something Aiden hadn't heard from her in a few weeks. "You're here because you feel obliged to spend time with me, not because you like it."

Under all that bragging and bravado, there's a lot of insecurity and self-doubts, Aiden realized. *She can't believe anyone would want to spend time with her and like her just for who she is. She can't believe we're here to stay because everyone else in her life walked away sooner or later. How do I reassure her?* She wished Dawn were here to take over or give her advice but knew she had to deal with it on her own. *Honesty,* she finally decided. *Evan will sense it if I try to bullshit her.*

"Maybe it was like that when I first met you," she admitted. "You didn't make a very good first impression, and I jumped to conclusions about you. Only after a while did I realize the problem wasn't with you—it was with me. I was thinking like a stubborn cop, not like a caring sister. I learned how to be a stubborn cop, and I'm good at it. I know nothing about being a caring sister, and I suck at it."

Evan stared at her and then laughed. "Yeah, you do! You didn't leave a stellar first impression either. I couldn't figure out what made the doc want to be in a relationship with you."

They ordered their coffees and took the paper cups with them on their walk around the block.

"Could? Past tense? Does that mean you figured out what she likes about me by now?" Aiden asked with a playful grin.

"Must be your good looks. You look a lot like me, you know?" Evan preened.

Aiden wildly shook her head. "No. You look like me." Then Aiden remembered where their similarities were coming from, and she sobered.

Evan stopped laughing too. "Did you ever meet your... or our, I guess, father?" she asked with such subtlety that Aiden, who had searched for an inconspicuous way to broach the subject for hours, heard the alarm bells ring.

She knows! Aiden was suddenly convinced. "No," she said over the roaring in her ears, "I never met him. What about you?" She wanted to be sure before she went any further, but now she knew her decision. If Evan didn't already know about their father, she wouldn't tell her. She didn't want to put her through all the self-doubts, the shame, the anger, and the guilt that she had been through. But if Evan already had her suspicions, she had to get them out in the open and talk about it.

"Never met him either," Evan mumbled.

"But you know a few things about him," Aiden made it a statement, not a question. She was almost sure now that Evan knew their father was a rapist.

Evan turned her head. They stared at each other. "What do you know about him?" Evan asked cautiously, clearly not willing to give up any information before Aiden had done so.

Aiden took a deep breath. *Here it is: the moment of truth.* There was only one thing Aiden knew for sure about their father. "He raped my mother." There was no way to make this seem better, so she just said it.

She had almost hoped to see shocked disbelief on Evan's face, telling her that Evan hadn't known, that Evan hadn't grown up with the knowledge that she was a child of rape. Evan's jaw clenched, but there was only anger and helplessness in her gaze, no surprise.

"You already knew that," Aiden said quietly.

Evan chucked down her coffee, acting as if it was a shot of something much stronger. "I suspected. Once a rapist, always a rapist. It's in the blood. You can't change it," Evan's voice held bitter resignation.

Aiden knew she was mostly right. There was no cure, no accepted therapy for sex offenders. Still, Evan's words had held so much more than just that scientific fact. *It's in the blood,* she mentally repeated and heard Dawn's voice again. *It's about making assumptions about yourself.* "So you think he raped your mother too? Are you sure?" Aiden had hoped for another explanation, a one-night stand or a short fling.

"Oh, yeah. No doubt about it." Evan took another sip of coffee even though Aiden knew it was still too hot to drink.

"How do you know?" Aiden asked quietly.

"I eavesdropped on my grandmother. Not that I had to eavesdrop because she was shouting at my mother over the phone, trying to get her to see me," Evan said, her lips a thin line.

Aiden frowned. "To see you?" She realized she didn't know anything about the way Evan had grown up. She only knew Evan had been in the foster system for many years, being shuffled from foster family to foster family until something else happened that made them send her away. "She didn't live with you?"

"She wanted nothing to do with the 'spawn of that devil.' If my grandmother hadn't been against abortion for religious reasons, she would have aborted me without a second thought." Evan's eyes were hard and emotionless.

This is something she knew for a lot of years and accepted as a fact, Aiden thought, feeling the sadness and hurt Evan had buried deep within herself. *I had a lot of hard times with my mother. The drinking binges, the arguments, the loneliness when she hid away in her studio for days... but still, at least I had one parent who cared about me, who cared about whether I lived or died.* She sent a silent prayer of thanks to her mother. "So you never even met her?" she asked, trying to understand how life had been for Evan and how it could have been for her.

"No. But the disinterest is mutual," Evan answered, pretending not to care. "The other kids in the foster system always dreamed about their 'real parents' coming and taking them with them to live in a luxurious mansion." She gave an ironic half grin. "I was the only one who never harbored that secret hope. Their dream was my nightmare."

"How old were you when you learned why she didn't want to see you?" Aiden asked, almost afraid of the answer.

Evan didn't have to think about the answer. Aiden was sure she had never forgotten about that day. "It was shortly before my grandmother died. I was six." Once again, Evan kept her voice matter-of-fact. "How old were you?"

Six! God! We really do have a lot in common. I wished that was one thing Evan didn't have to share with me. "Seven." Aiden hadn't understood the meaning of her mother's angry words back then, but she had begun to understand that her father was a very bad man—and that she reminded her mother of him in some ways. When she was sober again, her mother had always taken back her angry words and praised her for being a "good girl." Evan hadn't even had that balancing influence in her life.

"Is that what made you become a cop?" Evan asked frankly. "Because you wanted to catch him?"

Aiden shook her head. "I spent a lot of time trying to find out more about him, to catch him, but no, I didn't become a police officer because I wanted to catch him. Others like him, maybe. Mostly, I wanted to prevent it from happening to women like our mothers. I identify with the victim, not the perpetrator." It was an important distinction.

"Has he ever been caught? Do you know who he is? His name? Why he did it?" Evan had a lot of questions, but Aiden couldn't answer any of them. At least not the way Evan probably wanted her to.

Aiden slowly shook her head. "Once or twice I thought I had a lead, but it was never him."

"Are you still searching for him?" Evan asked.

Am I? Aiden wasn't sure how to answer that question. She hadn't thought about it before. "Not really," she said, trying to figure out when she had slowly ceased her efforts to find the man who had raped her mother and fathered her. *I haven't looked at the file in almost a year,* she realized. "Other things have become more important in my life, and there was never a new lead... until I learned that I have a half sister."

"Do you think there are others? Other women he raped? Other 'spawns of the devil'?" Evan asked, using her mother's words.

"I don't know. The only thing I know is... you're not a 'spawn of the devil.' Neither am I. Don't let yourself believe that." Aiden threw her half-full coffee cup into the closest garbage can and turned her full attention to Evan.

"We were born from an act of hate and brutality. We carry the genes of a rapist," Evan said as if that explained everything about them.

Aiden stopped and put both of her hands on Evan's shoulders, forcing her to stop too and look her in the eyes. "It doesn't mean we're bad people."

There was no spark of acceptance in Evan's gaze. After years of being told she was a good-for-nothing scoundrel, Evan had started to believe it. She thought the circumstances of her conception were her unchangeable fate.

"Look around," Aiden ordered. She was not about to let her sister believe bad things about herself. She gestured to the other people walking up or down the busy street. "How many of them do you think were born to parents who are thieves, thugs, wife-beaters, murderers, or people with an otherwise criminal past? How many do you think were conceived during emotionless one-night stands, meaningless short flings, break-up sex, or attempts to patch up a doomed relationship?"

Evan furrowed her brow, looking very vulnerable in her confusion. "I-I don't know. Some of them, I guess."

"Do you think it reflects on their personality? Do you think they'll automatically become criminals or uncaring people?" She stared at Evan, still holding on to her shoulders. People had to walk around them, but Aiden didn't care.

"N-no, of course not," Evan stammered.

Aiden continued to look into Evan's eyes. "Then why do you assume the worst about yourself?" Aiden didn't wait for an answer. "We're not helpless victims of our genes, Evan. Our mothers didn't have a choice. We do. We can make a choice not to be like our father."

"I don't know," Evan said with a self-deprecating smirk. "I'm practically famous for making bad choices."

Aiden saw things very clearly now. *Dawn had the right idea—this is all about making assumptions about yourself.* "Because you let yourself believe that you are bad and acted accordingly."

"Hey, why is this suddenly all about me?" Evan protested, clearly uncomfortable. "Are you telling me being a product of rape didn't affect you and your life at all?"

"It affected every aspect of my life. It still does. That's why I want it to be different for you," Aiden said honestly. She finally stepped back a little and regarded Evan silently.

Evan looked doubtful. "If even you can't make it work, why should I be able to?"

"I didn't say I can't make it work. It just might take me a little longer," Aiden said, hoping that time would prove her right. She wanted a happy life. She wanted a committed relationship with Dawn. She knew she was standing in her own way. On a rational level, it was clear to her that what she had tried to make Evan realize—that there was no danger, no darkness lurking inside her, if she didn't give that thought any power—was true for her too. She hoped that one day she could make herself believe it, instead of just understanding it.

They walked side by side without talking for a few minutes. Aiden could sense Evan had enough of this particular topic for now. "Come on." She softly clapped Evan on the shoulder. "Let's go back to the car and find out who can park the best."

CHAPTER 34

"WHAT NOW?" Del grumbled and stepped out of the shower when the doorbell rang. She hastily dried off and pulled on a shirt and a pair of pants before she hurried barefoot to open the door. A quick glance through the peephole revealed a familiar and very welcome face. Del quickly pulled open the door.

"Hey!" she greeted Kade. "What are you doing here?" She hadn't expected to see Kade so soon. Since returning to the city, Kade had been up to her neck in work. Del had given her space, knowing Kade probably needed some time to come to terms with the many things that had happened within the last few days. She had made sure that she, Aiden, or Ray were watching Kade from a distance, keeping her safe from the stalker without interfering with her life.

Del was giving her space now too. She wanted to greet Kade much more passionately than with a simple "Hey," but Kade made no move to establish physical contact, so she contented herself with drinking in the sight of Kade in one of her power suits.

Kade held up a bag of Chinese takeout. "Two birds with one stone. I wanted to see how you are and make sure you ate something, and I'm avoiding my mother's calls. She's been calling my apartment nonstop since we left Ashland."

"At least she's not breaking off contact with you," Del tried to console her while she led Kade into her apartment. "What does she say?"

"Not much. My answering machine keeps interrupting her." Kade smirked. "She's raving and shouting, demanding that I call her—but I won't. Not until she can talk to me more calmly. I won't let her treat me like a child who did something wrong."

Del nodded with a satisfied grin. She was glad Kade was taking responsibility for her life and demanding more respect from her mother.

"Have you heard from your family?" Kade asked as she followed Del into the living room.

Del shook her head.

"Do you think they will call if... when your father... dies?" Kade asked.

"I'm sure one of them will call to let me know. My mother will probably make my brother Ricardo call again." Del's mother didn't like to deal with things on her own.

Kade turned and softly touched her arm. "Will you go to the funeral?"

"No." Del had known that before she had even left the hospital. Her family probably wouldn't understand, and some people might think her cold and unforgiving, but she had her own reasons, and she didn't need their approval. If there was one person to whom she wanted to explain her reasons, it was Kade. She wanted Kade to know and understand her. "I've already said my good-byes."

Kade gave a quick nod. She didn't need to ask a lot of questions to understand. "How do you feel about it? Seeing your father, both of your parents, after so long... after everything that happened?" she asked gently.

"It'll always hurt," Del admitted to Kade and to herself. She saw no reason to lie. Kade was one of very few people whom she trusted with her vulnerabilities. "But it's not a festering wound anymore. I won't let it poison my life."

Del padded into the kitchen, gesturing for Kade to follow her. She stretched to reach the bowls on the top shelf that she always used for Chinese food. When she turned back around, she noticed that Kade was staring at her—or more precisely at the way her shirt clung to her still damp skin. "You know," Del said, setting down the bowls, "if you want to kiss me, you can."

She wasn't sure what she had expected Kade to do or say in reaction to the teasing words, but Kade's smooth move forward, right into her personal space, surprised her a little. Kade hooked one finger into the neck of Del's shirt and tugged her down.

For a second, Del marveled at the confidence Kade displayed in a situation that couldn't be familiar to her at all. Then Kade's lips met her own and all thoughts ended.

Kade kissed her slowly, leisurely, inserting a teasing nibble of her teeth here and there.

Del wrapped both arms around her and pulled her closer. With Del being barefoot, Kade's high heels almost brought them to the same height. They stood thigh to thigh, breast to breast.

Kade's thigh daringly slid between Del's legs. Del's back hit the kitchen counter, and she grunted a little in half-pained, half-pleasant surprise but never moved away from the increasingly passionate kiss.

Finally, they had to stop simply because of a lack of air.

"Jesus," Del gasped, making a show of wiping her brow.

She wasn't the only one who was surprised at the passionate abandon of Kade's kisses. It seemed Kade hadn't known she was capable of such passion either. Kade stood leaning against the counter next to Del, blinking dazedly, shaking her head as if trying to process what had just happened.

"And here I was worrying about how you are doing with all of this." Del gestured between them.

"Obviously, I'm fine with it," Kade said. She seemed to have recovered from her surprise, the famous Matheson smirk now firmly on her lips. "Del, the concept of two women together is nothing new to me."

Del's eyebrows shot up. A wave of surprise and unreasonable jealousy almost made her dizzy. "You mean...? But I thought..."

Kade rolled her eyes in amusement. "I said the concept, not the reality. Just because I've never slept with a woman doesn't mean I have to be totally ignorant about what to do with a woman. I have a few lesbian friends; I read a lot, and I've supported LGBT rights for years."

That wasn't what Del had been worried about. She had always known Kade was too self-assured to fumble when it came to kissing or making love, regardless of who her partner was. She knew the sexual element wasn't the hard part for Kade. "I know that," she said. "I was just wondering how you're dealing with the emotional and social consequences." Kade seemed okay as long as it was just the two of them, but when others were around, she carefully guarded her emotions and her actions.

Kade leaned back against the counter and studied Del thoughtfully. "Well, for the most part, I'm not. I'm avoiding the emotional and social consequences," she admitted. "If I start thinking about it in any depth, I'm not sure I can go through with... this."

"What worries you the most?" Del asked. She wanted to help Kade overcome her fears, but she also wanted it to be Kade's decision. If Kade came to the conclusion that the price was too high, she wouldn't try to convince her otherwise.

"I have my career to think about," Kade said. "You know I'm aiming high." She gave a confident, but also self-mocking smile.

I should have known she would pick the subject of her career and ignore what a relationship with me would mean for her emotionally. "You think being a lesbian would destroy your career plans?" Del asked neutrally.

"Being an out lesbian certainly wouldn't help them," Kade answered.

"Things are slowly changing," Del said. She had done some research on lesbians in legal and political positions. "There are about half a dozen openly gay or lesbian judges in Multnomah County and even a lesbian Oregon Supreme Court judge."

Kade shook her head. "Yes, but there's only one openly lesbian federal judge in the whole country, and there's never been an openly gay district attorney in Oregon."

It seemed Kade had done some research too, and her arguments were as sound as ever. "Yet," Del simply said.

"What?" Kade's smooth brow furrowed.

"There's never been a gay or lesbian district attorney in Oregon yet," Del said. "Someone needs to be the first. Why not you?" she asked with a smile.

After a second, Kade's tense expression relaxed into an answering smile. "Thanks for the vote of confidence."

Del nodded. She could sense that the topic was closed for now. Kade needed time, and she was willing to give it to her. "I think we need to reheat the food," she said.

"No, it should still be fine. Besides, cold Chinese food is one of the main food groups of us lawyers," Kade said with a straight face.

Del grinned and handed Kade the bowls. "And here I thought you were high maintenance." She jumped when Kade reached out and pinched her ass. "Hey!"

"Just for that little comment, you're opening your best bottle of wine," Kade decided.

"Oh, I am?" Del put up token resistance. Secretly, she loved being teasingly ordered around by Kade.

Kade nodded gravely. "I'll be in the living room, awaiting my glass of wine." With that, she strode from the room.

Del watched her go. Grinning, she reached for the corkscrew.

* * *

Kade leaned back against the soft cushions on Del's couch. She was glad she had decided to come here instead of heading home after her hectic day at work. At home, only her mother's increasingly upset calls, thoughts of the stalker who might lurk outside her apartment, and more work waited for her. Here, with Del, she could relax and forget about everything else for a while. She slipped out of her high-heeled pumps and listened to the sounds coming from the kitchen.

She heard a bottle of wine being opened, and then the microwave started to hum as Del reheated the food anyway. Over the other little noises in the kitchen, she heard Del begin to sing along with the radio still playing in the background.

Kade grinned as she recognized the song. The female singer was serenading a lawyer, telling him she was falling in love. Del didn't have the trained singing voice of a professional singer, but her low voice sent pleasant tingles through Kade nonetheless. She closed her eyes and listened as the singer professed her love for the lawyer's clever mind.

At first she thought Del was just mindlessly singing along while she worked in the kitchen, but then she noticed Del was changing the original lyrics. *Girls with a clever mind? Wasn't that men?*

The microwave dinged just as Del sang the last lines, telling the now suddenly female lawyer in the song to open her heart to her.

Kade's eyes shot open. *Was she singing that love song to me?* She stared at Del as she walked into the living room, balancing food and wine on a tray.

"Everything all right?" Del asked when she saw the stare.

It would be so easy to just let it go, to ignore it. Matheson women were masters at ignoring things they didn't want to deal with. *No,* she decided. *No masks. Not with Del.* "Um... that song you just sang..."

"Yeah?" Del tilted her head. "Not your kind of music?"

"The song is fine, but its sentiment... It's a little too much for me right now," Kade said honestly.

Del set down the tray and perched on the couch next to Kade but didn't try to touch her in any way.

Kade appreciated the space Del was giving her even if physical space was not what she was concerned about.

"It's a song, not a marriage proposal, Kade," Del said. A slow, lopsided grin danced over her face. "I know we're lesbians—"

"Speak for yourself," Kade quipped, already relaxing a little. Del always managed to reassure her with just a few words.

"Okay," Del conceded with a smile, "I'm a lesbian, and you are a woman interested in a lesbian." She waited until Kade gave a nod of agreement before she continued, "But that still doesn't mean we're going to move in together right away."

Kade felt a rare blush creep up her neck, and she cursed her fair skin. "I didn't assume that we would," she quickly said.

"You assumed that's what I want." Del looked at her with a knowing gaze. "Why else would the song scare you just because I changed one noun?"

"I'm not scared," Kade said. It was almost a reflex.

Del leaned forward and gently kissed her. "Liar," she whispered.

"I'm not scared," Kade repeated stubbornly. "I'm just not ready for love songs. I know you want what you just sang about— letting loose, opening our hearts, falling in love." Del had been so insistent, so unwavering in her "courtship" and open admiration for Kade that it was hard to believe she would suddenly be so casual about it.

"I won't deny that," Del said, openly gazing into Kade's eyes. "But I don't need to have it all at once. For now, we're dating—if you want to."

Her head, everything she had been taught to be and to want, screamed "no." She had always been in control of her life and had kept her emotions tightly under wraps. Controlling her emotions was a prerequisite for being a good lawyer—and a good Matheson. She had never let her emotions make her decisions. "What if I find out this is all too much for me?" she asked, voicing her doubts. "I don't want to end up hurting you."

"I'll be fine," Del said.

"Now who's the liar, huh?" With a faint smile, Kade brushed her lips against Del's.

Del laughed. "Okay. Maybe I won't be fine for a while. No one would be fine after getting dumped by a woman like you. But I'm willing to take that risk."

The question is: am I willing to take the risk? Kade wordlessly understood. "Just dating, huh? No commitment? No public announcements for now?"

"Yeah. Just dating. I'm fine with that—as long as it includes making out on my couch." Del waggled her eyebrows at Kade.

Over the rim of her glasses, Kade stared her down in mock disapproval.

"What?" Del played innocent. "A woman has to take what she can get. If you're not yet ready to give me your heart, I'll take your lips as a temporary substitute."

Kade laughed. Del was the only one who had that effect on her. She could make Kade laugh about her own limits and weaknesses. She could make her not take herself so seriously all the time. It was a gift, Kade realized—one she'd never had in her life. She wasn't willing to give that up.

"So?" Del prompted when Kade didn't say anything.

"It might be worth a try," Kade finally said.

Del tilted her head and grinned down at her. "What? Dating or making out?"

Kade couldn't help returning the grin. She never smiled or laughed as much as when she was with Del. "Well... both."

"Good." Del slung one arm around Kade and pulled her closer for a kiss.

Kade pressed her hands against Del's shoulders, holding her at a distance and enjoying the warm skin and the slender muscles she felt under Del's shirt.

"What?" Del lifted a questioning eyebrow. "I thought you agreed to the terms of the deal?"

"The food is getting cold again," Kade said.

Del bridged the remaining distance between them, with Kade's arms surrendering willingly. She playfully nipped on Kade's bottom lip. "I thought cold Chinese food is one of the main food groups of lawyers?"

"Good point." Kade surged forward and claimed Del's lips in a firm kiss. For once in her life, she was happy to lose an argument.

* * *

Still thinking about her evening with Del and what it meant for her future, Kade walked toward the door of her condo. She wasn't looking where she was going. Her hands and her eyes were busy searching for the keys in her purse.

She jerked to a halt when a tall figure suddenly blocked her way. In a rush of adrenaline, her fingers groped for the small semiautomatic Del had given her.

"Kade?" a familiar voice stopped her.

She looked up.

Aiden Carlisle stood in front of her, uncomfortably shuffling her feet.

"Aiden!" She let go of the gun. "What are you doing here?"

"I hope this is not a bad time? Your doorwoman let me in," Aiden said instead of giving the reason for her unexpected visit.

Kade suppressed a sigh. "No, it's all right. Is this about a case? Why didn't you try to reach me on my cell phone?"

"No. This has nothing to do with work. Well, not really. I mean... I..." Aiden shoved her hands into the pockets of her leather jacket. "I need some advice."

"From me?" Kade could hear the disbelief in her own voice. Giving advice about anything but work was not her forte.

Aiden nodded. "Can I come in? This is not something I want to discuss out here."

"Of course." *Letting a guest stand in the middle of the hallway... Your mother would be appalled,* Kade told herself. *But then again, your mother was appalled about a lot of things lately, and this would be the least of her worries.*

She led Aiden into her apartment and offered her a seat. "So, what's going on?"

Aiden took the time to look around the apartment.

"Aiden..." This visit was beginning to worry her. She knew Aiden had never visited her apartment before if she wasn't there on business.

"I need some advice," Aiden finally said.

She had already said that before. Kade gave her an impatient nod.

"I understand there are some legal documents..."

Ah. Kade relaxed a little. This was something she could deal with. She could give advice on legal documents without any problem. "Yes?" she prompted. "What kind of documents?"

"Documents to help protect our relationship... mine and Dawn's," Aiden explained. "I think it's time to make some steps of commitment."

Oh. So this wasn't really advice on legal things at all. This was about relationships. Never in a million years would Kade have believed that she would ever have this kind of conversation with Aiden. She had always known that Aiden's relationships—like her own—had mostly ended before breakfast the next morning. After her rape, Dawn Kinsley certainly wasn't up to being just another notch on Aiden's bedpost. She needed love, tenderness, and trust, something that was hard for Aiden to give. Kade would have bet her entire trust fund that Aiden would shy away from a relationship with her.

Fortunately, I didn't. Mother wouldn't have liked all that Matheson money going to a blue-collar cop. "Well, you should draw up a living will and a testament and give each other health care and financial power of attorney and of course a hospital visitation authorization," Kade sought refuge in the familiar legal terms. "I can give you the name of a good lawyer who specializes in things like that."

Aiden nodded but didn't react otherwise. She seemed as tense as before.

Kade suppressed a sigh. "So... commitment... how do you feel about that?"

"Happy, confused, scared... you name it, I've probably felt it," Aiden said.

Kade could understand what she meant only too well. A few months ago, she'd had no clue about the levels, ranges, and nuances of emotion one person could make another person feel, but now... "What scares you most?" she asked.

"Hurting Dawn, getting hurt, finding out I'm not good at this commitment thing..." Aiden ruffled her hair with both hands.

"And you're only starting to worry about it now?" Kade asked, surprised that it hadn't been an issue before. She had only just agreed to date Del, and she was already worrying nonstop.

"Yeah, well, Dawn is starting to talk about moving in together and having kids—and I'm not sure I'm ready for that," Aiden admitted.

Kade still couldn't see it clearly. "But what's so different from before? Wasn't this where your relationship with Dawn was going from the start? You knew who she was and what has happened to her from the first moment. You knew she's not the one-night-stand kind. Yet you still never hesitated to get involved with her, despite all obstacles. You were committed from the start—and you're clearly good at it. I mean... look at Dawn. A blind man could see she's happy with you."

Aiden tilted her head and looked at her with a hopeful glance. It was clear that she had never thought about it this way. Suddenly, she chuckled. "Getting advice on lesbian relationships from Kadence Matheson. Who would have ever thought we'd end up here, huh?"

"Certainly not I," Kade said, not laughing.

"What is it, Counselor?" Aiden asked with a teasing smile. "Afraid of commitment?"

Kade was afraid of so many things, but she had never voiced her fears to anyone in her life. It just wasn't done in the Matheson family. "Last year... before Dawn and Del came into our lives... did you ever think that maybe I was a lesbian or bisexual?"

"You mean besides wishful thinking?"

Kade gave a mild smile. She had been taught at a very early age to pay attention to how other people were looking at her, so she had always been aware of the admiring glances Aiden had thrown at her. They hadn't bothered her because she had somehow sensed Aiden would never act on that attraction. It was safe to wallow in that kind of admiration. "Besides that, yes."

"I never thought you were a lesbian," Aiden said, "but I always had the impression if the right woman came along..."

"Did anyone else think so too?" Kade asked.

Aiden stared at her. "I don't know. I didn't exactly start a survey about people's thoughts on your sexual orientation, Kade. Why is it so important what people thought?"

Yes, why? Kade suddenly asked herself. "Maybe it's not," she admitted.

Aiden reached across the coffee table and lightly touched Kade's hand. "Just be yourself—whatever and whoever that is. The rest will sort itself out."

Kade looked down at the fingers touching her own. For a moment, she curled her fingers and gave a short squeeze, then she let go and straightened. "And here I thought you came to get my advice."

"Well, this friendship thing works both ways," Aiden said with a smile.

Kade returned the smile. "Yes, it does."

Aiden stood. "I better go. It's late."

"Wait. I'll get you the card of the lawyer I mentioned."

"It can wait until tomorrow," Aiden protested. "You don't have to search for it now."

"I don't need to search. I know exactly where it is." Kade walked over to her desk and after just a few seconds, she handed Aiden the business card.

Aiden whistled. "Wow. You kept that handy, huh? Any plans of commitment you want to tell me about?"

"Out!" Kade ordered, pointing to the door.

With a laugh, Aiden pocketed the card and crossed the room. "Goodnight, Kade."

CHAPTER 35

RAY YAWNED. "I need coffee," he said in the same desperate tone of voice a man dying of thirst would have used to call for water.

"I need a new pair of eyes," Aiden said. She leaned back in her chair but kept her eyes on the TV screen. A black-and-white recording of the courthouse's entrance hall flickered over the screen.

They watched people pass through the metal detectors and cross the marbled hall to reach one of the courtrooms. They had already fast-forwarded through most of the security tapes that had been recorded on the days Kade had been in court back in October.

Investigating former suspects had led them nowhere, so they were now trying to find out if anyone had sat in the gallery during Kade's cases on a regular basis, showing an unusual interest in Kade.

"Stop!" Aiden shot up from her chair. "Go back a little. Yes... there!" She pointed at the frozen picture.

Ray squinted. "Isn't that...?"

Aiden nodded. "That's the doorwoman of Kade's apartment building."

Ray pressed "play" again, and they watched as the doorwoman confidently strode past one of the security guards and disappeared around the corner, walking in the direction of the courtroom in which Kade's case had been tried. "It could be a simple coincidence," Ray said hesitantly.

"Yeah, it could be." But Aiden couldn't just write it off as coincidence. Like most cops, she had developed a sixth sense for these things over the years, and it was working overtime now. She had learned the hard way that it wasn't smart to ignore that instinct. She rummaged in the box full of security tapes and came up with another tape, which she quickly put into the VCR.

Ray fast-forwarded, and again, there was the doorwoman, passing through the metal detectors to get into the courthouse.

Aiden picked a third tape from the box. It was the tape from the morning of the closing statements in the Ballard case.

"There's Kade," Ray said as they watched Kade stride confidently past the metal detectors. "And there's the doorwoman. She's following Kade!"

Aiden sucked in a breath as she compared the dates of the tapes. "She watched Dawn's trial."

They looked at each other with growing alarm. "Well, if she's the stalker, it would certainly explain how the flower deliveries and the letters got to Kade's apartment door without anyone seeing anything. And it would explain how the stalker knew Kade's unlisted phone number and was always aware of when she was home," Ray said.

"Yeah. And why we had no luck investigating suspects from Kade's old cases," Aiden growled. "She gave us a bogus description. She completely fooled us!" She snatched the phone from its cradle and punched in a few numbers.

"What are you doing?" Ray asked.

Aiden pressed the receiver to her ear. "Calling her employer. I want to find out her name."

When she put the phone down a few minutes later, she looked up and grimaced. "Tracey Sheldon," she said to Ray, who was waiting for the name with his fingers hovering over the keyboard of his computer. "Guess when she applied for the job as a doorwoman?"

Ray was busy hacking away at the keyboard, so she answered her own question, "Last October. Kade winning the Ballard case must have created an instant admirer. She got that job to be closer to Kade."

"This is not good," Ray mumbled, staring down at his screen. "There's a restraining order out against Tracey Sheldon, filed by a Melanie Riggs. Seems Kade wasn't the only recipient of her unwanted affections."

"Shit." Aiden's head jerked around at hearing the name. "Melanie Riggs? Are you sure?"

Ray looked at his screen again. "Yes. I know that name from somewhere, don't I?" He slapped his palm against his forehead when he remembered. "She was one of the victims in the Ballard case. Do you think Gary Ballard has anything to do with —?"

"No. My gaydar tells me Tracey Sheldon is a lesbian, and so is Melanie Riggs. Sheldon was probably her girlfriend or at least wanted to be. That's why Sheldon watched the trial—until she found a better object for her attentions in Kade." Aiden reached for the phone again. She tried Kade's office, her apartment, and her cell phone.

Kade didn't pick up.

"Where is she?" Ray wondered aloud.

There was only one last place Aiden could think of. She quickly dialed Del's number. "Del? Hey, it's Aiden Carlisle. Is Kade with you?" she asked as soon as Del picked up.

"No. Should she be?" Del asked, surprise coloring her words. "I assumed she's still at work, where she's safe with all the security guards around, or she would have called one of us to escort her home."

"Well, apparently, she didn't," Aiden mumbled, cursing Kade's stubborn independence and their lack of coordination. They had dropped the ball.

"What's going on, Aiden?" Del demanded to know.

"We think she might be in danger." Aiden had no time to beat around the bush. "The stalker... it's her doorwoman, and we can't find Kade."

Ruben, already on his way home, looked up from putting on his jacket. "You're searching for Matheson? When I handed in the arrest report for the Richards case over half an hour ago, she said she would head home in a few minutes."

Home, where Tracey Sheldon is waiting for her! "Shit, shit, shit!" Aiden said again. "Did you hear that, Del? Meet us at Kade's apartment!" She threw the phone down, grabbed her gun from the bottom drawer of her desk, and sprinted to the door. "Come on, Ray!"

* * *

Kade stuck another note to Ruben's arrest report. Instead of going home on time for once, as she had originally planned, she had decided to stay and look through Ruben's report. She had made no plans with Del for tonight, and at home, only her mother's demanding voice on her answering machine awaited her, so she had decided to stay a little longer. She would go through some reports, and when she was through with them, she would call one of her unofficial bodyguards and let herself be escorted home.

Her phone began to ring, then her cell phone. She had told Ruben she would head home soon. With the ever-efficient rumor mill, each and every one of her detectives probably assumed she was at home by now. That made it easy to guess the identity of the caller without even looking at the caller ID. *Really, Mother, this is going too far!* She picked up another report and ignored the ringing phone.

CHAPTER 36

*D*AWN SHIFTED THE food containers she carried to her left arm, trying to get one hand free to open the door to the Sexual Assault Detail's squad room.

The door opened before she could succeed.

"Ah." Jeff Okada grinned down at her. "Gracing our unworthy halls with your presence again, Doc?"

Evan and most of Aiden's colleagues had taken to calling her "Doc," and Dawn liked how affectionate it sounded. "Aiden and Ray are stuck with an investigation all night," Dawn said, without clarifying that they were investigating Kade's stalker, "and I wanted to make sure they're not starving."

"Oh. Bad timing, Doctor. They left in a hurry about ten minutes ago, and I'm not sure they'll be back tonight. I'm the last one out," Okada said.

Dawn hadn't expected that, but she quickly adjusted. Growing up in a family of cops had made her good at accepting sudden changes in plans. "In that case, this is your dinner." She handed Okada one of the containers.

Okada took it without hesitation. "If one of my ex-wives had been more like you, I might still be married. You don't happen to have a sister of marriageable age, do you?" he joked.

"I have a widowed mother, but I think you should talk it through with your accountant before I introduce you," Dawn teased, picking up a joke she'd heard from Aiden about all the money Okada had to pay his ex-wives.

Okada smirked. "Sound advice, Doc." He tipped his hat and said good-bye, leaving Dawn behind with another container of food in her hands.

* * *

"Hey, Sheldon, you in trouble?" Gus Bailey asked as he handed Tracey the clipboard to sign in for her shift.

Tracey looked up from signing her name and threw an impatient glance at him. She didn't want to make small talk with her colleague. Kadence had spent a lot of late nights at the office lately, but Tracey hoped she would be home soon, and she wanted him gone by then. Tracey wanted to be alone with her. "Trouble?" she repeated. The only trouble she had was the damned Latina cop who was sniffing after Kadence, ignoring her warnings to stay away from her girlfriend.

"Yeah. The boss said the cops called him, asking about you," Gus said.

Looks like that cop is doing everything to take Kadence away from me. That's not gonna happen! "Probably got one parking ticket too many," she lied. She waited until Gus had finally left, then hurried to her car.

She wouldn't wait until Kadence came home from one of her late nights at the office. With all of her cop friends who were constantly hanging around Kadence, they would only be disturbed at home anyway.

Tracey quickly got into her car.

The tenants of the South Waterfront condo building would have to make do without her. There was just one resident to whom she would offer her services tonight.

CHAPTER 37

𝒦ADE LOOKED UP from the report in which she had been engrossed when the door to her office opened. Normally, her visitors knocked before they entered, but Kade had often been surprised by unsuspecting cleaning ladies who had thought Kade had long since gone home.

This time, however, the face that appeared in the doorway didn't belong to someone from the cleaning staff. "Tracey?" she said in surprise. One of her mentors had taught her to always know the name of each member of a jury, and since then, she had made it a habit to practice by memorizing the name of the girl who wrapped her groceries, the boy who delivered her Sunday paper, and the doormen—and the doorwoman—of her apartment building.

"Surprised to see me?" Tracey asked with a smile, firmly closing the door behind her.

Kade furrowed her brow. She could feel her heart begin to beat loudly, echoing in her ears like a warning. Working with cops for so long, Kade had developed her own instincts about situations and people. She remembered that Tracey, the doorwoman, had always been a little too eager, a little too interested in her. *She was the one who told Laurie where Del lives,* she suddenly remembered. *Why would she remember the address? She must hear dozens of people give their cabbies an address each day, and I bet she doesn't remember any of them. Why remember Del's?* "Yes," she said cautiously, "a little."

"I thought so. You've been avoiding me lately," Tracey accused.

"Avoiding you?" Kade repeated. She didn't need to act confused. She didn't understand to what the doorwoman was referring. The only person she had avoided lately was her mother.

Tracey stepped closer until she was right in front of the desk. She put her hands to the left and right of Kade's file and leaned forward, looking into Kade's eyes from just a few inches away. "Yeah, avoiding me!" Anger sparked in the dark eyes. "You've barely been home for the last few days!"

Home? She sounds like I'm living with her. Kade realized with growing dread. *Damn, I think I just found out who my stalker is!* She eyed the phone and the door, any means to flee or call for help, while Tracey continued to rant.

"You even left the city without telling me. Where have you been? With your other girlfriend? I've warned her to stay away from you!" Tracey shouted. Her fists crashed down on the desk, making Kade flinch.

Shit, what do I do now? The crazy doorwoman was blocking her way to the door, and she would immediately stop her if she tried to reach for the phone on her desk or her cell phone. The gun Del had given her was in her purse across the room, too far out of reach to be of any use now. *Talk to her. Play along. Talk her out of it. Words are your weapons, remember?*

"She's not my girlfriend," she told Tracey, keeping her voice gentle. "I work with her. That's all."

Tracey towered over her. "Don't lie! I've seen you two together!"

"But it's over now," Kade said quickly.

"Prove it," Tracey demanded, still suspicious.

Kade stared up at her. "How?" she asked, already afraid of the answer.

"Leave her. Come with me right now." Tracey held out her hand.

Oh, shit. So far, playing along, acting as if she agreed with the delusional woman, had been her safest bet, but Kade knew that it was getting more dangerous now. She knew if she got into her car with Tracey, she would lose any chance of getting away. Tracey would take her wherever she wanted, somewhere quiet and deserted where she could do whatever she wanted to Kade without any interference.

Slowly, thinking feverishly, she stood from behind her desk. She took Tracey's hand and felt the rough strength. *Think, Kade, think!*

Tracey led her to the door, acting like the gallant admirer now.

"Wait," Kade said quickly, pulling her hand away. "Let me get my purse before we go." She took a step toward the coatrack, where her coat and purse hung. Her hand shot forward, aiming for the purse and the gun in it.

Tracey reached out one long arm and snatched the purse away. "I'll take this," she decided.

Kade stared at her empty hand. *Damn. She probably saw Del giving me the gun right in front of my apartment building.*

She watched Tracey empty the contents of the purse onto the floor. The semiautomatic clanked down on top of a small perfume bottle. "Is that what you were looking for?" Tracey asked with dangerous calm.

"No. No, of course not. I just wanted to freshen up a little before we go out on our date," Kade said, pointing to the perfume bottle.

Tracey narrowed her eyes but finally nodded. She bent down and picked up the gun, shoving it into her waistband.

Kade grimaced. *Great. Now she's armed. Brilliant, Kade.*

Tracey gallantly held her coat for her while Kade slipped into it. "Come on." Tracey waved toward the door. "Let's go."

Kade knew if they stepped through the door, this would end ugly. Her crazy stalker would try to take her away to some cozy little love nest. If the security guard tried to stop her, she would just shoot him and anyone else who tried to interfere.

People will die. You could die. Kade clenched her fist in her coat pocket and realized her fingers were wrapped around her car keys. An image of Del flashed through her mind—and with it Del's parting words from their very first meeting: *Next time, aim for the eyes.*

"Tracey," she said, giving her voice a seductiveness she knew Tracey couldn't resist.

Tracey turned around to look at her.

In one quick move, Kade pulled the keys from her coat pocket. She jabbed the biggest key into Tracey's face, aiming for an eye.

At the very last second, Tracey turned her head.

The key scratched along her temple. She stumbled back a step and pressed her hand to her head. Slowly, she took her hand away and looked down at it.

Blood glistened on her fingers.

Roaring, she advanced on Kade. "I gave you every chance to admit to our love, but you're still too stupid to realize what we have is so much bigger, so much better than anything that goddamned cop can give you!" She roughly gripped Kade's arm.

Kade tried to use the key as a weapon again, but the moment of surprise was gone now, and the other woman was much taller and stronger than she. Tracey grabbed her with both hands, forcing her back with her superior weight, height, and strength.

She struggled in Tracey's grip and kicked out in desperation.

A well-aimed kick to the knee made Tracey reach out with a curse, holding on to the nearest file cabinet for balance.

This freed one of Kade's arms, and she began to struggle and fight in earnest. She hit Tracey's nose, making her howl, and pulled out of the weakening grasp. As soon as she was free, she raced to the door.

She had almost reached it when Tracey's arm wrapped around her throat from behind, stopping her. Tracey roughly jerked her back against her body. "Hold still!" Tracey hissed into her ear.

Of course, Kade didn't. She stomped on Tracey's foot, trying to get her to loosen the stranglehold around her neck.

Tracey moved back an inch to avoid another attack on her toes, and Kade got one arm free. She rammed her elbow back into Tracey's stomach.

Tracey doubled over, gasping for breath.

Kade whirled around. She tried to reach over Tracey and get her hand on the gun sticking out of the back of Tracey's pants.

Before she could reach the gun, Tracey straightened and backhanded her.

Pain exploded in her cheek. The force of it made Kade stumble back until her back hit the desk.

Angrily, Tracey pulled the gun from her waistband and pressed the muzzle against the side of Kade's head as she continued to struggle.

Kade froze but refused to close her eyes and admit defeat. She looked right into the burning brown eyes and spoke in her calmest voice, trying valiantly to hide her shaking. "You don't want to hurt me. You love me."

"You don't deserve my love!" Tracey raged. "You betrayed me!"

Kade's heart raced. Sweat ran down her back.

She could practically feel Tracey's finger tighten around the trigger. Still, she didn't look away. "Don't," she commanded in a voice that got even the most stubborn jurors to listen.

Tracey hesitated.

Then, suddenly, the pressure of the gun's muzzle was gone from Kade's temple.

Tracey slumped forward.

Kade quickly jumped aside and watched in astonishment as Tracey landed on the floor in front of her.

"Jesus Christ!" Dawn Kinsley stood staring down at the fallen woman, one of the massive law books from Kade's bookshelf held in both of her hands. "What's going on here?"

Kade bent down and took the gun from the groaning doorwoman, who was slowly coming to life again. "That's the person who has been stalking me," she said. It took some effort to keep her voice from trembling. She aimed the gun at Tracey, hoping she wouldn't fully regain consciousness before help arrived. "Call security!" She jerked her head at the door, using both hands to hold the gun steady.

Before the baffled Dawn could move, the door swung open.

Aiden, Ray, and Del stormed into the room with their guns drawn, a horde of security guards behind them.

"Great! Now that the fight is over, the cavalry arrives," Kade mumbled, hiding her frazzled nerves behind a joke.

Ray quickly cuffed the groaning woman and dragged her from the room with the help of two security guards.

Del approached Kade slowly. She slid her hand along Kade's arm until her fingers rested on top of Kade's on the gun. "You can let go now," she said gently.

Kade dropped the gun with a sigh of relief.

Immediately, Del wrapped her arms around her and pulled her close.

Kade held on tightly, sinking against Del's comforting warmth, but then she became aware of the glances resting on her and Del.

Dawn, Aiden, and the remaining security guard watched their intimate embrace with interest.

Kade stiffened. She almost pulled back in reflex until her gaze fell on the gun that had been pressed to her temple just a few moments ago. *You could have died. It wouldn't have mattered if you were gay or straight or bisexual then. Is what they might think about you more important than feeling alive and safe in Del's arms?* she asked herself. Stubbornly, she ignored the curious gazes of the security guard and remained where she was.

Aiden was no longer looking at her anyway. She was preoccupied with holding on to Dawn. "What are you doing here?" Aiden asked Dawn.

"I wanted to bring you something to eat, but Jeff Okada told me you had already left. I didn't want my food to go to waste, so I thought I'd see if Kade was still in her office," Dawn explained. She had let go of the law book to wrap her arms around Aiden.

"What happened?" Aiden asked. She looked from Dawn to Kade. "You didn't shoot Tracey Sheldon, did you?"

Kade threw a conspiratorial glance at Dawn. "Let's just say that the full weight of the law hit her."

CHAPTER 38

AIDEN STOPPED IN front of the door to Dawn's apartment. A giant bouquet of flowers lay on the doorstep, rattling her already tense nerves even more as she thought about Kade's flower-sending stalker. Carefully, she picked up the flowers and regarded them from all sides, making sure there was nothing dangerous about the bouquet itself.

There was a small card, but the envelope was closed and she didn't want to open it without Dawn's permission. Wrapping one arm around the bouquet, she unlocked the door. "Dawn?" she called.

No answer.

"Dawn?" she called again, this time more loudly.

"I'm in here." The answer finally came from the bathroom.

Aiden relaxed a little as she opened the bathroom door just a few inches and saw Dawn lounging in the bathtub. "Can I come in?" she asked carefully. She knew there were still days when Dawn hastily covered herself when she was surprised like this.

Today, Dawn didn't cross her arms over her bare chest. Aiden had expected her to be a little upset about finding Kade held at gunpoint by a stalker and potential rapist, but to her surprise, Dawn didn't appear to be any the worse for wear. She just grinned up at Aiden. "Of course."

Aiden left the flowers, her badge, and her gun outside and slipped into the bathroom. Steam filled the air, rising from the bubble-covered bathtub.

The sight of the wet, glowing skin of her partner made Aiden's heartbeat quicken, but she held herself back. "There were flowers on your doorstep," she told Dawn.

"I know. The delivery guy called through the door, but I was half-naked, about to jump into the tub, so I told him to leave them outside," Dawn said. She lifted one slightly wrinkly hand from the water to wave Aiden a little closer.

Aiden obediently bent down to kiss her hello but didn't allow herself to linger for too long. She was too keyed up from the events of the last few days and her eventful shift. She felt as if she would somehow sully Dawn's purity by coming too close now. "Any idea who's sending you flowers?" she asked to cover the awkward pause as she interrupted their kiss.

Bare shoulders appeared from under a mountain of bubbles when Dawn shrugged. "I think they're from Kade. She called me earlier and said to expect a delivery."

Aiden whistled. "My, my, our DDA is getting really daring!" she said with a laugh. "First, she embraces Del in full view of the security guard and half of her detectives, and now she's sending flowers to other women!"

Dawn flicked a bit of the foamy bubbles at her. "She's saying thank you. She thinks I saved her life."

"You probably did," Aiden said seriously. She had battled a mix of emotions about Dawn's involvement in the arrest of Tracey Sheldon. She had been shocked and scared when she burst into Kade's office and found Dawn there. She had worried that it would cause nightmares and flashbacks and destroy some of the progress Dawn had made after her rape. She was even a little angry that Dawn had just risked her life without much thought, attacking an armed, crazy woman with nothing more than a thick compendium of laws. Most of all, though, she felt proud. "You are a hero," she declared and placed a crown of foam on top of Dawn's head.

Dawn wildly shook her head, making the foam crown crumble. "I'm not a hero," she said with an incredulous laugh.

"You are my hero—and Kade's and Del's," Aiden insisted. The situation held a certain irony. She and Del had been in an unofficial competition over who held the place of Kade's number one cop and protector. In the end, it had been the gentle Dawn who had done the rescuing while they had both been in the wrong place.

The whole incident had given Aiden a new perspective on a lot of things. For one, she realized Dawn was no longer a helpless victim. She had taken control of a very dangerous situation and had come out on top of it. She didn't need Aiden or anyone else to protect her.

At first, realizing that neither Kade nor Dawn needed her as a protector had made her feel like a failure. Now, after thinking about their slowly changing roles, she realized it wasn't quite so black-and-white. While Dawn didn't necessarily need her protection all the time, she would still want it on occasion, and Dawn was strong enough to protect and support her too. Dawn didn't need her to be perfect and strong—she just needed her to be herself.

"You are the hero in the family," Dawn objected. "I was just lucky enough to have been at the right place at the right time."

She sees me as her hero... and as her family, Aiden realized again.

"So what did you do today?" Dawn asked while she lifted one of her legs out of the water to scrub her foot. "You're a little late. Did something happen?"

"No, just the usual stuff," Aiden said. The "usual stuff" in this case included arresting a serial rapist, storming his apartment with the Special Emergency Reaction Team, Portland's SWAT unit and then interrogating him for seven hours straight.

Dawn reached out and tugged on Aiden's belt with one damp hand. "Oh, I can imagine your 'usual stuff.' It probably sounds like a script from a cop show, with you as the heroine."

"I told you I'm not a heroine," Aiden grumbled playfully. "And if this was a cop show, I would have been home hours ago. They always edit out the grueling hours of paperwork."

Dawn laughed. "You look like you could use a little pampering. The water is still hot, so come on in and take a bath with me," she invited and moved back in the tub until her back rested against the edge of the tub.

"No, I'm fine. Enjoy your bath. I'll just take a quick shower later," Aiden said hastily.

Dawn didn't take no for an answer. "I would enjoy the bath more with you in here." She looked up at Aiden with a sensual smile. "Come on."

Aiden reached for her belt, but then hesitated again. "Do we have the time? I thought you said we have to babysit Jamie and Tim tonight?"

"Change in plans," Dawn said with a grin. "My mother is taking care of Tim, and Eliza found another pair of babysitters for Jamie."

"Who?" Aiden asked. She knew Dawn's sister-in-law didn't trust just anyone with her ten-year-old daughter.

Dawn smiled up at her. "Your sister and Laurie are taking Jamie to the skate park and will watch her until Eliza and Rick are back from their party."

"Evan?" Aiden asked in surprise.

"Unless you have another sister you didn't tell me about," Dawn teased. She sobered when she realized what she'd said. "I'm sorry. I didn't want to—"

"It's okay," Aiden said. A few months ago, the teasing answer would have made her flinch. Now she was slowly learning that having siblings, even if they had been fathered by a rapist, was not necessarily a bad thing. "I'm a little surprised," she confessed. "I didn't think Evan would take anyone skating so soon. She felt so guilty after what happened with Laurie. She doesn't trust herself not to hurt the people in her care... and now she agreed to babysit?"

Dawn reached down and tugged a shoe, then the other, and finally the socks off of Aiden's feet. Her damp hand caressed the sensitive skin of Aiden's ankle. "I think she's starting to see herself in a different light. She's beginning to realize she doesn't have to keep people at arm's length not to hurt them. Having you for a big sister has been good for Evan."

"You think so?" Aiden wanted to believe it but wasn't sure how she could help Evan with the same issues with which she was struggling herself.

Dawn seemed to know exactly what she was thinking. "Evan would never admit it, but she admires you. She got to know you and realizes you're a good person. Seeing you struggle with the same fears and doubts she has... It makes her realize how basically irrational they are. I mean... they're real and understandable, but they don't reflect who you truly are. Evan is too close to her own problems to realize her father holds no power over her life and her personality—none that she doesn't give him. She can look at you and your struggles more objectively. She knows deep inside, no matter how you came to be, you're not a bad person."

Aiden was beginning to realize the same thing—about Evan and about herself. Wordlessly, she opened her belt and slid her pants down her legs. She could feel Dawn's gaze on her as she continued to undress. Her blouse followed and then her T-shirt, which was creased from wearing the bullet-resistant vest over it for half of the day. Finally, she opened the tiny clasp of her chain with the St. Michael's medallion and carefully placed it on the ledge beneath the mirror.

Naked, she turned back around. She climbed into the tub on the side that Dawn didn't occupy and sank belly-deep into the bubbles.

Dawn shook her head at her. "That's the way you bathe with your siblings when you're three years old, not the way you bathe with your lover," she gently chided.

"Oh, excuse me. I must have missed that page in the superlover handbook." Aiden playfully nudged Dawn with her toes. "So what is the required way to bathe with your lover?"

Dawn made room for her between her spread legs. "Come here, and lean back against me."

"Wouldn't it be better if I sat in the back?" Aiden asked, gesturing at Dawn's smaller body.

"Next time," Dawn said. "Now come here."

Aiden turned around and moved back until she was sitting between Dawn's legs.

Dawn's arms wrapped around her from behind and pulled her back until she reclined against Dawn's chest. "Now, isn't that much nicer?"

"Hmm," Aiden agreed, finally starting to relax for the first time all day, "and much softer than having the edge of the tub and the faucet in my back." She grinned back over her shoulder.

Instead of answering, Dawn cupped her hands and poured warm water over Aiden's head. It took some time to get all of Aiden's hair wet this way, but Dawn obviously didn't mind.

Aiden closed her eyes as Dawn shampooed her hair. Gentle fingertips massaged her scalp, and Aiden's head lolled back against Dawn's shoulder. It was soothing and relaxing, but there was also something very erotic about the experience.

She almost groaned in disappointment when Dawn finally took her hands away. Dawn cupped her hands again and let warm water run through Aiden's hair, rinsing it.

Aiden started to turn around, about to offer Dawn the same treatment, when she felt Dawn's soapy hands slide up her arms, lovingly cleaning every inch of skin with slow, circular motions.

Aiden leaned back again. For once, she would just enjoy this. Dawn washing her was a cleansing experience in more than just one way. It felt as if Dawn was washing away all the guilt, anger, frustrations, and self-doubts of the last few months.

Dawn's hands trailed down the outside of her thighs, circled her knees, and then bent one of Aiden's legs up to reach her calf. Aiden watched soapy suds slide down her leg, followed by Dawn's hand. Her skin tingled, and a tension of another kind began to build as Dawn's hand slid past her knee, more caressing than cleaning.

Dawn stopped at her upper thigh, though, and gave the same treatment to Aiden's other leg.

Frustrated, Aiden let out a groan.

"Relax," Dawn whispered into her ear.

"What you're doing to me isn't conducive to relaxing." Aiden groaned.

Dawn pressed her lips to the nape of Aiden's neck. "Are you complaining?"

Am I? With other lovers, Aiden knew she would have ended this little game of loving pampering and seduction a long time ago.

She would have turned around and initiated a passionate round of lovemaking or would have whisked her lover away to bed. It wasn't that she didn't like a slower buildup every once in a while. The issue wasn't even that she was suddenly the one on the receiving end of this masterful seduction. But sitting here in the tub, being cradled in Dawn's arms without being able to see her, forced her to let down all of her defenses and made every touch so much more intimate and intense.

"No, I'm not," she finally answered, realizing she was no longer so afraid of letting down her defenses. Not when she was with Dawn.

"Good." Dawn nipped the rim of Aiden's ear. Her soapy hands trailed over Aiden's hips, tenderly stroked her stomach, and then circled her breasts.

Aiden gasped.

Dawn leaned forward to peer over Aiden's shoulder and into her face. "Was that an 'ouch' gasp or a 'do that again' gasp?"

"A little bit of both," Aiden admitted. "I'm a little sore from wearing the bulletproof vest for most of the day." She hadn't wanted to tell Dawn about the ugly details of her workday, but now that it had come up, she realized that trying to hide it was stupid and unnecessary. Dawn was not fragile. She could deal with the dangers and the ugliness of Aiden's job.

"So that was the 'usual stuff' you did today, huh?" Dawn teasingly nibbled on Aiden's ear. Her touch on Aiden's breasts gentled but never stopped.

Aiden didn't answer. Her interest in the conversation was rapidly waning. The water and the bubbles made Dawn's touches feel like warm silk on her skin. Shivers raced up and down Aiden's body even though she was submerged up to her chest in hot water. She braced her arms on the sides of the tub, getting ready to turn around and capture Dawn's lips in a passionate kiss.

Before Aiden could execute her plan, Dawn wrapped her legs around Aiden, holding her in place.

Aiden was totally trapped now—and for a change loving every second of it. Feeling Dawn's whole body wrapped around hers was intoxicating. Dawn's breasts pressed intimately against her shoulder blades; her smooth legs were wrapped around Aiden's hips, and her center rubbed against Aiden's butt in a slow rhythm that made the water ripple around them.

Dawn craned her neck and rained a string of slow, sensual kisses from Aiden's jaw to the corner of her mouth. Her tongue teasingly danced over Aiden's bottom lip. At the same time, one of her hands slid down from Aiden's breast. Her fingertips dipped into Aiden's navel before they trailed lower.

Aiden surged around as much as she could in Dawn's intimate embrace. She captured Dawn's teasing tongue between her lips, playfully battling for dominance in a deep kiss.

With her arms and legs around Aiden, Dawn hadn't been holding on to the edge of the tub. The sudden change in position pressed her back and down. Gasping for breath from their kiss, she swallowed a mouthful of water. She sputtered and struggled to sit up.

Dazed, Aiden quickly moved back and let her sit up. She turned around and held Dawn loosely until the coughing stopped. "You all right?"

"Yeah." Dawn wiped soapy water from her eyes.

Aiden pulled her closer, enjoying the feeling of their warm, slippery bodies sliding against each other for another moment. "Come on," she said then. "Let's get out of here before one or both of us drown."

"This always sounds so romantic in romance novels," Dawn complained, nodding down at the tub.

Aiden kissed a few bubbles off Dawn's nose and cheek. "Oh, it is romantic, just not practical. Making love in the tub means that the person on top always gets cold from being half out of the water. Lubrication can also be a problem."

"So you've done this before?" Dawn asked. Her cheeks were a little flushed from more than the hot water or their passionate foreplay.

Sometimes Aiden forgot that Dawn had only ever been with two other people. It certainly hadn't felt as if Dawn was lacking experience a minute ago. Rarely had Aiden been seduced so masterfully. "You haven't?" she asked instead of giving details about her own sexual past.

"No. I never felt comfortable enough to experiment like this." Dawn shrugged with a hint of embarrassment, her naked body sliding against Aiden's with the movement.

Aiden was glad Dawn felt comfortable enough with her. She realized it went both ways. She had never felt as comfortable with any of her other lovers as she felt with Dawn. *Tell her. She needs to hear this,* she urged herself. "I feel safe with you too," she murmured with the side of her cheek pressed against Dawn's temple.

Dawn moved away a little and softly touched her fingertips to Aiden's face. "I want you," Dawn said, looking intently into her eyes. "Now."

A wave of heat shot through Aiden. Desire seethed through her blood. Dawn seldom had any problems communicating her wants and needs, but very rarely had she expressed her desire so directly. It was a powerful aphrodisiac.

For a moment, Aiden felt her emotions and her passion rage out of control, and she fought to rein them in. She closed her eyes. When she opened them again, she looked into Dawn's eyes and saw the same passion reflected back at her.

Dawn gave her a nod. It held a silent message—one that Aiden had begun to understand more and more during the last few weeks. Dawn didn't want her to rein herself in. She didn't need her to. Dawn loved her for what and who she was, not in spite of it.

Blood roared through her ears. Aiden stepped out of the tub and wrapped her arms around Dawn, half lifting, half steadying her as Dawn climbed out too. Her lips were on Dawn's the second they were both on steady ground.

Their naked, still wet and soapy bodies pressed against each other, and they both moaned into the kiss.

Dawn blindly reached for one of the fluffy towels. When her groping hand found it, she tore her lips away from Aiden's and gently shoved her back against the sink. She began to dry Aiden, softly rubbing the towel over Aiden's overly sensitive skin.

When the towel teasingly circled her breasts, Aiden surged forward and tried to capture Dawn's lips in another kiss. Her hands covered Dawn's and drew them against herself with more force.

"Not yet," Dawn said. "I have to dry your back first."

"Not necessary," Aiden answered breathlessly. "You make me so hot that every drop of water should have vaporized by now."

Dawn directed her to turn around despite those protests. Instead of using the towel to dry her back, Aiden felt Dawn's lips kissing away every droplet of water still lingering on her skin.

A hot tongue chased a drop that trailed down her spine, and Aiden had to grip the sink in front of her with both hands as her knees threatened to buckle.

Dawn's fingers slid over Aiden's sensitive sides, traced the outsides of her breasts, and then kneaded Aiden's muscled buttocks.

With a groan, Aiden tightened her grip on the sink and widened her stance.

Dawn took immediate advantage. One of her hands slipped down and brushed the heat between Aiden's legs.

"Jesus!" Aiden gasped. With all the passionate teasing in the tub, she already felt ready to explode. "This will be over in a second if you don't slow down," she warned.

"Oh, yeah?" Dawn rasped into her ear, pressing her whole body against Aiden's. "Let's see." She slid one finger into Aiden with an aching slowness.

Aiden let go of the sink with one hand and reached back to pull Dawn closer, hoping to get her to move just a little faster. She could feel Dawn's hardened nipples trail paths up and down her back as they moved against each other.

Careful teeth nipped at a tendon where Aiden's neck met her shoulder.

Aiden threw her head back, giving Dawn more access. The movement pressed her belly against the sink, and she shivered at the contrast between the cool porcelain and Dawn's heat against her back.

Dawn's tongue traced the rapidly pounding pulse in Aiden's neck. Aiden moaned as Dawn's free hand slid around her hip, followed the tense muscles of her stomach, and then tenderly cupped one of her breasts. Dawn's thumb rasped lightly over an erect nipple.

Aiden's hips bucked.

Dawn met each trust, no longer insisting on a slower rhythm. "More?" she asked, her hot breath washing over Aiden's ear.

"Yes!" Aiden struggled to get out that single word.

Dawn sucked at the skin of her neck, making waves of heat shoot down Aiden's body. At the same time, she added a second finger.

Aiden groaned deep in her throat. She felt the heat spreading. Her stomach tightened, and her legs trembled. Her eyes fluttered shut.

Immediately, Dawn took her lips off of Aiden's neck. "Aiden," she said, her voice tender but commanding, "open your eyes. Look up."

Aiden dragged open her eyes. She lifted her head from between arms that were tightly gripping the sink. Glancing in the mirror, Aiden watched herself move against Dawn with a total abandon she had rarely experienced before. Then she met Dawn's intense green eyes in the mirror.

Without breaking eye contact, Aiden let go of the sink with one hand and roughly pressed Dawn closer against her as she felt her orgasm build.

Dawn stopped the movement of her fingers. The hand that had been on Aiden's breast slipped down and softly brushed over Aiden's clit.

"Dawn!" Aiden gasped. The first wave of orgasm hit, and she collapsed back against Dawn.

For a few seconds, Dawn tried to hold her up, but the weight of Aiden's suddenly boneless body was too much for her. She gently withdrew and let them both slide to the floor.

Aiden lay with her cheek pressed to Dawn's chest. She couldn't tell if it was Dawn's heart beating so frantically—or her own. Her body was still shuddering.

Finally, her breathing calmed. She noticed Dawn was trailing her hand down her back in a gesture that was now soothing rather than arousing. She became aware of the damp bath mat they were lying on. Goose bumps covered her rapidly cooling skin. Groggily, she lifted her head and looked down at Dawn's tenderly smiling face. "I think," Aiden murmured and pressed her lips to Dawn's, lazily kissing her, "I need another shower."

CHAPTER 39

"...*A*ND THAT WAS when the detectives and security came stampeding into the room and arrested Tracey Sheldon," Kade finished recounting Friday's events. She leaned back in her chair and regarded the two women sitting on the other side of her desk, knowing her boss wouldn't like this mess. Senior Deputy District Attorney Althea Coltrane wanted the DA's office to fight crime, not provide victim and crime scene.

But to Kade's surprise, it wasn't Althea Coltrane who spoke first.

"Great!" Stacy Ford, the DDA who would take the Tracey Sheldon case to trial, groaned. "Another lesbian who turns out to be a nutjob and a criminal, contributing to the stereotype that gives us all a bad name!"

Us? Kade mentally echoed. It was an open secret that Stacy was a lesbian, and Kade was a little disconcerted, feeling as if Stacy was putting her in the same category. *Calm down. She wasn't talking about you. She couldn't possibly know, could she?*

The Senior DDA didn't pay Stacy's comment any attention. She fixed Kade with a stern gaze. "Can you please explain to me what Dawn Kinsley, a former victim and key witness in one of your cases, was doing in your office?"

Internally, Kade grimaced. *She wanted to bring me something to eat is probably not a good answer.* She looked at Stacy, hoping she would maybe provide a harmless explanation for her.

Stacy just looked back at her with a neutral, if mildly interested expression.

Does she know Dawn is Aiden's girlfriend? Kade wondered. With the very effective courthouse rumor mill, it seemed unlikely that she hadn't heard. Then again, Althea seemed clueless about it. If Stacy and Althea didn't already know, Kade didn't want to out Aiden by telling them Dawn was her lover. Not only was it

Aiden's and not her decision to make, but she also didn't want Stacy and Althea to start wondering why one lesbian had been trying to kill her while three other lesbians had come to her rescue.

"Yeah, Kade," Stacy agreed with their boss. "That's something we need to know. I don't want it to hit me from out of left field in court."

Traitor, Kade silently grumbled. Of course she knew that she would have said the very same thing if she were in Stacy's place. In fact, she had said the very same thing to Del when she had first met her and Del had wanted to testify against Gary Ballard. It seemed like a million years ago to her. On the surface, nothing had changed, but Kade knew her life would never again be as it had been just a few months ago.

Kade looked from one woman to the other. They were still waiting for an answer.

Should I lie? Come up with a plausible excuse? She shook her head at herself. *Is that how you want to live your life? Do you really want to spend your life in the closet, always afraid to be outed? Always hiding, lying, making excuses?* Kade knew it wasn't what she wanted, but neither did she like the consequences of the alternative. Still, there was more than just her job, her career, and her reputation at stake. *Do you want to force Del to live like that too? Del deserves so much better than that—and so do you. If a life trapped in the closet was what you wanted, you could have stayed in your family's golden cage.*

She took off her glasses and looked directly into Althea's eyes. "Dawn Kinsley is my friend," she answered simply.

"Your friend?" Althea repeated. It was easy to see that she wasn't very pleased with that answer. Her chair creaked under her as she leaned back and regarded Kade with irritation. "Kadence—"

Kade held up her hands. She didn't want to hear this. She already knew what Althea wanted to say anyway. "I know you think it's not 'appropriate' or professional." *Frankly, Althea, I've come to realize that in the grand scheme of things, propriety is overrated*, Kade thought. She was smart enough not to say it to her boss, though. "She became my friend long after her case was closed and the trial ended. There was never a conflict of interest," she told Althea.

"I'll meet with her to discuss her testimony if the case should go to court," Stacy said before Althea could answer.

Dawn will have to testify. Kade swallowed. *Of course she will. You're a lawyer. You should have thought of that.* She clearly remembered how scared but determined Dawn had been the last time she had been on the stand. She didn't want to put her through that a second time. "If you can get Sheldon and her lawyer to accept a plea bargain that doesn't let her off with a slap on the wrist, do it," she ordered.

Stacy stared at her. "Are you sure you want me to do that? You have a couple of very reliable witnesses and—"

"Stalking is never easy to prove," Kade interrupted. She didn't want her private life or that of her friends paraded around in open court for a conviction that wasn't guaranteed.

Stacy looked at Althea, waiting for her decision.

Finally, Althea gave a tense nod. "The DA's office doesn't have any interest in making this public knowledge either," she said, obviously guessing Kade's true reasons.

The two women stood and headed to the door. With her hand already on the door handle, Althea turned back around. "For what it's worth, I'm glad Ms. Kinsley came by at just the right moment." Before Kade could react to the unexpected sentiment, Althea added, "I would have hated having to take over your caseload."

* * *

Kade looked at her watch again.

Del was late.

Del had never been late to one of their "dates."

Kade knew perfectly well that a thousand things could have happened to make Del late, most of them totally harmless. One last report to review, one last form to log, a last-minute request from another unit to help out in an arrest or an investigation... *Del is a lieutenant. She has a career and a life of her own. She doesn't have to explain being five minutes late to you.* In the past, Kade had always hated the possessive behavior of her boyfriends or the men she dated. She didn't like the feeling of owing them an explanation for what she did and when she did it. In return, she had never been overly interested in how they spent their time away from her. If one of them had been late for a date, she would have pulled one of her files out of her attaché and put the time to good use, or she would have just gotten up and left.

With Del, there was no thought of leaving or working. Kade glanced at her watch again, then at the phone.

She jumped when it began to ring. Blowing out a breath, she reached for the phone. "Hey," she said with a relieved grin. "You stuck at work?"

Her caller cleared her throat. "No," came the surprised answer.

Kade rubbed her temples. *That'll teach me to answer the phone without even glancing at the caller ID.* "Hello, Mother. I thought you were... someone else," she said.

"Yes, that was quite obvious," her mother said haughtily. "If you had known it was me, you wouldn't have picked up the phone."

Kade sighed. She didn't defend herself, because they both knew her mother was right. "I would have called you when I thought you were ready to talk."

"I am ready to talk. Why else would I have called you?" Sophie objected.

"You might be ready to talk, but are you ready to listen?" Kade asked frankly.

"I'm ready to listen to reason," Sophie said. "And I hope you are too."

Reason? Kade thought about the implications for a moment. She had lived her life listening to nothing but reason, rules, sensible expectations, and rational plans. It had made her content but not happy. "Mother, my attraction to women isn't something that can be changed by listening to reasonable arguments. It's a part of me."

"It's never been a 'part of you' before," her mother said, repeating Kade's words with a distancing sarcasm, "and it doesn't have to be now."

"That's what I believed for a long time too. But life is too short to ignore whole parts of yourself. I almost died without ever having the chance to explore this part of me," Kade said, mostly talking to herself. With all the chaos Tracey Sheldon's attack had created—having crime scene specialists wander through her office, explaining things to her boss, and giving statement after statement—it had taken a few days until she had finally found enough time to think about what had happened—and what could have happened.

"What?" Sophie's refined detachment was gone. "Did you just say...?" She let out a strangled gasp.

Kade sighed. She hadn't intended to tell her mother. She had stopped telling her mother anything about her life when she had been a teenager. There was no way back now, though. If she didn't tell her mother, Sophie would hear it from one of the many friends she had in high places. "I've been stalked since October. Last Friday, the stalker attacked me in my office," she said as matter-of-factly as she could. *I don't think telling her the stalker is a mentally unstable lesbian who deluded herself into thinking she's in a relationship with me would help here.*

For a few seconds, there was only silence on the other end of the line.

Kade leaned back against the couch. Resignedly, she waited for the inevitable "Why didn't you tell me sooner?"

"Are you... are you all right? Are you hurt?" Sophie asked instead.

Kade blinked in surprise, then lowered her gaze to the bruises on her wrists, where Tracey Sheldon had grabbed her. "No, Mother. I didn't get hurt. I'm fine." She tugged on the sleeve of her blouse until it covered up the bruises again.

"That never would have happened to you if you had gone into private practice," Sophie blurted out.

There it is—the "I told you so" I've been waiting for. "This had nothing to do with my job," Kade protested. "Even if it had, it's not your choice to make. This is my life, not yours. If you're not prepared to support me in my choices—"

"How can I support you if you don't tell me anything?" Sophie interrupted. "You spent almost a week at home with me and yet you never thought it necessary to tell me your life has been threatened."

Kade knew her mother was right, but she refused to feel guilty about it. "Well, considering how my other revelation went over with you, I thought I'd leave that for the next visit," she answered.

Sophie was stunned into silence again. "I don't recognize you anymore," she said after a few moments of tense silence.

"How could you recognize me? You never knew me, Mother," Kade said quietly. "You only saw the things about me you wanted to see."

"I can only see what you let me see," Sophie defended herself.

That much was true, but it didn't take into account that Sophie's lifelong behavior toward her was the reason Kade had never been comfortable enough to be herself around her mother. "After some less than stellar reactions from you and Father when I did let you see things that are important to me, I quickly learned not to bother. You didn't like me taking the job with the DA's office; you didn't like me moving to Portland, and you certainly didn't like finding out I'm bisexual."

"How can I like it if I don't understand it? I don't think any of these choices was in your best interest, Kadence," her mother said.

For now, Kade chose to ignore her mother's lumping in of her sexual orientation with the other things as a choice. Understanding the finer points of sexual orientation was clearly beyond her mother right now. "You don't have to understand it, Mother, but a little bit of motherly support would have been great. Trust me to know what's in my best interest and what's not; that's all I'm asking." It was the first time in her life Kade had ever openly demanded support and respect from her mother.

She heard her mother sigh into the phone. "I'll try, but... all of this feels so wrong... so surreal to me."

*Surreal? Try living my life, Mother! Starting a lesbian relationship, being outed to my mother, and almost being killed by a crazy admirer... all within a week! **That's** surreal!* Kade didn't say anything. She knew her mother needed time, and getting into another argument wouldn't help.

"Do you... do you want me to come to Portland and stay with you for a few days?" Sophie asked carefully.

Kade removed the phone from her ear and stared at it in shock. "No!" she said quickly and then added more politely, "No, that's not necessary, Mother. I'm fine, really."

"Do you have someone to... someone who stays with you?" Sophie asked reluctantly.

Del was right. She's worried I'm alone and lonely, like she is, Kade realized. It was a strange, yet nice feeling to suddenly have some motherly concern in her life. "I'm fine on my own," she said. "If I don't feel like being alone, I'm sure Del would stay."

"Oh." That effectively silenced Sophie.

She doesn't want to think about what Del staying at my apartment might mean. Kade knew it didn't have to mean sleeping together. Not if she didn't want to. Del wasn't putting any pressure on her, and it gave Kade the freedom to explore her own feelings.

Sophie awkwardly cleared her throat. "Delicia... she's a good person. Very loyal and genuine," she said softly.

What? Kade hadn't expected that. She had been sure her mother would blame her sudden interest in women on Del and wouldn't have anything even remotely positive to say about her. Instead, Sophie had described Del very accurately. "Yes, she is," Kade answered cautiously, not sure where her mother would go with this.

"I'm glad you had a friend like her be there for you while you were dealing with being stalked," her mother said. It sounded sincere, not like one of the well-chosen, polite phrases Sophie usually delivered so smoothly.

Kade felt a little bad about it, but she couldn't stop herself from distrustfully waiting for the "but" in Sophie's sentence. "But?" she prompted when it didn't come.

Sophie sighed. "But I'm sure she would have been there for you and would have been just as loyal and supportive if you were nothing but friends. Why does it have to be more?" She clearly couldn't wrap her mind around the concept of attraction and love between two women.

Why didn't you stay just friends with Father? Why did that have to be more? Kade wanted to say, but in her opinion, her parents' relationship was not a good example to make her point. She had never sensed any true love and passion between them, just polite respect and mutual interest. "You mean why don't I keep Del and every other woman who might interest me as a strictly platonic friend and date men instead." She didn't make it a question because she knew that was exactly what her mother meant. "Because I've already done that for years, and it didn't make me happy. At this point of my life, I'm more attracted to women. Well, one woman, to be exact, and I owe it to myself not to ignore it any longer."

"But—"

The doorbell interrupted any further objections from Sophie.

Del! Finally! Kade stood from the couch. "I'm sorry, Mother, but I have to go." For now, she had said enough. Only time would tell if her mother had actually listened. She quickly said good-bye and hurried to open the door. Her hand was already on the door handle when she remembered to look through the peephole.

The distorted image of Del was the best thing she had seen all day. Kade quickly opened the door.

"Hey," Del said. "Sorry I'm late." She closed the door behind herself. "Stacy Ford intercepted me just as I was about to leave the precinct."

Kade, who had been about to step closer and kiss Del hello, abruptly stopped. "You already gave your statement, and I told her to work out a deal with Sheldon's lawyer. What did she want?"

Del flashed her a grin. "Oh, she just wanted to give me my new toaster oven. Reward for a job well-done."

"Jerk," Kade muttered. She glared at Del but couldn't stop herself from returning Del's grin.

Del laughed. "Okay, okay. She wanted to ask me a few more questions about when Tracey Sheldon attacked me in front of your apartment. I think dropping the charges on assaulting a police officer is going to be the carrot Stacy wants to dangle in front of Sheldon's lawyer to get him to accept a deal," she said.

"Are you okay with that?" Kade asked. She didn't like letting Tracey Sheldon get away with her attack on Del. As a DDA, she knew it was a promising legal tactic, but as a woman, she wanted revenge. She wanted Tracey Sheldon to pay for hurting Del.

"As long as Stacy makes sure Tracey Sheldon never comes anywhere near you again, I'm fine with it," Del answered. Her voice was calm, but the fire in the dark eyes told Kade that Del would do anything, risk anything to keep her safe.

Del stepped closer and studied Kade intently. "Hey, you okay? You look a little..."

This time, Kade wasn't even tempted to give her standard "I'm fine" answer. When it came to Del, she wanted to retire all standard answers. "I finally talked to my mother," she said with a grimace.

Del took her hand and entwined their fingers in a gesture of silent support. "And? What did she say?"

"Well... she likes you," Kade said.

Del lifted a skeptical eyebrow. "I've been in this situation before." She had dated women who had just discovered their sexual orientation and revealed it to their none too pleased families before. "The families of my newly out love interests called me a 'conniving little slut,' a 'lesbian recruiter,' or a 'temporary confusion,' but never once has a mother told her daughter that she actually likes me."

"The Mathesons are not like other families," Kade declared.

"No," Del affectionately squeezed Kade's hand, "you're special. But are you sure she didn't say she'd **like** me to disappear off the face of earth?" she asked with a small smile.

"No. She does like you and basically told me it's okay if I like you too." Kade gave her a meaningful glance.

"Ah." Del nodded. "Just not 'like that,' huh?"

"Exactly." Kade walked over to the couch and let herself fall into the cushions. She curled one leg under her and steadily regarded Del. "The problem is I already like you 'like that.'"

Del's eyes widened. She gazed at Kade, visibly surprised at her open words for a few seconds, before a big grin spread over her face. She sat down on the couch next to Kade and turned sideways to face her, laying a hand on her hip. "I like you 'like that' too."

"Good," Kade said with a satisfied grin. "I'd hate to have this all be for nothing." She gestured toward the phone, indicating the coming out to her very traditional family.

"It's not," Del said. She gently cupped Kade's cheek and looked deeply into her eyes. "It's something you had to do for yourself."

Kade gently threaded her fingers through the dark hair that fell onto Del's neck. With Del's hand on her hip steadying her, she leaned in to kiss her. What started as a gesture of affection and gratitude for Del's support quickly escalated into a passionate meeting of lips and tongues.

As the kiss continued, Kade disentangled her right hand and slowly trailed it down over Del's chest, curious to explore more of Del and to test out what responses she could evoke.

When she experimentally cupped one of Del's breasts, Del grunted and broke the kiss. "What are you doing?" she gasped.

"You couldn't tell?" Kade gave her a mischievous smile. "And here I thought you were the experienced one who already earned a dozen toaster ovens. I'm trying to find out if you're wearing a bra."

"Oooh, is that what you were doing?" Del grinned. "And? What's the verdict?"

"The jury isn't in yet. I'm still in the middle of my investigation," Kade answered. She slid her other hand under Del's shirt and slowly let it trail up her stomach.

Del swayed slightly. "Kade..." she murmured. "You better be sure about this. I usually have great self-control, but once it gets past a certain point... You don't want to torture me, do you?"

"I'm not a tease," Kade said with mock indignation. "I usually follow through on my threats... and my promises."

Del put her hand on Kade's, trapping it in place under Del's shirt. Her eyes looked directly into Kade's. "Do you really want this? Now?"

"Why not? If I have to take the heat from my mother, it should at least be about something that I actually did and got to enjoy. Do you really want to stop?" Kade gave back Del's question. She didn't want to discuss this. She didn't want to start thinking and analyzing. She just wanted to follow her impulses and instincts, without letting her thoughts and emotions catch up and possibly stop her.

"Hell, no!" Del chuckled roughly. "I want you, but I want more than just casual sex with you. If you can't give me that yet, I'd rather wait."

Kade sighed. She knew what Del was saying. Del wanted sexual intimacy, but not without emotional intimacy. "Women!" she said with an exasperation that was meant to hide how out of her depth she felt. "If you were a man, we'd already be having the 'cigarette after.'"

"You're not a smoker," Del said, "and I'm not a man."

"I know," Kade said seriously. "If you were, you wouldn't be here."

Still holding on to Kade's hand under her shirt, Del regarded her. After a few moments of silent communication, she finally let go of Kade's hand.

Kade leaned forward and kissed the soft skin that peeked out from above the neck of Del's shirt, silently thanking her for letting it go and not starting another discussion. She trailed her hand over Del's side, exploring the arch of her ribs. She felt Del suck in a breath.

"Why don't we take this to the bedroom?" Del suggested. "The couch is for teenagers."

Kade felt a little like a teenager, but she stood and tugged Del up from the couch. Her heart pounded as she led Del by the hand over to the bedroom. *Come on. Don't act like a scared virgin. This is not that different from being with a man.* But when she stopped next to the bed and looked at Del, she realized that it was very different. It wasn't only the differences of Del's body in comparison to her previous, male lovers. What made this so different was what she felt when she looked at Del.

Noticing Kade's momentary hesitation, Del stepped closer and wrapped both arms around her. She didn't offer to stop or ask if Kade was okay. She just held her, waiting for whatever Kade would decide to do.

Kade slid her arms around Del's waist and pressed her hands against the solid back. She buried her face against Del's neck, deeply breathing in her scent. She concentrated only on Del's presence, the body that was pressed tightly against her own, and blocked out everything else.

Finally, her churning emotions calmed, and she turned her head to press her lips to Del's neck, teasing it with little nips and kisses. She felt Del's pulse beat a frantic staccato against her lips. With one last kiss, she lifted her mouth away and looked up into Del's face. "Am I that good to make your pulse race with just a few little kisses, or are you nervous?" she asked with a teasing little smile.

Del looked down at her with eyes that were even darker than normal. "Both," she said with her characteristic honesty.

The contrasting mix of Del's tough, confident exterior and her emotional openness was one thing that Kade liked and admired so much about her. "Don't worry," Kade said with a glint in her eyes. "I've had plenty of mediocre or even bad sex in the past. I'm used to it. There's no need for performance anxiety."

"You!" Del growled at her. She tightened her arms around Kade, lifting her a few inches off the ground. She took one long step and threw Kade down on the bed.

Kade bounced on the mattress.

Before she came to a halt, Del pounced like a lithe big cat and covered Kade's body with her own. She balanced part of her weight on her elbows, but Kade could still feel her lower body press against her. "And here I thought you were a bottom," Kade joked, trying to hide how out of breath and out of control she felt.

"What? A bottom? Me?" Del's body pressed against Kade's even more intimately as she playfully glared down at her. Then she gave Kade a droll smile. "Althea Coltrane wasn't supposed to tell you all my secrets," she complained deadpan.

Kade threw her head back in helpless laughter. "Ewwww!" She shook herself at the thought of Del with her boss.

Del shrugged innocently. "Having a close, amicable relationship with the DA's office is important in my line of work."

Kade laughed again. *Sex... making love has never been this much fun,* she thought to herself. *It was fun and enjoyable in some ways, but never like this.* "Well, you can't get much closer or more amicable than this," she said, gesturing down at their entwined bodies.

"True." Del slowly leaned down and kissed the base of Kade's throat.

Kade shuddered as she felt Del's breasts press against her own and Del's teeth rake gently over her skin. "Sit up," Kade ordered.

Del lifted her head and looked at Kade with one raised eyebrow, but she complied without comment.

When Del sat astride on her hips, balancing on her knees, Kade grasped the edge of Del's shirt and lifted it up. For a second, she saw the surprise in Del's eyes before she lifted the shirt over her head and lost sight of her facial expression.

"So no bra, huh?" Kade commented as she let the shirt drop to the floor.

Del grinned. "I went au natural today."

Kade sat up too. Holding on to Del's hips, she rolled them over until she was leaning over Del, looking down at her.

Kade trailed the tip of her index finger up Del's stomach. She studied the contrast between her own pale hands and Del's smooth, café au lait skin. Impulsively, she leaned down and placed a gentle kiss on Del's belly button, nuzzling the soft skin. Her hands slid up the flat, defined planes of Del's stomach, feeling the muscles vibrate under her touch.

Finally, her exploring hands reached the soft underside of Del's breasts. Kade paused. She looked down at Del, letting her gaze roam over her whole body.

Some of the Latin women she knew were voluptuous, the epitome of the sensual, luscious Latin lover. Del wasn't. Del's body was sturdy and athletic, yet still unmistakably feminine. Kade had caught glimpses of Del's body in shorts and T-shirt before, and she'd seen her in her underwear twice. Still, the sight of Del lying naked on the sheets in front of her made Kade's heart race.

Kade knew Del was used to being in control, used to being the one to take the lead when it came to relationships and to sex, but Del lay under her without moving, gazing up at her with an expression of trust that took Kade's breath away as much as the sight of Del's body did. Deeply in thought, she rubbed her thumb over the underside of a small, firm breast, a little overwhelmed with the whole situation.

"Hey," Del said, letting her hand rest on the small of Kade's back. "Want me to give you a few directions?" She looked up at Kade with an affectionately teasing grin.

Kade shook her head. What was so overwhelming for her wasn't necessarily the thought of making love to a woman for the first time although that was challenging enough. What made her uncomfortable were the emotions she could see in Del's eyes and feel in the chaotic tumble that raced through her—nervousness, fear, doubt, desire, curiosity, affection, awe, and a deep need to please Del. "No, thanks. I have some ideas of my own." Kade gave her a sexy little smirk. "But I could do with... well, a little feedback. As a prosecutor, I'm used to it. If I do something the defense lawyer or the judge doesn't like, they instantly let me know."

"We're not in court, Kade," Del gently pointed out.

Kade knew Del wanted her to let go of her usual roles. Del wanted honesty and true emotions, not roles or masks. Del wanted much more than all her other lovers had wanted—not just her body, her family's influence, or a beautiful woman on her arm. Del wanted all of her. Kade wasn't used to giving all. She had always held back a little, never giving her emotions free rein or allowing herself to get fully attached to someone.

"But I can do feedback," Del agreed with a wink. "This," she let out a sensual moan, "means 'nice, please continue.' This," a longer moan, "means 'very nice, do that again.' And this—"

Kade didn't wait for further explanations. She leaned down and closed her lips around one of Del's nipples, feeling it instantly harden against her tongue.

Del sucked in a sharp breath. Her hands clutched at Kade's back, pulling her even closer. "And... this... means..." Kade felt a throaty growl vibrate through Del as her hand covered Del's other breast. "This means... Jesus, Kade, you don't need any feedback!"

Kade reluctantly lifted her mouth away from Del's breast. She stroked away the wet marks she had left there, loving how responsive Del was and how much pleasure she seemed to get from her touches. "Take off your pants," she told Del, wanting to feel all of her.

Instead of rolling out from under Kade, Del slid a hand down between them, making Kade moan as the back of Del's fingers pressed against her center for a moment. Then Del worked open her belt and the buttons of her jeans, and Kade moved back a little to help her take them off.

She slid her hand over the impressive muscles of Del's thighs.

Del reclined back against the bed. "Now you," she said. "Take off the slacks and the shirt. Tit for tat... so to speak."

Kade laughed and got off the bed. *She's making this so much fun.* She pushed her slacks down over her hips and quickly stepped out of them. Straddling Del, Kade pulled her shirt over her head. She looked down and studied Del's reaction. She had always been confident, even as a teenager, never experiencing awkward shyness and self-doubts when she undressed in front of her lovers. But now she found herself holding her breath while she felt Del's gaze rake over every inch of her.

Del sat up under her. Instead of cupping Kade's breasts, as most of her other lovers had done, she slid one strap of the bra down Kade's shoulder and gently kissed the skin underneath, then did the same with the other shoulder.

The gentle reverence of the gesture took Kade's breath away.

"Can I take it off?" Del asked. The eyes looking deeply into Kade's were almost black now.

Kade swallowed and nodded.

Their breasts pressed against each other as Del reached around Kade to open the clasp of her bra.

Kade captured Del's lips in a passionate kiss. Tightly pressed together, they sank back onto the bed. Del pulled the bra out from between them. Kade felt Del's breasts sliding against her own as they moved against each other. The sensation made her a little light-headed, and she slid lower to kiss Del's breasts again.

Her glasses collided with one of Del's nipples, making Del shiver. Kade quickly reached up to take off her glasses.

Del was faster. She gently lifted the glasses away from her face and leaned up to kiss the bridge of Kade's nose. She carefully folded the earpieces and set the glasses down on the bedside table.

Every little gesture, every touch, was so full of meaning, so full of feelings, that it made Kade's head spin, adding to that out of control feeling. Pausing to take a deep breath, Kade tried to calm the wild beating of her heart. She lowered her face and kissed the smooth underside of Del's breast, hiding her expression and at the same time taking control. Del's physical reactions to her touches were something over which she had complete control.

Del's long fingers slid into her hair, directing her up a little until Kade closed her lips around Del's nipple again.

Giving an experimental little lick, she listened to Del's low moans and watched closely for any indications of what Del liked and didn't like. At the same time, she learned how she liked to touch Del. When she slid up to place lingering kisses on strong shoulders, Del's hands trailed lower and cupped her butt, encouraging Kade.

"What do you want?" Kade whispered against Del's lips.

Del leaned up. Her hot breath on Kade's skin made Kade shiver until her lips were claimed in a passionate kiss.

Both of them were breathing heavily when Del finally broke the kiss. Del lifted Kade's hand to her lips and kissed every finger, the palm, and the sensitive inside of her wrist. Slowly, keeping eye contact with Kade, she directed Kade's hand down her body. When their joined hands reached the edge of her panties, Del stopped and kissed Kade again.

Kade rolled partially off of Del, lying more on her side. She needed to see what she was doing as she slowly slipped her fingertips under the edge of Del's panties. She directed a questioning gaze up Del's body, taking in the quick rise and fall of her breasts as Del struggled for breath.

Del gave her a quick nod. She bent one of her legs and wrapped both arms around Kade, holding her loosely.

Kade slid her fingers lower. She carefully combed through damp curls and started a slow, methodical exploration, savoring every new sensation and closely watching Del's flushed face to see how she reacted to each touch.

"Jesus!" Del hissed as Kade circled her clit, first clockwise, then, just to be thorough in her exploration, in a counterclockwise movement. "You're killing me!"

Kade tried a more direct stroke with a little more pressure. Immediately, she felt Del's hips buck under her, lifting her up a little so that their breasts slid against each other again. This time, both of them moaned. "Do you want me to —?" she asked, not sure where Del's boundaries lay and what was expected of her.

"Whatever you want to do," Del said breathlessly. "As long as you don't stop in the middle of things." She gave her a meaningful glance.

Kade chuckled and moved her fingers again.

Del's short nails rasped over her skin, making shivers race up and down her body. She nuzzled Del's breasts but didn't do much more because her concentration was on what her fingers were doing. She made small circular motions, guided by what she knew she liked and by Del's groans of approval.

Suddenly, touching was not enough. She wanted to see all of Del. Del's protest as she took her hand away quickly died down as Kade dragged the panties down over her hips. Kade moaned as her own center pressed against Del's leg, and she quickly moved back up, not wanting to be distracted. Her hands slid over Del's skin, caressing as much of it as she could. A haze of arousal swept away the last remnants of nervousness and doubts.

Kade slid two of her fingers through Del's curls and brushed them on either side of Del's clit. She looked back up, watching the play of Del's muscles under glistening skin as she moved restlessly on the bed. Slowly, her fingers dipped lower. She circled Del's entrance, sliding in about half an inch before hesitating. She didn't want to hurt Del in her inexperience.

Del's groan was not one of pain, though. She clutched Kade's body to her. Her thrusting hips drove Kade's fingers deeper.

Intoxicated, totally overwhelmed by emotions and sensations, Kade simply followed the rhythm Del set. She could feel the slight tremor in the muscles straining against her. Her own body trembled with excitement. She watched the pulse beat quickly in Del's neck, matching the pulsing she could feel beginning around her fingers.

Del moved faster against her. A long, shaky groan escaped from her parted lips. "Kade," she gasped, opening eyes that had closed in pleasure. "Can you...?"

"What?" Kade asked, almost as frantic as Del to bring her pleasure.

Instead of answering, incapable of speech, Del slid her own hand down. Her fingers brushed against Kade's before they found Del's clit.

Jesus! A wave of heat shot through Kade at the sight.

Del tossed her head from side to side. Her thighs clenched around Kade's hand. "Kade," she whispered roughly. Her body froze, then surged up one final time against Kade's fingers before she collapsed back onto the bed.

Kade protectively covered the heaving, shivering body with her own. Humbled by this powerful experience, not knowing what to say or do, she held still until she felt the contractions around her fingers stop.

Del wrapped her powerful arms around her, clutching Kade so tightly against her that it almost hurt. Finally, her grip loosened a little, and she opened her eyes. "I have some serious doubts about that toaster oven," she said, her words rumbling through Kade.

"What?" Kade had half expected the first words from Del's lips to be a declaration of love or undying devotion. Her mention of a toaster oven was a relief but confusing nonetheless.

"I don't think I deserve a toaster oven for this." Del indicated their naked, sweaty bodies. "You've clearly been with other women before to have mastered the art of lesbian lovemaking like this."

"Liar." Kade kissed the breast her cheek was resting on, tasting the salty skin under her lips. "We both know I'm a rank amateur. I didn't even understand what you wanted when you..." She gestured at the hand that Del had used to touch herself.

Del tilted her head. "I hope you don't mind me taking over a little. It just wasn't the best moment for long explanations." She grinned.

Kade freely shook her head. "It was fun," she said. With other lovers, she would have taken it as a criticism of her skills as a lover, as a slight on her ability to bring her partner pleasure on her own, without any assistance. With Del, she hadn't thought about any of that. It hadn't been important. Her focus had been on Del, not on anything else.

"Fun?" Del rolled around, covering Kade's body with her own. "Is that the highest word of praise in your vocabulary?"

"It was hot... and intense," Kade said honestly. She leaned up and kissed Del.

* * *

Del brushed a strand of damp hair off Kade's forehead, tenderly sweeping it back behind one cute ear. "Want to try to expand on that description?" she asked with a smile.

She had gladly relinquished control over their lovemaking to Kade, knowing it would make her more comfortable. Because of Del's natural authority and being older than most of her sexual partners, the women Del had been with tended to expect her to take the lead, and Del had happily taken it. Now she found it was a nice change of pace to relinquish control to Kade. There was something very erotic about giving herself to Kade completely. Still, she wanted Kade to show the same kind of trust in her.

Kade nodded and bit her lip.

Del could already feel Kade begin to close herself off, trying to hold back and keep control of her emotions. She was determined to make Kade feel—not just the physical sensations but also their emotional connection. "Any special requests, or am I free to act out some late-night fantasies?" she asked with a wink.

The sexy smile that appeared on Kade's face made Del's heart beat faster. "Oh, so you fantasized about this? About me?" Kade drawled.

"Well, yes," Del admitted without embarrassment. "Me and every other cop with an intact libido. The only difference is that I'm lucky enough to get to act on it." She gently kissed the bruise that Tracey Sheldon's attack had left on Kade's checkbone. Seeing the marks on Kade made her stomach churn with anger and guilt. She had spent a sleepless night, almost driving herself crazy thinking about how close Kade had come to being shot with the gun Del had given her for protection. Resolutely, Del shoved that thought aside. Anger and guilt weren't what she wanted to feel tonight. *Tonight, I just want to be happy and make Kade happy too.* She wanted to take away all the pain, hate, and fear in Kade's life and replace it with tenderness and affection. Her lips caressed a scratch on Kade's temple and the dark marks on her throat, then trailed soft kisses over the finger-shaped bruises on Kade's shoulders and upper arms. She kissed the bruises on the fair-skinned inside of Kade's wrists. When she looked up, she met Kade's gaze. "Turn around," Del whispered.

Kade hesitated. "What...?"

"Trust me," Del said, never breaking eye contact. She lifted up a little, silently indicating for Kade to turn around and lie down on her belly.

She knew it meant a lot when Kade slowly turned around and settled her head on her folded arms.

Del trailed a single fingertip over the elegant line of her spine. "You're beautiful," she said. Never in her life had she meant it more. One of her legs slid between Kade's when she kissed the bruise on Kade's back, where Tracey Sheldon had shoved her against her desk. She could feel goose bumps erupt under her lips.

Kade's fingers clutched at the sheets as Del tenderly swept Kade's red hair aside and kissed the nape of her neck. Del trailed her tongue across the warm skin to taste its saltiness. Her hands caressed Kade's flanks, teasing the sides of her breasts. She nipped at her shoulder, explored the dips of her shoulder blades, and rained kisses down along her spine.

Cupping Kade's hips with both hands, Del pressed one openmouthed kiss to the small of her back. The black lace of Kade's panties provided a sudden barrier. Del loosely trailed her hands over the fabric, but then decided to leave the panties in place for now and moved down the bed. With gentle fingers, she kneaded one fair-skinned foot, then the other. She nipped and kissed her way up the smooth, shapely calves she had admired since she had first met Kade.

Kade squirmed under her as she licked the sensitive skin behind her knees and then let her lips and hands slowly trail higher. When she reached the black panties again, she gently hooked her fingers under the waistband. "These are in the way," she said, giving a little tug.

"Then take them off," Kade ordered, turning her head to meet Del's eyes. Her voice was smoky and low, tinged with desire.

The sound alone sent an answering rush of heat down Del's body.

Kade lifted up on her elbows and knees, and Del pulled the black lace down over her hips. When Kade lay back down, Del slipped the panties down her legs, trailing her hands over Kade's thighs and calves on the way down.

Gently holding on to two firm thighs to keep her balance, Del leaned down and kissed one smooth ass cheek, then the other. She felt Kade's thighs flex under her touch. Pulling away a little, she put her hands on Kade's hips again, getting ready to turn her over. At the last moment, she stopped. She didn't want to "handle" Kade. All of this meant nothing if Kade didn't trust her—and herself—enough to let go of her tight control and allow herself to experience the full force of her desire and her emotions. "Turn over," she whispered against Kade's skin.

Kade's fingers slowly let go of the sheets. She turned and looked up at Del, who hovered over her.

Del stopped all movement and just looked at Kade. Kade's face was flushed, and her ice blue eyes glittered with equal parts desire and anxiety. Del quickly reached for one of the hands that had immediately taken hold of the sheets again. "Hey, everything all right? Do you want me to stop?" she asked.

She had known this wouldn't be as easy for Kade as Kade had probably thought. Kade was a confident, goal-oriented woman. She was liberal and well-read and had probably thought she knew exactly what making love to a woman would be like.

She hadn't been clueless about the "mechanics," but Del suspected Kade hadn't been prepared for the emotions it evoked.

"No," Kade answered roughly. She wrapped her legs around Del and drew her closer against her body.

Del groaned when she felt Kade's wetness against her stomach. She forgot her concern and desperately sought Kade's lips for a long kiss.

Kade began to rock against her as their tongues slid against each other.

Gasping, Del broke the kiss. She sucked at the damp skin of Kade's neck, gently at first, and then, when Kade threw her head back to give her better access, more strongly until she had added a mark of desire and affection to the bruises caused by violence.

Del moved her lips down Kade's chest in quick, feathery kisses. She cupped one of the full breasts in her hand and studied its beauty for a second before she lowered her head to kiss it. Her tongue drew circles around the nipple, teasing, but never touching it.

Kade slid her fingers into Del's short hair. Tingles started in Del's scalp and continued down her body. Kade's hands spasmed against the back of Del's head as she lowered her head and drew one hard nipple into her mouth.

A stifled moan encouraged Del to suck a little harder.

Kade's hips bucked under her, and Del had to force herself to go slow and savor every second. She lifted a hand to Kade's neglected breast and started to gently stroke and knead it.

Finally, when Kade thrashed under her and could no longer hold back her moans, Del gave one last kiss to her breast and moved lower. She placed kisses on the flat, yet womanly stomach and ran the tip of her tongue around Kade's belly button.

"Del!" Kade gasped. "Do you want to kill me on my first night with a woman?"

Del rested her chin on Kade's hip bone. "I was thinking more along the lines of giving you a 'little death,'" she answered with a grin. Resting both of her hands along the insides of Kade's thighs, she slowly lowered her head, giving Kade every opportunity to stop her.

Kade's fingers in her hair tightened but didn't hold her back.

Only inches away from Kade's wetness, Del paused and breathed in her scent. Her hot breath washed over Kade, making her groan in anticipation.

Del turned her head. She placed a few butterfly kisses on one inner thigh, then gently scraped her teeth over the other.

Kade writhed under her as she traced the tip of her tongue up the inside of her thigh.

Del brushed the fingers of one hand over the copper-colored curls and left her hand in place to help hold Kade open. Slowly, carefully, she swept her tongue over the swollen folds. When she heard nothing from Kade, she looked up the flushed body and into her face.

Kade had covered her eyes with her forearm and caught her lower lip between her teeth, trying to hold back.

"All right?" Del asked, her lips only an inch from Kade's skin.

Kade swallowed convulsively. She moved her arm away from her face and looked down at Del. Her eyes had darkened and were now a smoky gray. "Fine," she panted. "Just stop... teasing."

"Oh, because you didn't tease me at all, huh?" One more glance back up into Kade's flushed face made her take pity. She lowered her head again and moved her tongue back and forth more firmly against the sensitive flesh. Her hands reached up, taking hold of Kade's hips as they began to buck uncontrollably.

Kade was helpless to hold back her moans. Her legs tightened around Del's head, and her heels dug into the bed, pressing her up and against Del's tongue.

Del pushed the tip of her tongue into Kade.

"Oh!" Kade's fingers clawed at the sheets, at Del's shoulders, at anything she could get a hold of, trying to maintain some last semblance of control.

"Kade..." Del waited until Kade's half-closed eyes opened with difficulty and made contact with hers. "Let go. Don't hold back, Kade. You're safe with me." She closed her lips over Kade's clit and sucked gently.

Kade's guttural cry was muffled as her thighs clamped around Del's ears.

Breathing hard, enjoying the aftershocks she could feel rippling through Kade in her intimate position, Del waited until Kade's legs dropped weakly to the bed. Quickly, she crawled up Kade's body, sliding against the damp skin until she could take Kade into her arms.

Kade lay with her eyes open, staring at Del with an unfathomable expression.

Del kissed her, wanting to evoke some reaction she could figure out.

Kade's arms that had fallen limply to the bed suddenly wrapped tight around Del. Kade broke the kiss and wiped her lips with a trembling hand. "What a mess," she mumbled, her voice a little hoarse.

Mess? Del silently repeated as she wiped her mouth and chin too. She wondered if Kade was talking about the damp sheets and the sweat and fluids that were beginning to dry on their bodies, or if she meant the emotions their lovemaking had evoked.

Del knew that Kade's head, her sharp mind, had always kept control over her heart. In the past, Kade had gotten physically involved, yet had always kept an emotional distance. She had never allowed herself to love with all the consequences and vulnerabilities. For a woman like Kade, the emotions Del hoped she was now feeling were certainly a little messy and perhaps even unwanted. "It's not messy," she said gently, meaning both their lovemaking and the feelings that went with it. "It's beautiful."

She kissed Kade again, and this time, Kade kissed her back with more animation. "Say something," Del pleaded when the kiss ended. She felt the urgent need to establish some kind of connection with Kade and learn what was going through her busy mind.

"Wow," Kade said.

Del couldn't help her smile. "Wow? Here I am with the DA's office's most eloquent, articulate DDA, and all she can say is 'wow'?"

Kade turned on her side until she was fully facing Del. She reached out a hand and, with a very thoughtful expression, traced Del's eyebrows, then the rim of one ear with her fingertips. "You're not here with the DDA," she answered quietly.

Del's eyes, which had closed in pleasure at the gentle touches, shot open again. She stared into Kade's blue eyes in wonderment. Kade had said exactly what she had tried to get her to see since she had first expressed an interest in Kade—that Kade could be more, was more than just a talented lawyer, confident DDA, and future politician. She was more than her cool, calm, and collected façade. She was a woman with feelings, passion, insecurities, and vulnerabilities, and Del loved her even more for it.

Love, Del repeated, raising a brow at herself. *Careful there. It's a little soon for that.* "I'm glad about that," she said, finally answering Kade's statement.

"You should be," Kade replied with a grin, "because what we just did is probably illegal in some states."

"Not in this one," Del said, never looking away from the shining blue eyes.

Kade shook her head. A strand of red hair brushed over Del's naked shoulder. "Not in this one," she agreed. "But if we venture out into public like this, it could be considered negligent bodily injury by offensive smell." She indicated their sweat-glistening bodies with a smile.

"Yes, that could be... sticky," Del deadpanned. She was glad Kade felt relaxed and comfortable enough to joke around with her after their intense, emotional experience.

"We could easily prevent that. This apartment comes with a shower, you know," Kade informed her, sounding so regal that Del had to laugh. Kade rolled out of bed and stood on legs that seemed a little wobbly. "Jesus, Del! What have you done to me?" she complained, only halfway joking now. "I can't even walk straight!"

Del slid out of bed on Kade's side. "Then don't walk." She spread her arms invitingly. "Let me carry you."

Kade looked at her. They both knew it was more than just a means of transportation to the shower. Del offered trust, affection, and loyalty—if Kade could overcome her fear of emotional closeness and losing control. The blue eyes looked directly into Del's for long seconds.

Del swallowed but didn't blink, never looking away from Kade. Kade's answer meant a lot to her.

"All right," Kade finally said.

With a delighted smile, Del stepped closer and reached out to sweep Kade into her arms.

Kade stopped her with a quick touch. "On one condition," she bargained.

Maybe she should have been wary of that condition, but Del secretly loved that Kade wasn't giving up her fierce independence altogether. "Which would be...?" she prompted.

Kade folded her arms and took a challenging stance.

Del suppressed a smile. That familiar Matheson stance was much more intimidating when Kade wasn't naked, with tangled hair and a big hickey on her neck.

"That I get to carry you on the way back from the shower," Kade demanded.

Del didn't point out that she was taller and heavier than Kade. She had no doubt that, if she was determined, Kade could carry her back to bed. "Deal," she said, shaking Kade's hand and then kissing it. "That is... if, after helping each other get clean under the shower, we're both not too weak to carry each other anywhere."

Kade took one confident step, so close now that their noses were almost touching. She quickly nipped Del's bottom lip. "Then I'll just have to make sure that you are the one emerging from the shower with wobbly legs," she decided.

Laughing, Del swept her up into her arms and carried her off on legs that were already beginning to feel a little wobbly.

CHAPTER 40

"*I* LOVE SLEEPING with you," Aiden whispered into Dawn's hair.

Dawn lifted her head off Aiden's chest. Her cheeks were still flushed and her lips swollen from their kisses. "Oh, yeah, that was very obvious a minute ago," she said with a smile.

Aiden chuckled. "No, that's not what I mean."

"No?" Dawn looked up at her questioningly.

Aiden leaned down to kiss the tempting lips again. "I do love to make love with you. After the last..." she turned her head to look at the alarm clock, "...three hours, there should be no doubt about that. But I love sleeping with you too. Holding you when we go to sleep, having you be the first thing I see when I wake up..."

Dawn snuggled closer and closed her eyes. "I love sleeping with you too," she murmured against Aiden's shoulder.

"I never liked sleeping with anyone before. I always needed to have my own space," Aiden continued. Deeply in thought, she painted circles on Dawn's back with her fingertips.

Dawn's eyes snapped open. She lifted herself up on an elbow and looked down at Aiden. "What are you saying?"

"I'm saying that a lot has changed for me in the last few months. I have changed, and so have you. It's only natural that our relationship would change too." Aiden swallowed. "It scared me a little. Things are going great between us, and I'm happier than I've ever been in my life. I want to hold on to that and not risk doing anything that could screw it up." She exhaled and sank back against the pillow. Finally, she had admitted it, said it out loud to herself and to Dawn.

Dawn trailed her fingers through the hair at Aiden's temple. "Why do you think you'd be the one to screw it up? My history says I'm equally capable of screwing up relationships, you know."

"Meeting Evan and trying to help her deal with her past made me realize I've been making assumptions about myself all my life too," Aiden said, openly looking into Dawn's eyes.

"You're not scared of commitment. You're scared of yourself," Dawn voiced what Aiden hadn't said. "You think that if you let me even closer, let me see all of you without holding anything back, I'll discover something inside you that might hurt me or scare me away."

Aiden nodded slowly. She looked down at her hands that were still stroking Dawn's back.

"Aiden." Dawn laid her palms along both sides of Aiden's face, forcing her to look directly into her eyes. "I've faced evil twice in the last year. I know what it feels and looks like. What I see in you isn't anything like that. You love me, and I love you. If one of us gets hurt, it won't be because of evil lurking inside of you." There was an unshakable conviction in her voice.

Staring into Dawn's eyes at such close range, facing the intensity of her gaze without blinking, made Aiden's eyes tear up.

Before she could wipe her eyes, Dawn leaned down and kissed the tears away.

"If you told me that every night before we go to sleep and every morning when we wake up, I think I could start to believe it after a while," Aiden said, already starting to believe.

"You mean...?" Dawn stared at her with breathless hope.

"The lease on my apartment runs out at the end of next month." Now that Aiden had said it, she was actually starting to feel a little giddy. She knew her fears and worries were still there, but they didn't feel so overwhelming anymore.

Dawn stared at her with a happy grin. "Would you feel comfortable living here?"

"Let's see. I already discovered that I like the bathroom and the bedroom." Aiden winked at Dawn. "Not sure how I feel about the kitchen and living room yet, but you could help me find out."

Dawn pinched her. "Sounds like living with you might be quite the adventure."

Aiden grinned impishly. "I can't promise it'll always be easy, but at least it will never be dull." She studied Dawn expectantly. "So, what do you say?"

Slowly lowering her face until her lips were almost covering Aiden's, Dawn whispered, "Yes."

The End

About The Author

I GREW UP AMIDST the vineyards and gently sloping hills of southern Germany. I spent most of my childhood with my nose buried in a book, earning me the nickname "professor" before I even finished elementary school. The writing bug bit me at the age of eleven. The very first piece of fiction I ever wrote was a thirty-page western story that I still have somewhere (well-hidden because it alternately makes me cringe and laugh when I read it today). I wrote two dozen mostly novel-length stories (westerns, adventure stories, historical fiction, fantasy, science fiction - you name it, I've probably written it) in my "baby years" as a writer, but no one but my poor twin sister ever got to read them.

That changed when I discovered the Internet and the wondrous world of FanFiction and online stories. My parents belatedly got their wish - I took my nose out of my books and started to spend my time glued to the computer screen instead. Soon after, I wrote my first FanFiction, a Star Trek: Voyager story. Don't bother to search for it on the web; even if there was still a copy in circulation somewhere, it's in German. Back then, I would have taken a thousand oaths that I would never, ever be able to write more than a grocery list in English. Then I took an intensive, free online language course - almost eight years of constant fanfic reading. Let's just say that I learned some words I later had trouble explaining to my friends why I would know such expressions.

So in the beginning of 2006, I finally put my newly acquired knowledge of the English language to good use and wrote a series of three Law & Order: SVU fanfics in English. As my confidence grew, I wrote a longer FanFiction and then my first English historical fiction. In some ways, I've come full circle, because "Backwards to Oregon" takes place on the Western Frontier. Other than the setting I promise that it doesn't have much in common with my first childish attempt at writing.

I still live in Germany, where I work as a psychologist. When I'm not working or writing, I like to spend my time reading, cooking for a bunch of friends, spending time with my nephew and niece, and watching way too many crime shows. I also enjoy learning new languages (Russian is my latest project. I haven't found any lesbian online stories using the Cyrillic alphabet to help me learn, though).

Other Titles By This Author

Backwards To Oregon – Lesbian: Historical Fiction, Romance

Summary

"𝓛UKE" HAMILTON has always been sure that she'd never marry. She accepted that she would spend her life alone when she chose to live her life disguised as a man.

After working in a brothel for three years, Nora Macauley has lost all illusions about love. She no longer hopes for a man who will sweep her off her feet and take her away to begin a new, respectable life.

But now they find themselves married and on the way to Oregon in a covered wagon, with two thousand miles ahead of them.

Conflict of Interest – Book I – Lesbian: Romance, Crime

Summary

WORKAHOLIC detective Aiden Carlisle isn't looking for love... and certainly not at the law enforcement seminar she reluctantly agreed to attend. But their first lecturer is not at all what she expected.

Psychologist Dawn Kinsley has just found her place in life. After a failed relationship with a police officer, she has sworn to herself never to get involved with another cop again, but she feels a connection to Aiden from the very first moment.

Can Aiden keep from crossing the line when a brutal crime threatens to keep them apart... before they've even gotten together?

* * *

Next of Kin – Sequel to Conflict of Interest

Summary

SEX CRIMES Detective Aiden Carlisle is slowly getting used to being in a committed relationship with Dawn Kinsley—a relationship that isn't always easy since Dawn is not only a psychologist but also a former victim in one of Aiden's cases. Aiden's private and professional lives collide when Dawn's newest patient gets in trouble with the law. Will she be able to stay objective enough to solve the case without pushing Dawn away?

The same case also throws Deputy District Attorney Kade Matheson's well-ordered life into chaos. In the last few years, Kade has taken case files and law books, not lovers, to bed. She has been focused only on her career and fought hard to win cases like Dawn's, but now the case forces her to finally face her attraction to women. She suddenly finds herself with two secret admirers—but which one is more dangerous, the threat to her life or her heart?

*T*hank **You** for Purchasing and Reading

Next of Kin.

CPSIA information can be obtained at www.ICGtesting.com
Printed in the USA
LVOW090912070212

267482LV00001B/20/P